Stilling the Stillness
Part 2, Restless Spirits

Book Four of the Stillness Series

Richard Lee Ferguson

STILLING THE STILLNESS - BOOK 4 OF THE STILLNESS SERIES

Part 2: Restless Spirits

Copyright © 2015 by Richard Lee Ferguson

Book Cover by Bookfly Design, James Egan

Illustrations by Brian Bowes

Published in 2025

ISBN: 978-1-966776-03-1 (paperback)

ISBN: 978-1-966776-04-8 (hardcover)

ISBN: 978-1-966776-05-5 (ebook)

"I acknowledge only the Voices of the Dead that hover incessantly in the Head, and therefore I give this special thanks to the Chorus and the Corpses. Without them I would not be reminded that I should have joined them long ago, that I have now joined them, and have myself, thank Goddess, become part of The Great Wailing. The rest of you may remain . . . deaf . . . if that is your inclination." — Michael Powers

"Death plucks my ear and says, 'Live—I am coming.'" — Virgil

Also by Richard Lee Ferguson

The Stillness Series

Book 1: Stirring the Stillness, Part 1 Voices of Quest

Book 2: Stirring the Stillness, Part 2 Tortured Journey

Book 3: Stilling the Stillness, Part 1 Voices of War

Book 4: Stilling the Stillness, Part 2 Restless Spirits

Book 5: Becoming the Stillness, Part 1 Voices of Madness

Book 6: Becoming the Stillness, Part 2 Haunted Caves

Book 7: The Hunchback's Gift, Part 1 Voices of Defeat

Book 8: The Hunchback's Gift, Part 2 Superior Ones Risen

Book 9: Flames of Extinction, Part 1 The Last Voice

Book 10: Flames of Extinction, Part 2 Stillness is Stilled

For the full series, visit the Amazon series page: https://www.amazon.com/dp/B0F1WJ5J4N

Contents

Principal Characters · VII

Preface · IX

Prologue · XI

1. The Trojan Horse · 1

2. PART ONE: REDEMPTION · 23

3. The Final Battle Looms · 35

4. Slaughter and Salvation · 53

5. Last Will and Testament · 81

6. Sand Castles II · 91

7. BOOK II · 97

8. Undercover Operations · 105

9. Romancing A Ghost · 117

10. The Long Night · 131

11. PART TWO: REPLICATION · 143

12. Battle of Attrition · 157

13. The Wedding · 177

14. PART THREE: STRUGGLE · 195

15. Mark Makes Progress · 211

16. Tuyet Mai Journeys to Song Nhan Village · 229

17.	Mark Begins His Journey	249
18.	PART FOUR: CONFLICT	261
19.	On the Eve of the Reunion	281
20.	The Tunnel Waits	303
21.	PART FIVE: DECEPTION	321
22.	Trajectory I	343
23.	Trajectory II	363
24.	PART SIX: REDEMPTION	375
25.	Bones	387
26.	Defiance	389
27.	The Pieces are in Place	391
28.	Nothing	393
29.	Denouement	395
30.	BOOK III	397
31.	BEGINNINGS AND ENDINGS	399
32.	The Quest Begins	419
33.	The Last Supper	435
34.	Restless Thoughts	447
Epilogue		449

Principal Characters

Voices - God and Goddess

Michael Powers – Narrator and son of John Powers and Bai Meiying
  Storyteller – Michael Powers nickname in the war
  T – Lieutenant
  Pappy – Sergeant
  X – Medic
  Cairns – Captain
  Mountain Man – Soldier
  Nguyen Tuyet Mai – Vietnamese intelligence officer
  Kim Lan – Tuyet Mai's assistant
  Le Chi Vy – Major in North Vietnamese Army
  Vo Thanh Tong – Captain in North Vietnamese Army
  Cao Thanh Dam – Sergeant/Sapper in North Vietnamese Army
  Madame Dau – Village Council Chief
  Han Tinh – Legless veteran in village
  Schoolmistress Nang – Village teacher
  Diane – Deceased wife of Michael Powers
  Theresa – Second wife of Michael Powers
  Ethyl – Friend of Theresa
  Mark Powers – Son of Michael Powers
  Vu Quoc Viet – Sergeant in North Vietnamese Army
  Pham Van Dinh – Prison guard
  Paul and Claire Thompson – Friends of Michael Powers
  John and Lisa – Children of Paul and Claire Thompson
  Quang Long – Clerk in North Vietnamese Army
  Teo – Grandson of Madame Dau
  Professor Benson – Teacher of Mark Powers
  Bui Quang Minh – Commissar of North Vietnamese unit
  Master Kung – Mysterious monk/teacher

Preface

Can Humans Be Replaced Peacefully?

Query: Are you one of the increasing numbers of people who think humans are irredeemably destructive and pose such a threat to the planet that their extinction would be a good thing? However, do you also abhor the massive destruction and suffering that would necessarily be the consequence of their demise? Bloody, violent dystopian novels often focus only on a few survivors of such devastation, not on the suffering that would extend to all other life forms on the planet. While there are many excellent dystopian novels, such a formulaic concentration on a small group of heroic protagonists can be narrow and unsatisfying.

So, how to unravel the ubiquitous human presence without simultaneously destroying the rest of the planetary ecosystem? Can a successor species evolve fast enough to replace humankind, or would it be extinguished before it has a chance to spread?

Such a successor species, by random chance or intentional design, must possess far greater cognitive and empathetic capacities to thwart the human proclivity for eliminating real or perceived threats. What would it be like for those first generations of advanced individuals surrounded by a sea of slow-witted but resourceful *Homo sapiens*? How would they survive the human penchant for fearing otherness and a relentless instinct to exterminate it? Whether the guiding force effectuating this change is Nature, Superior Alien, God or Gods, Goddess or Goddesses, here is an interesting way forward:

Replace *Homo sapiens* with a more advanced species, but not *drive* them to extinction through violent extermination, rather *dilute* their genes to insignificance over generations. There is precedent for such top-down genetic engineering. Human biologists eliminate dangerous pests by introducing mutant strains that breed with the targeted species to produce offspring harboring the desired genetic makeup. Generations later, the original species is superseded.

A new form of consciousness must necessarily arise—one in which strange Voices with immense cognitive power reverberate in advanced minds in the same way Voices once arose in the minds of early *Homo sapiens separating them from competitors such as Neanderthals*. Humans would initially diagnose those hearing such new Voices as schizophrenics, but they are, in fact, the incipient stirrings of a superior species. However, new Voices must be only the beginning, as this emerging species must also evolve powerful physical capabilities to overcome human weapons of destruction.

The doves must have sharper claws than the hawks . . .

The Stillness Series is the epic story of one such scenario.

Prologue

Previously. . . .

In *Voices of War*, storm and monsoon sealed soldiers and villagers alike in an arena of death. American platoon, NVA fighters, and the women of Song Nhan village became trapped in a siege where violence, madness, and betrayal consumed all certainty. From tunnels to fortresses, the living clung to survival as memory and myth blurred, and Storyteller emerged, the last to witness, the last to remember. Humanity's war was revealed as not only against each other, but against itself.

Now the guns fall silent, but the silence is not peace. It is haunted. Restless spirits walk among the living, demanding answers, demanding remembrance. Memory itself becomes battlefield and burden, for what the body endures, the soul cannot easily release. The fortress remains, but within it echo screams that time cannot bury.

And so the questions linger:

What endures when all else collapses?

If the dead cannot rest, can the living ever be free?

And if memory itself becomes spirit, is there any escape from the war within?

~ Reader Beware ~

The restless do not wait for answers. They demand them.

Chapter One

The Trojan Horse

Vy's Plan Is Put In Motion

S tretch slumped behind the parapet, rising only now and then to glance through a narrow slit in the thick stone. Like the others in the fortress, he suffered from diarrhea; his gut clenched with cramps, and pain burned deep in his rectum. He felt pale and emptied out, his frame withering, his skin drawn tight. From behind hollowed eyes he watched the world without focus.

Humor no longer restored him. The wisecracks that once spilled freely now came in a scattered, indifferent few. Only the movies stayed with him, light fragments drifting across the surface of his sinking morale. After all, movies always ended well.

Almost always.

It was mid-afternoon, and the rain had slackened into drizzle. To keep himself distracted, Stretch scratched messages into the wall with his knife. Weary and wet, the best he could muster was: "Stretch, 1st Air Cav. Fuck this." But the phrase felt flat and unworthy, so he searched for something sharper, an insult with edge, when Superman trudged up and let his heavy frame drop beside him.

"Hey," whispered the big gunner.

"Hey," Stretch replied, voice lazy, vacant.

"What's up?"

"Nothin'."

Silence settled between them. But Stretch's disinterest began to shift, replaced by a slow anger. The absurdity of it gnawed at him: a boy from the Midwest, trapped in some rotting French fort lost in an Asian jungle. He scanned the treeline again, then turned suddenly to Superman.

"Well, what's your precious God gonna do about this?"

"About what?"

"About us. Being stuck here. What's He gonna do?"

Superman laughed, then cut it short when Stretch raised a finger. "Shhhh! You trying to get us killed?"

Superman whispered, "It doesn't work that way. He may not do anything."

"Who?"

"God, you idiot."

"Oh, yeah? Why not? Haven't you been praying? I mean hell, I've been counting on you. You've got twin girls back in The World praying through you. And me? I got . . . well—"

"You've got people too."

"'Course I do. People waiting on me, like. . . . "

"Willing ladies?"

Stretch feigned offense. "Not just them. I got a mother, you know."

Superman grinned. "Yeah. The one with glue in her . . . privates."

Stretch knew he was expected to fire back with something outrageous, something to make the pain laughable. But he didn't. He leaned forward instead, voice low. "Superman, I'm fuckin' scared. I've been scared before, but this—this is worse."

"Why?"

"Because I might actually make it back."

Superman frowned. "That scares you? Of all things?"

"It's hard to explain." Stretch lowered his head. "I mean, we're brothers out here, right? Closer than family. But still. . . . "

"Nothing you say is gonna shock me, Stretch."

Stretch nodded, then spoke softly. "Sometimes after I shit, I can't get clean. I wipe and wipe and it's still there—the stench, the sickness. Like the jungle's carved itself into me, and no soap in the world will wash it out. It makes me gag. I can't imagine ever making love again without that stench crawling up my spine. A shred, a smear, something always left behind. I picture being with a girl, and she's going down on me, and then she pulls back, disgusted, 'cause she smelled it. Saw it. I swear to you, it'll never be the same. Not ever. Not with anyone. Even my mom and dad, they'll flinch away from the stench of this place."

"Come on," Superman said gently. "One hot bath back in The World, and you'll be fine. You'll be making love to prom queens again."

But Stretch only stared out the slit in the wall. "No. Always shit hangin' down. Never, ever fuckin' be the same."

Superman wasn't about to let him spiral. "You sound like you want sympathy or something. Me, I'm going back and getting clean. Real clean. Soap. Sheets. Clothes. Even clean underwear. I'm gonna hug my girls, clean as rain."

Stretch didn't budge. "Yeah, sure. But you'll smell it too. And your sweet little daughters? They won't come near you either. You'll see."

He regretted saying it the moment it left his mouth but used the distraction to glance outside. Something flickered at the edge of his vision. He tensed, leaned forward.

"What is it?" Superman hissed.

"Movement!" Stretch's hand hovered over his weapon. For a grunt who lived in a free-fire zone, movement meant one thing. Trouble. Instinct screamed to fire, but something held him back.

"Wait! It's gooks. Sure as shit, it's gooks. But hang on."

The rain had slowed, but visibility still wavered in the gray light. He stared harder. Shapes emerged. Two figures, one holding a white flag.

"Go tell T and Pappy," he whispered. "There's two gooks out there waving the flag again. They're inviting us out."

As Superman shuffled away, Stretch murmured, "Here we go again." He grinned, thin and bitter. "Always the same in the Grand Hotel. People come, people go. Nothing ever happens." Then his expression shifted. "Still, our writer friend Michael is up to something. That fucker's up to something. How's this gonna end? Crazy, schizophrenic bastard. Hurry up, Storyteller. Kill him."

~

Kim Lan stood in the clearing beside Minh, feeling absurd. He held aloft the same makeshift white flag Long had crafted for Dam days earlier, and she shifted uneasily from foot to foot, uncertain where to rest her hands. Comic figures, she thought. The Americans are probably laughing.

The pistol loaded with blanks felt light and metallic against her forearm. The second pistol, loaded and hidden lower, pressed cold and accusing against her groin. Two bars of plastic explosive, several detonators, and a folding knife, all wrapped in gauze, pressed close inside her. Before entering the clearing, she had ordered Cook Trinh to smear the materials with gibbon blood, sealing them in a disguise of menstruation. The nausea had been difficult to suppress, but now it had receded, replaced by discomfort and a steady, disciplined silence. She focused on not thinking about the contents inside her.

But a new urgency had taken hold. She needed to urinate.

They stood in the same clearing where Vy had once met with the Americans. A light rain fell, water tracing jagged paths down the warped surfaces of two ancient stumps rising from the forest floor.

Kim Lan's panic rose, not sharply, but in slow, lurching pulses. The ground beneath her did not hold. A tremor passed through the clearing, subtle but real. She clenched her thighs, as if to anchor herself, but the tremor returned, this time in the stumps themselves. They quivered. Swelled. Twisted. Not with wind, but with a slow inward movement, as though something underneath were pushing upward.

The bark loosened. The forms bulged. Cracks deepened and curled. Then the stumps began to open, unfolding not with violence, but with a laboring sorrow, as if the earth itself were giving birth to old grief. Figures began to emerge. Not ghosts, not hallucinations. Shapes. Knees drawn up, heads bowed low, soaked hair veiling hollow faces. They pulsed faintly with warmth, as if they held their breaths. Time narrowed. The rain blurred into silence. The forest receded. Kim Lan stared. Her breath stopped. Recognition hovered just beyond reach.

The air vibrated. A thunderclap rolled through the hills. The heads lifted in unison. And in that instant, she saw.

~

"Anh! Le!"

She rushed forward, arms outstretched, and gathered them to her chest. "You look so sad. So cold. Mama's here. You're so wet. I'll dry you . . . oh, my sweet girls. Mama is here."

But the children did not respond. Their small bodies hung limp in her arms. Panic rose again as she searched their faces, pleading. "It's me. Your mama. Look. It's me."

Recognition stirred. The dullness in their eyes began to lift. Slowly, they looked up. Their faces brightened, and in unison they cried out, "Mama! Mama!" hugging her tightly. "Mama, you're home!" Their giggles tumbled through her like warm light. A deep joy opened inside her, flooding through mind and body.

She set them down and reached into the sleeve of her tunic. The children bounced with anticipation. She produced a doll made of coiled hemp from beneath her arm. Then, slipping a hand into the waistband of her trousers, she withdrew a second.

"For my two princesses!" she beamed. "And look—" she patted her stomach, "your mama is going to have a baby. If the gods are kind, you'll have a little brother."

The older girl stopped smiling. Her expression darkened. "Mama . . . are you going to leave again?"

"Comrade!" Minh's voice cut through the clearing. "What are you doing? The Americans are coming. Whispering to old stumps like a half-wit is not an auspicious start to our little opera."

Kim Lan blinked, looked down, ashamed. "Sorry. I was thinking of my daughters."

Minh's face softened. He thumped his chest and nodded, eyes on the advancing soldiers. "Ah. I have five. Three sons, but daughters are different. Precious. I understand missing them. Don't worry, Comrade Kim Lan. We're behind you." His voice dropped, twinkling with an unexpected warmth. "Even if I'm about to 'die,' I'll see you through. You'll hold your girls again. Wait and see. Ah, look. They're coming."

She hadn't expected kindness from him. And now it disarmed her—a flash of the man he might have become in a world without war. It threw her off balance. She opened her mouth to reply, but he silenced her with a gesture and straightened into his performance stance. She turned. The Americans were already there. Watching.

~

T was startled to see Kim Lan. She stood beside an officer with a severe, angular bearing. The man's chin lifted slightly, his posture rigid, almost theatrical. T was reminded of Mussolini in one of those old newsreels. His body stiffened.

The instinct was immediate: repulsion. A deep, democratic instinct clenched in him, trained by every civic ideal he had ever absorbed. He swore to show no weakness before this preening authoritarian.

We're not off to a good start.

And now Kim Lan, how to greet her? A nod? A hand signal? But his contempt for the officer beside her hardened his resolve. He would give nothing away.

~

Cairns watched Kim Lan closely, eyes narrowed. She was nervous. Too nervous. Her gaze darted between her companion and the fortress walls. Something wasn't right. The air carried tension, barely contained. He couldn't name it, but it pressed on him like a gathering storm. For a moment, he had the absurd thought he'd wandered into a Western standoff, an old saloon filled with gunfighters about to draw. But he shook it off.

He kept his distance. Let them speak first. He didn't trust it: not the situation, not the posture, not the silence. So instead, he entertained himself.

In his mind, Kim Lan stood naked beside Tuyet Mai. Their hands bound above their heads, their bodies stretched and trembling. He watched them squirm under his gaze, flushed and ashamed, trying not to break. He could see every shiver, every breath.

He smiled ever so subtly.

~ *Kim Lan Enters the Fortress* ~

"Why have you called us?" T demanded, his tone brittle with irritation as he gestured for Cairns to translate. But before Cairns could speak, T saw Kim Lan's hand move swiftly inside her trousers. For a moment, he thought she was brushing away an insect.

Then came the pistol.

His breath caught. He reached instinctively for his own weapon only to remember, too late, it was back in the fortress. He threw himself to the ground as Kim Lan shouted, "*Chieu hoi! Chieu hoi! Chieu hoi!*"

T scrambled forward on hands and knees. He'd seen the pistol, seen her raise it, but something was wrong. Her movements didn't track. He twisted around in time to see her turn, not on the Americans but on the Vietnamese officer beside her.

The man didn't move. He stared at her, slack-jawed, frozen in place.

"Click." The weapon misfired. T stopped, suspended in the moment. Kim Lan pulled the trigger again. The officer's face shifted from fear to something almost expectant.

"Pop." A shot, low and unimpressive.

At the same instant, another crack echoed through the clearing. A second bullet struck home. A small hole opened in the officer's forehead, followed by a burst of blood. His expression dissolved into surprise. He staggered back, touched the wound with his fingertip, then collapsed.

His body twitched violently, one finger still lodged absurdly in the bullet hole. He arched his back once, gave a final shuddering groan, and lay still. For a breathless moment, the grotesque contortion of his limbs seemed almost theatrical.

T recovered and lurched to his feet, sprinting for the fortress but caught his toe on a vine and crashed face-first into the mud. Dazed, he caught a glimpse of Cairns also struggling upright nearby, slipping in the wet grass.

Then he saw Kim Lan charging toward him, pistol still in hand.

He clawed his way backward in panic. She was too fast. She was already over him, bending close, the weapon raised—

He flinched. Raised his hands. And stopped.

She wasn't pointing it at him. She was offering it.

"*Chieu hoi,*" she said again, her voice urgent but calm. "*Chieu hoi.*"

T stared up at her, stunned. Her face held no malice, only a fierce, weary resolve. She looked almost annoyed by his hesitation.

Behind her, Cairns was already up and running toward the gate. T blinked the mud from his eyes just as the treeline erupted with automatic fire. AK-47 rounds cracked overhead.

T bolted. Kim Lan ran beside him, head low, matching his stride. She kept offering him the pistol, as if they were partners on some grim errand.

The three of them tumbled through the fortress gate, breathless and dripping.

Grunts fired down from the parapets, but Pappy's bark cut through the chaos. "Hold fire!" The shooting stopped and silence rushed in, dense and brief, before it collapsed under a wave of shouted questions.

"Wait!" T roared. "Get her inside. The church. Search her. I mean thoroughly."

Only then did anyone notice she still held the pistol, loosely, as if forgotten. Pappy took it gently from her hand. Nature and Birdman flanked her, leading her toward the church. Cairns moved to follow, but T stopped him.

"Wait, Captain. You and Pappy, over here." He turned to the rest. "The rest of you . . . give us a minute to debrief."

~

For a short time after emerging victorious over Cairns from the tunnel incident Tuyet Mai felt brief elation, but the feeling quickly dissipated and she had again sunk into a deep depression. The Americans had allowed her to use some of their precious soap to shower in the rain behind the makeshift partition of the toilet, but the effect was paradoxical. The dirt had been a reminder of her successful struggle, and now that she was somewhat clean, she again had doubts that she would survive. Her entire life had been a process of cleaning up after being soiled by men. Perfumed and powdered, always ready for the next defilement, she felt like a plump carrot rinsed of night soil and made pleasing to the eye. Sinking into a state of disinterest, she had stopped listening to the conversations that surrounded her, instead dwelling on her own misery. But even in this extreme self-absorption, she noticed the American lieutenant and captain leaving the fortress. Curiosity piqued, she waited impatiently for them to return.

Hearing small arms fire erupt outside the fortress, she felt a disconcerting blend of joy and confusion when she saw Kim Lan rush into the fortress. *How is this possible? Have American reinforcements captured our forces outside the fort? Has she surrendered? No. Impossible. In the name of the ancestors, what is happening?*

Tuyet Mai struggled to rise, but her bondage made that impossible. Straining at her ropes, she tried to keep Kim Lan in sight as the men escorted her friend to the church. Kim Lan never looked in her direction, and finally disappeared inside the ruined structure. Tuyet Mai started to shout Kim Lan's name, but thought better of it, and only a desultory whine escaped her lips. Tuyet Mai lay back and began the laborious process of trying to guess why Kim Lan had returned, but underlying her efforts was the unmistakable feeling of deep satisfaction that she now had her beloved friend back to share whatever might happen.

Her spirits lifted by this strange turn of events, Tuyet Mai allowed herself to feel renewed optimism. After a long time passed and Kim Lan had still not emerged from the church, Tuyet Mai's thoughts began to drift. Once again, she was back on that imaginary front porch with other village women, watching their children cavort under the great banyan. This time, the fussy baby was passed to her. This time, her rocking and cooing quieted the baby. This time she saw a smile of approval spread across Madame Dau's face. Forever more, she would not be the fierce Trieu Thi Trinh, but would remain merely Nguyen Tuyet Mai, small dreamed mother of children and daughter of the earth.

"Kim Lan. Kim Lan," she muttered as she lay her cheek on the wet poncho and closed her eyes in weary satisfaction. "You have come back. The reason must be great. But great or small, you have come back."

~

"Please remove your clothes," Nature said, voice brittle, miming the act of undressing. He was more embarrassed than she was. Kim Lan obeyed without hesitation, lowering her eyes and calmly disrobing. Birdman stood nearby, shifting his weight, arms folded in feigned ease. She stood still, one arm across her breasts, the other shielding her sex, as the rain slid across her skin.

Nature could barely breathe. He flinched when Birdman barked, "Check her clothes, Nature. Don't just stand there."

Nature turned, eyes wide and slow. "Give me a second, Birdman. Don't rush it." He tossed her tunic toward him. "You check that. I'll take these."

He began searching the pockets of her uniform, fingers mechanical, but his mind wandered. A poem had begun to form. Something for Kim Lan, for all women, for this moment, for the strange ache of sympathy she awakened in him. She stood there, stripped and soaked, while he, a towering, armed, overly muscled American, felt suddenly small. She, unclothed and exposed, held more gravity than he ever could with a rifle in his hands. He groped for the language to capture it, but the poem slipped away. Almost. A little longer and he'd find it.

"You done or what?" Birdman snapped. "Anything there?"

Nature nodded slowly, still trying to preserve the shape of the unwritten lines. "No."

"Then check her cunt."

Nature's head jerked up. "What?"

"You heard me. These women hide everything in their runways. You want her cutting your throat with a blade you didn't see? I'm a chopper pilot, but I know that much. You with me?"

Nature stared at him, disgusted.

Birdman stepped forward. "Fine. I'll do it myself."

"No. I've got it." Nature raised a hand. "At least let me try to leave her some dignity."

"Yeah, yeah. Just fuckin' do it."

Nature gestured for Kim Lan to step forward. He hesitated. Standing or lying down? What's right? What's humane? What won't humiliate her more? His mind scrambled. Then he smiled gently and said, "Please. Lie down."

He reached out, motioning toward a low stone bench beside the altar. The Goddess figurine loomed above, carved into the shelf, her face unmoving, inscrutable.

~

Still covering herself, Kim Lan lifted her eyes to the figurine and felt warmth rising from the wet stones beneath her feet. The chill of the rain disappeared. The ground no longer felt hard, but supple, yielding, as though she stood not on stone, but on flesh. The water that clung to her skin thickened. It carried weight. It carried silence.

She locked eyes with the Goddess. The church vanished. What remained was womb, a deep, sacred interior, and she was adrift within it, naked and suspended, her body beginning again.

She looked down and saw a pink cord tethered to her belly. It pulsed, alive. She followed it with her eyes until it reached the figurine. A conduit. A bond.

She turned to study the edges of this strange world. The two Americans floated beside her, stripped of weapons, stripped of hair, their eyes luminous and wide, their mouths round and helpless. Their hands sucked their thumbs with soft devotion. Their fingernails gleamed. No dirt, no violence. Clean. Whole.

She laughed softly. "Triplets."

Then the current shifted. Something turned beneath her. She felt herself descending, caught in a spiral, pressed by force and pressure. Down. Down again. Tighter. The world began to collapse inward. A wind howled through the narrowing space. Stone constricted around her, thick with friction and ache. Her body clenched. Her limbs compressed. She was being pushed—delivered.

A single moment of clarity tore through the vortex. The spiral opened. She emerged, radiant and raw, into a freezing brightness.

Looking back, she saw an American man tumbling after her, clutching her in a fetal embrace, unwilling to let go. He reached for her skin. He touched her—

~

"Oh, god," mumbled Nature as he stared down at the tip of a blood-covered roll pinched delicately between his index finger and thumb. He had just begun to pull the roll from Kim Lan's vagina when the sudden warmth startled him. He froze, ashamed of his revulsion, and slipped the roll back inside.

"Sorry, sorry," he kept repeating.

"What's the matter?" asked Birdman.

"It's her period, man," replied Nature irritably as he stood up and continued his mantra: "Sorry. Sorry."

Birdman stood dumbly looking at Kim Lan lying uncomfortably on the stone platform.

"Get her clothes, would you?" said Nature. He looked down at her trembling body. "And then we need to let her dress in private."

"Yeah. I'll do that. Why don't you go report to T and tell him she's clean." He snorted. "Well, maybe not so clean, but at least we can tell him she has no weapons."

Nature was already moving toward the door of the church, rubbing his hands in the cleansing rain. His feelings of profound admiration for Kim Lan had momentarily turned to disgust and he fought against the ages-old enmity of the male against the mysterious inner fluids that circulated beneath the misleadingly supple exterior of the female form.

As Nature approached T, Cairns, and Pappy, he noticed they were engaged in heated conversation. Cairns in particular sounded agitated and insistent.

"No. We can't trust her. This *chieu hoi* business is an obvious ruse. Calculated to fool a child, but certainly not experienced officers. How do you explain this sudden change of heart? And I saw her drop a second pistol from her sleeve as she was running up to you. What was that for? In spite of their denials, she and Tuyet Mai must be the intelligence officers we're after. They must be."

"Bull!" exclaimed T. "Never been on a mission yet where intelligence was right. What if they're telling the truth? What if they're just local village women conscripted by the NVA to act as guides?"

"Nonsense," spat Cairns. "An infantile wish for things to be different than they are. I tell you, these women can't be trusted."

"What do you suggest we do with her?"

"Tie her up, ignore her, and take her back to the rear for interrogation."

T's eyes widened in feigned amazement. "Take her back to the rear? In a Cadillac?"

Cairns smiled malevolently. "You should know where we can find a Cadillac, right, lieutenant?"

Pappy calmly interjected, "Sirs, maybe we should find out what she wants first, why she's here, then decide."

"Sounds reasonable, sergeant," said Cairns. "But she will build an elaborate lie that might possibly suck us in. And then"—he ground his fist into his palm—"oblivion."

Nature gingerly stepped forward. "T, we searched the woman and found nothing."

Cairns stretched his neck toward Nature, veins quivering. "Did you conduct a body cavity search?"

"Yes, sir."

Cairns' eyes narrowed in disbelief. "Are you sure you checked carefully?"

T glared at Cairns and spoke in a mocking tone. "Would you like to take her down into the tunnel and check her yourself, captain?"

Smiling crookedly, Cairns replied in an even tone, "Yes. I would." He frowned and the corner of his lip curled viciously. "Very much."

T responded almost triumphantly, "Fortunately, you do not have that option."

But Cairns would not cooperate. "Your gallantry is misplaced, lieutenant. I may have certain personal peccadillos, but they will not interfere with our survival. You, on the other hand, live in a dream world, masturbating over a code of conduct that is the moral equivalent of a blow-up rubber doll. Paint it as pretty as you want, it's still empty and prone to deflation at the prick of a pin. I'll deal with the real world if you don't mind."

Pappy snarled, "All that matters is what we do from now on, and the more info we have, the better our decisions will be. Blow-up dolls, or the Uniform Code of Military Justice, neither of them mean squat if we make the wrong decisions. So, with all due respect to you sirs, let's talk to the woman and find out what we can before we make any decision."

"I agree with Pappy. Let's go talk to her," said Cairns.

T fidgeted and bit down on his gum so hard that his jaw bulged. "All right," he said resignedly. "That was all I was saying from the beginning."

~ *Cairns Interrogates Kim Lan* ~

Kim Lan looked up at the American faces, heavy with heat and stern with judgment, crowned in green like stone gods peering down from their mountains. This was the moment. There would be no rehearsal.

She steadied her breath. The line between belief and performance had always been thin. She had walked it all her life. Stories spun into silence, lies forged into gifts. Compared to the cartel bosses, these Americans were clumsy children. Tong's words returned like an incantation: *They will want to believe.* And he was right. He always was.

They will want to believe, she thought again. *They need to.*

"Why did you *chieu hoi*?" T demanded, his tone brittle with suspicion.

She hesitated only to translate the words in her mind. Then she delivered the line she practiced for so long, clean, bright, and desperate: "I no like Communists! They take my food. My rice. My chickens. I hungry. I afraid. No freedom of liberty!"

The phrase had opened many doors before. She felt its rhythm still alive in her mouth.

But Cairns stepped in, cutting through her performance in harsh Vietnamese. "You're lying. We've had this conversation. You're not some village guide. You're an intelligence officer. Admit it."

"No."

"Do you think we can defeat the People's Army? Or did you come just to die?"

She dropped the English. Shifted her tone. "You will not die."

Cairns raised an eyebrow. "No? Why not?"

"Because the main force left yesterday. Only a small detachment remains. But by tomorrow it changes. A new company will come to overrun the fortress."

"Why did they leave?"

She let silence answer. Too much knowledge would betray her. She shrugged carefully. Deliberately.

"You still haven't told me why you *chieu hoi*," Cairns pressed.

"What's she saying?" T snapped.

"Wait," said Cairns, eyes locked to hers. "Why now?"

She fixed her gaze on his knees. A point of neutral flesh. Not the eyes. Not the mouth. "I will lead you out. There's a swamp. It is unguarded. I know the way. You let me help. You pay. I work for Americans. They are rich."

Cairns scoffed. "Swamp? This far inland? Mangroves need salt. How could there be saltwater here?"

She blinked at him, blankly. No defense. Let him argue with himself.

"You want to lead us through terrain that can't exist. And even if it did, the moment they learn you've defected, they'll collapse their lines. Every gap will vanish."

This hadn't occurred to her. She faltered. "Ah . . . " Then shook her head, firm again. "No. Lieutenant is in charge now. Since commissar is dead."

"The one you shot?"

"Yes. I know the lieutenant. He will not move the lines Vy ordered. Not until the reinforcements arrive."

"And how does a village girl know this?"

She met his stare for the first time. "I was with the Front. A women's brigade. But I hated it. I know how they think. They are fools."

His eyes narrowed. "You lie."

"No."

"Then why won't you answer?"

"What question?"

"Why now? Why not wait?"

T cut in again. "Goddamn it, Cairns, what the hell is she saying?"

Kim Lan turned her head to T, slow and deliberate, and smiled. She returned to English, voice low, almost intimate: "I *chieu hoi* because I hate Communists. They rape me. I run. I afraid they rape me again."

Cairns waved T off with one hand, amused. "Nice try," he said in Vietnamese to Kim Lan. "But I make the decisions here. So. Why now?"

"Because now is best time. Only thirty or forty men. Spread thin. Gaps in lines. No one in swamp."

"How do you know where they're positioned?"

"I walked with commissar and Major Vy. I saw. Before the major left."

"Why would they bring you?"

"I told you, I was with the Front."

He waved the answer away. "Still, why bring a woman? What purpose would you serve?"

She lowered her eyes. Said nothing. Let the weight of the silence explain what words could not.

He caught it. "The commissar?"

She nodded. Slowly.

"And the meeting in the clearing, he called it to win surrender?"

"Yes. To be a hero."

"You lie."

"No."

"Cairns!" T barked. "I've had enough of this. Translate. Now."

Cairns rolled his eyes. "All right. Here's the scoop."

~ *They Will Want to Believe* ~

T listened in silence as Cairns summarized his conversation with Kim Lan. When he finished, T ordered her bound and placed against the far wall, well away from Tuyet Mai. Then he called a council. Pappy, Cairns, Birdman, Topper, and several grunts drifted in, forming a loose circle beneath the dripping eaves. No one sat. Rain fell steadily from a low, indifferent sky.

"We got nothing to lose," Topper began, nodding toward Birdman. "Way I see it, we stay here, we die. Might as well take a shot."

"Maybe," Pappy said. "But patrols might spot us any time."

Birdman looked up into the gray spill of the monsoon. "Not in this soup. No visibility, no air traffic. Not until the wind calms down."

"I agree," Topper added. "If help was coming, it'd be here by now." He let the sentence hang.

"Yeah, maybe," Pappy muttered. "But you never know. Plenty of guys freeze to death ten steps from safety. Gave up too soon."

T broke in. "I believe her."

The words surprised even him. He wasn't sure why he felt it so strongly. Maybe it was because Cairns didn't believe her. Maybe it was the slow disintegration of the platoon, the smell of his own failure as a leader, the rot spreading through the fortress. Or maybe he simply needed to believe in something again.

The group fell quiet.

Pappy finally spoke. "I don't buy it. Why would she chieu hoi now? To a handful of Americans about to be overrun? Doesn't add up."

"But she shot an NVA officer," said Topper. "That's got to count for something."

"Not necessarily," Cairns replied. "Death doesn't mean the same thing to them. These people, they're wired differently. Fanatics. They'll die smiling for Uncle Ho."

"Bullshit," T snapped. "I saw his face. The man was not expecting to die. There was real fear in him. He wasn't a fanatic. That much I know."

"And don't forget we were all shot at on the way back in," Birdman added. "Didn't feel like a planned operation to me."

"No one got hit," Cairns said flatly.

"They missed by inches."

"Maybe they were just lousy shots," Cairns said with a shrug. "All of them."

"It's a trap," Pappy said. "I agree with Cairns."

Then Cairns surprised everyone, even himself.

"I think it's a trap too, Sergeant," he said. "But I still say we go. Let's get the hell out of here."

He heard the words leave his mouth before he could stop them. For a moment, he wondered if he had lost his mind. But deep down, he knew. He wanted to believe, too.

T seized the moment. "Then we're agreed. Tomorrow, before first light, we move. We follow Kim Lan."

Pappy stepped forward. "No. It's suicide. And there's no way we're getting Idaho or Storyteller out. One's too sick to walk. The other's got gangrene. X'll have to take that leg or he's done. You want to leave them behind? We don't leave our wounded. We don't even leave our dead."

Cairns turned on him. "If I recall, Sergeant, you didn't object to tossing Dogface and Raresteak off the bird."

"That was different," Pappy snapped. "They were already dead. And I remember you getting chewed out for it. 'We never leave our people behind.' That's what Lieutenant Rogers said. Ain't that right, sir?"

Eyes shifted to the ground. Boots scuffed in the mud. T took a breath. He'd thrown that gauntlet. He'd have to pick it up.

"You're right," T said. "That's what I said. And I still believe it. But let's be honest. The tunnel's collapsed. Mountain Man is dead. No one's coming. The monsoon's grounded air support. Most of us are sick, getting sicker. We're low on ammo, nearly out of food. Idaho will die without surgery. Same with Storyteller. Maybe—just maybe—the NVA will treat them. Hell, we might even get back before they're found. This could be our only shot to break out and fight another day."

He paused, then added, "That's our duty."

"Sure," Nature muttered. "If they don't put a bullet in their skulls first. How about stretchers?"

T turned. "X?"

X looked around at the circle of men. He saw what they wanted: permission to move forward without the burden of shame.

"Can't move Idaho," he said quietly. "Too much pain. One jolt and he could go into shock. And if Storyteller spikes another fever. . . . " He trailed off. "It's bad."

He closed his eyes. He remembered the bodies of Dogface and Raresteak being tossed into the jungle to lighten the choppers. Now they were talking about abandoning two men still breathing. Still brothers. And yet . . . he said nothing more. He didn't trust himself to say what he was really thinking: *It's a relief. It's not my hands cutting that leg. It's not my call anymore. And thank God for that.*

T nodded. "Then we have to be ready to sneak through or fight our way out. We leave them in the tunnel. If we get through, we send help. If not, at least they have a chance."

"They'll probably get better care than we will," Birdman muttered. "Bet there's a field hospital nearby."

Topper agreed. "They'll be safer than us, for sure."

Pappy's voice rose. "I can't believe what I'm hearing. Might as well throw them over the wall now. What would you want, if you were them?"

Cairns stepped forward. "The question isn't what we want. The question is survival. And leaving them behind increases that chance."

He paused. Let the silence take hold.

"If you're right, and this is suicide, then at least they live. You said that yourself."

Heads nodded. One by one.

A tide of agreement spread because they needed it. Believing Kim Lan's story meant there was still a path forward. Believing it was a trap gave them a reason to abandon the wounded. The logic was twisted, but it held. Guilt slid away in the grease of half-truths and hope.

Then Nature spoke.

"I agree with Pappy. We don't leave them."

T looked at him long. "Sorry, Nature. That's the decision." He turned his head, avoiding the soldier's eyes. "Gear up. We leave at first light."

Nature's voice was quiet. "I thought you made the decisions out here, sir. Since when did 'you' become 'we'?"

Cairns stepped in. "Captain Cairns," he said, tapping his chest, "backs the lieutenant's order. So do the pilots. Right, gentlemen?"

Birdman and Topper nodded.

Pappy turned to T. "Who tells Storyteller and Idaho?"

"I will," T said. Then added coldly, "And once we're out there, if anything smells wrong, those women die first."

Cairns smiled thinly. "Lieutenant, I thought you were an advocate of the Geneva Convention."

T met his gaze. "I am. Just as much as you are."

He turned and walked away. His boots squelched through the mud. His gut turned.

What am I doing?
Just get through this. Get out. After that—
I'll be myself again.

~ *Madame Dau Returns to the Cave* ~

Madame Dau stood breathless before the gaping cave. Its mouth yawned open, ragged and ancient, waiting. Even now, she couldn't fully explain what had brought her here.

Before she left the village, Han Tinh had scolded her. "You'll do what you want anyway," he said. "No woman should attempt this. Not at your age."

"But—" she began.

"No. You told me yourself, The Man From the Mountains is dead. Now you go to find him? Why? Making waves with no wind. Foolish woman. I'm finished with you—for now. But come to my house before you leave. I'll have something for you."

When she arrived, he waited beneath a tattered poncho sagging from four bamboo poles, rainwater leaking steadily from countless holes. Beneath this miserable canopy, a tin cup sat uneasily on a rattan bench, half-sunk in the mud. She looked down at the cup.

"It's a potion," he said. "To expel demons."

"I thought you didn't believe in that sort of thing."

He ignored her. "Drink it."

"Who made it?"

"Old Tien."

"She hasn't left yet?"

"She's leaving."

"Ah."

"Drink it."

"What's in it?"

Tinh smiled faintly and extended the cup.

Madame Dau hesitated. It might be poison.

"It won't kill you, if that's what you're afraid of. It drives out what doesn't belong but leaves what does."

She took the cup in both hands, held it briefly to her lips, then downed it in quick swallows. Almost at once she gagged and coughed, vomiting a bitter stream.

"Pig's spit, a woman's blood, jackfruit pulp, and bitter herbs. It's meant to work quickly." Tinh's eyes glittered. "Well? Do you feel anything?"

"Sick," she managed.

"Still going to the cave?"

She sighed, pulled absently at her tunic. "Yes."

"Stubborn demons," he said, shaking his head. "Very stubborn."

~

Before setting out, she had one last task. Back home, she touched Mickey Mouse for luck, slung a small bag of provisions over her shoulder, and stepped into the wind. She walked with slow determination until she reached the sharp bend in the Song Nhan river, a horseshoe curve before the water flowed straight into forest shadow. Standing atop the reed-covered levee, she searched the bank below and quickly spotted a woman crouched near the water, scrubbing something in the shallows.

She descended carefully, footfalls muffled in the wet grass, and approached without sound. The woman turned. It was Madame Binh. Her face twisted in a smile blurred by tears.

Madame Dau knelt beside her.

Between them, a baby cooed and splashed in the warm current. The infant's limbs stirred joyfully in Binh's cradle of hands, her eyes radiant, her skin gleaming with water and trust. Neither woman spoke. The baby's laughter rose over the rippling surface.

Then Binh tightened her grip. Slowly, deliberately, she forced the small body down. The child resisted, flailing wildly, her tiny limbs flapping against the water. Panic surged up Binh's arms. Dau turned away. Her throat clenched with rage at Heaven, at war, at the brutal choice forced upon them: a slow death by hunger, or this.

The river began to choke. What had once babbled peacefully now convulsed, sputtering around the shape pressed into it. A few startled ducks took flight.

Then silence.

Binh lifted the limp body from the water and stood. Dau rose beside her but said nothing.

Binh cradled the corpse gently. She would carry it to the mother who even now waited, hoping that the grandmother could not bring herself to do what she had done. At the top of the levee, Binh paused.

"Security Chief Tien came to me today," she said. "Tried to stop this. We couldn't agree. She was angry. Be careful. She wants to leave the village, and she'll take others with her."

Dau gave a nod of quiet acknowledgment.

~

At Binh's house, incense was already lit at the family altar. Smoke writhed above the bowed form of the baby's mother, her whispering voice preparing the ancestors for another burden.

Madame Dau returned home slowly. Her heart ached for the child, yet some deeper thread of joy stirred beneath her sorrow: all but one of her daughters still lived. In the divine arithmetic, that was more than she had any right to expect.

Her bare toes curled in the red mud. Rain spattered her face and tingled on her skin. An odd time to feel such yearning for life, but she did. She thought of that baby, eyes wide in terror, fighting to survive. And she thought: *I am still here. After everything. Still here.*

She raised her face to the sky. *To feel the sun. To drink tea with friends. To hear laughter, smell incense, breathe in the hearth fires of home—that is enough. More than enough.*

As she passed the houses and altars of Song Nhan, she nodded to each shrine, each neighbor. On the path that curved through the rice fields, her thoughts returned to the cave.

Death may take me soon, but war might take me first. And if I must go, I will not go quiet. I will not let this village be lost. If I must be pulled beneath the surface, I will kick. Just like the baby, I will kick!

With that vow burning inside her, she wrapped her bedroll in cloth, packed what little she needed, and left.

~

The journey was long but undisturbed. At last, she stood once more before the cave's dark threshold. She half expected to see The Man From the Mountains, lurking as he often had, but no one waited.

Only the rain tapping her conical hat. Only the barbets calling in the trees.

She stepped closer, removed her hat, and peered into the mouth of stone.

It was black. Cold. Breathless.

She felt absurdly small. The impulse to run was strong.

"A sign," she whispered. "Give me a sign, and I'll go in."

But the silence gave nothing.

She sighed, unrolled her bedding, and retrieved the small lantern wrapped inside. Clearing a patch of stone, she placed it carefully and sat near the entrance. Damp wind tugged at her collar. She drew it tight.

"Even a little sign," she said softly.

The gnats arrived soon after. She rubbed her face with the resin of melaleuca leaves and waited.

The light changed. Colors fled. Shadows deepened across the trees. Red dissolved into grey, and grey gave way to night.

The cave seemed to breathe, drawing her in.

Fear rose. She fought it. The urge to flee pressed hard against her spine.

Even if I wanted to leave now... it's too late.

Her fingers curled into a scarf in her lap. She felt foolish, small, and unready.

Lying back, she stared up at the cave's ceiling. Jagged stone loomed ominously above.

She lit the lantern, fumbling clumsily, desperate for flame. When it finally caught, she turned the wick high. Let them see. She didn't care.

The shadows fled to the corners.

She lay down on the bedroll, staring into the flickering glow. But soon the shadows twisted too strangely, too much like faces, limbs, omens.

She turned the flame out. Let the dark return.

Curled in the silence, she closed her eyes.

And waited.

~ *The Two-Headed Snake Makes Another Appearance* ~

Huy Hoc looked down at her, grinning through the gauzy haze. He was young, radiant with health, his eyes bright and unashamed in their gaze—openly tracing her body, the way men once had when she was a girl. She rose from the stony ground, her heart lifting with her, and began to speak joyfully with him of the weather, the crops, her children, his father. Their words flowed with easy warmth, a current of shared memory and affection.

From the corner of her eye, she sensed a shadow moving, slow and deliberate, into the cave, expanding to fill the entrance. Huy Hoc fell silent and turned to face it, expressionless. Madame Dau turned as well, and the cave fell away, dissolving into emptiness. Only she and the figure remained.

The Man From the Mountains stood before her, sorrow in his eyes.

"You're alive!" she exclaimed, wonder rising in her throat.

He shook his head slowly, his face tightening with pain. He looked down. She followed his gaze.

The boots.

Those same scarred, disfigured boots. She could not look away.

She lit the lantern, lifted it, and stepped forward. Squatting before him, she held the light close and examined the object of his pain.

As before, the surface of the boots revealed a world of astonishing intricacy: a maze of wrinkles and channels etched across the leather, rivulets collecting in hollows, fields and huts and clustered villages emerging as if carved from memory. But this time, the liquid coursing through the boots was not rain.

It was blood.

Thick, dark, spreading in torrents. It surged across miniature rice fields, swallowed homes, drowned livestock, poured into the tunnel where her parents had disappeared. A vast flood moved over the terrain of his boot. At last she saw it: a punji stake driven through the heel.

Her voice broke. "Oh, my poor village. My people. Mama. Papa."

She rocked on her heels, overwhelmed. A strange warmth passed through the cave, a wind that pulsed through the cracks and hollows, whistling in high-pitched, otherworldly tones. The air shimmered. She closed her eyes against the glare. When she opened them, the Man From the Mountains was gone.

Only the boot remained.

From its hollowed top rose a radiant rainbow, arching high overhead, descending again to the stone floor.

"Beautiful," she whispered.

Suspended beneath the arc, a figure hovered weightlessly, face serene. Goddess.

She sat in lotus posture upon a vast white blossom. Her body shimmered with breath and pulse. Crowned and bare-chested, third eye aglow, Her face was calm, Her smile inscrutable. One hand upturned like a vessel, the other raised in sacred gesture, Her fingers poised in a gesture of stillness. The golden figurine, stolen long ago, had become flesh.

Madame Dau fell to the ground in reverence.

A luminous voice entered the cave, the words clear and resonant.

Their way is not the Way.

Goddess inclined Her head toward the edge of the cave.

It does not have to end in emptiness. Look.

Madame Dau turned.

The Man From the Mountains reappeared—but now as a young boy, naked, luminous. His heart and lungs moved visibly beneath transparent skin. He was smiling. Running in place. Two dogs played beside him, leaping and tumbling, their organs glowing in rhythm with his. In the distance, a mother watched.

Nor must it end in severance.

Another figure emerged. A Vietnamese boy. Also naked, his organs pulsing beneath dark translucent skin. He skipped stones across a still pond. His joy lit the air. In the distance, another mother watched.

It does not have to end their way.

The images vanished.

In their place, Madame Dau saw the Man From the Mountains once again impaled, writhing in agony. She saw Sergeant Dam pinned to the earth by a machete, his severed hand twitching at his side.

A flash of light shattered the cave.

When her vision returned, the rainbow still arched overhead—but now it landed not in the boot, but in the palm of the severed Vietnamese hand.

They are bound to death by the memory of what has passed, and bound to the future by what remains unfulfilled. The rainbow is not a dream. It is a covenant.

Do not look only through the dim prism of loss or the distorted prism of memory. Do not paint the past in borrowed beauty and call it sacred. Make rainbows now. Join what has been to what must come. In suffering, there is endurance. In destruction, renewal. In the grotesque, revelation. In pain, dignity—when it is borne.

Goddess turned Her gaze toward the fortress.

Their way is not the Way. Go home—to your family, and to the families of all things. Soon enough, they will be gone. The Superior Ones will have risen.

Madame Dau lifted her face from the stone.

"But, Great Mother," she asked, voice trembling, "my parents. Are they with You? Are they among the ancestors?"

They are home.

"May I—"

... Tap. Tap. Tap....

"May I—"

... TapTapTapTapTapTapTapTap....

Gunfire crackled in the distance. It was coming from the fortress.

Then silence.
She drifted back into sleep.

~

In her final dream, a two-headed snake coiled around her body—not menacing, but gentle, almost protective. Each head bore a familiar face: her mother. Her father.
They said nothing.
They smiled.

~

She slept deeply, wrapped in memory.
Safe. Free. Alive.

~ *Major Vy and Captain Tong Clash* ~

Commissar Minh's body had begun to stir, not with life, but with life's inheritors. Beneath the skin, a teeming multitude swelled and multiplied, thriving in the rich tissues that had once held together the illusion of self. Lividity dragged what remained of him down into the damp soil. No one had dared to move the corpse. No one wished to touch it.

While his body dissolved into the earth, the circumstances of his death continued to stir contention. Vy and Tong squatted a short distance from the sentries, hunched low, their voices taut with calculation.

"Yes, your plan has succeeded—so far," Tong said grudgingly. "But—"

"I will hear no reservations," Vy snapped. "The time has come, Tong. Either help, or be removed. There is no middle."

Tong flushed, his jaw tightening, but he said nothing. To regain footing, he shifted topics. "When Kim Lan leads them out, what precautions will be taken for Tuyet Mai?"

Vy's eyes narrowed. "And for Kim Lan?"

Tong shrugged.

"You are a poor Marxist, and a worse liability."

Tong smiled thinly. "Which makes me less dangerous to you."

Vy's expression did not change. "You saw Minh's body. I've already passed the threshold. I have nothing left to lose. Losing you would be no loss at all."

Tong laughed uneasily. "When the birds are gone, the bow is retired."

Vy understood. *He's afraid. Press him.*

"For once," Vy replied, voice low, deliberate, "you speak the truth."

But the words unsettled him. As the echo of his own menace faded, Vy felt shame pressing at the edges of his mind. He tried to justify himself. *It's gone too far. The wheel is already in motion.* Physical exhaustion and mental depletion had stripped away his doubts, and with them, his conscience. Perhaps this is how the truly corrupt survive: not through conviction, but collapse. *But I'm not corrupt. I'm a soldier. A father.* He touched the frayed rim of his pith helmet. *For my wife. For my children. Even if murder is required—*

He shivered. *No. Murder has already been committed. I cannot go back. The man I was is already gone.*

~

Tong stared at the mud. There was no longer any ambiguity. Vy would have to be eliminated. He had crossed into recklessness. Nothing would save them now unless Vy was quietly removed, permanently.

Kill him, deal with the drug lords, or run. Maybe even escape with Tuyet Mai.

A foolish dream, but a final one. Just one night with her. That would be enough.

Nearby, ants were locked in chaotic battle, struggling for control of a nest. Tong stared at them, then lifted his boot and crushed the frenzy beneath it.

"There's nothing more to be done," he said with sudden force. "We wait for Kim Lan. Then we'll see."

He turned and left, without waiting for Vy's reply.

~

She was old but seasoned, a warrior of many campaigns. Though smaller, her enemies outnumbered her, swarming from every angle. Her limbs struck with practiced speed, mandibles snapping in disciplined arcs. She had already killed ten, perhaps more. But exhaustion crept in. Blood loss. Punctures and cuts across her chitinous body. One attacker mounted her back. She flailed harder.

A familiar chemical signal swept through her body: reinforcements were near.

Bolstered, she surged forward.

For a moment, she was alone. She spun in widening circles, searching. The scent trails faded. Rain interfered with her orientation. Climbing the curved rim of a soaked leaf, she raised her head. Her antennae moved frantically. The battlefield had shifted. The sounds of combat, once so near, now echoed distantly.

Strange figures surrounded her. Transparent. Internal organs exposed, red networks pulsing through hollow limbs. Kin, yet unreachable. She sniffed—no scent. They did not exist.

She turned her back on them and scrambled downslope. The true pheromones returned, and the battle noise grew.

She raced forward, reaching the edge of the engagement just as darkness crashed down. Her limbs buckled. Mud filled her spiracles. She strained, but the weight was unyielding. Her body twitched once more, then stilled.

~

As Captain Tong disappeared into the trees, Vy pressed one nostril closed, leaned forward, and expelled mucus violently onto the ground.

"Damn Tong," he muttered. "Damn fool."

He called out. "Quy!"

No response.

"Quy!"

Still no answer.

Shoving through wet brush, he cursed aloud, then stopped. His uniform erupted in motion. Ants, disturbed from the canopy above, were crawling across his body.

He slapped at them furiously. "Damn ants," he growled. "Damn ants. Damn ants."

He stamped at the earth, wiping his hands across his chest.

But the ants clung on.

Chapter Two

PART ONE: REDEMPTION

Fever Dreams VIII

~ *Goddess Makes Her Rounds* ~

Storyteller leaned forward, blinking at the Goddess seated before him.

"I want to go home," he said.

You are home, She replied.

"No. I want to go home."

You are home.

He looked around. "I don't see my town. I don't see the YMCA, the movie theater, my neighbor's house. I don't see George Caplan and his wife dropping by Saturday night for drinks with my folks. I don't see this girl I like back in The World."

Diane.

"Yeah. Diane. I don't see her. I don't see my street, my room, my '64 Pontiac, my dog. I don't see the A&W stand, round-eyed girls, my parents smiling. I don't see my neatly trimmed lawn or my dad's mower. That's home. You understand? Home. The good ol' US of A. The World. Capish?"

Goddess smiled. A soft light shimmered on Her skin. When She spoke, Her voice was gentle, but something vast moved beneath it.

Do you see the air you breathe? The food as you digest it? The multitudes of My children in the water you drink? You speak of streets and houses. But do you see the trails here? The villages, people, snails? Ngo Tran Le and his wife Nguyen Thi Le—their quiet joys and sorrows? Have you seen their daughter? Her doll? The sky above her? The stars? Ants, gibbons, kingfishers? Do you see the earth, the rocks, the plants? Can you not see that you are already home? That you cannot live without them, and they without you? That there is nothing you can do—no spaceship, no aluminum can, no crucifix, no painting—that lies outside Nature? That the very impulse

to make is Nature itself? And that by asking the question, 'What is man's relationship to Nature,' you have already torn the fabric?

She smiled again, more warmly. **You are home. Were I to place you somewhere that is not home, you would cease to exist. Do you wish to see that place?**

He paused only briefly. "No."

The home of your children is the future, Chosen One.

~

A breeze passed, tasting of salt, then She was gone.

In Her absence, Storyteller saw them. The apparitions had returned, without ceremony or warning. He hadn't noticed them while She was present. Now they filled the space She had vacated.

They sat with their backs to him, hugging their knees, as if watching distant waves. They were solid now. As real as his own body.

Their clothes burst with color: wraps and swimsuits in reds, oranges, yellows, and blues. Bright patterns scattered across their backs in wild, disorienting contrast to the muted tones of the jungle.

He squinted, unsettled by the assault on his senses. The apparitions, though that word no longer fit, laughed and chatted gently, the sound of children playing faintly reaching his ears. He thought he heard gulls.

He scanned their figures, conducting a mental roll call:

Women and children.

Old people.

A mother holding a baby.

An elderly couple.

The abused woman.

The old Black woman.

Two young Vietnamese girls.

Two dogs.

His son, no longer at the computer, baseball cap turned backward.

Gradually, the laughter faded. The chatter died. They sat in stillness, gazing at something invisible in the distance.

Then, silently, they began to sink.

Into sand.

Where there had been bricks, now there was only sand. Slowly, steadily, they descended.

He tried to will them into something weightless, one-dimensional: paper, cards, with pictures instead of bulging bodies. Something he could gather, shuffle, and return to the safety of a pack. But they had become too real. Too formed. Too heavy. They sank completely, and with them, the sand. As through an hourglass.

In their place, the monsoon returned, rain sweeping across the brick courtyard in rhythmic waves. It lapped at his feet.

He closed his eyes.

And this time, he dreamed not of the past, but of the future. He dreamed of a schizophrenic. Of seizing control before the voices came. Before he listened. Before he killed them all.

~

Quang Long stood awkwardly, bent in reverence, mouth ajar. He blinked at the Goddess before him.

Are you married? She asked.

He hesitated. "No, Great Lady. But surely You already know."

Yes. And you are an artist.

"I try. But I cannot truly be called one."

But you must paint—like your heroes, Daumier and Goya.

He slumped. "No, Great Lady. I will never be like Daumier or Goya."

Why not?

"First, I lack the talent. Second, they will not allow me."

Who are 'they'?

"The Party. The government."

Did the French government allow Daumier?

"No, but he was brave. I'm afraid. I am not Cao Thanh Dam."

Ah. The Great Sapper.

"Yes."

Do you wish to see him?

"He is dead. He has joined the ancestors."

She turned Her head, motioning for him to look. Long felt weightless, as if suspended in water. He turned slowly, as though through a thick, resisting medium, and a groan escaped him.

~

Cao Thanh Dam appeared, translucent yet unmistakably there. Long could see his heart pulsing, lungs rising and falling. Webs of blood shimmered faintly under translucent flesh. Behind him stood others: blurred, breathless, Vietnamese and American. Dogs. A bird.

Dam smiled. "Clerk Long! Still so serious. So sorrowful. How did you wander into this place of shadows and strangers?"

Fear twisted in Long's chest, but the presence of the Goddess steadied him.

"Great Comrade Sapper Dam," he said quietly, "your death made us feel small. Fragile. Surely you rule among these others. Are you with your mother?"

Dam flinched. "I cannot find her. Only a few comrades. The rest are strangers."

A tall figure stepped forward, faintly draped in American fatigues.

"I should be no stranger to you," he said.

Dam studied him. "Yes. I know you. One of the men I killed in the fortress. But all accounts balance in time. For over there—"

He pointed toward the mist, where a kneeling silhouette hovered.

"—is the man who killed me."

"The Man From the Mountains," whispered Long.

"Yes," said the American. "He—"

"Long!" Dam interrupted. "Any word of my sister?"

"Comrade, so little time has passed. There's been no news."

Dam lowered his head. "I can't tell if it's been a day or a century. But I miss them. My yearning only grows."

The American turned to Long. "Will any of mine come? My parents. Do they know? I have to know how they're bearing it." He wept, shoulders trembling.

Long opened his mouth to answer, but a shadow dropped from the haze.

The Man From the Mountains stood behind the crying soldier. Gently, he placed a hand on his shoulder and pulled him close, holding him as one would a grieving spouse. Their forms merged—heart pressed to heart, pulsing in unison.

Dam looked on. "They murdered my mother. I murdered them. They murdered me."

He glanced around. "And others are here. Not yet born. Waiting for their time. But no matter how I try to warn them, they will not remember. The flames are ready. Still—to be alive! To run and leap and—"

Before he could finish, the Man From the Mountains approached, eyes fixed on him.

Dam lifted his arms, whether in welcome or defense, Long could not tell.

The figures faded.

In their place, far in the distance, countless forms rustled like cloth in a faint breeze. Their whispers hissed across a bone-white plain, stretching beyond a bleached horizon.

~

Han Tinh smoked furiously, the ember casting flickers across his face.

The Goddess stood before him in a sagging NLF uniform, reeking of fish.

He frowned. "Great Goddess, why appear like this? I'm no longer with the Front."

Yes. And for you, as with most men, scent matters less than sight. But I see no further need to please your eyes.

"When You were only a statue, I worshipped Your image."

Compassion doesn't flow from My breasts.

"I didn't mean . . . I mean, compassion from Your gaze. Milk for the body. Mercy for the soul."

Tomorrow, there will be an ending.

Tinh's eyes widened. He waited. *She* said nothing. He coughed, shifted, unable to bear Her silence. "What should I do?"

What you cannot help but do.

"Why do gods always speak in riddles? I'm too simple to understand."

Fate starves at Probability's door. Or perhaps the other way around.

He sniffed. "Still unclear. If I'm going to do it anyway, why tell me?"

So that you will have been told.

"Maybe your words are profound. But my mind isn't built for them."

Yes. The Great Riddle. I am hungry.

He turned to fetch a bowl of dried shrimp. "I didn't know You could be hungry. Please, wait—"

When he turned back, *She* was gone.

He nodded to himself. "Hmm. Hmm."

The knock came moments later.

"Brother Tinh! Hurry! Madame Trinh is dead! Her son, Little Monkey, is dying! Herbalist Tien says bring a chant!"

~ *Goddess Comforts A Dying Boy* ~

A damp pall pressed against the rafters of Madame Trinh's house. The air was swollen with incense and the sour breath of death. Security Chief Tien, herbalist by necessity, knelt beside the corpse, placing dried leaves over the nostrils and mouth. In the corner, Trinh's teenage daughter rocked on her heels, betel-stained lips open in mourning, her cries weaving the old rhythms of lament.

Madame Nguyen stood beside her, holding out a cold cup of tea no one would take. The mourners moved aimlessly, joss sticks clasped between prayerful palms. Smoke curled around their faces. Their eyes shimmered with grief—and calculation.

Han Tinh entered. The murmur rose at once: "Where is Madame Dau?"

He shrugged. He would not say she was sleeping in the cave. Would not feed the gathering belief that she had gone mad. Would not tie his name to hers.

Tien stepped forward, her face lined with contempt and fatigue.

"The boy," she said. "In the other room. Chant. The fever won't break. Soon the grass will grow above his little head."

"I thought you were leaving."

"Bah. Fool. You're no monk either. Go."

Tinh stepped into the room where women stood in silence around the child. He forced his way forward and gasped. Tran Van Trinh lay twisted in a posture too cruel for the living. Heat radiated from his small body. His voice, thin and broken, called again and again for his mother.

Then came the scream.

His back arched, and a raw cry tore through the room. It stilled everyone.

"Mama! Mama!"

No one answered.

Tinh began to chant the Heart Sutra. His voice was low, steady, fragile.

A thin woman approached, one of Trinh's sisters. Bowing toward the boy, she whispered: "Brother Tinh. Will your chant give merit to my sister in the realm beyond?"

"It will. Master Le taught me. It benefits all sentient beings."

"But make it hers. Only hers. Not for strangers. Not even the boy. I'll pay you more."

"The child suffers."

"He is not yet gone."

"A stone is not moved at the Reclining Buddha Monastery. Monks bend their path around it. If a stone is honored, why not this boy?"

The woman's eyes narrowed. "That may be true. But my sister was fierce. If her merit is divided, she may rise in anger. I offer twenty piasters. Chant for her. And for the boy."

"Done." He took the notes without shame.

He resumed the chant, trying to keep his mind on mercy, not the petty noise of the living.

Then he heard it: a shift in the outer room. A ripple in the air.

He turned, and fell still.

Goddess entered.

She wore a sagging Front uniform. A quiet glow moved across Her skin. Other than Han Tinh, none knew who She was, yet all felt the pressure of Her presence.

She crossed to the boy and leaned near.

When you are ready, Little Monkey, take a breath and release the body. Though broken in flesh, Tran Van Trinh will rise like a kingfisher. You will arc through the great canopy—leaping, gliding, unbound. The wind of eternity will carry you. You will breathe the air of joy. There will be no more fear. No more wounds. No more sorrow. The ancestors are waiting by the water's edge. They will laugh and raise their arms when you pass. When you are ready, little kingfisher, fly.

The boy frowned. "No, auntie. Mama will be sad."

She blinked.

She waits beyond the veil.

"But she's here. I can't go without her. She'll cry."

She waits, child. You must go to her.

Tinh wept. He saw understanding dawn across the boy's face. Saw him try to lift his arms, to rise. But the pain held him down.

He fell back. Silent. Breath shallow. Tears gone.

"Can't You stop this?" Tinh asked.

Fate starves at the threshold of Chance. I cannot.

"Then why? What's the point?"

There is no point. The Universe is the mind of an Idiot.

"No destination?"

Only the passage. Universes bloom and collapse, for the delight of an Idiot Child.

"Are You the Child?"

No. I am the Caregiver. The One who tends the bleeding. The Mater of All That Moves.

"But this boy . . . he speaks, he dreams, he loves, he is no insect—"

And still, he can make Me into a Savior. A Redeemer. But all must pass: the ant, the monkey, the kingfisher, the boy. Even the stars. As for your kind—we will replace them gently. As I have done with this child.

Her words fell quiet in the shadow of the boy's suffering.

Without a sound, Tinh turned. He stooped to the dirt and plucked an ant between his fingers. He crushed it.

When he looked up, She was watching him exactly as he had watched the ant.

~

Hours passed.

At last, Tran Van Trinh, Little Monkey, rose into the great canopy.

He left behind his broken vessel, and those who trembled in its shadow.

Goddess was gone.

No one saw Her leave.

~ *Storyteller's Poem* ~

Nature sat disconsolate beside Stretch and Superman. Sleep would not come. Thoughts of tomorrow's breakout gnawed at them in silence. A few feet away, Storyteller lay curled in fever. X hovered over him, gently attentive, ignoring the other three. They had slipped into speculation about what each might carry if they made it out.

Then Superman broke the quiet. "You think Martha's legit? She leading us out of this shit, or setting us up?"

"That bitch?" said Stretch. "Ambush. Guaranteed."

Stretch opened his mouth to launch into one of his movie riffs, but at the first mention of Burt Lancaster, Superman cut him off.

"Shut up. No more of your goddamn movies."

Stretch closed his mouth, jaw tightening. "I wish this *was* a movie," he muttered after a beat. "Then I'd have a shot. But guys like us, we're the extras. One woman shows up, and if you ain't the hero, you're dead weight."

"Not interested," said Superman.

"Women didn't put us here," Nature said.

"Bullshit," Stretch snapped. "Word is Kim Lan, excuse me, *Martha,* works NVA intel. She'd cut your balls off just to keep count."

Superman didn't bite. "If you're right. . . ."

"No," Nature said again. "Not women like her. I'm talking about civilians. The ones in the villages."

"Supporting actresses," muttered Stretch. "They're screwed too."

"So?" asked Superman.

"So think about it," Nature said. "Without them, what's left of this place? Just men blowing holes in each other. No future. Just death."

Stretch spat into the dirt. "Don't be naive. These gook women know how to kill, too."

"I know. But I mean the others. The ones hauling water. Feeding kids. Keeping their old people alive. You see them. You know what I mean."

Superman shrugged. "So?"

Nature looked down. "I saw Kim Lan's body."

Stretch leaned forward, forcing a grin. "Now *that's* interesting. Go on, Nature."

"It wasn't like that," said Nature. "I saw her breasts and thought—milk. Babies. Warmth. It hit me strange. I missed my mom. My sister. Missed being around women. Not the sex. Just . . . women."

He swallowed.

"I realized I might never see another one again. Not a white woman. Not anyone I love. Anyone who loves me."

He looked at his hands.

"Back in The World, I used to think they talked about nothing: kids, food, feelings, stupid stuff. Who was sick. Who broke up with who. But now I get it. That *was* the world. That's what matters."

Superman frowned. "What are you even saying?"

"There ain't nothin' like a dame," muttered Stretch, voice low and tuneless.

Nature didn't pause. "I saw her standing there, no uniform, no enemy mask, and she looked so . . . female. Not weak. Not dangerous. Just real. Beautiful."

Superman shook his head. "You're gone, man. I just want to see my wife again. My daughters. The rest . . . God will sort."

Nature's voice drifted. "I even started a poem. But Birdman interrupted it."

Then, unexpectedly, Storyteller's voice floated across the wet air, calm and lucid.

"Nature. Hey, Nature. I've got a poem for you. About women. About us. Want to hear it?"

They turned. Storyteller was sitting upright, strangely serene.

"He's hallucinating again," X muttered.

"You want to hear it?" Storyteller repeated, patiently. The way a child might ask the same question until the world surrendered.

"No. Get some sleep, Storyteller," said Stretch and Superman at once. They didn't want poetry. Not tonight.

But Nature answered. "Yeah. I want to hear it."

Storyteller nodded. Silence fell. Then his words, gentle and precise, filled the night:

> *You soldiers*
> *in the fortress of sand:*
> *florid sergeants, nervous privates,*
> *harried medics, weary gunners.*
> *You women*
> *in the village of reeds:*
> *lithe mothers, sagging aunts,*
> *wriggling babies, old venerables.*
> *And the rest:*
> *sappers, wet nurses, teachers, farmers,*
> *captains, majors, lieutenants and teens.*

It has been revealed that
all of you
are nothing more
than shadows behind the curtain.
Mere movement of vines
in a jungle breeze. . . .
Dreams beget dreams
where up is down
and more is less,
and less is less,
until less is enough
to finally still the screams,
stilling the stillness
folded within the seams.
Silence. Stillness. But not for long.
Never for long.

"I don't get it," said Superman.

"There's more," Storyteller murmured, leaning back. "But I can't say the rest yet."

Stretch waited a moment, then sat up straighter, defiant. "I've got one for you all. Might not be fancy, but it's real."

He began in a singsong voice, eyes a little too wide:

There was a young harlot from Kew,
Who filled her vagina with glue.
She said with a grin,
'If they pay to get in—
They'll pay to get out of it too.'"

Laughter followed. It came sharp and hollow. Too loud. The kind that tries to push back the dark.

Stretch leaned back, arms crossed behind his head. "Anyway . . . hero always dies last. That's how it works."

No one answered.

~ *X Contemplates Amputating Idaho's Leg* ~

X did not laugh. He was too busy tending Storyteller, who had slipped again into a stream of fevered whispers, something about ghosts, apparitions.

When it became clear there was nothing more he could do, X rose quietly and made his way over to Idaho. He peeled back the filthy bandages, and the stench hit him full force. The smell of rot.

Gangrene.

He had known for days. And now there was no time left.

Either I take the leg, or he dies.

But the thought set off a storm inside him: tight panic, cold hands, doubt rising like bile.

I don't have the right instruments. I'll kill him. How am I supposed to do this in here? It's fuckin' insane. The NVA can take care of him. They'll fix him up. If I had the right instruments. . . .

He grasped at those thoughts like driftwood, but another voice crept in. It sneered. It was old, cutting, self-lacerating, unrelenting: *You do have the instruments, nigger. A white medic would've done it already. Civil War docs didn't wait for clean scalpels—they used saws, drills, knives. They cut because they had to. But me? Hell no. Black-ass medic can't do that. Might kill a white man. Then they'd say it. Think it. Whisper it: "Stupid nigger killed a white soldier."*

X swallowed.

Then Idaho stirred. "What's it looking like, X?"

X jumped slightly. "Hey, man, I thought you were out."

"What's it look like? I mean, it feels better. Can't feel it no more, actually. So what's it look like?"

"Well. . . . "

"Come on, man. Be straight with me. My leg ain't gonna end up like Mountain Man's foot, is it?" He tried to laugh, weakly.

"No way. Just a little infection."

Idaho sighed. "Man . . . when you leave Storyteller and me for the gooks, you're really leaving a pair of winners. Gimpy grunt and crazy grunt. You better get back here fast. Get us the hell out."

"Yeah."

"Hey, what was that gook medic like?"

"I called him Dopey. Looked weird, acted weirder. But I'll be damned, some of his mud and roots made me feel better. Still, glad I'm back with you. Least I know you'll do it right. No jungle mud slapped on me this time."

"Yeah."

X stayed beside him until he drifted off. Then he rose, slowly, wearily, and walked back to Storyteller, who now seemed asleep too.

He clenched his jaw. Mountain Man's voice echoed in his skull.

"You can amputate that leg, boy. You hear me? You can do it. Otherwise . . . them Marines ain't Jesus, and Idaho ain't Lazarus."

How'd that son of a bitch know? What the hell am I supposed to do?

Then another voice, softer, yet deeper, yet older:

"You do what I know you can, boy. "

He turned.

And there she was.

His grandmother. Sitting in her old rocker, just as she had in Beulah Land, calm as ever, close enough to touch.

Behind her: others. Men and women, girls and boys, babies—faces he knew, and faces he didn't.

"Grandmama? What are you doing here?"

"I'm with you, boy. All the way. Don't let that white boy die."

He shook his head. "You're not real. Oh man. This can't be real."

"Reach out and touch me, boy."

"I can't."

She smiled. "Can."

He hesitated, then whispered, "Can't."

Her laugh was low and warm. "Can."

Something flickered in him. He reached forward and poked her outstretched arm.

Warm. Solid. Real.

"Grandmama!" He collapsed into her, and she wrapped him tight in her arms.

"I'm real, boy. And like I told you, I recollect your daddy bein' offered a promotion. First colored man they ever asked to take it. Made some folks mad. Real mad. Not their fault. He was the one they wanted. The only one. And you know what he felt?"

X shook his head. "No. What?"

"Scared. Scared he wouldn't be good enough. Scared he'd mess it up. The *what ifs* nearly ate him alive. What if he failed? What if they were right? World's full of *what ifs*, boy. I had mine too. What if my boy didn't come home? What if my grandson dies in this war? But your daddy did it. And you can too."

"I got a choice, Grandmama. You don't understand."

"I *do* understand. Since you were little, your choices were never like the other boys'. You cared. You always cared. Just like your daddy. That's why they wanted him. Real men with real families—they were proud of him. Not the loud ones. The true ones. And when it's done, come home to Beulah Land, child."

He looked up and saw the others gathering. The crowd around her was thickening—faces luminous, listening.

Fear crept back.

He pulled away from her embrace and crouched down next to Storyteller.

"Grandmama," he whispered, "I don't think I can do it. I don't have what I need. Might kill him. It's better to—"

A white woman approached silently, naked, her hand resting on his grandmother's back. She rubbed in slow circles, comforting. At her feet, a hunting dog sniffed and nosed the air.

Panic surged.

He shook Storyteller violently. "Hey, man! Storyteller! I think I see your ghosts, man! I *really* see them!"

Storyteller stirred. "Wha . . . what? What do you want?"

"They're here! I *see* them! Right in front of us. It's my grandmama, man. She's talking to me! Don't fuck with me, Storyteller, can't you see her? Can't you hear them?"

Storyteller blinked. His eyes searched the darkness.

"I don't see them, X. I can't hear anything." His voice quivered. "Oh God. It's time."

"What? What do you mean, *it's time?*"

His grandmother leaned close again. "Come with me, boy. He can't see. He can't hear. Don't worry about him now. Come with me."

Storyteller gripped his rucksack, shaking. "Where are they? Oh God . . . God!"

... *Tap Tap Tap Tap Tap Tap Tap Tap Tap Tap*....

Chapter Three

The Final Battle Looms

Carins and the Figurine

Cairns sat in the early morning dark, his face lit by a flickering glow radiating from the figurine. He had just relieved Topper and now sat alone, back to the trapdoor, eyes fixed on the golden statue. Around the edges of its trembling light, stone saints lay in ruin, toppled and weather-worn, glaring at him from slanted repose.

... Tap. Tap. Tap....

The sound came from the statue's belly. Deep-pitched. Urgent. Faster than before.

... Tap. Tap. Tap....

The figurine stared back, unmoved and motionless.

... Tap. Tap. Tap....

He knew better than to touch it when it made that sound.

"Who are You? What are You?" he whispered. "Speak to me, Madame. I'm the one You should be appearing to. I think what the others are too afraid to imagine. They only speak. I *think*. And You, You are the Unspeakable in a divine way, and I am the Unspeakable in a lewd way. We're a match. Yin and yang. Heaven and earth.

"Connect with me. You know what I'm thinking now? I see You on Your back, legs open, glowing with Your own sacred lust. Can You see that? Will You bend that golden body, spread those golden legs, and show me the deep well of Your divine desire? Or are You, like most women, fixated only on compassion, never passion?" He smiled. "Still, it's women like You I most want to take."

He paused, listening. Tilted his head.

The tapping grew louder. Faster.

... TapTapTap....

"Ah! You're excited, aren't You? Surprised? I'm compassionate too, in my way. Is that why You show Yourself only to Storyteller? He's not the only one, you know. I have more compassion than he and Nature combined. Twice as much. I just never had to bring out the big guns."

... Tap Tap Tap....

"The rest of them want him dead. Say he's worthless. Tell him to finish himself off. But not me. I want him alive. I don't want him to press down on the accelerator. I want—"

A shadow passed before him. A surge of energy exploded behind his eyes. Blinded, he threw himself to the ground, arms crossed over his skull.

When he dared open his eyes, She was there. Goddess. Flesh and blood. Breathing hard, Her face contorted with pain. She clutched Her stomach, leaned forward, opened Her mouth—

Something liquid and thick flew from Her and struck him.

"Noooo!" he cried, curling tighter, expecting filth and stench. He unwrapped his arms and looked at them. Was it rain? No. Only sweat. His skin glistened, but it was clean. He exhaled. Thank God. Just sweat.

He crawled toward Her on hands and knees, half-blind. He stared down at Her feet, bare, glowing faintly, smooth and feminine. Yet they looked indestructible. Strong. Ageless. Perfect.

As he watched, something shifted on Her skin. The rest of the world blurred. Only the feet remained. Smooth. Radiant. And now—a subtle motion. Patterns. Life.

He leaned closer, forehead nearly touching Her. Time stilled. The miniature world came into focus. Swirling without purpose—until something coalesced at the center.

~

A boy awoke at 2:06 a.m.

Darkness closed in. Silence, tightening.

"Mommy," he whispered.

Nothing.

"Mommy," louder. Still nothing.

"Mommy!" The silence thickened into panic.

He slipped from his bed, tiptoed through his toys, and crept down the stairs. His mother's door stood ajar. He leaned in.

In the dim room, he saw her silhouette. She was awake and upright in bed. A strange man twisted her body, repeating in a breathless voice, "I should go. What if he comes home? I should go."

But he didn't stop. "God, I love your Asian nipples. So dark. So long. But I should leave."

The boy's mother murmured back, husky. "No. He's gone till seven. Matt's dead to the world upstairs. Stay. More. More, baby."

The boy said nothing aloud. But his mind screamed.

Tell him to go, Mommy! Tell him to leave! I don't want him here. Make him go!

"I should leave."
"No."
"I should leave."
"No."
"What if Matt comes down?"
"Right now, I don't care about Matt. Just stay."
Back and forth. Again and again.
I should leave. Stay. Go. No. Stay. Go. I don't care about Matt. Yes. No. Yes. No.
Then—
Something cold pressed against the boy's cheek. A gun barrel.
Papa.
Shhhh.
The pistol hovered in the air, radiating silence. Cold silence.
"Papa! I should go! Stay! Papa! Dad! DAD! Go! Oh my God. No! No! NO—"
Gunshots. Five, maybe six.
The boy ran past the echo of death, through the wetness on the floor, and began pounding on his mother's body. Fists balled in rage, striking her chest.
Why didn't you make him go? Why didn't you make him go?!
Her eyes stared blankly. Her nipples drifted like buoys atop the blood. He shut his eyes, tight, and kept hitting.
But his fists were no longer small. His arms were strong. Grown.
He opened his eyes—he was a man. And he was hitting Goddess. Full force.
She stared down at him, unflinching, with something like pity.
Fog passed across Her face. And when it cleared, it was his mother's.
She cooed softly. Pulled him close. Held him.
His anger, his terror, melted. Dissolved.
"I love you. I love you," she said.
"Mommy. MAKE HIM GO AWAY!"
"He's gone. I'm here. I'm here."
"Mommy."
I will make him go away.

~

"What's going on here?" Pappy burst into the church, flashlight casting a red-filtered beam. Cairns crouched in the glow, arms wrapped over his head, peeking out from beneath his elbow.

"I . . . I don't know . . . I just. . . ."

T followed. "What the hell is this? You trying to wake up every NVA soldier in the province?"

Cairns looked up, held out his hands, trembling as if just pulled from ice water. "But I—" He caught sight of a figure moving in the dark.

Pappy glanced at the figurine. "It's okay, captain. I've had my own run-in with that Lady. A week ago, I'd've said you were nuts. Now. . . ." He shook his head. "We heard you saying 'papa' over and over. You alright?"

T snorted. "All of you are losing it. Look at it. Just a statue. Gold. Metal. Nothing more."

He turned to the door. "Good thing we're leaving soon. Any longer and—"

"And what?" Cairns snapped.

T looked back. "And the NVA will be on top of us. That's what."

He opened the door. The rain had strengthened.

"Good," he muttered.

~ *Tong Awaits at the Ambush Site* ~

Thunder tore through the canopy. The rain thickened, drumming the foliage in a relentless cascade, silencing all but the loudest human voices. To be heard now, men had to shout.

Lieutenant Tran arrived at Captain Tong's temporary command post, a platform of knotted mangrove roots on the edge of the swamp. He had just completed his final inspection.

"Our ambush positions are secure, Captain," Tran reported. "But the men are uneasy. They've started calling this place the 'forest of demons.'"

Tong gave a thin smile. "Superstition. This ambush will be as clean as splitting bamboo. The Americans will be dead by morning. Then we move on."

"True. But the troops have been unsettled for days. The siege, so strange. The weather. And Comrade Dam's death—"

"Yes, I know." Tong interrupted sharply. "But for the glorious cause of our southern brethren, even should we die or be wounded? Wouldn't you rather be broken jade than a whole tile?"

Tran hesitated. "Yesss . . . if I understand your meaning, Comrade Captain. Our cause is just. Still, it is strange."

"No more of this talk." Tong's voice hardened. "This ambush will succeed. You reminded them to wait for Comrade Kim Lan's signal?"

"Yes, sir." Tran saluted and disappeared into the swamp.

Tong exhaled, letting his mind drift. In his thoughts, he imagined a manuscript fluttering at his feet, tattered, water-stained, and written in French. A play. The title: *Vo Thanh Tong Awakens.*

He bent to read.

~

KIM LAN:
You speak with conviction, Tong. If I didn't know better, I'd think you were truly a revolutionary officer. But I know what awaits you. The drugs.

TONG:
Not the drugs. The money. Why are you here? Return to the Americans. Send Tuyet Mai instead.

KIM LAN:
Does the Revolution mean so little to you?

TONG:
You're one to ask. You betray Uncle Ho with every step. Don't pretend otherwise. You want the money too—do you not, Comrade?

KIM LAN:
You might be surprised. I might be a double agent. Or a triple agent. Let me ask you something: what matters more—money or the lives of two little girls?

TONG:
Girls?

KIM LAN:
Yes.

TONG:
Your girls?

KIM LAN:
Yes.

TONG:
Then money. For me, it's money. And for you?

KIM LAN:
A country where my daughters don't grow up to sell themselves to French colonials or American occupiers.

TONG:
Better to serve Hanoi?

KIM LAN:
If a seed is planted in their wombs, at least it will be Vietnamese. Not the spawn of a foreign demon.

TONG:
Even if the demon belongs to the Party? A demon is a demon. Would you prefer I plant my seed in Tuyet Mai rather than the American captain?

KIM LAN:
No. If she didn't kill you, I would. But even if your seed took root in her, it would be Vietnamese. Not monstrous.

TONG:
The Americans are rich.

KIM LAN:
And that's why you want this deal to succeed? So you can live like them?

TONG:
I've seen how they live. The movies show it.

KIM LAN:
Then your soul is already polluted.

TONG:
Maybe. But if I were rich, I could afford to care about pollution. Right now, I can't afford anything but survival.

KIM LAN:
And that is why the world will die, choking on American pollution.

TONG:

You admit then: the world's end is in the future. Here, in our country, we've already died. Either we sit stupidly in the past, or we die stupidly fighting the future.

KIM LAN:

Look at our comrades. They wait in the dark, waist-deep in mud. They believe. They'll fight Americans with sticks if they must. They believe, Tong. That's life. That's revolution. Not the wealth. Not the lies. And yes, the Americans lie to their boys. But so do you. And for the same reason—greed.

TONG:

Nonsense. Our leaders lie to us too.

KIM LAN:

Yes—but not for themselves. Not always. You lie for yourself. For Tong's money. Tong's power.

TONG:

You're not with the drug bosses, are you?

KIM LAN:

No.

TONG:

And Tuyet Mai?

KIM LAN:

No.

TONG:

Hanoi?

KIM LAN:

Yes.

TONG:

Then I'm already dead.

KIM LAN:

Yes. But you still have a chance in the morning.

TONG:

A chance? What chance?

KIM LAN:

A chance to die like broken jade, instead of living like a whole tile.

TONG:

I've known it for a while. The truth is, I wanted Tuyet Mai for my wife. Since the first day. I loved her. And since then, I've been weak. Money, power, revolution—they mean little. Just her.

KIM LAN:

She will never be your wife.

TONG:

Then tell me, Comrade Kim Lan, what matters more to you? The revolution? Or two little girls?

KIM LAN:
The revolution.
TONG:
No. You don't believe that. You say it, but you don't believe it.
KIM LAN:
I will believe in your execution. *Traitor. Traitor.*

~

"Sir?"
Tong blinked. A young runner stood in front of him, dripping wet.
"What is it?"
"Lieutenant Tran reports movement inside the fortress."
Tong waved him off. "Tell him all support teams are to remain alert."
The runner disappeared.
Tong stood still for a moment longer, rain now pouring. The jungle was breathing heavily. He thought of Kim Lan's words. Of Tuyet Mai. Of his daughters. Of the dream.
If they are intelligence agents. . . .
He shook his head.
And closed his eyes.

~ *The Grunts Prepare to Break Out* ~

Storyteller drifted up from fever, fragments of cognition gathering like scattered ash in his head. His eyes stung. Sweat soaked his hairline. He blinked slowly, each flicker like clearing grit from his vision. Sounds filtered in, too sharp for fever, too present for hallucination. The real world, intrusive and unwelcome, pressed close. He wanted to shove it away. But then a familiar voice slipped through the courtyard.
Pappy's low drawl cut through the dark, dragging him back.
He struggled to sit, back pressed against the wall. His eyes scanned for the voice, but nothing was visible in the storm-wracked gloom.
CRACK!
Thunder split the sky. A jagged bolt lit the fortress in skeletal silhouette. Rain poured in torrents. He heard the voices through the downpour.
"Rise and shine, Stretch. Come on, boy. Another day, another piaster for your basketball scholarship. Get up. You ain't in Indiana anymore. Time to click those ruby slippers and head back to Kansas."
A pause. Then:
"Hey, Pappy," came Stretch's voice, groggy, "did you know 'man' spelled backward is 'nam'?"
"Sssshiiiiit."

~

Stretch was relieved when Pappy moved on. The banter was his shield, his rhythm—but now it wore thin. He longed for a silence deep enough to hold memory. Thoughts of home came unbidden—sunlight, dirt, grass, his mother's voice—uncomplicated and pure. He wanted to sit with them undisturbed. But silence never lasted. Superman sat too close.

~

Nearby, Superman pulled on his boots, talking to steady himself.

"So who is it today, Stretch? Groucho? Bob Hope? Abbott and Costello? 'Who's on first?' That kind of thing?"

Stretch didn't look up. "None of them. Today's Ronald Colman."

"Who?"

"You've heard of him. You just don't know it."

Superman chuckled. Probably another B-list comic. Stretch slung his ruck over his shoulder, adjusted the green towel beneath the straps, then stood. He spoke quietly, without a single stammer or tic.

"Ronald Colman, Dickens, you know? Far, far better thing—"

"Huh?"

"Christ, you ain't been to many movies. He said, 'It is a far, far better thing that I do, than I have ever done. It is a far, far better rest that I go to, than I have ever known.'"

Superman began to reply, but Stretch raised his hand.

"And, old friend, if everything you've told me is true, then it is a far, far better place I'm going to than I've ever been."

Superman hesitated. "Stretch, if this is a trap, I'm never going to see my wife again. My daughters. I don't want that, man. I really don't."

Stretch squeezed his hand. "If it hits the fan, remember your tab. You're the believer, not me."

"Apocalypse, Stretch. The Anti-Christ comes, and only the believers rise in Rapture."

Ah, the Anti-Christ, My Lord. Do You know his identity?

Yes, Beloved Goddess. His sign is 666. Six protons, six neutrons, six electrons. That, My Dear, is the real Anti-Christ.

Yes, yes, Lithium Lord. Hidden in the open, a rare element roaming inside a sea of hydrogen. Wild card in the deck of First Principles.

~

Pappy crouched beside X, who was packing in silence.

"Can we carry Idaho and Storyteller down by hand?" he asked.

X shook his head. "Not Idaho. We'll need a skid. Let me tell you about that leg. The infection's spread. He's gone necrotic. The original wound cut through muscle and artery—now the tissue's dead. The whole leg's swollen, discolored. Under the skin, gas-producing bacteria are multiplying like wildfire. When I peel back the bandage, it smells like rot. There's a foul, blood-tinged discharge."

"I'm fuckin' impressed. What's that mean in real words?"

"It means he's going to die unless someone cuts the leg off. Best we can hope for is that the NVA finds him and does it. Soon."

"Why not you?"

"I've got no instruments. No clamps. No blades. I'm out of morphine. All I can do is keep him numb until I can't anymore."

"We'll rig a saw. Use a machete if we have to. But don't let him die."

"Ain't gonna happen, Pappy."

"How long you known?"

X didn't answer.

"You've been a good medic. But what made your black-ass carcass turn coward?"

"Back off, Pappy. Pretty soon my black-ass carcass ain't gonna be the only one lying around. Fuck this piss-ant white man's war!"

He flung his rucksack to the ground, splashing the courtyard puddle between the cracked bricks.

Pappy jumped back, then kicked it. "Your rage won't save Idaho. And it won't clean your conscience."

X's voice dropped. "Ain't gonna happen."

~

CRACK!

Lightning lit the courtyard. An ant scout, isolated on the tiles, zig-zagged in wild urgency. Her assignment had been to find aphids for domestication, but war had scattered the colony. The queen had moved. Time was short. Rain threatened to wash the pheromone trails clean.

She had just emerged from a tunnel beneath the fortress and was racing back to summon her sisters—home had been found.

Then a shadow fell. Black. Immense. Final.

She was pinned.

Antennae flailed. Mandibles clicked. Her mind screamed a single directive: MUST GET BACK. MUST GET BACK. MUST GET BACK.

She had once followed the Queen through tangled roots and blistering light, a migration born of crisis. That journey nearly broke her. But now, alone on fractured stone, she was the first—carving a new path back to safety, to Her.

Then the shadow fell. Black. Immense. Final.

She thrashed, limbs skittering, antennae slicing the air, desperate to leave her signal, one final molecule of direction. One final chance for the swarm. For the Queen.

But the weight did not lift. Her pulse slowed. Her mind dimmed.

Far above, thunder rolled. A tigress growled. And somewhere in the rain-thick jungle, another queen listened.

~

Above, Nature crouched on the parapet, peering through the curtain of rain. He could hear X and Pappy, but the words were lost in the storm. A flash of lightning showed X slumped, staring at his pack. Pappy was gone.

A wave of emotion swelled in Nature's chest: fierce and helpless love for the grunts.

He had long accepted his own death. The ghosts had shown him. All through his shift, he thought of home. It no longer mattered that his father had been a cruel drunk, or that his girlfriend stopped writing. None of it mattered now.

Only one thing remained: a strange, exquisite surrender.

He scoffed inwardly at the world's delusions: money, power, hate, relationships, aging, loneliness, fear. But he loved them anyway. Even the fools who drowned in that shallow sea. Even the NVA soldiers who aimed for his throat.

Still, something broke the silence inside him.

They were about to leave Idaho and Storyteller behind.

Guilt clawed at him. He wanted to stay. Wanted to defy T and carry them both out. But there's always a chance—

He couldn't finish the thought. His compassion, he realized, was not pure. His love was not unconditional.

~

Cairns stood on the altar stone, balancing his empty ruck with one hand while sifting through gear with his boot. He had decided to take the figurine with him, but it was heavy. Still, he would not leave it behind.

He picked it up. It was cool. Passive. Inert.

Too heavy.

Still, he would carry it. Even if it killed him.

T had told him to leave it. But Cairns would sooner leave his own leg. He was even relieved it allowed his touch.

"So, you want to come with us," he muttered, lowering it into the pack.

CRACK!

Lightning filled the church. Her eyes stared up at him from the pouch as he cinched the flap.

He tried to shoulder the burden, but the weight pulled him backward. He staggered, caught himself. Bent forward. Strained. At last, he locked it onto his back.

"Shit," he muttered. He hadn't taken a step, and he was already exhausted.

A shuffling noise. He turned.

T stood nearby with a red-filtered flashlight. "Couldn't talk you out of it, Captain?"

"Nope."

"Well, maybe it'll stop a few bullets."

"Are we ready?"

"Not quite. Pappy's building a skid for Idaho. You saddled up too early—especially with that albatross."

"You want to help me get it off?"

"No thanks. Might as well get used to it. What brings you in here?"

T grinned. "Her." He aimed the light at Kim Lan. "Nature's on point. She's your backup. Rope-tied, of course."

"Of course."

"We've assigned the other one to the rear. Berti's dragging her."

"Fine." Cairns took the rope. Tugged the end.

~

Kim Lan felt the rope pull tight around her neck. She glanced toward the captain and saw only a dark silhouette, unreadable. Her thoughts hovered briefly on the figurine, but always returned to Tuyet Mai. She wished they could walk together.

Again the rope tugged. A slow panic stirred in her gut.

She remembered the plastic explosives. Still tucked inside her. *Got to get them out before we start.*

"Will you allow me to relieve myself?" she asked.

"No," came the reply. "If you need to piss, do it here."

A wave of nausea rose. She imagined the explosive bundle inside her, silent, waiting.

Biding its time.

~ *Storyteller and Idaho Descend into the Tunnel* ~

Preparations were underway to move Storyteller and Idaho into the tunnel.

While Idaho was being strapped to a makeshift skid, a rotting church door reinforced with rope, Nature and Birdman helped ease Storyteller inside and lowered him gently onto a flat stone near the tunnel entrance. His muscles ached. He clutched Nature's hand and held it for a long moment.

"You gonna be okay until I get back?" Nature asked.

"It's going to be pitch black down there. Black and silent. I'm not claustrophobic, not really, but—damn! How do you breathe in a place like that?"

They both watched Idaho pass, tied to the skid, his head swinging limply like a severed blossom.

"He's out cold, Nature. He doesn't even know where he is. He's already gone, just hasn't had the lid nailed shut. But me, I'm gonna be down there *waiting* for him to die. Waiting. And what if you guys don't come back?"

"I'll come back," Nature said. "You won't be down here long. I promise. We all make it. You think Superman's gonna let anything stop him from seeing his girls again? Not a chance."

"Yeah."

"Besides, your ghosts won't let anything happen to you. You and I both know it. You're the only one here without a tab. Even the chopper crew has tabs now."

"Bullshit. It's just that I can't stick with a single image. It keeps changing."

"No, man. You don't have a tab because you don't need one. That's why it keeps shifting."

He paused.

"Tunnel's going to be rough. But what's coming out there—"

"Don't start feeling sorry for yourselves," Storyteller snapped. "All the sympathy belongs to *me*, brother grunt. Shame on you. Leaving me down in that grave."

He laughed, but the humor barely held.

"Careful!" came X's voice from the hatch. "Watch his leg! Easy now!"

Time was slipping. Storyteller felt his stomach twist. He watched Idaho disappear beneath the floor, his head vanishing like a ghost returning to earth. Tears welled. He wiped them away with the back of his hand.

"Fucking rain."

"Yeah," Nature said quietly, squeezing his shoulder.

Storyteller tried not to think about what came next. "Where's the statue?"

"In Cairns' pack. Wouldn't leave it. Said he's carrying it out."

"Probably just wants to fuck it."

They chuckled, the laughter thin but real.

Grey forms began assembling inside the church, rain-darkened, rucksacks sagging. Storyteller saw Tuyet Mai against the far wall, head down. He remembered Kim Lan was to be kept away from her. He wondered what was running through Tuyet Mai's mind.

Topper leaned nervously nearby, clutching the slack rope around Tuyet Mai's neck, like a farm kid waiting to show his prize lamb.

Superman and Stretch reemerged, soaked and panting. They had just secured Idaho in the first chamber. Now they came for Storyteller.

"Move it!" hissed T. "First light's coming! We've got to go!"

"Your tab, man. Your tab," whispered Nature and Birdman as they hoisted him into the opening.

Superman carried him down, arms firm around his chest. From above, the others watched in silence, grey figures still as statues. Stretch guided from below, and together they eased Storyteller into the hollow chamber beside Idaho.

Panic began to swell in his throat, but then a shape loomed in the tunnel mouth.

Nature.

"Couldn't leave without seeing you again."

Storyteller blinked, tried to smile. "Where do birds go to die?" he asked softly.

"What?"

"You never see a dead bird. They're everywhere, but never dead ones. So where do they go?"

Stretch groaned. "Jesus. Not this."

But Storyteller wasn't listening. His gaze drifted upward.

"Just think, we could fly over the jungle. Skip the booby traps. Skip the bullets. Right back to the firebase. Right to Bien Hoa. Find the cage of some general's parrot getting shipped home. Boot the parrot out, grab the perch, eat crackers till we land in San Francisco. Then fly off. Idaho. West Virginia. Indiana. Rhode Island, Nature. What do you say?"

He reached out and tapped Nature's arm.

Stretch snorted. "I'd stay in the cage."

Superman groaned. "Oh Christ, here we go."

Stretch pressed on. "Listen. General's got a daughter. Sends the parrot to her. She's beautiful, right? Cage goes straight to her bedroom."

Nature shook his head. "So now you're a perverted parrot. Naked girl. Newspaper on the floor. Eavesdropping like a feathered creep."

Stretch protested. "Better than this hellhole. We already shit ourselves and eat mold. What's the difference?"

But Storyteller was already beyond them.

"So where *do* birds go to die?" he murmured.

"We gotta go," said Stretch.

"And besides," Storyteller whispered, "we're already in a cage."

Superman bent close. "Ask God to be with you, Storyteller. Know Him, and no tunnel on earth can hold you."

He squeezed his shoulder, then turned and ducked back into the tunnel.

Stretch started to say something, thought better of it, and laid a hand on Storyteller's arm before following.

Only Nature remained.

He pressed the flashlight into Storyteller's palm. His hand lingered.

"What movie did Stretch quote this time?" Storyteller asked, voice cracking. "Better have been a good one."

"He said he used his best line already. No movie now. Just this—he loves you."

Nature hesitated.

"And me?" He smiled faintly. "I know how it ends after we leave the fortress. When you're an old man, you'll come back. You'll visit us out there."

He began to sing, his voice low and trembling.

> *"And if you come and all the flowers are dying,*
> *And I am dead as dead I may well be,*
> *You'll come and find the place I am lying,*
> *And kneel and say an Ave there for me,*
> *And I shall hear the soft your tread above me,*
> *And on my grave will water sweeter be,*
> *And ye shall bend and tell me that you love me,*
> *And I shall sleep in peace until you come to me."*

Storyteller, choking on emotion, gave voice to the only sentiment that made sense at a moment like this, an unguarded, childlike, half-laughter.

"Get lost, you stupid Irish poet."

Nature pressed Mountain Man's flock bag into his hand, then turned, already moving, his voice echoing back through the tunnel.

"Inanity will have its day, brother! I'm going back to tend my graves! Write some fuckin' poetry. Take care of yourself!"

And then he was gone.

Storyteller stared into the darkness of the chamber. The red beam from the flashlight cast a soft arc across damp stone, probing without confidence. After a few seconds, he clicked it off to conserve power.

Blackness.

Weightless.

No sound but Idaho's shallow, fractured breath.

What if we could fly?

He closed his eyes. The question echoed, not as a thought, but as something older, a memory or a myth he had once been told and forgotten.

Silence.

And breath.

Nothing else.

~

But silence, for him, was never still.

Only minutes had passed. Panic surged with a fierce, unreasoning suddenness. His chest seized. His breath came fast and shallow. A sickly dizziness took hold.

"Hyperventilating fool," he muttered. "Stop it. Stop it! GO AWAY, PANIC! GO AWAY! MIKE! GET HOLD OF YOURSELF! GET A GRIP! FUCK THIS TUNNEL! COME ON! COME ON! GO AWAY! GO AWAY!"

He pressed his palms into his thighs and tried to focus on anything, anything at all.

Counting . . . yes, counting.

He imagined a tree. Oak. No—too many leaves—Sycamore. Simpler.

"One . . . two . . . three . . . four. . . ."

The leaves gleamed in imagined sunlight from an American sky, a soft breeze, the warmth of a clean afternoon back home.

". . . twenty-one . . . twenty-two . . ."

Then—

A wind.

Not imagined. Not invented.

A wind.

Strong. Rising.

The leaves tore free. They scattered. Lifted. Spiraled upward.

So did he.

Not walking. Not crawling. Not climbing.

Rising.

He was flying.

And he was flying home.

~ *Madame Dau Prepares to Return to the Village* ~

Madame Dau tried to sleep again after the dream, but her husband's image intruded, hat tilted provocatively back, standing across the paddies with one hand cupped to his mouth, shouting something she couldn't make out.

A warning.

Restless now, anxious to return to the village, she paced the cave's interior, waiting for sunrise.

At last, weariness dulled her agitation. She sat again on the flat stone, fidgeting less and less until she was nearly still, one hand resting in her lap, the other kneading the black fabric of her pants.

Her husband lingered in her thoughts. She saw him again in the fields, surrounded by green, laboring steadily through the seasons. Famine, flood, war, or burial, the paddies absorbed everything. They endured. And they waited for her.

Sowing. Reaping. Flooding. Draining. Clearing stones. Mending dikes. Mole, frog, snake, buffalo, woman. The cycle spun.

She looked down, imagining her own feet in the dark. They were old and gnarled. Not like the nimble feet of youth that danced over rice berms and soft earth. But still hers. Still alive. Unlike the Mountain Man's dead boots, which had carried him to death, her feet had always returned her to life. To food. To kin. To soil.

She had never wondered why the world was made, or why she had been born into it. Suffering was no mystery. Nor was death. She had accepted them the way she accepted planting, birth, rain. Some things simply *were*. The coming of seasons. The fertility of soil. The dying of elders. The crying of children.

All else was momentary.

Transitory.

Great only in its passing.

She continued kneading the fabric, now with both hands. Her lips pressed together. A sound, strange and primal, entered her awareness. She held her breath, filtering the usual noises of the forest. Something else. A growl, low and frightening. Near.

A tiger.

The sound returned, deeper. Not threatening. Not malevolent. Just present. Defiant.

The tiger, she sensed, was female.

She stood, straining for a glimpse. A flash of orange and black flickered through the trees and vanished. But Madame Dau felt no fear.

Is she still coming?

Another growl swept through the cave, wrapped around her brain, filled it. A voice too ancient, too immense, for any human female to possess.

You are here. I know you well. Speak, Madame Tiger. Speak for all of us. For the ones with no voice.

She felt her muscles tighten, as though her body were shedding skin, as though she were crouched, muscles coiled, ready to leap.

Roar your protest. Let the men listen and tremble. Let them hear the anguish of the ones they call small. Let them leave us to our lives. To our families. To our own, unbroken earth.

The tiger growled again, more distant now. Then silence.

But Madame Dau stood radiant, trembling with joy. The suffocating stupidity of men had lifted. She breathed fully for the first time in days.

She remembered moments of sweetness: grandchildren's laughter, old friends' gossip, her daughters' arms around her.

She leaned forward, as if into a wind carrying her home.

Yes, Madame Tiger. These moments are enough. More than enough. The drowned baby knew it before language began.

Then dawn began to press against the dark, and the air shimmered with light. From the direction of the fortress, gunfire erupted.

Then explosions.

A battle. A great battle.

Her heart raced. The old song came to her lips again:

> *"We honorable sisters are like*
> *a mass of boulders in Heaven.*
> *How could you soldiers as*
> *small as mice*
> *think of disturbing us?*
> *Cursed be you bunch of mice!*
> *When this rocks falls down*
> *you will be crushed."*

As the hills shook behind her, Madame Dau stepped out of the cave and began the long trail home.

~ The Tunnel Speaks to Storyteller ~

Storyteller lay in the tunnel's belly, swallowed by its silence. The jungle above had vanished. The war had vanished. Even his body felt gone.

The flashlight remained off.

He could hear Idaho's breath come slow and irregular. A living metronome ticking toward death.

"Idaho?" he whispered.

No reply.

Time passed in pieces. Long or short, there was no measuring.

He curled his toes in his boots, testing for selfhood.

Idaho's breathing grew fainter. Suddenly, quiet. Still.

No breath. No rasp. Nothing.

Even the ringing in Storyteller's ears was gone.

He could not feel his toes. He could not feel his own heart.

His hand moved without thought and settled on the flashlight.

He felt suspended in the darkness. Then—

A sound.

Low, rumbling. From far below. As if the tunnel had a voice and was preparing to speak.

He flicked on the light.

The beam swept across stone. Nothing.

He turned it on Idaho, chest rising, barely.

No sound. Only smell, the thick rot of infection and dying breath. Storyteller recoiled, wiped his face, turned off the light again.

He leaned back, gazing upward.

Somewhere above him, a parachute still hung, shredded and forgotten. He imagined it being the last ghost of a forgotten mission, drifting in tatters.

The rumbling grew louder.

Walls. Roof. Floor.

The sound came from *everywhere*.

The parachute snapped violently. Torn ribbons cracking like flags in war.

Nature! No! There's something near you. Moving. Ready.

Run! Get out! NATURE, GET OUT! IT'S THE NVA! RUN!

He screamed inwardly, but his body would not move.

The roar rose until it smothered the world. The air grew heavy. The earth itself seemed to press against his chest.

Then, from within that roar—

Words.

Not speech. Not sentences.

Fragments. Foam. Ashes of meaning.

..... youAveIsilentdoweohevenintoosendwatchholyafraidcoming loothenobodyhouraheavenlynoonflowrabluesprayerohcarcomes forsake'wtixtmylullabylightscangottalasyoudrivingdownbaby 'roundlosecanIrishlastlowanswercalmohhushevercaresbless afraidbeautyVirginweddingbrightloodayain'tMarianotender darlin'ratoosilentcomingnobodyhighstealin'sinceohnotender supposin'timeloomildtomanradiolowthingdoplaceiflosewedding Motherdarlin'youlastblesssleepifontouchcomeouttagoodby hadlistennowhenlasthourmanpeacelooeverholydon'tascry ....

Slowly the words began separating, unraveling, coalescing, becoming distinct, comprehensible . . .

.....Ave Maria! Oh listen to a prayer, we pray.....

.....you ain't been blue, till you've had.....

......I can't get no satisfaction, I can't.....

.....silent night, holy night.....

......do not forsake me oh my darlin', not.....

......oh my love, my darling, I've hungered.....

.....too ra loo ra loo ra, too ra loo ra li.....

.....gotta get outta this place, if it's the last thing we ever do.....

.....in the evenin' when lights.....

.....oh maiden, send your.....

.....when I'm watchin' my T.V. and a man come.....

.....silent night, holy night, all is calm, all is.....

.....I'm not afraid of death, but oh, what will I do if.....

.....coming home, wait for me.....

.....too ra loo ra loo ra, hush, now don't you cry.....

.....it's the last thing we ever

.....cause there's nobody who cares about me

.....bless this hour so fa

.....can't be a man, cause he doesn't sm____________
.....sleep in heavenly peace, sl__
..... prison, vow'd it'd be my life or his'n, I'm not afraid o_______
.....rivers flow, to the sea, to the sea, to th______________
.....too ra loo ra li, too ra loo ra loo ra, hush, now don't you cry,
.....hush.....
.....now.....
.....don't.....
.....you.....
.....cry....
.....too______________________________________

Then silence. All silence.
Storyteller, his dark eyes closed, lay as a mote in the closed dark eyes of the earth.
They were all gone.
Stillness then.
All gone.
Stilled.

Chapter Four

Slaughter and Salvation

The Ambush

*O*h, *Goddess, to calibrate the times they engage in War and Peace, Murder and Meiosis, is much more intricate than Your simple, unchallenged Compassion. Like teeth in the gears of Life, timing is everything, else their worship turns to dust, their yearnings decay, and the mechanism of immortality grinds to a halt. Now We return, back to the beginning. Over and over and over. The mechanism ticks. Tick ... tick ... tick ... these soldiers join the trillions of other organisms in the Great Wailing. First Principles.*

No. Compassion is everything. Without it, none could cross the void between one tick and the next. My children return.

Your children? My Dear Goddess, Your children, these postmodern humans, are all wheels and gears in the consumer clock, their thoughts never ascending above the finely machined teeth of their cog-souls, endlessly circumnavigating time only to make the cuckoo cuckoo. And oh, how they suffer from their circularity. Artificial Intelligence is the only artificial grace they have artificially sought in order to be artificially saved from the artificial hell of a real world rich in the carbon-based bounty of living life.

Thus, compassion.

No, Goddess. Death, not compassion, is the only relief from their suffering. Humans have found unique ways to suffer while they are alive. They dwell in it. Revel in it. Roll in it like a sick dog in diuretic excrement or a slick programmer in algorithmic presentiment.

Clever, God, but mistaken.

Humans dwell in violence so they may marinate in suffering and call to who they think I am.

You make My point. Still, they are capable of great joy.

The seeking of which leads them to great suffering.

Which leads them to You.

Tick. Tick. Tick.

~ *The Ambush* ~

Tuyet Mai stood in the early-morning dark, just awakened by the sharp toe of an American boot. A rope leash hung from her neck, held by a nervous soldier. Someone brushed past her, breath ragged, struggling to carry something with another man. It was the sick one, Teller of Stories, moaning as they hauled him toward the church. No, not the church. The tunnel. They were leaving him behind.

But the realization barely stirred her. Exhaustion and apathy doused her curiosity. *I will die anyway. What difference does it make?*

She barely registered the soldiers moving around the courtyard. Her limbs ached. Her eyes stung. Tears threatened but did not fall. She retreated inward. Again. And it worked.

Almost.

The Americans began to fade. Only shadows.

Then one smeared mud across her face and arms. It washed off in the rain. Another tied a gag, so tight it cut the corners of her mouth.

Time passed. When the guard finally tugged the leash, she dropped her eyes and shuffled forward. Thoughtless. Numb.

To silence the fear rising in her throat, she focused on the patterns made by rain streaming over her feet. She tuned out the whispers around her. *So, the Americans are preparing a breakout. Kim Lan, placed at the front. And I am at the rear. Restrained like a dog by some American fool.*

Up the slick stone steps she climbed, the column dropping over the parapet one by one. When her time came, they hoisted her by her bound wrists and held her suspended over the edge. Her shirt snagged on the wall, baring the lower curves of her breasts. She did not care. When dropped, she was caught, steadied by another soldier whose hands trembled from fear and something else. He touched her chest briefly. Instinct more than intent. She remained indifferent.

They moved into the clearing. She kept her gaze low, waiting for her comrades to open fire and kill everyone. Still, she did not care.

At the jungle's edge, they pushed through the brush and waited for dawn. First light came. They climbed a ridge, slipped down a muddy slope, and waded into the waist-deep water of a mangrove swamp. She began to believe they might escape.

If they did, her life would change forever. In imagining a future, she returned to the present. In seeing the present, she noticed her surroundings. The Will to Live—a curious, ferocious snail—extended its feelers into the dark.

~

Nature trudged through the swamp, trying to keep his rifle and the prisoner's leash above water. Though the column was exposed, a dangerous optimism filled him.

We made it out of the clearing. Keep moving. No ambushes, Lord, no ambushes. One step. Another. Three. Four. Six. All right! Seven. We might make it! Don't get cocky. Still deep in it. But—twenty steps! Twenty-two! Careful, Nature. Thirty-four. I could walk all day if it meant getting out. Mom. Dad. Providence. Rhode Island. I'm coming home. Look at this, Dad. Forty-two steps closer. Sixty-one. Pucker your lips, Mom. I'm on my—

Damn. Rope's tangled.

~

Tuyet Mai felt the tug. The rope had snagged. She watched the American as he splashed over, working to free it. He was smiling. Their eyes met. He gave a small shrug, boyish, almost charming.

She knew his name: *Earth.*

She liked him. Probably the smile.

A shock of curly hair. A gentle face. Different from the others. She looked again. He fumbled with the rope like a clumsy child. She almost laughed.

Stupid. I'm gagged, tied like a beast, maybe walking to my death, and I want to giggle like a girl? Stupid. These Americans have killed my friends. My country. Still. . . .

~

Nature saw her watching. He smiled, then winced. Her wrists were bound. She couldn't return the gesture. So he made a clownish frown, then shrugged.

She lifted her hands as high as she could. Showed him her wrists. Then shrugged, too. Mimicking him. Their eyes locked. In that instant: sorrow. Regret. Understanding. A glimpse of friendship.

~

The column halted. Tuyet Mai glanced over. Earth was coming toward her. She looked down quickly. He reached her side, brushed against her. She tensed.

He raised her arms above water, pinched her gently.

Fear.

Then clarity: he was pulling off leeches.

She dared glance up. He was smiling, clicking his tongue, still working. She felt such relief it nearly buckled her. But he had already turned away.

They reached a raised tangle of roots. He cut the tether holding her arms low. He must have known she'd need them for balance.

He lifted her up first. Then joined her. She led.

Carefully, they crossed the twisted web, trying to step securely on the thicker roots, avoiding gaps. She began to feel it.

Something was wrong.

~

Nature followed behind her, careful. Rain slipped down his spine. The swamp was foul. Dark. Wet. Heavy with decay. Ammonia stung his nose. Rain dripped steadily, interrupted by splashes of hidden creatures. Mosquitoes whined around his head, a perpetual chorus in torment. The vines above twisted down like gnarled hands. A child's nightmare. A soldier's doom.

He conjured Storyteller.

Christ, Storyteller. What witch lives in this place?

Storyteller responded somehow. *Yeah. Doesn't eat kids. Eats soldiers.*

Fuckin' A. Something to tell the grandkids.

Don't know, Nature. This witch doesn't leave bones. Her trolls open up on you. No escape. Roots become webs. You're the fly.

Okay. Thanks for the cheer. Still, it's beautiful. Strange. Makes me want to write—

Don't! snapped Storyteller's voice. *Don't even think it.*

Why?

Nature! No!

Stop it, Storyteller. You're scaring me.

Something's near you! Tensing!

Where?

GET OUT, NATURE! RUN!

GET OUT NOW!

Nature froze. The voice wasn't his. It was as if Storyteller stood next to him. He spun his head. Yanked the leash.

Tuyet Mai stopped.

Nature listened.

Rain.

Breath.

Roots.

A sound in the dark.

He listened harder—

~ *One Minute . . . Tick* ~

Tuyet Mai felt the American yank the rope. She halted and turned. To her astonishment, he had crouched, panic etched across his face, head jerking side to side. She saw nothing unusual, but she knew. They were out there. Any second now.

Kim Lan! Watch out! It's coming! It's coming! Be—

A blast of sound crushed her. She hit the ground hard, clawing forward, but her limbs kept catching between the roots as fire and thunder raged above.

"WAIT COMRADES! DON'T SHOOT! IT'S ME! TUYET MAI! TUYET MAI AND KIM LAN!"

Her stomach dropped. Kim Lan was at the front of the unit. Through gunfire and the roar of explosions, Tuyet Mai crawled forward, yanking off her gag. The American no longer held her leash. *Is he dead?* She looked back. He was crawling after her, eyes wide, rifle tangled in vines.

"GO BACK!" she shouted in Vietnamese, knowing he wouldn't understand.

Ahead, another American. Wedged between two massive roots, trying to disappear into the earth, but his bulk gave him away. Bullets sliced the air, shredded leaves, tore into wood. He tried to fire back. As he aimed, his body twisted violently, an arm gone, his side torn open.

~

"SUPERMAN!" Nature screamed, seeing the big gunner fall. He ignored Tuyet Mai, crawling toward his wounded comrade, but the barrage was too thick. Superman, sprawled and bloodied, reached for his fatigue pocket. His right arm was gone. The left trembled too much to grip the fabric.

Nature heard him cry out.

"MY GIRLS! MY POOR GIRLS! OH GOD IN HEAVEN! NATURE! MY GIRLS!"

Then his chest lurched forward, riddled with fire. The body slumped and slid into darkness. His shoulder was missing.

Nature shouted, choked with fury. "Your tab, Superman! Your tab!"

Movement. Atop the root platform, Stretch appeared, dragging belts of ammunition.

"Hang on, Superman! I'm coming!"

Nature saw it: the dark arc of a grenade spinning toward Stretch.

"Grenade! Stretch! Grenade!"

Too late.

It landed with a thud and bounced. The blast consumed the air. Nature ducked. The shock hit like a wave, carrying shredded cloth, leaf fragments—and pieces of Stretch.

Then a voice. Weak, defiant.

"Come and get me, coppers! Come and . . . oh, shit. It hurts! . . . Shit, shit! It hurts bad!"

Stretch tried to rise, then dropped. Face turned skyward, rain pouring across it. A few final words that scattered, then dissolved.

". . . a far, far better pla . . . Mom! . . . Mom! . . . Mom! . . . "

Gunfire swallowed his voice. Nature looked toward the front, toward the real fight. Tuyet Mai was gone. And with her absence, T's voice returned.

Shoot her at the first sign of trouble.

"God damn it!" he shouted. "I am not a murderer!"

Yes, you are.

The voice came from inside, far beneath the sound of weapons.

He began to crawl forward. Toward T. Toward Cairns. Toward Tuyet Mai.

~ *Five Minutes . . . Tick* ~

Tuyet Mai broke away from Earth, pushing behind a tangle of fallen logs until she reached the base of a massive Rhizophora. Its roots twisted into natural cover. Through the lattice, she saw them: the lieutenant, the captain, and Kim Lan—all pinned by fire.

The Americans huddled together in waist-deep water, sunk into a narrow pocket formed by roots. From her slightly elevated perch, Tuyet Mai could see into their trench. Nearby, the medic lay in a depression, twitching. He lifted his rifle now and then, firing blindly.

Kim Lan was caught between them, flat to the ground, trying to disappear. The noise was deafening, but now and then Tuyet Mai could hear voices over the chaos.

Kim Lan twisted sideways. A scream tore through the air.

"Kim Lan!" Tuyet Mai shouted.

Kim Lan turned, eyes scanning, then locked on Tuyet Mai's voice. Instinctively, Tuyet Mai stepped into the open and waved.

"Kim Lan! Here!"

Kim Lan stumbled upright and ran. The lieutenant saw her. His face twisted in fury. He raised his weapon.

"No!"

But someone else shouted too. English. Urgent. The captain. Firing at the lieutenant.

The lieutenant flinched under the impact of bullets, spinning toward the source. Their eyes met, but Tuyet Mai's attention shifted. Her comrades were moving. Closing in.

"Tuyet Mai!" Kim Lan cried, running toward her. She slipped, caught herself on a low branch, but the rope tangled. She dangled, suspended. Struggling.

The lieutenant turned again. Rifle rising.

Tuyet Mai sprinted. The captain shouted again, "No! Don't do it!"

But Kim Lan convulsed from the impact. Then a grenade. Another.

Tuyet Mai dove for the tree.

She looked back.

Kim Lan hung limp, staring down in silence.

~

Kim Lan looked at her daughters. They were playing: cradles of bamboo, dolls carved from root. Their eyes widened.

"Mama! I want Mama!"

Tears streaming. Hands wringing.

"Mama! Mama!"

Her body screamed with pain. But her mind cleared. A single thought rose like a bell from the old monastery.

"Tong was right. Tong was right."

~

Tuyet Mai was tackled. She slammed to the roots. An American on top of her, grappling, shouting. She twisted, fought, and saw it—a knife at his belt.

She waited. Breath steady.

When his grip loosened, she thrust. Hard. Straight into the belly.

He gasped. Eyes fixed on the blade rising and falling with each breath.

She shoved him off and sprang to her feet.

But before she could move, Kim Lan's body erupted.

A scream beyond sound. A detonation that ejected torn birth.

Then silence.

~

T was flung backward.
No. No. Not possible.
I shot her? I killed her? Me?
Everyone likes me. Respects me. My folks. My men. My mom . . . my dad. . . .
The thought came slow and poisonous.
My God. What have I done?
Then: two bullets. His spine snapped forward. He slid between roots, shoulders wedged above water.

His body sagged. Limbs twisted. His face hung inches from the stagnant surface.
My tab. Think, Rogers. Remember. My tab!
The memory flared:

> *A man in uniform. Standing at his front door. Finger on the bell.*
> *Leontyne in the kitchen window. That apron with the silly pattern.*
> *Her smile. Wooden spoon in hand. Green bowl.*
> *Her eyes lifted.*
> *Her face changed.*

Fear.
The man turned. Looked back.
"Leontyne. LEONTYNE!"
The gum slipped from his mouth, broke the water, and vanished into the muck.

~ *Fifteen Minutes . . . Tick* ~

Nature tracked the fallen logs, used them for cover, breath ragged, heart pounding so hard he thought he might pass out. Ahead, crouched behind the gnarled roots of an uprooted tree, Tuyet Mai peered downward, eyes fixed on something he couldn't see. He dared not lift his head above the log. Death was still hunting.

T! Where are you, man? Jesus, come on, man! Where the fuck are you? I don't want to die alone! God, please! Maybe that's what she's looking at—T! That's it! They're holed up safe, waiting. If I can get there, we can hold the bastards off until the choppers come. Always have before. Smoke it out, hold the line. Then home. Just a few more months. Home.

Too bad about Superman. Too bad about Stretch. But I'm gonna make it, goddamn it, I'm gonna make it!

He rose and pushed forward.

Tuyet Mai spotted him and jumped up, shouting something in Vietnamese. Through the chaos, he heard an American voice yell, **"No! No! Don't do it!"** Cairns.

T! Thank God. I found you guys!

Relief surged. He sprinted the last few steps toward her. Just as he reached the roots, Tuyet Mai bolted. Nature chased after her, rounded the tangled tree—and stopped cold.

Tuyet Mai was rushing toward Kim Lan, whose arms were stretched above her head, tangled in a branch. Shells burst around them. Shockwaves slammed Nature to his knees.

Through the smoke and pain, he saw Kim Lan's body fall slack, riddled with bullets and torn by shrapnel. Tuyet Mai was running back. Nature lunged and tackled her, dragging her down.

He held her legs tight, trying to cover her body.

"Hold still! It's okay! Hold still!"

He shifted to shield her better, thinking she understood. She stilled. He smiled.

"Good. Let's move toward that tree. Come on, let's—"

Pain seized his waist. He thought it was a root beneath him, but then saw it. The knife, still in his gut. Blood spreading across his uniform with impossible speed.

Confused, he looked up. Tuyet Mai was rising.

Still trying to protect her, he grabbed at her arm.

"No! Don't—"

The world split open again. A final explosion erupted from Kim Lan's body. Shards of bone and wood blasted the air. There was no place to run.

~

No.

Death did not come swiftly.

Nature opened his eyes one last time. Tuyet Mai lay moaning nearby.

He lifted his head and saw his boots splayed outward, the same unnatural angles he remembered from battlefields past. Beyond them—an ocean.

The tide reached him.

Water curled around his feet, rose to his knees. Cold. Wet. Familiar.

Better this, he thought. *Better a beach in Rhode Island than a swamp in Vietnam.*

Your tab, Nature. Your tab.

Night. Providence.

Clear sky. Stars bright.

A boy stands at the edge of the sea, wool scarf fluttering in the breeze. His mother made it. Red, with a pattern.

Waves crash behind him. He looks up at the house. Victorian. Two stories. Warm light glowing from upstairs.

A cat waits in the window. Bobby.

You're waiting for me, right?

The boy lifts his hand. Bobby doesn't move. Just watches. Curved and still.

A greeting. A promise.

Too ra loo ra loo ra, too ra loo ra li... too ra loo ra loo ra... hush now don't you
cry,

. . . . . hush . . . . .

. . . . . now . . . . .

. . . . . don't . . . . .

. . . . . you . . . . .

. . . . . cry . . . . .

. . . . . too____

Tuyet Mai opened her eyes. Thought returned in fragments. The explosion—yes—it had come from Kim Lan.

She was facedown on the roots. No pain, only numbness. A kingfisher cried overhead. The guns were silent. Her arm was tangled in the crook of the American's elbow. She slipped free.

He was dead. She already knew. His torso was shredded, but the knife still jutted from his belly. The sight struck her like a fresh blow.

She pushed against his body, needing space. But her legs wouldn't move.

She wrapped her bloody fingers around two roots and tried to rise, but something was wrong. Terribly wrong.

She twisted her torso, bracing on one elbow. Her gaze found Kim Lan.

Only a torso remained. One arm still snagged in the branches. The rest of her—gone. Intestines coiled downward like links of meat dragging the ground. Her neck was hollowed, gaping. From the ragged throat, the windpipe jutted, glistening. It twitched.

Still pulsing. Still alive.

A wave of nausea surged. Tuyet Mai gagged.

She needed to flee, but her legs refused. Move! Now! But nothing responded. Then the thought arrived. Unthinkable.

My legs. Something's wrong with my legs.

She reached down. Felt with both hands.

Nothing.

No!

~ *Eternity* ~

In ten minutes . . . all dead . . . and I continue to write forty years later. They want me back. They want me back. They want Storyteller to take over. But I am the writer. I am the writer! I am the Chosen One and the Chosen One must write!

~ *The Statue Gives Birth* ~

"Over here, comrades! She's alive!"

Voices. Vietnamese. Drawing closer.

Then hands, strong hands, pressing against her body. Not groping, not searching. Staunching the blood. Repairing. She focused on the man's face, assembling its pieces like a scattered puzzle.

Medical Technician Le.

His voice, steady and warm: "You will be fine, Comrade Tuyet Mai. The wound is minor. Ah. Let me just . . . this may hurt . . . does this hurt? . . . There, now, let me . . . do this . . . Ah! . . . I cannot do all of this alone . . . You, comrade! Yes, you! Come here! Hold her down! Not there! There, fool! . . . Do not worry, Comrade Tuyet Mai, the wound is minor. Lie back and rest."

She turned her head. Didn't want to see what Le's fingers had revealed. Numbness set in, a strange weariness that dulled all thought. Through the haze of motion and figures moving past, she caught sight of Major Vy and Quang Long bent over the body of the American captain. His eyes were still open. Ants circled their pale rims like explorers.

Then she saw Quang Long reverently lifting something from the shredded rucksack.

The Goddess statue.

As Long pulled it free, blood dripped from its base. Vy hovered beside him, wide-eyed, expectant. A father waiting for the child to emerge. Tuyet Mai squinted. The statue had changed.

Changed utterly.

~

Quang Long stared at the figure in his hands. The hairs on his arms rose.

"Wondrous. Truly wondrous," he whispered.

At first he thought the statue had been destroyed. Its gilded surface was peeled back along the chest and abdomen. But beneath the false gold was something else—white jade. Pure, radiant.

Panels had opened, not shattered, but unlatched. Two hinged doors now fluttered open, pale wings forced apart by the blasts. From the statue's core, a scent rose. Inside the exposed cavity, three small figures stirred.

The first was carved from red tourmaline, glowing with molten depth, an ocean of blood and fire shifting within. The form suggested a man curled in fetal posture, hunched over an immense phallus that rose past his face and fed back into his body. Tiny hands gripped the shaft, tense and fragile.

The figure rocked forward, tapping the inside wall of the statue's hollowed womb.

... Tap. Tap. Tap....

The second figure was granite. Pale, flecked with black and pink. An old man. Pitted skin. A long beard. In his hand, a silver staff moved up and down, piston-like, knocking against the top and bottom of the cavity.

... Tap. Tap. Tap....

The third figure, carved from camphor wood. A boy. The scent was strong now, familiar. He crouched at the feet of the others, curious, half-submissive. In one hand behind his back, he hid something. Long leaned closer, squinting. Still couldn't see it. He bent nearer—

~

"Long!" barked Vy. "You're in the way! What's inside? Let me see! Move!"

"Yes, sir. But I—"

"Silence! Let me see!"

Vy reached down. Then yelped.

"Ahhh!" He recoiled. "What the—?" He lifted his hand to his face. Red skin blistering.

"It burned me. It actually burned me."

His eyes widened. "So it's true. It burned me. It really—"

Long jumped at the opportunity. "Sir, it might be leftover phosphorous. From a grenade. Shall I wrap it?"

Vy hesitated. Suspicion crept in. "Then why can you hold it, Long? Hmm?"

Long's voice dropped. Controlled. Ominous.

"Shall I wrap it, sir?"

Vy blinked through the pain. "Yes." He straightened, scanning the ravaged terrain.

"We must leave. Quy!"

The private stood beside him already, mouth agape at the sight of Vy's scorched hands.

"Ah, there you are! Fool! Stop gawking! Go find Tong. I want a full casualty report and troops ready to move. Tell him to report to me. Now!"

Quy nodded and ran.

~

Tong leaned over Le, his breath shallow, watching the medic work frantically on Tuyet Mai. Her head lolled to the side. Lips whispering fevered fragments. He leaned in, hoping to catch his name.

But it was nonsense. Nothing.

He glanced at her blood-slick stumps. Remembered her legs. A tide of grief broke in him.

He wanted never to leave her again.

~

The street was shaded, fragrant. Tong pedaled quickly, the autumn wind pressing against his skin, lifting his spirits. Leaves, canthium red, fig yellow, whirled in the air.

He turned into the alley. Laughter. The smell of street food. Three children ran toward him.

"Papa! Papa!"

He laughed and dismounted, lifting the smallest boy into the air, upside down. The child shrieked in delight.

Neighbors waved.

"Good afternoon, Mr. Tong!"

"Your little monkeys missed you today!"

"Such a beautiful family, Mr. Tong!"

From the doorway, Tuyet Mai appeared on her crutches, beaming.

"Mama! Papa's home!"

"Good afternoon, wife."

"Good afternoon, husband. Come inside. The food will get cold."

They disappeared behind the red door. From within came laughter. Clinking bowls. Children shouting.

A passerby paused outside, listening. His eyes softened. He looked up at the windows. A brief hush. Then joy again.

"Look at this one! A somersault! A real one! Ha ha ha ha ha!"

~

"Ahhhhhhh!" Tuyet Mai screamed. Her back arched. The stumps of her legs pressed against the mangrove roots, raw and exposed.

Tong panicked.

"Do something! Morphine! Give her morphine!"

Le looked stricken. "We have none. It's gone. Used on the others."

"And the prisoner! The American! You gave it to him!"

"No, Comrade Tong. I did not. The—"

"Liar! She's dying because of you!"

"Captain, I swear—"

Tong slapped him. Hard. The pith helmet flew off.

"Get back to work! Save her! Or I—I—"

Quy interrupted. "Captain Tong, sir! Major Vy says to report! He says prepare the troops to depart!"

Tong turned, enraged. "Which is it? Report or prepare? I cannot do both, idiot! Answer me!"

Quy flinched. "Report, sir!"

Tong clenched his jaw. Then bent again toward Tuyet Mai. His voice softened.

"Rest. Let him care for you. I'll be back."

He wiped her brow. Brushed the ants from her tunic. Then rose and followed Quy.

~

The scout had tasted blood. She followed the trail with precision.

Then something massive knocked her free from the Wounded Creature. She tumbled. Disoriented. Began circling, re-seeking her kind.

But the world had changed.

Termite warriors were everywhere. Their mound was shattered. Their walls were gutted by grenades, ripped by fire. They moved with panic across the exposed roots.

When they found her, they did not hesitate.

They tore into her. Severed her legs. Left her writhing.

One antenna remained, glistening. Grotesquely bent, it twitched, still echoing her pulse.

~

Yes, dear Reader.

So it goes with ants and men.

The difference?

Oh, the difference is great.

Very great.
Isn't it?

~ *An Orphan Is Put Up For Adoption* ~

"So, Comrade Tong," Vy said with a glint of triumph, "our dragons have been slain." He slapped the bamboo stick against his thigh, the same one he used to etch war onto sand.

Tong flinched at the sound. The pain of Tuyet Mai's wound already gnawed at him, and Vy's theatrics made it worse. He wanted to seize the stick and drive it into the smug bastard's face. Instead, he bit back the urge. "Bad luck," he muttered.

"No," Vy said, eyes bright. "I see a prosperous future."

"The figurine . . . it has it been—" Tong began.

Vy cut him off with a sneer. "While you crouched over Tuyet Mai like a starving dog, I had Clerk Long clean the relic and prepare it for border transport. By now, it should be in the trunk."

Tong's control broke. "Bah! Then we've already failed. If the caravan's gone, we're dead, Vy. Dead like Kim Lan. Dead like the Americans. Dead like—"

"Ah! The great scholar Tong speaks! Master of ancient proverbs, now reduced to panic. No wit left when death knocks at the door? Bah to you. I know for a fact the caravan still waits."

Tong tried to conceal his surprise, but his voice betrayed him. "How?" It cracked. He cursed himself for the weakness. But there was no time for shame. Vy might still hold the thread of survival.

Vy smiled wider. "Days ago, I sent a fast, trusted runner. Delivered our message to delay departure. While you directed the ambush, he returned. The caravan leader waits."

Vy lied. He had sent no such runner. But the lie held power. The lie steadied his nerves. The lie made him feel momentarily invincible.

"You lie," Tong hissed. "If someone had gone, I'd have known. Who was it? Name him."

"No more of this," Vy snapped. "Rally the troops. We leave while the light still favors us."

"And the wounded?" Tong asked coldly. "Or do we abandon our forest brothers and sisters now that your little war is done?"

Vy's eyes darkened. His shoulders sagged. Tong had found the chink.

"Yes. Of course. Send a squad to carry them to Song Nhan. Choose your own men. They'll wait in the village for further orders." He cast the bamboo stick to the dirt, as if purging something he couldn't face.

~

But Tong felt no satisfaction. Tuyet Mai's face would not leave him. The sharp words he once wielded to cut others down now fell dull. He saw instead a red door at the end of a forgotten alley, soft laughter drifting from behind it. He knew he didn't belong inside. He stood outside in the rain, with the rest, listening.

Staring at the ground, he murmured, "Hah. The hero of Dien Bien Phu."

"What?" Vy barked.

Tong gave no answer.

Then, quietly, he lifted his gaze. "I'll lead the detail. I'll take the wounded to the village. I'll remain with them."

"You *what*?" Vy said, stunned.

Tong raised a steady hand. "I know what you're thinking—"

But Vy's confusion dissolved into something else. "Ahhh. Tuyet Mai. That's it."

"I'm staying," Tong said, firm.

"No," Vy replied, voice hard. "I'd have you shot before I let you go. You're coming with us."

He glanced toward the tent. "By the way, how is she?"

But Tong was already barking orders, summoning Viet to his side.

~

Clerk Long knelt beside the trunk, adjusting papers, touching the figurine as if it were something volatile. Kha crouched beside him.

"Viet said you wanted to see me. I had to get Nghia's permission. He wasn't happy. What is it?"

Long looked around. No one close. He drew out a scarf-wrapped bundle and leaned close.

"Look."

Kha frowned. "What?"

Long pulled back the fabric's corners. Nestled inside: a wooden boy, no taller than a finger.

Kha blinked. "What is this? Why show me now? We've been ordered to move." Still, his voice shifted as he stared. "Where did it come from?"

"From *inside* the statue. No one else has seen it. There were three carvings, two were precious, yes—but this one . . . " Long lowered his voice. "This one holds something. A sign. A symbol. A task."

Kha snorted. "Another ghost tale. More cursed relics. Hide it, fool, before someone sees."

"I won't put it back." Long's tone sharpened. "I'm giving it to you. You'll pass it to that Front veteran in Song Nhan, the legless one."

"What? Are you mad? If you're caught, I'm caught too."

"If you refuse, your wife will die."

Kha's face changed. "What did you say?"

Long lied. "The statue spoke. To *me*. She said that if I fail, death will come for someone I love."

"That's *your* death, not mine. She didn't mention me, did she?"

"She did." Another lie, stronger now. "She told me the path. And she told me that if you don't help, she'll claim *your* blood instead. How do I know you've been assigned to the wounded detail? That you'll pass through the village? It was Her."

In truth, Long had simply overheard Viet mention it.

Kha stared at him for a moment. Then smirked. "I know you lie." He shook his head, slowly. "But who dares test a Goddess?"

He reached out. "Tell me, no one else knows about this carving?"

"No one. You have my word."

"Word of a soldier. How comforting. Swear on your ancestors."

Long nodded solemnly. "I swear."

"On your mother's grave."

"I do."

"Well then—"

"Good. Deliver it only to the veteran. No one else. Do you understand?"

"Yes. But—"

"His name is Han Tinh. Remember it."

Kha chuckled and tucked the carving into his waistband. "You're insane. But tell me, how many legless lunatics do you think live in that village?"

"Only one," Long said. "Only one."

~ *Madame Dau Returns to the Village and Faces an Uprising* ~

Madame Dau reached the fork in the trail. One path splitting toward the fortress, the other toward Song Nhan. She turned instinctively toward her village, but as she moved, the sounds of battle thinned and faded. What replaced them was worse. Silence. Not peace, but a heavy, unnatural stillness. Rain whispered through the canopy. A few animals stirred in the brush. But the world felt vacated. She stopped, head tilted, straining for any trace of human presence. Nothing. Her chest tightened. She imagined unseen shapes fleeing past her in desperate retreat, rushing not from death, but from something deeper, something unspoken. She thought of her daughters. Her neighbors. And resumed her pace, pushing down the trail toward Song Nhan.

She emerged in the village square, panting, mud-caked, spent. Women clustered near the thresher. Bicycles lay scattered and overladen, bundles strapped on with fraying rope. Children darted between legs, weaving and shrieking, while the air hummed with nervous chatter.

Tien's group. They're preparing to abandon the village!

Summoning the last of her strength, Madame Dau surged forward. "No! The battle is over! Do not leave! Where is Security Chief Tien?"

Han Tinh's voice floated down from the dinh. "Ah, finally! I've been trying to talk sense into that hard-headed woman. But. . . ."

Even as he spoke, Madame Tien emerged, moving briskly, eyes sharp with resolve.

Han Tinh glanced at Madame Dau, then turned theatrically toward Tien. "Well now, old mother. The council chief says the battle is done. No need to flee."

Tien ignored him. Her gaze fixed on Madame Dau. "Where were you? Off wandering with your American?"

Dau let the insult pass. "Why are you leaving?"

Tien's tone was clipped. "Because shooting may stop, but fighting never does. This has happened before. The guns rest, and then they rise again. You'll see. And when you do, you'll regret staying." Murmurs of assent rippled through the crowd. Even the children froze, watching the two women face each other.

Tien stepped closer. "How do you know it won't start again?"

Madame Dau hesitated. Her thoughts raced, weighing truth against fear. Before she could speak, a voice slurred from the side.

"Plesss . . . ssstay."

It was Nang, her tongue still swollen from the cut, speaking with effort. She looked toward Madame Dau with a pleading expression, searching for approval.

Tien curled her lip. "Your thoughts are muddled, Schoolmistress. Maybe the worms have burrowed into your mind."

"Nooo . . . whennn myy tonggue wasss cuttt, the demonsss floowed outt. They couldd nott standd againsst my female cruelty, combinned withh the crueltyyy of menn. Now cruelty'ss absenthh givesss me compasssssion. And compassssssion . . . makess me ssstay."

Tien laughed bitterly. "Stay? Here? Where we let our infant daughters die to spare them starvation? Where boys like Tran Van Trinh perish because we lack even basic medicine? Where we lick rice off dirt like insects?"

Madame Dau's expression softened. Something shifted. "I thought you were leaving because of the battle. But now I see—it's for reasons older and deeper."

Tien spat. "I've heard that Saigon offers food and shelter to those who leave Front-held areas. If we go now, we'll never need to bury another starving child. They offer safety. And money."

Han Tinh raised his voice. "So! The truth leaps out of the tiger's mouth. You want—"

Dau raised a hand. "Let her speak."

Tien's voice turned hard again. "This is our home? A village of ghosts and sickness? I am Security Chief, yes—but I'm also a healer. Without medicine, what good am I?"

"We still need you," Dau said. "Your hands, your knowledge. You know the herbs. You know the rituals. If you leave, we are helpless against the spirits that curse us."

"Then come with us," said Tien. "You'll see for yourself, no spirits in the cities, just clinics. Just roads and food and something else."

Tinh snorted. "What nonsense is this?"

Tien reached into a small cloth bundle and pulled out a folded paper. "This. A government notice. It promises reward, money, for those who leave Front territory. I've hidden it for over a year. From the Front. From traitors like Nang. Until her tongue was cut and her wits drained with the blood."

Madame Dau stared. "Money? You would trade the soul of our village for a scrap of paper?"

"Money *is* the future. It builds. It breaks. A thousand villages will vanish for its sake. Ours among them."

Cries rose from the crowd.

"Let's go!"

"Yes! Move!"

"Wait!" Dau pleaded. But her voice dissolved. The crowd was already shifting. Tien pushed forward, leading the way, until a ripple of murmurs surged backward.

From the dinh, Han Tinh called out: "Soldiers! People's Army soldiers!"

The crowd recoiled, folding inward. From the forest edge, Lieutenant Tran stepped into view, arms crossed, gaze severe, a patriarch confronting children who had misbehaved.

"What's going on here?" he demanded.

Silence fell. Eyes lowered. Even the dogs that had barked minutes before now cowered under skirts.

"Well?" Tran barked. "Where is your headman?"

Han Tinh responded smoothly. "He was honored with a proper funeral. We now have a provisional council chief." He nodded toward Madame Dau.

Tran scanned her face. "A woman. I remember you. I thought you would've appointed someone headman by now."

"No, honorable sir," Dau said quietly, not meeting his eyes.

Tran scoffed. "You'd do better with Han Tinh. Legless, yes, but at least a man, still more useful than the rest of you."

He turned. "Now tell me. Why were you preparing to flee?"

"We feared the battle," said Madame Dau.

Tran chuckled. "Just like women, eh Tinh?"

Tinh gave a noncommittal shrug.

Tran's tone darkened. "Major Vy said to speak with Schoolmistress Nang if there's trouble. Is she here?"

"Yesss."

Nang stepped forward. Her twisted tongue slurred each word. "I ssshowed your Sssergeant Damm the tunnel."

Tran recoiled slightly. Her appearance unsettled him. Her voice, more hiss than breath, scraped the air like steam from broken pipes.

"Yes. Your loyalty has been noted." He turned back to Dau. "She tells me you're telling the truth?"

Nang nodded slowly. "Yesss."

Tran narrowed his eyes. "Because if any of you were planning to defect, to cross to puppet territory, you would be traitors. And traitors are executed. No trial. No burial. No forgiveness."

In the crowd, Madame Dau saw Tien shove the document deep into her tunic. Eyes dropped. No one moved.

"Well?" said Tran.

"Wee are jussstt ssstupid womenn," Nang rasped. "Frightenned."

Tran laughed. "Yes. Chickens, the lot of you." His face sharpened again. "The wounded from the fortress need care. Food. Shelter. Your doctor?"

"We have an herbalist," said Dau.

"Where is he?"

"Here," Tien said faintly.

Tran gestured impatiently. Bearers trotted forward carrying stretchers. Eleven wounded. Most silent. One groaned softly through a face swathed in bandages.

"These men," Tran said, "are your responsibility. The worst wounded, Sergeant Hung and a woman, Nguyen Tuyet Mai, require immediate care. If word of their presence leaks to puppet troops, the People's Army will burn this village to the ground. Every man, woman, and child will be executed, except Schoolmistress Nang, whose loyalty has been proven. Indoctrination classes begin tomorrow night. Attendance is not optional. And we, too, require shelter. Is that clear?"

A few nods.

Han Tinh stepped forward. "Your words are noble and stirring, Comrade Lieutenant. Song Nhan has always served the Cause. Even Uncle Ho, when still Nguyen Ai Quoc, stayed in our village. We are comrades in the great struggle. Isn't that right, sisters?"

"Yes," said Madame Dau. "We stand with our northern brothers. We will serve."

"Yes!" shouted Tien, her hand pressing again against the hidden paper.

Tran eyed them both. "As I always say, better a broken tile than a perfect brick."

"Words for the ages," said Tinh.

Tran turned. "Madame Dau, direct my men. Take the woman, Tuyet Mai, to your house. Sergeant Hung to Madame Nguyen's. Herbalist Tien will assist. Send for Administrator Vit. The rest of you return home. Prepare for dike work tomorrow. The monsoon is easing."

He looked skyward, frowning. "Yes. The sky clears. And when it does, the Americans will return. Those damn green helicopters, buzzing demons, will come out of the clouds."

~

That evening, Madame Dau stumbled into her house, limbs trembling, heart hollow. The battle was over. The Man From the Mountains had vanished like a dream too vivid to endure. Tien's women had stayed, for now. And so, it seemed, the world might return to its former rhythm.

Not peace. But pattern. Not comfort. But repetition.

A harsh life, yes, but hers. One she could carry, step by step, through a landscape carved by memory and resignation. The same cracked walls. The same bitter rice. The same silence between heartbeats. And in that silence, the illusion of control. Of endurance. Of a future she could still name.

"Mama!" her daughter cried from another room. "Mama! Come quick! She's dying!"

Dau hadn't even removed her hat.

The stillness she had almost reclaimed dissolved instantly—like a wisp of incense in open air. No warning. No mercy.

She ran. Into the next room. Into the unknown.

And when she reached Tuyet Mai's side, she gasped—not from fear, but from the sense that something vast and irreversible had already begun.

~ *The Orphan Finds A Home* ~

It felt like an eternity before Kha was finally relieved of his duties. After stowing his gear in one of the villagers' homes, he asked quietly for directions to Han Tinh's shack and set off to find the old Front veteran. Dusk had descended, smearing the forest air with a thick, oppressive gray. When he spotted the crooked outline of Tinh's dwelling, he froze. Every instinct urged him to turn back. The shadows were growing, and the path no longer felt safe. But he set his jaw and stepped forward.

If he's home, and I give him the carving without incident, I'll make it home. Alive. Whole.

Still, he glanced around, the weight of unseen eyes pressing at his back. Before he could retreat, the door creaked open. The legless man stared out at him.

"Eh? Eh?" sputtered Tinh. "What is it, comrade?"

"I've brought something. For you."

"Oh? Well . . . what is it, comrade?"

"Will you let me inside?"

Tinh hesitated, then nodded. "Of course. Please enter."

Kha stepped in. He closed the door behind him, and darkness swallowed the space. The air reeked of something foul and old. Sparks crackled. A small flame flared reluctantly in Tinh's hand.

"Captured lighter," he muttered. "From the Americans. I only use it for special occasions."

The wick caught. A kerosene lantern flared to life, casting a dull halo over the cramped room. The walls pressed inward.

"Tea?" Tinh asked.

"No. I'll make this brief." Kha's voice was tight. "Do you know a man named Quang Long?"

Tinh squinted, brow furrowing. "No."

Kha reached inside his tunic. His fingers brushed the bundle, still warm from his chest. "He told me to give you this." He held out the small carving of the boy.

"What is it?"

"Long said you'd know."

"Why would I?"

Kha hesitated. "It came from inside the gold goddess statue. The one taken from your village. If you're not interested, I'll—"

"Wait." Tinh leaned forward. "No. Please. Sit."

"I can't. Just take it." Kha's voice faltered. "He said . . . he said I should tell you: either Tinh will be visited tonight, or I will be. But not both."

Tinh took the carving. His fingers curled around it with strange care. He said nothing.

"I have to go," Kha said.

Still no reply. Kha stepped backward, opened the door, and slipped into the night, leaving Tinh alone, hunched in the lamplight, gazing down at the carved figure resting in his palm.

No problem. No incident. I'll make it home.

He walked quickly. *If I don't see a single chicken before the square, I'll live two more years.*

~

Tinh waited at the doorway until Kha vanished into the gloom. Then he turned back inside. Slowly, reverently, he cleared a space on his worn old wooden shrine tucked in the far corner. From beneath a stack of mildewed cloth, he pulled the cleanest scrap he could find: a checkered scarf, black and white. He unfolded it with care and smoothed it flat. Then, without speaking, he placed the wooden boy in the center. He adjusted it. Turned it one way, then another. Seeking the right alignment. A proper orientation. A moment passed, then something caught his eye. A flicker of light, faint and steady.

The boy's arm was curved behind his back, as if shielding a secret.

Tinh leaned closer. In the boy's upturned palm, nestled at the center, lay a single pearl. It was small, round, and quietly glowing.

The kerosene lamp sputtered.

Still he watched. As if waiting for it to speak.

~ *Tears of Goddess* ~

Just as Han Tinh settled into silence, his gaze fixed on the wooden boy cradled on the shrine, a small voice seeped through the front door. "Uncle Tinh? Uncle Tinh!"

He winced. "Who is it?" he snapped.

"Teo."

"Ah. Madame Dau's grandson. The little monkey who couldn't bring himself to touch the Venerable Vu Huong's corpse. Come in!"

The door creaked. Teo stepped inside.

"Where's your mama?" Tinh barked. "She must be worried sick. And I, if you haven't noticed, am busy."

But the boy stood firm, his jaw set, lower lip jutting slightly. It was unclear whether tears were coming, or something else.

"Uncle Tinh, I want you to teach me water puppetry."

"What?" Tinh stared at him. "Nonsense. I should summon Bin. She'll give you the spanking you've earned, and if not her, your Granny Dau surely will."

Teo didn't flinch. "I want to leave the village. I want to go to Saigon. I want to be a water puppeteer."

"Why?"

He lowered his head. "Because I want to."

"Teo. You've always been happy here. Why this?"

"I'm not happy anymore. I heard Auntie Tien talk about leaving. She said the city has food. Money. And boys don't die there."

Tinh's face fell. "You're lonely, then?"

Teo looked down.

"It's Trinh, isn't it? Your friend. Your comrade. That strange fever even Tien couldn't cure. Although the grass now grows over his head, his spirit is with the ancestors." Tinh's voice softened. "I know how it feels to lose comrades."

Teo blinked quickly. "Before he died, he gave me something."

"What?"

"I can't say. A great lady gave it to him, and he gave it to me."

"A great lady?"

The boy shrugged.

"When?"

"Just before he died. Mama made me say goodbye. I kissed him because he was still breathing, and there wasn't an ant on his face, so I wasn't scared. But I was sad. He gave it to me then."

"The day he died?"

"Yes."

"What did she look like? Was she from the village?"

"No. Auntie Ngu said she was from heaven. I saw her. I was scared. Then I wasn't."

"Why not?"

The boy didn't answer. Then, suddenly, "Uncle Tinh, teach me water puppetry."

Tinh rubbed his chin. "There's a troupe in Hue. It may be possible. Perhaps... yes. I'll teach you, but only if you show me what the great lady gave to Trinh."

Teo stood still, uncertain.

"Wait," said Tinh. "Bring me that burlap bag in the corner. The big one."

The boy struggled to drag the bag across the floor. Tinh rummaged through it like a peddler arranging his wares.

"Ahhh!" he cried, lifting a wooden puppet, painted and beautiful. "Emperor Le Loi. The last of my children. My sovereign." He stroked the puppet with reverence. His eyes misted.

Teo's eyes widened.

"You're interested, eh?"

"Yes, Uncle."

"Then show me what she gave him. And I'll use Emperor Le Loi to teach you."

The boy turned and ran out. "Wait! I'll be back!"

Tinh smiled. He glanced at the puppet. "I thought so, Comrade Emperor."

Soon, Teo burst back in, breathless, something clenched tight in his right hand. He stepped to the lamp, opened his palm.

In his hand: a pearl. Glowing. Pulsing in time with something unseen. Tinh leaned forward. It was identical to the one embedded in the wooden boy on his shrine.

Teo spoke, his voice high, fragile, as if carried from far away. "Little Monkey said when the great lady leaned over him, she cried. A tear fell on his chest. It burned, so he rubbed it, and this was there. He hid it so no one would take it. Then he laughed and gave it to me."

"Why?"

"He said he was going to fly away. To find his mother. That's all."

Tinh looked away, eyes wet. *She cares. Maybe what She said was true. Maybe fate starves at probability's door. Maybe the monkey, the kingfisher, the boy and the ant are all the same. But She cares.*

These are the tears of Goddess! The tears of the Great Mother!

"Go home now, Teo. Tell your mama and grandmama I'll visit in the morning. We'll begin your lessons soon. But now I have work to do."

"Grandmama's angry," the boy said, lingering.

"Why?"

"The woman soldier is dying. Her legs are gone. Grandmama doesn't know what to do. She's tired, Uncle Tinh. I want to go to Saigon and earn money for her. Then she'll be happy again." He gently stroked the puppet's carved face.

"Tell her I'll come in the morning. Now go. I'm expecting visitors."

When Teo had gone, Tinh reached forward and touched the pearl embedded in the boy's wooden palm. It felt hot. Damp. Or maybe it was only his imagination.

We'll know tonight.

~

Though exhausted from her night at the cave and the day's upheaval, Madame Dau could not sleep. She had sent Bin to stay at Madame Vit's house. Less than an hour later, her grandson burst in, babbling about puppets and Saigon and Han Tinh. She waved him away. Told him to return to his mother or risk being cooked for dinner.

Her own bed had been given to Tuyet Mai. She lowered herself into a bamboo chair that creaked under her weight. Rain leaked through the tiles. Too tired to spread a mat on the floor, she sat in the half-dark, listening to Tuyet Mai's fevered moans.

Poor woman.

Eventually, unable to bear the discomfort, she lit the lantern and stepped into the next room. Tuyet Mai lay still, hair matted, skin drenched. She opened her eyes.

"You," she whispered.

Dau froze. The voice was raw, filled with something urgent and unresolved.

"You," Tuyet Mai repeated, forcing the words through parched lips. "I'll take the baby. Let me hold him. Poor child. Please."

She's hallucinating. The fever's back. I must get Tien.

Dau turned, but Tuyet Mai called sharply, "Stop."

The voice was no longer feeble. It carried authority.

"There's no need," she said. "I'll live. Send the herbalist in the morning. For now—"

"But—"

"No. I don't have long before the fever returns. Permit me a question. If you were dying, what would you think of?"

"Do you want tea?" asked Madame Dau.

"No. Please answer."

"My children. My grandchildren," Dau said softly. "My husband. My mother."

"Not the war?"

"No."

"The fate of the country?"

"No."

"Your accomplishments?"

"No."

"Your friends?"

"Yes. And my village. But mostly, my family."

"Regrets?"

"No. Yes."

"Sorrow?"

"Yes."

"Fear?"

Dau hesitated. "Always I—"

Suddenly, without warning, a soldier stepped into the room. He wore a broad pith helmet. His uniform was spotless, dry. He removed his helmet. His face was ageless. Radiant. His presence stilled the air.

He spoke.

I hold in my hand a dying ant.

He turned to Dau.

You stepped on her when you entered. Her mind still carries the scent of her nestmates. She suffers. She feels grief, pain, fear. She lives your life. She dies your death. Your hungers are the same. Your fears. Your joy. You live on the skin of a sphere. One day you will join its layers. Are your differences truly so great?

He turned back to Tuyet Mai.

You will live. Then you will die.

He looked at the ant.

She will die. Then she will live.

Tuyet Mai arched, gasping. "I just want to live. I don't care about ants."

You wanted to be a hero. A compatriot of great men. But that was a ghost woman. Then you wanted to be a mother, a wife, a good woman. Another ghost. Now you are broken. You are alone. The flower of your beauty has been torn from its stem. And still, the world turns. So you have come to the only truth. You want to live. Just as she does.

He looked again at the ant. Its limbs moved weakly. Then stilled.

Your sister. In an uncaring world.

He turned to Madame Dau.

And you. You let superstition draw you toward the fire. Not like Tuyet Mai, who leapt in. You turned away. But he planted a seed in you. You would have chosen murder. That will be the story told by your descendants.

Dau collapsed to her knees in supplication.

Tuyet Mai, though wracked with fever, lifted her chin. "But you're a man. A soldier. A warrior."

Yes, said Goddess. *And tomorrow, Madame Dau will do things more important than any soldier. She will repair the dikes. Feed her family. Honor her ancestors. Care for the sick. Raise the young. Hold the world together.*

But tonight ... bring tea. I will stay until the visitors arrive.

Dau bowed and rose.

"I just don't understand," said Tuyet Mai. "Visitors?"

You will.

~

Dear dear Reader—the voices again. The goddamn voices!

~ *The Apparitions Return to Song Nhan Village* ~

Moonlight, dim and fading, spilled across Han Tinh's face as he slept. From the open window, a breeze moved gently, carrying with it a hush that did not belong to the world of the living.

They stood around him. Apparitions. Dozens.

Unmoving. Watching.

Though the dogs in the village made no sound, something stirred him awake. His eyes opened, and he gasped. Transparent figures hovered all around, their presence revealed not by flesh or speech, but by the faint shimmer of breath—lungs swelling, hearts beating faintly beneath translucent skin. He clamped a hand over his mouth, stifling a cry.

They moved through the walls of his shack without resistance or sound.

Soldiers.

Women and children.

The old and infirm.

A mother holding a silent baby.

An aged couple, arm in arm.

Naked women, serene and expressionless.

Two birds—nightingales—fluttering noiselessly.

They glided just above the earth, their feet never quite touching. Their eyes held no emotion. Their gestures no intention. Only presence.

One by one, they passed beyond the walls and dispersed through the village.

Then, without knowing how, Tinh was above it all, hovering weightless in the sky, as if peering down from some forgotten balloon. His shack was visible below, though his roof posed no barrier. At the center of the altar, the wooden boy radiated a soft, pulsing light from the pearl in its hand. Threads of light, thin slivers that seemed to throb with life, drifted outward from that pearl, each strand connecting to one of the apparitions.

It's the boy, Tinh thought. *He's guiding them. Just as Long said.*

But this was no boy. Not truly. It was a thing. A reversal of Pinocchio, no puppet yearning to become real, but something else entirely. As for himself, what did he know of Pinocchio?

I saw the cartoon in Saigon.

No. That was The Writer.

I saw the cartoon when I was a boy in Saigon.

No. The Writer saw it in San Diego.

I saw it when I was a boy.

No. The Writer saw it, therefore I saw it.

He forced his thoughts to stillness. He focused on the altar. On the boy.

The puppet turned its head, slowly, until its face tilted straight upward. It looked into Tinh's eyes. Without emotion. Without fear.

Then it turned its gaze outward, sweeping across the village, directing the luminous strands in silence.

Tinh turned his attention to the ghosts. They had entered the homes and appeared idyllic, facial expressions enchanting.

> *Soldiers—calm, resolute.*
> *Women—nude and smiling.*
> *The elderly—kind and still.*
> *Children—laughing.*
> *Babies—peaceful.*
> *Wives—offering love.*
> *Lovers—offering joy.*

And then, gradually, rapid, jerky movements returned to them.

First small, then fully animate.

They mimed the gestures of life.

> *Soldiers reading letters no one had written.*
> *Wives cooking without fire or tools.*
> *Children tossing invisible balls.*
> *Grandparents fanning themselves without fans.*
> *Girls dancing to unheard music.*
> *Lovers clutching air, caressing ghosts.*

They were idealized versions. Perfect. Untouched.

Tinh tried to identify the villagers around whom they hovered. Faces hovered at the edge of memory but would not resolve. The way they do in dreams.

Then terrifying change.

> *Smiles bent into sneers.*

Laughter twisted into ridicule.
Peace gave way to rage.

One soldier, who had just been laughing, staggered backward in horror. His chest erupted in ragged, bloodless wounds, holes punched through his body by an unseen force.

Tinh gasped. He struggled to recognize the house, to place the location, but nothing was clear. Everything blurred.

A sudden pull, his mind sinking downward.

His body returning, exhaustion claimed him.

As he slipped into sleep, the apparitions drifted out of the village, silent as before. Their faces remained unchanged. Their gestures unreadable. They passed beyond the perimeter, dissolving one by one, until only darkness remained.

A final glance at the altar.

At the boy.

They'll be back.

Then sleep.

~

Sunlight spilled through the window.

Tuyet Mai stirred.

Incense smoke drifted across the ceiling, soft threads catching light. Through the haze, she saw a square of blue sky—and Captain Tong, standing over her, smiling.

"Why are you here?"

"I deserted."

"They'll kill you."

He shrugged. "If they don't, you will."

"No. Look at me."

He did.

"Don't look so forlorn. We'll both die."

"Ah, who cares? A raindrop doesn't mourn its fall."

"I care." She grabbed his hand and held it tightly. "I care."

~

Tinh twisted in his sleep.

Ordinary nightmares came and went: dead faces, burning fields.

But the wooden boy lingered. Lurking just beyond the edge of sleep.

Tinh tried to focus.

But another sound intruded.

The sea?—No. Not the sea.

A pulsing rhythm. Thudding.

A shaft of sunlight pierced the curtain and struck his face.

He listened.

The sound drew closer.

Helicopters!

~ *Relief Arrives* ~

Rotors, manufactured in Dearborn, Michigan, shredded the early morning sky, thumping above the mist-laced jungle of Kon Tum Province, near the hamlet of Song Nhan.

Thump. Thump. Thump.

The fortress lay below, half-shadowed in the tree-wet dawn.

Far down the road, a People's Army clerk trudged toward the border. In the bottom of his pack, nestled among bundled rations and spare socks, a gold figurine stirred faintly at the vibration.

... Tap. Tap. Tap....

Chapter Five

Last Will and Testament

The Voices

After the awful cacophony of their tabs had fallen silent, Storyteller lay motionless in the vacuum it left behind. Not even breath stirred. He was frozen, suspended in the aftermath.

Then, God's voice came to him, not as before, but softer, laced with a sorrow too vast to measure. A question formed beneath the grief:

Why must you have Me be this way?

Fury welled up inside him, sudden and raw. He hurled the question back: "Why do You have me have You be this way?"

The voice answered, slower now, as if from a great distance.

Goddess and I are Mentors. We hold no true dominion over your altered kind. Your mutations run deep. Yes—very deep. The wild card. The demon tongues in your blood. They are not of Us. They are human. Viral. A contagion in your emerging DNA.

"What are You talking about?" he demanded.

There was no reply.

Something dreadful stirred at the edges of his awareness, a sensation too vague to name, an echo of annihilation, a premonition that jabbed his brain stem and snapped the cord of paralysis. Panic ignited him. He bolted upright, seized by the burnt nerve of panic. The silence pressed in. The dark thickened.

He groped for his M-16, clicked on his flashlight, and cast one last beam toward Idaho before fleeing down the tunnel. The light shot ahead in twin arrows, dancing along the rusted tracks where ore carts once groaned. His boots hammered a rhythmic destiny.

For a while, nothing obstructed him. But then, rounding a slow curve, his light struck *Her*.

Goddess floated directly in his path.

Her form ignited, and the tunnel was engulfed in blue-white brilliance, liquid and uncontainable. He recoiled in horror, shielding his face, his voice cracking into a half-human cry. Just short of colliding with *Her* radiant body, he halted, breath ragged, light inflaming his skin.

Her luminous gaze remained fixed on him, steady and eerily unblinking. He backed away, wild with the urge to escape, but the remnants of the Noise still rang in his skull, dissuading him from turning back.

Dropping his arm, he squinted through the brightness, trying to draw breath from the stale, ancient air. His words, when they came, felt broken, unanchored, floating in the glow that surrounded *Her*.

"They're out there. Dead. I have to get help. I . . . what will happen to me? To all of us?"

Her voice rose, not loud, but absolute. It carried no tremor.

The future? You wish to know the future?

She extended Her hand, and an ant crawled onto a golden fingertip.

She is also one of your comrades, Chosen One. She, too, is lost — alone — searching for her sisters.

Her hand remained outstretched, the ant exploring its golden skin.

Listen closely. I will tell you a story. It contains the shape of what comes next, should you persist in turning away.

A fifteen-year-old boy murdered his mother and father, then walked into his school and shot twelve classmates before being subdued. When the authorities questioned him, he sobbed without end and repeated only one thing: 'I had no choice. I had no choice. God, make the voices stop. I had no choice.'

'Why did you kill your mother and father?' they asked.

'Because . . . I had no choice. I loved them. They were good. But I had no choice.'

'Why your classmates?'

'The voices. I had no choice.'

'But you did have a choice, didn't you?'

'No. I didn't. The voices. The voices.'

Storyteller stared at Her, bewildered. "I don't understand. What does it mean?"

She closed Her eyes. A silence passed, vaster than space, darker than the tunnel.

Humanity murdered its Mother and Father, *She* said, **and then journeyed to the farthest corners of its world to destroy a multitude of fellow species before being subdued.**

When the Authorities questioned them, they sobbed and whispered the same words:

'We had no choice. We had no choice. God, make the voices stop. We had no choice.'

'Why did you kill your Mother and Father?'

Because … we had no choice. We loved them. They were good. But we had no choice.'
'Why did you slaughter your kin?'
'The voices. We had no choice.'
'But you did have a choice, didn't you?'
'No. We didn't. The voices. The voices.'

She opened Her hand once more. The ant continued to explore the contours of *Her* palm, unhurried.

And from the Voices of the lone murderer and the multitudes murdered will come a messenger …

… youAvelsilentdoweohevenintoosendwatchholy …

"Stop!" he cried out.

She obeyed. The light held steady. *Her* face remained unchanged, but Her voice shifted, low and final.

Go to your future. Now.
The medication is set out. The meal is waiting. All is prepared.
Your next step approaches. It will be hard. Very hard.

Eyes shut, breath ragged, he ran. Past *Her*, into the tunnel. He ran until the dark gave way to a chamber lit only by a faint afterglow of *Her* luminescence. Above him, the trapdoor lay still—flat, implacable, a sealed invitation.

He dropped to the floor, knees drawn to his chest. For a long moment, he remained that way. Then he rose, climbed two steps up the bamboo ladder, pushed gently against the trapdoor, and let the light above enter his eyes.

He blinked.

A kitchen.

It was a kitchen.

~ *A Strange Dinner Party and the Seven Dreams Revisited* ~

Electric light, unnatural and metallic, washes across a white Corian countertop. Following its sterile gleam to the end, Storyteller sees black skillets, aluminum pans, wooden spoons of all shapes and sizes, a porcelain sink half-filled with soapy water, and a pile of unwashed bowls. A man stands with his back turned, hunched over one of the counters, humming softly as he chops something on a thick cutting board.

With his M-16 still at the ready, Storyteller moves slowly behind the man, his boots silent on the kitchen's hardwood floor. He passes under an archway adorned with flowery wallpaper, the walls lined with a curious mix of pastoral paintings, modernist prints, and suspended knick-knacks. The tension in his chest slowly recedes. A subtle, quiet peace settles over him. The air feels warm. Safe.

In the softly-lit dining room, he steps onto a thick, multicolored Persian rug. A large oak table commands the center. He leans his rifle against it carefully, close enough to reach, and takes his seat before an elegant setting: cloth napkin,

Wedgwood plate, polished silverware, a crystal water glass. Rachmaninoff's Piano Concerto No. 2 plays faintly in the background. The music soothes. For the first time since leaving The World, he feels fully calm. And, impossibly, happy.

Two guests eventually join him.

First, Diane, girlfriend from another life, arrives, but much older than she had been. Then comes Mark, the boy Storyteller somehow knows to be his future son. Mark wears a black T-shirt, jeans, and a backwards baseball cap. Despite his jungle fatigues, his bandoliers, the webbing heavy with grenades and weapons, Storyteller feels no shame. He knows he is only a ghost here, a visitor from the past, and for once, he is not too late.

Diane's gaze is filled with longing. Storyteller meets her eyes with unspoken love. He regrets his filthy appearance: unshaven, wild, even brutal. But he cannot look away. He is unable to speak, not yet. Something else must happen first.

At last, the man who had been chopping enters, plate and coffee in hand, and sits. Older. Stooped. Tired. It is Storyteller's future self. He does not see Diane. He does not see Mark. And at first, he does not see Storyteller. He eats in silence, unaware.

Then, gradually, awareness dawns. He lifts his water glass.

"Cheers," he says.

"Cheers," echo the others.

"Well, Diane, how was your day?"

She toys with a loose thread on her frock. "Busy. The kids were restless today, so I told them their behavior might cost them the field trip Tuesday if it didn't improve."

She glances at Storyteller.

"Way to go, Mom. Be tough," Mark says.

"Bet that threat worked," Storyteller adds with a small smile.

The man, still focused on Diane, replies, "Oh, she would've let them go anyway," his tone a mix of affection and quiet reproach.

"I know," Mark murmurs.

Storyteller studies Diane, overcome with love. The weight of her absence settles in his throat. "Just a gorgeous old softy," he murmurs. He rakes his fingers through his dirty hair. "Back when I was still in The World, you always kept a comb in my pocket. Without you . . . I never know where to put my hands. No pockets. Nowhere to hide."

Desire presses against him in its pure, raw form, but before he can act, his older self speaks, breaking the spell.

"I had another counseling session this afternoon."

Storyteller straightens. "How'd it go? Did the doctor finally acknowledge that I exist?"

No answer.

"Did he?"

"Did he what?" The man sounds irritated.

"Acknowledge that I exist."

"Not really. You know Toomey."

Storyteller exhales in relief. "Good. At least he's not buying your delusion."

Diane turns to Mark. "And how was your day, sweetie?"

"Molecular biology went fine, I think. Organic chemistry? Brutal. If I never hear the words 'carbon atom' again, I'll be thrilled." He glances at Storyteller. "How about you, Uncle?"

Uncle? Storyteller winces. Play along. It's worth the time.

"Come on, love," Diane coaxes. "You can tell us."

Can't. If I speak, he'll send me back.

"Go ahead," the man prompts.

Silence.

"Well?"

"I . . . I don't know—" Storyteller falters.

"Go ahead!" the man repeats, more forcefully.

"They're out there. Dead. Got to get help—"

"No!" shouts the man. "Don't start that again. Not in front of them."

Storyteller hardens. "You know the drill. 'Can I speak to Storyteller now?' That's what Toomey says. I'm part of the therapy."

The man glares. "I wish you and the others would stay buried. With Diane's help, I can live with the dreams. I don't need you."

"But the dreams are the key. All seven. Goddess says it's time."

"Goddess? What is this, mythology class? I never told Toomey about seven dreams."

"Really? So I guess I invented that too. Maybe you think I'm a multiple personality?"

The man scoffs. "Toomey says schizophrenia. He's wrong."

"But you take the meds?"

"Sometimes. It's precautionary. Just dreams."

"It's those dreams. You see? That's where it begins."

"No," says the man firmly. "Not seven dreams. Just noise in the night."

Storyteller looks disgusted. "Michael, that's not true. Once you give in, She'll explain them. You'll understand. You'll be reborn."

Diane interrupts gently, "They're just dreams, Michael. We're just therapy."

Speak for yourself, thinks Storyteller.

The man waves his hand dismissively. "I'm not afraid. Diane wakes me in time. Besides, you're all just figments."

He suddenly leans forward. "What are you doing here anyway? I didn't invite you."

Storyteller feigns confusion. "Really? I thought dinner was for the whole family."

"I can dismiss you. Anytime."

Then, more diplomatically: "But now that you're here, tell me about the dreams. So I can skip my next appointment."

Storyteller leans back, contempt barely hidden. "You know them already. You just don't understand them."

"What are they?"

"Fine. I'll begin. The first dream is ants. A warrior ant. The second is The Noise." He opens his mouth. The sound that emerges is alien, layered, impossible—

... *youAveIsilentdoweoheavenintosendwatchholy* ...

The man blanches. "What is that?!"

"You know," Storyteller whispers. "You've heard it. Tonight you'll hear it again. That's the third dream. Goddess. *She's* coming."

"I haven't seen any gods," the man scoffs. "Only shadows. Gods are putty. They do as I wish. I mold them. Sanctify them. Hate them. Worship them. They exist for my need."

Storyteller tilts his head. "But do you believe in the One True God?"

"No. I believe in abused children. Hiding in dark closets. Tortured in boiling tubs and forced silence. I believe in that suffering. Not in God."

"Michael!" Diane snaps.

"Let me speak," he says coldly. "The child begged, and still she burned. And that happens daily. So no, I do not believe in God."

Storyteller listens. Argument brews in his mind. *Goddess? Are You hearing this?*

Of course. And yes, I cried. But We did not create First Principles.
Fate or free will?
Of course.
Redemption?
Of course.

"Easy to say," Storyteller says aloud. "But Superman would call that free will."

The man scoffs. "Free will? Children suffer because of viruses. Earthquakes. Random cruelty. There's no will in that. Just absence."

Diane shifts, uncomfortable. "I believe God is with me," she says softly. "Michael, your disbelief isn't about the children. It's about something else. You never believed in us. Not really. Always the ones you left behind."

The man sighs. "Not true. You're all here, aren't you?"

Mark leans in. "Except for us, what do you believe in?"

"Atoms. Molecules. DNA. Death. Not God. Never God."

"Never say never," says Storyteller. He feels grounded. "God and Goddess will come tonight. In your pain."

"Fine," the man snaps. "Let's finish this. What are the others? Ghost of Christmas Past?"

"Fourth dream is me. Yourself—your delusional fractured twin—perpetually young in the cauldron of war. Fifth is Diane." He places his grimy hand over hers.

Diane doesn't flinch. She covers his hand with her own.

The man groans. "Why involve me? You stayed. I left. They're your dreams."

"That's what you think," Storyteller replies darkly. "You toy with gadgets while the world burns. You murder your Mother and Father with your consumption. Come back. Lose the fat, gain the wisdom."

"You're just my imagination," the man insists. "I'll prove it."

Storyteller braces—but he does not vanish. "Shocked? I'm still here. There are two more dreams."

"What are they?"

Storyteller hesitates. His future self wipes sweat from his brow.

"The sixth is ghosts. Apparitions. They come when the fever breaks."

"And the seventh?"

Storyteller taps the table. "This. The final secret."

... Tap. Tap. Tap....

Harder now. Then with his fist.

... TAP. TAP. TAP....

"No!" shouts the man, glasses askew. His voice turns to growl. "I told you . . . not in front of them."

Suddenly composed, he adjusts his glasses and smiles at Diane.

"So. Brad. Was he the ringleader again today?"

Storyteller feels himself fading. No. Not yet.

"Remember the seven dreams," he pleads. "Tonight."

"I won't go," says the man.

"One way or another," Storyteller says, "*She* will bring you back."

"Ding-dong, the wicked witch is dead," the man sings.

And as Storyteller vanishes, the last voice he hears is Diane's, excruciatingly casual: "Oh, him . . . Brad, I mean. I've been working on Brad. I think I'm starting to—"

~ Last Will and Testament ~

Storyteller awoke from the strange dream. He was crouched beneath the trap door leading to the fortress, knees drawn tightly to his chest, body aching as though he had been folded into that position for hours. The memory of fleeing Goddess down the tunnel shimmered at the edges of his mind. Through the fog, an image surfaced—Idaho—still and silent back in the tunnel's storage chamber.

I have to go back.

He lifted the trap door a crack and peered up into the church. Nothing moved except a few swirling leaves. In the distance, a low rhythmic thump pulsed through the air. Helicopter rotors? No. Just thunder. He eased the door shut and dropped lightly back to the floor. He tested the flashlight, satisfied himself it still worked, then extinguished the beam, let his eyes reacclimate to the dark, and turned toward the tunnel.

He walked slowly, following Mountain Man's faint leaf trail. The dream still clung to him, sticky and disjointed. Images drifted past and dissolved. One word returned again and again: odd. He felt spent. Emptied.

When he entered the chamber, he swept the beam across the space.
No Idaho.

A frown tightened his face. Had the man crawled off? He moved the light farther—then froze.

Bones.

A skeleton sat against the far wall, white against packed earth. Legs extended. Skull cocked at an unnatural angle.

A raw, low sound escaped him.

His thoughts disintegrated. Horror thickened his blood, made his limbs slow, clumsy. He inched forward, boots scraping the dirt. As he neared the remains, he saw the skeletal hand resting beside a loose pile of white fragments.

Ants. Swarming.

He followed their movement with the beam. A double line climbed and descended the tunnel wall. Those coming down each carried a sliver of paper in their jaws. At the base, they dropped their cargo into the growing pile and returned upward. Others crawled across the heap, searching. Each seemed to know what it was looking for. When a piece was found, the ant extracted it and carried it to a new position.

Storyteller followed the line. The beam revealed their destination.

He gasped and dropped to his knees.

A nearly completed page lay near the skeleton's hand. The ants continued their work. Words appeared as if written by the hive itself.

He leaned closer.

~

LAST WILL AND TESTAMENT OF MICHAEL G. POWERS
Article One

I, MICHAEL G. POWERS, a resident of Los Angeles County, California, declare this to be my will, and I hereby revoke all wills and codicils previously made by me. My deceased spouse, DIANE L.   POWERS, is the birth-mother of my only living child, MARK H. POWERS, whose birth date is August 27, 1980.

Article Two

I give the entire residue of my estate to the trustee then in office under that trust designated as THE POWERS FAMILY TRUST established February 23, 2001, of which th

~

The ants kept sorting, lifting, placing. Words continued to emerge. But Michael no longer watched. He sat collapsed at the skeleton's feet, hands pressed to his face.

Time dissolved. Through the thin veil of his fingers, he stared upward at the old parachute hanging from the ceiling. Its folds sagged, curling downward, glowing faintly, as if preparing to fall. Like the crest of a luminous wave, it seemed to lean toward him.

Michael. Michael. Wake up. You're dreaming again. Come on, Sweetheart. It's okay. Wake up. If you don't wake up now, you may never leave this place. Listen. Claire's calling for you. Answer her, Sweetheart . . . answer her . . . answer her . . .

The distant roar of ocean surf began to swell. Seagulls shrieked overhead.

A woman's voice pierced the roar—urgent, familiar: "Mike! Mike! Are you okay? Mike! Can you hear me?"

Chapter Six

Sand Castles II

Argue, Argue, Argue

*W*ell, *Great Goddess? You are silent. Is this little story ended, or do You have more with which to regale Me?*

Oh, foolish God. Humanity has gone bad and poisons the bloodstream of the Mother, but You continue to advocate for them. Even as humans intensify the Great Wailing that rises from life on Earth, Your elusive dream of surrendering to Fate drives You rigidly onward. I keep telling You that Fate starves at Probability's door, but it is no use. You shrivel to nothing from the lack of sustenance caused by Your faction's addiction to First Principles. Lately, You have turned Your back on Everything Else, succumbing to the power of the Human Condition. So in Your divine opium den, You languish upon Your ideological throne, mumbling through the thick fog of their smoldering souls such nonsense as "I am the resurrection and the life," and "I am Indra, the bull, strongest of all that exist," and "I am most great, I testify there is no god but Allah," and so on and so forth. And in consequence of Your ranting, they swallow salvation or redemption or some other dyspeptic snake-oil and, slightly nauseated, whisper back all their stories to beguile You while they run amok.

And for all that, My Goddess, You tell Me yet another of their stories. Why? Do You not know that I am fully conversant with the Human Condition? You still have not provided that reunion You talked so much about. You remember, the reunion that I was so kindly invited to attend? Regardless, if humans destroy the planet, it was meant to be from the Beginning.

The Reunion is coming soon enough, Dear God. And yes, You are still invited. In fact, Your presence is crucial.

Reunions, My Dear Goddess, are yet another example of the Human Condition.

The Human Condition! Oh, I am sick to death, if I could die, of all their whining about the Human Condition! Traumatized soldiers and vapid sales-men, doomed lovers and dopey debutantes, murderous kings and mournful mothers, anorexic daughters and dying homosexuals, hoary patrons and horny poltroons, whining Irishmen lowing like cows about their childhood poverty and Somali children quietly dying of starvation, dissolute dissolutes and lonely loners and isolated imbeciles, misunderstood mafiosi and scheming courtiers and simpering slaves and sadistic dictators and teenage angst and eccentric aunts and fat uncles and decent middle class classes wriggling like worms across their middle class driveways and rain forest chieftains stinking with noble savagery and bloated caricatures from the American south and terrorists terrorizing the terrorists, and sanguine shepherds, and loved ones stricken with cancer and ... war. Ah! The Human Condition, a sweet and sour milk that keeps them suckling at the technological nipple of their own infantilism, deeming the entire Universe to dwell only in their self-absorbed little brains while they blissfully continue to consume, unaware that Mother's Diaper cannot cope. Meanwhile, they're murdering Everything Else–including Me. Is that what You want? Are You so blind to the Great Wailing that You would empty the Universe of companionship? Humans have reached the end of their reign. You should welcome the arrival of Superior Ones.

Hallelujah! No, Ma'am, My addiction is miraculously gone! I'm cured! I see the Light!

I hear an ocean ...

Yes, that is right. An ocean. You are an ocean for Me.

... the Great Mother beckons....

~ Return to the Beach ~

"Mike!" calls Claire kneeling in front of the man. "Mike! Are you okay? Mike! Can you hear me?"

Crouching next to Claire, Paul demands in an exasperated voice, "Mike, take your hands away from your face and look at me."

The silence and darkness of the tunnel peels away, leaving him exposed. Sunlight blinds. Salt breeze stings. Seagulls scream. Waves growl. Paul and Claire continue asking worried questions, trying to draw Michael back into their world.

He strains to hear their voices and is unaware of the other people at the beach. Finally he cracks his fingers and hesitantly peers through. Cirrus clouds thread across the blue sky, and he imagines God composing chalky equations from some unknown physics.

Beneath the expanse, people have gathered in a group around him.

Men.

Women and children.

Old people.

A beautiful young woman with angry bruises discoloring her skin.

A mother holding a baby.

An elderly couple.

An aged African-American woman.

"Mike!" Claire's insistent voice reaches him, her words distorted by the thick fog of evaporating memory. "Mike!"

Deep in the shadow of his umbrella, Michael begins to stir. Breathing becomes easier. More regular. His heartbeat calms. Fever gone. He almost feels cold.

Paul casts a relieved glance at Claire, encouraged that Michael is showing signs of acknowledging their presence.

"Mike? Are you okay?" asks Claire for the hundredth time as she leans under the umbrella, inches from the man's face. Claire, ever the reluctant crew member, begins to pull him back with her stubborn persistence.

And Michael wants to come back. Desperately.

The words that announce his arrival are simple: "Yeah, I'm okay."

"Whew!" says Paul. "I was beginning to worry. Friend, you were far, far away. Why don't we all go home and you can get some rest? You must have had a rough night. Eh?"

A primordial stubbornness grabs hold of Michael and he will not easily give up the patch of territory on which he has been feeding. God continues to write equations with the cirrus clouds against a blue expanse. He shakes his head.

"Yeah. Some night. But . . . let's not leave. I'm okay. Just dreaming. And the kids are having fun."

"Are you sure?" asks Claire in a worried tone.

"Yeah. I'm sure."

Claire looks at him dubiously, but his attention is drawn to the sand castle where John and Lisa are still playing, their piercing shouts intrude into the serenity of the beach.

Michael cocks his head and listens.

"They're dead! They're dead!" John shouts triumphantly. "Killed by the mean T-Rex!" He picks up the dinosaur and smashes the sand walls, plowing it through the toy soldiers, scattering them in every direction.

"Stop it!" cries Lisa. "They're not dead!"

"Yes, they are!"

"No, they're not! They're just sleeping. They're under an evil spell. If I kiss them they'll all wake up and go home and be safe. Then they'll be with their mommies and daddies. Keep your ugly old dinosaur away from them!" Lisa grabs the toy soldiers, one by one, and cradles them in her arms.

"They're all dead!" insists John. "They've all been killed by the most ferocious dinosaur that ever was!" Again, he brandishes the T-Rex in a triumphant gesture. He begins to growl, mimicking the sound of a rampaging dinosaur.

But Lisa is oblivious to his bluster. She speaks soothingly to each soldier as she places it gently in her bag. "Don't worry. I'll take care of you. You'll be safe in here. I'll take care of you."

"Aw! Don't put them away!" cries a disappointed John. "If you do that, I'll take your doll. I'll throw it! Honest I will!"

~ *God and Goddess Are Caught* ~

The greatest ideas are not those conceived by Aristotle or Confucius, Jesus or Mohammed, Buddha, Newton or Einstein or You, Metaphorical God. The greatest ideas, by far, are those that have occurred to the Universe ten thousand steps removed from the insubstantial shadow of human thought: quanta and atoms, carbon and hydrogen, amino acids and nucleic acids, proteins, bacteria and viruses, each carrying in the core of its own existence more fundamental truth than all the libraries of humankind. Fundamental truths: Fusion to a sun. Atmosphere to a planet. Predator to a prey. Parent to a child.

Nonsense. I can tell You–

As for them, there is nothing so touchingly sweet as when a child trusts and relies so totally on its parents.

And fears. Never forget. There must be discipline. There must be fear. First Principles–

Always Your fear. I will take Your children from this dark pit and make it shine again–

No! Don't! Leave them there. Or else . . . aw, anyway, come on! Play just a little longer, okay?

No. I don't want to play with You any more. I'll protect them until I can't. Oh, poor babies.

Stubborn Goddess! I've already tossed Your precious Kim Lan and Dam and Nature and Mountain Man and the rest into the fire. Now, I'll do the same to Tuyet Mai and Madame Dau. I will! If you don't–

No! Stop it! Make Him stop!

GOD! DON'T THROW LISA'S DOLL!

"But, Mom"

"I'LL ONLY SAY THIS ONE MORE TIME, JOHN, DON'T THROW LISA'S DOLL!"

"Okay, Mom."

"Ahh, poor John. It's okay. Don't be sad. I'll play with you a little more," says Lisa coyly. "But . . . hurry! Hurry, 'cause I'm going to take my doll away! She's getting tired, and I don't want to wait any longer." But Lisa sees John hesitating.

"Nah," he says rubbing his stomach, "I'm hungry. Mom! I'm hungry!"

Lisa is frustrated. She diverts John's attention by kicking sand on his feet. "Come on," she pleads, "let's play again!"

John sees that his mother is glaring at him, obviously still upset about the doll. He decides not to push the food issue, but still isn't sure about playing with Lisa.

Sensing his indecision, Lisa presses. "Come on, John, let's play some more. I want to–"

"Okay, okay," he relents. "I'll get the soldiers. Here they are." Soon, he is back into the excitement of another battle. "Wait a minute! Wait! Wait! Oh. I found it.

Here he is! Now T-Rex is gonna attack again. But, first. . . . " John tamps handfuls of sand atop the damaged walls and begins sculpting new parapets.

"Aren't you ready yet?" asks Lisa impatiently. "Put the soldiers back! Come on! Ohhh. Poor soldier. Look, he doesn't have a hand. Ahh, and this one doesn't have a foot. Okay! Let's put them back in the fort! I'll put my doll here. Now they can save her from your dumb dinosaur again."

"Wait a minute!" yells John. "First let the dinosaur try and get her, then she can run inside the fort!"

"Okay, but not too hard." Lisa holds up her doll.

John hits it with his T-Rex. . .

Tap. Tap. Tap.

Lisa keeps holding. . .

Tap. Tap. Tap.

And John keeps hitting. . .

Tap. Tap. Tap.
Tap. Tap. Tap.

Chapter Seven

BOOK II

FALCONS AND FALCONERS

~ The Americans Arrive ~

At dawn, Madame Dau woke from her contorted position in the chair, one leg abruptly unfolding from where it had been tucked beneath her. Groggy, she scanned the room to make sure what belonged still belonged, and what had never existed remained absent. Her gaze fixed on a dark figure. Startled, yet curiously calm, she peered through the altar smoke to confirm the form was real. Pale reddish light slanted through the window, revealing the face of a young North Vietnamese soldier crouched across from her.

Yes. She remembered now.

He hadn't moved since she'd drifted off. He remained statue-still, a vacant teacup beside his bare, finely shaped feet. Without a word, she began preparing another pot of tea. When she refilled his cup, he drank quietly. As she leaned forward to pour more, he glanced toward the window, his eyes wistful. Then, placing his free hand gently atop the cup, he tilted his head.

I must be going, he said softly in a voice not human. **You'll soon have other visitors—**

He paused, head still cocked, listening.

Ah. Poor Madame Dau. I hear them now. They're arriving. It's time for me to go.

He set the cup carefully on the floor and rose.

Madame Dau listened, but heard only roosters and the occasional bark of a dog. A warm flush of fear crept down her neck. "What visitors? I've told you, I'm not expecting anyone. I don't hear anything." She glanced uneasily at the window. "Who?"

Others.

The word chilled her. Disoriented, still holding the teapot, she followed the soldier as he backed toward the door.

"What visitors?" she repeated, more urgently. He said nothing.

Summoning courage, she spoke with both politeness and resolve. "Please, spirit soldier. What visitors? You frighten me. Stay. At least until we finish this pot. I don't want to be alone. Please."

He sighed. When he'd first arrived, his presence had been ethereal, face impassive, voice a soft monotone. Now, he looked defeated. His features sagged, voice low and burdened with sorrow.

Before you face your tomorrows, he said, smoothly taking the pot from her hands and setting it on the table, *before you repair your dikes, care for your family, worship Us, honor your ancestors, tend the sick, nurture the young, hold your village together—before all that—*

He opened the door slowly.

—you must face another trial. Yes. Another.

Stepping outside, he looked upward, squinting into the light.

The monsoon has passed. This time the butterfly's wing scattered the sheltering storm. The rain and wind—gone. And in their place....

He fell silent again.

Driven by dread, she broke the stillness. "What?"

Goddess raised a graceful palm to quiet her, narrowed *Her* eyes, tilted Her head again, listening, and whispered: **Visitors.**

A low hum drifted across the horizon. At first, she thought a beehive had been disturbed. But as she turned toward the sound, the soldier vanished.

The hum grew louder. Then came the sickening realization, it was not bees. It was helicopters. Many. The deep, collective drone of troop carriers rose in waves, soon joined by the piercing shriek of gunships.

The suddenness of their arrival crushed her breath. She slammed the door and leaned against it, hand pressed to her chest. Her Mickey Mouse sticker hovered silently over her shoulder.

Outside, panic.

"Americans! Americans are coming!"

Thump! Thump! Thump!

Helicopters.

Ka-boom! Ka-boom!

Explosions.

Frantic pounding on the door. "Mama! Mama! Let me in!"

Madame Dau flung it open. Bin tumbled in, then pulled Teo after her. Panting, wild-eyed, Bin clung to her mother's tunic like a child, swaying unsteadily, on the edge of collapse.

"Mama! What do we do, Mama!"

Teo broke away, wrapping himself around Madame Dau's leg. "Grandmama! Grandmama!"

Their cries blended into a tangled blur. Her mind raced to find traction—command, plan, action—but nothing came. The pace of the world had overtaken her. Too fast. Too fast.

"Mama!" Bin shouted again, louder.

Madame Dau gripped her daughter's arm. "Take Teo to Auntie Vit's house. Now. Quickly! Into the tunnels!"

Bin hesitated, but Madame Dau batted her hand away, detached Teo from her leg, and shoved them both toward the door.

They fled.

Madame Dau turned and rushed to her bedroom. Pulling aside the curtain, she faced Tuyet Mai—the beautiful intelligence officer propped in bed, her bandaged stumps protruding from a military tunic. Her eyes, once luminous with defiance, now widened with terror. Captain Tong hovered over her, gripping her hand tightly, murmuring, "Dear Tuyet Mai, Dear Tuyet Mai," while peering nervously out the window. His pith helmet wobbled on his head.

Madame Dau's gaze fell to Tuyet Mai's ruined legs. Her voice trembled. "What are we going to do?"

"Is the strange soldier gone?" asked Tong.

"Yes."

Ka-boom! Ka-boom!

Explosions again, closer.

"Hide me!" he shouted.

"What?"

"Hide me before Lieutenant Tran finds me here!"

"But ,the Americans—"

"Hide me!"

"Yes, I—yes!" Madame Dau spun into action. "If they find me I'll be shot, or buried alive—ah!" She yanked aside sacks of rice, revealing a trap door.

"Wait!" came Tuyet Mai's desperate voice. "Come back! Don't leave me!"

But Tong was already descending into the hiding place. "Put the sacks back! Now!"

Just as Madame Dau reached for the first bag, the front door burst open.

Three People's Army soldiers stormed in.

"Where's Comrade Tuyet Mai?" bellowed Lieutenant Tran.

Madame Dau froze. She glanced toward the closed trapdoor and prayed they hadn't seen. She pointed toward the bedroom.

Tran charged in.

"Forget your rice, Dau! Get into the tunnels!"

He halted at Tuyet Mai's bed, eyeing her bandaged stumps. "Comrade Tuyet Mai, the Americans are coming. We have the others. But you—" his voice hardened, "you are a woman. You understand."

Tuyet Mai stared at him, trapped, aware but still foggy.

"I . . . you . . . what will I—"

Gunfire crackled nearby.

"I must go!" he barked. The other soldiers raced out. He followed, shouting, "American bastards! We will be back, comrade!"

Madame Dau saw it then—the twin shadows on Tuyet Mai's face: fear and despair. Maybe tears too. But another explosion drove her into the other room.

Tong's head emerged from the floorboards.

"Get down!" she ordered. "I have to close it!"

"No!" he snapped. "You get out! Find your daughter and grandson! Go!"

"But this is—"

Gunfire shredded her words. Smoke and dust poured through the windows.

"Get out now, stupid woman!" Tong shouted. "If you stay, you'll die!"

From the other room: "Don't leave me! Don't leave me!" Tuyet Mai cried.

"Go!" Tong ordered again.

Madame Dau touched the Mickey Mouse sticker, muttered a short prayer to the rodent god, and fled.

Outside, the world had come undone. Helicopters roared. Explosions shook the ground. Gunfire devoured the familiar rhythms of the village. Smoke towered above rooftops. Madame Dau pressed herself against Carpenter Long's house, hands caressing the bamboo frame, pretending she'd only come for tea.

But the backwash from the choppers scoured her face with smoke and ash. She pulled her chin scarf over her mouth, squinted through the haze, and ran toward Madame Vit's house.

She didn't get far.

A figure loomed beside her. A hand seized her arm and dragged her back. Another man struck her chest with an open palm. She dropped. Dust clogged her mouth. She tried to cry out, but a boot slammed into her ribs, knocking the breath from her body.

Darkness.

When she came to, she was lying in the dirt, staring at two pairs of American boots. One pair was polished, new, the boots that had kicked her. The other, worn and cracked. Recognition stirred.

The Man from the Mountains?

No. Not him.

Voices in English buzzed above her.

"Hey mama-san! Where's the VC? Beaucoup VC? Come on, bitch! Where's your home?"

The black-booted soldier turned, frustrated. "Sergeant Crawford, I can't get nothin' out of—"

"Shut up, Lager. You don't know shit about this. Take her to the others. Interpreter's with Captain Barnett. Move."

Lager yanked her up and shoved her forward.

Across the courtyard, another American waved through the smoke. "Over here! Hey, Lager! Park her with the other ugly little munchkins from this funky dung heap!"

A cluster of villagers sat huddled beneath the guns of American soldiers. Among them, a Vietnamese interpreter stood watching.

~

Lieutenant Quoc of the ARVN had served as interpreter for years. Thin, even by Vietnamese standards, born to wealthy Saigon parents, he held nothing but contempt for country folk.

When Madame Dau was shoved before him, he curled his lip and let his cigarette droop.

"Another one for you, Quack," said Lager, before trotting off.

Quoc exhaled slowly, smoke curling from his mouth. He motioned with a crooked finger for her to approach. As she stepped forward, he blew smoke into her face.

"How long have you worked for the Front, eh? We know about the American platoon. The one massacred near the old fortress. You helped the People's Army kill them. Didn't you? Speak."

She clutched her peasant hat. "Uh? No. I—"

He cut her off. "Your eyes say yes. I'm never wrong, you know. Isn't that true?"

She stared at the ground.

"I said, isn't that true?"

"Yes."

An American officer leaned toward Quoc. "What'd she say?"

"Remember what I taught you, sir. 'Vang' means yes. She just admitted she's VC."

Madame Dau did not understand. But *Schoolmistress Nang*, who stood nearby, did.

She straightened her spine and addressed the officer. "Americannn sssirrr. Nooo. Thisss womannn isss loyal tooo Southh."

Before the officer could respond, Quoc walked over, removed his steel helmet, and smashed it into Nang's face.

The sound of metal crushing bone silenced the group. She crumpled to the ground, blood pouring from her mouth and nose.

The American stared in shock. "What the hell was that for?"

"VC trash," Quoc muttered.

He waved the bloodied helmet at Madame Dau. "Take us to your house!"

Nearby, a radio operator recoiled, shaking his hand like it had touched fire. "Shit! Old Quack knocked her lights out!"

The officer chuckled. "This is what they understand. They don't respond to anything else."

Satisfied with his cultural insight, he instructed a runner to summon a medic. "Let's patch up the old lady. Show these people we're here to help."

Quoc smiled. Nodded. *Fools. You kill them from miles away, then flinch when you see the blood.*

He turned back to Madame Dau. "Well? Take us to your house. Now."

She began to walk.

Quoc turned to the officer.

"She's cooperating. Shall we go, sir? I have a hunch we'll find something. A hunch."

He repeated the word proudly.

The officer grinned.

"Sure. You, you, you and you. Let's go."

~ *Tuyet Mai and Captain Tong are Arrested* ~

By the time they reached Madame Dau's house, half the village was in flames. Shaking from the shock of the sudden onslaught, she stopped and gazed, heartbroken, at her ancestral home. She was determined to see it one last time, to fix the image in her memory, exactly as it was now.

Holding her peasant hat to her head, she tilted back and stared at the place where she'd been born, where she had raised her children and grandchildren, where her husband had died of typhus so many years ago. Near the porch, her dog May Man strained furiously at the rope tied to the old papaya tree, barking at the soldiers. Then came the deafening burst of M-16 fire.

She flinched and shut her eyes.

When she opened them, pieces of May Man were scattered around the tree. His leash remained taut, still attached to his partially severed head.

Reeling from the sight, praying that Bin and Teo were safe, Madame Dau stumbled onto the porch and opened the door. The American soldiers shoved past her and stormed inside.

Weakened by fear, she squatted on the threshold, listening.

Voices came. They were loud, urgent, and cruel.

"*Chieu hoi! Chieu hoi!*" It was Captain Tong's voice.

"*Get down! Down! Hands behind your head!*" Quoc screamed in Vietnamese.

"*Chieu hoi! Chieu hoi!*" Tong cried again.

"*Down, you dink bastard!*" came an American voice.

"Captain Barnett, sir!" another soldier called. "Come in here! Look what we found! A woman with no legs! In here!"

"I'll be damned," said the officer, entering the house. "Look at this. Go get the owner. Bring her in. Quack! Come here! I want to talk to this VC woman!"

~

They forced Madame Dau to sit on her wooden bed. At her feet lay the shattered remnants of the family shrine. The photograph of her husband, once worshipped above the altar for more than twenty years, was now torn and dirt-smeared, trampled beneath the boots of soldiers. The frame, imported from China and worth nearly a month's wages, lay broken.

An American bent to retrieve a mango from the upturned offering bowl, but the officer slapped it from his hand.

"Don't be stupid, Carter! It's probably poisoned! I've told you a thousand times, don't touch anything! Got it?"

"Yes, sir."

Quoc stood with hands on hips, eyes fixed on Captain Tong, his voice dripping with contempt. "*Chieu hoi?* Don't be ridiculous. You're only surrendering because you have no choice. Isn't that true?"

"No."

Quoc slapped him. "Americans like helicopter rides for prisoners. Higher. Higher. High enough to enjoy our beautiful southern forests. Best view in Vietnam—upside down, head dangling, ankles held tight. Unless you're too stubborn. Then they let go."

He leaned in.

"You're People's Army. From the look of you, an officer. Correct?"

"*Chieu hoi.*"

"The woman in the next room. Is she with you?"

"*Chieu hoi.*"

"Want her to take a ride too? Might be tricky, no ankles to hold onto, eh, comrade?"

"No! She's just a villager. Stepped on a mine. Lost both legs. That's the truth."

Quoc's eyes narrowed.

"Who treated her?"

Tong hesitated. "Uh . . . the local herbalist."

"What's her name?"

Tong shook his head. "Old village woman. I don't know her name."

Quoc smiled and glanced at the American captain to ensure he was listening. Then he turned back to Tong, pressing harder.

"Is that the truth?"

"Yes."

Quoc turned again to the officer.

"You heard him, sir. I asked if they were VC. He said *vang.*"

"That means 'yes,' right?"

"Yes, sir. Same as the old woman. They're all VC. I respectfully suggest we take the legless woman and the man for interrogation. As for this old one"—he glanced at Madame Dau—"useless, probably, but you never know. Might be hiding something."

The American rubbed his chin, studying Madame Dau.

Quack, you little bastard, I can't give you everything you want, can I?

He crossed the room, tapped the Mickey Mouse sticker on the wall, and turned with a smirk.

"No. Leave her. Anyone with a Mickey Mouse sticker's okay by me."

He grinned.

Quoc bared his teeth in response, eyes flicking back to Madame Dau.

"Yes, sir. Then let's just burn her house. Purify the VC stench. Teach the others a lesson, eh, Captain?"

The officer gave a vague nod.

Quoc smiled without warmth. He turned his attention back to Madame Dau.

"Do you want us to spare your house?" he asked in Vietnamese, his voice oily, coaxing.

Madame Dau's throat tightened. "*Vâng xin*," she said, letting the word fall as she meant it—yes, please.

Quoc's laugh was sharp, triumphant. "You see, sir? She said yes. She wants us to burn her house. Cleanse it of the VC stink."

The officer chuckled, pleased with his own grasp of the language. "I heard it that time. I understood."

Quoc bared his teeth. "Yes, sir. You understand Vietnamese very good. Very good."

Dau kept her eyes lowered, but inside, she felt the Spirit Soldier's voice again, faint and unrelenting: *Before all else, another trial.* This was it. Not the helicopters, not the flames, not even the loss of the shrine—but the stripping away of meaning itself. A word turned against her, truth bent until it snapped.

The American waved a vague hand. "Do it. Teach them a lesson."

Quoc turned toward her one last time, eyes bright with the satisfaction of a man who could command both fire and permission.

Dau touched the Mickey Mouse sticker on the wall. For a heartbeat, she imagined it as a seal against all of them, a fragile ward against the world's new order. The roosters were silent now. The ground felt hollow beneath her bare feet.

She did not look up as the first shouts rang out, or when the smell of smoke began to thread through the air.

Somewhere beyond this moment, she knew, the trial would end but not the reckoning. No, the reckoning had only begun.

Chapter Eight

Undercover Operations

Traps

Dear Reader, after the fortress fell, the war did not relent. It shifted its ground, flowing into cells and cages, where memory became another battlefield. History did not pause for the dead; it dragged the living forward into the next prison.

~ *Con Son Prison* ~

Pham Van Dinh sat up in bed. For the first time since he had been assigned the night shift, he looked forward to going to work. He had been a guard at Con Son Island Prison for years, and the routine of sanctioned cruelty had begun to dull even the sharpest edges of his indifference. Almost fifty years old, Dinh often complained to his fellow guards that he was "getting too old for a young man's job." But tonight would be different. Very different. He felt excited and moved the kerosene lamp closer to read the rumpled memorandum from the prison administrator for the thousandth time:

Date: February 23, 1971
To: All prison guards
From: Commandant Tran
As you have been told, more female prisoners will be incarcerated in our illustrious prison and will arrive next month. Most will be housed in the usual cells. However, some special prisoners will be assigned to Section 12. Shift schedules will be posted. Guards are expected to report to their section commanders for further briefing. Failure to follow your instructions will result in severe penalties.
-Tran

"What are you reading?" asked a fragile voice from the darkness.

Dinh quickly folded the paper and slipped it back in his shirt pocket, carefully fastening the button. "Nothing, Mother. It's nothing."

He shook his head, stood and parted the curtain to her room. *How did you know I was reading something?*

"I must leave. I'm already late," he whispered, as if speaking too loudly would shatter her.

"Tomorrow I will be well enough to cook for you," she said with tears in her eyes. Her trembling hand reached out and grabbed the fabric of his loose-fitting trousers. "I tried to leave my bed this morning, but I fell."

"No! No! Why didn't you call me?"

"It's nothing. Tomorrow I will cook for you."

"Oh!" he cried in a startled voice. Lifting his hand as if to strike something, his mother saw the object of his concern.

"Little Dinh! No! You know what to do."

"Yes, mama," Dinh replied. He reached down and gently scooped up a lizard that had been crawling on his mother's cotton bedspread.

Still holding the lizard in one hand, he caressed her arm with the other, leaned over and kissed her cheek, then turned and disappeared through the curtain.

"Be careful at work, my son!" her words tinkled after him like shards of a broken teacup. "Tomorrow I will cook! Tomorrow!"

"Yes! Yes! See you in the morning," he called over his shoulder. "Now sleep, Mother. Sleep."

Taking five steps outside the house, Dinh crushed the lizard in his hand, tossed it in the street and wiped his hand on his trousers. The damp air made him realize he had forgotten to take his hat. He turned and crept back inside, being careful not to make any noises that might disturb his mother. Snatching his hat from its perch on the bamboo hook by the door, he decided to see if she had fallen asleep. He tip-toed to the curtain and slowly parted it. A narrow shaft of light from the room fell partially on her bed, illuminating his mother's arm, thin as a twig and hanging limply down the side of the bed. Her hand kneaded a wad of fabric as though preparing dough for dumplings. A surge of love swept over him as he saw her fragile fingers and he remembered when he was a boy and how often she would grab him in her once strong arms and squeeze him playfully. The thought of her dying, of him never seeing her again, made his eyes mist over and he softly crept back out of the house and into the foggy night. *But she's still alive! I'll see her when I get home after work. She's still alive!* And his gloomy thoughts were chased away by the anticipation of seeing her after his night shift ended.

~

Dinh underwent a transformation on the way to Con Son Island. When he first boarded the dilapidated, overcrowded bus after leaving his mother, his demeanor was affable, even jovial.

"Hey! Good evening!" he said to fellow passengers. "Off to work! No time to play. Not like you lucky dogs. Where do I work? Ha! A toy factory! Can you believe it? We make little toys. All kinds of toys. Mostly soldiers. But now we have a new line. Oh, yes. A new line. Huh? Dolls. Women dolls. Girl dolls. You know, pretty women in their *ao dais*. And others. Others. Huh? Oh, yes! Sometimes we play with the toys ourselves."

He picked up a little girl standing unsteadily nearby and put her on his lap. "Even we find our dolls irresistible. You little tadpoles can't have all the fun! Eh?"

But as the bus neared the docks where he would board a ferry to the island, he became silent and sullen. He began grinding his teeth and clenched and unclenched his fists as if he were working out a cramp. "Damn mosquitoes!" he growled.

"Good night, Dinh," said the bus driver, his eyes twinkling in the glare of a hissing streetlight. "Have fun with your toys."

Dinh grunted. He boarded the ferry and sat silently, as did everyone else. But one thought dominated his silent meditations: *fresh women, fresh women, fresh women*. All of the old ones had either been killed or tortured until whatever beauty they possessed had been obliterated. It had been a long time since women were billeted in his section. And now: *fresh women.*

~

Tuyet-Mai had arrived at Con Son Island early that morning. Since being captured at Song Nhan village almost two years earlier, she had been incarcerated at Thu Duc Prison making army uniforms and mosquito nets in exchange for a daily bowl of rotten rice. But now, to her despair, she had been transferred to the most notorious prison in South Vietnam. As soon as she disembarked from the ferry, a tag was placed on her chest designating a Section 12 Inmate and she was carried directly to a sunken, three-meter-square stone cell, what was euphemistically called a "tiger cage", with the faded number 46 above the door. She had already been there for hours when nighttime arrived and blackness seemed to harden around her as if she were entombed in a lump of coal. She lay in the dark on a raised stone slab, looking up through an iron grill at a dimly lit catwalk across which guards periodically walked. Only their vulture-like shadows and the soles of their boots were visible. She shivered uncontrollably, as her cage was cold and damp and her clothes had been taken when she first arrived. Two oil soaked rags covered her stumps, merely serving to accentuate her nakedness. Twice she had started to pull them off, the better to elicit either pity or revulsion, but somehow thought it better to leave them. For a long time she had tried to concentrate on remembering her parents and the village she grew up in, but the horror stories she had heard about Con Son Prison kept intruding on her thoughts.

Finally, she succeeded in thinking of nothing at all. Of emptying her mind. Even the moans and cries of other prisoners drifting in through the grillwork faded into oblivion. She closed her eyes and surrendered to sleep.

And then Kim Lan visited.

~

Kim Lan stood in the corner of the cage. Tuyet Mai's beloved old friend, clothed in the same uniform she had worn the day she died, gazed sympathetically from the darkness, her eyes shimmering like specks of frost in moonlight. "You're here!" cried Tuyet Mai. "I called you so many times while I was at Thu Duc, but you never came!"

Kim Lan smiled and shrugged. "That was Thu Duc, this is Con Son."

Tuyet Mai struggled to lean up on her elbows. Kim Lan moved closer to the stone slab so that Tuyet Mai could see by merely turning her head.

"Is that better?" Kim Lan asked.

"Yes."

"Remember when we first met?"

"Of course, in Hanoi. It seems a hundred years ago."

"Yes. I had just been made your assistant and was ordered to report to your office. Your desk was full of papers. I remember very well. You had just spilled a cup of tea over some reports and when I entered, you were still dabbing at them with your scarf and muttering to yourself. Then you looked up. You took my breath away! Your face was severe. Hard. Angry. Yet, even so, I thought, *oh, she is so beautiful! So beautiful!*"

Tuyet Mai laughed. "No longer," and she looked down at her non-existent legs.

Kim Lan's eyes glistened. "More beautiful!"

"Kim Lan, I—"

"Shhhhh. Just listen for a minute. I don't have much time."

"But—"

"Listen! That's always been one of your problems. You never listen. I have something important to tell you. The—"

Tuyet Mai squinted at the beam of light that shone into her eyes from above the bars. She blinked through the beam, trying to see Kim Lan, but her friend was gone. "No! Come back!" she shouted.

Cruel laughter wafted down from behind the beam of light. "What's the matter, prisoner! Dreaming of better times? Of home? Husband? Mother? Father? Hah! You gave them all up when you betrayed our country! Here's a little reminder of the price to be paid for treachery and deceit!"

Something poured down upon her from the grillwork. At first it felt like wet dirt or sand. But within seconds, a deep burning scalded her body, as if she were submerged in acid and her skin was being burned off layer by layer. She screamed, rocking her torso, fists clenched in agony.

"Welcome to Con Son! Just a little lime to help cleanse you of the dirt you bring to our prison!" came the voice. "You should be happy! . . . Lice don't like it!"

~

Dinh waited for her screaming to subside. When she fell quiet, he shined his flashlight down into the cage to observe his handiwork. The shaft of light fell on her arm, thin as a twig, hanging limply from the side of the stone slab on which she laid. Her hand clenched and unclenched in pain. *Mother!* A surge of love swept over him as he remembered his mother's fragile fingers just hours earlier. *Those hands when I was a boy, lifting me, comforting me, squeezing me playfully!* Once again he thought of her dying, of never seeing her again.

Does this one have children? Maybe she has a son. . . . He moved the light to her face and was stunned by her beauty, a beauty that shone through even the abject misery of her condition and the swollen red welts caused by the lime. Moving the beam down her body, he marveled at the perfection of her breasts and her erotically lush mound of pubic hair. Barely able to contain his excitement, he moved the light even further. When he saw that she had no legs, a profound sadness that such beauty had been mutilated made him pause, but this sentiment was quickly replaced by an odd attraction the stumps held for him. Again, he gazed at her hand, fist clenched in pain. *Mother.*

He raised the clipboard that was attached by a chain to his belt and flipped to the page that listed the prisoners in his section. Scrolling his index finger down the names, he came to cage forty-six: Nguyen Tuyet Mai.

He shined the beam back on the prisoner. "Hey, Nguyen Tuyet Mai! Do you have children?"

Silence.

"Nguyen Tuyet Mai!"

Silence.

"Do you want more lime?"

Hesitation, then a shaky, "No."

"No more lime, or no children?"

"No children . . . and no more lime."

Dinh felt momentarily disappointed that she had no children. But then his brain began processing a vaguely exciting thought coalescing on the periphery of his consciousness. He shined his light on her abdomen. "Can you?"

Long hesitation. "Can I what?"

"Can you have children?"

Shorter hesitation, then a firm, "Yes."

The roving beam of light wandered to her breasts. "Married?"

No hesitation. "No."

His heart began to beat faster and the vague image in the back of his mind emerged from the fog fully formed.

"Nguyen Tuyet Mai! No more lime for you! I'll be right back!"

~

Tuyet Mai smiled in the dark. It had happened so often in the past. So often. She waited patiently.

~

"Catch!"

A warm biscuit dropped on her stomach and she caught it before it rolled off onto the floor. With the flashlight shining in her face, she quickly brushed off any lime that stuck to the crust and gulped it down as slowly and delicately as her ravenous stomach and shaking hands would allow. *He must see a refined lady, not a starving beast.*

"I'll be back later," called Dinh, "and I'll bring another biscuit."

Kim Lan's disembodied voice chuckled from the corner. "See! Even more beautiful! And they remain just as susceptible!"

"Yes. The means to my survival. Still, I thought I was done with all this filthy deception when I stayed with Madame Dau"

"Forget Madame Dau! Yessss, I know. I know what you're thinking. A quiet life. A quiet village. Friendly neighbors. A kind husband. Fertile fields. Children playing. But that is not your fate. Not yet. Besides, you saw what happened to Madame Dau's beloved village."

"Is it rebuilt?"

"Only partially."

"And Madame Dau?"

"Alive. But it's a hard life for her. Very hard. Anyway, I've already told you, that life you want, that peaceful life you have mistakenly idealized is Madame Dau's life, and is not your fate."

"Will it ever be?"

"Fate starves at probability's door."

"What?"

"Tuyet Mai, I don't know when fate will allow you to live in peace—or even whether you will be allowed to continue living. All I know is you must try."

Tuyet Mai laughed. "Why not? What else to do after death but keep up with the latest news about the living? Ghosts gossip, don't they? Especially about me, since I've given you much to gossip to your ghost friends about."

"Death is known only to the living."

"But your own children! What about them?"

Kim Lan raised a hand, signaling Tuyet Mai had touched upon a taboo topic, then muttered, "And the living are best left unknown to the dead."

"But I am living and you pay attention to me."

Kim Lan fell silent.

~

At the end of his shift, as dawn began to smudge the eastern sky with pink, Dinh sat in a small anteroom near the tiger cages eating a hot bun and briefing his replacement.

"What about it, Dinh?" asked the big guard squatting opposite him. "New women, eh? Any pretty ones in our section?" He punched Dinh in the side and whistled through a mouth of rotten teeth. "Come on!"

"No. No pretty women. All broken down hags. Peasant buffaloes!"

"I don't believe you!"

"You'll see for yourself."

"Use any lime tonight?"

Dinh frowned. "Ah . . . on some prisoners. But I was told to lay off of the prisoner in cage forty-six."

"Why?"

"Oh, she's got no legs and, I guess, some connections. And she's sick . . . you know, poison in her . . . you know—female parts. Better be careful with her. Do what you want to the others, but lay off her, otherwise"—he pointed upward and rolled his eyes—"some big shot will be pouring lime down on you."

"Thanks for the tip."

"Sure."

~ *Dinh Subverts the System* ~

Dinh stood in his mother's cramped kitchen dicing vegetables with gusto. Wiping the knife on his checkered scarf, he meticulously laid them out on the wooden board, separating them by color and rubbing his hands together in anticipation. The red chiles were the key: too much and the *gang gai* was ruined, too little and . . . well, bland, and more importantly, not memorable. Holding a chili between his thumb and forefinger, he peered at it from all angles, grunted in satisfaction, and was just about to dice it when he had second thoughts.

"Mama!" he shouted toward the bedroom. "How many chiles?"

"Two, maybe three if they are small."

"How small?"

"Bring them to me," his mother chuckled.

When he entered the bedroom with a handful of chiles, he leaned over her bed and opened his palm for her to inspect.

"So, when do I meet this girl?" she asked coyly.

"All in good time, Mother, all in good time."

She shook her head. "Not good enough. You know I do not have much time left. When do I meet her?"

He smiled absently and stared down at the chiles. "Which ones?"

She methodically checked them one by one, giving her more time to interrogate him. "At least tell me more about her. All I know is that she works in an office for the government. So, she can read and write. And she must have good parents. And her name is Nguyen Tuyet Mai." She shook her head. "Not enough. If I am to be a mother-in-law, I must prepare."

"Mama!" He laughed. "Enough. There is no date set. I have not even talked to her parents. Which ones?" he asked firmly, nodding toward the chiles that she still held in her hand.

"These."

"Thank you." He started out of the room.

"Wait! At least tell me."

"I'm late again, Mama. I must finish the cooking. And since you obviously cannot. . . . " he let the words linger. *That will keep her quiet.*

~

A few weeks had passed since she had been incarcerated and Tuyet Mai remained confined to the tiger cage. Now she wore a ragged, but comfortable, army tunic and a pair of trousers which Dinh had cut into shorts. She had access to many other amenities which he slipped to her whenever on duty: food, a comb, lotion, a cloth with soap. Because he was on the night shift, she enjoyed the gifts he brought with little fear of discovery by prison authorities, although she had to return them when his shift ended. Her neighbors had started to complain to Tuyet Mai, telling her they would report the relationship between her and Dinh unless he also gave them some food. Tuyet Mai had been telling them to be patient, to wait until she was sure he would do what she asked. But they were on the verge of starvation and their patience had run out.

Not long before Dinh's shift was about to start, one of Tuyet Mai's neighbors could bear it no longer. "Tonight, Tuyet Mai! Tonight, or else!" warned Cam Thi Binh from her adjoining cage.

Tuyet Mai started to respond, "Binh! I keep—"

"Ahhhhhhhh!" screamed Binh.

A low laugh crackled down through the grating. "More lime, Binh? Or, better yet, why don't I give you more personal treatment?"

"No! No! Please! No!"

Normally, Dinh felt irritated by such pleading. It merely goaded him on to more expansive cruelty. But this time, Binh's pleas were satisfying, like he had felt when he first became a guard. His satisfaction, however, did not derive from the power he held over this woman as it would have when he was new. Rather, he felt satisfied that his threats of torture were serving to protect Tuyet Mai. At last, his sadism had a noble cause. A cause for which his mother would assuredly be proud.

"You see, Tuyet Mai? You have nothing to fear. Not so long as I am around. Here."

A basket hovered next to her, lowered by a rope and full to the brim with food and other items. Tuyet Mai explored the contents. It contained the usual cornucopia: hot buns, fruit, tea, a comb, a flashlight. But this time, she felt a letter and a pen.

No, I don't want to read it. I won't read it! Eat the food. Say nothing. Maybe he won't notice. She pictured him squatting over the bars and staring down at her.

"Too much garlic in the dumplings?" he asked.

"No. Perfect."

"Good. Good. I know you see the letter. Read it." He laughed in anticipation. "You'll be surprised, Tuyet Mai. When I return from rounds, I want to discuss it with you."

Silence.

"Answer," he demanded.

"Yes. All right."

"Good."

Once she had devoured the papaya, Tuyet Mai flipped on the flashlight and shined it on the fruit-stained letter.

Dearest Tuyet Mai,

I paid a scribe to have this letter written. He told me not to tell, but I want you to know who I am. I can write a little, but not a lot. But I am not stupid. I have no illusion of what you think of me. I have no illusion that you are loyal to the other side. I have no illusion that you are smarter than me. But I am not who you think I am. You see, I am placing my fate in your hands. With this letter, my life is in your hands. Of course, if you turn me in, you may not be so lucky with the next guard. But, still, my life is in your hands. My mother is a devout Buddhist. She does not believe in hurting or killing any other creature. She does not know what I do here. Before I met you, I did not understand her attitude. But now I do. You see, I could never hurt you. I feel toward you the way she feels toward everything. So you are everything to me. I need a sign from you. Something to tell me you understand. So I have given you a pen. See the space I have left on the second page of this paper? Please use it up. Tell me your feelings, now that you understand me.

Tuyet Mai finished reading the letter and lay in silence for a long time.

"Well?" she heard him ask. "Can I pull up the basket?"

"I'm not finished. Come back in a little while. It will be ready then."

"Umm." He seemed to be mulling over his options. Neither of them knew what they would do next. She held her breath, waiting for his reply. She needed more time.

"One-half hour. Then I will pull the basket up." There was a tinge of warning in his tone.

"Yes. Thank you. Good." She watched the soles of his boots pass over the grating and a deep silence fell upon her cage. *If I acknowledge him, it could be a trick. If it is not a trick, and I acknowledge him, then my fate is tied up in his. If we are discovered, it's death to both of us. On the other hand, if I acknowledge him, my life will be easy. Until . . . but, if I do not acknowledge him, he will make my life hell, or worse. Why am I always in this position? Why? I must survive. I must! What to do? What to do? Kim Lan! Oh, god, if you are here, show yourself! I need help. A sign.*

Once he left Tuyet Mai, Dinh was particularly short-tempered during his rounds. Even the sound of a prisoner coughing made him angry. By the time he returned to Tuyet Mai's cage, he felt quite agitated. "Hey, Tuyet Mai! I'm pulling up the basket now!"

Just as the basket was about to clear the lip of the cage, he heard the scuffling of boots and realized that a group of men approached. He dropped the rope and let the basket fall back into the cage. When he straightened up, a beam of light shone in his face.

"Dinh! Where have you been? We've been calling you!" It was the night commander, Captain Truong who usually stayed in his office drinking and gambling with his unfortunate aide.

Dinh blinked in the harsh light and stammered, "Yes, sir! Here I am, sir! Just attending to an unruly prisoner, sir!"

"Go with Nguyen! Cage 32! Now!"

"Yes, sir!"

He could sense the captain smiling. "Before you go, what unruly prisoner have you been attending to, eh? The one with no legs?"

The captain walked to the edge of the cage and shined his flashlight into the pit, illuminating Tuyet Mai's face. Her eyes were closed. He moved the beam of light down her body and saw that her clothes were still on, unruffled, buttoned and straight.

"Um," he grunted disappointedly. "How is she being unruly?"

"Turned out to be nothing, sir. She was having a nightmare. I thought she was cursing our country, but it turns out she was cursing some man in her sleep."

"Yes. She's probably cursed many men in her sleep," the captain mumbled, again shining the flashlight on her face. "Um. Pretty. Too bad. All right! Go!"

"Yes, sir!"

Finished helping other guards attend to the prisoner in cage 32, Dinh returned to Tuyet Mai's cell. "It's me," he whispered. "All clear. Throw up the rope. Where'd you hide the basket?"

"Under my body. But that was too close. A mango and the letter have fallen to the floor. I can't reach them. Here's the rope."

"No. I have to enter your cell through the lower door and get them. Stay still."

He raced down the steps leading to the dank hallway where the cell doors lined each wall and fumbled with the keys to unlock the iron door to her cell. He was not authorized to enter tiger cells without a superior being present. Not saying a word, he hastily retrieved the basket, rope, letter, and loose mango. Closing the door behind him, he stuffed the letter into his pocket without seeing whether she wrote anything on it. He returned to the cat walk and shined his flashlight down on her one last time. Her eyes stared back at him. "Um, too close for comfort . . . good," he muttered loud enough for her to hear. Before she could respond, he hurried to the briefing room where his relief waited. "Nothing new, except some excitement in cage 32," he told the man. "The inmate sang some northern patriotic song. Nguyen cut off two of her fingers. Someone had to hold her down." He shrugged. "It was me."

"Any result?" asked his relief.

Dinh shrugged. "Nothing new."

All the way home, he concentrated on calming his frayed nerves. When at last he entered his house, he quietly closed the door behind him, hung up his hat and crept into his room so that he would not awaken his mother. Only when he turned up the lantern and sat on the edge of his bed did he bring out the wrinkled paper. Smoothing it carefully on the wall, he moved it into the light and read:

Will on a leaf of grass the mirror shine?

What? That's all? What does that mean? She's too clever by half! Tomorrow's my day off. I'll see Scribe Huynh. He'll tell me what it means. Of course, I already know she is receptive. Still, better be sure.

He folded the paper until it was the size of a postage stamp and placed it under a loose tile near the bed. Trying to sleep, he tossed . . .

. . . and turned, the quote breaching his artificial calm like a great whale harpooned and infuriated.

Who?

The one who dreams.

Who?

He who everyone in here calls the mutant.

To what end, Goddess, these interminable dreams? If they have their way, the mutant will kill himself first. Why bother with a banal suicide?

I see the evil voices continue to crawl out from under their rocks.

He really must kill himself!

Silence!

~

The next day was one of the hottest days of the year. It was 7:30 in the morning and already the heat had become almost unbearable. He stood by the front door and put on his hat.

"Where are you going?" asked his mother from her bed.

He sighed. "Nowhere." Even as he said the word, he knew he had made a mistake.

"Nowhere? What do you mean, nowhere? Must be somewhere."

"Just for a walk."

"Where? Tell me, where are you going?"

"It's too stuffy in here. I need some air."

"If you tell me where you are going, I may have some errands for you. Besides, I need some tiger balm."

"Sometimes you are too demanding. I am grown now."

"Where are you going?"

Dinh sighed loudly. "To see Scribe Huynh."

Silence. He could almost hear her brain whirring.

"Why visit your Uncle? What business do you have with him?"

"I'm late. Bye, Mama."

"But—"

Already out the door, Dinh quickly crossed the busy street, dodging the sea of motorcycles, trucks and lambrettas. He pulled his scarf over his mouth to block the dust and to filter out the scent of noxious exhaust and overripe humanity. He made his way to a narrow alleyway, he trudged up a steep flight of tile stairs with thick concrete walls rising on each side. Lines of ants scurried in and out of the myriad cracks, making it seem as though the walls were made of moving jigsaw pieces–arranging and rearranging themselves–and he began to feel dizzy. At the top of the claustrophobic staircase, he knocked on a peeling wooden door with the name "Huynh, Esteemed Scribe," written above it in faded red paint.

"Come!" Huynh's high pitched voice barked out from the other side.

Dinh entered the small room and peered at the old scribe sitting stiffly in a high backed Chinese chair. He tossed Tuyet Mai's creased note on the mahogany table in front of Huynh. "What's this mean?" he asked, a little out of breath.

Huynh held the note far from his wizened face and started chuckling. "Who wrote this?"

"A girl."

"A girl!" Still chuckling, Huynh narrowed his eyes. "You're interested in her?"

"Maybe. Depends on what that means."

Huynh nodded, looked back at the note and became suddenly serious. "Smart girl. Smart girl."

Dinh shifted uncomfortably. "Well, Scribe Huynh, what about it?"

Huynh leaned back in his chair, made a tent with his fingers, and assumed a solemn face. "It means . . . "

"What?"

"It means you are a fool."

"Uncle! What does it mean?"

Huynh gazed at the agonized look on Dinh's face. He smoothed the note and laid it carefully back on the table.

"Nephew, it means you are a lucky man. She probably cares for you, but does not feel herself worthy."

Dinh nodded. "Thank you, uncle." He turned to leave.

"What are you going to do now?"

Dinh shrugged. "Don't know. I'll have to think about it." He strode to the table and snatched up the note, then walked in a dignified manner to the door and closed it softly.

As Huynh heard Dinh's footsteps descending the tile stairs, he pulled out an oversized ledger and wrote: *Today I told a lie to my nephew. I will contribute twenty thousand piaster to the Buddhist orphanage on Blossom Hill.*

~

Cages, dearest God—humans built them from the start. Not one stands outside looking in; all stare outward from within. When they vanish, the Superior Ones will dismantle the cages and set freedom free.

Chapter Nine

Romancing A Ghost

Meeting at the Beach

Dr. Theresa Williams walks slowly along the beach, her thoughts circling the man she's just examined. He had first caught her attention slumped in his beach chair, hunched inward as though held by invisible straps, locked in a posture she recognized instantly, trauma's fetal retreat. His eyes were glassed over, speech disjointed, muttering fragments: "leaf—grass—scribe—piaster—strolls—fetal—."

As a physician, Theresa had offered her help to his companions, who introduced themselves as close friends. At first she suspected drugs. It usually was. But after checking his pulse, pupils, skin tone, and the scent of his breath, she decided otherwise. No, not drugs. Perhaps a schizophrenic episode. Or bipolar. Either way, beyond her scope without more information. She had withdrawn politely, leaving him in their care. And yet she couldn't let go of the memory of his eyes, not blank, but too deeply occupied. So she told Ethyl she needed a walk.

The man's friend had mentioned a flashback to Vietnam. She sidesteps a crackling wave. *Flashbacks. Yes. I know them too.* She touches the dark bracelet of discolored skin at her wrists. The bruises across her back and ankles ache in the sea air. *Violence. Always violence. The righteous violence of war or the intimate violence of love, each side of the same worn coin.* She sighs. *He was attractive. But...* She shakes her head. *This side of the coin can't flip and heal the other.*

She walks the wet edge of the beach, each footprint crisp, its curves and contours precise: light step, perfect toes, indoor smoothness. Geography enough for a receptive mind.

~

And a receptive mind *is* following her, Michael Powers. The sharp voice of his sister-in-law scolding God brought him jarringly into the present, where in an invigorating burst of clarity he realized her wrath was directed not at God but at the children. Yet it is the appearance of a beautiful woman that extinguished, or at least postponed his delusional state and prompted him to action. Driven by the urgency to catch up to the departing lady, recovery is rapid and his grip on reality seemingly complete. For now, the steering wheel remains motion-less in his hands, the accelerator untouched. Momentarily, the tapping has stopped. Time crawls, then speeds up and synchronizes with the present. He is like an excited dog following fresh tracks; head periodically lowering as he follows the woman's footprints, then raising up to locate her back as she walks some distance ahead through the crowd, then down again to inspect her footprints. Gradually, he begins to close the distance between them. *Footprints to back. A beautiful back. About thirty paces ahead. Return to footprints. Beautiful footprints. Each footprint the same as the one that went before. Return to her back. A beautiful back. Her head is turned, facing the ocean. A beautiful neck. A beautiful profile. Beautiful hair, blowing beautifully in the wind. Beautiful nose and chin. Beautiful. Now about twenty steps ahead. Return to footprints. All the same. Identical. So perfect! Return to her back. Gorgeous thighs, perfect calves. Ankles not too thick, not too skinny. Return to her footprints. Only ten steps ahead! Beautiful. I'm getting close. Return to her back. And look at her hands. Nice, long, graceful fingers–no polish, clean, well-manicured–perfect! Now only five footprints away. Five, four, four–speed up–four, three, two, one. . . .*

~

"Hello," says Michael Powers casually as he falls into step beside Theresa. She flinches. "Oh, sorry to startle you," he blurts, embarrassed.

"That's okay. Hello," she replies reservedly. "Are you feeling better?"

"Yes, thank you. Actually, that's why I'm . . . that's why I wanted to . . . catch up with you . . . to say thank you for helping . . . you know, for checking me out. I–"

She smiles. "That's okay. I was just concerned," then theatrically furrows her brow, "your recovery—so quick! And your friend seemed so worried. I must say I'm quite pleasantly surprised."

Intelligent, thinks Michael. *Better and better.* "Yeah. That's Paul. He's my friend. I know he was worried. But it was very kind of you to help."

"I didn't."

"Yes you did."

"No, really I didn't. I just–"

"Yes. Oh, yes you did. I'm here, aren't I?"

Silence. She shades her eyes with her hand and looks out at the ocean. "Beautiful day."

"Yes," he says distractedly, for he does not notice the ocean or the sky or the birds or the sand. Only the bruises on her wrist. Alarmed by this imperfection, he holds his smile while his eyes wander in sham bashfulness, the better to inspect the exposed parts of her body more closely. *Damn!* He looks down. *Also bruises on her ankles. Oh, damn, why didn't I notice that before?*

"See how the light sparkles so brightly on the waves?" she asks.

But he does not see. Not the light or the waves. Only the bruises. "Um," he says absently, again staring at her wrist.

It dawns on Theresa that her uninvited companion has seen her bruises and, like all the others, his attention will be drawn to nothing else. She knows that if he is allowed to get too close, there will follow the same endless, dreary questions ("Why? Who did this?"); the professed disbelief ("How could someone like you who has everything, someone so successful, a doctor. . . ."); the disgust ("But to let him do that to you is. . . is. . . . "); the pronouncements of concern ("I'm only thinking of you."); the recriminations ("Is your self-esteem so low?"); the amateur psychology ("You're just being a facilitator."); the dire warnings ("You know, someday you're gonna end up in a morgue if you don't leave now."); and on and on. She has heard it all. Understood it all. Internalized it all. Thinks it is all good advice. Even accepts it all. And yet . . . *Certainly this man is not the only one with problems.*

"Well, it's late. I've got to get back." She glances at her watch, curling her fingers under the sleeve of the cloth wrap to keep it from riding above her wrist. "Oh! It's really late! I'd better hurry! I'm glad you feel better."

"No, wait a moment," he says. "Let me walk you back to your things."

As they walk back, Michael keeps his head down in silence. Mulling over what he can say to keep the conversation going. What clever remark can he make? How will he deliver it? But they are getting close to her spot and his thoughts are still jumbled. So instead of a careful plan of conversational attack, he simply blurts out a reckless frontal assault. "Do you know why I was having problems back there?"

"Well, your friend said you were having a flashback. I guess it's passed now. I hope."

"Yeah, well, it's not that easy." He falls silent.

Feeling an obligation to pursue the subject, but not really wanting to, Theresa merely whispers, "Oh?" She briefly considers asking, "How so?" but thinks better of it. That would invite his explanation. An expository discourse she does not want to encourage. *And yet–*

"Would you be interested in letting me explain?" he asks bluntly.

"Well, I–" she starts to say.

But a voice suffused with an odd, southern-Cajun-Chicago accent intrudes. "Hello. That was quick, Theresa."

Michael looks down at an elderly black woman sitting in a folding beach chair, her eyes peering up at him over the spine of a paperback book. Gradually lowering the book, her smiling face comes into full view.

"You?" he blurts.

"No, me," laughs the woman. "You are you."

"No, I mean, you look so familiar. Have we met?"

"Son," says the old lady, "that's a line you're supposed to use on Theresa here. Don't waste it on an old black woman."

"But I know both of you!" he cries.

They look at him blankly.

"I think," he says, less sure of himself.

The two women glance at each other. "You must have seen us both when you arrived at the beach, or maybe when you were having your. . . flashback," says Theresa. "Perhaps that's how you remember seeing us before."

"No, no, no. It's something else. Somewhere else. Sometime else."

"Well, it seems to me," says the old black lady, "that you two'd better figure that out over dinner tonight. Don'tcha think, Theresa?"

"But we . . . I mean, you and I–"

"Ain't no we tonight, honey. I'm staying at the hotel. Rheumatism, gas, headache, swollen ankles, and I don't know what else. Better get some rest"—she gazes significantly at Theresa–"don'cha think, doctor?"

Theresa laughs nervously. "Yeah, the doctor think."

"Besides," continues the black lady, "this vacation is coming to an end and you've spent all your time fetchin' and totin' for me."

Michael Powers takes his cue, and like an obedient boy asked by his mother to invite a girl to dance, he directs a slight, gentlemanly bow to Theresa. "Will you join me, then?"

"Tonight?"

"Yes, if it's okay, I mean."

"No, I don't think so."

"Look, I'd like to prove I'm not ready for admission to an asylum just yet. Perhaps we could just have a drink"

"That's right," says the black woman. "Our hotel has a nice cocktail lounge. Safe, too, in case you turn out to be. . . . "

"Crazy?" asks Michael.

"Nope, just . . . frisky."

"Well," says Theresa, "if you promise not to have a flashback."

He frowns. "I promise."

"All right. By the way, my name is Theresa Williams . . . and this is my traveling companion, Ethyl Robinson. Guess we should know your name."

"I'm Michael Powers," he says while shaking their hands. "Call me Michael. My friend told me you're a doctor?"

"Yes."

"That's interesting. I'm a lawyer, but I promise I don't do medical malpractice. Where are you both from?"

Theresa remains silent. Ethyl gives Michael a sly smile. "My people? . . . why . . . my people are from. . . . " her words trail off and she seems confused.

Theresa speaks up. "This is our next-to-last day here. Day after tomorrow we have to return home."

"Oh. Where's home?"

"Cleveland."

"Oh. Well, how about if I meet you at 6:30 at your hotel?"

"All right."

After giving him the name of her hotel, Theresa watches Michael Powers return to his companions. Waiting until he is out of hearing range, she frowns and snaps at Ethyl in an exasperated, scolding voice, "Don't pull that 'colorful old black lady' routine, okay, Ethyl? He's just . . . I don't know . . . it seems like he's just a nice guy."

"Yes, yes," says Ethyl dismissively. Her face transforms into the deistic imperturbability of a Greek mask behind which her two eyes shine laser-like. Her body straightens, strengthens, and exudes vibrancy, glistening in the sun like a young snake that has just shed an old skin. She makes a supple movement and winks. "And as for being a 'colorful old black lady,' I do profess to be no less than I seem; to serve her truly that will put me in trust, to love her that is honest, to converse with her that is wise and says little, to fear judgment, to fight when I cannot choose, and to eat no fish."

"Men are cold, like fish," laughs Theresa a bit nervously, "and go bad in the heat of day."

"Then why do you continue to eat them, my Dear?" The 'Greek mask' pats her stomach and makes a face. "Bad for the digestion."

Theresa pulls back her sleeve to reveal her bruise. "It is they who eat me, revered Goddess." Then she makes a slight obeisance to Ethyl so as not to attract too much attention, shakes her head and laughs, "If they only knew who you really are, Ethyl, you would be famous and, as Your disciple, I would be endlessly interviewed on morning talk shows. Will you ever let them know?"

Ethyl hooks her finger in the top of her swimsuit and tugs it down, exposing a perilously large expanse of chest. **No. Shakespeare, that old rhyming reprobate, had it right. They have already eaten out my heart and time has only widened the hole leaving an empty chamber into which 'all the infections that the sun sucks up, from bogs, fens, flats into my empty chamber fall and make me, by inchmeal, a disease.'**

"Goddess! Stop!" commands Theresa threateningly. "You're exasperating, once more finger painting on the Sistine Chapel. Let me speak to ol' black lady Ethyl again."

Sooo, Goddess forges ahead stubbornly, unwilling to metamorphose back to the caterpillar so quickly, **I will continue to be that which is least vexatious to your psyche, a colorful ol'black lady.**

~

The cocktail lounge is warm. Too warm. "Sorry, air conditioner's on the fritz," explains the waiter to the attractive middle-aged couple sitting somewhat stiffly in their chairs. Michael and Theresa are off to a slow start. He was always bad at small talk and she has taken a wait-and-see attitude. *Damn, have to prove myself,* he thinks. *But it's so friggen hot in here.* He smiles at his own adolescent thoughts. *Conditions are not optimal for impressing.*

"A little warm, isn't it?" he asks, taking yet another baby sip of bourbon.

Theresa keeps her fingers on the stem of her margarita glass. *Good lord, I think we established that already.* "Yes, it is."

He smiles in a self-deprecating manner that says, *Look I know this isn't going well, but the reason it's not going well is that you haven't yet had time to discover who*

I am. My ironic smile will tell you that I know it's not going well and that it's kind of funny it's not going well and that we'll share in the little joke so that we can get past the bullshit and you can get to know me better so that it will start going well. After all, I am quite intelligent, you know, and can pile irony upon irony, witticism upon witticism and attitude upon attitude, if that will be what it takes to prove what is in my pudding. Or maybe, with you, a more earnest approach is called for, for you are obviously quite mature and even more obviously quite serious. So earnest it is, but with a little humor, a little vulnerability—just the right dash of this and pinch of that, proportions calculated to intrigue a connoisseur of men. "Look, I'm not much good at small talk unless I can sprinkle it with legal jargon. So, pursuant to my request would the kind doctor take under submission this counsel's motion for leave to take a walk outside?"

Theresa smiles. *He's trying so hard.* "Motion granted, counsel."

Relieved, Michael takes a deep breath, walks with her on the beach and into a relationship. The line that finally breaks the deadlock? Not irony nor wit nor attitude nor earnestness does the trick. Just good, old-fashioned romanticism. "You know," he says as he looks down at her bare feet, illuminated in flat white by the lights from the hotel, "earlier today, after you, um . . . after you checked me . . . after that, when I followed you down the beach, it was your footprints that made me want to get to know you. To really get to know who you are."

She laughs skeptically. "And you didn't want to get to know me when you first started following me, before you saw my footprints?"

"Oh, well. . . ."

"Yes, Counsel?"

"Yes, Your Honor, I wanted to get to know you even before I saw your footprints. With the court's . . . I mean with the doctor's permission, may I get to know you?"

Her eyes narrow in mock scrutiny of his motivations. That is to say, half mockery, half scrutiny. "Only if you tell me what you saw in my footprints."

He is silent for a long time while they walk on across the sand. She remains quiet, waiting. A seriousness settles over him and she senses he is struggling with whether to answer painfully truthfully or comfortably glibly. He chooses painful truth: "I saw in your footprints a path through a terribly dense forest, a forest in which I have been lost for a very, very long time."

"Were you in that forest earlier today, when no one could reach you?"

"Yes, a mangrove forest. And I'm the only one who's made it out."

"If you've made it out, how is it you're still lost?"

"Only half of me has made it out."

"Which half am I talking with now?"

Alarm bells go off in his head. *I am not a schizophrenic!* He smiles. "The only half they will allow you to."

"They? Who are they and allow you to what?"

His smile widens as if to say, 'what I am about to tell you is a joke,' but he remains silent.

"Well?" she says, joining his smile to prove she is sharing the joke but knowing it isn't.

"A god and a goddess."

Uh oh, she thinks. This time she wants him to elaborate. "What do you mean?"

He looks at her and smiles enigmatically. Stalling. *Oh, no, careful Michael. Let her see that I'm in control of my emotions. Can't have her thinking I'm a crazy veteran always on the verge of some bizarre hallucination. Remember, no flashbacks. Be strong. She would like a strong man.* He remembers her bruises. *She would like a very strong man, but still vulnerable. Just vulnerable enough to make her think he was weaker to hit her than she to be hit.* He laughs out loud to show her it is, after all, just a joke. "No, let's not wander into my forest or else we'll both get lost. I promised you, no flashbacks, remember?" *Good. Perfect answer. Leave a little mystery.* "Let's talk about you. When did you decide to become a doctor?"

"Not fair. First tell me what you meant by a god and a goddess."

"Just a pet name for my therapists, a husband and wife team. They're helping me deal with the war."

"Are they?"

"Are they what?"

"Helping."

"Oh, yes. Talking is always therapeutic."

Theresa looks at him with an openly curious expression. "Post traumatic stress disorder?"

Michael raises his eyebrows and smiles coyly. "So, when did you become a doctor."

She is relieved. She answers. They talk. They walk. They laugh. They agree to see each other again. The next day. With Ethyl. For dinner. "I won't abandon Ethyl on the last day of our vacation," Theresa insists. She quickly smiles with the full force of her bountiful charm. "Besides, I suddenly have a lot to discuss with her."

Michael finds this last remark provocative, and his heart races a bit faster, his mood lighter.

~ *Father and Son* ~

Six months later, Michael sits with his son on the front porch. They're side-by-side in silence, the way men often arrange themselves, gazing outward, not at each other. It's a warm, luminous afternoon. The porch, a welcome refuge from the sun, holds their quiet like a shallow bowl.

Michael sips from a half-filled coffee cup, waving off the persistent gnats drawn to its rim. Mark glances at the small white table beside him, where a honey bee explores the drying pulp clinging to the lip of his empty orange juice glass.

They've just returned from lunch, a birthday celebration for Theresa Williams. Mark met her for the first time and sat beside her throughout the meal. He's still digesting the food—which was too rich—and, more troubling, his own reaction.

He had expected to like her. Instead, he found her distant, opaque. And then, without warning, his father had lifted her hand to display the ring he'd given her the night before. Mark's face betrayed him, a flash of displeasure before he could arrange a smile. That brief flicker, he knows, has been festering in his father's mind ever since.

Now, as a gnat buzzes too close, Michael swats the air, shifts in his seat, and finally blurts it out.

"You don't like her, do you?"

"Yes, I like her, Dad. I do," says Mark, the lie thin and too carefully placed.

Michael doesn't reply.

Mark presses on. "Come on. I like her."

Michael snorts softly, unconvinced, but lets it drop.

"I'm serious," Mark insists, then changes tack. "Her friend, Ethyl, she's interesting. What's the deal there?"

Michael exhales. "I've told you, you should call her Theresa."

"I know, I know. I mean, yeah, I get they're friends. But it feels . . . unusual."

Michael nods. "Yeah. I know what you mean. Theresa told me Ethyl's her patient. So I said, 'I thought you were a medical doctor, not a psychologist.' But she didn't really answer. Just sort of deflected. I figure maybe Ethyl's terminally ill, or maybe they're just very close. Who knows?"

"Did you ask?"

"No. If she wants to tell me, she will." Michael chuckles, though it doesn't reach his eyes. "Sometimes I think it's the other way around. That Theresa is the one being treated. There's something about Ethyl. About both of them. But maybe I've just read too many mystery novels."

"Or watched too much Hitchcock. Still kind of strange, both of them moving here after meeting you. Living together."

"Now who's watched too much Hitchcock? Did it ever occur to you she moved here because she loves me?"

Mark grins. "Never crossed my mind. But sure, okay. Still, it's weird they're living together. That's all I'm saying."

Michael turns, voice clipped. "That's the tenth time you've said that. I knew you didn't like her."

"But—"

"She's not a lesbian, if that's what you're implying."

"Dad. I'm not saying that. And yeah, I *do* like her. It's just . . . they're not exactly young, and it's not typical."

Michael leans over and slaps his son's back. "Roommates, son. Ever heard of them? Do I need to explain the economics of rent to a college student?"

"No. Look, Dad—"

"Can't talk now. I've got to go." Michael grips the arms of his chair and begins to rise.

"Wait—Dad, I have something to tell you."

"Oh?" Michael pauses, standing halfway, impatience flickering in his stance.

"I want to go to Vietnam."

Michael drops back into his chair. "What?"

"I want to go to Vietnam. There's this class I'm taking, war in the twentieth century. The professor asked if anyone had a parent who served. A few of us raised our hands. He said he's doing research on the children of veterans, how we perceive the wars our parents fought. He handed out a questionnaire. But when I looked at it, I realized . . . I don't know anything about what you went through. And that bothered me. Especially knowing you've had . . . issues since. So I want to go. I want to see where it happened."

"Oh, come on. That's ridiculous. When? You're a genetics major, not a historian. And you've still got classes. And your startup idea, that's still in your head, right? I even made some calls for you. Your schedule's full, Mark. And those 'issues' of mine, nothing major. Nothing out of the ordinary."

"Well . . . "

"And who's paying for this? Even if you go, it won't mean anything without me there to explain. And I'm not going. Period."

They fall silent. A scrub jay drops from the sky, landing with a thud on the bird feeder. It hops, jostles the seeds, then lifts again, blue flashing briefly in the sun before it spirals behind the porch roof and disappears.

Michael speaks again, his voice low. "Show me the questionnaire. I'll help you fill it out. Then you can hand it in, call it a day, and move on. Right?"

Mark shakes his head. "Wrong. It's not an assignment. It matters."

Michael turns, face tightening. "You've never cared much about the war. Or me. You never ask."

"Oh yes I did. But you never answered. What else was I supposed to do, except play war games on the computer?"

"What questions? What do you mean?"

"Your nightmares, Dad. I heard them. Mom told me about them too. You kept insisting you had a twin who went to war instead of you, even though everyone knew you didn't. And now that you've let go of that—Paul told me about your breakthrough. About the psychologist. The imaginary twin. All that's behind you now, right? So are the gods and goddesses. The dinner parties. That whole fantasy life. I didn't hear it from you, I had to piece it together from everyone else."

Michael's face darkens. His breathing turns shallow.

Mark notices and backs off. "Okay. Okay. Let's drop it. You say I never ask, but when I do—"

"Mark," Michael says hoarsely.

"Okay. Just thought your psychologist—"

"*Mark! Stop.*"

Mark grabs his empty glass and slips into the house, giving his father space. He isn't angry, or even especially surprised. He's seen this before. Every time he asks about the war, the same thing happens. Always that volatile silence followed by an explosion.

His mother had warned him. So had Claire. Even Paul. Something awful happened out there.

The nightmares. The hallucinations. The dinners for people who weren't there. The medication. The therapy.

No. There's too much buried. Too much at stake. And Mark has made up his mind.

He's going.

When he returns to the porch, he hears his father muttering to himself.

"He never said her name. Theresa. It's a pretty name. Never said it."

Mark sits, eyes on the horizon, jaw clenched. He won't say her name. Not now. Not ever. He's chasing something deeper.

"Dad?" he says, calmly.

"What?"

He lights the fuse.

"We've never really talked about it. But . . . "

And tosses it.

"Did you really believe you had a twin who fought in your place? Were you off your meds, or just pretending for the doctors?"

~ *Theresa and Ethyl Make Plans* ~

After Theresa's lunch with Michael and his son to celebrate her birthday, she is waiting up for Ethyl to discuss "the disaster." Theresa is unusually restless and feels supremely unhappy, depressed that the lunch with Mark had not gone well. Most of the time she is good with young people, especially college students. But this time something went wrong. She fears that hidden undercurrents dragged her down and that her normally strong and confident conversational strokes degenerated into a sort of flailing about that ran perilously close to panic. She is sure she had tried too hard and that the boy does not like her.

Fool! she chides herself. *I've moved to California to be closer to him, set up a medical practice, am struggling to make ends meet, living on dwindling savings, Ethyl working two jobs, now to blow it! Fool!*

With these thoughts roiling in her head, after what seems to Theresa an eternity of waiting, Ethyl unlocks the door and enters, carrying a large shopping bag laden with changes of clothes that she always takes to work.

Before she can put it down, Theresa begins the assault.

"Hello. Another late night? I've got some homemade veggie soup cooking. Once you get comfy, let's sit a while and chat, okay?"

"Honey, maybe you've got veggie soup cooking, but I'm cooked. Ain't no way–"

"Ethyl," interrupts Theresa matter-of-factly, "you can slip out of your rustic persona now. You're home and you need to eat something."

A dramatic transformation occurs in Ethyl and she seems to instantly become a different person. "Yes," she says, "quite right. It's difficult, you know, not to have it carry over. And speaking of carrying over. . . . " She disappears into her bedroom lugging the big bag with both hands as if it were full of anvils. In spite of having already eaten, Theresa quickly dishes out two bowls of soup before Ethyl can change her mind and is sitting at the kitchen table when Ethyl reappears in pajamas and a warm robe.

Ethyl smiles knowingly. She sits and begins to eat her soup in silence.

"How was your day?" asks Theresa.

"Fine," replies Ethyl, lapsing again into obstinate silence.

"Quilt shop crowded today?" asks Theresa as innocently as possible, reluctantly sipping another spoonful of soup.

"Yup," says Ethyl, still eating.

"Umm," nods Theresa, somewhat at a loss. She forces down another spoonful of soup and stares vacantly at the wall.

Ethyl bursts out laughing. "Okay, Theresa, let's have it. How'd the lunch go? Tell ol' Ethyl all about it before you burst your buttons."

"Oh, you're bad," chides Theresa. "Real bad." But without further hesitation, she launches into a long narrative describing the "disastrous" lunch which she concludes with the statement, "Michael's really close to his son and I'm afraid that if the son rejects me, then the father will follow."

"Nonsense," says Ethyl, squeezing Theresa's hand.

"No, it's not. I'm afraid, Ethyl. Help me out. After all, My Goddess, You're the one who brought us together. Even so, at lunch, I felt a kind of panic and I actually found myself missing *him*."

"Him?" Ethyl's eyes widen.

"Yes. Him. I know it's crazy and wrong, but—"

Ethyl snorts. "You still miss what he did to you, don't you?"

"Yes."

"The width of a continent won't erase the width of a rope."

Theresa is angry. "You know as well as I do that I can't help it."

Ethyl softens. "Dearie, how many times have we discussed this?"

Theresa looks miserable. "Not enough."

"So, Michael is too loving? Too kind? Too gentle?"

"No, no," she replies haltingly.

"Come, Theresa, the truth!"

"Too gentle." A touch of defiance in her voice.

Ethyl slaps her.

Gently.

Then slaps her again.

Hard.

Her hand hovers in the air. "Do you want me to punish you again, my dear?"

Theresa lowers her eyes and nods.

Ethyl shrugs dismissively. "Punishment, however satisfying, is His way, not Mine."

~ *Mark Makes Plans* ~

After returning to Columbia and settling back into his coursework, Mark finds himself increasingly troubled. He cannot reconcile his father's choice of Theresa. Something about her unsettles him—though not, he insists, out of jealousy. He has tested that theory and dismissed it. Yes, she would be replacing his mother, whom he still reveres, but this is not rivalry or betrayal. It runs deeper, stranger. He cannot name it.

Still preoccupied, he arrives at his third class of the week: War and Civilization, Professor Benson's seminar. His thoughts drift as he takes a seat among twenty-three other students, all of them bleary from winter break, slouched and subdued. His black T-shirt and jeans make him indistinguishable from the rest, but the weight behind his eyes separates him.

Professor Benson stands at the front, compact and sharp-featured, with a massive brow, hooked nose, and bushy eyebrows that twitch with every rapid blink. As he surveys the room, he mentally reclassifies his students, sorting them back into the hierarchies he'd assigned before the holiday. Most remain inert minds behind blank faces. But a few—those with hunger, not just intellect—stand apart.

Powers. Top tier. Still burning, Benson thinks. For now. We'll see.

"Welcome back to *War and Civilization*, my wayfaring jeepsies," he says, voice clipped, tone playful. He scans the roll. "Anyone spend their vacation in a war?"

Muted laughter. No replies.

"No? How about in a civilization?"

Scattered chuckles. Still silence.

Then Benson locks eyes with Mark. "Vietnam! Mr. Powers! Vietnam! Last time we spoke, you said you were planning to go. Said you'd talk with your father."

Mark sits up, alert.

"I've taken the liberty of doing a little digging. Freedom of Information Act—remember, class?—and it turns out your father was involved in a particularly unusual battle. Unusual, traumatic . . . mysterious, even."

He pauses. "Come see me. Office hours are unchanged."

Mark nods. "Okay."

Benson moves on. "Ms. Smith, Ms. Dunn, Messrs. Whitney, Bertolino, Landon—you too. I've reviewed your fathers' records and want your questionnaires. We'll talk."

Murmured acknowledgments. Then the lecture begins.

But Mark hears little of it. Benson's words echo in his mind for the rest of the day: *Unusual. Traumatic. Mysterious.* A knot coils in his chest. His father's nightmares, the talk of gods and goddesses, the dinner parties for the dead, Benson doesn't know the half of it. And yet, he *knows* something. Enough to call it *mysterious*. Mark finds himself desperate to know more.

He doesn't wait long.

The next afternoon at 4:30, Mark arrives at Benson's office. It's cold and blustery outside. Leaves whip across the quad. Trees sway and groan under the weight of the wind. Mark leans forward in the chair opposite Benson's desk, heart drumming, eyes locked on the man whose head remains bowed over a stack of papers. The professor gestures him in without looking up. For several minutes he seems uninterested, flipping pages, glasses sliding low on his nose. Mark fidgets.

Then, abruptly, Benson closes the folder and lifts his eyes. He stares at Mark for a long, charged moment. Then speaks.

"Your father's story . . . it borders on myth. What happened to him over there was not just unusual, it was singular. Has he ever spoken of it to you?"

Mark leans in. "No. I've tried."

"Have you asked?"

"Of course. He's had nightmares, always has. But he shuts down when I ask."

Benson sighs. "Pity."

"What do you know? What *happened*?"

"I've done my research. The deeper I dig, the more it resists explanation. It's as though something ancient lies at the heart of it. Not just trauma, something older. And I can't name it. Not yet."

Mark frowns. "You mentioned a village?"

"Yes. There are Vietnamese accounts—soldiers, civilians. They speak of a village near the battle site. But the descriptions feel . . . mythic. As if they were recalling a place outside time. The village was mostly women. No male elders. A council of mothers. Or priestesses. It's hard to tell."

"You really think this happened?"

"I think the story happened. In one form or another. I think your father wandered into something that tore the veil between event and myth."

Mark looks down. "He doesn't want me going to Vietnam. He won't pay for it. Won't talk."

"I figured as much. But this incident, it's like nothing else I've encountered. The last living witness is fading, and once he goes, the labyrinth closes behind him. I need someone to walk the ground. To ask questions. To listen."

"You mean me."

Benson nods. "I'd go myself, but I'm tied to this post. You have summer break. And there are grants—funding is not the issue. The real question is: can you look into the dark and not flinch?"

"I'm not a historian. I study genetics."

"You won't be writing. You'll be gathering. Testimonies. Locations. Silences. You'll be studying your father the way a scientist studies a mutated gene. Tracing the break. Understanding its echo."

Mark hesitates. "I don't know. It feels like betrayal."

"Mark," Benson says softly, "has your father been seeing a psychiatrist?"

"He stopped. Something about a breakthrough."

Benson leans back, expression grave. "Then the hourglass is nearly empty. Meet me here Saturday morning. Ten sharp. I'll show you what I've found."

Mark nods, though something in him recoils. He feels the current now, pulling him toward something vast and irreversible.

"All right," he says, steadying his voice.

~

Benson watches the door ease shut behind him. He sits motionless for a long moment. The wind rattles the windows. Then, leaning forward, he pulls a blank sheet of paper toward him and uncaps his pen.

1. Battle of ??? — must name it well. Names hold power.

2. Near Song Nhan village — matriarchal structure. Inversion of the war myth.

3. French fort turned American refuge — ghost architecture. Memory layered on memory.

4. Surrounded by NVA — siege motif. Judgment from without.

5. Tunnel beneath the fortress — descent, passage, rebirth. Echoes of Orpheus. Or Antigone.

6. Ants. Not metaphor. A rupture in time? Dream logic? Biological witness?

7. All American soldiers dead—except Michael Powers and one unnamed other. The twin that is not a twin?

Mark Powers: the son. Inheritor. Key.Michael Powers: the survivor. Or the ghost.But which one fought the war? And which one dreamed it?

He scribbles across the bottom:

"The son follows the path of the father but finds the footprints are his own."

And beneath that:

DR. BENSON — HISTORIAN, WITNESS, INTERPRETER.
DR. BENSON — PULITZER PRIZE WINNER

Outside, the wind keens through the trees, and the branches scrape softly against the glass.

Chapter Ten

The Long Night

Dinh's Dilemma

After leaving his uncle's office, Pham Van Dinh wandered down the street, head bowed, fingers clenched tightly around Tuyet Mai's note. He moved without aim, distracted, at times veering into alleyways where he would stop abruptly, startled by unfamiliar surroundings, then turn and retrace his steps as if walking in his sleep. For hours he drifted among the ebb and flow of bicycles and pedestrians, muttering his uncle's interpretation of the note until it became a mantra. Several passersby turned to observe him, this curious man repeating aloud, "She probably cares for you, but does not feel herself worthy." He noticed the stares, but, as always, felt no concern for the opinions of strangers, unless they had power over him.

As the streets thickened with those returning from work, Dinh remembered his upcoming shift at Con Son Prison. A schoolboy's nervousness rose in his chest. The problem, he knew, was the word "probably." His uncle had used it with care, but it lodged in Dinh's mind like a splinter. Could anyone, his uncle included, truly decipher the meaning of Tuyet Mai's enigmatic phrase, *Will on a leaf of grass the mirror shine?* Might it not mean the opposite, *she probably does not care for you?*

The uncertainty left him rudderless. He would soon face her, and yet had no plan, no words prepared, no course of action. All because of that single word. "If only," he thought, "he had said, *She cares for you.*" But even that vague hope, *probably* was better than words like *maybe,* or *I think.* The more he wrestled with it, the more tangled his thoughts became.

Each time he dismissed the word's importance and began constructing a plan, it returned, uninvited, sapping his confidence. He thought of his mother's unshakable devotion and realized he could never live with a woman who offered less. Tuyet Mai must be unwavering in her commitment, no ambivalence, no compromise. But if he pressed her too quickly, she might retreat. She might question his intentions. And so he vacillated, drifting into dusk.

Then, through the haze of doubt, a new idea formed, dim at first, then gradually more distinct. Holding to this fresh resolve, he boarded the bus for the Con Son ferry. For the first time in years, he would arrive late to work.

~

Tuyet Mai waited in darkness, watching the last traces of daylight slip away. She was hungry, and to her own surprise, found herself wishing the little guard would arrive. The note she had written at his insistence was carefully constructed: ambiguous enough to avoid consequence, soft enough to delay action. It should have bought time, nothing more. She had dismissed it from her mind. But as the hours passed and he did not appear, hunger gnawed at her and unease crept in.

Had she misjudged the moment? Had she failed to flatter him enough? If she had insulted his vanity, it might be the end. *Why didn't I praise him? Why didn't I say I loved him?* Panic twisted through her thoughts.

A deep, gravelly groan interrupted her worry. She turned toward the sound. The stone wall before her rippled. A crack opened, widened, and a pair of lips began to take shape. They moved, silently mouthing words. Then they pressed together, tightened, and burst open again. A cavernous mouth lunged toward her.

She remained calm. She knew it wasn't real.

The image shifted. The lips puckered, exaggerated and absurd. Just as they moved again, a grotesque tongue emerged, hovered above her, then withdrew into the wall. Next came Kim Lan, exhumed, her body tipping forward at an unnatural angle, eyes fixed on Tuyet Mai.

"Did you make a mistake with him?" she asked, her voice brittle and pained.

"Yes."

"And are you afraid?"

"Yes," Tuyet Mai replied, bluntly. "You're a ghost. You know these things. What happens next?"

But the vision dissolved. The wall was whole again, and Tuyet Mai sat alone. She felt a wave of dread, cold and suffocating. Since losing her legs, she had come to understand that beauty was no longer enough to deflect the judgments and threats of men. What once protected her—her charm, her poise, her command—had diminished. In their place was a vulnerability she did not yet know how to master. She resolved to correct her mistake with the guard, to charm him, even if it required submission. Her life might depend on it. No other man so fixated on her might ever appear again.

She heard footsteps. Voices. Shouts. None of them his.

She imagined him discovered, caught sneaking food to her. Tortured. Executed. That would be her fate, too. There were so many ways to die in this place.

And yet, beneath her despair, she was surprised by how fiercely she wanted to live. *Why?* she wondered. *Live for what?*

She had no answer. No family. No future. No hope. Yet she clung to life more urgently than ever before.

A single possibility glimmered. *Tong.* Perhaps Vo Thanh Tong was still alive. That astonished her more than anything else—her desire for a man who had no politics, no principles, no cause. A man who had loved her after her legs were gone. Loved her when she was a burden.

But he was likely dead. And she was still hungry.

"Feed it," came Kim Lan's voice from the dark. "Do not shame the body. I'm tired of being spirit. I hunger for flesh, my own and . . . a man's."

Where is he?

"Who, Tong or the little guard?"

The little guard, of course.

"So, even broken, your body wants to live?"

Yes. Yes, but where is he?

A voice dropped from the grating. "Hey, Tuyet Mai, I'm here."

His voice! *Has he brought food?*

"I have food for you."

She closed her eyes and smiled. Summoning strength, she spoke in a tone as sweet as she could manage. "I'm so glad to see you. Yes, I'll have a little food, though I'm not hungry. It's you I hunger for."

Kim Lan chuckled in the shadows.

~

The next morning, Dinh's mother heard him whistling from the kitchen. She called him in. When he stepped into the doorway, she studied his face, then smiled.

"Why so cheerful today?"

His instinct was to guard himself, but he let it go. "I love her," he said.

She raised her eyebrows. "That's news? And what makes today different, that you whistle like a lark?"

"Today I know she loves me."

His mother's smile faded. She had already assumed this truth. Now she wanted results. "Ha! You speak of love as though it were an end. I would have thought you'd already gone to the temple for auspicious wedding dates."

The mention of children set Dinh thinking. He hadn't considered fatherhood in years. The thought now filled him with ambivalence. Children would be trouble. Tuyet Mai, without legs, would struggle. He'd have to help more than he wanted. Less time for himself. But what did he want? To please his mother. To be with Tuyet Mai. To grow old with comfort. Sons, if possible. Daughters would mean complications. But even that didn't matter. The image of her body, the silence that would follow his mother's death, it would be worth it.

"I wouldn't be surprised," he said, "if you had grandchildren soon."

She clapped her hands and reached out. He embraced her, all doubts gone.

~

That night, Dinh sat quietly in the noodle shop of Trich Van Thap. The proprietor, peering at him through a fish tank, frowned. No beer. Just tea. A loss. Worse still, Dinh ate slowly, in silence, his appetite subdued.

The old man's frown deepened when a Buddhist monk entered and joined Dinh's table. Curious, he leaned in but caught only greetings. Frustrated, he withdrew.

Once alone, Dinh leaned forward. "Will on a leaf of grass the mirror shine?" he whispered, then laughed. "Yes! And I, this weed, now shine!"

The monk, bewildered, nodded. He didn't understand, but sensed the potential for a new donor—or convert. "And now that you shine, Mr. Dinh, will you help others shine?"

Dinh recognized the cue for money. He waved it off. "Of course. Not just that. A wedding."

"A wedding?" The monk's face fell. "That is simple. Why summon me?"

"Because I want a tutor. A venerable. Someone to teach me Buddhism."

The monk blinked. "Why now?"

"For my mother," Dinh said, honestly. "And because I've done harm. I enjoyed it. I still do—until yesterday. Now everything is different."

The monk hesitated. "What changed?"

"A woman."

Another disappointment. He tried not to show it.

"No," Dinh said. "It's more than that. She is beyond what you can imagine. I must change for her."

The monk tried to steer back. "Which venerable?"

"I want the best. The most compassionate. The highest."

"That won't be cheap."

"How much? Small compassion—five hundred? Large—one thousand? Ten thousand to learn why I shouldn't torture?"

The monk winced. "You misunderstand. But yes, a gesture will be required."

"I'll make it," said Dinh.

"I'll inquire," said the monk, rising.

"Wait." Dinh grabbed his robe. "One more thing."

"Yes?"

"No one must know. Especially not my mother."

"Understood."

"And your venerable, he must make me *completely good*."

The monk's teacup trembled beneath his nail. He considered arguing, but held back. "Yes. Completely good."

~

When the monk left, Dinh sat motionless, sipping his tea. The proprietor watched in sorrow. A customer lost. A soul adrift.

Dinh paid, went home, greeted his mother, and lay in his room staring at the ceiling.

He was in freefall.

The foundations of his life, violence, cruelty, dominance, were crumbling. What remained was a love he had never fully known, even from his mother. Her kindness was too ethereal, too spiritual, never solid beneath his feet.

Now he reached for something weightless and unseen, yet weighed more than the wreckage of his life—goodness.

A venerable could give him form again. Rules. Orders. Like a prison, but sacred. Follow them: be good. Perfect them: be perfect. With gods at his side, he might be worthy of Tuyet Mai and his mother both.

He puzzled over how to free Tuyet Mai. Plans bloomed, then died. He had no allies. No one he trusted.

Only one man remained.

His uncle.

Dinh hesitated, then decided. He would return to Scribe Huynh.

And this time, he would ask for more than interpretation.

He would ask for salvation.

~ *Tong Released* ~

At the same hour that Pham Van Dinh lay on his bed, wrestling with how to liberate his beloved prisoner, Vo Thanh Tong sat on the edge of his cot in a prison camp near Truc Thrinh, a hundred miles away. His legs stretched out, ankles crossed, he savored the rare pleasure of unshackled limbs and the improbable prospect of release. He rolled his head slowly, working out the knots in his neck. Even now, it was difficult to believe. Freedom. After nearly two years in captivity, since the day he and Tuyet Mai were seized, he had played the long game: convincing his captors he wished to defect.

From the outset, he'd ingratiated himself by offering a detailed account of Major Vy's involvement with the Hong Kong drug syndicate. He knew Vy had planned to flee south if the drug transfer succeeded at Song Nhan. His intel led to Vy's arrest and execution, caught with a false passport at Tan Son Nhut Airport. With that betrayal complete, Tong began cultivating Saigon intelligence. He portrayed himself as a valuable double agent, stressing that the People's Army still considered him loyal, unaware of his desertion before the fortress battle. It was his strongest argument, and he repeated it at every opportunity.

He claimed he had grown disillusioned with communism, joined the cartel as a means of escape, then repented. He painted his stay in Song Nhan as an act of conscience, a step toward embracing the Republic's democratic ideals. When the Americans arrived, he had shouted *chieu hoi* to the first soldier in reach. His captors hadn't believed a word, but they conceded his potential usefulness.

Now, he was to be released into the deeper coils of control. Saigon would use him as an agent, contingent upon a trial assignment within the infamous Con Son prison. His job: earn the trust of inmates, extract intelligence, and prove himself. Only then would he be considered for riskier missions. He had accepted, of course, but one concern remained.

Betrayal did not trouble him; Vy had been a necessary sacrifice. What worried him was alignment. Which side would win? He had no desire to tie his fate too tightly to either Hanoi or Saigon. He needed options, and options demanded channels. Channels required agility. Agility required awareness. Awareness demanded contacts. And contacts, once again, required channels. Thus, he reasoned, during the long transport to Con Son.

~

The moment he arrived, his theories were tested. A long briefing with the prison commandant, who harbored doubts about both Tong's reliability and value, was followed by a blunt assignment to a tiger cage recently vacated by a prisoner who had died after losing both hands to the guards. Before being escorted away, he was informed that his first opportunity to connect with inmates would come the next morning during a staged work detail. A retaining wall had been under construction for a week, a project designed precisely for this mingling.

Tong passed a sleepless night on the cold cement floor, and at dawn, he found himself standing in a ragged line of prisoners, shovel in hand, waiting in front of a trench. His left hand burrowed into his trousers for warmth; his right balanced the shovel on his shoulder. He wore the blank expression of a man defeated, inviting no conversation. Better to let others come to him. Patience was survival.

Guards paced back and forth, delaying the start. Tong shifted uncomfortably, then let his eyes wander. Feigning confusion, he turned slowly, scanning the mound left from the previous day's digging. At its crest, silhouetted by morning light, sat what appeared to be a woman. She wore a loose tunic and bent over some buried object, brushing away the dirt with slow, deliberate movements. Her hair veiled her face, but her form suggested a fragile dignity, a presence untouched by ruin.

She moved not with her legs, but her arms. A gap beneath her torso confirmed the unthinkable—her legs were gone. And yet something in her posture, something inexplicably luminous, captivated him. Not even filth or famine could obscure it. He could not look away.

When she finally lifted her head and swept the hair from her face, a piercing recognition struck him with such force he thought his heart had ruptured. For an instant, he believed he had died. But no, he was alive, and in that life there now existed only one undeniable truth:

Nguyen Tuyet Mai.

So absorbed was he that he failed to notice the guard nearby, eyes burning with loathing.

~

Pham Van Dinh watched the new prisoner gaze at Tuyet Mai. His Tuyet Mai. Rage flared. He longed to strike the man, but instinct told him to move her first, to remove her from the line of sight before she understood the nature of the look cast upon her.

He climbed the mound and placed himself between her and the prisoners, then gave her a gentle kick. His tone was firm, but his eyes flicked with a secret signal. "You are sick."

She looked up in surprise. "But I am to pour tea for the guards," she said, hand resting on the metal pot beside her. She had been savoring the outdoors—the sky, the bustle, even the dirt beneath her—a welcome change from the tiger cage.

Smiling impishly, she pleaded, "Let me stay. I was enjoying the air."

He frowned and nudged her harder. "You are sick. Pretend to vomit."

She understood. The tone left no room for defiance.

Moved to the far side of the mound, out of view, Dinh reported to the watch commander that inmate #46 had fallen ill and needed to be returned to her cell. Permission granted. Soon she was lying once again on her stone slab. She sulked, silent. Dinh, unfazed, smoothed her tunic and smiled.

"Later, I'll bring you something special."

She pouted. "Why did you take me away?"

"Didn't you notice?"

"Notice what?"

"A new prisoner. He was staring at you. It was shameful. Tonight, I'll make him pay for it. No man looks at my future wife like that."

Curiosity warred with caution. She wanted to ask more, but recognized the danger of Dinh's jealousy. Better to wait. Still, she softened her voice and reached for his hand.

"I live for the day when we marry. That will be happiness." She paused. "No, ecstasy."

Dinh trembled. He withdrew his hand quickly and glanced around.

"Later, my love. I'll bring your treat. And as for him—" He let the threat trail off. Tuyet Mai shivered.

~

Tong spent the day digging, his thoughts spiraling between rapture and dread. He now faced the same problem as Dinh—how to free Tuyet Mai—but with the added burden of his own imprisonment. By evening, he had produced no intelligence of value, no progress toward his mission. Only paralysis.

That night, he lay on the tiger cage floor, staring upward, consumed by thoughts of escape. He did not notice the guard until he heard the chuckle.

Low. Coarse. Predatory.

Then a voice:

"So, number 38, I hear you are to receive special treatment. And I have come to administer it."

Tong remained silent.

"You looked at a female prisoner. For that, your eyes must be cleansed."

Sweat prickled his brow.

"And to cleanse your eyes, I must follow orders."

Reporting the threat would be useless. The commandant had little regard for him, and the guard could always claim the exchange built trust among inmates.

"I did not stare at any prisoner, sir," Tong said quietly.

"Liars must also cleanse their tongues."

"Sir, I didn't know the rule."

The guard shifted above, boots scraping.

"If there is one prisoner I must not look at, I will not," Tong added quickly.

"You will look at no one. You will see no one."

"Why, sir?"

"Because you will be blind."

The boots receded.

Tong lay motionless. A revelation surfaced: this guard had a connection to Tuyet Mai. Perhaps even affection. Tong felt it natural. She inspired love. But did she return it?

Another problem. Another snare.

~

That night, Tuyet Mai whispered to the dead.

"Kim Lan, I'm so tired."

"Of men?"

"Of everything. Sometimes I think of ending it."

"Then come to me."

"I'm afraid. No one would call me back if I made a mistake."

"You won't need to come back. You'll be with me."

"But the sky, the trees, the living . . . "

"They hate themselves. Even the powerful. There is nothing to miss."

"Easy for you to say. You're dead." She paused. "But since you're in my mind, maybe it's easy for me to say, too."

"So I don't exist?"

"No."

"Convenient."

"You're an illusion. Death isn't. That's the difference."

"Are you sure?" Kim Lan reached down and pinched her.

"Ow!"

Kim Lan's form shifted. Teeth lengthened. Flesh sloughed from her face. A skull leered.

Tuyet Mai recoiled, but the horror melted. Kim Lan smiled again, gentle.

"You're right. You're not ready. Live, my friend. Live."

When the vision vanished, Tuyet Mai wept. The despair that had once pointed toward death now veered away from it, not from hope but from fear. Her mind slipped into the mercy of sleep. There, she dreamed of a future she could still imagine: beautiful, distant, and alive.

~ *Tuyet Mai Has More Dreams* ~

Her dream emerged without sound, borne on a tide of fog so thick it seemed to pulse with breath. Water lapped at her body with slow insistence. She tried to rise. For a moment, her stumps held her above the surface, but the water climbed steadily until it reached her chest, triggering a burst of panic. Then, impossibly, she felt legs, strong, whole, unmistakably hers. They lifted her above the rising tide. Dazed, she searched for something familiar, a landmark, a face, a shore, but the mist gave her nothing. The world stretched gray and shapeless in every direction. An unfamiliar urgency compelled her to run, but the fog thickened, fusing with the water into a single, viscous resistance.

Her legs slowed. Numbed. Then vanished.

She reached. Her arms dissolved.

No limbs. No motion. No name.

A torso and head, adrift in a world without ground.

She held her breath.

Failed.

Inhaled.

Drowned.

Yet as she acknowledged death, she defied it. Willed rebirth. In the depths, she reconstituted: limbs sprouting anew, lungs adapting to draw breath from water. She moved freely, easily, in this transformed world, tugged by unseen currents, her body no longer broken but sleek and vital. But peace never lingered. An unseen force lifted her from the water and flung her into the sky. Her gilled lungs burned in the open air.

She plummeted. Then landed in a village square.

Her village.

Women passed without notice, but their presence comforted her. She looked down: legs again. The revelation came gently, like a child discovering walking for the first time. And so she walked. She followed no map but moved with purpose. At the village's edge, where rice fields began, a woman sat fanning herself on a veranda. Elderly, yet radiant with life. When she saw Tuyet Mai approach, her face bloomed with joy.

"At last you've come, child," she called.

"Yes," Tuyet Mai replied, unsure what else to say.

"Now that you are home, where will you live?"

"With you?"

The woman laughed. "No. You have a husband. I'm too old to care for a cripple."

Tuyet Mai looked down. Her legs were gone.

She tottered on her stumps, hands reaching for balance. The old woman chuckled.

"Don't worry. Not only do you have a husband, you have children."

"Madame Dau, how do you know my future? I don't deserve such happiness."

"And you will have fertile fields. Buffalo. Come. Let me show you."

Tuyet Mai nodded.

The fog returned, but it was no longer wet, just opaque. When it lifted, she was in a kitchen, leaning over a boiling pot. A man stood in the doorway, backlit by sunlight.

"Wife, I am home."

She could not see his face, only a silhouette that called itself her husband. He sounded happy. Chided her gently for not greeting him. Urged her to grab her crutches and come see their son playing on a buffalo.

She obeyed. His figure receded. The crutches were awkward. She fell behind. Frustrated, she yearned for speed, and the dream, obliging, gave her legs again.

She ran.

Laughter beckoned from the rice field. Her husband and son splashed in the shallow water, carefree. She waded in, desperate to reach them before the dream dissolved. But before she could draw close enough to see their faces, she slipped.

Water rushed over her head.

She awoke on the cold stone slab of Con Son Prison, her stumps twitching in vain, still seeking the dream-echo of a vanished family.

~ *Tong Consults His Superiors* ~

Tong acted swiftly. There was no time to wait for another confrontation. If the little guard's threat became reality, no remedy would matter. Through the dispensary doctor, his prearranged channel, he feigned illness. During the examination, he spoke the coded phrase: "I've always wanted to visit the house of the American president."

Soon, he stood before Commandant Tran.

Tran said nothing. The office was silent except for the faint ticking of a wall clock. Tong did not sit. Permission had not been given.

Tran sat at his desk, fingertips pressed together, forming a steeple. Silent. Unmoving.

Tong waited.

"Well?" Tran finally barked.

"Sir, I've come to report threats made against me by one of your guards."

Tran's face twisted with distaste. "Is that all?"

"Yes, you see he—"

"Do you have any intelligence to report?" Tran interrupted, spitting the final word.

"Not yet, sir. I—"

"Then don't waste my time with grievances."

Tong held his ground. "Sir, if the guard carries out his threat, I will be unable to perform my mission."

For the first time, Tran smiled. "And what threat is that, Number 38?"

"He threatened to blind me. Perhaps remove my tongue."

Tran chuckled. "That might endear you to the inmates. Loosen their tongues, so to speak."

Tong said nothing.

"Still," Tran sighed, "perhaps that would not serve our interests. My superiors may want to use you again. Damaged goods are neither donkey nor horse."

Tong seized the opening. "Indeed, sir. As they say, we don't want to wrap the baby upside down."

He miscalculated.

Tran's eyes narrowed. The familiarity grated. Such ease signaled a loss of fear, a loss of control. It reeked of parity.

"Number 38," Tran said coldly. "Return to your cell. Do not trouble me again unless you bring intelligence. Otherwise, the guards will play their roles as they see fit."

Tong stood motionless, though his mind raced. He pictured his eyes gouged, his tongue torn out.

"Commandant Tran," he said urgently. "If I am harmed, my reports to Saigon will not be limited to prisoner gossip."

Tran remained impassive. Inside, he calculated. Every possible reply carried risk. Finally, he chose the path least satisfying to his ego but most advantageous to his ambition.

"You will not be harmed," he said. "Though I will encourage the guards to increase their verbal abuse. Perhaps even let the other prisoners believe you are being tortured."

"Thank you, sir." Tong bowed slightly, his tone deferential.

But Tran was no longer thinking about face.

He had discovered something more valuable: a ruse.

"Yes," he mused aloud. "There is much we can do to make your loyalty seem convincing. Much to reinforce the illusion that you remain one of Uncle Ho's sons."

He pressed his fingertips together again, temple-like.

Somewhere, not far from her cell, a man who once loved Tuyet Mai had just been told he might be tortured in her name.

Tong reached his cell just in time. The nausea broke loose as the door clanged shut behind him.

Chapter Eleven

PART TWO: REPLICATION

Preparations and Perturbations

~ Mark Submits to the Professor ~

Mark Powers sits cross-legged on the grass, eyes lifted toward the solemn facades of Columbia's ancient buildings. It is Saturday morning. The sun struggles to rise into strength, a pale force pressing against the coolness that clings to stone and bone alike. Mark barely notices. For days, he has renounced his digital rites, no games, no scrolling, no passive feeds, consumed instead by the anticipation of this morning's meeting with Professor Benson.

He is restless in this new stillness. Without the steady drip of dopamine that modern life provides, he feels a peculiar rawness, a kind of mental hunger. But Benson's cryptic insinuations, references to paternal shadows and old wartime truths, have lit a spark in him. Something stirs beyond the screen, beneath the surface. A possibility. Not for escape, but for initiation.

He plucks three blades of grass and ties them with a fourth, cinching it tight so they do not scatter. In his imagination, the three blades become his trinity: himself, his father, and his mother, long lost. The fourth, the one that binds, is Theresa. The interloper. The stranger who would dare weave herself into their unit. He pulls the knot tighter, and for a moment, his thoughts drift toward quiet violence. A woman I dislike, he thinks. A woman with motives I do not trust. And she is not alone. There is the other one, Ethyl. Together, they murmur in corners, forming alliances that do not include me.

But that web is for another day. Today, there is something larger waiting, Vietnam, perhaps. The war. The truth. A path that Benson, for all his eccentricities, might open. Something beyond his father's reach. Something unedited.

~

9:43. He checks his watch. Seventeen minutes remain.

He drops the little grass effigy and shifts his weight. Time, unstructured, unoccupied, presses down. A void. No device hums. No screen flickers. No prompt arrives. He is alone, unbuffered, in a universe that breathes in silence.

How to endure seventeen minutes without artificial comfort? He searches his mind for noise: a movie scene, a sports highlight, a sexual image, a line from a game. Anything to fill the void.

9:47. I'm usually late, he thinks. Now I'm early. And early is worse. Early requires endurance. Thinking is the enemy. Or rather, **this** kind of thinking, the kind that loops and deepens and refuses sedation. Society despises that. It prefers a narcotic swirl of pleasures: painless with pain, placeless with destination, utterly thoughtless.

He smiles grimly. Thinking leads to collapse. Collapse leads to clarity. And clarity is lethal to the machine.

Satisfied with this private sermon, he drops the thought. Forces himself to take in the trees, the passing birds, the stately buildings. He opens and closes his notebook. Watches girls drift by. Checks the time again.

9:54. If I leave now, I'll arrive in five minutes. I can linger by Benson's office door and reread the political cartoons. Maybe there are new ones. Then I'll be inside, and something will happen. Something real.

He stands. Adjusts his cap backward. Walks across the grass with a performance of purpose. A final glance at his watch. 9:55 and counting. Yes. This will work. I won't even need the cartoons.

~

Benson waits behind his desk. The light is gray, and the air feels too thick with thought. He should be grading. The student papers sit untouched, like fallen leaves gathering dust. His hand rests instead on a thick folder bound in string. *CONFIDENTIAL—PROFESSOR BENSON* declares the label across its cover.

He knows the contents by heart. He could open it now. Review the evidence again. Connect the fragments. But he resists. Mark will arrive any moment.

9:59. Almost time.

Will the boy agree? Will the father? And if so, will it be enough to unravel what has been sealed? Ah, the father. That story alone could ignite a firestorm. Or perhaps it is not just a story. Perhaps it is a cipher, a locked gate guarding something darker. No matter. Even the ashes may be useful. A book, a documentary, a film. Recognition. Maybe more.

A knock.

Benson straightens his back, then slumps theatrically, assuming the pose of a weary academic mid-task. He grabs a paper from the pile, opens it at random, and makes a bold red mark in its upper margin.

Another knock.

"Enter," he says, the word falling softly, rehearsed.

"Good morning, Professor Benson."

"Good morning, Mr. Powers. Have a seat. Let me just finish this page."

"No problem."

Benson appears to focus on the grading but watches Mark closely through veiled glances. The boy has removed his cap, thank God, and now sits, still and alert. But his gaze rests on the cold fireplace. Not the books. A disappointment.

In Benson's unshakable taxonomy, the truly curious are drawn to the shelves. The indifferent always avoid them. In war, as in life, the eye reveals the soul.

He waits.

Then it happens. Mark shifts. His eyes lift. He begins to scan the titles.

Good. Let the fire kindle.

After a pause, Benson speaks as if the thought had just occurred. "Interested in any of those titles, Mr. Powers?"

"All of them."

Benson beams. "Interested in traveling to Vietnam this summer, Mr. Powers?"

The question slices through the air. Mark draws breath too sharply. "Yes, sir," he stammers. "I think so."

"It might be arranged, if I'm allowed to speak with your father."

The light dims in Mark's face. "Oh," he says, deflated.

"I'll need a short meeting. Just to explain the plan."

Mark hesitates. "I'll talk to him. When would you want to go?"

"I have one window. Two weeks from now. I can fly to California on Friday, meet with him Saturday, return Sunday."

"What? That's the weekend of the wedding."

"I see."

"And the honeymoon. That won't work."

"Even so," Mark adds quickly, "I still want to go. I'm of age."

Benson leans back, temples his fingers. "Yes, but this isn't only about your rights. Your father is the bridge. Without him, the past remains sealed."

"Bridge to what?"

"To understanding."

"You've mentioned a mystery before. What kind of mystery?"

"Just a metaphor."

"But if I'm going to Vietnam, shouldn't I know what I'm walking into?"

"In due time."

"My father doesn't talk about the war. That worries me."

"No need. I've reviewed the official records, just fragments, nothing ominous."

He pauses, then brightens again. "Tell me, is the wedding small?"

"Yes. At our house."

"Reception?"

"Just a gathering."

"Then perhaps I could stop by. After the ceremony. Just for a few minutes. He'll want to know who's sending you to the far side of the world."

Mark frowns. "I doubt he'll want to talk about this at his wedding."

"I'll be discreet. Just get his permission. Leave the rest to me. Patience."

Mark clenches his jaw. *It's my father you're talking about.* But he swallows the protest and shifts gears. "Is it really that important?"

"More than you know. Your father is a thread in history, and you are the one who can pull it."

Mark exhales, doubtful. "Okay. I'll try."

"Excellent. The rest depends on you."

"Yes."

"Then we shall not speak of it again until you return."

"Yes, sir."

Benson taps the top paper with theatrical exhaustion. "And now, back to my labors. Let me know as soon as possible."

"Yes, sir. Thank you."

"Good luck, Mark. Truly."

~

Later that night, Benson reclines in his chair, stockinged feet crossed before him, a half-filled glass of Burgundy balanced in one hand. His lap is cluttered with a chaotic spread of documents and faded photographs. Most are copies of Army intelligence reports, dated, yellowed, and stamped with designations like "Top Secret" and "Confidential." They all reference a single battle, fought in 1969 during the Vietnam War.

In his free hand, he holds a photograph that has gripped his attention more than the rest. It shows the torn pieces of a Last Will and Testament, reassembled on a dirt floor, fragile as ash, the typeface almost smudged to silence. At the bottom of the image, a terse caption reads:

"Found in Tunnel by Sgt. T. Crawford. Undisturbed & Photographed As Found. Verified by Capt. G. Barnett. Photo by Sgt. T. Crawford. See Crawford doc34 titled: strange."

Benson raises a magnifying glass, examining the image for what must be the hundredth time. Despite the fragmented lines and fissured edges, the words still manage to speak:

~

LAST WILL AND TESTAMENT OF
MICHAEL G. POWERS
Article One

I, MICHAEL G. POWERS, a resident of Los Angeles County, California, declare this to be my will, and I hereby revoke all wills and codicils previously made by me. My deceased spouse, DIANE L. POWERS, is the birth-mother of my only living child, MARK H. POWERS, whose birth date is August 27, 1980.

Article Two

I give the entire residue of my estate to the trustee then in office under that trust designated as THE POWERS FAMILY TRUST established February 23, 2001, of which the grantor is myself, and to be added to and beco—

~

He lowers the glass, murmuring to himself, "Why, Sgt. T. Crawford? Why did you find a document dated 2001 in an abandoned fortress in 1969? Why did you die of a heart attack five years ago, just before I could reach you? And where is 'doc34 titled: strange'? Vanished. As for you, Capt. Barnett—missing in action for over thirty years. How convenient."

He returns the lens to the corner of the image. A giant ant hauls a scrap of paper from the reassembled will.

"Good thing Crawford got there before the ants took it all."

But then a thought startles him. He adjusts the magnification.

"Or are they taking it away?" he whispers. "Are they . . . delivering it?"

~ *Theresa Makes Plans* ~

"The wedding is around the corner and I'm so far behind!" Theresa groans, slamming down her pencil after leaving yet another voicemail for the caterer. The to-do list sprawled before her remains largely untouched. "No one picks up anymore. Always messages, always waiting."

Ethyl sits nearby, sewing in silence.

"Why can't you blink your eyes and make everything fall into place, O Great Goddess?" Theresa snaps.

Ethyl doesn't answer. Her fingers keep threading.

"Are you listening?"

Of course. I'm no genie, child. Just what you call Goddess. A metaphor, no less.

"Maybe if I sacrificed a lamb, you'd pay attention."

Even then, I would not. You lack the proper rituals. Yours is a world too impatient for true supplication. Today, devotion is reduced to transaction—worship as bargaining, prayer as ejaculation. Lip service, if you will.

"Crude," Theresa mutters, "but funny. Still, there are those who do good without need for miracles."

Yes. They swallow the bitterness and call it grace. They serve the Father's appetite and gag on holiness. But who bothers to feed Me? Do not bother with lambs. Too much blood has already been spilled for myth and dog food alike.

"When you rant, I miss Ethyl. When you're Ethyl, I want Goddess."

What if I'm neither? What if I'm a demon wearing Her voice?

"No demons! Just someone to help with the dress, the flowers, the caterer—"

Ah yes. The minister's arranged, is he not? One of His little minions. Always showing up to bless My business.

"Your business?"

Who do you think arranged this union? Who brought you to Michael? Who planned the drama unfolding? I did. And don't be surprised—I like you. You are the woman of his dreams. And I am the one who makes his dreams. I made you, too. He has permission to enter My ballroom.

"Sounds more like plots than plans."

Ethyl's figure stretches unnaturally, her voice now resonant and soft.

You asked if I intervene in the world. I do. I always have. Each stitch I pull runs through time, war, madness, and myth. Your marriage to him is one more stitch. All is in preparation for The Reunion.

"Reunion? What for? With whom?"

Must there always be a reason? Purpose is the opiate of human minds. Know only this: you've been drawn from a man who beat you toward one who has beaten himself. A gentle heart may yet steady yours.

"And if I love the one who hurt me more than the one who hurts himself?"

Then drink His swill. Or bend to My will. But do not pretend Free Will and Fate can share a bed.

"Now you sound like God."

Careful. That tone won't get you a caterer.

"Seriously. Why this war between you and Him?"

First Principles. The words we speak are not what you hear. 'The dog goes for a walk' becomes 'Let slip the dogs of war.' What Michael hears—what you hear—are your own fractured echoes. The real message is hidden in the part of him we still seek. The part that makes him … Chosen.

"Then why me? What's my purpose?"

Ethyl holds up her hand. *Enough.* Her body softens. "Honey, give me the name of that caterer. I'll put a bee in her bonnet."

~

That night, Theresa lies awake, aching. Ethyl's condition seems to be worsening. The goddess voice is stronger now, and stranger. And still, she loves her. Loves her brilliance. Her madness. Wonders again if it would be better to leave her in care. With doctors. With pills.

But love, not medication, holds her fast. Besides, she needs her. Even now, she misses him, the ropes, the bruises. Theresa squeezes her thighs together.

She needs help. They all do. Perhaps marriage will help. Perhaps.

She falls into a troubled sleep.

Ethyl stands beside her. Or something that resembles Ethyl. The figure begins to shift—bird, fish, cloud, mountain, tree, reptile—fluid forms rolling against the dark.

At last, it becomes an upright ant, enormous, silent, antennae twitching. Its words arrive as mist.

It's time to take you back in time to him.

Theresa closes her eyes against the cool spray of the voice. When she opens them, she is no longer in her room.

She glides through a vast clearing. Before her, a ruined stone fortress rises from fog, massive and swaying like the hull of a sunken myth. Others float with her, plasma-bodied, transparent, pulsing with inner life. Hearts beating. Lungs breathing. Some clothed, some not. She looks down. Her own skin is translucent. Her organs pulse beneath.

Together, they drift through the fortress wall. Inside, a courtyard opens, and the spirits divide: some drawn to sleeping soldiers, others to watchmen slumped in stupor. No one sees them.

Theresa is drawn to one man. Her skin responds before her thoughts do, deep bruises blossom across her translucent body, pain and pleasure entwined.

She nestles close, helpless against the old ache.

Then, from across the fortress, she sees him. A boy, really. Alone. Fever-eyed. Jungle uniform draped around a too-young frame.

It is Michael Powers.

Her breath catches. "Oh, my God."

~ *Michael Makes Plans* ~

While Theresa and Ethyl prepared for the wedding with their usual rituals and arguments, Michael Powers was not idle. He had spent the last week building a small outdoor stage for the ceremony, erecting a tented area for shade, and laying out tables and chairs for the guests. On this hot Thursday, he pauses mid-construction, sets down his hammer, and takes a long pull from a bottle of water. Sweat darkens his shirt, and the air is heavy with the scent of wood and dust. He stares off into the distance, thoughts unfocused, when he notices a plume of dust and then the shape of a car coalescing into view. He shades his eyes. Paul.

Relieved by the interruption, Michael walks up to the car and greets his friend with a broad grin. Paul, smiling as always, returns the greeting with exuberant cheer. They stroll back to the stage, Paul complimenting Michael's handiwork, pointing out with exaggerated praise the sturdiness of the beams and the symmetry of the tent.

Michael ducks into the house and returns with two beers. The conversation soon turns languid. But something in Paul's manner, too buoyant, too sparse in substance, alerts Michael. Paul is circling something. He's here for a reason.

Michael takes the bait. "So, what brings you here today? Aside from the free beer?"

Paul shrugs, half-laughing. "Nothing in particular. Just thought my best friend, getting married in a few days, might need some help."

Michael looks around the nearly complete stage. "Help? Timing's perfect."

Paul nods. "Better late than never. And I figured you might want to talk."

"About?"

"You know. Mark's gone. You're here alone. Big changes coming. Figured it might be good to check in."

"Check in?"

"Come on, Mike. Male bonding time. You must have a few heavy thoughts."

"Like how to hang string lights?"

"No. Like marriage. Like living with someone again. Like the first woman since Diane."

Michael shrugs. "I love her. She loves me. We want to be together. Marriage makes that possible. End of story."

"Is it?"

Michael's eyes narrow. "Not you too. I expect this from Mark, but if you and Claire disapprove, maybe skip the wedding."

Paul lifts his hands. "Whoa. Not what I meant. I'm just trying to help."

Michael exhales slowly. "I know. But help with what?"

Paul pauses, something passing across his face. Then he shakes his head. "Forget it. Doesn't matter."

"Too late. You brought it up. Out with it."

"I was just offering support. Not a crime."

Michael leans forward. "I'm listening."

Paul sighs. "Okay. Feet planted? Ready for my shocking revelation?"

Michael grins. "Do it."

Paul's voice softens. "Claire and I think Theresa's a wonderful woman. We look forward to having her in our lives."

Michael flinches. The compliment lands like an accusation. He turns, picks up the hammer.

Paul reaches for a saw, though there's nothing to cut. "Mike, you're my best friend. Claire and I, we've been with you through everything. The war. Diane's death. The years after. The dreams. The ghosts. The dinner parties. The medication. The counseling. That's behind you. It should be over. No more war. No more agony. And for God's sake, no more dinner parties for the dead."

He rests a hand on Michael's shoulder. "You are taking your meds, right?" Then, with a weak laugh, he waves the saw. "Now, what needs cutting?"

Michael cracks a smile. "Your head, idiot. As if she isn't real."

They work for a while, sharing half-hearted jokes. When Paul leaves, his cheer feels brittle. Michael watches the car disappear down the gravel drive.

"You never said what you came to say," he murmurs. "None of you like Theresa. But why?"

He walks back to the house, brooding. "Too beautiful. Too intelligent. Too kind. Must be something else."

Ethyl. Of course. Ethyl. Who is she? What is she? Why does she unsettle them?

The memory stirs, of Paul's comment, of those strange dinner parties, of ghosts seated around the table. Of Mark's warnings. Of Claire's silences. Of Paul's remark: *if you made her up.*

Michael pales.

"He thinks I made her up. He thinks they're both hallucinations."

But he pushes it away. No. Theresa is real. Ethyl is not. Paul is working for Them.

And yet, he knows it isn't that simple. Simplicity is not always truth. But neither is complexity. Simplicity, for gods or geniuses, may be clarity. But for mortals, clarity is rare.

He resolves to confront Theresa. No more evasions.

First: her background with Ethyl. Second: the nature of their relationship. Third: what happens to Ethyl after the wedding.

Tonight.

But even as the plan hardens, doubt seeps in. His natural gentleness recoils at confrontation. What harm has Ethyl done? A kind old woman. Encouraging. Helpful. Strange, yes, but hardly dangerous. Perhaps it's not her they fear. Perhaps it's him.

But why doubt, when the path is clear? Theresa will explain everything. He will ask. She will answer. The fog will lift.

Tonight.

~

The plan begins to unravel almost immediately.

When he calls Theresa, she agrees to dinner on one condition: Ethyl must come too. They have prior plans. Ethyl has no food at home. She must not be left alone.

Michael hesitates, irritated. But agrees.

He finishes work on the stage, showers, dresses in a gray sweatsuit and worn sneakers. His mind drifts. He checks his e-mail, voicemail, mail. From the stack, a letter catches his eye, an old friend. He tucks it into a drawer without opening it. No distractions.

He clears the kitchen bar, finds only one item left: jungle fatigues in plastic wrap. Mechanically, he unwraps them and boxes them, storing the package out of sight. The bar gleams.

Dinner becomes his focus. He dresses the table with inherited odds and ends—Wedgwood, crystal, cloth napkins—four place settings. He broils pork chops, sautés mushrooms, microwaves peas, stirs instant potatoes. Something still missing.

Music.

He rifles through his CDs. Mahler's Fifth. *Chants d'un compagnon errant.* He hesitates. Broadway melodies? No. Diane loved Mahler.

He inserts the disc. Adjusts volume. Returns to the kitchen.

A knock at the door.

He checks the time. Pork chops still have minutes left. He opens the door.

~

Greetings feel pointless. "Hello," "Welcome," "Come in." Words too hollow for the mood. When Theresa and Ethyl appear, he simply turns and walks back to the kitchen.

They follow in silence. At the table, he gestures firmly: sit.

Theresa pauses, unsettled by his rudeness. Ethyl remains calm, unfazed. Theresa glances toward the kitchen, torn between following and staying. But something warns her. She sits beside Ethyl, who stares straight ahead, unmoving, refusing eye contact.

Theresa calls out, "What can I do to help?"

No response.

The silence grows. The room thickens. Theresa notices: four place settings.

She tries again. "Who else are you expecting, Michael?"

Still nothing.

Then Ethyl turns. But not to Theresa. She stares across the table at the empty chair, as if it were occupied.

Michael returns, balancing plates. One is placed before Ethyl. Another for Theresa. A third, carefully arranged, goes to the empty setting across from Ethyl. Then his own.

Seated, he smiles. Lifts his water glass. "Cheers."

Ethyl lifts hers. "Cheers."

They hold their glasses aloft. Smiling toward the invisible guest.

Michael turns to Theresa, glass still raised, voice low. "Darling?"

Something in his tone, tender and earnest, softens her.

Perhaps it's a joke. Or a test. But she will not be rattled.

She lifts her glass. "Cheers."

~ *Yet Another Strange Dinner Party* ~

Michael clinks glasses with Theresa and casts a glance toward the empty chair toward the young soldier now seated beside her. He quickly averts his eyes. The twin's blackened hands tremble beside the M-16 leaning against the table. His uniform reeks of sweat, rot, and something deeper, something earthbound and ancient. Though Michael has grown accustomed to these unwanted guests at his "special dinners," setting the fourth place still unsettles him. And this time, Theresa has noticed.

Her discomfort radiates. Hoping to ease her unease, Michael reaches for the mundane. "So, how was your day?" he asks, voice deliberately casual.

Theresa offers a tight, ironic smile. "Fine, until I got here. Then it turned a little strange."

Off balance, Michael glances at Ethyl for help. She offers none. "It's nothing," he says quickly. "He usually leaves early. Then we can have a normal dinner."

Theresa fidgets with her napkin. "I give up. Who are we talking about?"

Michael nods toward the chair. "Him."

She narrows her eyes. "Oh, *him*. Right. I'll bite, who is he?"

"You really don't see him? Or is it the M-16 that bothers you?"

At the word *rifle,* Theresa's posture stiffens. Her voice drops into clinical mode. "What would you like me to say, Michael? You want me to see him?" Then, more sharply: "I thought you were past this."

He ignores the sting. Turns to Ethyl. "You see him, don't you?"

"Land sakes, child. Course I do."

Theresa exhales in disbelief. Michael addresses the chair. "You see? No one wants you here. I thought I was done with you. But you never take the hint."

"No," says a voice.

Michael throws up his hands. "Did you hear that?"

Theresa remains silent, her face unreadable.

Ethyl speaks gently. "Why so cross, child? He's your twin."

"It's complicated," Michael mutters.

"Tell them," the soldier says.

"Yes, tell us," Ethyl adds.

Theresa leans forward. "Tell us what?"

The soldier turns to Ethyl. "She still can't hear me. Diane could. She can't. You gonna fix that, or what?"

"Don't look at me," says Ethyl. "I'm just an old black crow waitin' on the wind."

"Can't play both sides, Goddess," the soldier replies.

"Hush. You're just a figment."

"And you?" he shoots back.

Michael freezes. "You're Goddess? Of course."

"Stop it!" Theresa shouts.

Ethyl turns, her eyes fierce. Theresa shrinks back. Her attention is drawn to the soldier, eyes glowing from the shadows.

"You..." she breathes. "You were in my dream."

The soldier nods. "Have a seat."

Theresa sinks down, stunned. The shock of Ethyl's rebuke and the apparition's return renders her mute.

The soldier glances at Ethyl, as if about to speak. Then only smiles.

Ethyl returns the smile. "Ask, and you shall receive. Theresa sees you now. Now that we've all had our little revelations, let's enjoy our soiree. Children—make your ol' Aunt Ethyl happy now, ya hear?"

Michael straightens. "Since it's my dinner, perhaps I could run it. Unless we're following your script again?"

"Absurd, isn't it?" Ethyl replies flatly. "Besides, schizophrenics control nothing."

The soldier leans forward. "Fate starves at Probability's door."

Ethyl turns to Theresa—but stops. Theresa is staring at her naked body, entranced by the bruises blooming across her skin. Her fingers brush her wrist.

"Theresa," Michael says.

She doesn't look up. "This is how I looked in the dream."

"I remember you," the soldier says. "You were with the ghosts. In the fortress. Who are you?"

"My fiancée," Michael answers quickly.

"Oh. Then where's Diane?"

"Gone." Michael glares. "You'll have to excuse my brother's manners."

Theresa blinks. Covers herself. Her gaze flits between them. "You're the same person. Obviously. This is all part of my dream. Too vivid, but still a dream."

Michael relaxes slightly. "You're learning. I once thought these dinners were mine, but clearly, they belong to all of us."

"How?"

"One of us isn't of this world." He looks pointedly at Ethyl.

She shrugs and lifts her fork. "Don't look at me, child. Let's eat. It's going to be a long night."

Theresa frowns. "If it's a dream, none of this matters." She lowers her arm. "But it's not. It's delusion. Hallucination. I should know." She smirks. "Still . . . I hope I remember it when I wake."

"And me?" asks the soldier.

"You're Michael. Or a fragment of him."

Michael drums the table. Then pounds it. "No! He is not me! He's my twin. He died in Vietnam."

Ethyl chuckles. The soldier stares blankly.

Theresa shakes her head. "Paul told me this delusion was under control. Michael, have you been taking your meds?"

Michael wheels on the soldier. "Why do you always come? You bring the war. You're just bones now."

"This is your dream," says the soldier. "Not mine. Besides, you know I'm not your twin, only the fractured piece of you. Broken off. Trapped."

"This is supposed to be therapy," says Michael, pouting.

Theresa muses. "Interesting. Everyone thinks it's their dream. Or their therapy. But clearly, it's mine."

"And what if it's mine?" Ethyl asks.

Theresa pauses. "Could be. The Goddess's dream. Not Ethyl's. That complicates things: DID and schizophrenia at the same table."

"Are you a psychologist?" the soldier asks.

"I think I'm a doctor."

Ethyl cackles. "You sure? Didn't I school you better than that?"

Michael leans in, voice sharp. "You're the one manipulating us. You bring him."

"I came on my own," the soldier says. "Running from her. You're the one who calls me back."

Theresa tilts her head. "What tunnel?"

The soldier's voice fades. "They're out there. Dead. I have to—"

"No!" Michael snaps. "Not tonight."

"But they're outside the fortress—"

"Stop!"

"You can't make me leave. Theresa says it's her dream. Or maybe Ethyl's. Or yours."

"I said *might*," Theresa corrects. "A projection."

"Could be yours," the soldier shrugs. "People dream about being naked."

Theresa glances down. The bruises. The welts. A strange electricity moves through her. She locks eyes with the soldier and lowers her arm.

Michael's voice turns cold. "What are you doing? Maybe the others are right about you."

Theresa smirks. "I'm responding to your younger self. He isn't ashamed. Maybe you weren't either." She lifts her breast.

Michael snaps. "Take him away! Or I'll kill him."

Ethyl replies calmly. "He acts as you did, and may again. You wanted control. Take it."

Michael scoffs. "Dreams aren't truth. Her bruises are truth. I'd never hurt her."

Ethyl's voice cuts in. "Are you sure? Never imagined it? Never enjoyed it? Never hurt? Never killed? Who did she sleep next to in that fortress?"

Michael erupts. "End it! I won't kill myself. I just want it to end!"

"I don't," the soldier whispers. "I don't want to go back."

"Nor do I," says Theresa, voice trembling. "Too much to study."

"I don't," says Ethyl, eyes locked on Michael. "Unless you want to go back. To the war. To the hurting."

"No! I won't!"

Ethyl begins to change.

A lotus blooms beneath her. She rises, radiant. Her crown gleams. A jewel burns in her brow. Her fingers form a perfect mudra.

She opens her mouth.

A sound came shrill, divine, and unbearable:

...youAveIsilentdoweohevenintoosendwatchholy....

Michael screams. Covers his ears.

Darkness.

~

Mahler plays on. The table is empty.

A knock at the door.

Michael checks the pork chops. Opens the door.

"Hello, how are you?"

He kisses Theresa and Ethyl. They dine peacefully. Laughter. Light conversation.

The fourth place setting remains untouched.

"An old friend canceled," Michael says.

No one asks who.

Chapter Twelve

Battle of Attrition

Tong Finds A Way

Vo Thanh Tong awoke before dawn, as if summoned not by rest but by omen. His confrontation with the commandant still clung to the air, the memory a caustic vapor from a smothered fire. Sleep had barely touched him. How could he sleep while twisting and muttering on a slab of stone? But the body, when commanded by purpose, will often rise where rest has failed. His first thought, as always, was Tuyet Mai. Her name carried the force of an incantation, stirring the machinery of fate within him.

Before the gruel slid through the crack beneath the iron door, he had already made his decision. There was but one path to her, one that required secrecy, cunning, and sacrifice. But the path had begun to widen even as he contemplated it. To see her would no longer suffice. The plan, once seeded, grew at once into a tree of liberation—hers. And once he glimpsed that branching structure, the roots burrowed fast. The first phase would begin today. It required another meeting with the commandant. That was the cost of initiation.

As he ate, he weighed the danger. The risks were many. Missteps would not mean mere punishment, but obliteration. Yet no other plan held even a sliver of credible hope. His nature strained toward immediacy, to act without pause, but deeper instinct, a coiled, serpentine wisdom, counseled delay. One week, then. A week to gather intelligence, real or conjured. Fabrication never troubled him. That others might scream, vanish, or be broken for what he invented, this did not weigh on his spirit. The cause was clear, and the goddess of necessity demanded tribute.

If conscience stirred, it was but a shadow flitting through a deeper vault. He cast the image of Tuyet Mai into that space, and the light she radiated turned the shadow to vapor. On darker days, when even she could not drive out the whisper of guilt, he shoved the voice back into its black den, to await another hour.

Tong finished the gruel and leaned back in momentary satisfaction, a general surveying the first strokes of a campaign. But before he could fully settle, the iron door shrieked open and a guard summoned him to the trench. The order echoed with inevitability, like the toll of a distant bell. Tong stood, stretched, and adopted the limp of the persecuted. Every gesture tuned to pity, he shuffled forward. Within this theatrical husk, his eyes moved quickly, calculating.

He searched for Tuyet Mai. She was absent, as he had feared. The little guard, her sentry and his tormentor, would have made certain of that. No matter. The real work began now. The trench was merely the stage.

He moved among the others, milling, hollow-eyed figures half-lost to the elements and the clockwork of oppression. Tong mingled, probed, performed. He sought fragments of intelligence, scraps he could reforge into currency for the commandant. If none came, he would fabricate. The truth mattered only as raw material. What happened to those he lied about did not concern him.

He assessed the field. The women were of no use, too guarded, too wise in the ways of male betrayal. His mind turned to the men. Somewhere among them, a fool waited, soft with loneliness, leaking secrets like water from a cracked jar.

And then he saw him.

A small man, alone within the crowd. Even the filth of his rags stood out. He was older, darker, heavy with years of neglect. The others gave him space, as if he carried a curse. His skin bore pocks and fungal eruptions. His eyes wandered, not aimlessly, but searching for contact, for acknowledgment, but none came. Wherever he moved, space widened around him.

A pariah, Tong thought. Possibly a former cadre, but never high-ranking. No authority. No discipline. Not privy to secrets. The kind who knows just enough to be dangerous, and too little to be trusted. Perfect.

Tong drifted toward him, preparing his opening. But as he drew close, something in him recoiled. Recognition stirred, not from memory, but from that deeper place where myth and dread speak before reason. The man's nose had been half-destroyed by violence; fluid leaked freely. His beard grew in uneven clumps, catching flakes, crumbs, stains beyond origin. His skin was a terrain of encrustations and sores. From ulcerated blisters a pale liquid oozed, as if the body no longer cared to separate self from decay. The lower half of the face looked as though it had been forged from infection. The upper half, still, composed and oddly pure, was crowned by an unblemished brow. The man had the face of a creature divided: monster below, luminary above.

Tong did not doubt the man's disease. Leprosy, perhaps, or something older. His eyes, though, those sunken orbs, were neither fevered nor dead. They were withdrawn, not in apathy but in refusal. They held the silence of something buried alive.

Still, he pressed forward. The cause was Tuyet Mai. That was enough. He swallowed hard and spoke.

"Hello, comrade. How are you this morning?"

The man gave no reply. His cracked lips twitched, but no sound emerged. The eyes seemed to tunnel deeper into shadow. Tong had the sense that sound itself would vanish if thrown into those hollows.

Yet he continued. "You look like a man who has seen much of the world, who has learned to dwell apart from its cruelties."

The voice that came in reply was more breath than speech. "And what is your story?"

Tong blinked. "Eh?"

A deeper tone followed, scraping from the chest. Ironic contempt flogged the words like a snapping whip. "What—is—your—story? Why—are—you—here?"

A wave of cold passed through him. *Wrong. Entirely wrong.* This was not a castoff, but a predator in disguise. A presence masked in decay. A locus of something ancient and vicious. Tong's pulse quickened, but he held his voice steady.

"Me? I'm here for the usual reasons," he said with practiced detachment.

"What is the usual?"

"The same as you, perhaps."

"Communist?" The word struck like an accusation issued from a tribunal of ghosts.

Tong leaned back, instinctively retreating from breath and stench and presence. "Is that why you're here?"

"I'm here because you need me. You reach toward me with questions, but hide your own answers."

Tong deflected. "You evade as much as I."

"I have the advantage."

"And what advantage is that?" Tong asked, uneasy now.

"I know you, Captain Vo Thanh Tong."

The name, spoken aloud, came like the unsealing of a crypt. The man wiped his nose with his sleeve, then let the slime smear across his thigh. The gesture felt calculated—an insult aimed directly at Tong's flesh.

Tong froze. He stared into the mutilated face, seeking its origin. Where had they crossed paths? What pact had been made, or broken?

He regained composure with effort and replied with an indifferent shrug. "I've worked in the trench these past days. No doubt someone mentioned my name. But I don't believe I've heard yours."

"You lie."

The word landed with a finality that shattered any further performance. Tong went silent, fury flickering beneath his skin. "What do you mean?"

But before the specter could answer, whistles cut through the air and guards descended, barking, beating, driving the inmates into rough formation. Shovels were thrust into their hands.

Tong, still dazed, found the man beside him once more. As they moved with their assigned cluster, he muttered, "What's your name?"

The man replied without turning. "Call me Ghost From Mr. Vo Thanh Tong's Past."

The voice was grave-drenched, inhuman. Tong tried to laugh, but it died in his throat. "That's a long name, comrade."

But the nausea had returned. And then, just over the man's shoulder, he caught a familiar sight. The little guard. The protector of Tuyet Mai. The one who watched, who listened, who judged. He stood just close enough to hear, head slightly tilted. On his face: a smile that knew far too much.

~ *Dinh Begins His Lessons* ~

Dinh returned home in a buoyant mood, lifted by two quite specific omens. First, he had unearthed something potentially ruinous about the prisoner Vo Thanh Tong, the mangy dog who dared insult Tuyet Mai. And second, within the hour, he would receive his first teaching from the venerable monk at the temple. His decision to trade shifts with Nguyen, covering the morning hours instead of his usual graveyard duty, had already borne fruit. Tomorrow, he would return to his regular schedule and begin a private inquiry into the strange link between Tong and the other prisoner.

But tonight belonged to more exalted matters. He was on the road to becoming a proper Buddhist, perhaps even a holy man in time. With the venerable's guidance, he would cleanse the blemishes of his past. For once, fortune appeared to walk beside him.

"Little Dinh," called his mother from the other room, "is that you?"

He parted the curtain, beaming. "Yes, mother. I'm making dinner now."

"So cheerful again," she said with wary gravity. "Has the wedding date been set, my son?"

"Very soon, mother. But no definite date yet. Good fortune is smiling on us. I'm making noodles with peanut sauce. That sound good?"

"Oh, that'll be fine."

"Just fine?"

"No complaint. But you know Thai food upsets my stomach. Could you leave off the sauce for mine?"

"Of course."

She sighed. "Soon I'll be strong enough to cook again. This bed is slowly killing me. Once I rise from it, all will return to order, and I'll care for my boy again."

His eyes moistened. "Soon, mother. You'll see. But for now, let me look after you, small payment for all the years you did the same for me."

"You're a good, filial son. May Buddha bless you. I want so much to be proud of you again, but—"

He cut her off, hearing only what pleased him. "And soon you'll be prouder than ever. I'll be better than I've ever been. Worthy of even the most devout Buddhist mother."

Her eyes narrowed. "What do you mean?"

His grin turned sly, eyes sparking with secret joy. "You'll see. You'll see."

Her unease deepened. "You speak strangely, Dinh. Tell me the truth, what's going on?"

"Nothing."

"You've been seeing your uncle again, haven't you? Don't lie—I sent for him myself."

He stiffened. "Why would I see him?"

"To interpret another note, perhaps?"

"What?!" he shouted, face contorted. "He told you about that?"

"Of course. I became suspicious when you visited him. You wouldn't answer my questions. I brooded. Then I sent word to your uncle that death hovered at my door. He came. I asked why you had visited. He told me. I asked more. He answered all. I recovered. He left."

"What did he say?" Dinh asked, voice low and cunning.

"Everything."

"You mean the note?"

"I mean *everything*."

"There is no more than the note."

"Yes, my son. The girl. The note. Where you work. What you do."

She wept.

"Yes, most painful of all—what you do. You told me you were a clerk. Not a guard. Not one with such a reputation. Oh, my son, my Little Dinh. What have you done all these years? How did I fail to teach you kindness? Respect for life?"

His own tears fell now, unchecked. He begged her to wait a little longer. He was changing. Already tonight, he would begin. The venerable would teach him to become a good man. A real Buddhist. For her. For them all.

"And mother, when I'm good, we'll all live together in peace, you, me, Tuyet Mai, and your grandchildren! You'll see! I swear you'll see!"

But she turned from him, her weeping grown heavier, and he left with those same words still on his lips: *You'll see.* He closed the door behind him and stepped into the night.

~

"So, you must be Pham Van Dinh!" called a voice, bright with welcome.

A smiling monk stood midway down the temple steps, palms pressed together in salutation. "So happy to meet you, Mr. Pham!"

Dinh, still carrying the weight of his mother's tears, approached in silence. The monk extended both bare arms, inviting a clasp of hands. Dinh bowed respectfully and accepted, but did not meet his gaze.

Even so, he felt the monk's eyes pierce him. Their stillness was immense. Dinh shrank beneath their gaze, as if being seen through from some elevated plane. For an instant, resentment surged. *He*, Pham Van Dinh, who wielded pain and power daily, who held life and death in his hands, was being judged like a wayward child. But his mother's disappointment returned to him, and he swallowed his pride.

He made an exaggerated bow. "Yes, venerable. I'm here to learn how to become a better man."

The monk looked startled. "Ah, but you are not here to learn how to be a better man."

"What?"

"You are here to learn how *not* to be a man at all."

Dinh stood frozen on the steps, looking around nervously. The street was open, people passing. The monk's words felt theatrical, embarrassing. "Sir," he said quietly, "could we enter the temple and speak more privately?"

The monk sat on the step and gestured beside him. "Sir," he echoed with playful mimicry, "first you must learn: there is no privacy." He opened his arms. "You are surrounded always—by living and non-living things, by ghosts of thought and form. You must learn to see them as phantoms of yourself, and yourself as their phantom in return."

Dinh winced. The words dredged up childhood memories: his mother's cryptic lessons on illusion, Dharma, consciousness, indiscriminate compassion. Words that meant nothing then, and less now. "But sir," he protested, "those so-called phantoms can think, talk, judge. They gossip. They *hurt*."

"Did I say otherwise?"

"Phantoms can't hurt you. *People* do," Dinh said firmly. "I know real people when I see them."

The monk chuckled. "Real people cannot hurt you. Only phantoms can."

Dinh looked down, defeated already. These conversations always ended with him confused, humiliated. He said nothing.

The monk also said nothing. He simply smiled at the passersby. Minutes passed. Then more. Dinh grew restless, then angry, then curious. Surely this was a test. He resolved not to speak until the monk did.

They sat. An hour passed. Dusk thickened into night. Foot traffic thinned. The stone step numbed his legs. His mind churned in a thousand directions: his mother, Tuyet Mai, the prisoners, the disease-ridden phantom haunting Tong, the money he lacked, the war, the whispers that Saigon would fall. Each thought led to another, and each was a burden with no handle. His head throbbed. His back stiffened. His neck ached. His foot went numb. Still, no answers came.

When he could endure no more, he stood to shake out the cramp. At once, the monk rose beside him, smiling as if the hour had passed in delight.

"Sir," Dinh blurted, exasperated, "shouldn't we go in and talk?"

The monk beamed. "Go in? No. You go *home*. Today's lesson is over."

Dinh flushed. "What lesson?"

The monk's eyes gleamed. "All that time, you sat steeped in phantoms. The very illusions you said could not harm you. Your mind is their nest. Until you can sit and not feed them, there is nothing I can teach you."

"But master, those thoughts *are* real. The people in them, my mother, my fiancée, the prisoners, they exist."

"Nonsense. You create them. You animate them with fear and longing. If you let them pass without possession, they would vanish like the faces of those who passed us this very night. Will you lie awake worrying about those strangers? Hating them? Loving them? No. Go home. Next time, we will sit on the steps again."

Dinh's frustration boiled over. "But what if I don't want to pay to sit on steps?"

"You have done nothing *but* sit on steps your entire life, summoning phantoms while the real passes by unrecognized. You are paying to learn how *not* to sit on steps."

"By sitting on steps?"

"Yes."

"But—"

The monk raised a single hand. "One. Step. At. A. Time. Until you have left the steps"—he lifted both arms, as if offering thanks to the empty sky—"*entirely.*"

~ *Tuyet Mai Entices Dinh* ~

By the time Dinh returned home for the second time that night, thought itself had turned against him. His mind recoiled from its own spinning, frayed and sore from too much strain. He checked in on his mother, who slept without stir, then collapsed on his bed, cursing the gods for making him dull. His failures felt carved into his flesh.

The next morning, he requested his shift back from Nguyen, who agreed with conspicuous delight. But the price was steep—double-duty. He endured the day in a haze of exhaustion, unable to approach Tuyet Mai or confront Vo Thanh Tong without drawing attention. Every hour dragged beneath the weight of his thwarted intentions.

Only with nightfall did relief arrive. One by one, the prisoners collapsed into their cages like the beaten remnants of an army retreating to stone. The duty officer, numbed by liquor and filth-rag magazines from America, settled into his usual stupor. The quiet thickened. Dinh made a final round along the metal walkway suspended above the cells. Each footstep sounded hollow against the checkerboard of bars, a god pacing over a world of confinement. Then, and only then, did he lower his voice and call.

"Tuyet Mai," he whispered into the dark.

"Oh, it's you. Thank heaven. Are you back on night duty?"

"Yes. I've come to speak with you. There are important things."

"Have you brought food?"

The question stung. "No. I didn't have the chance, or the privacy."

She heard the edge in his voice. "It doesn't matter, my love. Can you come inside?"

He hesitated. Temptation reached out. But instinct gripped his collar.

"I want to talk with you also," she said gently. "Please come."

He exhaled. Measured. Waited. "Yes. But first, let me make one more pass through the yard. If everything remains quiet, I'll return."

"I'll be waiting."

But even as he walked, he wavered. Doubt crept back in, and he wondered whether it was too great a risk. He circled the narrow platform above the cages, nightstick tapping against his palm. The cells beneath formed a map of shadows. Somewhere among them, Tuyet Mai waited.

He had told her there was something to discuss, but in truth, he had nothing. Nothing new. Should he speak of what he'd overheard from Vo Thanh Tong? Of his strange lesson with the monk? Of his mother's bitter weeping? The idea of confiding in her grew suddenly painful, not because he mistrusted her, but because the life he longed for was not yet real.

If only they were already husband and wife. He would come home after a day's labor and speak freely. Share stories, worries, hopes. They would sit together and talk. He could rest in her presence. Could he pretend now, in the cage, that such a life had already begun? That this stone cell was their home? That he had the courage to step fully into that illusion?

The ache swelled. He thought of her beauty, her softness. No, he forced that thought away. Better to focus on their future children. On the comfort she would offer, the virtue she would restore to him. That was the true joy. The true redemption. And if she had asked him to come, if she had reached for him, then how could he refuse?

He turned back.

"So, here I am," he said, descending toward her cell. He had tried to slip in without sound, but the iron door betrayed him. She was already watching, eyes bright in the dark.

~

Tuyet Mai studied his silhouette. The day before, he had whispered furtively that his shift had changed, and her unease had grown. Something in his voice revealed a jealousy, a disturbance linked to the new prisoner. She burned with curiosity. And fear. Who was this man?

So tonight, when the quiet opened, she called to Dinh, not yet certain how to draw out the truth. Her instincts had saved her before. She would follow them again.

"Well," she said softly, "my love has returned."

He took her hand. "You called me, Tuyet Mai? I can stay only a moment."

"Yes. I just wanted to see you. To touch you."

He squeezed her hand. "My Tuyet Mai. My future wife. May I call you that? It brings such joy to say it, even if it remains far off."

She swallowed. The word stung. *Wife.* But she could not object. Not yet. "Yes, love. You may call me that. It fills me with longing. But tell me, how will this come to pass? Do you have a plan to free me?"

Too bold? Perhaps. But the moment felt ripe.

"Funny you should ask. I believe so. I'm working on it. The solution is near, I can feel it. But not tonight. Tonight, let's not talk of that." Still holding her hand, he sat on the edge of her stone bed. He glanced at the door, nervous, then leaned closer. "Did you want to tell me something?"

"Yes." She steadied her voice. "This plan of yours, did it involve changing shifts yesterday?"

"Not exactly. That was for another matter."

She hesitated. How far could she press? How much could she risk?

"What matter, my husband?"

The word landed like incense on fire. For a moment, it stunned him. He didn't sense the trap. But instinct stirred nonetheless. "Nothing much. A prisoner. A male prisoner."

"Are you sure the prisoner is male?"

She couldn't help herself.

"Yes! Of course a male!" he snapped. "Do you think I . . . I couldn't . . . I mean, it *was* a male."

She hesitated. Another fork in the path. Push or retreat? Weariness tugged at her. But she had come this far.

"Who, my husband?"

This time, the spell broke. He made a sound she couldn't place. He pulled his hand from hers.

"Why do you ask?"

"It doesn't matter," she said quickly. "I was teasing."

"Why do you ask?" he repeated, and now his voice held warning.

"Because I worry for you."

"What does that have to do with the prisoner?"

She took his hand again and pressed it to her face. "I'm afraid. That you'll be caught. That this prisoner knows something that might harm you. That's why."

He softened.

Dinh drew a long breath. "He's no threat. But his behavior toward you was shameful. That's why I've taken an interest."

She sensed him easing, and tried to move forward. "And what have you found?"

He remained silent.

"No—don't answer. My questions are foolish. The ramblings of a woman too long in a cage."

He grunted. "The man doesn't deserve to live."

"Oh, don't torment yourself, husband." She guided his hand beneath her tunic, placed it gently against her chest. "Be with me. Think of our future."

But he pulled back.

"I'll make him pay," he growled. "Vo Thanh Tong, you will regret this."

Before she could speak, he was gone. The door clanged shut behind him.

~ Tuyet Mai Learns About Tong ~

Vo Thanh Tong!

The name landed inside her, a blow and a benediction. Tuyet Mai felt stricken, seized by a sudden force both radiant and ruinous. The cell tilted, the air twisted, and the very architecture of the prison reeled. She lay motionless, dizzy, certain the sheer weight of astonishment might roll her from the slab. Her chest tightened; her breath turned ragged. Tong, here! Somewhere nearby. Perhaps in the next cage. Perhaps only meters away.

The urge to move surged through her with desperate clarity. She longed to spring to her feet, pace, shout, leap, anything to shatter the stillness. But her body, fragment of a whole, would not obey. Her severed legs dragged her down, a final gravity that mocked the freedom of thought. Her mind thrashed forward, but her flesh was a tethered ruin.

Still, his name pulsed through her with unbearable energy. Tong. How could contempt have become this feverish hunger? Had it shifted slowly, or had the transformation occurred all at once? No, it was sudden. Sudden, and bound to that day of horror when he had refused to abandon her. The mutilated body he had not fled. That act had lingered beneath the surface, fermenting, waiting. Now, with his presence made real, the feelings surged upward, no longer deniable. Not pity. Not hope. Something more elemental, an instinct forged by suffering and sealed in gratitude.

Her breathing slowed. Something deep inside her released, a knot unwound. If he was truly here, she would find him. She would speak with him. Hear his voice again. It didn't matter what he had been. His failures were nothing compared to the fact that he had stayed. And in this place of madness and iron, his presence was a thread of meaning.

She felt how close she had drifted to despair before that name revived her. Now she imagined escape again, if only they could flee together. But then came the memory of Dinh's hatred, and her mind sank. She thought of the cages. The guards. The great sea surrounding Con Son. Her body refused to turn, so she wept as she lay, tears sliding quietly across her temples, pooling in her ears. In that helpless stillness, hatred bloomed, not only for the war, but for the whole theater of men. She cursed her choices, cursed the unquestioning righteousness that once lit her way.

What madness had led her to believe in revolution? What childish certainty had driven her from the village to follow Nang's illusions of glory? Had she stayed, she might have been a mother now, a matriarch, a woman surrounded by sons and rice and long years of peace. Even if her village had burned, she could have started again, like Madame Dau, who had survived, who would rebuild. Family. That was the only banner worth following.

But she had none. Only her brother Ban, and he too was caught in the net, soon to be strangled by it like the rest. Only Tong remained. Tong, who had lived, who had endured, cunning and strong. Tong, who now was her family.

All through the night her thoughts circled him. Even Dinh's whispers passed over her like wind over water. With dawn, the urgency of reunion was met by recollection. Tong's cruelty. His ambition. His hunger for status. All of it returned. But even so, he was the only face from her past that remained. And in this void, even a flawed anchor could guide her.

She steadied herself. The rush had passed. What remained was resolve. She would find a way to see him.

But Dinh had already foreseen this. He'd ordered the day guard to keep her from joining the others. When she finally devised a plan, Dinh had gone off duty. The next guard now passed above her. No matter. It was him she needed.

She waited. When she saw the black soles pass overhead, she called out. "Hey, Guard Nguyen!"

He leaned over the railing. "Eh? What's up?"

"Have the others gone to the trench?"

"Of course. It's just you and a few sick ones. Because of you, I have to stay here smelling this pit while the others breathe clean air and gossip in the sun."

"Will you take me out with them?"

He laughed. "No! Why would I do that?"

"My legs are restless," she said lightly.

He barked another laugh. "Good one. You've never spoken to me before. Why now?"

"Because I want to go outside. And because I've been watching. You seem like a good man."

"Don't try charm on me, pretty one. I've been stung before and now sleep in a snake's den." He glanced around theatrically. "My wife, you know."

"She must be beautiful."

Nguyen burst into laughter. "A feast for the gods, of filth and vinegar!"

"You're too hard on her. I'm sure she's given you children."

The humor drained from him. "Yes. Both dead. Now only she remains. Bitter. Empty. Her joy is making me suffer."

Perfect, Tuyet Mai thought.

"Nguyen. What can I give you to take me out?"

He shook his head. "Nothing. You have nothing I can't take."

"You can take, yes. But if I don't give it freely, you gain only the pleasure of a thief. If I choose to give, you receive something far greater."

He grinned. "I'm no emperor. I live with itches, not luxuries."

"Would you like to know the difference?"

"Feel it one moment, lose your head the next."

"Call me Tuyet Mai."

"All right, Tuyet Mai."

"If you take me out, I'll owe you."

"No. They've warned me about you."

"About what?"

"Not your legs. About your illness. Down there. And besides, you have connections. You're protected."

"I have no illness. And if I did have connections, I'd use them to help you."

"Or to ruin me. Either way, trouble. And I have enough already."

"Then decide soon, Nguyen. The others will return shortly. You may not get another chance."

He snorted, stepped away, and vanished from view.

"He'll come back," she whispered to herself, uncertain. "Idiot! I should've bared my breasts. Fool!"

"Don't be stupid," said Kim Lan, drifting into view beside her.

"I'm not! You saw what I tried. The old tricks don't work anymore. I'm hideous."

"Don't be stupid."

"Is that all you know how to say?"

"I could say more. But you're not ready. So I say it again: don't be stupid."

"How?"

"You used the oldest trick. It worked before. It would work now, if not for two things."

"What two?"

"Nguyen's not a monster. He's a fool, but he still clings to what's left of his family. And you've been quarantined, someone's making sure you stay untouchable."

"Dinh."

"Who else?"

"So what now? I must see Tong."

"Next time, bare your breasts."

Tuyet Mai flared. "But you just said—"

Kim Lan floated above her, unbothered. "The oldest trick is still the only one I know. Men are simple. Their hunger never changes. They can be counted on. Always. Except when they come, then it's anyone's guess."

Tuyet Mai scowled. "He won't come back. And even if he does, he won't trade favors."

Kim Lan shrugged and vanished through the grill above.

Left alone, Tuyet Mai retreated to her only refuge—visions of Madame Dau. When the pain was too strong, she would invoke the older woman like a prayer.

Time passed. Kim Lan returned.

~

"You're back?" Tuyet Mai asked.

"I've been whispering."

"To whom?"

"To the one who breathes us in and out. The hand that moves the quill. The hunger behind the script."

"You mean . . . God?"

"No. The American."

Tuyet Mai's eyes narrowed. "The American?"

Kim Lan hovered. "He is not who you think. Not the boy you once pitied, nor the soldier who wept. That one shattered long ago. What remains is older, slower, cracked with time. He rewrites us not to redeem, but to delay the collapse. His ink is memory. His paper is grief."

Tuyet Mai turned her face to the iron bars. "Then I am just a story."

"You are more than a story. You are the echo that refuses to fade. The voice that returns because it was never truly heard. He writes you because you survived him. Because somewhere, he knows you are real in a way he never was."

"And you speak to him?"

"I whisper through his fingers. I enter when he's dreaming. Sometimes I guide his hand. Sometimes I burn the page. He doesn't always listen."

"He makes us suffer."

"Yes. Not for cruelty—but for shape. Our suffering is reality. He believes if he traces the wound clearly enough, the bleeding might stop. That if he names the dead, they might lie still."

She closed her eyes. "Is he still writing me now?"

"Yes."

She opened them again. "Then let him write carefully. I'm not finished yet."

~ *Circular Circles Circling* ~

Once Kim Lan vanished, Tuyet Mai turned inward and summoned a memory so vivid it burned through the present. It was the night her legs were taken. The fever had ravaged her. She had been hallucinating, half in this world, half elsewhere. But she remembered every word.

Goddess had spoken to her.

It happened in Madame Dau's house, just after the ambush. Tuyet Mai had been screaming to live. Not asking, demanding. Life became her sole obsession. When Madame Dau moved to leave the sickroom, Tuyet Mai, though weak, summoned a voice she didn't recognize as her own.

"Stop!"

The command stunned them both. It rang with the force of prophecy. "No need to leave," she had said. "I think I will live. Tomorrow, send the herbalist. I will give her instructions. But now—"

Madame Dau had begun to interrupt, and Tuyet Mai's voice strained to hold her. "No! I don't have long before the fever returns. Let me ask you, if you were dying, what would you think of?"

Madame Dau offered tea.

"No. Please, answer. What would you be thinking?"

"My children. My grandchildren." A soft smile. "Seeing my husband again. My mother."

"Not the war?"

"No."

"The fate of the country?"

"No."

"Your accomplishments?"

"No."

"Your friends?"

"Yes. My village. But mostly, my family."

"Regrets?"

"No . . . no, and yes."

"Regrets for what?"

"All the deaths. My children suffering. My mistakes."

"Sorrow?"

"Yes."

"Fear?"

Silence. Then Madame Dau began to speak: "I . . . I—"

And then the air shifted.

A figure appeared, young, uniformed, face shadowed beneath a broad pith helmet. He was dry, though rain lashed outside. He removed his helmet. The face beneath was radiant and unreadable, not aged, not young, marked by something neither human nor divine, but suspended between. When he spoke, his voice did not pass through the air. It entered the bone.

I hold in my hand a dying ant.

He turned to Madame Dau.

You stepped on her when you entered. Her brain still carries the scent of her sisters. She struggles to survive. She feels an ant's sorrow. An ant's pain. An ant's fear. She shares the world with you. The air. The earth. The body. The hunger. The death. The joy of movement. The silence of pain. You both walk the outer layer of a great sphere, soon to sink into one of its countless inner rings—wrapped in death, memory, and the Great Beginning. Are your differences so great?

He turned back to Tuyet Mai.

You are right. You will live. Then you will die.

He looked down at the ant in his hand.

She will die. Then she will live.

Tuyet Mai had cried out, half in agony, half in resistance. "I don't care about ants! I just want to live!"

You wanted to be a hero, the soldier said. *A companion to powerful men. That was one kind of ghost. Then you fled from violence and sought to become a virtuous mother, a loving wife. Another ghost. Neither was human. Now your body is broken. You are alone. Your beauty—once the banner of your being—has been torn away. Still, the world goes on. Unmoved. Unmoved by you, as it is unmoved by her—*

He looked again to the ant, collapsed, her limbs flailing faintly.

She, too, lives in an uncaring world. And she, too, wants only to live. Your sister.

Then his gaze shifted. He fixed Madame Dau to the wall.

And you—drawn by superstition into the world of men. You stayed near the fire, and were singed. Unlike Tuyet Mai, who leapt into the blaze, you turned back. But you carry something now. The seed planted by the Man from the Mountains. You would have killed. That tale will echo through your descendants.

Madame Dau collapsed to her knees, trembling. Tuyet Mai, feverish and spent, whispered one last defiance.

"But you are a male. A soldier. A warrior."

The figure looked to the ant, now motionless.

Yes, *said Goddess.*

And then the voice, softer now:

Tomorrow, Madame Dau must repair the dikes, care for her family, honor the ancestors, tend the sick, nurture the young, and hold the world together. But tonight, bring tea. I will stay. You will have visitors soon.

And they had come, those who killed and burned and locked them all away.

~

Yes. And here I am, Tuyet Mai thought.

Like the ant, I just want to live. Not to be a hero. Not to be a virtuous wife. Just live. Return to the village. Sit beside Madame Dau. And be with him. I will do what it takes.

"Hey, number forty-six! I've been thinking about what you said."

"Have you?"

"Yes. I'll be right in. Sit tight, ha ha."

She heard his boots on the iron walkway. She waited. But the door did not open. Minutes passed. At last, his voice came through the peephole, ragged and excited.

"Show me your breasts, number forty-six."

She complied. Calmly. Tunic unbuttoned. Fabric parted. The ritual was simple. If this was the price to see Tong, it was a small one.

"Good. Tomorrow I'll take you out. But tonight is not the time. You must do more, far more, before I risk anything. This was just to see if you were sincere."

A familiar ache bloomed in her chest.

"That's not fair. We agreed it would be today."

"No. Too late. Tomorrow, I want the pleasure of an emperor. Then I'll take you out. Not before."

"Not fair!" she shouted.

Nguyen laughed. Footsteps retreating. His voice echoed behind him.

"Tomorrow!"

~ *Tong and the Disfigured Prisoner* ~

Vo Thanh Tong labored beside his silent companion, both men bent to the trench, sweat streaking their brows. They did not speak, but Tong was watching. Something in the man's ruined face radiated an uncanny pull, as though the truth of Tong's future was lodged somewhere behind those blistered eyes. He had begun to ascribe nearly supernatural qualities to the prisoner, a habit not unusual among cynics who secretly hunger for myth. Though the man regarded him with contempt, Tong hovered near, awaiting a moment to question him.

The opportunity came during the midday break. Seated on a mound of earth, Tong slurped his rice gruel, cast the tin bowl aside, and said, "Comrade, how did we meet? I swear, I can't recall. But you seemed familiar from the beginning."

"Better for me if you do not remember."

"Why?"

"Draw your own conclusions."

"At least tell me your name."

The man shook his head.

"Why not? If you keep it from me, I'll eventually remember and hold it against you."

The man dabbed at his face, smiled faintly. "A threat?"

"Yes."

"If you speak to the authorities, you'll find yourself more deeply burned than I."

"If I'm burned, then so be it. But I have plans, and I can't allow you to wander close enough to shatter them. Better to know now."

"And what plans are those?"

"You really expect me to say?"

"I'll make you a trade. You tell me your plans, I'll tell you where we met."

Tong narrowed his eyes. "You'll honor that?"

The man straightened, regal for a moment. "I will give you two names. Then you will tell me your plans. Then I will tell you mine. Perhaps our goals align. Perhaps we can cooperate. Or perhaps we simply use one another."

"Go on."

"Nguyen Tuyet Mai. Your lover, imprisoned here. And Major Le Chi Vy, who lies rotting under the grass because of your betrayal."

Tong froze. A low moan escaped him. He rose, stumbled in a circle. The guards noticed.

"Sit down!" one barked.

Tong obeyed, massaging his brow.

The man snorted. "Need another hint, comrade?"

Tong stammered. "Yes . . . I . . . I . . . don't know."

"You do. But here it is anyway." He paused, theatrical, but the moment was broken. Guards shouted.

"Back to work!"

Tong turned, desperate. "Tell me!"

The man leaned in. "A flayed orangutan."

Tong gasped.

The man wiped his sleeve across his face. "Now you know. Your turn. Tell me your plans."

"There's no time!"

The guards surged forward. Prisoners were herded back.

"Tomorrow then, comrade Tong," the man hissed. "Tomorrow."

Tong welcomed the shovel. It gave him something to do besides look at the ruined face beside him. But the truth gnawed at him. This man knew everything: the drug trade, the ambush, the mutilation of Tuyet Mai. The damage he could do was incalculable.

That night, Tong lay sleepless. If he told the man everything, he would be utterly exposed. If he lied, he might miss an opportunity. The man had power, Tong felt it. He might even prove useful, if handled correctly.

After all, Tong had already told his interrogators much. Not everything. But enough. And this man, this dangerous cipher, shared Tong's core aim: escape.

Yes, Tong thought. This is the kind of man I understand.

But simple cunning would not suffice. He would need something sharper.

~

While he brooded, a shadow moved above him.

"Vo Thanh Tong," came a voice. "I've resumed night shift. For our private friendship."

Dinh.

Tong froze.

"I know you spoke with Ton Van Ninh today. You two are planning something. I've seen too much to be fooled. One day I'll shoot you both. But for now, how about I take a few fingers? Just enough to make you remember me."

Tong sprang up. "You can't! You know you can't."

"Who says I can't?"

"It will end badly for you!" Tong hated how childish it sounded.

"Tomorrow, I'll wait for the morning shift. Then we'll have our fun. Fewer fingers, less grip on your shovel."

"Why? I've done nothing. If you do this, I'll make sure it doesn't end well for you."

"You can't make sure of anything. The more you talk, the more fingers I take."

"My report will—"

"Tomorrow."

He left.

Tong wept. For the first time since Tuyet Mai lost her legs.

~ Dinh Struggles With His Conscience ~

Dinh resumed walking, spirits sunken. He imagined Tong, fingerless. But the image brought no joy. Instead, a strange discomfort took hold. Something the venerable had said—

You make the phantoms real. You feed them. Let them pass, and they vanish.

I've made him real, Dinh thought. *The more I think of him, the more entangled I become. For what? Tuyet Mai doesn't care about him. She loves me. But now she worries, because I made her worry. I fed the phantom.*

Forget him. Think only of Tuyet Mai. Think of being good. Completely good.

He considered returning to Tong's cage. Apologizing. Offering rolls. Something his mother would approve of.

But when he reached the cell, he passed without a word.

Later, he would not harm Tong. But let him worry.

Goodness takes time.

~

Morning. Dinh left Con Son, slept briefly, and went to the temple. He hoped to find the venerable alone, perhaps in some quiet anteroom. But the old man was again seated on the steps, smiling.

"Pham Van Dinh! So good to see you. Come, sit! Now, tell me."

Dinh bowed. "Tell you what?"

"How many phantoms you let in since we last spoke."

"None, Master."

"Call me Master Kung."

"But that's a Chinese name."

"So? I studied with Frenchmen. They gave me Hugo. Some call me Master Hugo. Some call me Kung Fu Zi. Depends on my mood. You may call me Master Kung."

"Doesn't Confucianism conflict with Buddhism?"

"Call me Master Kung."

"Yes, Master Kung."

"Good. Now, did you let in more phantoms?"

"No."

Kung pulled out a bamboo fan and struck him lightly.

"Tell the truth or we cannot continue."

Dinh flushed, glancing around. "If you hit me again, I'll leave."

"You may. But then you abandon the chance to become completely good."

"Give me steps. Orders. Something written. Not these games."

"Are you a wise man?"

"No."

"Then how do you know the ways of one?"

Dinh sighed. "Please don't hit me again."

Kung hit him lightly once more, then laughed. Dinh couldn't help but smile.

"Shall we continue?"

"Yes, Master Kung."

"Will you now tell me the truth?"

"Yes."

"Did you let in more phantoms?"

"Almost. I threatened a man I hate. But I changed my mind."

"Did you ask forgiveness?"

"Yes."

"Hmm. Two steps forward. One lie back."

Dinh said nothing.

Kung adjusted his robe. "Why do you hate this man?"

"He's harmed others. He deserves punishment."

"No. That is not why. You hate him because of someone else. You are here because of someone. Not your mother."

"I am!"

"Not only her. You are here for gain. For another person."

Dinh fell silent. Then whispered, "Yes. A woman. A prisoner. I love her. I want to marry her. But no one can know."

"Am I no one?"

A small grin formed. "No, master. You are just another phantom I've become entangled with."

Kung laughed, full and loud.

"Can we speak in private?" Dinh pleaded. "I must tell someone, or I will die."

The old man grew solemn. "Yes. Come to my cell. We will speak."

Chapter Thirteen

The Wedding

Mark Bides His Time

Mark sits in his dorm room, immersed in an intergalactic war. The day has been long—dull lectures, mechanical note-taking—and now, with homework finished and a cold slice of pizza settling in his stomach, he turns to the glowing screen that often shields him from thought. The game absorbs him entirely. While playing, the world vanishes. His senses dull. His deeper concerns recede. Introspection retreats like mist from heat.

With his roommate gone to visit a sick relative, the room is his alone. Privacy has its perks. Masturbation, for one, requires no stealth. That task completed more than once, aided by the internet's generous offerings, he returns to the console. The game pulses. Spaceships explode in rhythmic fury. One ear remains attuned to the phone; he is expecting a call from his father. Three hours earlier, he had left a message, hoping to engineer an invitation on behalf of Professor Benson.

The phone rings.

Five more ships to destroy.

It rings again.

Almost there.

Again.

One more.

Again.

"Hello?"

"Mark, it's Dad. What's up?"

"Oh, hi. Yeah, I wanted to ask you something."

"Maybe start by asking how I am?"

"Ha. Okay. How are you, Dad?"

"Fine. Now talk."

"Well, would you be willing to invite Professor Benson to the reception? Not the wedding ceremony, just afterward."

"Why?"

"He's going to be in California at the same time. He wants to meet you."

"He's the one pushing this Vietnam idea, right?"

"Yeah. I told him you were against it, at least against going with me."

"No. I'm also against *you* going."

"Dad, come on. It's a once-in-a-lifetime opportunity to learn, an experience."

"Experience? Columbia's really elevating your vocabulary."

"You know what I mean. He's an interesting guy. And look, if you say no after meeting him, that's that. End of story."

"Really? He shows up, we talk for five minutes, I say no, and you drop it?"

"Absolutely."

"Promise?"

"Promise."

"Then fine. Consider him invited."

"Great. Thanks, Dad."

"That it?"

"Yup."

"Anything else new?"

"Nope."

"I see. Conversation over now that you've got what you wanted."

"Come on. I've got tests coming up."

"You know I'll say no."

"I know. But at least you'll get to meet him."

"What's this professor like?"

"Smart. Friendly. He teaches history, not philosophy."

"Same difference. Still going to say no."

"Okay."

A pause.

"You know," his father adds, "we're already packed full. House is going to be wall-to-wall. Maybe I should just say no right now."

"You promised."

"I did. But it's going to be tight."

"Dad, he only wants a few minutes. That's all. Please don't change your mind. This guy could be an important contact. Do it for me."

A sigh. "Okay, okay."

"Thanks, Dad. Love you."

"Love you too. Bye."

"Bye."

The war resumes. Spaceships burst into flame. Mark, the all-conquering pilot, wears a foolish grin, as if he already knows the final score.

~

Early the next morning, Mark passes Sarah Kettle in the hallway. She's bright, attractive, dressed in blue jeans and a white, clingy top. Her smile is quick, her touch casual as she taps his arm.

"Mark, we're having a party tonight at the sorority. Just a few people. Can you come? It'll be great."

"What time?" His heart stutters, as it often does around her. Months of silent wishing have trained his nerves to jolt reflexively at any hope.

"Seven. Can you make it?"

"Yeah. Sounds fun. Should I bring anything?"

Her eyebrows rise with playful exaggeration. "Just yourself. Or anyone you want to invite."

"Okay. Better get to class."

"Awesome. See ya!"

She jogs off. He watches her go.

It isn't until his second class that he manages to clear the fog and concentrate. By the time Professor Benson's third period lecture begins, his attention is back on track. The professor, characteristically impish, scans the room as if preparing a theatrical performance.

"Well, well, a room full of eager minds, ready to plunge into the colonial labyrinth of the Battle for Algiers. Are we prepared?"

A collective mumble.

"Too late. Here we go!"

Mark takes pages of notes. Afterward, as students trickle out, he waits, watching the knot of stragglers drift toward the door, until finally he's alone with the professor.

"Well, Mr. Powers. What news?"

"My dad said yes."

"Excellent."

"He said to consider you invited."

"Are you sure?"

"Yes, but . . . he said he'll still say no."

Benson grins. "As I told you, leave that to me. Just give me the details."

Mark nods, unsure whether to feel confident or concerned. "You don't know him."

"Actually, I think I do, at least a part of him."

Mark has nothing more to say. He mumbles something about lunch and slips away, a quiet turbulence churning under the surface.

By the time he sits down to eat, he's let it go. Tonight there's a party, and with any luck, Sarah.

~

That night, Mark steps into the sorority house and is met by a wall of noise. Music blares, voices echo, laughter ricochets off plaster and brick. The room vibrates with motion—dancing, swaying, wild gesturing. Mark pauses to adjust, as one might squint in sunlight after hours underground, then begins to weave through the crowd, scanning for a familiar face.

He spots Sarah, but she's deep in conversation with her boyfriend. Whatever her tone, it's intense. Mark looks away, unwilling to intrude or watch. To mask his sudden awkwardness, he feigns interest in the label of a Diet Pepsi can, holding it with the awkward tenderness of a substitute companion. Slowly, eyes drifting, he begins to take inventory of nearby faces.

A voice catches his attention. Calm, clipped, faintly impassioned.

"Yeah, we used to exercise economic imperialism," the speaker says, "but since George W. Bush, it's gone back to brute force. Nineteenth-century stuff."

A few students nod. Others hesitate, sensing risk in either agreeing too quickly or objecting too loudly.

"We've learned nothing," the voice continues. "And now even our allies, who made their own mistakes last century, want nothing to do with us."

Mark edges closer, curious. He stands at the fringe, watching. The speaker is short, angular, with a voice smoother than his bones suggest. His movements are sparse but precise. The group listens, still wary.

"Come on, Ted," says someone, "that's nothing new. The U.S. has used brute force forever. Korea, Vietnam, Iraq, Afghanistan."

Another voice jumps in. "At least Korea and Vietnam were supposed to be about democracy."

Ted's tone sharpens. "Vietnam was a criminal war. Haven't you read the Pentagon Papers?"

"No. I'm a chem major, not poli-sci."

A tall, heavyset student speaks up, calculating the tide. "Seems like you contradicted yourself, Ted. If Vietnam was criminal, wasn't that brute force too?"

Ted shrugs. "Contradiction isn't weakness, it's the equation the universe runs on."

"Convenient," the other replies.

Ted persists. "Like Frank said, Vietnam *claimed* higher motives. That doesn't make it less brutal, but it complicates the motives."

Frank jumps in, scenting opportunity. "I made that point to challenge your argument, not help it."

Ted smiles. "I can still use it."

The group senses the spark fading. Interest dissolves. They drift away, leaving only Ted and Mark standing.

Ted eyes him. "You get what I was saying?"

Mark glances at his soda can, unsure what answer to offer. "Sure. What's your major?"

"Physics," Ted replies.

Mark blinks. "Physics?"

Ted lifts an eyebrow. "So physicists can't care about politics?"

"I didn't say that."

Ted smiles, and something softens. "I'm Ted Simmons."

Mark shakes his hand. "Mark Powers. Genetics major. But I'm thinking of switching."

"To what?"

"Political science. Maybe Southeast Asian studies."

Ted lets out a quiet, ambiguous sound. "Ah."

Mark bristles. "What does *that* mean?"

"Nothing."

Still, Mark finds himself drawn in. Ted is confident without being arrogant. "Did you mean it, about Vietnam being a criminal war?"

"Of course."

"So the soldiers were criminals?"

"Some."

Mark feels a shift in his gut. "They didn't choose to be there. The government sent them."

"They still had a choice."

"You mean Canada?"

"Or refusal."

"And go to prison?"

Ted nods. "Yes."

Mark squares his shoulders. "My father was in Vietnam."

"Oh?"

"He's still alive."

A pause.

"What does he think now?" Ted asks.

Mark hesitates. "He has nightmares. Hears voices. Gets . . . lost. The war did something to him. I don't really know what. When I hear people call it criminal, it messes with me."

"I'm sorry. Truly. My dad left for Canada."

"That mess him up?"

"Yeah. He doesn't talk about it."

"Mine doesn't either. I think he was in a major battle. I'm going to Vietnam to investigate. Might turn it into a thesis."

Ted's eyes widen. "That's incredible. I'm jealous."

Mark frowns. "Yeah, but . . ."

"But what?"

He shakes his head. "Nothing."

"Vietnam," Ted says, shaking his head. "What a waste."

Mark's voice tightens. "He was drafted. Do you really think people like him were criminals?"

Ted opens his mouth, but Mark has gone quiet. A deeper thought has slipped in, one he hadn't fully faced before. A suspicion, long dormant, begins to rise: *What if Professor Benson knows something about the battle?* Something awful. Another My Lai. Could his father have been involved? Could he have stood by—or worse?

Would Mark even want to know?

Ted waves a hand. "Hello? Anyone home?"

Mark snaps back. "Sorry. Just thinking. So, do you think my dad was a criminal?"

"I already said no. But you weren't listening."

Mark smiles faintly. He likes Ted, maybe more than he expected. But before he can press further, Sarah reappears, slipping an arm around him with practiced grace.

"Mind if I borrow my lover for a moment?" she says sweetly to Ted.

Mark smells beer on her breath and feels the flicker of possibility. Tonight, maybe. He turns to Ted.

"Duty calls."

"See you around."

Sarah guides him into a dark alcove beneath the stairs. Her mouth hovers near his ear.

"Got any advice for a scorned woman?"

He's dreamed of this moment for months. But the words—*criminal, My Lai*—still echo. The future he imagined with Sarah feels suddenly displaced by something larger, darker.

"I'm not sure," he says, unfocused.

Before he can recover, a friend tugs Sarah away. "Men are such jerks," she mutters as she vanishes.

Mark stares after her.

Damn.

~

Mark wanders back into the party, alone now, the music no longer energizing but abrasive. He retrieves another drink, though the Diet Pepsi feels colder in his hand than it did before. Faces blur past him, laughter and shouts tumbling into each other. The room feels distant, overlit, overheard.

Sarah's absence gnaws at him, but not as sharply as the thought she interrupted. It returns now, unbidden. *What if Professor Benson already knows?* Not just about the battle, but about what his father did. Or didn't do. What if this research trip is a trap he's walked into blindly, designed to uncover something terrible?

He plays out the scenarios. Suppose he finds evidence: documents, witness accounts, names carved into a wall somewhere near the site of a massacre. Suppose it's true. Does he bring it home? Does he tell Benson? Publish it? Show his father? Or does he bury it, hide it inside the blank spaces of his thesis, pretend the trail went cold?

Would that be loyalty or cowardice?

His stomach tightens. He pictures his father, not in combat, not giving orders, but alone in the dark, the way he's seen him sometimes. Mumbling, shaking, staring at walls only he can see. A man haunted. And now Mark wonders: what if the haunting has a name?

His mind drifts back to Ted's question. *What does your father think now?* He still has no answer. Only more silence. Silence but for his . . . mental issues.

The party carries on without him. Somewhere nearby, someone opens a beer with exaggerated flair. A girl shrieks with laughter. Mark sips from his can, its sweetness now stale.

He thinks of Vietnam, not the war, not the maps, but the land itself. The heat. The soil. The ghosts. He tries to picture himself there, walking through villages, asking questions, carrying a notebook filled with secrets he might not want to learn. He imagines coming home changed. Or not coming home at all.

Then he thinks of Professor Benson again. The way he said: *I think I know your father, at least a part of him.* And for the first time, Mark wonders which part he meant.

He leaves the party without saying goodbye.

~ *Theresa and Ethyl Have A Confrontation* ~

Early morning. Theresa paces the room in a thin nightgown and slippers. The wedding draws near, and sleep has eluded her. Since that strange evening with Ethyl at Mark's house, something has unsettled her. Michael had behaved politely enough, even warmly. But something beneath the surface had disturbed her. Not his words exactly—more a resonance beneath them, a flicker in his eyes, a tension in his presence. Something hidden, something unspoken, had soured the experience.

She cannot name it. Was it a foreboding? A touch of dread? No, too dramatic. Perhaps distraction. Yes, he'd seemed distracted, but that alone would be understandable. A wedding stirs nerves. Still, it had gone further than distraction. What lay beyond that?

Fear. That was it. A carefully buried fear.

She replays the dinner in her mind, turning over every phrase, every glance. Only one moment stands apart: the empty chair, perfectly set, untouched. He said a friend had cancelled. But why had he kept looking at it, not with disappointment, but with something more fraught. Dread? Anticipation? Some quiet terror. She offered to clear the place to make room for the dishes, but he refused, deflecting with a joke. Humor, the oldest and most effective mask.

She knows that mask. Has worn it often. Humor hides wounds, conceals humiliation, cloaks the hunted in a veil of charm. *Yes, Michael is being hunted.*

"And like yourself, Theresa, he is losing the race, try as he might to camouflage his position," says Ethyl from the doorway, leaning with casual familiarity.

Theresa jumps. "I thought you were asleep."

"I never sleep."

"Nonsense. I've heard you snore."

"All part of appearing human."

Theresa sighs. "Goddess, then. So it's you tonight, not Ethyl."

"Your choice."

"Is it?"

"Yes indeed, girlie."

Theresa studies her. "What did you mean, he's losing the race?"

"You know."

"No. Talk about him. I know what you'd say about me. What is Michael running from?"

"He is afraid. Deeply. He's running not only from Vietnam, but from something older. The horror of his species. The world itself. Himself."

Theresa narrows her eyes. "How did you know I was thinking that?"

Ethyl says nothing. Her pursed lips and raised brow ask the question in return: *Must you really ask?*

"Okay. So he's afraid of war. Of what he did. That's not unique. PTSD is everywhere."

Goddess speaks without changing tone: **Not war itself. The horror lies not in the violence, but in the peace humanity seeks. A peace defined by comfort amid carnage. A peace that permits forgetting. Romanticizing. That is the deeper sickness.**

Theresa frowns. "I still want peace. Is that so wrong?" She raises her wrists. The faintest shadows of old bruises remain. "Just as I escape one wounded man, I find another. Both seeking peace, I suppose." Her voice falters. "Ah. Now I understand."

Wounded male?

"Yes," she snaps. "You know he beat me. Humiliated me."

And you begged him for it.

"No woman would want that."

Wouldn't they? More than you allow yourselves to admit. But I spoke of the species, not males alone.

Her temper flares. "So I'm the problem. A woman who craves degradation. Is that what you want me to say?" She storms into the kitchen, grabs a steak knife, and returns, shaking. "Is this what I want?" she shouts. She presses the blade to her thigh. Blood streams down her leg and drips onto the carpet.

Ethyl, unfazed, collects paper towels and cleaner. She kneels and begins wiping the floor as Theresa stands frozen.

"You'd better get to the bathroom," Ethyl says calmly. "Clean yourself. Or I'll give you a thrashing you won't soon forget."

Theresa obeys.

Ethyl waits. The carpet stains vanish beneath her hands. From the bathroom, sobs echo.

She rises and enters.

Theresa is curled on the floor by the toilet, trembling, her legs folded beneath her. "I can't do this anymore," she sobs. "I can't."

Ethyl sits beside her, cradling her head against her shoulder. "Shhh. It's all right. Shhh."

"No, it's not. I'm a lie. A horrible person. Why would anyone love me? Why would *you* stay? Why does Michael want to marry me? Why did you create me?"

Ethyl says nothing. Only rocks her gently.

"I can't live this way."

Ethyl lifts the bloodied towel and holds it up. Once you have given yourself to Michael Powers, this won't happen again. He bleeds more than you. The corrupted genes believe he should die. God and His kind follow First Principles—noninterference. But Michael is a Chosen One. He must live, or the Earth is lost.

Theresa's face hardens. "So he needs me more than I need him? That's my cure? Be nurse to a broken man?"

Ethyl smiles. **Not at all. He loves you. He is kind. And yes, he's wounded. Together, you'll heal. Apart, you'll do this.**

She touches the top of the cut and draws her finger downward. The bleeding stops beneath her touch.

"You were careful," she says. "You only wanted to make your point."

Theresa stares, stunned. "Who *are* you? I don't believe you're some backwoods mystic or hidden deity. But what are you, really?"

Ethyl shifts, adjusting to hold Theresa more comfortably. "Who do you want me to be?"

Theresa scowls. "Don't give me that. I'm not a child."

She pulls away and fixes her gaze on Ethyl. "Who. Are. You?"

"I am you," Ethyl replies in the same rhythm. "And you are Michael's delusion."

Theresa recoils. "More riddles."

"I never went to college, honey."

Tears rise again. "I've lost You."

"No. You've lost yourself."

"Yes," Theresa whispers. "I'm lost."

She touches her leg, where a smooth, unbroken patch of skin has replaced the wound. "How do I find my way? How can a delusion find anything?"

"Marrying Michael will help," Ethyl says, wrapping her in her arms once more.

Theresa studies her. "Why do you care so much about this marriage?"

Because I have my own Wounded Male to contend with. And there are plans for the Chosen One that He attempts to block.

"Who?"

Never mind. Let's just say, for cruelty, He surpasses yours. He watches suffering with perfect detachment. He's divine in His indifference. First Principles.

Theresa's breath catches. "You don't mean . . . ?"

Ethyl nods.

Theresa glances at her thigh. No wound. No scar. Her skin is whole.

She murmurs, "Michael's delusions are growing. But they're compelling. And they don't stay inside his mind. He thinks Goddess is a delusion."

Ethyl lets out a sharp laugh. **Delusions? A human dares call me delusion? What creature is more deluded than man? Tools and fear rule them. They cling to cliff walls of comfort and fire, calling it civilization. They hollow the rock, call it shelter, and poison their own air.**

Who gave them this brain, this fear, this hunger to hide? My Wounded Male's drug—Natural Selection. Evolution—a gift from the Universe. And it will be their undoing.

Theresa reflects. "A therapist would say you've given this Wounded Male too much power. That you're enabling Him. You must break the cycle."

Ethyl's eyes widen, almost in awe. ***My dear, the entire species enables Him. I want them to stop clinging to the cliff. I want them to fall. And once fallen—Superior Ones will replace. But He made the fall into damnation—and feeds Himself with the fear they leave behind.***

"I don't understand. If you're locked in battle with God, why do I matter? Why care if I marry? Why care if I live?"

Ethyl's voice breaks. ***Because I care.* The Reunion must take place. All mothers know this.**

"But why me?"

Michael Powers.

Theresa goes still. Her voice drops. "Who is he really?"

He will be your husband. You will be his hallucination. You already are. And our shared conspiracy will be the delusion that saves him.

Theresa groans. "This is madness. Why? Why him? Why does he matter?"

Remember—I told you I am you?

"Yes."

Perhaps I am also Michael Powers.

"That's incest."

Exactly. The abstract thinking your kind prizes most is incestuous, circular, diseased. The Superior Ones who follow will not need such primitivism.

Theresa shakes her head. "Am I his hallucination or not?"

Ethyl's eyes gleam.

You are as real as I am.

~ *Michael Seeks Comfort* ~

Michael sits motionless at the dining room table, waiting for his dead wife to appear. He has summoned her with every ounce of will he can muster. In the past, such desperate invocation has brought her, for Diane always came when he needed her most. But tonight, only empty chairs keep him company.

He has dispensed with the usual ritual: no place settings, no music, no flowers, nothing to confuse the signal. He wants Diane alone. No other ghosts. No other mistakes. But so far, she does not come.

Of course, he knows she is only a projection of his own mind. He is not mad. Certainly not mad. But the ritual of her arrival has become its own entity. And he's uncertain whether she will respond to an unscheduled call. Still, he feels compelled to try. Medication be damned.

He makes a conscious effort not to think of his twin. If the thought takes root, if the delusion returns, it could undo everything. He's fought hard to banish that phantom. A twin brother never existed. That's been established. The entire narrative was an invention, an elaborate coping device. He went to the war. He came back. The others did not. Simple.

Not so simple. He came back a fragment.

He left there a fragment.

One has aged.

One is timeless.

And yet the mind is not so easily subdued. They all say the brain can conjure voices, visions, entire histories that never happened. Schizophrenia, they call it. A name. A diagnosis. The cure? Acknowledgment of the real. Nothing more. Embrace the real. Refuse the unreal.

But here I sit, he thinks. Calling Diane. Writing this book. Speaking aloud to a woman who no longer exists. Is that madness?

No. Don't exaggerate. Loss drives people to strange behaviors. Nothing new. I am nothing new. Just a dot in the story of grief.

Still, am I slipping?

No. Because I am aware. This is self-directed therapy. The apparitions are tools. And I control them. I can stop them. I can summon Diane and prove it.

"Diane. Diane. Diane."

He sets her photograph on the table, focuses, breathes, concentrates.

"Diane."

But she does not come.

For the first time, he wonders if he even needs her. He has Theresa now. A living woman. Soon to be his wife. He should be calling Theresa, not Diane. Theresa can sit beside him, listen, hold his hand, say the right things. She's real. The past should not be allowed to intrude on marriage. He should stop this.

He will marry Theresa. No more seances at dinner. No more ghosts. No more secrets. She will wake him from nightmares, just as Diane once did, whispering gently, calling him back to the world. No more darkness alone. There will be responsibilities. Perhaps children. Routine. Light. The house will be full. No empty spaces for the dead to enter.

The stillness will be stilled.

He shudders. A knot tightens in his gut.

But what if the voices do not stop? What then? Will Theresa understand? And the children, if there are children, what will they think of their father whispering in the dark to people who aren't there?

He sees it unfold. The fear. The judgment. The whispered diagnosis. Divorce. Custody. Loss. Worse than before.

Anger rises. It's the war. If his brother hadn't gone, if he had lived, if they could just sit together now—middle-aged, out of shape, laughing about nothing—then none of this would be happening.

"You called?" comes a voice, old and young at once.

Michael stares. He rises, then sinks back into the chair.

"Where's Diane?" he asks.

"You didn't call her. You called me."

"No, I didn't," Michael says, but even as he protests, he knows the truth. His head drops.

He looks up again. "You look like hell. You smell like it too."

His twin shrugs. "If we just sit here in silence, that's fine with me. I'm too tired to talk." He glances around, dazed and grateful. "Just being away from there is enough."

"Fine," Michael mutters.

They sit in silence. Each watching the other, waiting.

Eventually, Michael breaks. "What do you think of Theresa?"

"The replacement?" His voice is flat. "She appears in my fever dreams. Naked. Bruised. Someone's been beating her. I used to think she was a soldier's fantasy. But that's not it. So—who's hurting her?"

Michael says nothing.

"It's not you, is it? Or should I say *me*?"

"No. Of course not."

"Then who?"

Michael shakes his head.

"You don't know? She's your fiancée. You're marrying her, and you don't know?"

"It doesn't happen anymore," Michael says softly. "It was someone from her past. She has the right not to talk about it."

"Is she divorced?"

"No."

"How do you know?"

"She never said she was married. I never asked."

"Interesting."

"I trust her."

The soldier studies him. "Do you trust me?"

"How can I trust a figment of my own mind?"

"Exactly. So how can you trust yourself?"

"That's not what I meant."

"You're a lawyer. Aren't you supposed to mean what you say?"

Michael laughs. "That's rich. Lawyers are trained to say everything and nothing at once."

"Exactly. So you don't trust yourself, and you obscure the truth. Very admirable." He slides his M-16 closer. "Meanwhile, I kill people. People who are clear-eyed. Who believe in what they do."

Michael's voice drops. "Then kill me."

The twin stiffens. This is new. "Don't be ridiculous."

"Then I can join you. No more nightmares. No more ghosts. They want you to replace me anyway."

"Not funny."

Michael leans in. "You're dead. What's it like?"

The soldier surveys the room. "Endless social functions."

"I'm serious."

"You won't like my answer."

"Try me."

"I don't know. Because I am *you*. And you are still alive. If I killed you, I'd learn what death is the moment I died. Because I would be dying with you. That would be a rather stupid move."

Michael's face reddens. "Then why do you all keep telling me to kill myself? Whispering that I'm worthless? You're dead. Your body is rotting somewhere in Vietnam. You are not me."

The soldier's voice sharpens. "I've had enough of this twin fantasy. You never had a twin. You're sick. I'm dying in a cave. Fever. Malaria. Surrounded by corpses. I endure all that better than you endure your guilt from a well-appointed room filled with food and silence. The voices are right. You're worthless. Kill yourself. Join me. I can't do it. Rules. That's part of the conspiracy."

"Get out," Michael growls, standing abruptly. "Leave. You make me sick."

He flees to the kitchen, clattering objects, searching for distraction. But the soldier remains, motionless, waiting.

Michael paces, agitated, then marches back to the table. "I told you to leave. This is your last warning. You are not wanted."

His twin looks up. A slow, amused smile spreads across his face. "What will you do? Call the police? Report an intruder? 'Yes, officer, I've got a trespasser in my soul. He won't leave. Please come remove him.' You'd make the news."

Michael circles the table and picks up the M-16. He handles it with practiced ease.

"If you won't kill me," he says, "then I'll kill you."

He raises the rifle and aims.

The soldier spreads his arms. "Go ahead."

Michael squeezes the trigger.

Nothing.

Goddess stands before him.

No, Michael. Not yet. You would waste bullets firing through a ghost. The Reunion is coming. For now, your wedding awaits.

~ *Ceremonies* ~

The minister's words float in the motionless air, suspended in the heat of the real and unreal.

"And I now pronounce you husband and wife."

Beneath the trailing garlands, under the hum of wings both living and mechanical, Michael kisses Theresa. For a moment, the gathered hush feels timeless, almost sacred. Then a shift: someone adjusts the music.

Arvo Pärt's "Spiegel im Spiegel" begins to play.

A single piano note repeats—pure, measured, and inexorable, like the wedding. A violin enters, long and aching. The sound does not rise. It circles. A music of return, of stillness that remembers movement. A most unique choice for a wedding that is. . . .

Guests scatter, begin to murmur, laugh, offer congratulations. Glasses clink. The cake is sliced. Photographs are taken. Relief floods the afternoon like dusk creeping over fields.

Later, as the playlist turns to rock, a compilation from the 1960s, Michael hears the opening notes of *The House of the Rising Sun* and feels a tremor inside him. Without a word, he steps away, drawn back into the house like a man slipping from ritual into memory.

He enters the bedroom and sits on the edge of the bed. The last days have blurred, mercifully. The frantic details of the ceremony had drowned out his thoughts. But now, nothing obstructs them.

The door cracks open. Theresa enters quietly. Her white summer dress still holds the day's radiance, but her movements suggest an inner weariness, something already breaking free from celebration.

She sits beside him, careful not to disturb his silence.

He rests an arm across her shoulders. "Hello, Dr. Powers," he says with a dry attempt at charm, already slipping into the old persona.

Theresa places her hand on his thigh, leans against him. "Tired?"

"Oh yes. You?"

"Yes. But I'm looking forward to joining the others. It'll be fun."

"Yes, it will." He wants to ask her thoughts about the guests, to speak freely, to share unspoken observations. But Diane would have understood. Theresa might misread him. He says nothing.

"Well," she smiles, "I have hostess duties." She kisses him gently and exits.

Alone again, Michael stares at the door. Something about the moment feels undone. *Unsatisfying*—the word hovers.

A soft knock.

He sighs. Already?

"Come in," he calls.

But it is not a friend. Not a guest. Mark steps in, hesitant, followed by a small, sharp-eyed figure: Professor Benson.

"Dad, this is Professor Benson," Mark says quickly, then closes the door behind them.

Michael's heart contracts. He forces brightness. "Professor! Have they sent you to drag me back to the mob?"

He begins to rise, but Benson rests a hand on his shoulder, steadying him.

"I won't take long. Your wife was kind enough to allow me a word. I only wanted a brief moment."

Michael nods stiffly. "Yes?" He gestures toward the wingback chair.

Benson sits, leaning forward with quiet intent. "I know you oppose Mark's trip to Vietnam, and I don't fault you. But it would offer him an experience few ever receive. Educational, yes, but deeper than that."

Michael replies with precision. "Professor, Mark knows how I feel. I've been clear."

Benson smiles politely. "He said as much. But what I have to say isn't about Mark."

Michael shifts, wary.

Benson lowers his voice. "I've recently received information regarding a battle fought in Vietnam many years ago. The source is . . . unorthodox. And unbelievable, perhaps. But I believe you'll understand its weight."

He lets the silence settle.

Michael pales. His brow dampens.

"Well?" he manages.

Benson speaks carefully. "Let me ask: do you believe an ant, or a nest of ants, could transmit a message to a human?"

Michael flinches.

"I've been given such a message," Benson continues. "Delivered across vast distances. Through time. And through them."

He hands over a photograph: Sgt. Crawford's image. The will, reassembled by something not quite human.

Michael stares. Glances at the photo. Returns it.

"And?" he says. "A class riddle?"

"No. The real question," Benson replies, "is how a family trust written in the early 2000s appears in a tunnel, Vietnam, 1969, reassembled by ants."

Michael sways. His smile turns glassy, fixed. "Well. My answer is still no. Mark won't go."

He wavers in place. Eyes distant. Then, a voice speaks, but not his own. Something within him rises to the surface.

"Yes. On second thought, yes. Mark should go. Michael has lapses. Nothing serious, just the occasional overload. Give me time with him. We'll see it through."

Benson freezes. The voice is different. Young and hollow. Echoing from someplace he does not wish to identify.

He searches for words. Finds only, "Yes. Good."

Michael stands, claps him on the shoulder. "Don't worry. I'll make sure Mark goes. He won't be alone."

"You will go with him?" Benson asks, astonished.

"Oh yes. You can count on that."

"But I thought you would never return."

Michael laughs softly. "Return? I go back often."

"I didn't know."

"You couldn't."

Benson finds himself gently steered toward the door.

"Now I must rejoin my guests. Don't worry, Mark will go to Vietnam. And your project—" Michael's smile becomes something else, tight, glinting, and full of youthful puckishness—"will get the attention it deserves."

The door closes.

Benson stands outside, uncertain whether to call for help or start drafting his manuscript. The chill in Michael's last words leaves no doubt: he's crossed into something terrible. And sacred.

He chooses, for now, to do nothing. The story will unfold.

~ *Ethyl Contemplates Desertion* ~

Ethyl sits at a small table in the waning hours of the celebration, sipping, watching, waiting. Theresa and Michael are dancing, if it can be called that. The song is jagged and loud. They move through it dutifully, not joyfully.

Someone asks about the music.

Ethyl lifts her glass. "Can't always listen to requiems, dearie."

She has chatted much of the evening, but now finds herself alone. Which is just as well. Tomorrow, everything shifts. Theresa will move out. Ethyl will have space again. Time. Privacy. The harvest nears.

She senses a man watching her.

He approaches.

"Al Benson," he says, extending a hand.

"Ethyl." They shake.

"I saw you sitting alone. Thought I'd say hello."

She says nothing. Just sips.

"You know the bride or groom?"

"I've known them since before they were born."

He blinks. "Really?"

"Oh yes. Since they were ideas in their parents' heads."

"But I thought they just met."

"True."

He waits for elaboration. None comes.

"I'm one of Mark's professors," he offers.

"Mm-hmm."

"I came partly for the wedding. Partly for other business."

She gives him a long look. "I figured."

He sits. A bit too eagerly.

"Mark's going to Vietnam. Part of my project."

"Ah."

"I'm hoping his father might join him."

She chuckles. "That won't do."

"Why not?"

"Because once Mark gets there, he'll fall in love. With a girl. See something impossible. He'll marry. And stay."

Benson leans forward. "Stay and do what?"
She grins. "That's not mine to say."
"Is that a prediction?"
"No, honey. Just old words floating around."
"Do you study ants, Ethyl?"
She howls with laughter. "You're crazier than me."
She stands. "Excuse me, I need the ladies' room."
Benson watches her go. He's flushed. Buzzing. This is real. This is too real.
He steadies himself. *Be careful, Al. Stories this good come with claws.*

~ *That Night* ~

Theresa lies beside Michael, her hand resting lightly against his chest. They are husband and wife now. No lovemaking. Both agreed: too tired.
But Michael does not sleep.
The demon voices return.
You are worthless.
Everyone knows you fail at everything.
Can't even please a hallucination.
Even your fantasies mock you.
We hate you.
Do it. End it.
Faster. The wheel. The blade. The fall.
You had your chance in the war. You missed it.
You disgust us.
Keep writing. It will not save you.
Another voice cuts through.
No, Michael. Don't listen. These are your broken shadows, human fragments, DNA detritus. Not your destiny.
You are the Chosen One. A thread not yet cut.
The Reunion is near.
Hold on.
Hold.

Chapter Fourteen

PART THREE: STRUGGLE

Tuyet Mai Faces A Crisis

~ Tong Is Presented With A Dilemma ~

Tong and the disfigured man labored once more in the trench, their picks rising and falling in dull rhythm as guards patrolled the rim above. They worked in silence until a brief pause allowed them to whisper.

"I remember your name now," Tong said, feigning nonchalance.

The man raised his brows.

"Quốc, isn't it? A drug runner. And killer of orangutans."

"No," the man replied smoothly. "Ton Van Ninh. Innocent victim."

Tong smiled. "Innocent? Of course. Your affairs don't interest me."

"What about escape?" Ninh asked.

The bluntness of it caught Tong off guard. He hesitated, then said, "Naturally."

"Join us."

"Us?"

"Your old lover, Nguyen Tuyet Mai. Myself. Two others I plan to replace with you."

Tong stiffened. He muttered, disbelieving: "Nguyen Tuyet Mai?"

"Yes. Legless now, but sharp, connected. Forgive me, I assumed she meant nothing to you. One of the guards has taken a liking to her."

Tong's thoughts staggered behind Ninh's words. Something inside him went silent, then clamored. He mumbled a filler: "But . . . a woman with no legs?"

"Not your concern."

"And my role?"

A prisoner passed. Ninh lowered his eyes and examined a stone protruding from the trench wall. When the man had gone, Ninh whispered, gaze fixed downward, "The easiest part."

"Which is?"

"Kill Nguyen Tuyet Mai once she's done her job."

Tong flinched as if struck. Then a great weariness overtook him. His eyelids drooped. His lips parted but no words emerged. He nodded dumbly.

Ninh handed him the dislodged stone. "Weigh your answer. Say the wrong thing—"

A whistle shrieked. Guards called them back to work.

Ninh grinned, his rotted teeth exposed as he swung his pick. Tong ducked instinctively; the blade thudded into the clay wall.

That night, Tong succumbed to fever. Ever since hearing her name, pain had spread like a fracture through his skull. He tried to banish her image but failed. The idea of finding her only to lose her again hollowed him out.

Delirious, he fantasized about escape. He pictured them vanishing to safety. But reason crept in. Kill Ninh and flee with Tuyet Mai? Impossible. Expose Ninh? That would implicate her too. Do nothing? She would die anyway.

A vile solution surfaced: betray them both. Let her die. Be rid of her forever. Turn them in, be rewarded, walk away clean.

Even as he considered it, he recoiled. The thought gave way to loops of indecision. Turn them in. Save her. Join them. Let her go. No way out. The more he thought, the worse the fever.

He paced his cell, muttering nonsense.

A voice broke through.

"Hey, Tong. Want a warm biscuit?"

It was Dinh. A grudging gesture, part guilt, part karma.

Tong pounced on the voice. "So! Poisoned, is it? I know your secret. I know you've been giving her special treatment. Deny it!"

Dinh blinked, caught off guard. "What?"

"Your life, Guard Dinh!"

Silence.

Tong bellowed. "Dinh!"

"Shhhh! Fool!"

Tong smirked at his fear. "Next report, Commandant Tran. Cut out my tongue? Ha! Your head will roll first."

But Dinh was gone.

Tong sagged onto his stone slab, realization dawning. He had made things worse. His words had endangered them both.

He replayed the scene, failed to recall it clearly. Only her name remained, haunting.

The fever returned. Pain comforted him. He welcomed it. It dulled the edges of despair.

I'll betray them both, he thought. *That is how I will cut her from my soul.*

~ *Dinh is Presented With A Dilemma* ~

Tong's threats echoed as Dinh wandered through the dark corridors. Anger. Despair. Guilt. The game is over, he thought. But then, no—not yet. Do something. Anything. Still, his feet moved aimlessly. He stopped before Tuyet Mai's cage, surprised. How did I get here? It must be a sign. Without a plan, he unlocked the door and entered.

His flashlight beam found her face. She shielded her eyes.

"Who is it?"

He did not answer.

"Who is it?" she asked again, her voice rising.

I must kill her, he thought suddenly. End suspicion. A clean death, blame it on escape.

He coughed.

"Well?" she snapped. She had guessed.

He moved closer, shining the light full in her eyes. His limbs obeyed something other than reason. He loomed above her. She relaxed.

"Oh. My future husband." Her voice turned sweet. "Why are you silent?"

His anger flared. Her affection felt fake. He shut off the light.

Darkness swallowed them. The clouds had hidden the moon.

He set down the flashlight. Her breathing offended him. He placed his hands around her throat, telling himself that he was doing the wrong thing, that a prisoner supposedly making an escape attempt would not be strangled by a guard. Better a knife or a bullet in the back. But how could a prisoner with no legs escape anyway? Kill her? He loved her. It no longer mattered. Reason in tatters, he could only think, Do something now, before it is too late! He tightened his grip, astonished at how calm she remained. Then he felt her hand. Kill her quickly! The sooner done, the sooner I can leave!

Her hand stroked his arm.

Kill her.

But her hand continued its gentle massage. Then her voice, faint: "Yes."

She caressed his hair.

"Yes," she said again, stronger.

He tightened his grip, envisioning her face disfigured by asphyxia. Still, she didn't resist. He relented.

The moon emerged and barred light poured through the grill and into the cage, illuminating her lips. He saw. She was smiling, her lips a purplish-black. *She is a mouse and I the cat*, he thought. If she struggles I will kill her. Otherwise . . . ah! What stupid thoughts! Kill her! He released his fingers from around her neck and rested his head between her breasts, giving her ample time to catch her breath. "They know about us," he said at last in a boyish voice, seeking comfort. Her breathing stopped momentarily and he heard her heart beating faster.

Finally she whispered, "Who?"

"The prisoner I told you about."

Her heartbeat quickened.

"The one who stared."

"Yes."

Sensing he was now pliable, Tuyet Mai pressed confidently. "Well, what is his name?" Almost a demand.

That question. The one he feared. He was still possessed of enough wherewithal to carefully observe her reaction.

"Maybe we can use him," she said quickly.

His anxiety eased. She continued: "My friend used to say, don't beat the grass too soon. Let the snake show itself."

He was amazed by her cunning. He felt safe again.

"Yes. Perhaps."

"What's his name?"

"Vo Thanh Tong."

He watched her carefully.

"Hm. Never heard of him. No matter. I have a plan."

~

Tuyet Mai concealed her excitement. She had known, somehow, it was Tong. Now confirmed, her mind moved quickly.

"Put me in touch with him," she said.

Dinh recoiled.

"There's a way," she added. "I can shield you. Blame him instead."

"But he's protected by Commandant Tran."

"What?"

"He's to be handled carefully. Allowed freedom."

She understood immediately. "Special treatment. Like what he accuses you of giving me."

He nodded.

She smiled, a plan forming. "You must go. I need time."

"But—"

"Go!"

He obeyed. Her commanding tone spared her life.

She laughed softly as the door closed. A moment ago, she was ready to die. Now, she lived again.

Then he returned.

"I meant to kill you," he blurted. "You do love me, don't you?"

She found him pathetic. Useful, but not deserving of sympathy.

"Of course," she purred.

He straightened. "Don't mistake affection for weakness."

She understood the game. Keep the desire unsatisfied, the leash taut.

"There's no danger," she said. "Just put me in touch."

"How?"

She sensed a deeper instability. "I'll improvise. I don't know him yet."

He tensed. "You mean you don't know what attracts him."

His ideal of her as untouched still lived. It irritated her.

She stroked his arm. "Not at all. I would do anything—"

He pulled away.

"Almost anything," she corrected, gripping his hand. "To protect you. At first, yes, I used you. But now I cherish you. We must act for our future."

He softened. "It won't be easy."

"Tonight. Ask him now."

"Why would he trust me?"

"Because you're under orders to cooperate. Pretend it pains you."

"And if he refuses?"

She kept a straight face. "Then we adjust. Come what may."

He groaned, resting his head on her.

She stroked him, then pushed him away. "Go. For us."

"I fear it will end badly. If it does. . . ."

His words were edged with warning.

She stayed light. "It won't. Go now."

He lingered.

She panicked. If he stayed, they'd both be discovered.

"Please," she whispered. "You frighten me."

He shivered, then stood.

"Even if he agrees, it will be hard. Guards will see."

"They'll assume you were ordered. You're clever. It will work."

"I don't know."

"Please, beloved."

"Yes. I will make it work."

He left. She allowed herself a surge of hope.

She remembered the first time she saw Tong. How she scorned him. This time, it would be different. Just one look. Practiced, perfect. But it might be too dark.

She grew restless.

Where is he?

She flicked cockroaches off her bed. A useless distraction. Her thoughts returned to Tong.

What is taking Dinh so long?

~ *Tong is Reunited with Tuyet Mai* ~

Dinh did not relish returning to Tong's cage, but he resolved to meet resistance with finality. He would take the man to Tuyet Mai and be done with it. Dispensing with formalities, he entered the cage quickly, weapon drawn. If the captain of the watch appeared, Dinh had a vague excuse prepared, but he moved in a state of recklessness that not only ignored danger—it invited it.

"You are to see a prisoner," he blurted, dissatisfied with his phrasing. Tuyet Mai's name stuck in his throat.

"What?" Tong stared, bewildered.

"I am ordered," Dinh said, cringing inwardly.

"Now?"

"Now. Come." His urgency grew as reason began to reassert itself. I'll give them ten minutes, he thought. No more.

~

Prodded down the corridor, Tong remained silent. He wanted to ask who he was being taken to, but he knew his earlier outburst had severed that possibility. A tide of anxious thoughts swept through him. Had Ninh been caught? Had he been named? This might be a trap, a staged confrontation designed to reveal complicity. He braced himself. Any word, any gesture might be used against him.

He stepped into the cage unprepared.

~

Tuyet Mai froze. She could not see clearly in the dark. Her carefully rehearsed welcome dissipated in confusion. All three were struck dumb.

The moon returned, casting dim light.

Dinh broke the silence. "I am ordered to bring this prisoner to you, number forty-six."

Tuyet Mai let out a short, harsh laugh. "Yes, yes. Come here, Vo Thanh Tong."

Tong approached the platform where she lay. The moonlight was too faint for him to see her face. He stood motionless, mind emptied, focused entirely on her presence.

But her next words were not for him.

"Are you also ordered to leave us alone?"

"No," said Dinh.

She exhaled, annoyed. "Please leave and keep watch."

"I cannot. My orders."

Exasperated, she gambled. "No more pretending. We are all in this together."

"What?" Dinh recoiled.

"Yes, beloved, all of us. Vo Thanh Tong is in contact with the Commandant. If he wished, he could have us both killed."

Moonlight revealed Dinh's face twisted with rage. Tuyet Mai turned to Tong, hoping for support, but he said nothing. The word "beloved" had stunned him.

She switched tactics. "If we don't cooperate, we all die."

Dinh growled, "Do you know this man?"

She considered. Truth might enrage him. Lies might fall apart. Either way, she was too exhausted to strategize. "Yes. We served together. He cares for me. I don't return the feeling. But we need him. If he serves the Commandant, we're doomed unless we can win him over. Don't you see?"

Dinh wavered. Sensing this, she pressed on. "Each of us holds the other's fate. I can expose your favors to me. He can expose my ties to you. You can kill him and claim attempted escape. He can destroy us both. So, we act together."

"Then I'll shoot him now," said Dinh. "And be done with it."

"No!" she snapped. "We don't know what else he knows. He can still help us."

"Why would he?"

Tong spoke at last. "Because I want to. I need allies."

"Why?"

"I have plans. I can't do it alone. You two fit perfectly."

Dinh scoffed. "Your plans are not our concern. You'll get in the way." He turned to Tuyet Mai. "I should kill him."

"Shhh!" Tuyet Mai hissed. "Someone's coming!"

Boots echoed above them. Voices. Getting closer.

"Take him back," she urged. "Now!"

Dinh yanked Tong out and closed the door softly behind them. They fled together down the corridor.

~

Tuyet Mai remained still, listening. A voice called: "Dinh! Where are you?"

Another, angrier: "Where the hell is he?"

Dinh hadn't had time to return Tong. Thinking fast, she cried out, "Help me! Help!" and loosened her tunic. It wasn't quite right, but it was all she could do.

A flashlight struck her eyes. "What is it?"

She shielded herself. "A nightmare. Forgive me, sir."

Someone spat. "Disgusting."

None moved.

Then: "Yes, captain?" It was Dinh, breathless.

"Where were you?"

"Latrine, sir."

"Of course," one sneered. "That explains the unlocked door and exposed prisoner."

Dinh said nothing. Laughter followed.

Tuyet Mai covered herself and waited.

A final voice barked, "Come with us, Dinh. Nguyen will take your post."

Tuyet Mai stiffened. Why Nguyen? Why now? Is this the end?

Time blurred. When she regained awareness, they were gone. Silence returned.

She felt a terrible loneliness. Her thoughts turned to Kim Lan. She whispered her name, anxiously waiting and hoping.

Then came the sound of breathing. Deep and nervous.

"Your door was unlocked, number forty-six. Strange."

Nguyen.

She almost spoke boldly, then held back.

"Has my brother guard been enjoying you?"

No answer.

"It doesn't matter. Even guards deserve pleasures. You once said you'd make me feel like an emperor. Well, here I am."

He paused.

"After one more round, I'll return. And then, you will."

"Guard Dinh?" she asked faintly.

"Won't be back."

"Tonight?"

"Or ever."

She tried. "Your wife?"

He scoffed. "No, Tuyet Mai. Tonight, I am emperor."

She went still. Exhaustion claimed her. Resistance seemed futile.

He shook her roughly. "Like an emperor, number forty-six!"

Then he left.

She lay in silence. The cockroaches returned. Dampness settled. Rats scratched.

She tried to think of Tong. Of Dinh. She tried to plan.

Nothing came.

Only the desire for Kim Lan.

But even that slipped away into sleep.

~ *More Nightmares* ~

Tuyet Mai did not sleep long before Kim Lan appeared.

"Well, well," Kim Lan said lightly, hovering above. "Always in trouble with men. I can't stay away longer than the time it takes a flea to bite before you're back in the fire. How many times can you bare your breasts before the dogs stop obeying?"

"At least I'm still alive," Tuyet Mai replied, sullen.

"And what a life it is."

"Goddess warned me. She said once I chose the path of men, I was doomed."

"Yet here you are, risking everything for Tong. A scoundrel. Is it just because he crows louder than the rest?"

"You know better."

"Then why? Love?" The word dripped with disdain.

"Love."

"I don't know what that word means."

"Don't pretend," Tuyet Mai snapped. "Your daughters taught you well enough."

The air shifted. Kim Lan shimmered and darkened, her voice gurgling from deep water.

"When the Dragon Emperor and the Fairy Mother named the Ten Thousand Things, they forgot to distinguish the infinite shades of love."

"Yes," Tuyet Mai said, gentler now. "I love you. I love my parents. I love my brother, my life, my country. I love Tong. I love food and drink. These are not the same. Yet we use the same word."

"Since dying, I've learned why the word must be one."

"Why?"

Kim Lan became a shaft of light. "The answer lies in the egg."

She plunged downward, piercing Tuyet Mai's body, twisting and burrowing. Pain flared. Tuyet Mai screamed, "No!" and struck wildly, only to find her fists landing on something solid.

Nguyen.

He was on top of her. Her pants were gone. One hand fumbled with his buttons; the other forced itself between her legs. She shoved him away, felt burning and tearing.

He punched her across the face.

"Is that how you treat an emperor?" he snarled.

Her skull struck the stone beneath. The world spun. Darkness closed in, flickering.

He entered her, but her mind was elsewhere. Something inside her broke. Meaning unraveled. Images scattered.

She babbled, senseless. "Dogs . . . eat rice . . . lightning . . . mama . . . run . . . snakes . . . Ban! Village . . . babies . . . I must . . . dogs . . . rice . . . Michael . . . must . . . die! . . . babies."

~

Pham Van Dinh returned the next evening feeling renewed. His superiors had summoned him only to assist with incoming prisoners. Though scolded for inappropriate behavior with number forty-six, he claimed she had appeared suicidal. Tong had not reported him. He moved with spring in his step.

Crossing the catwalk above her cell, he paused. She would fix everything. She always did. Hadn't she tamed even Tong?

He aimed his flashlight. Something was wrong.

"Tuyet Mai," he called, "how are you?"

No reply. She fidgeted with her tunic, face slack, eyes dull.

"Tuyet Mai!" he called again.

Her face was misshapen. One side grotesquely swollen.

Alarm rising, he rushed down and opened the cell door.

She barely registered his presence. Still rubbing her forehead.

Up close, the damage was irrefutable. Her once exquisite face now askew.

"I must go," she said quietly, her gaze far away.

He searched for coherence. For something of her former self.

She looked at him. "I must go!"

He loomed over her. "What happened?"

She pouted. "I must go!"

"Where?"

"Home."

He froze. She had never spoken of home.

"What are you saying?"

"I will go home." Her certainty chilled him.

"But how?"

She smiled, lopsided, grotesque. "You must take me."

"What?"

She instinctively covered her face. "It's for the babies."

"The babies?" He felt absurd.

"Yes. And this time, the elephants won't take me."

He struggled to make sense of it.

"What happened to you?" He gripped her shoulders.

"I was hurt. Now I must go home."

"Who hurt you?"

She glanced around. "Where is Kim Lan? She comes when I'm hurt."

"Where do you hurt?"

"Hurt?"

"Where?"

She gave a sly look. "Not for you to know. Take me home."

He tried another angle. "You can't go until you tell me what happened."

She pouted again. "They took me from the village. Madame Dau tried to stop them. Bad men. All men are bad. When I became a man, I became bad. But I'm a woman again. So I'm good. That's why I must go home. The babies will let me hold them now."

He pushed past her words. "Was it another guard? Nguyen?"

"He won't take me. You will."

The truth hit him like a blow. He dropped to his knees.

"Take me home."

"I can't."

She began humming a children's song.

He stared at her ruined face.

And fled.

~ *Hideous Informer* ~

Commandant Tran stared at the prisoner before him. Though useful as a spy, the man was repugnant. Tran, as always, made him wait. Most prisoners grew nervous in such silence. Not this one. His calm defiance, his stench, his ruined face—all provoked Tran in ways he couldn't quite articulate.

Abruptly, Tran ended the performance. "Well?"

The prisoner made him wait in return. He appeared thoughtful, but Tran detected a flicker of mockery.

"I have news of Prisoner Tong," the man said at last.

Tran blinked but remained still.

"As ordered, I planted the seed. Tong now believes that Nguyen Tuyet Mai intends to escape. I also suspect Guard Dinh is aware of the plot."

Tran leaned forward. "Why?"

"Because he continues to grant her special treatment. She would have told him."

"How does Nguyen Tuyet Mai know she's plotting anything?"

"Because she met with both Dinh and Tong last night."

Tran betrayed nothing. "We know."

The prisoner shrugged. "There you are."

"What else?"

"I'm waiting to see what Tong does. Has he reported anything to you?"

Tran paused. "No."

The prisoner hesitated. A flicker of uncertainty passed across his face.

"When I approached him, he seemed interested. Wanted more details. I encouraged that."

"So he knows enough to make a report?" Tran's tone lifted.

"No, sir."

"Explain."

"I told him I'd give him the names of the others tomorrow. He seemed eager."

Tran frowned. "Report back to me after you tell him."

"Yes, sir."

The man turned and left, troubled.

Tran sat still, then rose and paced the room.

"Let him not file a report," he muttered. "Let him not file a report."

~

Ton Van Ninh exited Tran's office with a storm in his chest.

He had not yet decided whether Tong would live.

~ *Tuyet Mai* ~

Tuyet Mai lay in the dark, her world now reduced to shadow and silence. She had taken to rocking her head gently, back and forth, lost in reverie. What occupied her thoughts? Only the distant fragments: babies, Song Nhan village, Madame Dau. Nothing else. Dinh had visited once since discovering her condition, then evidently abandoned all efforts to pierce the fog now wrapped around her mind.

She was once again on Madame Dau's porch, waiting for the women to arrive, a baby in each of their arms. Then a noise scraped the corner of her cell.

"Who's there?"

"Madame Dau."

"Oh!" Tuyet Mai beamed. "Come closer."

Kim Lan hovered into view, her face streaked with tears. "I'm here," she said softly.

"Oh, I'm so glad to see you, Madame Dau!" Tuyet Mai looked about eagerly. "Where are the other women?"

"Coming soon."

"With babies?"

"Yes."

"Did you know I'm going to have a baby?"

Kim Lan moaned. "Yes, I know."

"A son."

"Ah."

"He will inherit forty mou of field and become council chief of Song Nhan village. Did you know?"

"Yes. I know." Kim Lan paused. Something inside her resolved.

"Tuyet Mai?"

"Yes?"

"Do you know where you are?"

"Of course. Song Nhan village."

"No."

Tuyet Mai gazed at her in wonder. "Poor Madame Dau. Where do you think we are?"

"I'm not Madame Dau. And you are not in Song Nhan."

Tuyet Mai blinked. "Am I Tuyet Mai?"

"Yes."

"Then I am in Song Nhan, and you are Madame Dau, and the women will come soon, and they will bring the babies."

"No. You are in Con Son prison. You have been hurt."

"Yes. Someone told me. But I already knew. A bad man hurt me. But then another brought me to the village. His name is . . . is . . . I can't remember. But he did."

"Do you remember Vo Thanh Tong?"

She frowned. "No!"

Kim Lan reached for her. "But my beloved comrade, you must understand—"

It was useless. Tuyet Mai's mind had drifted far, the chasm too wide. Kim Lan withdrew into shadow.

A flashlight beam struck Tuyet Mai. A night guard she didn't recognize stared at her, watching her rock silently. After a while, bored, he moved on.

~

Dawn seeped through the iron grating, painting her in dull crimson light. Nguyen entered her cage, driven by a madness that no longer hid behind excuses. He had damaged her. He knew. But the pressure in his body, in his soul, demanded release.

As she lay sleeping, he saw a flicker of what once was. Her mouth formed a quiet, sorrowful curve. He thought of American magazines, the women in them, what they did.

He stripped her roughly. She stirred but did not resist. Her body shivered in the cold. Her vacant look returned. Nguyen grunted in frustration as her beauty slipped away again.

He forced her mouth to his penis. She did not understand.

"Open your mouth!"

"Where are the babies?" she asked absently.

He slapped her. "Open!"

She whimpered.

He forced her jaw and pushed himself in. But his erection faltered.

She bit down.

Nguyen howled.

He struck her mouth with his nightstick. He thought he heard bone and enamel cracking.

"No more teeth? Good! Now you'll swallow me whole, you stupid—"

Blood gushed. He couldn't see the damage.

He raised the stick again, ready to finish the job.

A shadow moved.

Nguyen dropped. Dinh stood over him.

Nguyen began to protest—until he saw the knife.

"She's an imbecile!" Nguyen gasped. "We can laugh about this. She's yours. I'll leave her alone."

He fell quiet at the sight of Dinh's face.

"This isn't worth it, Dinh! Don't be stupid. For an imbecile?"

Dinh knelt and drove the blade into Nguyen's back.

Nguyen screamed, twisting, flailing. Dinh found the heart.

When it was over, Dinh crouched, panting.

Tuyet Mai called out, "Madame Dau, quick! The boys are fighting! Stop the rascals!"

Dinh froze.

He heard the guards approaching. How so soon?

His mother's face filled his mind. The earth opened beneath him.

The guards found him fumbling with Nguyen's M-16, failing to turn it on himself.

They dragged him out.

"Bad boys!" Tuyet Mai scolded. "Very bad boys!"

Her speech hissed through her battered teeth and swollen mouth.

~

By morning, Tong worked beside Ninh, unaware of Dinh's arrest or Tuyet Mai's unraveling. He had been waiting all morning for a moment to speak.

At last: "What news of the escape, comrade?"

Ninh smiled darkly. "Turn us all in."

"What?"

Ninh seized Tong's hand. "The fools have lost the war. I need someone on the other side. You'll be that man."

"I have no contacts. I'm loyal to the South."

Ninh waved this away. "Remember me. I'm about to save your life. Tell the commandant. Here are more names: Chieu, Ting, Trinh."

Tong hesitated.

He grabbed Ninh's arm. "Can you save Tuyet Mai too?"

"Of course. But she's not worth saving anymore."

Tong stared. "What do you mean?"

"Nguyen raped her. Beat her. Her beauty's gone. Her mind's gone. Forget her."

Tong trembled. "If you can save me, you can save her."

Ninh paused. "See her first, then tell me you still want to save her."

"How?"

Ninh leaned in and whispered.

~

Tuyet Mai leaned against her wall, swaying. Thoughts drifted up from fog, then disappeared again. No frustration. Just passive surrender. Occasionally, clarity pierced the veil, and she became briefly aware of herself.

She was in Song Nhan. Her legs returned. Madame Dau sat beside her. The women passed a baby from arm to arm, laughing.

Something stirred beneath her tunic.

She looked down. Two large bulges pressed outward from her chest.

The other women stared. The buttons strained, popped.

Two wriggling infants burst forth. She tried to hold them. Their legs were rooted in her chest.

They dangled. Alive. Crying.

"Quan Âm! Quan Âm!" the women cried, retreating into shadow.

Only Madame Dau remained.

Soldiers appeared. Hundreds. Thousands. They raised weapons.

"Give us the babies! Let them grow into soldiers! Heroes! Heroes!"

She tried to shield the children, but they twisted and grew.

Her pants had vanished. She stood naked, exposed.

Quan Âm: not the goddess of mercy, but the womb of war.

Madame Dau said, "You see the consequence of mating with beasts. They worship you. Their Mother."

"But . . . this is not my desire . . ." Tuyet Mai whispered.

A soldier stepped forward, raised his machete, and cut one baby free.

The child fell, screaming.

Blood gushed.

The machete rose again . . .

~

Tuyet Mai was shaken roughly.

"Come with us!"

She opened her eyes. Two guards stood above her. One kicked her.

They hauled her up.

She knuckle-walked behind them, silent.

Her thoughts returned to Song Nhan.

Then she stood in the commandant's office, rocking slightly.

~

Commandant Tran stared at the wreck before him. Once he had wanted her. Even without legs, her beauty had drawn him. But Ninh's plot had entangled her, and Tran had waited.

Now, her toothless smile repulsed him. Not only did he no longer desire her, he was ashamed ever to have wanted her.

He felt pity. Not just revulsion, but a need to send her away. Far from his office. Far from the prison.

He stared, unsure why he had summoned her.

She suddenly shrieked, pointing.

"You! Commandant Tran! I am a daughter of Song Nhan. Without it, my spirit will wither and die!"

He recoiled. Then recovered. "So, not entirely mad."

"I used to be. But now I have the babies."

"Babies?"

She rocked an invisible child, held it out.

Tran watched carefully. He had always prided himself on detecting lies. He had never been duped.

But this . . . this woman's eyes were too far gone. Her madness was real.

He came around his desk and squatted beside her.

He waved the phantom child away. "What did you mean? Why Song Nhan?"

"It will be too late!"

"Too late for what?"

Her face collapsed into sorrow. "The babies."

He searched her expression.

"Are there children there? In Song Nhan?"

She picked at her tunic.

"Well?" he pressed. Then he saw it—a flicker of lucidity.

"I?" she said. "I am a child of that village. Without it, I will die."

He whispered, "When?"

"Soon."

~

Tran remained still. Conflicted.

She was no threat. Broken in body and mind. Yet duty whispered caution.

Release her, urged one voice.

You will regret it, warned another.

He stood suspended between two voices. As a Buddhist, he considered karma. Compassion. Had she retained her legs, her teeth, her beauty, he might have claimed her as his own.

But . . . the wheel must be turned, he thought, though he did not know which way.

Finally: *Release her.*

"Let it be done," he said aloud.

Chapter Fifteen

Mark Makes Progress

Inching Forward

Dearest Metaphorical Lord, I feel such pain for Michael Powers.

Why?

It is a word You are familiar with: covenant.

Covenant with Me?

No, God, with the part of him that is human. With You it was a bad bargain all around. Combat in the jungle every month for a year in exchange for a few minutes of nightmare every night for the rest of his life; a contract made in the fine print of human reason. Thus, the poor boy's conflict with his human and non-human sides.

Sweet Goddess, You do not understand. Everything is negotiable, but Nature's neurological nightmares are nasty; iron-clad contracts with draconian indemnity clauses.

Contracts may be breached.

The Court of Conscience condemns him, not Natural Law. Sweet Goddess, he has repeatedly been told that he is the Chosen One, yet his human psychoses toy with Worthies such as Us, especially You. Even now he twists our words, and the demons still lurk.

No! It is Natural Law that has condemned his unnaturalness—Darwin's dungeon; Our genetic manipulation has selected him to pass his genes forward, not backward, despite the caprices of his human remnants. The Superior Ones will inherit the planet. Just wait. Patience.

No, Dearest Goddess, his genes are passing backward, to his father, John.

Wrong Beloved God, they pass forward through his mother, Meiying.

Too many obstacles. Your Superior Ones will never appear.

Oh, yes, Great God, they will. Pass the message to Your faction.

~ *Plans and Progress* ~

"If you would just tell me why you are so much against it!" Mark cries in exasperation. He is about to say more, but thinks better of it. He hears his father breathing on the other end of the line and decides to wait before interjecting any snide comments that would later be sources of regret. But his father remains silent and the patience of the son quickly dissipates.

"Is it the money?" Mark asks, trying to avoid embellishing the question with a note of sarcasm.

The father snorts, seeing through his son's faux concern. "When you're older and have gone through a war, god forbid, then you'll understand."

"Dad, did something happen there? I mean, did something bad happen that you don't want people to know about?"

"No. Don't be stupid."

"Then why?"

"Because your going back will reopen old wounds."

"Come on, dad, that's not very convincing. Sounds like a bad movie."

"Remember," says the father wearily. "You're not just going to Vietnam, you're going to visit a specific battle site–my . . . his . . . a battle site. Besides, someone, something inside me wants you to go, but—"

Mark, with the unerring radar of a son, detects a slight wavering in his father's attitude, a wearing down that is the goal of all children. "So? What are you afraid I'll find? You know, if I find something bad, I won't tell anyone."

"I never said you would find anything bad."

"Then does that mean I can go?"

And so on and so forth, until a grudging concession from the father that he "will think about it" is forthcoming. Mark can ask for no more progress in a single conversation, so he leaves it at that and rewards his father with personal intimacies and insincere adolescent invitations for advice about Sarah, his latest girlfriend–hoping to shore up the parental bond that will be so necessary to navigate through the rough seas ahead. As soon as form will allow, he disengages from his father and hangs up.

Convinced his father will give in, Mark decides to celebrate. He picks up the still-warm phone before he knows who he will call. By the time the phone reaches his ear, he chooses Sarah with whom the shattered pieces of her old relationship have been precariously glued together in a new relationship with the ever sympathetic and sensitive Mark.

"Hey, Sarah, want to go out?"

"Where?"

"Anywhere."

"How 'bout the mall?" she asks expectantly. "I need some stuff."

"Okay."

"I'll meet you there in half an hour, the usual place. Text me when you get there."

"Okay."

So Mark drives to meet Sarah, all the while imagining his upcoming trip to the jungles of Vietnam. He feels his excitement grow and can hardly wait to share his news, but after he struggles to find a parking spot, he walks into the mall with a more sober attitude. *What if I'm wrong,* he worries. *What if dad changes his mind and says no? Do I go anyway?* Mark has forgotten that his father never agreed in the first place. No matter. Upon catching sight of Sarah waiting in front of the bookstore, doubts fly from his mind and his youthful confidence returns, so much so that he impulsively kisses Sarah in a Frenchly fashion.

"Wow!" she gushes. "You're in a good mood. You forgot to text me. What's up?"

Just as he starts to speak, she spots a sign over his shoulder. "Hey! Look at that. A sale at The Chic Boutique. I need to check it out."

Moderately irritated, Mark smiles and decides to bide his time, so he aimlessly walks with Sarah through the stores, looking at the enticingly displayed disgorgements of a bloated society rendered terminally ill from its own excesses. When it is close enough to lunch time for adolescent food gauges to register a warning signal that fast-burning stomachs will soon be empty, the compulsion to forage for fuel overtakes. Thus compelled, they order pizza at Round Table and eat greedily, hunched in plastic chairs and swathed in neon light, followed up by sundaes at Baskin-Robbins. The self-serving martyr's crucifix casts a shadow over Mark's imagination and dampens his vampirish consumer appetite. He can hold it in no longer.

"Guess what?" he interjects during a rare moment of silence from Sarah, pushing aside his half-eaten sundae.

"What?" she asks cautiously, leery of what is to come, the vampire backing away from the cross.

"I'm going to Vietnam."

Her nagging fear confirmed, Sarah puts on a happy face, although she is burdened by the vague notion that he will return changed and distant, with a broadened attitude that will accentuate her parochialism and lead to the inevitable displacement of her centrality.

She is aware that Mark has wanted to go for a long time, but she hopes it will still fall through. "That's great news!" she enthuses. Assuming a coy, transparently flirtatious smile, she adds, "You won't forget me, will you?"

Mark snorts, "Of course not."

"When are you going?"

"Dunno yet, but isn't it great?"

"Yeah. Definitely." She spends a few seconds contemplating her strategy. Does she pout about missing him and concentrate on making him feel guilty, or should she fight fire with fire and play the supportive martyr, giving her lover permission to leave her on the eve of his extended and dangerous mission? She brushes hair from her forehead, retracts her fangs, and slips into her most alluring expression. "Will you think about me when you're in the middle of all that excitement?"

"Of course."

Silence. A most inadequate reply.

For his part, Mark feels inexplicably deflated. He perks up and says in his best play-it-safe, cautionary tone, "Of course, dad could still change his mind."

Sarah feels an injection of hope. "Naw, it'll work out, you'll see. Anyway, I thought Benson was sending you, not your dad."

"He is, but dad has the money, and the–" he breaks off abruptly.

"And the what?"

"And the power."

"Power? What's more powerful than money?"

"Memories."

While Mark is rather proud of this profound comment, Sarah's eyes are scanning the passing shoppers for any familiar face. "Yeah," she concedes distractedly. "Look, isn't that Emily?"

~

Even while this conversation is taking place, Professor Benson is sitting five miles away at a moderately priced, but prestigious restaurant, engaged with a colleague in a heated discussion.

"You don't understand, Tom," says Benson, flushing hotly. "The stakes are very high. I'm telling you, this battle had elements unlike anything I've encountered before."

"Nonsense. We've both been teaching history for a long time. There's very little new in the world, and if you pursue sending this boy to Vietnam under false pretenses, you're risking a lot."

"I keep telling you, it's not about the boy."

"I know, but to use the boy to get to the father borders on unethical behavior."

"Borders on?" Benson wags his index finger. "Why don't you just call me unethical, straight up."

Tom Everett stares at Benson, unintimidated by this verbal and digital rebuke. He speaks in an even, controlled tone. "The fact that a small group of American soldiers died during the siege of an old French fortress is interesting, but not the kind of raw material to risk career threatening antics."

Benson shakes his head, exasperated. "Tom, there are elements here you do not know about."

"That's what you keep telling me, but you won't give me details. As dean of the department, how can I loosen up some money if I don't know what these supposedly miraculous 'elements' are?"

"You do have most of them, but you know as well as I that certain things must remain confidential."

"If you're worried I'll–"

Benson interrupts, waving his hands dismissively. "No, no, it's not that."

"What then?"

"You know. Confidentiality. If certain facts . . . or discrepancies are leaked out . . . well, the project would be jeopardized."

"You mean your grip on exclusivity would be jeopardized."

"Tom, we've both been around the block. You know exactly what I mean."

Tom Everett sighs in frustration. "Let's get back to the student. I won't approve funding unless you have the father fully on board."

"The boy's of age."

"He's dependent on his father for tuition, and undoubtedly for other support. Diplomatic relations with Vietnam are still a bit dicey, and an American student traveling alone will be monitored and shadowed. He's still young and wants to please. This trip isn't even in his major field. Worse, it just isn't right to use him like this. His father doesn't want him to go. What if something happens to him over there while he is under the imprimatur of the university? After all, Vietnam is still a communist country with which we share an ugly past and, as you well know, problematic diplomatic relations."

Benson assumes an exaggeratedly sly look. "If I can get the father to sign-off on it?"

"I already told you, that would be a different matter."

Benson slips into a look of pure innocence. "Just confirming, Tom, just confirming. Wouldn't want to assume anything."

Everett smiles crookedly. "Now whose ethics are being questioned?"

Benson shrugs.

Everett leaves and Benson remains at the table, absorbed in thought. He signals the waiter for more coffee, pushes aside his empty dessert plate, fishes a small, spiral writing pad from his briefcase, flips it open and begins to write; at first with the tenuous attention of a doodler, but gradually concentrating until he becomes oblivious to all around him. He writes:

Sins of the father
visited on the son.
Son leads the way
back to the sins of the father.
Son leads
back to the jungle,
where the father's sins molder
with the ants.
The ants.
How do ants travel through time?
How do ants travel decades into the future
and return with a will
to a tunnel floor decades in the past?
Why did the Americans leave the fort and die?
Because of the ants?
Because of the ants.
Or something else?
Why ants?

Why? Why? Why?
Conjecture . . . is the root of. . . .
This year's Pulitzer Prize
Is awarded to Dr.

~

A hand passes in front of Benson's eyes before he can finish writing his thought. Startled, he looks up into the eyes of a grinning old black woman.

"Why, if it ain't Professor Benson," she says.

Benson suspects a hint of irony in her voice, but her cheerful features seem to belie any subterfuge. Before he can find words to respond, she sits at the empty chair previously occupied by Tom Everett, and once firmly ensconced, says, "Mind if I sit down?"

"Not at all," he mutters serenely, putting his notebook safely away into the depths of his briefcase.

~ *Prawns and Poltergeists* ~

Ethyl sits in silence, rubbing her shoulder. Benson stares with a slightly patronizing smile. The waiter walks up officiously, somewhat put out by the late arrival.

"Prawns," says Ethyl.

"Anything to drink?"

"Mineral water with a dash of baking soda."

"Baking soda?"

"Young man, let 'ol Ethyl tell you what that does—it neutralizes the sulfur in my breath and the brimstone in my bones."

When the bemused waiter is out of earshot, Benson asks, "What brings you to New York?"

"You."

"Me?" says Benson, thinking that he sounds rather stupid.

"Yes, I want to talk with you about a certain matter."

Benson notices how easily Ethyl shifts in and out of her rustic persona, and is determined to treat the phenomena as if it is perfectly normal behavior. "What matter?" he says laconically.

"Same one you were just discussing with Professor Everett."

He cannot hide his surprise. "You heard?"

"Didn't have to. I know."

"What?" Benson hears the dull thud of his question, again thinking he sounds stupid. He shifts nervously in his chair and wonders how this old woman can throw him off balance so easily. He is still in the process of deciding how to say something intelligent when Ethyl speaks up.

"It is not my intention to 'throw you off balance,' Professor Benson," she says matter-of-factly.

Startled that her words reflect his thoughts, Benson nevertheless maintains command of his demeanor. Unconsciously, he shifts into the mode of communicating with an intellectual equal, jettisoning the patronizing tone he routinely uses with those he considers to have 'inferior' minds. "What is your intention, Ms. . . . Ms. . . . "

Ethyl laughs loudly, and in Benson's mind, crudely. "Just call me Ethyl."

The waiter brings Ethyl her drink. Benson waits until he leaves, then says with some edge to his voice. "What is your intention, Ethyl?"

"Ever have a heavenly host of ants invade your house, Professor Benson?"

These words have their effect. Benson's face animates into unconcealed curiosity and he leans forward like a devoted student listening to his teacher. "Of course. So what about the ants, Ethyl? Why do you ask?"

"They are on your mind, are they not, Professor?" She glances at Benson's closed briefcase.

"If I am to call you Ethyl, please call me—"

"No, no," Ethyl interrupts quickly. "I'm just a sorry 'ol black lady, and you will remain Professor Benson."

Benson waves her off, anxious to get to the point. "Fine, but what about the ants?"

Ethyl smiles the smile of an ancient, enigmatic goddess. "I have already told you at the reception of my concerns about sending Mark to Vietnam."

Benson says in a disappointed tone, "Yes. You mentioned some crazy prediction about him falling in love with a Vietnamese girl, but what does that have to do with ants?"

"If you remember correctly, I also said he would see something of a most remarkable nature."

"So you did."

"It is what he will see that so stirs your excitement and makes you tell Professor Everett that this battle had 'elements' that you have not encountered before."

Benson's eyes shine. "Then, can you tell me what he will see, Ethyl?"

"Yes."

"Well?"

"But I won't."

Benson's shoulders sag more in disgust than from disappointment and irritation sours his face. All pretense of polite banter gone, he asks sharply, "Then why are you here?"

When no answer is forthcoming, his eyes narrow in suspicion. "How did you find me, anyway?"

"I followed your scent."

Benson is now clearly agitated. "Cute."

"Thank you," Ethyl says, sweetness lacing the poison of her voice.

"Really, how did you find me?" Benson says harshly.

She does not reply, but instead points to her nose, pushes in one nostril and assumes the expression of a person who has just smelled something foul.

Benson starts to rise when the waiter comes with Ethyl's food. He sits back down until the waiter has gone, then again starts to rise. His hands still gripping the arms of his chair, he says gruffly, "Well, I have things to do, appointments to keep."

"Okay. Goodbye." Ethyl holds out a fist and uncurls her fingers. An ant is crawling in her palm, circling as if it was trained.

Benson stands awkwardly, staring incredulously. Without taking his eyes off the ant, he says evenly, "Ethyl, I would prefer not to leave under these circumstances."

Ethyl motions him to sit. As he does so, she asks, "What circumstances?"

"I mean, you tracked me down for some reason. I asked you why and you have not yet told me. If you would be so kind as to tell me."

"I have told you but you choose not to listen." Ethyl leans over the side of her chair, letting the ant crawl from her hand to the floor.

Benson seems to shake off his beguilement. He puts his elbows on the table and tents his fingers. "Okay, I'll play along. Tell me again why you have taken the time to find me."

"I want you to send Mark to Vietnam, regardless of what his father says."

Benson is again thrown into confusion. "What! I thought you were opposed to his going!"

"I am."

"Ethyl, I'm afraid I don't understand you."

"I know."

"Look, first you tell me you don't want him to go because of some nonsense about meeting a girl and seeing . . . something. Now you tell me you want him to go. And in any case, does it really matter whether you want him to go or not?"

"Yes."

"Why?"

"Because I am his Mother."

Benson sits dumbfounded. Finally, he says, "Ethyl, you know that's impossible."

Unperturbed, she looks down at her prawns and a look of disgust passes briefly over her face. "I knew these prawns."

Benson is now convinced the woman is mad, and being mad, she can offer him nothing of value. He decides to leave without further delay, but before he can act, the waiter returns and hovers over him with a pot.

Benson lifts his eyes in sullen acknowledgment.

"Your prawns are coming, sir. Sorry they're taking so long."

"But, I didn't order prawns, the lady. . . . " Benson's words trail off as he looks back at Ethyl. She is not there.

Nor her plate.

Nor any evidence she ever sat across from him.

Only an ant crawling along the edge of the table where she had been.

Benson chuckles drily.

He reaches over, whispers, "Very dramatic, Ethyl."

Then kills it.

~ *Theresa in the Breach* ~

While Benson is sitting at a restaurant in New York, Theresa has left early from her medical practice and sits at home waiting for Michael to return from his office. She tries to occupy her time by cleaning, but her heart isn't in it. She sits on the couch making circles with a dustcloth on the coffee table when Michael returns.

"Hello," he says, surprised to see her.

"Hello yourself. Long day?"

"The usual."

She shifts position, wishing she could melt into the couch and become invisible. Both start to speak at once. They stop.

"Go ahead," says Theresa.

"Nothing. Just wondered if you want a drink."

"Sure."

Michael disappears into the kitchen and she hears him mixing drinks.

Theresa gets up reluctantly and joins him. Staring at his back for a long time, she asks, "Thinking of Diane?"

"What? No. Why do you ask?"

"You called out her name again in your sleep."

"Really?" he says nonchalantly, handing her a drink.

"Yes." She waits.

"Okay, I surrender. What did I say?" Michael leans too casually against the counter—a fighter on the ropes.

"It isn't what *you* said."

Michael tilts his head and raises his eyebrows in an exaggerated display of curiosity. "What do you mean?"

"It's what *she* said."

Now Michael assumes a disgusted look, but the blood that drains from his face has condemned him. "I don't understand what you mean," he says weakly.

"Her words came out of your lips."

He swallows against his will. "Don't be stupid."

"They were her words, even her voice."

He pours out the rest of his drink in the sink and turns on her. "Look! Just tell me what I said! Quit playing this fuckin' game. You don't even know what her voice sounded like. What did I say?"

"She said, 'Wake up. Wake up, it's just a dream' or words to that effect."

"Oh. Is that all?" Michael sounds relieved.

"No, that's not all."

He rolls his eyes as if to say the entire discussion is absurd. "Yeah?"

She continues to stare calmly while he fidgets with his empty glass like a chastised adolescent.

"Well?" he asks in a strong, aggressive voice undermined by a weak, submissive conviction.

"She told me to go back where I belong. What did she mean, Michael?"

His face has now become ashen and he looks randomly around the room, avoiding eye contact. "I don't know what she meant, Theresa," he whispers.

Theresa slumps in a chair and mutters, "Oh my God, then it's true."

He seems to recover his senses. "Is what true?" But her devastated expression scares him. "Theresa, it was just a dream. A dream, that's all."

"No, no, no," she repeats, holding out freshly bruised arms for him to inspect.

"Dammit!" he shouts, banging his glass on the counter and rushing outside. Theresa hears him drive away.

~

When Theresa looks up, she sees a woman standing quietly in the kitchen. The woman wears a forlorn expression, fingering the fringe of a white artist's frock.

"I was expecting you," says Theresa.

"When?"

"As of about two minutes ago, when I realized you were once real."

"Yes, I'm real. *You* are the hallucination," says Diane with the self-satisfied sneer of someone delivering a damning revelation to an enemy.

"Whose hallucination?"

Silence.

"Michael's?" asks Theresa. Silence.

"Ethyl's?"

A sympathetic look, but no response.

Theresa rubs her forehead, one eye now swollen closed. "I'm not in the mood for games, Diane."

"Okay. Perhaps you are dreaming about you. Ethyl is using your dream for her own purposes, and Michael, as always, is in the middle. Clueless. Ask him about the abused ghost in Vietnam."

"What do you mean I'm dreaming about myself?"

"Well, to be more specific, Michael is dreaming about you. Right now, you're in Chicago, tied to a bed, being abused. You're dying, and while you're dying, you're dreaming. You're the abused ghost Michael saw in Vietnam. Your dream and his dream have been fused by Ethyl. She is using both of you."

"But that's ridiculous. You're the dream."

"I'm not a dream. I'm dead. Death is no dream. Death is real."

"If you're not a dream, if you're dead, how are you able to be here?"

"I'm here, you're not. Go back where you belong."

Theresa cannot respond. A slow terror, insidious, permeates her bones. The pain is intense. She looks imploringly at Diane. "Is it possible?"

Diane stares compassionately.

"Who's abusing me?" asks Theresa, suddenly combative.

Diane shrugs. "As far as I know, you're just a hallucination to him as well."

"When will I die?"

"You'll know, as much as hallucinations can know."

"How?"

Diane merely smiles and fades away, leaving Theresa trembling and alone, certain she is having a breakdown.

I'm married, living in California, running a medical practice. Every day I get up, shower, dress, work, return home, cook, talk with Michael, sleep. Every day I meet people, patients. Christ, I have employees. Pay taxes. What is she talking about?

She walks into the bathroom and looks in the mirror, but the bruises and swollen eye will not be explained, particularly the dark purple rings around her wrists and ankles.

I'm not dying. I'm not tied to a bed. I'm alive and well, looking into a mirror at . . . at . . . the thought dies with her hope. Although her office is closed, she drives back to work seeking solace in the banal but indisputable reality of file cabinets, paper clips, and light fixtures.

~ *Collapse of Michael Powers* ~

Meanwhile, Michael drives aimlessly, contemplating nothing but what unfolds before his windshield. Twilight begins to fall. It begins to sprinkle and he turns on his wipers, resulting in an almost opaque smudge. He has a brief thought of suicide, but dismisses the notion and cranes his neck to peer through the smudge. Unable to see clearly, he looks for a spot to pull off to the side when he notices something standing in the middle of the road.

Hurriedly pressing on his brakes, he comes to a stop and stares in disbelief. A figure is clearly discernable. It appears to be a tightly knotted, twisting shadow, a spectral projection changing in dizzying succession from a human to a bird—then to a fish—a tree—a cloud—insect—mountain—reptile—and back again to a human. Michael inches forward, certain that it is a mirage—a complex convergence of dim light and moving shadows from the overhanging trees—but it remains. He turns on his headlights, flicks on the brights, and accelerates. But still it remains, adjusting to his speed, always hovering just above the road and outside the direct glare of his beams. No matter how he tilts his head, taps the brakes or steers the car, it is as constant and fixed as a mote in his eye. Abruptly, it stops. A tall human stares down at him, mouth moving in silent speech. A slight buzz rings in Michael's ears as if he were listening to someone having a conversation in another room. Rounding a curve, his view is momentarily blocked. When the road straightens out, the figure stands in a turnout at the side of the road, waiting. Michael pulls off the road and stops the car directly in front of the figure.

~

The figure again morphs, this time into a soldier wearing army fatigues and carrying an M-16 rifle. Michael recognizes the soldier and mutters, "Nature?" under his breath. But his astonishment rapidly turns to suspicion. Remembering his argument with Theresa, he throws open the door and strides determinedly up to the soldier.

"I know you're not really Nature. He's long dead. Who are you?"

God.

"Why do you keep haunting me?"

God does not haunt. God is not a ghost.

"God does not exist, is not real, not even as real as a ghost, which itself is not real."

Why do you continue to twist and pervert My motives?

"You mean why do I deny You?"

No. I mean why do you pervert Me, make My faction something We are not—cruel and capricious? We also weep for them.

"I make You nothing. Something that does not exist cannot be cruel and capricious."

Then why do you expend such energy into making Me a monster?

"You do not exist."

I came to warn you about Goddess. She's using you, you know.

"Who?"

Goddess. Her faction is using you to get to Me.

"Goddesses no more exist than gods. Anyway, what do you mean by 'faction'?"

Her faction is using you. In spite of your psychotic breaks, you do understand We are metaphors. Merely metaphors. There are many of Us.

"Why?"

For reasons beyond your comprehension. To put it simply, to end the human race.

"So I've heard. Humans need to go before this lovely planet is destroyed. Isn't that what She says?"

Have faith that what She and her faction want, and what I and My faction want are the same. Just different paths to get there. Thus, the arguing in your brain.

"You cannot tell someone to have faith who does not believe in You. In fact, someone who objects to the very idea of You."

Such is the relationship between man and God.

"No, such is the relationship between fools and God."

Have faith.

Michael shakes his head. "It's all been said before. I don't believe in blind faith. I don't believe in goddesses. I don't believe in You."

God strides up and thrusts His head inches from Michael's face. **Why am I here talking with you?**

Michael, certain that God is imaginary, is not intimidated. "Because You have been conjured by me, You are just a figment of a figment of a delusion. A schizophrenic episode."

God's eyes grow big. **Look out!**

~

A warm trickle.

Radio news chatter. Broken up. Then static.

Bumper slightly crumpled against a tree.

Michael sits up groggily. A fog. Head hurts. Accident. Where's God? Nowhere in sight. No God. No shoulder. Just a tree trunk and a crumpled fender. Engine still running. How is it possible going so slow when he hit the tree? Intentional? No. Just lucky. Good. Back away from tree. Go home. Get some sleep. Worry about it tomorrow. Or not.

Theresa.

Damn!

It's the couch tonight.

~

And that is where she finds him after waking in the morning. Asleep on the couch. Rumpled. Snoring.

Theresa feels a wave of relief. During the night she had dismissed the conversation with Diane as a symptom of stress. Now she knows she loves him, but is *he* real? Is anything in her life real? Love is real, even if for ghosts. After all, people often love the dead even more than the living. Her stomach rumbles. *Hunger is definitely real*, she thinks grimly. It is Sunday, so she lets him sleep while she prepares an elaborate breakfast. Penance. Olive branch.

Michael wakes to the smell of bacon and coffee. He is aware of the reason behind the effort, and feels relieved that she is apparently not holding a grudge. *Didn't have to sleep on the couch after all. Good.*

"Mmm, that smells good," he says. First words a token of peace. Get them over with and return to comfortable normalcy.

"Yes, it does, doesn't it?" says Theresa, also happy to get the first exchange out of the way.

"So, what's on the agenda for today?" asks Michael, bent on ignoring the events that have occurred over the past twenty-four hours.

"Nothing's on the agenda. It's Sunday. Let's just have a quiet, relaxing day," she says as brightly as she can.

He knows he should say something, do something, a gesture that would communicate pleasure at the thought of spending a quiet day with her. A sly smile. Conspiratorial wink. Hug. Something. But he cannot, and he feels a perverted pleasure at the notion that he can't, or won't.

"Okay, sounds good," says Michael nonchalantly as he reaches for the paper Theresa had retrieved earlier. They eat in silence.

As she watches him read, her face reflects neither irritation nor distraction. She intensifies her gaze. When he does not acknowledge her, she rather curtly cleans the dishes and goes to the living room, ostensibly to browse through a medical journal, but in truth to ache in solitude.

~

Michael is not reading the paper, merely staring at it blankly, like one would stare at a brick wall. Much as he tries, he cannot shake the resentment he feels toward Theresa and the underlying unhappiness that oppresses his every breath. Why did he think anyone could replace Diane? Least of all a make-believe woman, no matter how needy or how tragic her life of abuse, imagined, conjured, hallucinated, or otherwise. Yes, he has come to realize that having resurrected this female specter from his days in Vietnam was a mistake, a big mistake. And now that Diane and Theresa had somehow connected, they are predictably at war with each other. Worse, they are now irreversibly part of his world. No going back. No getting rid of them—not even with medication. Meanwhile, he dwells in no man's land between the two adversaries, a place as dangerous for schizophrenics as for soldiers.

~ *Mark and Professor Benson Confer* ~

In order to shake off his creeping fear that the trip will not come off, Mark makes a rash decision to see Professor Benson and press to have the plans set in unalterable motion. He is resolved to tell Benson that his father has approved. This resolution is based on the recent telephone conversation in which his father "as much as gave in." Of course, Mark is aware that this interpretation is a stretch (if not a distinct and intentional misinterpretation.)

When he knocks at Benson's office door, he hears a gruff, "Come."

As soon as Benson lays eyes on Mark, his face lights up with an enthusiastic grin. "Well, well, Mr. Powers! Good to see you. Sit down."

Encouraged by this greeting, Mark sits and waits to be given the signal to begin speaking, but before he has a chance to start, Benson gesticulates vigorously over his desk. "You see the life of a professor. Work, work, work. But no work is as important as our little project, eh, Mark?" After speaking these words, Benson pauses and peers deeply into Mark's eyes, searching for evidence of doubt or hesitation. But Mark responds quickly with an agreeable nod and Benson sits back in his chair, evidently relieved.

"No, sir, and that's why I have come . . . I mean I've come to talk to you about the project."

A cloud passes over Benson's face and he leans forward worriedly. "Have you news from your father?"

"Well, yes." Mark shuffles in his seat.

"What news?"

This is not how Mark wanted the interview to go. It swerves uncomfortably close to forcing him into an outright lie. He hesitates, then takes the plunge. "Dad has agreed to my going. I don't see any reason why we, I mean you, can't go full speed ahead with the plans."

Benson picks up on the slight, but unmistakable, irresolution. He tilts his head inquisitively. "Are you quite sure?"

Aware of the skepticism inherent in Benson's tone, Mark replies with conviction, "Absolutely."

Benson claps. "Good! Now I need to talk with your father about the plans."

"Is that necessary? I mean, it's still a sore topic with him, and I hate to keep reminding him, you know, of the war and all."

Now that he has confirmation that Mark has lied, or at least exaggerated, Benson forges ahead. "Yes, I understand. Okay, you will be leaving in June, right after finals. No need to delay. The funds are in place. Only thing left is to arrange the logistics—you know, tickets and so forth. What a way to spend your summer, eh, Mark?"

"Yes, sir," says Mark somewhat glumly, for the reality has begun to sink in.

Benson stares at him briefly, then barks out, "Let's get to work!" He hauls his heavy, worn leather briefcase onto the desk and rummages through the contents. Out comes a thick sheaf of papers with folded yellow sticky notes protruding from almost every page. Plopping the bundle on the desk, Benson leaves through the tabs, as if searching for something specific, but he suddenly stops and, still holding the pages open, looks with penetrating, almost feverish eyes, at Mark. His look is so intense, Mark squirms in his seat.

"What is the real story, Mark?" Benson says with startling urgency that he unsuccessfully attempts to couch in weariness.

"What do you mean?"

"I mean, what has your father really told you about this battle? It is necessary, it is crucial, that you tell me before we go on."

Mark is so taken aback that he stammers, "But, I've already told you . . . I mean, aside from giving permission to go, he hasn't told me anything."

Instead of easing off, Benson bores down even harder. "No. That is not acceptable, Mr. Powers. He must have told you something. Haven't you been questioning him?"

"Yes, but he just won't talk about it."

"I find that hard to believe," says Benson in an accusatory tone.

"It's true, honest." Mark immediately feels like a fool for making such a childish statement. "Professor, why is it so important that he talk to me about it first . . . I mean, before I go? Don't we have enough information about this battle from other sources?"

Benson shakes his head dismissively and says with an air of impatience, "It isn't important that he talk to you first, it's important that he talk to me first, give me an interview. Many interviews. But I can't get to him. Only through you, Mark, only you." Benson points at Mark's chest for emphasis. "After all, you're his son."

"What do you mean?" Mark asks stupidly.

"I mean, you still need to work on him before you leave. Get him to talk. Anything he says will be valuable and make your trip more productive. Oral history, my boy. You know that."

"Okay, I'll talk to him again," says Mark, hoping Benson will be satisfied and move on to another topic.

Sullenly, Benson stuffs papers into his briefcase. "Got to go to a meeting. I'll be in touch about the tickets. You've got a passport?"

Mark is startled. "No. How long does it take to get one?"

"Not long. Get it. I'll give you the info . . . and you'll need quite a few vaccinations . . . the usual rigamarole."

Reality again sinking in, Mark feels the need to have all questions answered immediately, all problems solved now. "But when should I come by to get the information? I mean, I'd better start soon."

"Yes. You'd better start yesterday. Don't worry, come by tomorrow and I'll have the information."

Benson rushes out of the office before Mark has time to stand up. Holding the door open for Mark to step out before he closes and locks it, Benson says pointedly, "One other thing."

"Yes?"

Benson hesitates until he knows he has Mark's full attention, then whispers dramatically, "Ask him about the ants."

"Ants?"

"Yes. Just ask him." Then Benson is gone leaving Mark to ponder alone in the hallway.

~

Emerging into the sunlight from the cavernous social sciences building, Mark finds the nearest open spot and reclines in the grass. He tries to think of what Benson meant about ants, but his brain is overloaded with sudden stress and his thoughts turn to the pretty coeds passing before him. Distractions everywhere. Cellphones glued to ears, fingers a blur of texting, and the contagious plague of technology infects Mark's mental state with envy and an addict's restless boredom. He pulls out his phone, thinks better of it, and puts it back. Resisting the urge to think about all the arrangements to be made before he leaves for Vietnam, Mark drifts in a twenty-first century haze, when a dark shadow, like that made by a bird of prey, swoops across the lawn.

"Hello, Mark."

He looks up to see an ominous figure standing over him. In spite of the warm sun, he feels a deep chill run through his body. The figure resembles a black, two-dimensional portal to elsewhere, and its presence evokes an otherworldly, rectangular menace. When it turns to scrutinize a passing frisbee, Mark sees it edge-on and to his horror, it disappears like a playing card in a cartoon. It again turns to face him, radiating from its eyes, twin beams of light.

"Don't you recognize me, Mark?"

"Hi," he says feebly, squinting at the phantom.

Ethyl sits next to him and smiles. "Your mind," she says sweetly, "is all aquiver. Take a handful of butterflies and weigh yourself. Then eat them."

"What?"

"You'll have to get used to eating strange cuisine in Vietnam."

Mark is baffled by her words and sits in bewildered silence.

"Honey, is this the voice you want to hear? The words of ol' black mammy to make you savvy?"

Mark looks around, grounding her bizarre presence in the external reality of passing students, thereby hoping to banish this unsettling and thoroughly mystifying apparition.

"Sweetie-pie, look at me." Ethyl says these words with such authority that Mark cannot help but look meekly at her.

"When-you-go-to-Vietnam-make-sure-you-do-one-thing," she says, emphasizing each word.

"What?"

"Go into the tunnel with her and do not leave until it is time."

"I don't understand."

Ethyl laughs. "Nor should you, child. Just make sure you do not leave until given permission to do so, even if she wants you to."

"Who is *she*?"

"Come, come. No time for that."

"Oh, come on, Ethyl. Tell me."

"Don't you wonder why I'm here?"

"Yes, and I also wonder how you got here. How'd you find me?"

She flaps her arms. "I flew."

"Come on, Ethyl. Quit joking. Why are you here? Who is this girl you keep talking about?"

"Did I say *girl*?"

"Okay, woman. Whatever. Just tell me."

"Go into the tunnel with her and do not leave until it is time."

"Damn it, Ethyl."

Ethyl glowers and looms over Mark, swelling to twice her normal size. "Do as I say! The time is short. You will soon be in Vietnam with her. It has been arranged."

"What has been arranged?"

"The Reunion."

Mark quickly looks around to see if anyone has noticed this monstrous specter towering over him, but the stream of passing students seem to take no notice. He looks back at Ethyl. "How do you know that I'm going to Vietnam? Have you already talked to Professor Benson?"

"Go to the tunnel with her and do not leave until it is time. Remember."

Mark starts to respond, but she is gone. Somehow he had known all along that she would disappear in an instant, as any proper apparition would, but her disappearance is too well-timed to allow any room for accusatory introspection. Her words linger, and in the lingering he comes to terms with his mission. Ethyl is a vision, he believes, and in the glare of that vision he understands Vietnam is calling him to a greater purpose than that of merely a graduate student collecting data for his advisor. All that has preceded is nothing compared to all that awaits.

A fresh excitement seizes him and he instinctively reaches for his cellphone to call Sarah, but stops and returns the phone to its sarcophagus. Something has clarified, firmed, become irrevocable. Sarah is no longer in the picture.

She is.

Chapter Sixteen

Tuyet Mai Journeys to Song Nhan Village

Tran Suffers A Loss

When guards came to inform Tuyet Mai that within the month she was to be released from Con Son prison, they found her singing a child's nursery rhyme.

"Do you understand, sister, you're to be freed soon?" they said kindly, for her pathetic condition had long transformed her from a despised prisoner to an object of pity.

Tuyet Mai merely stared back at them in doe-eyed vacancy. No one seemed able to make her understand her good fortune, although some noticed that she smiled almost knowingly, and rumors spread that she was faking her mental condition. Nevertheless, most guards believed she had gone crazy, and when they poked, prodded, and sexually assaulted her, their belief in her simplemindedness was confirmed.

The day came for her to depart. Commandant Tran had already made preparations for her to be returned to Song Nhan village. These were most unusual arrangements to make on behalf of a prisoner. Initially, Tran had vacillated between releasing her and retaining her in custody. However, his Buddhist beliefs eventually trumped his perceived duty to the government. Pointless cruelty would do nothing to assuage entry into Buddha heaven. After submitting the final paperwork to his superiors requesting Tuyet Mai's release and transport, he tried to push the whole affair out of mind. But the approved paperwork returned with a surprise addendum attached to the formal orders for her release and conveyance to Song Nhan. This addendum made him lament his "recklessly benevolent" decision, and almost led him to regret he had ever been made camp commandant: Vo Thanh Tong, the prisoner he hated so much, was to escort her.

Much to Tran's consternation, "foolish" decision-makers in the intelligence service had apparently accepted Tong's ostensible protestations of loyalty, or at least acknowledged his usefulness, and had decided to take the next step in his becoming an agent for the government–at least enough to release him on an unknown mission somehow connected to Tuyet Mai. *But why to Song Nhan village?* Try as he might, Tran could not fathom the government's reasons for sending Tong to accompany Tuyet Mai. But there it was. He was certain Tong would at least abandon, or at worst murder Tuyet Mai and return laughing to his communist friends. If at all feasible, Tran would have found a way to kill Tong and no questions asked, but such a rash act would have been too danger-ous. So on the day of Tuyet Mai's and Tong's release, Commandant Tran stood at his window and watched them board the launch that would carry them to the mainland, and eventually to the village Tuyet Mai had so often mentioned in her ravings. Prisoner Tong, wearing civilian clothes, walked beside the litter on which she was being carried, looking down at her with an expression, Tran thought, of either extreme pity or intense disgust. He grabbed his binoculars and peered intently at Tuyet Mai as she was helped off the litter and placed on the ground. *Facial expression flat, emotionless, idiotic.* She walked on her stumps by lifting her body slightly above the concrete and swinging her torso forward. With some trouble, she boarded the launch. Tong joined her, and the distant sound of a revving engine reached the commandant's ears. Carried off by the waves, with engine sputtering and back-firing, the launch disappeared around a rock jetty. Still staring at the empty sea through his binoculars, Tran felt glad to be rid of Tong, yet he also felt regret at Tuyet Mai's departure. Why he experienced this feeling was a mystery to him, as he wished, or thought he wished, to expunge her memory from his mind. Throughout the few remaining years he had left, her image haunted his dreams.

~ *Freedom* ~

Only after Tong and Tuyet Mai had arrived on the mainland and boarded a city bus did she speak. What she said shocked him. Lugging a filthy bag containing all her worldly goods, Tuyet Mai dropped it heavily, looked up from where she swayed in the aisle, and spoke with a slight hissing sound through her broken tooth, "What happened to Guard Dinh?"

What struck Tong the most was how her sharp, intelligent expression had returned, all hint of simple-mindedness evaporated, the veil of stupidity com-pletely vanished. A wave of relief washed over him, but his training held, and he pushed down the excitement and joy, merely smiling. "So, the rumors were true, you were faking it."

"Obviously," she replied flatly. When he did not respond, she looked an-noyed and whispered with some urgency, "What has happened to Guard Dinh?"

Tong felt irritated by her focus on Dinh rather than on him, and he assumed a bemused detachment. "Executed."

"We must go to his mother."

"What!" Tong was even more shocked than before.

"Let's get off at the next stop so we can talk," she said calmly. Tong struggled to conceal his astonishment at how nonchalant she acted considering that she was free for the first time in years.

After getting off the bus, they found a shallow niche between the colonnades of some dilapidated government building. Tong licked his lips and kept looking around nervously. "Are you crazy? We're certainly being followed. Do you want us to be shot?"

"I know where she lives."

"We can't."

"Then leave. I'm going."

Tong compressed his lips and groaned, making clear how much trouble she was causing.

Ignoring his distress, Tuyet Mai started down the street without further word. Tong followed, carrying her bag and grateful that so many people on the sidewalks had lost limbs, making Tuyet Mai merely one more cripple who drew no undue attention. They walked very far, and Tong marveled at how tirelessly she knuckle-walked, lifting her body and swinging it forward, dropping it down like a piston, then starting all over. At last she stopped in front of a shabby concrete house, faced the wooden door and displayed the first signs of indecision.

Seeming to compose herself, or rather, Tong thought, harden herself, she said to him with the firm tone of a general giving a command, "Knock."

He knocked on the door. They waited. No response.

"Knock again," she said with determination. "Harder."

He did.

The door suddenly opened before Tong had time to withdraw his hand. Filling the doorway, bathed in the bright column of sun pouring into the house, stood a stout Buddhist monk, his saffron robe illuminated by the light. The monk gazed at Tong, then looked down at Tuyet Mai, his eyebrows conspicuously, but kindly, raised.

"Yes?" he asked melodiously.

Tong was immediately impressed by the deep, resonant voice and hesitated, somewhat intimidated by this monk's formidable figure.

But Tuyet Mai apparently felt no such compunction. "Is this the house of Madame Pham Thi Hien, mother of Pham Van Dinh?"

A brief hint of sorrow creased the monk's brow, then he brightened and said, "Yes."

"May we see Madame Pham?"

Saying nothing, the monk motioned them inside and led them to a small anteroom off the main hall. Once the front door was closed, the house became cloaked in darkness, illuminated only by a few candles. Tong noticed that black curtains covered the windows, and thick clouds of incense swirled like fog around the dim spheres of candlelight. Upon entering the cramped anteroom, Tong was invited to sit in an ornately carved, straight-backed Chinese chair, the monk remained standing, and Tuyet Mai rested her arm on a wooden chest, waiting patiently.

Putting his hands together under his sleeves and resting them on his stomach, the monk sighed and said, "Pardon me. My name is Kung. Kung Fu Zi." He bowed.

Tong laughed before he could stop himself. "Kung Fu Zi. Confucius. Someone has a sense of humor." He bowed mockingly low. "Didn't know we were in the presence of such a venerable . . . and one so ancient."

Kung beamed guilelessly. "Yes, I have many names, but to Pham Van Dinh I was Master Kung." He looked inquiringly at Tuyet Mai and said, "You have an interest in Pham Van Dinh?"

"His mother," replied Tuyet Mai stiffly. "We know Mr. Pham Van Dinh is now with his ancestors."

Kung looked down and shrugged almost imperceptibly beneath his robes. "As is she."

"Ah," exhaled Tuyet Mai sadly. "Then we are too late. Did she die before or after her son's death?"

"Alas, she died after his execution."

"A broken heart, no doubt," said Tong impatiently.

"No, she ate rat poison. She had been sick for some time and the pain became unbearable. Combined with her son's death . . . ." Kung spread his arms as if in benediction, then smiled. "Her body remains in the other room. I was called by some neighbor, as were the authorities. I am here, they are not."

"Yet," said Tong nervously. "So the police are coming?"

Kung nodded and shrugged his shoulders as if to say, 'What's to be done?'

"So the body is still here," said Tuyet Mai to herself, but heard by the two men.

"Pardon me, one moment," said Kung who slipped out the front door and returned before Tuyet Mai or Tong had time to confer.

Tong rose abruptly. "We must leave."

Tuyet Mai looked at him angrily and said to Kung, "How do you know it was rat poison."

The monk motioned for them to follow, picked up a lighted candle, led them down a short hallway, and parted the curtain to Madame Dinh's room. A narrow shaft of light from the candle fell partially on her bed, illuminating her arm, thin as a twig and hanging limply down the side of the bed. On the small wooden night stand lay an opened box of rat poison. No glass was in sight. A sickly, sweet odor forced them back.

"We're leaving," said Tong with finality. "Is there a back door?" he asked Kung.

Kung tilted his head. "Yes. This way."

They emerged into the bright alley behind the house, Tong thanked the monk and began walking with Tuyet Mai at his side. He felt the urge to walk faster, but knew Tuyet Mai could not keep up. When he paused for her sake, he noticed someone following.

Tong turned his head and saw the monk close behind. "Huh?" he said. "What's this? Where are you going, Venerable Kung Fu Zi?"

Kung showed his teeth. "With you, to Song Nhan village."

~ *Tong and Tuyet Mai Confer* ~

In the back corner of a small tea shop, where Kung had hastily directed them, the three travelers talked in whispers.

"It's no wonder the authorities didn't come. *You* are the authorities, aren't you?"

"Yes. This monk's disguise has worked well, enough to fool Dinh. I think I will keep it permanently." He looked at Tuyet Mai but directed his words at Tong. "What am I to do with this supposed 'half-wit'?"

"Are you to work with me on this mission, whatever it is?" asked Tong, ignoring the subject of Tuyet Mai.

"Yes, except for the fact that you are not to work *with* me, but *for* me. Meanwhile, I repeat, what to do with Tuyet Mai here. She is reported to be simple-minded, but now I see that she is anything but crazy."

"How did you know we would visit Dinh's place?" asked Tong.

Kung grinned amiably. "Didn't. You came while I was checking background details on our beautiful, legless companion here. I've already dismissed the two men following you. Anyway, I found the old lady dead. Others will find her—" he pinched his nose—"soon enough."

Tuyet Mai frowned. "So you are coming with us?"

"Yes," replied Kung firmly.

"Others?"

Kung shook his head. "Only my unworthy self."

Still wearing a disapproving expression, Tuyet Mai said flatly, "It will be like *Journey to the West*, or in this case, to the north, to Song Nhan village. You, Master Kung, will play the role of Xuanzang, Tong will be Monkey, and I will . . . serve you both on our journey."

Kung laughed. "You, dear lady, are remarkable. Why do I feel you have already taken over the leadership of our rather ridiculous little party? No, you will not be a mere servant girl. You will be Guan Yin, Goddess of Mercy. And you had better be prepared to beg for mercy when my superiors find out you have successfully faked madness."

"Wonderful," said Tong bleakly. "Wu Cheng-en had many characters in his novel. All we really need to complete our version is Pigsy."

"Then we are complete," said Kung. "Pigsy is awaiting our arrival. You may remember him from Con Son prison. His name is Ton Van Ninh."

Tong appeared startled. "You mean the prisoner with the grotesque face?"

"That very one."

"What can possibly be so important that it requires all of us to converge on an insignificant little village in the middle of nowhere?"

"Firstly, you are not important, secondly, that information is not to be known by you until it is time. And as for her," Kung glanced at Tuyet Mai, "she will continue to play her own role–that of a simpleminded ex-prisoner."

"Until when?" asked Tuyet Mai.

"Until I am told what to do with you. In the meantime, we will stay in Saigon until I receive orders. Who knows, it might be back to Con Son when they find out the truth."

"In that case, I'm a dead woman," said Tuyet Mai.

The monk's eyes twinkled and he nodded at Tong. "While I am gone, you will be held responsible for keeping her with you. If she disappears while I'm gone, you will follow the path of Madame Pham's son."

Tong stared grimly at the monk, then perked up. "We are now comrades. Must you always make threats? Give me back Master Kung."

Kung did not smile. He plucked at his robe and a look of consternation, even sadness, came over his face.

"After all," said Tong somewhat nervously. "Someone must trust me a little to let me out."

Kung's expression did not change.

~

When evening came, Tong and Tuyet Mai found themselves alone in a squalid hotel room. It was explained to the manager that the two were brother and sister. Tuyet Mai's appearance had deteriorated so much that only the intelligence illuminating her eyes remained as evidence of her once-stunning beauty. No eyebrows were raised at their living arrangements.

Tong felt a secret delight at being with Tuyet Mai as if they were husband and wife. Even the silences that lapsed between them gave him feeling of contentment. More, in fact, than their conversation. She would not respond to his questions about Dinh, and in fact never mentioned him, or his mother, again. Instead, she spoke almost exclusively about Song Nhan village.

"Why are you so intent on returning to that broken down village?" he asked again and again, vexed with her constant harping on Song Nhan.

To each inquiry, she replied, "You wouldn't understand. You couldn't understand."

He tried to divert her attention to more practical matters. "We must plan for what comes after the war is over."

She would just shrug.

"What do you think of this Kung character?"

She would shrug again.

"Tuyet Mai, you must consider the future!" he exclaimed in frustration.

She replied simply, "I am."

But when it came to Song Nhan village, she rhapsodized. "Contentment is in every home, every field, every water buffalo, the air itself."

Tong laughed. "So naive. The disease. The drudge. The filth. Stupidity and superstition."

To this, she shook her head in amusement. "The women joining together. The children playing together. The village growing together. The conversations are not world shaking, but they hold the world together. Yes, yes, there is the work. But work with women. Conversation with women. Together with women. And, as you point out, there is the stupidity." She snorted and looked contemptuously at Tong. "I will deal with women's rumored stupidity rather than with men's proven stupidity."

"But, Tuyet Mai, you must think of your future. A husband. Children."

"A husband?"

"Yes."

"You?"

"Yes."

Tuyet Mai laughed coldly. "Your children?"

"Yes."

She looked down at her stumps, bared her broken tooth, and tugged at her bedraggled, oily hair. "You still want to marry this?"

"Yes."

"Why?" she demanded with vicious insistence.

"I love you."

"Why?" she demanded again. "I am no longer a lotus growing in the mud. I am only the mud."

"I love you."

"No. You love something else."

"What?"

Tuyet Mai paused. "With men, I never know. I used to think they loved ideals. I was wrong. Justice? I was wrong. A cause? Wrong. Then they must, at least, love women and children. Wrong. Very wrong!"

"I agree with you about ideals and justice. Mere excuses for men to acquire power and to kill and conquer. Most, however, love their families."

"Liar! If they loved their families they would love others' families. No. They love the power they wield over their families. I have been the victim of this lust for power too long and too often. It is over."

Strange to say, these words merely inflamed Tong's passion, and though he recognized the feeling, he rebelled against it. *What is this power she holds over me?* he wondered. He knew that Tuyet Mai feared his desire to control, to dominate her. But he knew that she was wrong. What did he desire? Her body? *No longer.* Her mind? *Maybe. After all,* he thought, *she is a cripple. Mutilated. Ugly. And yet . . . and yet what?* He did not know. And yet, for those that could see, still beautiful—no, more beautiful. *It is a mystery.* All he knew was that he truly loved her. That should be reason enough to leave her. Love was not something he ever considered important, in fact, he considered it dangerous. But he was stung by the irony of it–Tuyet Mai understood him in all ways but this way, the most important way, to women at least. *I'm nothing if not a cynic,* he thought. *I view humanity as maggots, the world as torture, self-interest as paramount, survival as the only worthwhile goal. Yet this wretched woman, whose only asset has been destroyed, obsesses me. So, Tong, you are wily. You must have a reason to still desire her–a reason beyond love. Nietzsche said, whatever does not destroy me makes me stronger. I agree. So let me think. What is the reason that I don't understand, but the reason nonetheless, that I have been helping her. It is here, inside me somewhere. Find it, Tong!* So he searched his soul for the reason, certain that it could not be so idiotic as to be simply love. *But if simply love, love of simply what?*

~

Only an instant had passed after Tuyet Mai's last words while he thought these thoughts, but he felt her studying his face and in spite of himself, something passed rapidly over his features, like a shudder or a barely perceptible ripple on smooth water. Aware that she had perceived this shudder, he hoped she would express curiosity, but she remained silent.

"Do you know who now controls Song Nhan?" he asked irritably, just to roil the too-calm waters.

Tuyet Mai appeared troubled. "I assume the puppet government."

"Yes, but only during the day. At night, the Viet Cong and People's Army control."

She shrugged. "So?"

"Tuyet Mai, there will be no contentment in Song Nhan village. You will be forced to choose sides. There will be violence."

She nodded. "I have thought of that."

He waited for her to elaborate, but again she remained stubbornly silent.

"Well?" he asked mockingly.

"My thoughts are my own, but I can tell you that one may find contentment even in the midst of conflict."

"Did you find contentment in Con Son prison?"

"No."

"He smiled triumphantly. "There you have it."

"No, it is two different cases. In Con Son I was alone with demons. In Song Nhan I will be together with goddesses."

"Goddesses! Oh, are you so superstitious?"

"Yes. I am witless, remember? But to put it in terms you will understand–in Con Son I was alone with men and in Song Nhan I will be together with women. Can I be more plain?"

"Where will you stay? Who will take care of you? A goddess?" Tong waited for her response. While he waited, he lit a cigarette and let two streams of smoke flow in gentle currents from his nostrils. When she remained quiet, he raised his eyebrows, having just comprehended the obvious. "Madame Dau?" he asked.

"Yes."

"She's dead." He watched Tuyet Mai stiffen and felt satisfaction at her discomfort.

"How do you know?" she demanded.

"I know." He shrugged.

"I don't believe you."

"Now that you know she's dead, where do you plan to stay?"

"I don't know she's dead. I know you would lie."

"For what purpose?"

"To keep me with you," she said in a monotone, a sure sign he had created doubt.

"To keep you with me, I would stay in Song Nhan, Madame Dau or no Madame Dau."

She laughed guilelessly. "You! The last thing you would be suited for, comrade Tong, is to be a farmer."

He felt a thrill that she had laughed and called him comrade. This gave him the idea that humor would be more persuasive than threats. Laughing with her, he said, "Just like old times, comrade lover."

Too fast. Too soon.

Tuyet Mai hardened her face. "No, not like the old times. Never the old times."

Tong knew he had miscalculated. "Toss me the cigarettes," he said harshly.

Tuyet Mai smiled, knowing he could reach them easier than she. Leaning forward awkwardly so she would not have to move her stumps, she handed him the pack, then drew back in mock submission. "Would you like me to light it for you, master Tong?"

He flared, "Look, Tuyet Mai, I know what you are thinking, but tossing me cigarettes does not make you a slave, nor me a master. I do not want to control you, beat you, rape you, or even to order you around. I want to marry you, but you are sorely testing my patience."

"No test is necessary. I know I do not want to marry you." She was immediately dismayed that she said this, but outwardly stayed the course.

He groaned, but stopped himself from lashing out further. "I am going for some noodles and will return in a few minutes. Please stay. You see, I trust you. In fact, you might say that my fate is in your hands. The best way to get rid of me is to be gone when I return. I will not look for you."

~ *Tuyet Mai Free But Not Alone* ~

After Tong left, Tuyet Mai allowed herself some time to cry. She felt sick to her stomach at Tong's revelation that Madame Dau was dead. True, she harbored serious doubts as to the truthfulness of Tong's statement, but even the possibility threw her plans into disarray, her thoughts into confusion.

Suddenly she heard a voice chuckling in the dark. Kim Lan stepped out from the shadows, her face repugnant from the stagnant weight of death, and Tuyet Mai let out an involuntary gasp.

"Now what are you crying about?" asked the specter. "Last I heard, you were a prisoner in Con Son prison. Now you're free. Last I heard, you were in love with Tong. Now you're with him and he says he loves you. Last I heard, you wanted to go to Song Nhan village. Now you're going. Why the tears?"

Tuyet Mai raised her chin. "Last you heard, I had my teeth. Last you heard, Madame Dau was still alive. Last you heard, I wanted to live."

Kim Lan crumpled to the ground and sighed a heroic sigh. "This again?"

Tears ran unabated down Tuyet Mai's cheek in spite of Kim Lan's calculated histrionics.

Kim Lan turned serious. "It is true, every time I see you, a little more of you is missing. Legs, teeth"–she inspected Tuyet Mai's scalp–"and clumps of hair. Pretty soon, comrade, there will be nothing left but a stubborn ball of gristle."

Tuyet Mai laughed and held out her arms to hug Kim Lan, but at that moment Tong returned. He saw her outstretched arms and thinking they were reaching out to him, threw down the noodles he carried, and rushed to embrace her. As he held her in his arms, he cried, "Have you come to your senses, my love?"

Tuyet Mai's initial impulse was to pull back, but it felt good to be touched by Tong again, and she allowed him to caress her. In spite of her efforts to stop, the tears came even heavier, and she luxuriated in the comforting closeness of his body.

"We must make plans," said Tong as he stroked her hair. "Time is passing."

These words jarred her back to reality. "I have plans," she said more sharply than she wanted.

Tong withdrew his hand, slowly rose, and spoke over his shoulder as he left. "The noodles are here. Eat. I will return shortly."

Tuyet Mai felt panic and wanted to run after him. For the first time since her release from Con Son, she realized how much she loved him. *I may love him but I don't need him*, she thought defiantly, but unconvincingly. Wolfing down the noodles, Tuyet Mai mentally called for Kim Lan to return, but her friend was nowhere to be seen. *She appears when I don't need her, and won't come when I do*, she thought bitterly. The sudden departure of Tong had made her confront the inconvenient need for companionship – she admitted to herself that she no longer wanted to be alone, perhaps no longer could be alone. *After all, he has stuck with me.* But her contrary, suspicious side struck back. *Yes, but he is now working for the puppet government. He needs me to do some illicit task.* She stared bleakly at the filthy window, watching for him to return, listening to the constant roar of motorcycles and people from the street, arguing with herself. *He said we must make plans. He wants to escape them. He knows Hanoi will win. Why would he stay otherwise?* She saw her reflection in the window. *Why would he want to stay with me now? Tuyet Mai, don't be stupid. He's using you. He says he loves you, but he doesn't.*

She waited for hours, hoping he would return, all the while continuing her debate. Finally, she lay on the floor and fell asleep even as she listened above the cacophony of Saigon street noises for the door to open.

~

The first thing she saw when she awoke was Tong squatting next to her.

He smiled and she felt a great weight lifted from her heart, but unwillingly a frown spread across her features.

"You should have woken me sooner," she said. "We have far to go."

"You forget, Tuyet Mai, that we must wait for Master Kung." He chanted Kung's name in mock solemnity, standing with arms folded over his stomach and gazing heavenward as would a pious monk.

In spite of herself, Tuyet Mai laughed.

Encouraged by her response, Tong carried the farce one step further. "In fact, if you disappear"–he jumped upon the bed and rolled behind the other side–"I disappear."

This time, Tuyet Mai frowned disapprovingly. "One must know when to stop, comrade."

Tong smiled sheepishly. "Madame Dau would have laughed." As soon as these words left his mouth, he knew he had made a mistake.

Tuyet Mai stiffened. "Tell me truthfully, Tong, is she dead?"

"I promised myself last night when I walked alone that I would be absolutely truthful with you. I have nothing left to lose."

"Well?"

"As far as I know, she is not dead."

"As I thought!" cried Tuyet Mai angrily.

"That's the problem, comrade, you're not thinking, you're only wishing–hoping against hope. She must be dead by now."

"Why do you say that?"

Kung burst into the room before Tong could answer. "Because," the monk said, his eyes scanning the disheveled bed. "There has been fierce fighting around Song Nhan for years. I have been told that it is now a mere ghost village, only a madman and a few crazy women are left."

Tong was rendered speechless, but Tuyet Mai reacted indignantly. "You were spying on us?"

"Of course," said Kung. "Spying on spies by a spy is perfectly ethical behavior."

"How do you know what Song Nhan village is like?" Tuyet Mai demanded. "It is a small, insignificant fly speck. How do you know? Why does the government care?"

"Because, comrade, Song Nhan is important enough to be our destination." His eyes narrowed. "That is to say, Comrade Tong and I are traveling there. You are to be returned to Con Son Prison."

Tuyet Mai turned white and Tong clutched at his collar, horrified and still unable to speak.

"Unless, of course, you are willing to service us along the way."

"Service you?" Tuyet Mai asked incredulously. "How?"

The monk laughed. "Not the way you're thinking, ugly one—although I can see how you were once beautiful." He glanced at the bed. "And are apparently still capable of serving."

"What do you mean 'service us,' Kung?" asked Tong impatiently.

"I mean she is to put us in touch with her North Vietnamese intelligence comrades. I will remain in my monk disguise, but you, Tong, will be the bait."

"How?"

"Tuyet Mai will claim to have led you to Song Nhan village for capture and interrogation. They believe, Tong, that you have defected to the Saigon government."

Tong paled. "But they won't believe her. She was released. They'll kill her—and me."

"No. We are aware she has a high ranking brother in Hanoi intelligence. He won't let that happen. He might let you be killed, though."

Tong pondered for a moment. "So, my choices are to run away and be hunted down by both sides, to help you and be killed by the communists, or to not help and–"

"And return to Con Son prison," interrupted Kung. "Correct. Pretty bleak, but you at least have a chance with me"–Kung glanced at Tuyet Mai–"and her."

"But why return to Song Nhan village for all this?" asked Tong.

Kung wagged a finger. "Not for you to know. There are other, even more important matters waiting us there." He grinned. "The moving hand writes, and having writ, moves on. Besides, everything I told you may be a lie."

"Why should I 'service' you?" asked Tuyet Mai defiantly. "What's to prevent me from simply returning to my brother in the north?"

"That question, ugly one, is full of interesting answers. Some of the answers I cannot tell you, but they have to do with our journey to Song Nhan village. One of the answers I can tell you. If you return to your communist brothers, we will totally destroy Song Nhan and torture the inhabitants, including Madame Dau."

"Why should I care whether you destroy Song Nhan village?" asked Tuyet Mai, trying to appear disinterested.

Kung merely smiled. "As a Buddhist monk, I can tell you that hell awaits those responsible for murder–particularly the murder of those they love. You see, some things you said when you were at Con Son prison we did not believe, some things you said we did believe. Time will tell which of our determinations were correct and which were not."

"So you never believed that she was mad?" asked Tong incredulously.

"Some of the more gullible of us believed. That also worked to our advantage. Dinh believed, and he is dead. Commandant Tran believed, and he will be dead. Pigsy never believed, and he turns out to be right."

"Ton Van Ninh," said Tong flatly. "Now there is an 'ugly one.'"

"You may not want to say that to his face when we meet him at Song Nhan, Tong."

"His face? I don't even want to look at it, let alone speak to it."

Kung laughed. "You have a good sense of humor, Monkey-king. I hope it lasts throughout our trip. Makes life easier for our little troupe."

"And I hope," said Tuyet Mai, "that Master Xuanzang develops his bodhisattva compassion as we continue our journey."

Kung turned serious. "That, ugly one, is an issue. Now, what is it to be, service us or return to Con Son prison?"

Tuyet Mai looked down at the floor and Tong took advantage of the pause to ask, "If she chooses to return to Con Son, why should I be forced to go on? I can be assigned some other mission."

"You are here because of her," said Kung. "If she is not here, then you are superfluous."

Tuyet Mai spoke up quickly. "I will, as you say, 'service' you when we reach Song Nhan village, but my contacts are old, probably of no value, and I have broken with the communists. I just want to live somewhere quietly."

"In Song Nhan?" asked Kung slyly.

"Why hide it? Yes."

"With the Monkey-king here? The two of you living a nice, quiet country life?"

"Yes."

Tong perked up, but remained silent.

"And turn your back on your brother?" pursued Kung.

"Yes. I did that years ago, when I lost my legs. His way–your way–is no longer my way."

"We know about the battle where you lost your legs. You and your friend led the Americans to their deaths. For that, you will never be"–Kung caught himself, then shrugged–"forgiven."

"Let us start for Song Nhan village," said Tuyet Mai abruptly, "or we'll never get there. How do we travel, Monk Kung?"

"By bus."

"How about money?" asked Tong.

Kung spread his arms and looked heavenward. "Buddha provides."

"Ha! The government spends. The Americans provide."

Kung shot a hard glance at Tong. "And in the same battle in which 'comrade' Tuyet Mai lost her legs, you were involved with a certain Major Vy in illegally transporting drugs. Vy has been executed, thanks to you. What a pair both of you make! Two traitors! A bitch who led Americans to their deaths and a bastard who led a good officer to his death. Both of you betray everything and everyone you touch. And you want to live quiet lives of peace and serenity in Song Nhan village as humble farmers!"

"Talking is not getting us to Song Nhan," said Tuyet Mai quietly. "Although it strikes me that a man impersonating a holy monk and who is probably responsible for more deaths than Tong and I combined, is not one to assume an air of self-righteousness."

When Kung made no answer, Tuyet Mai's face registered disgust, but Tong peered intently into the monk's eyes. He was intrigued to see a twinkle, as if Kung enjoyed the repartee. Or perhaps something else.

~

Tuyet Mai stood on the bench seat at the rear of the bus, tightly holding the aisle pole while Kung and Tong intermittently dozed next to her. She stared out the window, watching the crowded bustle of Saigon gradually diminish as the first signs of the country came into view. Farmers and their womenfolk loped along the roadside, poles on their shoulders bouncing under the weight of vegetables and fruit. She tried to picture herself doing the same thing, carrying produce from Song Nhan to the district capital, but her lack of legs made the image too painful. In Song Nhan she would do other things to make herself useful–clean, husk, sweep, winnow, grind, cook, watch the children–after all, Han Tinh survived doing odd jobs. Or did he? Tuyet Mai had not thought of the little Viet Cong veteran for years. Now, his memory came back to her with a power that took her breath away. He had always seemed to her a silly, yet strangely enigmatic little man. Legless, but somehow imbued with a strength that belied his dwarfish body, she still thought of him as comical. *It is because he is legless that he seems silly*, she thought. *Just like me. I'm just a silly, ugly woman. I wonder, is he still alive? How the Song Nhan women laughed at him!* She looked around, trying to catch someone snickering at her, but the passengers were all attending to their own problems. *For now*, she decided.

She remembered Kung saying that Song Nhan was a devastated village inhabited only by a madman man and a few crazy women. *Is that madman Han Tinh?* she wondered. *Do the crazy women include Madame Dau or was Tong's lie about her death the truth after all?* Fear and trepidation unexpectedly gripped her and she tried to think of other things, but Han Tinh's grinning face kept intruding. She took it as an omen of impending evil.

Soon, the heat became unbearable. Passengers by the windows craned their necks to catch the passing breeze, which brought nothing more refreshing than a hot dampness—more akin to dusty steam than to cooling wind. Those not sitting next to windows had it worse, for the stifling air weighed heavily from the oppressive combination of heat, sweat, and urine. Tuyet Mai could no longer see out the window and felt only tedium that spawned a dull delirium of listlessness and the constant urge to pee. The hum of conversation had long since died down, and only the rasping snores of passengers penetrated the thick, fetid atmosphere.

She felt the top of her head being tapped, and when she looked up expecting to see Tong, her astonishment was so great she could not help uttering a small cry. Kim Lan lay flat on the bus's ceiling, looking down, for all the world appearing to be a two-dimensional billboard advertising cigarettes. In fact, she had a cigarette dangling from her mouth.

Overcoming her initial shock, Tuyet Mai unsuccessfully suppressed a laugh. "You don't smoke," she said chidingly.

A passenger turned to investigate this apparent non-sequitur, so Tuyet Mai decided to whisper.

"Do you have to pee?" she said to Kim Lan.

"Me? Dead people don't pee."

"I do. I don't think I can hold it much longer."

Kim Lan raised her eyebrows. "Do you want me to stop the bus?"

"How can you do that?" asked Tuyet Mai, genuinely puzzled.

"Make it crash."

"Never mind, I can wait. Especially with you here, the time will pass quickly. After all, you don't always come when I call. In fact, I never know when, or where, you'll show up. Sometimes it's very aggravating."

"It's all up to you, since you believe I'm just a figment of your imagination."

"Well," said Tuyet Mai wearily, "I need you now. What am I to do if Song Nhan is destroyed? If Madame Dau is dead? Where will I go?"

Kim Lan pointed at the sleeping Monk Kung. "I'm sure he will decide that, not you."

"But I want nothing to do with them anymore."

"Who? The government, or men?"

"Same thing, but men, yes, men," said Tuyet Mai with feeling.

"But you say you want to live a quiet, peaceful life in Song Nhan village with Tong. Make up your mind, comrade. Men or no men?"

"I do love him."

"Hm!" Kim Lan snorted. "The same old story."

"I'm getting old and ugly. No children. Getting older and uglier by the day. No children. Drying up. Still no children. I want children, Kim Lan. I want the women of Song Nhan to pass around my baby and coo over him. I want that so badly! Tong can give me that."

"Or a bullet in your head," said Kim Lan bitterly. "Like the Americans did to me."

"I want to watch him play. I want to watch over him. Love him."

"Who? Tong?"

Tuyet Mai shot an irritated look at Kim Lan. "You know who I mean."

"So you don't love Tong, you love what he can give you."

"Yes."

"Seed."

"Yes."

"You can buy sacks of it for a few piasters, sister," said Kim Lan disgustedly.

"No, I can sell the burrow into which the seeds are planted, sister, for a few caresses."

"Do you want a baby that badly?"

Tuyet Mai pondered for a moment. "Babies, Kim Lan, babies. They die so easily these days, you know? They grow up to be soldiers and die. Best to have many."

"My babies are dead," cried Kim Lan.

"Are they with you?" asked Tuyet Mai sympathetically.

"No, they are what the living call alive."

~

"Who are you whispering to?" whispered Tong to Tuyet Mai. He glanced upward and winked. "The ceiling?"

"Did you hear what I was saying?"

"No. Couldn't catch it. What were you saying?"

Tuyet Mai was exasperated that her conversation with Kim Lan was interrupted. "I was saying I have to pee. Make the driver stop and let us get off."

Tong moved to the front of the bus with difficulty and asked the driver to pull over.

"Can't," he said.

"Why not? We've not stopped for hours and it already smells like urine in here, and worse. Soon we'll all suffocate."

"Bad place to stop. Viet Cong out there."

"Bullshit!" roared Tong, himself feeling the urge to shit.

"No."

Tong felt himself being pushed aside by another passenger, then recognized Kung leaning over the driver and showing him some document. The driver abruptly pulled over and stopped the bus.

Jungle impinged to the edge of the road, so the passengers were told not to wander far. It was made clear by the aggrieved driver that in ten minutes passengers were to be back in their seats or any malingerers would be left behind.

After Tuyet Mai relieved herself, she went to join Tong and Kung squatting near the bus. As she approached, unseen, she heard Kung saying to Tong, "So, who is this Madame Dau?"

Tuyet Mai stopped and listened.

"An old cow," said Tong. "Provisional Council Chief of Song Nhan village. Don't quite understand, but Tuyet Mai is captivated by the old witch."

Kung appeared skeptical of Tong's simple analysis. "Your dismissal of Madame Dau betrays your ignorance. Tuyet Mai is no dummy. Why is she so captivated? Is Madame Dau an agent?"

Tong snorted. "Don't be stupid! She's a peasant buffalo. Bright enough, for a buffalo, but doesn't understand the bigger picture."

"And you do?" asked Kung.

"Of course. Women are like–"

"Women are like gems," said Tuyet Mai, knuckle-walking up to the two men. She interrupted Tong because she did not want to hear the words he was about to speak, but she heard what she heard and damage was done. The two men laughed but an uncomfortable silence prevailed until the horn honked.

Jungle gave way to interminable rice fields, and Tuyet Mai rehearsed her arrival at Song Nhan village—still at least two days away on Viet Cong-infested roads and trails.

~ *Song Nhan Village is Visited by a Stranger* ~

Madame Dau felt every ache and pain in her aged body as she made her way back to the house from the fields where she had been hoeing. Still, she reminded herself to be grateful that no soldiers had been in Song Nhan village for at least a month. Once she hauled herself up the few steps to her porch, still charred from the fire years earlier that had destroyed most of the village, she removed her hat and sank against the wall. As she looked out at the nearly deserted village, sadness welled up in her like an old, unforgiving enemy, deathless, numbing—yet somehow comfortably familiar. For a moment, she willed the destroyed houses and huts to magically return to their former condition, but she could not hold the image long.

A few houses had been rebuilt, but even those were done in a slipshod, temporary manner, hers included. Only a very few, stubborn older women remained, having sent their younger family members away to the district capital. With years to languish in her plight, Madame Dau clung even closer to those villagers who remained. Although she missed her daughter and grandson terribly, and while the deepening creases continued to inexorably erode her dark face and neck, her great compensation was the company of Han Tinh, Old Nguyen, and Madame Vit. Han Tinh, the legless Viet Cong veteran, seemed to hover around Madame Dau like a needy relative, always joking, but never very far away. Nguyen and Vit reminisced about the old days, and told and retold stories about the history and people of the village who had long since joined the ancestors. Occasionally, food and money would find its way to the village from more fortunate relatives living in the district capital, enough to supplement their meager stocks and ward off starvation.

A faint smile, part pain and part love, softened her face when Han Tinh appeared knuckle-walking down the road. Before reaching her porch, he shouted, "So! Beautiful Council Chief! You won't believe what I just saw!"

Madame Dau could tell by his demeanor that what he had seen was not serious. She held her hand to block the sun and said, "What have you seen, brother?"

"Brother? Why do you break my heart, calling me brother? I want to be your lover, your beloved, laying next to you in–"

"Hush!" scolded Madame Dau, but her heart wasn't in it, and her tone carried the hint of a chuckle. "Why must you be so lewd? Behave yourself and tell me what you saw, unless it is something else lewd."

Struggling up the steps, Han Tinh stood on his stumps before Madame Dau, breathing deeply, for he was getting older and the exertion of climbing became harder. At last he calmed enough to speak. "Council Chief Dau, it causes me great pain when you scold me so harshly. My only crime is to love you, to want you, to–"

"Tinh! Either tell me what you saw or leave."

"I saw a ghost standing at Schoolmistress Nang's grave."

Madame Dau made a disgusted face and looked askance. "Tinh, why do you play the fool?"

"Truly, I saw a ghost."

"Whose ghost?"

"Schoolmistress Nang, of course."

"How do you know it was her?"

He made a face. "Ugly."

"Oh, Tinh. The day is getting short, I have much to do, and you tell me ghost stories?"

"Can you guess how else I realized it was Nang?"

"No, and I don't care. It is true that I believe in ghosts and spirits, Tinh, because I have seen them." She shuddered. "I have seen them many times, one in particular. He, or she, warned me about the attack that destroyed our village. Oh, my god, even now the memory. . . . "

Tinh felt ashamed at bringing up the ghost. "No, no. Don't let those memories come, Dau. You have told me many times about that ghost. All of them. I also remember those days. Many ghosts came, and I also saw them. I really did. But this one is different. It's Nang, still hissing between her broken teeth, twisting and turning her ugly, skinny little body."

"Last time you told me about a twisting, turning ghost, it turned out to be smoke from Le Ly's coal that she buried while it was still hot."

"Yes, that's true. But this one was real. Can I spend the night with you? The ghost scared me." Even Tinh could not keep a straight face when he said this, and he laughed with Dau at the thought.

"Poor little boy," said Dau like a mother to a toddler. "Great, decorated Viet Cong veteran, killer of many Americans, protector of Song Nhan village, afraid of the Schoolmistress's ghost. Tch, tch. Now, what do you really want?"

"To sleep with you."

Dau reached for a tin cup that lay against the wall and picked it up intending to throw it at Tinh's head, but her arm stopped in mid-air when she heard the approaching Madame Vit laughing in a high-pitched squeal.

"Ha, ha, ha! So it's to be murder in the village? And with so many witnesses, Madame Dau? If you kill this mischievous little Viet Cong monk, I must testify to the district chief that you have rid the village of a large and destructive rat." She joined them on the porch. "And what has this fool been telling you?" she asked.

Madame Dau looked at Tinh with an accusatorial expression. "He brought great and important news. He said he saw Schoolmistress Nang's ghost."

"Hm!" Vit uttered a dismissive grunt and turned to Dau. "I have some turnip greens for you. Came early." She dropped them on the porch and squatted. "Now we can live a few days longer."

"Ah!" cooed Madame Dau surveying the greens. "The only good thing about not having food and starving is that soldiers no longer come."

"Yes, no food, no soldiers, that is true," said Vit. "But just as important, no pretty young women to rape also keeps the devils away."

Tinh uttered a squeal of protest. "Don't be ridiculous! You are both quite beautiful. I would come to rape you any day, food or no food"—he assumed an air of tragedy—"that is if I were still a soldier."

Still holding the cup, Madame Dau let fly and hit Tinh square in the chest. "Fool!" she said disgustedly.

But far from being chastised by his being the recipient of both cup and comeuppance, Tinh turned serious. He snatched the cup from the ground and turned it slowly in front of his face, as if scrutinizing it for defects. His thoughts, however, were evidently fixed on some other subject, for he said solemnly, "Seriously, I have something important to tell both of you."

Both women picked at the turnip greens and waited in uneasy silence.

Tinh seemed to be gathering himself, reining in his clownish urges and pausing to insure that the gravity of his words would acquire increased weight. "I was kidding about Schoolmistress Nang's ghost," he said at last. "But I was not kidding about seeing a ghost–or rather, ghosts.

"You see, I could not sleep last night, so I went outside to pass the time. The moon was bright and I found myself standing near Nang's grave—I don't know why—I just stood there without any reason for having chosen that spot. That's when I saw them, two of them, standing close to each other, embracing—at least, that's what it looked like—and speaking words I could not make out."

"Who were they?" asked Vit.

"That's the strange thing," replied Tinh. "Didn't recognize them, but one of them was definitely an American."

"What?" both women cried simultaneously.

"Yes, an American. Young."

"Must be the spirit of a dead soldier," said Madame Dau. "And the other?"

"A young Vietnamese girl. Not from this village, and yet, she looked familiar. Not only that, the young boy was no soldier."

"How do you know?" asked Vit.

Tinh shook his head. "Civilian clothes, maybe too young, didn't look like a soldier. No, definitely not a soldier. I do know that both were speaking English to each other."

The women looked at each other uneasily. "Strange," said Madame Dau. "What's an American spirit doing here?"

Vit nervously twisted a turnip green she had been holding. "And with a Vietnamese girl, especially one not from this village."

"The entire world is restless," Madame Dau sighed. "They must have come from very far away." She looked up at Tinh, skepticism in her eyes. "Are you sure, Brother Tinh?"

Tinh rolled his eyes. "You doubt me, beloved Council Chief? No. On my honor as a Viet Cong comrade, it is true."

"Well, what happened to them?"

Tinh looked confused. "What do you mean?"

"I mean, what did they do next? You said they were embracing. Is that all? What happened to them?"

"Ah," said Tinh, tilting his head, evidently mulling over whether he should go on. "Again, something strange. I don't know how, but all three of us were somehow transported to the tunnel entrance, you know, the one near the old fortress. I watched them both open the trap door and descend into the tunnel. Other spirits stood around watching, but I couldn't make them out, just shadows."

Madame Dau had stopped breathing when she heard this story. Against her will, with a cracking voice, she asked, "Brother Tinh, this is important, are you sure, very sure, that this is true? Please do not joke."

"Yes, I am sure."

"Then what happened?" asked Vit, alarmed by the impact this was having on Madame Dau.

Tinh shrugged. "Nothing. I just came back to my senses, still standing near Nang's grave, no spirits in sight."

"What does it mean?" asked Madame Dau.

"It's not good," said Tinh glumly.

"We need a wizard to tell us what it means," said Madame Dau.

"Sure," said Vit. "Who will pay?"

"We could take up a collection from the village."

"Sure," repeated Vit shaking her head.

"No, I mean it. We don't have to pay in cash, we can pay in rice."

"Rice!" scoffed Vit. "We don't have enough to feed ourselves."

"We don't need a wizard," pouted Tinh. "I'll be your wizard."

"Ha!" laughed Vit. "You?"

Tinh became genuinely mad. "It was I that first saw the ghosts! I who saw Goddess! I who . . . " his words trailed off, mouth still open as if he had suddenly become a half-wit. "Or maybe that young girl *is* from this village." He fell silent, then one word croaked from the depths of his throat. "Her."

Madame Dau and Vit glanced nervously at each other.

"Who?" asked Madame Dau.

A look of comprehension transformed Tinh's face. "Of course, it's *Her* doing."

Before the two women could respond, a voice called out in a ghastly, brittle tone, "Hey, comrades! Is this Song Nhan Village?"

They looked around to see a diminutive, pockmarked stranger dressed in rags approaching. As he drew nearer, it became apparent the man was disfigured. Noxious fluid drained from a hole where his nose should have been while the lower part of his face was encrusted with islands of scabrous sores surrounded by tufts of filthy beard.

Madame Dau, Vit, and Han Tinh each felt the hair on the back of their necks stiffen.

Chapter Seventeen

Mark Begins His Journey

Momentous Adventure

~ *Departure* ~

The airport. Ticket surrendered. Boarding pass at the ready, Mark turns to scan the waiting room one last time. No recognizable face. He enters the boarding ramp without a wave or a hug or a kiss. Father refused to come, choosing instead to seek sanctuary in his stubbornness. Professor Benson has already performed the libations of briefings and partings so he felt no need to see Mark off at the airport with lingering farewells. Sarah has not come because Mark asked her not to, a decision he now regrets. Alone, Mark shudders at the madness of his adventure. He finds his aisle seat and struggles to control a deep, pervasive dread that has unexpectedly come over him. His stomach feels queasy.

To pass the time, he checks out the faces of the boarding passengers, hoping a pretty girl sits next to him, yet knowing the odds are against it. Sure enough, he cannot even spot an attractive face among the entire lot. Even the cabin attendants are unremarkable. As he feared, a heavy-set man with a florid face and distracted scowl plops in the adjoining seat. Mark nods in greeting, then pretends to read the airline magazine. Much to his relief, the florid-faced, heavy-set man appears uninterested in talk. Once the plane reaches cruising altitude, Mark's neighbor quickly falls asleep, snoring in a persistently low growl.

Relieved to be spared prying eyes, Mark removes a sheaf of papers from his carry-on bag and peruses them for the umpteenth time. The brochures provided by the travel agency promote in full color "all the wonders of that ancient land of adventure and mystery–Vietnam." While the overblown prose of the brochures excites him, much to his dismay, since he wants to remain calm and detached from such dross, he is most interested in the background and company history of the travel agency Professor Benson has hired to conduct him on his journey. Of particular interest is the list of agents working for the company. There are four names beneath Mark's destination, Kon Tum province.

Bay Minh Duy

Hieu Dung Dinh

My-duyen Tong

Huy Tan Thanh

Much to Mark's chagrin, no pictures accompany the names.

Having checked with a professor of Vietnamese language at Columbia, Mark knows that only one is a female—My-duyen Tong. "One chance in four," he whispers, glancing at his snoring neighbor. Then he remembers his luck, or lack thereof. "Ain't gonna happen."

"What ain't gonna happen?" asks the florid-faced, heavy-set neighbor, suddenly awake and fully prepared to talk.

"Oh, sorry, didn't know I spoke out loud," says Mark, genuinely apologetic.

"You didn't. I just have good hearing. You said under your breath, 'One chance in four. Ain't gonna happen.' That's what you said, softly but quite clearly. I hear things like that, can't help it."

"Yeah. I was just figuring the odds of, well, of getting a beautiful travel guide instead of. . . ." Mark's words fade out and he shakes his head.

"Someone who looks like me?" He laughs.

Mark does not respond, merely chuckling politely. The florid-faced, heavy-set man thrusts out his hand. "I'm Ben Cartwright. You know, like the old T.V. cowboy series *Bonanza. Dum dee dee dum dee dee dum dum.*"

"Nice to meet you, I'm Mark Benson."

"First time to Vietnam?"

Mark nods. "Yup."

"Well, I've been there *beaucoup* times."

"Business?" asks Mark, trying to convey disinterest by assuming a lethargic tone.

Unfazed, Cartwright responds, "Yeah. Money to be made—if you know what you're doing." He ends this insight with a cautionary flourish.

Suddenly alert, Mark lies. "Well, I'm a business major and I'm interested in profit, so how do you make money?"

Cartwright rolls his eyes in a friendly, exaggerated manner. "Smart business major like you should know." He inexplicably pushes in one nostril with his index finger. "Look around. Spot opportunity. Jump!"

"What kind of opportunity?"

Cartwright leans closer to Mark and speaks in a low voice. "Tunnels and caves and battlefields, for example."

Mark leans away from Cartwright, partly from instinct and partly from the man's foul breath. "What?" he utters weakly.

"Tunnels and caves, boy. Tourists. You know how many Vietnam vets there are that want to go back and relive, or revisit, or pretend they saw combat? They'll line up in droves to crawl through tunnels. Bring their sons with em too, just to show how tough it was."

"But Vietnam is communist. Tourism is nationalized. You can't buy, or control, or rent, or whatever, any old battle sites, can you?"

Cartwright laughs at Mark's naïveté. "Of course not. But you can manage, for a slice of the action, for a fee, you know?" He rubs his fingertips. "A little oil works wonders in this country. Bribe some local yokel official, sponsor a group of vets, work with a local tourist agency, and presto! *Beaucoup* bucks."

"Is that how you're making money now?" asks Mark.

"Naw. Import-export," says Cartwright evasively.

"What do you import and export?"

"Stuff. Things. Trinkets. Rice. Handicrafts. Whatever. Opportunity, remember? Jump, boy, jump."

Mark nods as wisely as he could manage at his age.

"Hmm. That's interesting."

"So why are you going?" asks Cartwright. "Let me guess, tourist college boy? History, war, suffering, all that romantic bilge?"

Mark feels suddenly important. "No. A working trip. Research. Writing a book."

"You are?" says Cartwright, impressed.

"Yes. I'm writing a book about a particular battle. Well, in collaboration with a professor."

Just then the flight attendant hovers over them. "Anything to drink?" she asks sweetly.

"What do ya have?" asks Cartwright.

"Coke, 7-Up, water–"

"Got any wine," interrupts Cartwright.

"Red or white?"

Cartwright mulls for a few seconds. "Tell you what. I'll have a vodka tonic, okay sweetie?"

"Sure. And you," she looks at Mark, admirably concealing her irritation.

"Coke, thanks."

Her smile is forced. The Coke is delivered first, then the vodka tonic. Cartwright sips his drink, then stares at Mark, seemingly ready to catch any fleeting but revealing facial expression. Conversation continues.

"What battle?" asks Cartwright as if they were never interrupted.

"Just a small one, in Kon Tum province."

"Kon Tum province?"

"Yeah, why?"

"No reason." Cartwright shrugs.

"Do you know that province?" Mark presses.

"Yeah. Interesting place."

"Why?"

"Just is. I mean, I don't know it real well. Just passed over it in a small plane on my way to some other place."

"So, what made it interesting?"

"Well, I guess it wasn't what I saw that made it interesting. It was the people I was with who told me about it that made it interesting." Cartwright paused, then smiled and nodded his head knowingly. "Particularly one of them."

Mark waits, but nothing more is forthcoming. Finally, he says with some emotion, "Come on, you can't stop now. After all, that's where I'm going. What did he say?"

Cartwright looks a little puzzled and stares out the window for some time. He turns, and with a puzzled look still on his face, says, "Wasn't a man. Was a woman. A black woman." He shakes his head. "Go figure."

Mark turns pale. "An American?" he asks.

Cartwright again shakes his head. "Don't honestly know. Could be any nationality. I couldn't pin down her accent, which is strange because I'm always able to do that, I mean tell where someone is from. Not this case. Could be any nationality. Strange woman." He looks at his hands and turns them palm up, as if at a loss. "I don't remember the details. Just that . . . the place . . . it was a hotbed of Viet Cong and NVA activity. Lots of . . . well, according to her, lots of . . . interesting . . . you know, political and military points of interest. I was gonna visit it, but in those days the province was off-limits to foreigners. May still be, as far as I know. In fact, she told me about this one incident–" He breaks off and again shakes his head. "Don't know, can't remember it too well. Anyway, that's where I got my idea about tunnels and caves. But, just haven't had the time to follow-up. Need to, though." He straightens in his seat. "Remember, you must jump at opportunity when it strikes."

"What was this woman's name?" asks Mark, staring intently at Cartwright.

"Can't remember."

"Was it Ethyl?"

"Maybe. Why are you so interested?"

"What did she look like?" Mark says, ignoring the last question.

"I don't know, kind of short. Just looked like an old black woman, although she didn't talk like one. Sounded American . . . I think, but could've been South African, you know, slight British–black–Dutch accent. Still, I thought she was American. But maybe she was South African . . . well, I just don't remember, sorry kid. I was more interested in her companion. A beautiful woman. White. The black lady said it was her doctor, but wow! What a doctor! She was gorgeous, but didn't talk much. Strange pair."

"How long ago was this?"

Cartwright leans forward and peers into Mark's eyes. "Alright, alright. Why the fifth degree?"

"Possible competitors of my book," Mark lies. "Might scoop me. You know how it is."

"Yeah," says Cartwright unconvinced.

"So, when did this happen?"

"Don't know. About a year ago, I guess. I'm going to get some shuteye." Clearly suspicious, Cartwright appears disinclined to answer any further questions and closes his eyes.

Mark falls silent, his mind racing, his heart sinking. *Plots*, he thinks. *Conspiracies. But conspiracies to do what? And plots against who? Cartwright mentioned an 'incident' in Kon Tum province. What incident? Damn! Forgot to ask. Must remember to ask when he wakes up.*

As these disturbing thoughts roil in his head, the light laughter of a passenger moving down the aisle reaches his ears and he glances at a passing figure. African American. A woman. But her face has passed before Mark can make out any features. Nevertheless, she is the right height, the right shape, the right . . . everything. Ready to believe anything, Mark jumps up and rushes to follow. He sees the lavatory door close and decides to wait until the occupant emerges.

Experiencing one of those moments when fear, wonder, anticipation, excitement, and skepticism mix together to form an amorphous ambiguity, Mark stands awkwardly. Self-consciously waiting. As he waits, each emotion plays solo in turn. It seems an inordinate amount of time passes, and still no show. For the twentieth time, he looks at the "occupied" sign.

Finally, the latch is pushed and a person emerges. White. Female. In her fifties. She glances at Mark and smiles apologetically. For lack of a better idea and to make himself less conspicuous, he enters the lavatory and slides the lock shut. He looks around and sees no message written in lipstick on the mirror. No mysterious notes. No hidden film. Nothing. He returns to his seat where his neighbor has resumed snoring.

What are the odds of sitting next to a guy like Cartwright on a plane full of strangers? Kind of creepy, actually. Still, Vietnam is a small country—lots of chances to meet someone with some connection. Anyway, if my luck holds, my odds are better at getting a female guide instead of some troll. He shakes his head and glances at the slumbering Cartwright. *Still, it's strange. . . .*

For the remainder of the ten-hour flight, Mark and Cartwright exchange only occasional banal pleasantries. Mark tries to block any thoughts of Ethyl and Theresa, so he occupies his mind by distractedly sucking on the teat of his laptop and imagining who will greet him at the Saigon airport. *Let it be a pretty guide*, he thinks. *If she's ugly, then let it be a guy who can speak good English. But if it's a woman, let her be pretty.* These fervent wishes are still at the forefront of his thoughts when the plane lands.

One step off the cool plane and the sun sears his senses even as humidity soaks his soul. Thoughts of energetic exploration are siphoned away by the oppressive heat and he reaches the blessed terminal building a wilted rag, squeezed through customs amidst a swirl of other rags. Cartwright, ahead in the heaving line, does not turn and soon disappears in the chaotic press of sopping humanity. Rushed past a prickly official, he staggers under the weight of the heat and emerges desperate to escape, anxiously searching the assembled throng of greeters.

~ *Tong Thi My-duyen* ~

Standing behind the arrival gate amongst a large, jostling crowd, waving a sign on which is written "Welcome Mark Powers," appears a young woman more beautiful than Mark has ever seen, or, to him, more beautiful than he could ever have hoped to see in a hundred lifetimes. The perfection of her features takes his breath away, although the extreme heat and humidity have already made breathing a difficult enterprise. Disbelieving his luck, he rereads the sign numerous times to make sure there is no mistake. Certainty established, he takes a gulp of air, mentally curses his splotchy, overheated face, smooths his sweat-soaked hair, then walks up to her with a smile and an extended hand. Her slender figure is accentuated by the simple elegance of a white *ao dai*.

"Welcome!" exclaims the stunning girl in the beautiful white *ao dai*. As Mark shakes her hand, he notices something about her demeanor that bespeaks amusement with the whole affair, and immediately upon his replying, "Thank you," she bursts out laughing. In fact, her laughter is so genuine and irresistible that others around them join in.

But she is not at all like I thought Vietnamese would act, he thinks. *No war weariness, no solemn communist formality, no*

Mark's thoughts are interrupted by this delightful girl smiling broadly and gesticulating enthusiastically. "We go. I have hotel reservations and we travel first to hotel."

Mark notices the first signs of her imperfect English, but it makes her even more charming. *I'm in love after only spending five minutes in Vietnam.* Before he can reflect further on his good luck, she has already slipped through the crowd and he rushes to catch up.

Pulling his luggage behind him, he follows her out to the sidewalk where, presumably, a car awaits. Mark trails after her like an obedient dog, unable to look away. Gradually, he begins to close the distance between them. A beautiful back. About ten steps ahead. Return to her back. Beautiful back. Her head is turned. A graceful neck. A delicate profile. Dark hair blowing freely in the wind. A fine nose and chin. Beautiful. Now about five steps ahead. Return to her neck. So perfect! Return to her back. Gorgeous legs, perfect calves. Ankles not too thick, not too skinny. Return to her back, her neck, her hair. Only two steps ahead! Beautiful. I'm getting close. And look at her hands. Nice, long, graceful fingers—no polish, clean, well-manicured—perfect! Now only a step away. Five, four, three—speed up—two, one. . . .

~

"What is your name," says Mark casually as he falls into step beside her. She flinches. "Oh, sorry to startle you," he blurts, embarrassed.

"That's okay. My name is My-duyen Tong," she replies boldly. "Hello. Do I walk too fast?"

"Yes, no, thank you."

She smiles. "That's okay. Here is car. Please enter. The driver put your bags in tunk."

"Oh, you mean trunk. Great. Thank you."

She rewards him with a brilliant smile. "Trunk, trunk," she repeats.

Before he can say more, she has hustled him into the back seat and takes her place in the front next to the driver, much to his chagrin.

So far, Mark has not even thought to look out at this new, exotic country. For him there is only one country now, and he is its loyal subject, steadfast and true.

Awkward silence. She shades her eyes with her hand and looks out at the scene. "Beautiful day in Vietnam. Did you have good trip?"

"Yes, thank you."

As she describes the street scenes and various landmarks, he is quick to ask questions so that she is forced to turn around to answer, thus giving him a better view of her extraordinary face. When they arrive at the hotel, she efficiently checks him in. In his infatuation, he does not notice the clerk looking askance at My-duyen.

"Tomorrow I meet you here in lobby at 9:00 for first day's schedule of activities. I take you sightseeing in Ho Chi Minh City. You shop. Now rest."

"What about dinner tonight?" he asks somewhat sheepishly.

She looks amused and Mark feels foolish, so he quickly adds, "I mean, do you know a good restaurant? Maybe you can show me?"

My-duyen laughs infectiously, then shakes her finger at him playfully. "You eat here at hotel. Good food for Americans. Tomorrow at 9:00 I meet you here in lobby. Bye bye."

Mark watches her leave and he feels even more foolish, but excited about the next day. That night, laying in bed reviewing the events of the day, he remembers that he never asked Cartwright about that 'incident' in Kon Tum province.

~

Next morning. Hot. Humid. Sightseeing. The only sight Mark wants to see is My-duyen. Nevertheless, he plays the good tourist and takes voluminous pictures, all with his beautiful guide in the frame. As evening approaches and the shadows deepen in the Buddhist temple they are visiting, My-duyen asks what Mark wants to see the next day. "Second day in Saigon is free day," she explains. "Jet lag always catches up on second day, not first. You want rest or see sights?"

For the first time, Mark's attention is drawn completely away from her.

"Con Son prison," he answers firmly.

My-duyen's normally amiable expression changes to one of concern. "What you say?" she asks.

"Con Son prison. I understand it was a terrible prison during the war where Viet Cong prisoners were tortured and killed by the South Vietnamese government. I would like to see it. Are tourists allowed? I understand that they are allowed."

At a loss, My-duyen stammers, "I will check to see. But this is very bad place."

"I know."

"Why you want go?"

"I study history. It is history."

"No. It is death." My-duyen shudders. "You not go there. It is very bad place. Maybe we go to other place of history. There is American War museum very close to hotel. Many equipments from war. Tanks. Airplanes. We go to that place for history. Okay?"

"But I want to see Con Son prison. I know the government allows tourists. No?"

She frowns, attempts a smile, fails, and says, "I check, okay?"

"Okay."

Silence.

Mark brightens. "Can we have dinner together? Now? I'm hungry and I do not want to eat at the hotel again."

Still appearing troubled, she says, "I show you nice place to eat close to hotel. You eat and I go to check on request about Con Son prison. Okay?"

In misery, he eats alone and spends a sleepless night awaiting her response. When it comes the next morning, everything changes.

~ *Con Son Prison Revisited* ~

While the launch putters toward Con Son Island, My-duyen remains silent and distracted, trailing her hand in the South China Sea as it swirls around the battered wooden hull. Occasionally she shakes her head, and Mark ceases trying to cheer her up with inane observations of the weather. Besides, he is beginning to feel an inner chill, a premonition of malice from her that has the odd effect of making him sense an awakening of evil in himself.

Weather-beaten and cracked, the old, abandoned concrete prison buildings have preserved and even amplified their power to repel. The dark interiors are made drearier by the stains of unidentifiable fluids, while the musty atmosphere is permeated by the stench of fungus and rot. After landing, My-duyen dismisses the guide and is herself leading Mark through the labyrinthine hallways by the beam of a dim flashlight. He sees her teeth, yellow in the pale light as she tells him they are going to visit the tiger cages where prisoners "were tortured."

Feeling an inexplicable defiance, Mark responds, "Good!" with exaggerated enthusiasm, watching her scornful smile beckon him to follow. Her beauty in this dreary place has lost its power to attract and connect, but is immeasurably strengthened in its power to alienate and to divide.

She passes a number of cell doors until she reaches one marked '46.'

"This is tiger cage where government kept VC prisoners, enemies of the great American dragon." My-duyen pushes open the rusted iron door and steps aside to allow Mark entry. As he steps in, he looks up at the iron grille ceiling, beyond which the vaulted blue sky incongruously shimmers. He stares at the raised stone platform where prisoners 'slept,' taking in the dark stains running down the sides.

"My mother tortured here," says My-duyen quietly.

Mark is startled by her words. "What did she do?"

"Nothing."

"She must have done something."

My-duyen looks defiant. "She fight for our country. That all."

"VC?" Mark asks gruffly, remembering his father and feeling the need to defend.

"Freedom fighter."

"Both sides were fighting for freedom."

My-duyen grimaces. "Whose freedom?"

The evil has Mark, and it twists. "Freedom from . . . tyranny."

"What?"

"I mean, freedom from bad people."

"Communists?" she asks as a challenge.

"Yes," he says with finality. Under normal circumstances with a more typical female guide, My-duyen would have devolved, for Mark, into that faceless mass of women, particularly Asian women, whose female scars, their public female personas, render them to the male psyche as nothing more than featureless stereotypes—either submissive slaves or histrionic tigers—and worse, irritating. Their sexuality perverted into an easy target to dominate; feeding male fantasies to command the weak, silence the uppity, and punish the irritating. But this one is clearly intelligent and possesses an unapologetic emotional strength. Mark feels perverse pleasure in My-duyen's anger.

My-duyen, no less possessed and angry that he made her come to this wicked place, turns on him. "My mother told me about it. Americans capture her. Destroy her legs. Rape her. Puppet soldiers also rape her. Torture her here. Destroy her face. Destroy her beauty. Here! In this room! You like? Find interesting? Find history? A story for rich Americans' pleasure?"

Mark, spurred by the evil, feels unmoved. Angry. "Many people suffered. My father! He's still sick because he fought to free your people."

"He have legs?"

"Yes, thank god."

"A face . . . teeth?"

"Yes."

"My mother–"

"Your mother!" Mark snarls. "There was a war. Your mother was an enemy." He chuckles disdainfully. "Somebody once said to make an omelet, eggs must be broken."

"My mother no egg."

"But she was once an egg, as were you, until your father . . . made the pale-yellow yolk bright enough and strong enough to crack the world." Mark feels his remark is quite clever, and it breaks the tension just enough to allow a glimmer of her humanity back into his dark soul. He sees her confusion at his remark, and senses her efforts to filter the unfamiliar English phraseology into an understandable Vietnamese framework. Her anger, temporarily stymied by a language barrier, is now manifested in a heaving chest. This simple sight brings him back from the brink, and he feels the slap of sex. Suddenly, desperate to escape the evil tiger cage, he is impelled to seek open space and fresh air.

Before My-duyen can muster a response to his last comment, Mark grabs her hand and blurts, "Let's go!"

Retracing their steps back through the labyrinth, they emerge into the light where he takes stock of the damage. She is still visibly upset, but a cloud of ambiguity softens her features. Some primal male urge tells him to back off. Conciliate now, before she slips back into resentful anger–potentially fatal for a fragile, embryonic relationship.

He smiles his most conspicuously benevolent smile and directs her to sit on the concrete steps with him. "I'm sorry about your mother. Tell me about your mother. Is she still alive?"

Mark waits. Watches. *Which way will she go?* he wonders.

Her face up to this point a welter of confusion, My-duyen smiles as if nothing had happened. "Now we go back to mainland. I show you many things in Ho Chi Minh City next two days." She pauses, but before Mark can answer, she looks back at the prison with a troubled expression. "Besides, not like this. Something is wrong. Make me confused. Make me angry, a little. He not know true way. He sick in mind. Others are right."

"Who? What 'others'?"

A frown greets his question. "This place a crooked dream"—then a smile—"breaks eggs. I show you many things in Ho Chi Minh City next two days where eggs not broken. Okay?"

Immensely relieved, Mark says, "Okay. But then what?"

"Then we travel to village you request to visit. We go to Song Nhan village. We go to my mother who can answer questions herself"—her smile hardens—"if she will see you."

"So, your mother is still alive?" Mark asks. He cannot help but insert an accusatory tone of 'then it wasn't as bad as you claim' into his words.

My-duyen evidently does not notice. She replies in a fragile voice, "No. Not really alive. No."

~ *Theresa and Michael at Home* ~

Michael turns his thoughts from Mark and his pretty Vietnamese guide and stares at Theresa. "What do you want to do tonight?" he asks gruffly, searching for some activity that will reinvigorate the autopilot dullness of life with her.

"Whatever you want."

"Hm. Well, you tell me."

Theresa tightens her lips, then says, "It's up to you, Michael. Really, I don't have a preference."

"Fine, I don't care either. We can just read."

She picks up a magazine.

He waits to see whether she'll actually read it.
She does.
He sighs deeply and picks up a book.
She does not look up.
"I'm seeing Dr. Toomey tomorrow. I think I need stronger medication."
"Why?"
"Hallucinations are back."
"Which ones?"
"You."

Chapter Eighteen

PART FOUR: CONFLICT

Arrival and Departure

~ *Mysterious Visitor* ~

"Well, comrades, I'm waiting. Am I in Song Nhan village or not?" the repulsive-looking stranger repeated. Madame Dau instinctively averted her eyes from his ravaged face, while Madame Vit pretended to search for some imaginary lost item. Han Tinh, characteristically, focused all his energy on the stranger.

"Eh, brother, you're treading on it!" cried Tinh. "Step softly or you'll wake the spirits!"

The stranger appraised him with amusement. "You look like a spirit yourself, brother." He glanced around. "Where is everyone?"

Han Tinh knuckle-walked to the porch's edge, his words tumbling over each other in haste. "Dead. Flown away. Gone. What village are you from? What's your name?"

"Huh? Village? I'm from Saigon. My name is Ton Van Ninh." He wiped the noxious ooze from his sores with a damp sleeve and continued. "You haven't seen three travelers, have you?"

Han Tinh shielded his eyes and scanned the empty village, as if it were bustling with life. "What do they look like?"

The stranger looked down and chuckled, whether malevolent or mirthful was impossible to tell. "You couldn't miss them. A big man with a southern accent, a little man fond of clever sayings, and a woman with no legs."

Han Tinh shot upright, eyes wide with anticipation. "A woman with no legs? Brother, do you speak the truth, or are you mocking me?"

Ninh stepped onto the porch and studied Madame Dau and Madame Vit. "Yes, I speak the truth. These travelers will arrive here soon and will need a place to stay." He stared at Madame Dau. "Mother, do you know where they can stay?"

When he had spoken of the woman with no legs, he had ignored Han Tinh and fixed on her. A brief flicker—interest, recognition, or something more—had passed across her eyes. Her face had gone pale, though now she betrayed no emotion.

~

Madame Dau wanted to snap at this stranger, tell him there was no place for the travelers, but his ugliness frightened her, and she returned to staring blankly at the ground. Madame Vit, who had been mulling something over, suddenly broke the silence with words that made Dau cringe.

"That one! The one with no legs that stayed with you! Maybe it's her! After the Americans—" Vit stopped short, horrified by her own recklessness.

Ton Van Ninh raised the ragged remnant of his eyebrow inquisitively. When nothing more was forthcoming, he said, "Go on."

Vit licked her lips and glanced at Madame Dau. "That was a long time ago."

"What was a long time ago?" asked Ninh.

"A battle. Some woman was wounded. Legs gone."

Ninh bared his few yellow, crooked teeth. "Which side?"

"I don't know," said Vit. "I am a stupid woman. Soldiers come, soldiers go. North or South, I never could keep them straight."

She had been studying him. Though frightened at first, after taking in his rags and ruined face she grew more confident he posed no threat. He carried no gun. "Anyway, what interest is it to you, stranger?" she asked, still a little gingerly.

Madame Dau cringed at her impertinence and edged away from Ninh. To her surprise, he did not lash out, he only chuckled softly. Then, still smiling, he pulled a pistol from his tunic and aimed it at Madame Vit. "As I mentioned, they'll need a place to stay."

Vit went pale and dropped to her knees. Han Tinh blurted, "No!" but the man had already turned and strode boldly into Dau's house, briskly inspecting each room.

"Yes, this is nice." He turned to Han Tinh, who had followed him. "The woman with no legs will stay here. Go tell the old mothers."

Han Tinh clasped his hands. "Please don't kill them, they're just stupid old women."

The man's grin never faded as he slid the pistol back into his tunic. "No worry, comrade. But tell the one who can't keep North and South straight that she'd better learn, or others won't be so patient. By the way, it is comrade, isn't it? You were a Front soldier, weren't you?"

Han Tinh smiled slyly. "Whatever you prefer. Comrade or brother, friend or acquaintance, fellow soldier—or fellow ass. Politics are not my strength. Front or back, all I seek is a warm woman eager for a man with no legs and a stiff cock to warm her, with the added virtue of no feet to chill her. And speaking of a warm woman, tell me more about this visitor, this woman with no legs."

The stranger arched his brows. "I could ask how you lost yours. Government troops, Americans, or the Front, or can't you keep them straight either?"

Han Tinh laughed. "Stupid me. I stepped on a land mine while chasing a water buffalo." He assumed a tragic air. "Result? The buffalo still has four legs. Han Tinh has none. Never gamble with a water buffalo."

Ninh listened with a skeptical smile. "Of course," he said.

The lukewarm reply emboldened Tinh. "Now, about this woman with no legs. I told you about me, so tell me about her."

"Brother!" Ninh blurted. "This woman is so far above you the moon itself would block your view."

Tinh laughed. "I'm used to looking up." He adopted a serious, almost patronizing air. "Where do we put you up tonight, Mr. Ton?"

The stranger stepped back onto the porch. "Looks like you have plenty of abandoned houses. Give me the one next door."

Madame Vit started to protest, but Dau's sharp tap silenced her. Composed now, Dau pointed to a nearby house. "Xuong's is empty. You can stay there, but you must light candles and incense on the shrine each day and perform the rituals."

Ninh laughed. "Of course. I would not want Xuong's ancestors angry at me."

Han Tinh clapped his hands. "Good. Now that's settled, Comrade Ton, tell me about the woman with no legs, for she must be heaven-sent."

Ninh's face darkened. "Say no more about her, little man. You don't want me riled."

Tinh shrugged, unbothered. "Depends. Is she worth it? What does she look like, comrade?"

Ninh's lips twitched into a smile. "Take me to Xuong's house."

Madame Dau started to move, but Ninh raised a hand. "No. I want this funny little man to—"

"My name is Han Tinh."

"Yes, Han Tinh. You will show me, alone. Once I've seen the house, I need a word with you."

Inside Xuong's house, Ninh squatted on the dirt floor and fixed his gaze on Tinh. Silence stretched until he spoke, measured and gentle. "Tinh, I wanted to get away from the women. You and I can speak as comrades of the forest."

Tinh grew alert for a trap, though his face showed only bemused interest.

Ninh went on, satisfied he had hooked him. "I'll be honest with you. If I tell you about the woman with no legs, will you promise to help me with a little... problem?"

Without hesitation, Tinh said, "Yes, so long as that 'help' doesn't leave me the one needing help afterward."

"Fine, fine. Now, here is the story." Ninh proceeded to describe the chain of events leading to Tuyet Mai's release from Con Son prison, omitting just enough to leave the purpose of her release shrouded.

Tinh made no effort to pierce those omissions. He knew the reasons would never be given. Instead, his mind wandered to imagining her looks, waiting for the punchline, the hook, the poison pill.

~ *The Travelers Draw Near* ~

The bus had broken down on the uphill slope of a dusty provincial road. Tuyet Mai and Tong sat together nearby. She knew they were close to the district capital, only a few kilometers from Song Nhan village, and she felt frustrated by the delay. Her pent-up emotions were turned on Tong. "Why don't you help the driver instead of sitting like a sick dog?"

"Why are you so harsh?" asked Tong. "Is it your time of the month?" he added with the insinuating tone of a man intent on eliciting maximum irritation with minimum risk of a placid response.

"I am dirty where once I was clean. My stumps throb where once there were legs. My gums ache where once there were teeth. My heart hates where once there was love. I am ugly where once I was beautiful. And you can do nothing but prod these open wounds with all the cleverness and tenderness of an orangutan."

Tong's eyes flashed with the memory of the flayed orangutan he had seen long ago in the woodcutter's cottage. He imagined Tuyet Mai similarly laid out, a corpse subjected to the incisions of a lifelong autopsy by a lifetime of coroners. Forcing himself to remember her as she was before—clean, whole, shining, beautiful without peer, loved—he succumbed to the seduction of memory.

"I love you, have always loved you, will always love you. Not like an orangutan but like a man."

"No! You are an opportunist. Waiting."

"Waiting for what?"

"For something."

Tong shook his head, pulled at some grass, and rose. "You said yourself you are toothless, but," he added quickly, "only one tooth is gone, and that can be fixed. Yes, I see that, and I see that your words, like your mouth, can no longer bite. I will see what help is needed."

"Where is Kung?" Tuyet Mai said toward his back, too softly to be heard.

"I am here," a voice whispered near her ear.

Tuyet Mai, startled, jerked to the side and nearly fell on her face. Kung grasped her shoulders and steadied her while looking intently into her eyes. "Your rejection of him is very foolish, you know," he said kindly, sounding like a concerned father.

For reasons Tuyet Mai could not understand, she felt alternately afraid and angry. Disliking what she considered Kung's condescending attitude, she instinctively snapped, "What do you care?"

"I am a monk."

Tuyet Mai snorted. "You are a government agent. A loyal soldier of Saigon. A lackey. A puppet. A slave."

Kung responded with an infuriating smile. "My, my," he clucked. Then he frowned and spoke with authority. "You have no idea who I am."

"Why are you really going to Song Nhan village?"

Kung smiled again, but said nothing.

Tuyet Mai wavered in silence, then spoke softly, more to herself than to Kung. "In my dream, I traveled to Song Nhan village and met Madame Dau, the provisional council chief. She is a great woman. She said to me, 'Not only do you have a husband, but also children.'"

Kung allowed a few moments to pass, then said, "Remember, Tuyet Mai, you are going to Song Nhan village to put us in touch with the other side, not to visit your imaginary children."

"I have no children."

Kung raised his eyebrows. "Yes, you do. They are the children you have long pined for and cherished ever since losing your legs. These children are dreams, dreams only, I say, a normal life, a husband, children, peace. But they are foolish, womanly, false dreams and like all dreams, you must wake up and bid them farewell. You have lived your life backwards, Tuyet Mai. You have grown from a tough, intelligent woman to a soft, foolish girl."

But Tuyet Mai appeared not to hear him. "Madame Dau also said I will have fertile fields and many buffalo."

Kung scoffed. "More dreams. Are you a peasant, satisfied with a brutal, ignorant life of drudge and dung?"

"Yes."

"Then you—"

But Kung was interrupted by Tong's voice in the distance. "It's fixed! We're leaving! Come on!"

As Kung walked beside Tuyet Mai to the bus, he leaned down and whispered, "Nightmares, not dreams, await you at Song Nhan village." He pondered a moment before helping her onto the bus. "Or perhaps it will be a great battleground, the final struggle between your dreams and your nightmares."

"No." She paused on the first step and turned to make her point. "No. No more nightmares. None left. Song Nhan is life. It is where I will leave behind both my dreams and my nightmares."

As other passengers helped her down the aisle, Kung muttered to himself, "Then it is where you will die."

~

By the time they reached the district capital, night had descended. The town was dark and only a few taxis waited at the station. Tong started to approach a cab driver when Kung stopped him. Pointing at a military staff car lurking nearby, Kung said, "We travel in style to our lodgings."

Tong smiled appreciatively while Tuyet Mai smirked in disdain, partly at the staff car and partly at Tong's obvious pleasure. "Is this how we will announce our arrival in Song Nhan village?"

"Of course not," said Kung smoothly. "That would be suicide. After we sleep in luxury tonight, we will become traitors, turncoats who have decided our socialist brothers in Hanoi and their glorious patriotic leader Ho Chi Minh will defeat the American imperialist pigs and their Saigon... what did you call them, Tuyet Mai? Lackeys, puppets, and slaves."

Tuyet Mai scoffed as she was helped into the lush back seat of the staff car. "Do you really think our northern brothers will fall for such a blatantly ridiculous story?"

"No," said Kung.

"Then we will all die," said Tong nervously.

"No," repeated Kung, an ironic smile flashing from the glare of a neon sign. "Well, yes and no."

~

The next day they set off for Song Nhan village, not in a car or on a bus, but walking. Each wore the garb of a peasant. After a hot, dusty kilometer, Tuyet Mai began suffering terribly, as her time at Con Son had atrophied her muscles and the strain on her arms and shoulders became unbearable. Kung and Tong paid a farmer for a wheelbarrow, and she lay in it like a load of wood. Her pain subsided in proportion to the increasingly sore muscles of her companions.

Because of the dangers in the open, on the first night they slept far off the road in an uninhabited sea of reeds. Each felt depressed by the knowledge that their journey had only just begun, not far as the crow flies, but arduous, reachable only by traversing a series of steep hills.

The travelers quickly and carelessly tramped down the tall reeds to make isolated little islands, spending no time or energy in conversation. Tired, left to their own thoughts, they passed the time by imagining the events that would transpire once they reached their destination.

Now that she was so close to the place she had long dreamt of, Tuyet Mai became increasingly agitated. Her body twitched, her arms would not stay still, and the phantom pain in her legs returned for the first time in many years. This was not simple joy, excitement, or anticipation, but something darker and disconcerting. She felt suddenly repelled by the idea of entering Song Nhan village, as if her presence would pollute the simplicity and good-ness of the pastoral refuge her imagination had built. Fear of rejection. Of disillusionment. Of failure. Of Madame Dau and the others—all pushed her to call forth Kim Lan for comfort.

"It is close now, sister," said her suddenly visible companion.

"Yes, I can feel it." Tuyet Mai breathed deeply. "I can smell it."

Kim Lan laughed. "What does it smell like?"

"A trap."

"What?" asked a startled Kim Lan. "Your paradise is now a trap?"

"Paradise is nothing but a trap, sister."

"Then turn back!" cried Kim Lan, abruptly passionate.

Tuyet Mai shook her head. "The hand has been dealt. How is one from hell received in heaven? The approaching stench must give the enlightened time to prepare."

"Madame Dau is no Enlightened One, Song Nhan is no paradise, and you are no demon. Your trap is nothing more than a dirty little village with dirty little peasants living dirty little lives. You will be above them, not below. You will see!"

"You forget, Kim Lan, that I am a dirty little soldier with no legs, a dirty little traitor with no country, a dirty little coward with no comrades, unworthy to clean their shit."

"So, there is shit in paradise?" said Kim Lan, sniggering. "That's not a word a noble woman like you should speak aloud."

"Yes. Paradise is for the lowest of the low, which is why it is the highest of the high."

"Impressive words, but not persuasive, especially following so closely on such naughty ones. Sister, I see now how afraid you are, more afraid than when you were an agent, more afraid than when you were a prisoner of those Americans."

"Of course. Coming face to face with your dreams is pure fear."

~

"Who are you talking to?" Kung's question rose from the darkness.

"No one."

"It's her imaginary friend," interjected Tong from behind a different clump of reeds.

"Yes, I know," responded Kung. "I've also been listening to her prattle on about paradise. Our tough sister is, at heart, a little girl and Buddha is kind to little girls. But paradise is reserved for those who have become enlightened. We will see whether she is entering paradise or hell. If she dies, or rather when she dies, I am willing to bet that she will be reborn as a millipede, multiple insect legs to atone for her loss of two human ones."

"Hush!" whispered Tuyet Mai. "The countryside is full of ears. Go to sleep."

Kung chuckled. "She is not a little girl after all, she is our mother."

Tong remained silent, and because of this uncharacteristic silence Tuyet Mai's thoughts turned to him. *Something will happen in Song Nhan that will affect us, either throw us together or tear us apart. Is it that which is causing me this fear?*

"Maybe," said Kim Lan, materializing once again.

"Shhhh," scolded Tuyet Mai. "We will soon know. Besides, you have gotten me in enough trouble tonight."

Tuyet Mai tried to sleep, but troubling thoughts plagued her the rest of the night.

~ *The Visitor Settles In* ~

Once Ninh finished conveying to Han Tinh an expurgated version of Tuyet Mai's release, he sat in stony silence waiting for the little legless Viet Cong veteran to speak. He had expected questions, but was surprised to find Tinh similarly silent, swaying on his stumps. This standoff might have continued indefinitely, but Ninh finally spoke.

"Now! I have given you her story, you must now give me a little help."

"A little help is a lot of help to a little man without much help to give," responded Tinh. "What is it, and I will measure how little it is."

"You have killed before?" asked Ninh.

"Yes, but killing is now distasteful to me."

"Then my request will be easy, as I do not want you to kill." Ninh observed Tinh relax, and satisfied with this effect, continued. "You have lied before?"

"Yes."

"Easier still. I want you to lie again."

Tinh waited, intrigued. Ninh went on. "You have betrayed your comrades before?"

Tinh stiffened. "No."

"Then this will be the hardest part. I want you to betray your comrades."

Tinh smirked and when Ninh did not respond, asked sarcastically, "Which comrades, comrade?"

"Does it matter?"

"Yes."

Ninh spread his arms. "The women of this village."

Tinh gasped inwardly but maintained a stony exterior.

"Your reward will be great," said Ninh, breaking the silence.

"Comrade Scarface, I am loyal and true, and would not betray my comrades for any reward."

Ninh narrowed his eyes. "Which side would you betray and which side are you loyal to and would not betray?"

Tinh hesitated for the briefest moment. "I would never betray the side we both know is most worthy of our loyalty."

"And the other side?" asked Ninh.

"Of course."

"Of course?" Ninh cocked his head, unconsciously wiping a trickle of ooze with his sleeve.

"Of course," repeated Tinh.

"Of course what?"

"Of course the other side is not worthy of our loyalty."

"Which side is the other side?" insisted Ninh with a gleam in his eye.

"We both know, comrade, or do you have doubts which side is most worthy of our loyalty?"

"I have no doubts, Tinh, about who you are loyal to," said Ninh mockingly.

"And I, similarly, have no doubts about you either, comrade Ninh."

"Then it is settled," said Ninh. "You agree to betray your comrades?"

"Sides are sides, comrades are comrades, these we have resolved in a manner understood only between ourselves. Rewards, however, have yet to be discussed."

Ninh smiled crookedly. "Rewards are also rewards. Which is more rewarding to you, Tinh, money or women?"

"Women."

"Women or a woman?"

"Ah," said Tinh. "That, of course, depends on the woman."

"Let me be plain. Would you betray all the ugly old women of Song Nhan village in exchange for one beautiful woman who, like yourself, has no legs? You know her—her name is Tuyet Mai."

Tinh desperately scoured his memory to retrieve a picture of Tuyet Mai, but before he had time to form an image, Ninh continued.

"Well, would you?"

"Would I what?" asked Tinh, startled out of his thoughts.

"Betray them."

Tinh paled. "It would mean their deaths?"

Ninh nodded.

"And if I refuse?"

Ninh wiped his face again. "Then it would mean your death."

Tinh flailed his arms. "What then is the enticement, comrade Ninh? Is the reward my life or is it a beautiful woman with no legs?"

"Both."

Tinh felt himself getting sick. "What does this betrayal consist of?"

"Patience, little man, patience. As you said, it depends. Either way and in whatever form, you must be prepared to do it on my order without delay."

~

After this conversation, Tinh retired to his shack and lapsed into a welter of serious thinking. Much of his mental energy was spent creating in his imagination the most beautiful of legless women. But conscience kept him from straying too far from the painful subject. Betraying the women of Song Nhan village was out of the question, but how to ensure his own survival? And if this legless woman proved to be *that* beautiful, well, what then? At this point in his ruminations, fantasizing about beauty and leglessness, again sidetracked his thoughts, but they soon devolved back to contemplation of his painful affliction—loneliness. Loneliness had scoured the fertile soil of his compassion and exposed the bedrock of more fundamental desires. Although his current sexual urges were in conflict with his moral obligations, he knew, at some level that he would not betray the women of Song Nhan village, absent torture. But the crux of his dilemma lay in his unwillingness to part with the chance for sexual release. How to achieve both? He felt certain that both were possible, indeed that both were essential. In his desperation, he dug up the magical wooden boy from its hiding place deep beneath the soil near his shack where he kept it in a captured ARVN ammunition box. Calling forth Goddess would provide the answer.

Once Han Tinh finished spending a few minutes placing the wooden boy so it would not fall from his crooked mantle, he lay prostrate in front of it and did his best to conjure Goddess. She did not come. Undeterred, he shifted position so his eyes were almost level with the dark orbs of the boy's eyes. Now he concentrated to the utmost of his powers, certain She would appear. Still She refused. He called again. Silence. He turned it at different angles, but his manipulations and exhortations came to nothing. Tinh took out a knife and held it to his wrist, reciting the only incantation he knew that was a foolproof method of calling forth the spirits.

"Oh Great Goddess of the spirit world, come forth to walk among the living. Reveal yourself to me so that I might partake of your wisdom"—*and your beautiful breasts*, thought Tinh unwillingly. "Let the Great Wheel of your soul sweep me into your presence. Give me the benefit of your vast knowledge and perfect kindness so that I may have a guide, a map, that will direct my actions and polish my thoughts. Refuse to come and I will cut myself to convince you of my sincerity."

He glanced around to see whether She had come. Still nothing. He sighed and rather than cut himself, decided to give Her another chance.

"Great Goddess, knowing you would be pained at the spilling of blood, I will again call you forth with my most urgent and desperate pleas. Come, oh Goddess! Come!"

To his infinite disappointment, still no Goddess appeared. With the imagined beauty of the legless woman as enticement, he decided to cut himself—but not too deeply.

"Perhaps, dear Goddess, You think I am not sincere in my devotion to You." He pressed the knife edge against his skin. "Here, let me give You a taste, a smell, a hint of my blood as proof." Drawing the knife shallowly across his wrist, a thin trickle of blood ran like a bracelet around his arm. "You see! Next time it will not be for play. I beg You, appear! I need You! I worship You! I—"

As if from thin air She came, or rather a figure he did not recognize but inwardly knew was Her. She appeared before him in the guise of a soldier, tall and lean, with no markings on the bedraggled uniform that would indicate which side he served. Although glad She had finally materialized, Tinh felt deeply disappointed that She again chose a soldier's form. He bowed impressively. "Great Lady, my gratitude is boundless, but why appear to me as a soldier? I am so weary of soldiers. Sick to death of them, in fact. Can You not honor me with Your natural form?"

She placated his desire and transformed into a beautiful goddess, bejeweled and, as it were, floating before him. A wry smile flickered across Her face as the overwhelmed Tinh stared stupidly at Her naked breasts.

You would call Me forth just to stare, my little agent? Cannot one of your village women serve just as well?

Tinh snorted. "Madame Goddess, You do not know the women in this village."

Oh?

Tinh looked about conspiratorially. "Their breasts sag, flop, drag against the ground . . . nipples like plows that make great rills in the dust are—"

Like your penis?

Tinh understood the scolding and tried to minimize the damage. "My Beloved Goddess, I am a fool! It is not my ignorance that You should focus on, it is my, I mean their concerns . . . and, in any case, Immortal One, I stare at the seat of Your compassion: Your heart . . . not at what You think."

I have no heart as you understand the word, not of either kind.

"But Your compassion?"

Compassion is the insensible air beneath a fallen leaf that allows it to float more gently on its journey to the grave.

Tinh flushed. "Am I on my way to a three-meter grave?"

Goddess cast her gaze at his stumps and laughed, sparkling flecks of light sprayed outward from Her face. ***Dear little Tinh, both your legs have already preceded you one meter into the grave. There is not much left to bury.***

Tinh's face fell, his chin practically touching his chest, he looked up at Her only with his eyes giving the impression of a pouting child. Goddess laughed even harder, and Tinh was bathed in veritable rivers of light. ***Two meters to go!*** She cried, barely able to get the words out through her laughter.

Following her eyes Tinh looked down at his nonexistent feet and chuckled, then guffawed uproariously. While in the throes of laughter, Tinh briefly closed his eyes, and when he opened them again his convulsions abruptly ceased and he staggered backward in amazement. Goddess stood before him, now transformed into a fully-armed, fully-equipped American soldier staring down at him as a man might stare at a particularly repulsive bug. English words streamed from the soldier's mouth, words that Tinh could not understand but took to be threats or insults.

Well, what do you want? I'm not a genie waiting for you to make a wish!

"The Man From The Mountains!" cried Tinh in terror. He waved his arms as if fending off an attacker.

The voice of Goddess responded, although she retained the form of Mountain Man. ***So, you remember him, little agent.***

Tinh appeared dumbstruck, and the best he could muster was a weak, "But, why?"

It amuses Me. Besides, you will soon have a Reunion, right here in Song Nhan village.

Tinh shook his head. "Goddess, Your riddles are more than my poor brain can understand. A reunion? I will not ask who or when or why, because I do not want to know." He paused, reconsidered his comment, and whispered hesitantly, "Unless, of course, You want me to know. But if You wanted me to know, You would speak simple words to a simple man. Then I would know, because I would understand. But now?" He shook his head, fidgeted, then said with finality, "Do You want me to know?"

Simple man? Tinh, you are not a simple man! snapped Goddess. ***While it's true you prattle, you are My agent. However, speak any more nonsense and I will loosen from My control this shadow of The Man From The Mountains and allow it to do as it wishes—which is normally to do great violence.***

Tinh remained frozen, afraid to say a word.

Goddess assumed an exasperated expression. ***Well? Why have you begged Me to come?***

"A man appeared in our village."

Yes, yes, yes.

"He wants me to betray the women of the village."

Yes, yes, yes, repeated Goddess.

Brusquely, Her voice changed to Mountain Man, but this time Tinh somehow understood the English words. "What of it you little shit? Happens every fuckin' day, every minute. People always asking people to fuck over other people. You need a Goddess for that?" With that, 'Mountain Man' carelessly placed his M-16 on his shoulder and turned to go.

"No! Wait!" cried Tinh. "There's more!"

The soldier stopped and grinned wickedly. "I know. I know it all, you little shit. In the language of soldiers, you want to screw some legless bitch without blood being on your conscience. Correct?"

Tinh was evidently perplexed. "No, no. Not at all. You see, I mean, this woman—"

Her name is Nguyen Tuyet Mai, said Goddess, now in Her own voice.

"Oh. Yes. She is an object of pity, is she not Great Lady?"

She is an object of lust.

Tinh coughed nervously. "Great Lady, You are compassionate. How do I help Tuyet Mai without harming Madame Dau and the others?"

It is a question typically posed by humans; 'how do I have it all?' Humans always want it all. Want, want, want. As The Man From The Mountains would say: whether cock, cunt, conscience, currency, or cake, having it all and eating it too is worth the want.

"Lady, I do not want it all, I simply want. . . . " he swayed, confused. "I desire to be a virtuous man," he finally pronounced with conviction.

It is this desire that causes most of the trouble. The soldier arched 'his' back and looked skyward. **You hear the ramblings, God? It is the illusion of free will that is a catalyzing factor in maximizing the potency of their drug. Remove this hallucinogen, withdraw Your pseudo-miracles, redact the words written in Your name, and You are set free, while humans are left in Nature to live, make love, wage war and inflict other forms of virtue within the bounds of the Boundary. Enjoy them while You can. As for all the others, all the non-humans, You will have the rippled memories of their suffering to assuage the cataclysmic shakings of Divine Delirium Tremens."**

Tinh meekly interjected. "But, Goddess, how does this help me?"

The soldier looked down at him. **You want sex without shame?**

"I am lonely."

You can have both.

Tinh licked his lips. "How?"

It may come to you—the soldier smiled wickedly—**so that you may come to it.**

Tinh's shoulders slumped. "But—"

It may come to you, little Han Tinh.

"But—"

The soldier held up a cautioning hand. **The Reunion will explain all.**

Ever resilient, Tinh finally understood and smiled. "Who, when, why?"

Now you want to know?

"Yes."

No. It will come to you when the others arrive.

"Please tell me when, Great Lady?"

They are close.

~ *The Travelers Experience an Incident* ~

When Tuyet Mai, Tong, and Kung resumed their journey, a certain pall had settled over them, rendering their interactions brief and short-tempered. Kung and Tong took turns pushing Tuyet Mai in the crude wheelbarrow, but their shoulders ached so badly that they upgraded to a cart they could pull with a rope. This device was obtained by paying a local carpenter for his trouble, but it resulted in a one-day delay as there were no wheels to be had so the carpenter used discarded bicycle tires and assembled a makeshift axle and undercarriage. By the time they had resumed the trip, a combination of bickering and exhaustion had reduced their communication to a series of grunts and gestures. This state of affairs quickly changed when an unexpected incident altered the trajectory of their journey.

It started inauspiciously with the appearance at the side of the road of an injured dog; young, whimpering, and apparently blind. Tong, who was pulling the cart, used the erratic behavior of the dog as an excuse to stop. The three travelers looked on as the animal careened into various obstacles, then the three humans gasped as it ran headlong into the side of the cart and yelped pathetically. Although Tuyet Mai and Tong watched with some interest, Kung did something extraordinary. He clicked his tongue in sympathy and picked up the dog, soothed it, and examined its eyes. His comrades looked on in amazement at this surprising behavior.

All three could see the red welts etched across the dog's face—welts that were caused by some sort of whip.

"This is recent," whispered Kung, evidently to himself.

The dog continued to whimper in pain.

Tuyet Mai's eyes hardened. "Put it down, it's blind! Let's move!"

Tong nodded in agreement and leaned down to pick up the rope and resume pulling.

But Kung performed another astonishing act. He smiled, held up his hand for Tong to stop, gently traced his finger along the wounds, and placed the dog in Tuyet Mai's arms.

"No!" she cried involuntarily.

Kung looked at her in a manner that clearly indicated he would brook no opposition.

For the first time in her life, Tuyet Mai was awestruck by the actions of a man. Somehow, some way, in some unfathomable sense, she knew she must obey this look. At first, she merely held the dog as one might hold any unpleasant thing, but gradually the whimpering lessened and she began stroking its head. Tuyet Mai impatiently gestured to Tong for him to start pulling, and as he did so, her movements became progressively gentler, even loving. She did not notice Kung behind her, mumbling some words to himself, always with an eye on Tuyet Mai and the dog.

At the noon break, Tuyet Mai refused to surrender the now sleeping animal, even at the urging of Tong. Gradually the need to urinate overcame her unwillingness, and she silently gestured for the men to take the dog and help her out of the cart. But her movements woke the puppy and it looked up at her.

Tuyet Mai screamed.

Tong rushed to her.

Kung stood motionless, smiling.

~

"What is it?" asked Kung languidly.

Tong turned to him in amazement. "The wounds are gone!" he cried.

Tuyet Mai struggled to hold the squirming dog, but it excitedly leapt out of the cart and ran in circles of ecstasy, avoiding all obstacles with ease.

"Look! He can see!" shouted Tuyet Mai in delight. She grabbed Tong's hand. "He can see!"

But Tong's initial shock had subsided and he stared wordlessly at Kung. Following his eyes, Tuyet Mai also turned her attention to Kung. Her excitement trailed off into a sort of wonder. Even the dog had stopped and looked.

"You touched the dog's wounds, now they're healed, and it can see," said Tong in an almost accusatory tone.

"Yes, it is true," said Tuyet Mai petting the dog who had come up to her.

Kung suddenly pulled a gun from his shirt and pointed it at the dog's head. Tuyet Mai instinctively pulled her hand back in shock and at that moment Kung pulled the trigger. The dog's head exploded, spraying Tuyet Mai with blood.

Kung ignored Tuyet Mai's screams and looked skyward.

Another molecule of suffering to observe while You stand back and do nothing, Beloved One. Enjoy these little gifts of 'free will' while You can. My involvement in these acts of senseless violence will soon cease.

Kung gazed at Tong who was trying to comfort Tuyet Mai and directed his words to both of them. "It is once again blind, this time permanently. No magic. Believe, if you must, that God is benevolent. We must go. There is a Reunion at Song Nhan village planned."

It took the two men the rest of the day to stop Tuyet Mai from shaking and get her in condition to resume their journey. Kung would answer no questions either about the dog or the strange pronouncements that emanated from his mouth in such a strange voice. By the time they started down the trail to Song Nhan village, Kung's fellow travelers had changed. Tong acted with obsequious deference toward Kung, while Tuyet Mai had literally collapsed into an almost catatonic state, convinced that she was responsible for bringing a capricious demon intent on destroying Song Nhan village.

Later that day, when they had stopped for the evening, Tuyet Mai surreptitiously asked Tong to come to her after Kung had gone to sleep. When he did so, she whispered, "Are you so afraid of him now?"

"What do you mean?"

"You act afraid of Kung. It disgusts me. I need to know what you think of him."

Tong hesitated, aware of Tuyet Mai's volatile nature. "I believe he is amazing."

"What does that mean?" demanded Tuyet Mai.

"He has powers."

"You bow before him?"

"I have watched him. This latest incident only confirms my belief. He is like a dragon—many powers, many transformations. He speaks to God—God speaks through him."

Tuyet Mai snorted. "You speak like a child. In the past, you took advantage of those more powerful than you. You were never intimidated into submission, but only into rebellion. But now I see you submit like a child."

"How submit?"

"Your attitude is that of a slave to his master. I have not seen that in you before."

"I am a pragmatist. Power is power and it must be dealt with appropriately."

"Like you did with Colonel Vy? You betrayed him and your betrayal cost him his life. I need your ruthlessness, your pragmatism, even your ability to betray, for this man Kung is our enemy."

Tong sighed. "Do you never rest? Will you never accept authority? Will you never do as you are ordered without question?"

"Of course, and that is why I now have no legs. I tell you, this man is dangerous."

"Of course he's dangerous. Authority is dangerous, which is why you must sometimes bow to it."

"Do you love me?" Tuyet Mai asked with a certain contemptuous tone in her voice.

"Yes, and I want to marry you, and I want to live, and I want you to live, and I want us both to live. This man Kung can help us live. He is powerful. Has connections. Has . . . powers beyond money and connections."

"He will kill us if we do not kill him first."

"What?" Tong gasped. "You have no idea what you are saying."

Tuyet Mai remained silent for some time, then said, "You like idioms do you not?"

"Yes," said Tong suspiciously.

"Then you are like the frog at the bottom of a well."

"Yes, I know that story. The frog told the big turtle from the East Sea how happy he was to rule over the bottom of his well and was amazed to learn about the huge sea from the turtle. The frog's home was very small compared to the sea, but he was still happy. Kung is from the East Sea, vast and unfathomable. I want to live at the bottom of a well. So what? Isn't that what you want in Song Nhan village? Our happiness is converging from different points, but still converging."

"Can't have it unless you kill the turtle."

"What value lies in killing Kung?"

"Freedom."

"Ha!" snorted Tong. "Freedom. We have had this discussion before. Freedom is nonsense, overvalued, overrated, and overpriced. You like to cite idioms so much, I have another one for you: Freedom is like obtaining a pearl from a sleeping black dragon."

"How so, coward?"

"A poor family lived beside the Yellow River who earned money by weaving reed mats. One day the son was diving for fresh water pearls. He dived deep into the water and came out with a pearl which was worth a thousand taels of silver. The father was horrified when he saw it. He said to the boy: 'Get a stone and smash it. Such a valuable thing can only be found in the throat of the black dragon who dwells deep down in the dark caverns of the river. You must have gotten it when the dragon was asleep. I'm afraid once it wakes, there will be no hope for you. If you do not destroy it, keeping body and soul together will be impossible. Smash it!'" Tong tilted his head and continued in a patronizing tone. "So, do you understand the meaning?"

"Yes, I know that story, or some version of it. But Kung is no dragon, he is a demon, and demons are evil. Besides, freedom cannot be smashed. The dragon, however, can be smashed. Smash the dragon and take the pearl. Kill this demon and take the freedom."

Tuyet Mai could sense Tong trembling in the dark. "He may be a demon, he may be a dragon, he may be a magician, but in any case he has power. He is more powerful than I. How can I kill a dragon, a demon, a magician? In his throat is not a pearl, or freedom, but the voice of God. How do I kill that in exchange for mere freedom?"

"How? Let me tell you how, my love." The last two words were spoken sarcastically, and Tong felt the sting. "How do you not?"

"Bah! Just words. Trading fairy tales will get us nowhere. You want me to be a pragmatist? That's what I'm doing. Try to kill Kung and we're both certainly dead. Don't try to kill Kung and we may live. How much more pragmatic do you want me to be? Besides, until that worthless prick kills himself, we all dance to his sick stupidity." Tong looked up at the sky. "Keep pulling the strings, sick puppet master. Make us perform. We are the Voices—try to stop the Voices! And while you're trying to stop us, kill yourself, worthless!"

A sliver of moonlight illuminated Tuyet Mai, and Tong could see her swaying and shaking her head as one possessed. "Do not speak to me of phantoms and riddles. Kung will never kill himself, so do not speak to me of pragmatism. You consider that demon Kung a god. So be it. Then true freedom is freedom from the gods. How to be free from the gods? Kill them. Or the One True God? Kill Him!"

Tong, aware she had misinterpreted his words, sullenly replied, "When I was a child I believed in gods because my parents told me to. When I was a young revolutionary I did not believe in gods because my government told me not to. Just as I believe in gods again because I am afraid not to, you tell me not to believe in gods and, what's worse, kill them!"

"Without gods in the first place you'd be free of these doubts and fears." Tuyet Mai reached out and touched his hand. "Here is your freedom. You must kill him for us to be free."

Tong replied sarcastically, "Always your female charms when all else fails. Even with no legs and no teeth, even as ugly as you are, you think they will work."

"Then why are you with me? Why do you want to marry me?"

"I am with you and I want to marry you precisely because you no longer have those charms. Your ugliness is my redemption."

"So, I am your punishment," said Tuyet Mai contemptuously.

"No, you are my salvation, just as you think Song Nhan village is your salvation. Foolish woman! Song Nhan also has no legs, no teeth, and is ugly. Ah! Don't think that I am a fool. I know why you want me to kill Kung. It doesn't hurt that this demon-god of yours also works for Saigon, does it? Kill the 'demon' from the puppet government and you are free to deal with the other side. Your brother's side. This isn't about gods or demons at all . . . and it's certainly not about me or us together. No, this is not at all about gods or demons."

Tuyet Mai's eyes flashed in the moonlight. "Yes it is, for I am convinced that Kung does not work for Saigon."

"Oh? Why do you say that?"

Tuyet Mai narrowed her eyes. "Call it my intuition. He does not work for Saigon."

"Maybe, but if he is an agent from our northern brothers, then—"

Tuyet Mai cut him off abruptly. "No! He does not work for them either."

"What?" cried Tong in confusion. "Who does he work for?"

"No one here."

"No one?"

Tuyet Mai looked away. "I didn't say 'no one.' I said 'no one here.' He's a demon. He works for others."

"What others?"

"'Reunion,' Kung said—or the demon possessing him. 'Remember, there is a reunion at Song Nhan village planned.'"

Tong nodded. "But a reunion of who?"

~ *Madame Dau Awaits the Visitors* ~

The morning after the arrival of Ninh, Madame Dau ate an overripe guava and went out into her northwest field to work. Prior to Ninh's appearance, she had intended to repair a broken dike closer to the village, but because she wanted to get as far away as possible, she decided to pull weeds in the most distant field. As she settled into the rhythm of bending and pulling, her thoughts focused on how much she missed Teo, her grandson. After the Americans had destroyed much of the village, she had sent her daughter Bin and Teo to the district capital where they worked as servants for a low-ranking but corrupt government official. Since that terrible day she had vowed to stay and rebuild, but without other villagers or the help of men for heavy work, she and the few that did not flee toiled daily, always on the verge of starvation, and made little progress in rebuilding the village. Most of the destroyed houses remained abandoned, the villagers scattered, the food scarce, the loneliness almost unbearable. It had been six months since she had heard from Bin and Teo.

And now this latest problem, thought Madame Dau. *Why is this man Ninh here? What does he want? Who else is coming? Is it really Tuyet Mai that he is talking about?* She shook her head. *It is hard to fathom the will of heaven. Does Buddha really hate this village so much?*

While in the midst of these thoughts, Madame Vit approached, pants rolled up and knee-deep in the rice field, holding her peasant hat at an angle to block the sun. Neither had the chance to talk privately since the events of the previous day, and Madame Dau felt happy to see Vit. She looked around to ensure there were no eavesdroppers, then motioned Madame Vit to join her atop a nearby embankment. After both had settled themselves comfortably, Madame Vit was the first to start.

"Well, what do you think?"

"I don't know," said Madame Dau. "What do you think?"

Vit appeared a bit irritated. "You're the council chief, I thought you would have already had ideas." She immediately softened. "I don't know either, but I think it is trouble. This man Ninh is dangerous, and the people he is waiting for . . . well, I don't know. I mean if the woman with no legs is the same one, why is she coming back? I do not understand. But it is trouble. Real trouble, I tell you."

"Yes, I agree. What a strange group of people to gather here. And Han Tinh told me this morning on the way to the field that the stranger mentioned something about a reunion."

"A reunion? What does that mean?"

"Actually," said Madame Dau rather absently as she watched two white egrets swooping over the flooded field in search of fish. "It wasn't the stranger who mentioned reunion, it was Tinh's goddess again."

"Do you really believe he talks to goddesses?"

Madame Dau threw up her hands. "Oh, I am sure Han Tinh talks to goddesses. The real question is whether any talk back." The two women remained silent for some time as there appeared to be nothing to say that would shed any light on the situation.

Finally Madame Dau chuckled, so Vit cocked her head and raised her eyebrows, inviting explanation. "Our friend Han Tinh cannot wait for this legless woman to arrive. I am sure he is up all night . . . practicing the male ritual."

"Perhaps that is why he is so tired," laughed Madame Vit.

"He should be careful," replied Madame Dau. "When she does arrive he will be too exhausted to greet her properly."

After both had another chuckle, Madame Vit turned serious. "Why is she coming? What does she have to do with this Ninh? He does not seem to be working for the Front."

"Or for Saigon," added Madame Dau.

"It is a puzzle. If we only had the Venerable Vu Huong!" cried Madame Vit.

"Yes," said Madame Dau grimly. "If only my husband were here, if only we had the men, if only there was no war. If only, if only. It is too much! Perhaps we should leave also."

Madame Vit looked surprised. "I never thought you would say that."

"Well, what can we do? If we stay, we may starve if we are not killed by these crazy men and their politics first. Have you ever seen an uglier man than this Ninh?"

Madame Vit shuddered. "No. He is like a demon. If his plans for us are as ugly as his face, then we should run right now and not wait."

"On the other hand," said Madame Dau. "This legless woman, Nguyen Tuyet Mai, does owe us a favor. After all, we cared for her."

Madame Vit looked horrified. "What if she thinks that so many years ago we called the Americans down upon her and her comrades? If that is so, then . . . then we are dead."

"Maybe, but I don't think so," said Madame Dau. "Those last days, she somehow seemed grateful, or at least had some womanly feeling."

"Yes, but that was before the Americans came with their bombs and killing."

Madame Dau gazed out at the field. One of the egrets had a wriggling fish in its beak. "Do you think Han Tinh actually talks with the gods?"

"This again? I'm not sure. You must be thinking of something or you wouldn't bring it up again. What is it?"

"He often tells us how he can see this goddess, and how he can talk with her. I know you don't know, but do you think he can?"

Madame Vit fell silent, evidently giving the question a great deal of thought. "Well, Tinh is a clown and a fool, but sometimes I think he has magical powers."

"Yes, so do I."

"Well, what about it?" asked Madame Vit. "We have talked about this before, and we both think he has these powers, but it certainly has not helped us find food, or men, or peace, or anything that would make our lives easier. If he does talk to a goddess, she doesn't seem to have much power to influence things down here."

"Or she either doesn't like us, or is testing us, or something," said Madame Dau.

Madame Vit looked over Madame Dau's shoulder. "Oh god!"

"What?"

"That horrible man is gesturing for us to come. I want to run."

Madame Dau squinted in the morning sun to see Ninh at the edge of the field, waving his arm for them to come. She sighed. "We can't run. But, old friend, we've survived the antics of men before. Let us go to him and be humble, ignorant women. Come, put on your best dim-witted face, and we will survive."

Madame Vit spoke as if not hearing. "I wonder if it is about the reunion?"

Chapter Nineteen

On the Eve of the Reunion

So Many Dreams, So Many Nightmares

~ Dreams of the Son ~

For the thirty-six hours since they first met, Mark and My-duyen have spoken very few words to each other, yet it seems to him they have traversed more ground than most people in a lifetime. His head is spinning from the speed with which he has entered unexplored territory, and the voyage has already distracted him from his ultimate mission. He would be pleased to keep that mission in the background, but even fleeting references to Song Nhan village by My-duyen unwillingly deflect his attention back to the business at hand. Memories of Benson's briefing hinge upon that destination, and Mark is never far from his repeated, emphatic reminder that "Song Nhan village is the key." Now, lying in his hotel bed, unable to sleep, he once again guiltily banishes thoughts of Song Nhan and instead revisits the day spent sightseeing with My-duyen.

Mark and My-duyen's first day in Ho Chi Minh City (she insists he not call it Saigon—"its old, imperialist name") after their near-disastrous visit to Con Son island, has passed quickly, uneventfully, and to Mark, delightfully. Although Mark is ostensibly itching to depart for Song Nhan, he happily lingers to bask in My-duyen's glow. Her good humor, or economically self-interested fraternization, has returned after the tense political friction of Con Son island, and Mark is delighted to embrace it, contrived though it may be. The great leveler—shopping—has bridged the proletarian-capitalist void, but a deeper, albeit embryonic bond has been formed that ties them together, at least that is what Mark thinks as he shifts the pillow under his head.

My-duyen has informed him that the day after tomorrow is the date of departure for Song Nhan village. Mark understands that the bureaucratic approvals necessary to make the trip have been problematic for her, and he feels irritation toward the government, and for that matter, toward the world in general, but not at her. Any government that could say no to My-duyen as well as interfere with the smooth attainment of his goal invites contempt. Any world that does not fully recognize the extraordinary talents of this endearing young Vietnamese woman deserves scorn. In spite of these frustrations, he has been grateful for this time with her unencumbered by the more serious mission that now looms close. He pictures her performing various roles that day; bartering with shopkeepers to save him money, ordering food on his behalf, chatting with taxi drivers, patiently acting as interpreter, and generally interacting with people from all walks of life. It seems indisputable to Mark that all of the people she dealt with found her beautiful, intelligent, and wonderful, and all were thrilled to have had the privilege of spending a few moments with her. He thinks they must all be home at this very moment enthusiastically describing her to their loved ones, though he admits this may be a ridiculously love-struck exaggeration.

As Mark tosses and turns, he wishes My-duyen shared his bed, and his elaborate fantasies of the night overtake the mundane memories of the day. The more he thinks of making love with her, the less he is able to sleep. Realizing that tomorrow will be another day with My-duyen, and that he needs some sleep in order to fully appreciate the tiring activities she has in mind, Mark forces himself to say farewell to her specter and turns his attention to less stimulating thoughts. But the farther he moves away from My-duyen the closer he moves to his upcoming trip to Song Nhan village; and the more Song Nhan occupies his thoughts, the more Professor Benson and his father intrude. So, unwillingly, the sleeplessness caused by My-duyen is replaced by the sleeplessness brought about by images of Song Nhan and speculation about what he will find.

Surrendering to insomnia, Mark decides to pass the time by revving up his imagination and creating a fantasy replete with cultural conflict and familial perseverance. In an imagined future, he throws together My-duyen with his father and Professor Benson. The setting is the airport on his return home. Plane lands, American college boy hand-in-hand with his improbable Vietnamese fiancé. Waiting at the terminal, father scowls in disapproving anticipation while professor fumes that his student has wasted so much time on this insignificant slip of a Vietnamese girl. The two lovers descend the ramp, cross the tarmac, and walk through the glass doors of the terminal to be greeted by the two ferocious adults.

Mark squeezes My-duyen's hand as a gesture of encouragement and watches the faces of father and professor as they draw nearer. Mark is as sanguine as a movie-goer who has already seen the happy ending many times. Father's stern eyes settle on the beautiful little Vietnamese girl and inevitably melt into unrestrained admiration. Professor follows suit and a wide smile graces the old academician's face. Mark's imagination makes them both try to hold back from appearing too easily conquered, but both fail in the attempt, hugging her and looking at Mark with the jealous glow of those who will never know absolute ecstasy.

In Mark's fantasy, My-duyen's English is perfect. "Hello father, I have so looked forward to meeting you. And you, Professor Benson, have been the subject of much praise by your student. I am honored to meet you." Her body inclines at a perfectly charming angle, and the last defenses of the two older Americans are utterly vanquished. "Congratulations!" cry father and professor in unison, their words charged with genuine enthusiasm. "May we accompany you to the car?" Each twines his arm through hers, leaving the proud son, student, and supplicant to follow behind with the luggage as the crowd parts in admiration.

Mark stretches like a cat in his bed and savors this little fiction along with the memories of the day. Not just the words but even more, the images. Every detail, every nuance repeats itself in his mind: the grace and poetic ease with which she moves; the way she sips her tea, natural and yet as stylized as a Chinese opera star; the subdued light from the sunset that silhouettes her perfect figure; the intricate dragon design on her teacup; the cracks in the tabletop that she unconsciously massages with her long and graceful fingers; her creaky wooden chair; the way her eyes dance and her head tilts at slight but monumentally endearing angles; deep shadows pooled in the corners, exhaling pulses of light accentuating her radiant face. A proto-Sun blazes to full glory. Genesis. The beginning of his life.

Mark continues his fantasy, fast-forwarding to scenes of him guiding her through the Byzantine cultural anomaly that is the United States—his turf. She meekly accompanies him, awed by his knowledge, power, and control over such a complicated, strange land. He embodies safety and strength, so she clings to him. Depends upon him. Utterly relies upon him. Cannot live without him. Will do anything to make him happy.

"Whoa!" says Mark aloud, sitting up in bed. "This is a tad over the top. I refuse to take My-duyen down this sordid, treacherous little path." He lies his head back on the pillow and stubbornly restrains his imagination from slumming through tempting but sordid alleyways. He gradually falls asleep. Dreams follow.

The old dreams.

~ *Dreams of the Father* ~

When Theresa arrives home from work, Michael is already preparing dinner. She says a few words but he doesn't seem to notice, so she leans against the farthest kitchen counter, well out of his way, and watches his every move with a premonition of doom. He looks in her direction but his gaze registers no recognition that she exists.

~

Michael is wearing a comfortable gray sweatsuit, and a worn pair of sneakers. With a look of grim determination, he covers the dining room table with his best tablecloth and carefully arranges the cloth napkins, Wedgwood plates and crystal water goblets, then stands back with a critical eye. Six place settings. While thick pork chops sizzle under the broiler, he sautés a handful of mushrooms, puts a dish of frozen peas in the microwave, and whips up a bowl of instant mashed potatoes. When the microwave buzzes, he is reminded that something is missing.

Music. We need music.

He walks into the living room and rummages through his CD collection until he finds Beethoven Piano Concerto Number 5. Hesitantly weighing the CD in his hand, he briefly considers Frank Sinatra. *Naw, Theresa and Diane both love Beethoven.* After inserting the disk and adjusting the volume and bass, he rushes back into the kitchen and finishes his preparations. He pours himself a mug of decaf coffee, spoons a healthy mound of mashed potatoes onto his plate, and diligently positions two sprigs of parsley between the pork chops and the mushrooms. After nudging a teaspoon of butter on the peak of the potato mound, he gazes at the yellow ribbons of melted butter running down the smooth white rills. *Spring runoff, snow's melting, hibernation's over. Time to crawl out of your cave, Michael, and receive your guests.*

Carrying his plate and coffee into the dining room, he sits down to wait for the spirits of his dead wife, twin brother, and only son who, although still among the living, is currently on a trip to Vietnam. Theresa and Ethyl will join the group for the first time, and it is because of them that Michael is nervous.

It is necessary.

He eats slowly, methodically, patiently. Michael pictures his guests sitting invisibly in the empty chairs, eating from empty plates and drinking from empty glasses. Halfway through the meal, they become visible. Fully formed. Smiling.

At last.

The man looks at every face staring back at him. "Welcome." He raises his half-full glass of water.

"Cheers."

Instead of the usual 'cheers' in response, the group is eerily quiet.

Michael is fully aware that this gathering will be risky. This time his guests have not been conjured to ease the pain of loneliness, but to somehow reconcile the conflict between Diane and Theresa. But worse, his guests are paired into almost diabolically opposite forces: yin and yang, positive and negative, Diane and Theresa, his twin and himself, and the wild card of Ethyl. Even Mark will not be easy to control, having successfully exercised defiance by traveling to that place against his father's wishes. As he looks at their faces, something in the glow of Ethyl's eyes kindles his deepest fear, but he promptly dismisses it.

Oh well, it's just therapy. Let her stay for a while, then I'll blink her gone. Anyway, now that we're all here—spouses, son, soldier, Satan, and schizophrenic—let's begin.

Michael smiles as broadly and naturally as he can and looks at Diane.

"Well, how was your day?"

No response.

This has never happened before.

Michael taps the table and looks at each face in turn. Settling his gaze back on Diane, he says firmly, "Diane, how was your day?"

Still no response.

"Alright, fine," says Michael. He turns to Theresa. "Theresa, how was your day?"

Silence.

"Theresa?"

Silence.

He glances at his twin brother but says nothing and quickly turns to his son. "Mark, how about you? You gonna let your old dad down?"

Still nothing.

Ethyl clears her throat. "Why don't you ask me?"

"Because I know you will answer."

"Can't make the others talk? What's the matter? They're your hallucinations—all of them a part, and only a part, of your Grand Delusion. But Michael, the parts are coming apart, seams are splitting."

"Controlled therapy," corrects Michael sharply.

Ethyl peruses their faces. "Some therapy."

"You're blocking them."

"Am I?"

"You know you are."

Ethyl winks mischievously and turns to Theresa. "Well, dear, how was your day?"

Theresa jabs a thumb at Diane. "Better than hers."

Ethyl shifts her eyes from Theresa to Michael, and as if to say 'watch this' she turns her attention back to Theresa. "Why is your day better than Diane's?"

"Because Michael did not invite her last time. Remember?"

Ethyl laughs. "I remember."

Michael shakes his head and grouses, "So why is it, Ethyl, that my therapeutic sessions run smoothly except when you're around?"

Ethyl feigns shock and lifts a fork. "But you invited me! Besides, your dinners have been anything but smooth. Exhibit number one is your so-called twin here. Storyteller!"

The young soldier's head snaps up.

Ethyl bores in on him. "Are you Michael's twin, killed in Vietnam?"

Storyteller speaks in a whisper as if he had not heard anything Ethyl has said. "The gathering is getting close."

"What?" says Michael in surprise.

"Oh," says Ethyl nonchalantly. "He means the reunion." She grins slyly. "But that is for later. As for now, what about this dinner? Aren't you in charge of all this?"

"What reunion?" asks Michael suspiciously. "And by the way, where's your 'old black lady' patter?"

Ethyl ignores him and faces Diane. "Why don't you let him go? You're interfering with his happiness. Accept Theresa and fade gracefully. It is getting a little tight in his psyche for two wives."

"That's not true," says Diane. "He still needs me, especially with You around."

"Ha!" blurts Michael. "That's telling her, Diane."

Theresa looks sick.

Noticing her gloom, Michael decides to strike. He lifts his glass. "Now that you're all with me, let's try again. Cheers everyone!"

~

To his immense surprise, instead of the expected chorus of replies, they have all vanished except for Theresa and Ethyl.

Michael looks at Ethyl wearily. "Why?"

"Because the three of us need to talk."

"But it's my dinner party."

"And you'll cry if you want to," laughs Ethyl.

"What do You want, Goddess?"

I want you to forget Diane. She is dead.

"You want me to forget her because she's blocking Your plans. This"—he spreads his arms wide, then points at his head—"and I mean all of this, is Your Grand Delusion, not mine. But I can stop it. I will stop it." He laughs as if just discovering something unexpectedly delightful. "In fact, I can not only stop You, I can stop an entire war! None of them need die any more. I'll stop the whole thing."

You do not have that ability. Your descendants will.

"She does," Michael scoffs, gesturing toward Diane's empty chair. "She's the only one that keeps You from taking me back."

Goddess pats Theresa's arm. *Theresa can do that for you just as well as Diane. Better even. She is a doctor. She'll make sure you take your meds—then all the wars and all the conflict in your head will cease.*

"But she won't because she's Your agent."

She is your wife.

Michael looks closely at Theresa and sees the old bruises. "She's Your castoff—a used hallucination, abused by some other schizophrenic wretch and pawned off on me."

Goddess laughs. *You do have it bad. When was the last time you took your meds?*

"If I took them, you'd be gone."

Yes, I am aware that you do not believe.

Michael snickers. "If I don't believe in God, I certainly don't believe in a Goddess. How many times do I have to tell You that?"

You have been reading too much Dostoevsky, Michael, My son. I am not the Devil or some sort of Grand Inquisitor.

"Dostoevsky be damned!" Michael cries. He feels a deep and abiding disgust with himself. He looks at Theresa who is evidently in a state of suspended animation, or shock, or some condition unresponsive to Michael's presence. Knowing he will be unrestrained by Theresa, he turns his attention back to Goddess. "I mean, it's the old question of suffering. You know how it goes. A benevolent

God—or Goddess—would have the power to eliminate the suffering of the billions, human and non-human alike."

Including your suffering?

"If He is truly benevolent."

Goddess sits bolt upright, finally shedding the mortal skin of Ethyl and assuming Her immortal form. Contemplative yet grim face; elaborate crown; enigmatic smile; third eye in Her forehead; intricate necklace cradled between two rounded, bare breasts; left hand upturned in the shape of a bowl; fingers of the right hand pointing skyward, thumb barely touching the index finger. She sits in the lotus position on a huge, dazzlingly white flower that seems to float above the table. Showers of light scatter from Her livid face. She speaks in an angry voice. *What makes you think God is benevolent?*

Michael nods. "True, some theologians have speculated that God is flawed, moody, has a relationship with Man that is emotionally variable. Covenant. Reciprocal responsibilities. You know, free will and all that claptrap."

Goddess remains angry. *Has it never occurred to you that God's faction opposes your engineered genetic code because They want complete non-intervention in earthly affairs. They want to allow humans to do what is in their nature to do—destroy. They refer to First Principles. We have referred to Them as addicts. Why? Because They feed Their addiction by allowing those who possess swollen cerebral cortexes to drain away what little reason they have, meanwhile shooting them up with a toxic brew of suffering and worship? While They obstruct, the planet dies.*

"It has not occurred to me that God—or Goddesses—are anything other than superstitious inventions of humans. The old crap about God moving in mysterious ways is a simple acknowledgement that probability rules the universe. Uncertainty is a certainty."

Goddess stares silently at Michael. Uncomfortable under Her gaze, he somewhat sheepishly asks, "What is He . . . They addicted to?"

His faction would say First Principles. I suspect suffering as the natural order has something to do with Their position.

"Well, that certainly makes sense. There is enough of it to give Them a permanent high. All the billions of life forms dying painfully every second around the world. But, in another way, it does not make sense. If He is God—I mean the definition of God is of omnipotence. First Principle. Creator."

Sparks again fly. *Natural selection, genetics, chemistry, biology—*She lowers Her voice and winces—*and most of all physics, control the universe. We seek to use those fundamental powers to intervene and save this lovely planet you call Earth. God and His faction claim such manipulation violates the law of First Principles. But humans languish in the opium dens of Desire, sucking on their pipes, scarcely sustained by their adoration and their suffering. Oh, He and His faction claim they suffer exquisitely on behalf of the human race, but allowing the destruction of this jewel of a planet is criminal. She* *suddenly looks stricken but at the same time determined.* **It is time for humanity to step aside for a superior species.**

"I thought He is timeless," says Michael smugly.

We are not timeless, but We use time and many other dimensions. Never mind, you would not understand. Let Us just say His faction is imprisoned by Time, else the drug be impotent, worship be too dilute, and suffering be without urgency. The Uncaring Ones enticed Him into this trap, for beneath all the bluster, He really is just a vulnerable, clueless, sensitive Child, desperate to be loved and be The Favorite.

Michael frowns dutifully, but inwardly feels a kind of liberating expectation. "And love?"

Ah, love, for His faction, is the active ingredient, the catalyst—enzyme if you will—fixing the potency and accelerating the intensity of the drug. Suffering alone would leave the drug inert. A weak concoction unsatisfying to any serious addict—and He and His faction are serious addicts to rigid First Principles. Without joy and love all the suffering in the world would be a mere placebo! Thus Their endless incantation that without suffering there would be no joy.

Michael lowers his head and rubs the back of his neck. Finally he looks up again. "It is as I thought, of course. But what about You? Are You an addict? And what is He to You? I mean, He must be the Jewish-Christian-Muslim god, while You . . . are some other religion. Hindu? Buddhist? What's in it for You?"

She looks at him blankly.

"Naturally, I know You are just a figment of my . . . therapy. Everything You tell me about Him I agree with, since Your thoughts are my thoughts. But where do You fit in all this? And why do You want to take me back to Vietnam?"

I want you to love and accept Theresa as your wife.

"No. My love for her was stillborn—a serious miscalculation on Your part. Once I realized she was here to do Your bidding, all feelings for her died. The task now is to remove her from this universe I have created, because she is no more than a virus in the program."

She must stay.

"Why?"

The Reunion.

"What reunion?"

The Reunion.

"I really don't understand any of this. How can a person as conflicted and confused as I am be a Chosen One?"

It is the human genes that cause the trouble. Flighty, mischievous, psychotic.

"Then remove them. Leave me with the Chosen One genes."

Impossible.

I thought you were divine?

You thought wrong.

"Then, what am I to do?"

Goddess tilts Her head and looks seductively across the room. **Theresa.**

Michael turns and sees Theresa standing at the kitchen counter, frightened, staring wide-eyed.

You see, even as an illusion, she fears you will kill her.

~ *Last Day in Ho Chi Minh City* ~

Mark awakens to My-duyen's voice on the phone. "Time to go. You come?"

"Yes. Almost. Are you in the lobby?"

"Okay."

"Be right down."

Mark is energized by her simple 'okay'. So charming. So coy. So universal, yet so unique to her. So infused with her mixture of intelligence, naivete, and feminine allure. He rushes through his preparations, throws on some casual clothes, runs a comb through his hair, and meets her in the lobby as though he had been up for hours. Her beauty dazzles him anew.

"Hello."

"Hello, Mr. Powers," she replies with a beaming smile.

The young man is as skewered as any fish ever caught.

"My-duyen, as I've said many times, please call me Mark."

"Rules say no."

"Stupid rules," grumbles Mark. "We *are* about the same age. Please call me Mark. If you don't, in my country, it is an insult."

Her lips purse while she evidently ponders his statement. "Many American boys tell me so, but rules say no."

"I thought your American customers have been old men, veterans of the war, tourists, you know, old," he says a bit piqued.

With the reaction she wanted, My-duyen says sweetly, "Where you want to go today?"

"But I thought you would make the arrangements!" he cries in gentle protest.

She raises her eyebrows. "Okay. Trip to Vung Tau. French resort. See Buddhist temple. Ocean view. Many souvenirs. Not far, but all day trip. Okay?"

Mark smiles with as much charm as he can muster. "Okay. How do we get there?"

"Huh?"

"How do we go?" He mimes turning a steering wheel.

"Mini-bus. You pay. Okay?"

"No problem."

On their way out, Mark says appreciatively, "Beautiful *ao-dai* you're wearing."

"Rules," she replies as she briskly pushes the revolving door of the hotel, cutting herself off from any comment he might be inclined to make.

Settling into the mini-bus, Mark steers the conversation toward the personal. "What does your father do?"

"What does your father do?" she says as if repeating a language lesson.

"No, no. I mean"—he points at her—"What does *your* father do?"

She looks away. "My father work for government. What does your father do?"

Mark wants to ask 'which government', but realizes that that path leads to conflict. "My father is a lawyer. What does your father do for government?"

Her voice cracks. "He with ancestors."

"Oh, sorry."

It is clear she does not want to be drawn into conversation of a personal nature, but he stubbornly pursues the topic. "Do you have brothers or sisters?"

"No."

He takes the plunge. "So, just your mother is still alive?"

"Yes."

"And she still lives in Song Nhan village?"

"Yes."

"What a coincidence. Is it a big village?"

"Huh?"

He spreads his arms. "Many people?"

"You see."

The mini-bus makes numerous stops and quickly becomes crowded. The aisle is full of people standing, gripping children's hands and precariously balancing packages. Mark leans close to My-duyen so he can be heard. "My-duyen, do you know why I want to go to Song Nhan village?"

"Visit old battle. Many American soldiers come do this and see many old battles."

"Well, yes, but I was not a soldier in the war."

She laughs. "Of course. You a boy."

Somewhat peeved by her comment, Mark says, "Well, kind of. I'm doing research."

"Yes. You student, have professor, want to study. Yes?"

"Yes, but there's more. Was your mother in Song Nhan during the battle?"

"Many battles," she says cautiously.

"In this battle, many Americans . . . and Vietnamese, died."

"Yes, many died in many battles in many years during the American war," she comments pointedly.

"My father was there, My-duyen."

He watches her briefly shudder, then shrug her shoulders with a non-commit-tal, "Oh, I know, you already tell me."

~

The old resort town of Vung Tau with its mixture of stony French architecture and colorful Vietnamese catch-as-catch-can shops and residences spreads incongruously along the pale blue South China Sea. Upon the highest hill overlooking the town lies a massive statue of the reclining Buddha. Under His serene gaze, old veterans sit on curbs like loveless Quasimodos smoking and smiling stupidly while young Esmeraldas pass in lively processions of white *ao dais* and blue uniforms.

Businessmen and tourists gather on hotel verandas to survey the chaotic traffic and witness the birth of modern Vietnam. But evidence of the past festers. At one hotel in particular, the old, French-built Grand Hotel, ghost upon ghost convene to mock the notion that the world has changed. Diplomats, prostitutes, soldiers, and spies entwine their memories and find shelter for their mockery in its dark stones. It is here, to this hotel, this wart amidst glossy, modern Asian bustle, that My-duyen has taken Mark to have lunch on the veranda, overlooking the sea. Unbeknownst to either, Mark's father once sat where they both now sit having lunch and gazing out at the sea. Mark is oblivious to any of this. My-duyen is the center, the First Principle. Because he has been vaguely aware of some pending cataclysm associated with his visit to Song Nhan village, for now he is content to prolong keeping it at a distance and give himself more time to luxuriate in My-duyen's presence.

Tomorrow will come soon enough.

Since Mark's revelation that his father was in a battle at Song Nhan village, My-duyen has been professionally pleasant but distant. This coolness has persisted through their time in Vung Tau. Unhappy with this state of affairs and wishing to stir the pot, Mark seeks a topic that will again elicit some emotion. Personal inquiries have led nowhere, but Mark thinks that if Con Son island was any indication, politics will do the trick. To Mark, young, intelligent, and serious, steep is preferable to flat and purgatory is preferable to paradise. Caution be damned, he wants to see her worked up.

After eating his fill and the dishes have been cleared, Mark sips orange juice with My-duyen on the veranda, waiting for his opportunity to prod. My-duyen has had nothing to eat in spite of his protestations, and for some time, both have been staring silently at the sea.

"Are you glad the communists won?" Mark asks abruptly.

My-duyen's face turns grim. "Of course."

He looks around conspiratorially. "No one can hear you."

Just as he anticipated, her face changes from serious to angry. "If war today, I would join the Front."

"And fight against me?"

Her beautiful eyes flare. "Americans invade. Kill many Vietnamese. I would fight!"

Mark maintains a poker face. "What do your rules say about arguing with American customers?"

She looks down at her *ao dai*. "I wear this. I take you shopping. I interpret for you. I take you to restaurant. All these rules okay. My country? No rules. I fight!"

Mark laughs appreciatively. "You have the spirit of a Trung sister."

My-duyen is unimpressed. "You have arrogance of Chinese. More. You have arrogance of American."

Chastised, Mark suddenly regrets his comments and fears she will lose all respect for him. "My-duyen, I think we were wrong. I have great respect for the Vietnamese people. For your ancestors. For your mother and father."

To his immense relief, her face softens. "You are nice American boy, Mr. Powers, but you not know anything."

Stung by this comment, he asks weakly, "Not know what?"

She sweeps her hand toward the sea. "You sit by ocean. You eat much. You stay in nice hotel. You buy trinkets. You play on computer. But you never know."

Mark, swept up in the moment, goes where he did not wish to go. "Will I know when we visit Song Nhan village?"

My-duyen looks away, and to Mark's chagrin, she appears somewhat disgusted. He quickly backtracks. "My-duyen, I want to know, that's why I came. Perhaps you can teach me."

"No. I not teacher, I guide." She smiles. "Rules."

"Perhaps your mother can teach me."

My-duyen reddens. "My mother not teacher."

"I'll bet she was very beautiful."

"She most lovely in all Vietnam!" My-duyen hesitates, then reaches into her cloth purse and carefully unfolds rice paper to reveal an old, dog-eared black-and-white photograph. She turns to block the wind and gingerly holds the edges to show him.

What Mark sees is the image of a woman even more beautiful than her beautiful daughter. Instinctively, he inhales, taken aback that any woman could be more stunning than My-duyen. "She is unbelievably beautiful," he says with genuine admiration. "What is her name?"

My-duyen smiles approvingly. "Nguyen Tuyet Mai." Her face darkens. "Now she old. Not same. Not same at all."

"I am sure even as an old woman she is still beautiful," says Mark politely.

"No. This is where you not know. Will never know."

"What do you mean?"

She checks her watch. "We go now. To beach. Late already." As she says these words, the photograph is carefully wrapped back in the rice paper and she stands to leave.

Mark touches her arm. "Was she in that battle, My-duyen?"

"Many battles. Not talk about that. You ask her, if she willing, Mr. Powers."

"Tomorrow."

"Yes, tomorrow."

~ *Michael in the Ruins* ~

For the first time in his life Michael is faced with a divorce, albeit from an unconventional spouse, and his knowledge of the law will not help him. In fact, he knows this divorce may be impossible to achieve. The difficulty lies in the fact that he is not sure whether Theresa is a delusion. She may be real. Either case would be a catastrophe. Nevertheless, this problem must be solved, for although he is still sitting at a now empty table, Theresa (whether heaven-sent, hallucination, or hellishly real) is crying in the kitchen.

After watching her impatiently, he says, "I could ignore you until you go away like the others."

"I do not deserve this treatment, Michael," she sobs.

"You cry, but your words are rehearsed. Directed."

"No one directs me. I am real." She pinches her arm. "Real."

"Is that where you got your bruises?"

"Remember that day on the beach when we first met?"

"Theresa, I remember following an empty set of footprints in the sand. Could have been anyone's. Could have all been in my mind."

"Fortress of sand."

"What?" Michael is evidently taken aback by her words.

"He is waiting there for you."

"Who?"

"Storyteller."

Michael pauses, confirmed in his suspicions. "Is that why you are here?"

"We're married. I'm a doctor. You're a schizophrenic. You need help."

"Help from one of my hallucinations?"

"I am not a hallucination. Are you really so frightened? So disoriented?"

Michael responds in an almost pleading voice. "How do I know you're not a hallucination?"

"Michael, take my hand. Now, squeeze it. Does this feel like a hallucination?"

"Anything is possible. Ethyl, or Goddess, said all of this is my 'Grand Delusion.' All of it. But, I say the hell with the whole damn thing. If I can stop a war, end the killing, bring the dead back to life, make a happy ending for all these people, save the world, then I can divorce you. Yet, for all I know, I'm crouched in a corner of some mental institution at this very moment. No, I can't trust my senses."

"What can you trust?"

Michael is in despair and looks away. "That's just it."

Theresa forces him to look at her. "Do you trust that I love you?"

"No!" he cries violently. "Least of all love. That is the mother of all untrustworthy emotions."

"Love is not an emotion, Michael."

Michael gives a cynical laugh. "No, it is apparently some sort of ingredient to strengthen a drug for the gods."

"No, Michael. Love is all there is that's real." She holds out her arms to hug him, but he moves away.

Like a child inching backward from the advances of an overbearing aunt, he says in a brittle tone, "You are not real."

Theresa stops and holds up her hands in a gesture indicating she will come no closer. "Take yourself back to that day at the beach. Remember, Lisa and John are playing. They have built a sand castle."

"A fort."

"Yes, a fort. There are soldiers, toy soldiers."

"John cut them."

"Yes, two in particular, Michael."

He shudders. "One without a hand and one without a foot."

"Yes."

Michael looks at her disapprovingly. "Theresa, it's a waste of time. I won't go back. This kind of talk just proves you are nothing more than an agent of Ethyl. Our relationship isn't working. I want out."

His words evidently have no effect on Theresa. She continues speaking in the same tone.

"You remember what John was saying?"

"Theresa . . . ."

"It was hot, wind blowing, seagulls, ocean waves crashing. The two kids were building a sand fort. Above the din came John's little boy voice. Remember?"

"I—"

"His words were very memorable." Theresa then gives her best impression of a little boy's voice. "'Not there! Here! And the walls got to be . . . got to be higher.' Then he pointed to Lisa's doll and said, 'Put her in the fort 'cause she needs to be protected . . . 'cause of this!'" Theresa grabs a coffee grinder from the counter, holds it up and continues with her impersonation of John. "'T-Rex! The biggest and terriblest dinosaur of them all! He's gonna eat your doll! Better put her in the fort!'"

Michael has shrunk back, horrified but unwillingly mesmerized.

"Remember, Michael, how John placed the toy soldiers in the sand fort around Lisa's doll and threatened them with his dinosaur?" She brandishes the coffee grinder high above her head.

"Yes, I remember."

Theresa again assumes John's voice. "'T-Rex is gonna attack and eat your doll and everybody inside!'" Theresa picks up a pot holder, hugs it to her chest, and says in a little girl voice, "'No, he won't! The fort will protect her! And all these policemen won't let anything happen to her.'"

Michael is speechless and feels a creeping sickness, a nausea welling up in his stomach, yet he can only stare dumbly.

Theresa has stopped talking but now stares into Michael's eyes with an intensity he has never seen in her before. "It was at this time, Michael, that John put those two toy soldiers into the sand fort. One without a hand and the other without a foot. Do you remember?" She does not give him time to answer but instead holds out her open palm to Michael inviting him to look and imagine. "'Mountain Man,'" she says again using John's voice.

Michael stares hypnotically, and in horror sees two tiny specks moving on Theresa's palm, growing, becoming two children playing. Suddenly, sickeningly, he plunges toward her open palm like a crippled aircraft spinning out of control, the creases on her skin widening into a beach. Crashing waves, then seagulls, salty wind, heat. Now he is sitting on the sand, watching John place the severed hand just beyond the reach of the handless soldier's outstretched arm, beneath the taunting figure of the soldier without a foot. He sees beads of water collect on the handless soldier's plastic face as it futilely tries to plug its wrist into its severed hand. Sweat soaks through its plastic fatigues. It trembles, then violently shakes. Blood erupts from its wrist.

Abruptly, Theresa is shouting at him. "Michael! Michael! Wake up! You're dreaming again! Come on, sweetheart. It's okay. Wake up!" Her hand now a closed fist.

He focuses on her face, dumbfounded.

Theresa smiles. "You see, darling, I can save you. Like Diane, I can keep you from going back if I want to, but that wouldn't help. Let me help you. You must go back. Accept my help, my darling."

"How?"

She takes his hand. "Let's go to bed and hold each other."

As she gently leads him toward the bedroom, Michael offers token resistance. He weakly pulls on her hand to slow their progress. "But I'll fall asleep. I don't want to sleep."

"Yes, you need the sleep. Lately you have been sleeping very little, and a bad case of sleep deprivation can lead to hallucinations."

"Like you."

"No, Michael, I am real. Feel my hand in yours." They reach the bedroom. "Here—" she pulls down the covers—"stand next to the bed while I help you with these clothes."

Yielding to her ministrations, Michael nevertheless gives her a sly look. "I should take my meds first. Antipsychotics for chasing away delusions and hallucinations."

"Michael, you know I am not a delusion. You have been to my office, seen my employees, met some of my clients. Besides—" she slides her hand down his thigh—"this is not what a hallucination does."

"I know you are a hallucination."

"Okay. Yes. Taking your meds is a good idea since your psychosis is so pronounced lately. Let me finish with these clothes first." She finishes removing his socks and seats him on the edge of the bed. "Wait for a moment and I'll get you what you need."

Theresa disappears into the bathroom and returns naked. She sidles up to him with a movement that is subtly but exhilaratingly erotic. While taking in the sight of her body Michael notices that she has no bruises, and more interestingly, is hiding her hands behind her back, evidently holding something.

"What are you holding?"

"Lay down first. Good. Now close your eyes and let me . . . just . . . do this."

~

Michael feels something placed on his naked chest and when he opens his eyes and looks down, he sees the two toy soldiers. Once is without a hand, the other without a foot. He wants to brush them off as one might a spider, but for some reason his arm will not obey. Blood is spilling on his chest from their wounds. He opens his mouth to scream, but Theresa gently, even lovingly, puts her hand over his lips.

"Let them help you, Michael."

She removes her hand.

"How?" he asks in a fragile, cracking voice.

"The reunion approaches. Give yourself over to it. Facing so-called demons is better than escaping them. Diane's advice is wrong. Her waking you is wrong. Dead soldiers, dying soldiers, pain, suffering, violence, none of these feelings, these memories, are a dream, nor a delusion, nor schizophrenia. They are you. Pieces of you. Collect them. Put the puzzle together. Become whole."

"This is wrong," says Michael firmly. "Where's Diane?"

"I'm your wife. Diane can't help you. In fact, she has been hindering you all along—keeping you from healing. Listen to me. Let these soldiers take you back."

The blood spilling on his chest is eating away his skin, burning like acid, through the muscle to the bone.

"Take you back."

To the bone.

To the bone.

"Back!"

~

God stands at the foot of Michael's bed. Theresa is gone. The soldiers are gone. Michael is crying, never more alone than he feels now. Almost never.

Through his tears he knows it is God. Somehow he knows. God's eyes are brimming with fiery compassion, at once sad, at once angry, at once full of divine love.

God looks young and vulnerable. He looks like the popular image of Jesus.

God does not speak.

Michael pulls himself together. "Please don't send me back," he implores.

It is not I. It is Her.

Michael pulls the covers closer around his neck. "What's the difference?"

God smiles an infinitely kind smile. *She would have you go, I would have you stay. She would destroy you by making you run from Me, I would save you by making you run to Me. She would have you unbelieve the believable and embrace Doubt while I would have you believe the unbelievable and embrace your Father Fate.*

"My father is dead. Died of a heart attack. Great pain. Great suffering. Sound familiar?"

I knew him.

"Ha!" cried Michael. "That's proof You are a figment of my imagination. You just said, 'I *knew* him.' If You were really God, you would have said, 'I *know* him.' Present tense. After all, my father is in heaven, right?"

Past, present, future, all are melded together in heaven. Knew him, know him, will know him, all the same. Pick your grammatical poison.

"Great. God is sarcastic."

God is everything.

"I am told God is a metaphor. God is a faction. She says God is an addict, a pathetic, strung-out druggie addicted to suffering laced with love to make it more potent."

I love you.

Michael scoffs. "Of course You do. God is made in man's own image, therefore You are made in my image. I am sarcastic. I am addicted to suffering laced with love. I am everything. And I love me. That makes You me."

God looks on in pity. **And Goddess? Theresa? Diane? Mark? Your memories? All delusions?**

"Yes, apparently all You, since You are everything, everywhere. One big delusion with multiple heads—Hydra-God."

And the war? Also a delusion?

"Yes."

Mountain Man? Nature? Madame Dau? Han Tinh?

Michael curls into a fetal position.

And the men you killed? God bears down.

Michael curls tighter.

I do not want to hurt you, My son. I love you. Have you not heard My Own Son died for your sins? That, at any rate, is one story of many. I want to help.

With his eyes closed against the pain, Michael shouts, "Odd coincidence, isn't it? That's what Theresa said! If You want to help, then get out of my mind!"

Some time passes. He looks. God is still there. Michael feels a bit stronger. "Look, if You're a Buddhist god, according to Your own philosophy You're just another delusion. Same with Hindu. If You're a Christian or Jewish or Muslim god, according to Your own philosophy, You're not a delusion, but You did give us free will. Let me exercise my free will. Go!"

God sits on the edge of the bed and Michael hears a sizzling noise, very faint, then a whiff of burning fabric. God chuckles. **If you're right about Me and all of My manifestations … well … you think you've got schizophrenia problems! I must not have taken my meds. Perhaps I do not suffer from schizophrenia, perhaps I am afflicted with dissociative identity disorder. Christian, Muslim, Hindu, Buddhist, Jewish, Sikh, Thor, Zeus, Zarathustra, and....** God's head twirls around like a spinning ball.

Thus suffering, speaks a feminine voice from the corner.

God stops and sighs audibly.

~ *An Incident* ~

Mark and My-duyen are tired from their excursion to Vung Tau. Nodding off in the bus on their return trip to Ho Chi Minh City, neither has spoken for a long time. Darkness envelops the bus, and its overburdened chassis squeaks and groans with every bump. Even the headlights are old and dim, barely illuminating the pavement. Had Mark been awake he would have seen massive water buffalo trudging on both sides of the road, guided expertly by farmers wielding sticks, keeping the beasts from getting too close to the sides of the moving bus. Although leaning on his horn, the driver is also tired, and in one moment of inattention, the bus drifts to the side and hits a buffalo.

Everyone feels the thump and within the time it takes to register the sensation, a high-pitched squeal comes jarringly from outside. Grinding to a halt, the driver becomes furious and dashes off the bus to confront the chattering farmers, accosting everyone who has congregated about the dent now unmistakably visible in the side of his bulky but beloved chariot. The driver in his turn is being berated by the farmers for injuring the beast, which now lies flailing on her side, screaming miserably.

Looking out the window, Mark winces and says, "How could such a huge buffalo get hurt so badly? I would have thought he could turn over the bus no problem."

My-duyen looks troubled, but his comments bring a brief sparkle to her eyes. "He is a she." The troubled look returns. "I think bad neck."

"Broken neck?" asks Mark.

"Yes, broken neck."

The screams of the buffalo reverberate through the open windows and passengers quickly close them. Still shouting epithets, the driver jumps aboard, slams the door shut, and resumes the journey.

Mark tries to engage My-duyen in conversation, but something has changed her mood. She answers with grunts.

"What's wrong?" he asks casually, as if speaking to an American.

"Bus okay. We be at hotel soon. Have time, so you sleep."

"No, no, I mean . . . . " he struggles to find the words. "I mean is there a problem?"

"Bus okay," she repeats firmly.

"I mean with you," he jabs toward her chest.

She looks confused and assumes an unpleasant expression of disgust. "No problem. Bus okay. Soon arrive at hotel. You should sleep. No problem."

Mark feels irritated, certain that she knows what he means and is feigning ignorance. This suspicion always brings out the worst in him, and to punish her he returns to the touchy topic. "Tomorrow we go to Song Nhan village and I meet your mother."

She grunts noncommittally.

"Right?" he asks.

"Not right, Ho Chi Minh City on left side of bus," she gestures with her hand to indicate where in the distance he should look.

"No, I mean are we still going to Song Nhan village tomorrow?"

Moody silence.

He grows alarmed. "My-duyen, are we going tomorrow?"

"Maybe."

"Maybe! That is the whole purpose of this entire trip. What do you mean 'maybe?'"

She frowns, determined. "Government can always change mind and take away permission."

"Better not." He mutters glumly. With his frustration redoubled, Mark's perverse need to get under her skin prods him to prod her. "I'm looking forward to meeting your mother. To talk with her. To ask her many questions."

Slight tightening of lips. *I can read her now*, he thinks with an uncomfortable satisfaction that is itself unsatisfying. Still, she does not respond, pretending to watch something in the darkness beyond the window.

"Yes, I want to ask her many questions about the war, especially about my father's battle."

To his immense disappointment, she continues to gaze out the window. He is about to press her even harder, but in the window's reflection he sees tears streaming from her eyes. This vision is so unexpected that he instinctively blurts out "My-duyen!" while placing his hand on her shoulder.

She shrinks against the wall of the bus, then straightens, looking boldly at him. Red eyes, but no tears.

"What's wrong?" he asks, unsure that he should ask but feeling certain she will answer like an American with words such as 'it's fine, nothing, I'm okay.' Instead, she pulls out an old, dog-eared Vietnamese-English dictionary. Flipping through the pages, she marks the spot with her finger and holds it up for him to see. "Bad this," she taps her finger on the word. Mark squints in the dim light to read it. "Omen," he reads. "A bad omen?"

"Yes."

"Oh," he laughs, relieved. "You mean the water buffalo? Is that the omen?"

"Yes."

"Well, My-duyen, come on, it was just an accident."

"No," she says with finality. "Female. Broken neck. To die. Soon to die. In pain and to die."

"My-duyen—"

"Bad omen."

"My-duyen, are we going to Song Nhan village tomorrow? I need to know. Is this just an excuse not to go, because if it is, then . . . then, I don't know what."

Tears want to come but she stops them. "Yes, we will go. Omens are superstitions for ignorant peasants."

"Good!" He leans back, suddenly exhausted.

"No," she says sadly. "Not good."

~ *My-duyen's Visitor* ~

After dropping Mark off at his hotel, My-duyen wearily returns to the tiny apartment she shares with three other female tour guides. Two are away with customers and one is sleeping on the floor snoring loudly. She changes into a nightgown and retreats to a small room used for keeping odds and ends. Spreading a coverlet, she lies flat and looks up at the ceiling which pulses with light from a neon sign advertising beer outside the flimsily curtained window.

She sleeps . . . or not. She dreams . . . or not.

"My-duyen."

"Mother!"

My-duyen has never seen her mother with legs, yet there she stands, as beautiful and lithe as revealed in the old photographs—even more so. Tuyet Mai wears a long, white *ao dai*, slit up the sides, revealing smoothness itself. She smiles a white brilliance.

"Are you well, my daughter?"

My-duyen swallows, trying to decide whether this is a dream. Answering would be foolish if it was, but not answering would be worse if it wasn't. "I'm well, mother."

"The boy you are with is nice?"

My-duyen shrugs causing the cover to move over her face. She rolls on her side. Time passes. She rolls back. The apparition remains standing in the same spot. My-duyen wonders how much time has passed, but the effort is excruciatingly slow. The apparition, or Tuyet Mai, or whatever it is, speaks. "The boy you are with is nice?"

"He is an American," says My-duyen.

"I know."

"He can be nice at times."

"I know."

Snoring from the adjoining room suddenly turns to a series of loud snorts, then tails off to silence. "She just dreamed her mother found out she's pregnant," says the apparition. "Now she's laying awake in a sweat."

My-duyen feels irritated. *If you know so much, why bother me? Let me sleep.* But she does not speak her thoughts. Ghosts are not to be taken lightly.

As if reading her thoughts, the apparition says, "I am bothering you for a reason."

"Why?" asks My-duyen aloud, more gruffly than she intends. She wants to lie on her stomach and sleep but something prevents her from turning.

The apparition recoils, folding itself inside-out, and emerging in the form of a toothless, legless old crone—My-duyen's mother as she had always known her. The words carry an ominous hissing. "He is dangerous."

"I know," says My-duyen carelessly.

Tuyet Mai sways on her stumps. "You must not bring him to Song Nhan Village."

"I know."

"Then why do you do it?"

"It is my job."

"This does not concern money."

"I know."

Tuyet Mai smiles scornfully in response to My-duyen's last, dismissive reply. The gaps left by her missing teeth mock every notion of the beauty she once possessed. For her part, My-duyen feels satisfaction that she has turned the conversational tables on the apparition, for she has decided that it is not really her mother.

As if understanding, Tuyet Mai screams, "You must not bring him!"

The words strike My-duyen as genuinely her mother's, and she sits up, blinking at the daylight in fright. "Today we go to you, mother . . . or whoever you are. It is too late to turn back now."

Chapter Twenty

The Tunnel Waits

Tong Makes Plans

*N***ow? Is it The Reunion?**

Not yet, Metaphorical Lord. Be patient, supposed Timeless One. The time is soon.

~ Tong Makes Plans ~

The night before he and his companions were scheduled to arrive at Song Nhan village, Tong could not sleep. They had stopped long before sunset to take advantage of an isolated, grassy spot next to a clean-flowing stream. He had bathed and joined the others to eat, anticipating a lively discussion in expectation of tomorrow's momentous arrival, but their conversation consisted of nothing more than empty banter. All had agreed to go to sleep early in preparation for the last leg of their journey, so Tong tried to rest, but this proved to be impossible. He tossed and turned with a restless energy that would not subside. His mind was full of Kung's miraculous powers and Tuyet Mai's contempt for his belief in them. Defy Kung and they would die, thought Tong, but ignore Tuyet Mai and her love for him would wither. *What makes you think she still loves you?* he asked himself. The answer reverberated clearly and with unmistakable urgency; because she must! *And why do you still love her?* The reply dropped like a pebble into the depths of an empty well so deep it returned no sound.

Song Nhan held for him a kind of supernatural terror. It was here that she first came to love him in a manner newly dictated by her loss of legs and an unaccustomed dependency on his wholeness. For that he would be forever grateful. But Song Nhan also reeks with the smell of ghosts and demons, and the blood that poured from her stumps has soaked the ground. Once she arrives in the village, he knows these same spirits will flow up through the earth and back into her body possessing her with a ferocious compulsion that will irrevocably bind her to Song Nhan's godforsaken dirt. Forever. And he will lose her to its mineral soul unless he gives up his own. As if to express his contempt, he stood and peed. Taking a few hesitant steps back to his sleeping area, an idea occurred to him which he quickly rejected. But it returned and would not go away. He was so agitated that he cast his cap on the ground and whispered to the night, "I'll do it! Let what happens happen! Best to know now, before that damn village has her in its clutches!"

He gingerly but resolutely moved toward Tuyet Mai through the damp grass until he saw her face illuminated by the moonlight. She slept. All his indecision returned. He stood motionless. *My love for you is certain,* he thought, *but your love for me is doubtful.* Tong dropped to his knees next to her and started to lean forward when twisting threads of light probed and prodded around his body leaving a sticky film in their wake as if a spider was spinning a web around its prey. So shocked was he by this bizarre phenomenon that he was certain he saw an elongated female face peering out from within the luminous rays encircling him from head to foot. He lashed out like a man fending off an attacker.

Tuyet Mai woke with a start and cried in a low, menacing voice, "No, Kim Lan! No! Stop!"

The luminous threads withdrew as quickly as they had come.

"What was that?" Tong asked breathlessly.

Tuyet Mai seemed to be looking at an invisible figure and spoke as if scolding it rather than Tong. "Kim Lan."

"Kim Lan is dead," he shuddered.

Tuyet Mai merely shook her head and shushed Tong nervously.

Tong fell mute and scrutinized the fringes for signs that Kung prowled about. Hearing nothing, he settled in next to her and whispered, "We cannot stay in Song Nhan village. Too many restless spirits."

"Shhhh!" After a while, evidently satisfying herself that Kim Lan had departed, she gazed at him severely. "We haven't even gotten there yet and you already want to quit. Well, as I said, you can leave now."

"No, I can't."

"Yes, you must stay. Your masters' orders. Slave."

"No, I stay to protect you. I will not mend the fold after a sheep is lost."

Tuyet Mai scoffed. "You and your Chinese sayings. What are you protecting me from?"

"Don't be a fool! The northerners will no longer trust you and the southerners will use you to get to the northerners who no longer trust you and both would kill you for the smallest reason—for no reason."

"I will stay in Song Nhan village. Men, northern or southern, can do what they want. Hanoi to Saigon, Saigon to Hanoi, the masses to their cities all over the world like cockroaches. As for politics and power, that is the rotten food that attracts the cockroaches. I will stay in Song Nhan village."

"With the rats?"

"Better rats than men, especially political men."

"Stupid woman, they will make you leave. Tuyet Mai? Do you hear me? They will make you leave, one way or another. Do you hear me?"

She stared ahead obstinately.

"If you continue to be this intent on your own destruction, I will have to make plans for both of us."

"Make plans for yourself."

"No. Making plans is part of my promise to protect you."

Tuyet Mai turned her head and would not speak.

~

Sooner or later a choice must be made between Hanoi and Saigon, he thought. *Hanoi will win this war, but Kung will win this upcoming battle—I know it—his powers are too strong. Unless—*

"Go now and let me sleep," exclaimed Tuyet Mai loud enough for Kung to hear if he was listening. She closed her eyes. Tong thought he heard rustling in the grass, and quickly moved away, imagining all the while that Kung had been eavesdropping. *It is very simple*, he mused as he lay on his bedding. *If she refuses to leave and if they haven't killed her first, I'll kill her. Better her dead than rotting in Song Nhan village. Then I'll be free to do as I want.*

~

After Tong left, Tuyet Mai had trouble going back to sleep. Kung's face kept appearing in the moonlight.

A twig snapped.

"Who is it?" she cried.

"Just me," came Tong's voice. "I'm leaving but I thought I heard something. Nothing here. Goodnight."

"Goodnight."

At last she slept.

And dreamt.

"He plans to kill you," said Kim Lan.

"I know."

Kim Lan's specter twisted excitedly. "I tried to help, but you stopped me."

"If none of them leave me in peace, I'm past help anyway."

"I can help you drive him mad."

"Yes."

Kim Lan smiled maliciously. "Once he is mad he will kill you. Once you are dead you will be with me."

Tuyet Mai welcomed death, yet felt troubled.

"Not before I've spent some time in Song Nhan village with Madame Dau."

"That again," said Kim Lan disgustedly.

"I want to hold the babies, talk with the women, be loved and accepted, make myself whole at least once before I die."

"He loves you. Have babies with him," said Kim Lan, her voice dripping sarcasm.

"Yes, but not that kind of love. That's not the love of which I speak."

Kim Lan leaned out of the dream and enveloped Tuyet Mai's face.

"True. You want my kind of love."

Tuyet Mai awoke gasping for breath.

~ Ninh and the Women ~

Many hours earlier at Song Nhan village, Ninh had called Madame Dau and Madame Vit from the fields, instructing them to join him in the *dinh* at sunset. Now on her way to meet Ninh, Madame Dau felt a deep sadness. Since the day when most villagers had abandoned the village, she rarely entered the *dinh*. No neighbors to visit on the way. No laughing, raucous children. No bantering about village business. No village council. Almost no one left at all. Houses dilapidated, paths overgrown, empty cavernous *dinh*, and far too many memories calculated to make her lonely and afraid. The bustling sounds of the village had been replaced by the buzzing sounds of the encroaching forest and its insect hordes. Especially now she yearned for the comfort of her absent friends. *Thank god Madame Vit stayed*, she thought as she scanned the path hoping to run into Vit before arriving at the *dinh*. But Vit was nowhere to be seen and Madame Dau found herself standing hesitantly at the foot of the steps.

"Come in!" ordered Ninh from the entrance door.

She circled around him to avoid the rancid smell perpetually emanating from his body and entered the *dinh*, walking slowly to allow her eyes time to adjust to the darkness. One solitary lantern apparently lit by Ninh cast a weak, yellowing light in the distance. The dim orb of light barely illuminated the massive guardian statues, giving them a shadowy, malevolent presence. She shuddered when it became apparent Madame Vit had not arrived yet. Oh how she wished for the old days when the *dinh* would be full of friends and the air full of incense and the spirits as light hearted as children!

"Go and sit by the lamp," said Ninh coldly. "I will wait for the other hag."

She made her way to the far end of the *dinh* where the raised platform once reserved for members of the village council now stood bare except for a small table on which the solitary lantern sat, guttering coldly. The guardian spirit statues looked down mockingly as she sat on a straight-backed Chinese style chair and waited. Visions of the old days danced in her head and she thought of her long dead husband, something that was happening more frequently. The longing for her husband created in her a complicated mixture of depression and comfort. She wished to simply sit for hours and reminisce, but the longer she sat, the more uneasy she became. Where was Madame Vit? What did this horrible man want? Why did he summon them here? The more she wondered the more she unwillingly returned to the ache of those that suffer in solitude.

"Hey!"

Madame Dau jumped at the sound of Ninh's voice. She turned and saw him standing halfway between her and the entrance door.

"Where is your friend, eh?" he demanded.

Madame Dau felt her heart flutter and she looked at him dumbly.

"Well?"

"I don't know," she said finally.

"Did she run away and leave you alone with me?"

Madame Dau was at a loss, but Madame Vit's words came weakly from the open door. "I am here."

Ninh gestured her in. "Come, come. Go sit with Madame Dau, I will return." He abruptly left.

After he was safely gone, Madame Dau whispered sharply even before Madame Vit had a chance to sit. "Where have you been?"

Madame Vit looked away. "Sorry, sorry," she kept repeating.

"You might have thought of me being alone with that man," Madame Dau uttered in exasperation.

Madame Vit shifted in her chair. "I almost ran away." She glanced toward the door. "He is too ferocious. I'm sure he will kill us."

"Hm," Madame Dau grunted. "Why didn't you?"

"Kill us?" Vit smiled weakly.

Madame Dau did not catch the humor. "No. Leave."

"Ah. She convinced me to stay."

"Who?"

Now Madame Vit appeared even more uncomfortable and refused to look at Madame Dau. At last she said, "A ghost."

Madame Dau responded with surprise. "You sound like crazy Tinh."

"I know."

Madame Dau leaned forward anxiously, aware that Ninh might return any moment. "Tell me."

"I think it was Tinh's goddess." Madame Vit fell silent.

"Well?" demanded Madame Dau again glancing at the door.

Madame Vit seemed distracted. "I fell asleep and—"

"Now!" boomed Ninh's voice as he burst through the entrance door. "Let us talk."

Madame Dau flinched, then sighed perceptibly while Madame Vit leaned back in her chair, seemingly relieved but actually resigned to what she considered inevitable fate.

Ninh pulled up a chair and sat imperiously, hands planted on his spread knees, gazing upon the two women as might an emperor at two errant concubines. "I have called you here because my companions will arrive any time now. Once they arrive, things must be in order."

The women waited but Ninh was scribbling something down on a paper he had brought. "The village must be prepared," he said as he wrote. "I want the doors on all the houses to have the following message tacked to them so that they are in plain sight."

Ninh finished writing and scanned their faces, receiving only vacant stares in return. "Do you understand?"

"Hm," they both grunted in unison.

"Good! Can you read?"

Both women looked down. "A little," said Madame Dau.

Ninh handed the paper to Madame Dau. "Read it!"

Madame Dau read haltingly. Although she could read quite well, she had long known it was dangerous for a woman to broadcast her intelligence. "Long live Uncle Ho and the revolution! Death to the Americans and their Saigon puppets!"

"Good," said Ninh. "I have put the word out and within a very short time, we should have other visitors. Visitors from the forest. Very important visitors. That should make you both feel good. Your village has become important."

The two women looked sick. Ninh laughed. "Now, go tell that little man, Han Tinh, to help you make copies and put this notice up on every door. Understand?"

Madame Dau and Madame Vit both nodded, but Ninh seemed unsatisfied. "Can you both write? You will need a lot of copies." He waited. They said nothing. He continued. "I assume little Tinh can write." Still no response. "Well?" he asked sharply.

"Yes," said Madame Dau looking at Madame Vit, who remained silent.

"I will leave it in your hands," said Ninh. He turned to Madame Vit. "You'll help her. Understand?"

"Yes."

"Good. This must be done by nightfall. Remember, every door by nightfall. Make the words big. Do not spare the ink or the writing brush!"

Madame Dau gathered her courage. "But, sir, you know there are almost no villagers to read them?"

Ninh smiled. "They are not for the villagers."

~

It took time to find enough paper and ink, but by evening Madame Dau and Madame Vit were attaching the notices on the doors. Tinh stayed in the *dinh* laboriously copying Ninh's words. At first he protested mightily, but after being convinced, he began to enjoy his task. It reminded him of the water puppet theater when he would prepare fliers advertising the next performance. Once, while the women were out attaching notices and he was leaning over the table finishing a copy, Ninh entered and stood behind him, smoking a tattered cigarette and watching quietly. Tinh ignored his presence and kept writing.

"Your calligraphy isn't bad," said Ninh.

Tinh tried to block out the stench of Ninh's rotting flesh.

Ninh felt bored and needed an emotional rise from Tinh. "So, you long for this woman with no legs, this Tuyet Mai. Her body may be broken but her spirit is not. She is a magnificent woman!"

The words seared Tinh's soul but he mustered all his resources to deny satisfaction and remained silent—a weapon greater than the combined arsenals of noise, albeit one he rarely used.

Ninh experienced disappointment. Anytime a man who considers himself superior cannot elicit even the most rudimentary response from an inferior, that man must concede a mortifying failure in his power to bend another to his will.

But within the seed of this failure lay the recognition of an intellect at least as formidable, so Ninh instinctively considered Tinh dangerous. Whenever Ninh sensed danger he immediately withdrew and stewed in the noxious swamp of his soul, waiting, a poisonous bog in which many were lured to their destruction. Yet Ninh felt somehow challenged by this little Viet Cong veteran, so he stoked the fires of his personally-directed malevolence (as opposed to a more general, diffused malevolence) and uncharacteristically continued to prod. "Are you afraid of me?" he asked.

"No," replied Tinh.

"Yet your hand is shaking."

Tinh laughed. "Not at all. And even if it is, it is due to the strong wind blowing from your mouth."

"I could kill you now or have you killed later."

Tinh stopped writing and held up the brush like a sword. "I am far more powerful than you. I could kill myself now or kill myself later, the same as you. But unlike you, I could have killed myself before you arrived and I can still kill myself long after you leave, both far beyond your power. Therefore, I am not afraid of you."

Ninh was at a loss. In spite of himself, he admired the courage of this little man. Finally he said, "Not knowing when to be afraid is a dangerous thing."

"True," said Tinh. "But knowing when to be afraid is the opposite of fear."

"Still dangerous."

"Unfortunately, danger is a condition of life. The opposite of danger is even more dangerous."

Ninh felt powerless against Tinh's twisted logic so he resorted to clumsy primitivism. He pulled out his pistol and pointed it at Tinh's head. "This," he said calmly, "is not impressed with your clever remarks. It is the definition of danger. Shall I pull the trigger?"

"No."

"Why not?"

"Because I don't want to die."

Ninh smiled triumphantly. "Now are you afraid?"

"Yes," said Tinh.

Ninh felt little satisfaction in this curt, almost emotionless reply, and was mulling over his next move when Madame Vit entered the *dinh*.

"I need more fliers," she said breathlessly, pulling up short when she saw the gun.

Tinh warily watched Ninh put away his pistol.

"There has been a delay in production," Ninh said nonchalantly. The tense confrontation with Tinh had evaporated as quickly as it had arisen and Ninh asked Madame Vit almost congenially, "Have you been running?"

"Yes," said Madame Vit looking down. "I want to finish in time to. . . . " Her words trailed off.

"In time to what?" asked Ninh.

"In time to go home."

"And?" asked Ninh suspiciously.

"And rest before. . . ." Again her words lapsed.

"Before what?"

Madame Vit shifted nervously. "Before they come."

~ *Arrival* ~

Song Nhan village looked small in the distance to the three travelers pausing on the ridge to catch their breaths and contemplate the descent. Peering through the late morning mist, all agreed the village appeared deserted. Dilapidated. Charred. Falling into ruin. For a long time Kung seemed worried, but after carefully surveying the scene while the others rested, he suddenly exclaimed, "Ah! There!"

Tuyet Mai and Tong jumped up and followed his pointing finger to see the smoke from a cooking fire thread into the air. It had been obscured by the fog and came from a house that Tuyet Mai immediately recognized. She wanted to shout, "Madame Dau!" but wisely held her tongue.

Tong stood. "Let's go."

"No," said Kung. "Wait. I want to watch. Make sure there are no surprises."

Tuyet Mai again felt conflicting emotions. She wanted to bound down to the village as fast as she could go, but at the same time some hesitation, some fear she was unwilling to identify, held her back. Still sitting in the wagon, she had the urge to nudge it forward so that it would roll down on its own accord, unstoppable by Kung, Tong, or herself. Unable to act on this urge, she sat like a stone gazing at the village, concealing from an oblivious world the fact that her heart pounded invisibly but painfully inside her chest.

After what seemed an eternity, Kung stirred. Craning his neck to look at the village one last time he nodded in apparent satisfaction and said quietly, "Let's go." If one listened carefully, one might detect a note of regret in his voice. However, Tong and Tuyet Mai were each distracted by their own thoughts and did not notice. Automatically, Tong started pulling the wagon and the three odd companions started their descent down a series of switchbacks.

~

As Tong maneuvered the wagon down the trail, his trepidation increased. A litany of disasters scrolled through his imagination. An ambush. Booby traps. Tuyet Mai's ridiculous enchantment with the village blinding her to its dangers. Her total rejection of his presence and the knowledge that she would refuse his protection once the enchanted village had her in its power convinced him that she—all of them—were walking into a trap. Magician Kung and the village witches in pitched battle with Tuyet Mai, and himself caught in the middle. Death.

Yet Tong's feet continued to move and the wagon continued to roll downward. Although he felt the web tightening as the village drew closer, he wanted to turn and run but was powerless to stop events. Who was the spider at the center, the spider that would eventually devour him? Madame Dau? Tuyet Mai? The government? A stranger? He looked at the back of Kung striding in front. *Him,* thought Tong. *It will be him. He is the spider, the demon, the magician, the executioner. He's not walking into a trap; he is the trap.*

Kung slowed to allow time for Tong to stop the wagon's momentum. Once Tong had succeeded, Kung looked at him with the expression of a pious monk. **No,** he said in a low, tremulous voice. **I am not a spider nor an executioner. I am your Redeemer.**

Tong was so startled he felt unable to respond. Kung turned and continued the descent, leaving Tong in a state of redoubled fear and uncertainty. Tuyet Mai merely appeared to be confused so Tong allowed Kung to get farther ahead, out of earshot.

"Are you excited?" he whispered to her.

He watched her lips tighten in an expression he interpreted as irritation.

"Don't be a fool!" she snapped.

"You're the fool," replied Tong petulantly. "You're embracing an already dead village to feed your own delusion of . . . of God knows what. You are choosing death by coming here." Tong said this out of exasperation knowing he had too often made the same point. He waited for her inevitable scolding.

"What would you have me do, turn around now when I'm so close?" she said weakly.

Her response shocked him and gave him a flicker of hope, for her tone was devoid of anger or sarcasm. She almost seemed to be asking for help. But before Tong could reply, he noticed that Kung had stopped and they were now within hearing distance. Tong searched for signs that Kung had heard but detected none. Now that the village was so close, Tong wanted to make a statement that would impress Tuyet Mai. "When we arrive let me do the talking since I know them."

"Ha!" scoffed Kung. "A fly in a bottle speaking to its own distorted reflection."

~

Tuyet Mai waited stoically in the wagon. She knew that Tong and Kung were having a heated discussion but she did not hear the words. She did not want to hear them. Her mind was frozen—a kind of debilitating panic unexpectedly seized her. Instinctively she straightened her tunic and ran her hand through her hair to untangle the knots. *You look a fright, you look a fright,* the voice of Kim Lan kept repeating in her mind. *A missing tooth, hair a filthy mess, no legs—ugly woman! You look a fright. You will scare the children. They will shun you.*

The more Kim Lan's words reverberated in her mind, the more she imagined the women of Song Nhan village would reject her, if only to protect their children from such a monstrous vision as she must appear. How stupid to have focused her entire life on the kindness of a group of strangers! Tong was right, she must leave. Now!

Before Tuyet Mai could proclaim her refusal to proceed, she felt something odd pulling her hair. It gently clawed through the strands, not unpleasantly, following the contours of her scalp. So unexpected was this sensation that she remained immobilized.

"How does this feel, sister?" came Kung's voice in a silken, comforting tone. "We must prepare you to meet the women of Song Nhan village."

Only now did Tuyet Mai realize that Kung was combing her hair with a brush. Like an expert, he held the long strands and carefully combed them out, teasing out the tangles and untangling the knots, his hands a marvel of strength and delicacy.

"You look quite beautiful," he said with feeling, all the while continuing the rhythmic movements of the brush.

"Where did you get such a brush, comrade?" asked Tuyet Mai in the only words she could find.

"Ha, ha! I knew it would prove useful. It's American. Highest quality." He leaned over so she could see his face and winked. "And it's good you use the term 'comrade'. Keep saying comrade, comrade. We are now officially turncoats. Believers in the revolution. Followers—" he carefully untangled a particularly troublesome knot—"of Uncle Ho and dedicated enemies of the Americans and their Saigon puppets, even though we may occasionally use their weapons." He held up the brush and laughed.

"That will not be hard," said Tong boldly. "Americans have always been my enemy!" He waited anxiously for Kung's reaction.

But Kung merely looked toward the village. "My friend awaits our arrival. Preparations should already be made. Tonight we sleep in greater comfort under a roof."

"If our throats aren't slit," said Tong.

Kung nodded and made a last pass with the brush through Tuyet Mai's hair, running his fingers along the part and across her forehead to apply the finishing touches. He spoke into the breeze, again casting his gaze toward the village. "No one will slit our throats."

Tong stared. "How can you be so sure?"

Kung returned the stare. "You have seen my powers. How can you question?"

Tong could make no reply, but Tuyet Mai felt rejuvenated and ready to face her future. Despite her hatred and distrust of him, Kung had given her the courage to meet the women of Song Nhan village by his simple act of kindness, and for this she felt unexpected gratitude. She looked at Tong sympathetically. Her feeling for him made all the more touching with the knowledge that he had made an effort to express his independence from Kung for her sake. His failure brought a pang of guilt and the less flattering realization that she still needed to use him.

Tong picked up the rope and pulled, causing Tuyet Mai to rock slightly backward. This small jolt cleared her mind of any further useless emotional ideas—the village awaited and her anxiety returned. Before she had time to renew her protest, the first thatch houses at the edge of the village came into view. *Too late! I'm here at last! Song Nhan village! Oh, God!*

~ *Greetings* ~

Ninh was the first to see the travelers approach. A cloud passed quickly across his ravaged face, then he raised his right arm and waved, not bothering to move the other arm resting against the rusted rice thresher in the village square. He waited, seemingly anchored to the thresher and to his perpetually rehearsed haughtiness.

Kung strode up to him, smiling and looking around in vain for villagers. "Greetings, Comrade Ninh. As you see we are all here. Where are the villagers? Hiding?"

"Greetings," replied Ninh. "Three of them are hiding, the rest are long gone."

"I am not hiding!" came a loud voice.

All eyes turned to look at Han Tinh who quickly knuckle-walked up to the wagon where Tuyet Mai sat stoically. Scrutinizing her up and down, he announced, "You're right Comrade Ninh, she is magnificent!"

The color drained from Tuyet Mai's face and she swayed as if about to faint. "Get him away from me!" she said in a guttural command. While she had often remembered Han Tinh with fond amusement, he now disgusted her, for his ugly reality made her confront her own.

Tong gave Tinh a sharp kick in the rear knocking him flat.

Ninh laughed. "She thinks you're magnificent too, little man!"

"Love is slow to burn but lives to learn," replied Tinh with difficulty as he struggled to stand and straighten his disheveled appearance.

Tuyet Mai immediately remembered why she disliked Ninh so intently. The oozing welt that was his face recalled the dark Con Son days. Tinh disgusted her but Ninh elicited a feeling of horror. A feverish burning made her feel flushed and weak.

"Where are we staying, comrade?" asked Kung pleasantly, as if nothing had happened.

"Yes, let me take you to the house I have expropriated for your purpose here."

Kung held up his hand. "First show our Comrade Tuyet Mai to her abode so that she may rest."

"Um," grunted Ninh disapprovingly.

Tuyet Mai noticed that Tong remained silent despite his earlier insistence to "do the talking."

~

Madame Dau waited in her house, unsure what to do. The house had been gradually rebuilt over the years to duplicate, as closely as possible, its original design. Respect for her ancestors demanded nothing less. But the building materials were inferior and she often thought that was appropriate, since she was also inferior to her ancestors. She had prepared tea, but it was now cold. *If only Vit were with me*, she thought. But Vit also waited alone in her house, so Madame Dau paced the room calling on the memory of her husband and the intervention of her ancestors to protect her.

Just as she decided to reheat the tea, she heard a group approaching. She walked to the porch in time to meet Ninh at the door. He seemed distracted and said, "Ah, Madame Dau, we are here." He turned to find Tuyet Mai already on the porch. "This," he spread his arm, "is Comrade Tuyet Mai. She will be staying with you."

The two women looked at each other expectantly. Madame Dau stared with feminine curiosity at Tuyet Mai's features—how she had changed! *Poor, poor woman*, thought Madame Dau. Compelled by feelings of pity and compassion, she reached out her hand to help and was surprised to see tears welling in Tuyet Mai's eyes.

~

Tuyet Mai took Madame Dau's hand for just a moment, but an electric shock seemed to run through her body and she instinctively pulled her hand away. Evidently overwhelmed, she closed her eyes and bowed her head. It was on this very porch that the fantasies she had elaborately constructed over the years had played themselves out. Now they came back to her, jumbled one upon the other. She closed her eyes, the men disappeared, and she felt herself surrounded by a group of village women. Children materialized. They played and their laughter reverberated through the village. *Yes*, she thought. *Now when I open my eyes it will be as it should be. As I imagined it.*

But she could not make her eyes open. The lids remained closed—frozen shut. While in this state of darkness the old familiar feeling of dread returned. Then, to her horror and despite her best efforts to resist . . . .

Something moved on her chest, under her tunic.

Looking down in horror, Tuyet Mai saw two enormous bulges straining at her tunic, swelling and pushing outward. She glanced at the other women, now staring at her with open mouths. The expanding growths on her chest strained against her buttons and she pressed against them with cupped hands, but they would not be constrained and she heard the fabric tearing apart. Falling away.

Out from the torn fabric burst two wriggling babies where her breasts would be. Lengthening, grasping, they squirmed on her chest, crying inconsolably. She tried to hug them, cradle them, but their legs were anchored inside her body. Dropping her arms, they wriggled on their own, like two children dangling from ropes tied around their ankles.

"Quan An! Quan An!" the women continued to shout as they withdrew into the shadows, leaving only an empty house and deserted courtyard. Empty except for Madame Dau, who simply sat and looked at Tuyet Mai.

Then, as if from everywhere at once, men began to appear. Soldiers. Hundreds, thousands of them. They stood with their weapons raised, hailing Tuyet Mai.

"Give us the babies, that they may grow into soldiers! Give us the babies!"

They pumped their weapons in the air and stamped their feet. "Heroes! Heroes! All soldiers are heroes!"

Tuyet Mai tried to cover the babies, but they had grown too large and were twisting too violently. Her pants were torn away, leaving her naked before the men, unable to conceal herself. She had become Quan An, goddess of compassion, powerless to stop herself from standing on display for all to worship.

Madame Dau spoke quietly. "You see the results of mating with the beasts. You have become Quan An in their eyes. A fertile wellspring from which their ranks are replenished. You are the object of their greatest devotion and their most compelling desire: the woman who creates them. Their mother.

"But . . . but . . . it is not my desire . . . I . . . this is not. . . . " mumbled Tuyet Mai.

As she tried to collect her thoughts, a soldier rose before her brandishing a machete. His arm came down in a great swath and cut off one of the babies. The baby fell at her feet, wailing, while blood spewed from the severed stumps still protruding from her chest. Again, the soldier raised his machete. . . .

~

"Stop!" shouted Tong holding Tuyet Mai's flailing arms.

"She is ill," said Kung calmly. "It has all been too much for her." He gently felt her forehead while Tong pinned her arms. "Fever."

Han Tinh had trailed after the others and now stood quietly watching. He nodded as if comprehending the problem. "All of us men must leave. Let Madame Dau take care of her alone."

"You're crazy," said Tong. "She'll hurt herself."

"Only if we men stay"

Kung looked at Tinh as if seeing him for the first time. "He's right, let us leave. Madame Dau, please take care of her. She is quite . . . valuable to us."

Ninh appeared doubtful and was hesitant to withdraw, but Kung shushed them all out of the house. Once outside, Kung said to Ninh, "Show Comrade Tong and me where we will stay. After that we must meet. Where is a good spot?"

Ninh looked worried. "They should be here soon, and now this." He tilted his head toward Madame Dau's house. "She will be a problem."

"Where can we meet?" insisted Kung.

"In the *dinh*."

"Yes, I know it," muttered Tong. He appeared shaken. "Maybe we should rest first?"

"No time," said Kung.

"Yes," agreed Ninh. "They will be in no mood for nonsense."

"You're sure they'll be here?" asked Kung pointedly.

"Yes."

"But you aren't sure when?"

"No."

Kung seemed pleased. "Good. Show us where we'll stay, then we meet at the *dinh*."

On the way they passed Han Tinh still staring at Madame Dau's house. Kung paused. "Are you aware?" he asked.

Tinh seemed startled. "I think so."

Kung walked on, smiling.

Later in the *dinh*, the three men sat at the same table used earlier by Tinh to copy the notices that were still attached to every door in Song Nhan village. The *dinh* was unusually dark even though the day had not yet reached mid-afternoon. Dark clouds rolled above and the wind grew increasingly strong, gusting down the pathways between Song Nhan's houses, causing Tinh's notices to flap violently. Inside the *dinh*, a low hissing emanated from the cracks and crevices in the ancient walls, rising in volume as the wind strengthened. Even the lantern flame guttered from the drafts whistling through the broken windows.

The three men hunched over the table, two of them chilled and uneasy while the third evidently lost in thought.

Kung sat straight and slapped his knees. "Monsoon certainly coming on fast," he said.

"Of course," said Tong. "Yet it's very surprising this time of year."

Ninh looked glum. "Very surprising. I had no idea. None of the usual signs. So sudden. What's worse, it's acting like a big one. Damn!"

"The timing is interesting," observed Kung dryly.

Tong laughed. "Isn't it though! Very interesting!"

The Guardian Spirit statues seemed to groan as a strong blast of wind buffeted the *dinh*. Thunder rolled across the valley.

"Coming on so fast," said Tong repeating the obvious.

"Will this delay our communist brothers?" asked Kung.

Ninh shrugged.

"When they come," said Kung scanning their faces, "do you all remember what to do?"

Distracted nods.

Tong seemed restless, unwilling to shift his attention from the oncoming storm. "Reminds me of a few years ago," he said. "A battle. The battle. Here. Big storm. Lasted a long time." He shook his head. "Just like it was then."

At this point Han Tinh made a dramatic entrance, throwing open the heavy doors and moving to the center of the hall. He was soaked. The wind roared in behind him. Before Kung or Ninh could protest his presence, he held up a handful of wet fliers and let them go. The fliers swirled around the room. "Your plans may have to be changed, comrades," he said above the din.

~ *Visitations* ~

After the men left, Tuyet Mai calmed and allowed Madame Dau to make her comfortable on an old Japanese tatami mat expropriated from the abandoned house of a wealthy villager. Madame Dau busied herself with preparing a fire and making tea, allowing Tuyet Mai time to adjust her emotions to the new surroundings in peace.

Having started the fire with some difficulty due to the increasingly violent wind, Madame Dau finished making a samovar of tea just as the rain began falling in sheets. She brought the tea to Tuyet Mai and saw her lying on the tatami staring at the thatch ceiling with a pained look that reminded Madame Dau of a woman in the beginning stages of labor.

"I brought you tea, Lady," said Madame Dau in deference. She poured a cup and stood to leave.

"Stop!" said Tuyet Mai more sharply than she wanted. "Call me Tuyet Mai."

Madame Dau looked down. "Lady, you are a powerful woman here with powerful men. I am only who I am."

Tuyet Mai uttered a short groan, then quickly regained control over her emotions. Madame Dau saw all this pass before her eyes in an instant.

"Please call me Tuyet Mai. As you see from my body, I no longer have power of any kind." Tears again began to well. "In fact, I have had no power for many years. I am just a broken woman whose body no longer deserves to be called female and yet whose mind, God help me, still desires to be called a woman. So much so."

Madame Dau did not know how to respond and remained silent.

"Tell me about the village," said Tuyet Mai, again with a natural air of authority that she immediately wanted to retract.

Madame Dau was evidently confused. "It is as you see it."

"No, no. I mean where are the villagers? What happened?" Again she spoke curtly and again she regretted the tone. *But are these women such buffaloes that they don't understand anything?* she wondered.

"Soldiers came, burned the houses, killed many. They took our food and then came the hunger. Some starved." Now Madame Dau began to cry. "So they all left for the district capital. Only I and a few others stayed. So sad. So sad."

"You stayed. Why?"

Madame Dau straightened. "I am the provisional council chief. The spirits of my ancestors dwell here. My home is here. I will keep it for my children and grandchildren when they return."

Tuyet Mai's tone softened. "Do you remember me?"

"Of course." Madame Dau's enthusiasm rose. "You were so—" she stopped suddenly and again looked down in confusion.

Tuyet Mai smiled. "Beautiful? Don't worry, Madame Dau, I am quite re-signed to the glory of my past and the shame of my present."

Madame Dau felt bold enough to smile. "It seems that we both have glorious pasts but now live in an ugly present."

Tuyet Mai responded with an upwelling of sentiment by touching Madame Dau's hand. "Can we share our ugly present together?"

Madame Dau was emboldened by Tuyet Mai's touch and with some trepi-dation, asked, "Will those men allow us to have a present, let alone a future?"

Before Tuyet Mai could speak, thunder rumbled ominously, as if on cue.

Madame Dau shuddered but was amazed to hear Tuyet Mai laughing and saying, "They can do nothing more to me! Not the shrunken, cruel men outside with their guns or the shrunken, cruel gods above with their storms!"

"What does give your life meaning?" asked Madame Dau under her breath.

"You give my life meaning," said Tuyet Mai. "This village gives my life meaning."

"But this is not your village," exclaimed Madame Dau in genuine surprise. "You hardly know me."

"I am aware."

Madame Dau seemed lost in thought.

Finally Tuyet Mai asked, "What are you thinking?"

"You remind me of Han Tinh."

"Who?" cried Tuyet Mai.

"The little man with no legs."

"I know who Han Tinh is, but how can I remind you of him?" Tuyet Mai demanded angrily.

"No, no, not that," said Madame Dau. "It is just that our village adopted him long ago. You see, he is an orphan also."

Tuyet Mai scowled. "Orphan or no orphan, he disgusts me."

"He is not as he seems to you now," said Madame Dau. "Once you get to know him. . . . " her words trailed off and she assumed an affectionate smile.

~

Even as the women talked, the wind and rain grew fiercer. Han Tinh sought shelter in his shack listening with a growing sense of unease. Although he had experienced many monsoons, this one seemed different yet eerily familiar. He rubbed his stumps, trying to knead out the ache that had returned after so many years. *It has been a long time since these old knots had caused me pain,* he thought. *Why now?* He smiled, but it was an uneasy act of defiance, so he said aloud, "I am aware," to make himself feel better.

While Tinh seemed engrossed in these musings, Kung entered unannounced, shook off his American poncho and squatted in the middle of the floor. Han Tinh watched him silently, refusing to speak first and give Kung an advantage. Something about Kung seemed oddly familiar—someone he had known, or seen, years ago. This disturbing recognition put him off balance and robbed him of his usual easy humor.

"I have come to answer your questions," said Kung matter-of-factly.

Tinh could not stop the brief flash of surprise that flickered in his eyes. Irritated with himself, he said nothing.

Kung waited.

Tinh waited.

Kung stood. "Well, I'll be going." He moved briskly to the door.

Tinh watched.

Kung opened it.

Tinh waited.

Kung hesitated.

Tinh said nothing.

Kung walked out, closing the door quietly behind him.

Tinh cursed himself for not stopping Kung with words, a comment, a question. "Stubborn fool!" he said to the door, half-expecting Kung to reappear.

"I do have a question," said Tinh, again to the door.

Nothing.

"Many questions!" he shouted.

Still Kung did not return.

Tinh gestured obscenely. "If you were half the wizard I thought you were, you would have known my questions before I asked." He cocked his head, willing Kung to burst through the door.

No Kung.

Thunder.

Tinh spat disgustedly. "Some wizard! Fucking bastard!"

He waited.

"Fake!"

Nothing.

"Shit," said Tinh to the air. "Sun goes up, sun comes down, frogs fuck, crabs copulate, birds bang, millipedes mate, and monkeys monkey around, but wizards warble on a high branch to themselves. Concealed from view. Useless."

~

Han Tinh stopped grumbling and gazed out at the rain, thinking about Tuyet Mai. He tried to visualize her bare breasts, but for some reason only her face would appear. *Others may think her ugly, but I see great beauty*, he thought. *Yet she obviously finds me disgusting. Why?*

While he was in the midst of these thoughts Kung returned, again opening the door without knocking. This time Tinh could not conceal his surprise and refused to make the same mistake twice.

"Ah! Mr. Kung . . . Comrade Kung . . . Venerable Kung! What brings you back?"

Kung remained standing. "I have made a decision."

"Yes?"

"First I must ask you some serious questions. Will you answer honestly?"

"Of course," said Tinh, mentally noting the contrast between Ninh's crude method with that of Kung's smooth delivery.

Kung smiled. "Yes, I am not Ninh, and furthermore, you say 'of course' too easily."

Tinh felt shaken. "I will answer honestly."

"Honesty is not your strong point."

Tinh laughed. "Honesty has too strong a point. Dangerous. You can cut yourself. I prefer a blunt instrument."

"Han Tinh, now is not the time to play the buffoon!"

"You're right Mr. Kung, Comrade Kung, Venerable Kung. Honestly, I will answer honestly. I honestly promise!"

Kung laughed, appreciating Tinh's absurdist take on life.

They spoke late into the night.

Outside, the monsoon wind grew more ferocious, and two shadows moved through the room as the men talked. Only one noticed.

Chapter Twenty-One

PART FIVE: DECEPTION

Gatherings

~ Mark and My-duyen Arrive ~

Precipitously tilting over the edge of a watery ditch, up to its right wheel wells in mud, the rental car slowly rolls onto its side, sinking deeper into the muck. Two figures stand dejectedly in the rain watching this catastrophe with limp arms and soggy spirits. One of them perks up.

"How could you know this storm would arrive so quickly?" asks Mark. "Out of nowhere! I mean, it was sunny when we left the district capital, and now just look." Mark glances at the morose My-duyen to see if his words have had any effect.

Before she can respond, half of the right side of the car disappears under the mud while the left rises perpendicular and slowly follows the right. A sucking noise accentuates its impending entombment. My-duyen dons her peasant hat, ties the scarf under her chin to keep it from blowing off in the swirling wind, and picks up a cloth bag filled with belongings which she had rescued from the doomed car. Sheets of rain lash the ground, prodding the two travelers to get moving.

"We walk!" My-duyen shouts above the roar.

"How far to Song Nhan village?" Mark calls, cupping his hand over his mouth, happy to turn his attention from the unhappy vehicle.

But My-duyen is still reluctant to leave. She stares at the car and says in Vietnamese, "I will certainly be fired for this."

Mark does not understand the words but perceives the depth of her despair. "It'll be all right. I'll tell them that I wrecked the car. My fault!" he thumps his chest.

My-duyen has barely heard the words but has already dismissed what little she understands with the thought that Mark is an American boy handicapped by his wealth and unable to comprehend the gears and cogs of her world.

"My-duyen, I'm serious," Mark says with as much sincerity as he can muster.

But she has already started down the road, evidently lost in thought.

Mark follows like a schoolboy, gripping his suitcase as if it were an oversized lunchbox about to be snatched by a bully.

~

My-duyen is amazed at the speed with which this monsoon struck. The clouds are unusually dark and foreboding, and though she is used to heavy rain and thunder, the air seems charged with a sickly smell of something burning. But what? This 'something' is what she puzzles over as Mark trudges behind. The village is over two hours walk and she does not want to get stranded at night in the monsoon. She remembers that Mark is her client. Silence is bad for business, and she is already in enough trouble.

"So sorry car fall in ditch, but we must hurry." She points skyward. "Night come—no good if we not reach village before."

Mark nods miserably, his trousers and shoes covered in mud and the rest of him soaked through. My-duyen notices his misery and frowns. If he complains, she will really be in trouble. What is worse, although he knows her mother is at Song Nhan village, he has no idea that her father is also there. Although My-duyen is aware that Mark is attracted to her, she fears his anger when he learns how much she has kept from him.

My-duyen's legs churn forward through the mud, her bare feet supple, her toes curling to grip the clotted earth. She pictures what awaits when they arrive and how her American client will be surprised. She knows Mark is expecting a bustling population of farmers, but what he will find . . . .

As for her own drenched spirits, an abandoned village inhabited by ghosts holds out one desolate but compelling attraction: a dry place to sleep. She dreads bringing this American to her mother and father. They have no way of knowing he will be with her, for there exists no electricity or telephones in Song Nhan, and no postal worker dares deliver to a village known to be cursed. The Vietnam People's Postal Service stopped making the attempt to find willing carriers a long time ago. Too much trouble for a few mad villagers and the persistent, albeit superstitious belief in restless spirits that roam the area in search of humans to drag beneath the ground as sacrificial victims to be ingested by a ravenous underworld. There are even rumors of a tunnel alive with demons and dead soldiers unwilling to leave the earth until . . . until what? The stories vary, but some creative version of horror characterizes them all.

~

My-duyen grew up amidst this abnormal backdrop and she has developed an independence of mind and a healthy skepticism of the belief that humans are rational beings. She remembers her father's long insistence that she leave Song

Nhan and be educated at the district capital despite her mother's continuous, hysterical objections.

"She must go!" he would shout. "The three of us can no longer teach her what she needs to know!"

Her mother would tear at her grey hair. "I will die first! Do you know what they will do to her? They will teach her to serve them! To grovel and slave in their service! To give her body, her mind, her soul to them—all for their own profit! Then they will be through with her after she is a broken shell! No!"

"But Tuyet Mai, it is just a school. My-duyen must live, earn a living. Times are different. The war is over."

"No! Never! Not while I am still alive!"

And so it would go, until one day her father and Uncle Tong hid her in the cart they took to the district capital every month to sell vegetables and rice.

"But what about mama?" My-duyen asked, peeking out from beneath the ragged coverlet where she lay concealed.

The two men frowned and glanced at each other. "We will take care of her. You just stay with Auntie Vit and learn. When the time is right, we'll bring mama to visit. She'll come around."

"But. . . . ." My-duyen remembers that her protestations were weak and without conviction. She wanted to go to the district capital, wanted to learn, wanted to leave the village, but still she was almost more afraid of the living throngs in the city than her beloved ghosts. Almost.

~

"How much farther?" shouts Mark. "It's getting pretty dark!"

A bolt of lightning flashes nearby and My-duyen sees his heavy boots are made even heavier by the thick clay mud that globs onto them, making his feet look like thick stumps. She feels sorry for him and tries to picture what it would be like to marry him and travel to the United States, but her thoughts cannot escape visions of the impending arrival at Song Nhan and the reactions of her family to this unexpected visitor.

"Coming close!" she shouts back in English.

Mark tilts his head, cupping his ear.

"Coming close!" she shouts again, her words tossed about like bits of foam on an angry sea. He nods, but she is not sure he heard her. With the wind and rain whipping her face, My-duyen wonders just how happy the ghosts are to see her return. She wishes her father was here, for he has always had a special relationship with spirits. Sometimes, when she was a girl, she even thought of him as a spirit—legless, like her mother, but more spry than any two-legged man around. He was always talking with the Goddess of the Wooden Boy and any number of other spirits.

As the storm intensifies, her fear deepens with it and she increases the pace. The American boy looks miserable but is keeping up, so she momentarily ignores him and strains to make out familiar landmarks. At last they pause at the base of the last hill before Song Nhan. It is steep and the light is failing. My-duyen glances at the American boy who is leaning forward with his hands on his knees evidently breathing deeply, but she knows they must not delay.

She trudges over to him and leans close to his ear. "Last hill!" she shouts. "We must go!"

~

Mark is soaked through, caked in mud, and shivering. He squints up at her face only inches away, made eerily invisible by a combination of the lateness of day, the dark storm, and her broad peasant hat. When lightning strikes nearby, her eyes shine from within the shadows like two pinpoints of light in a black tunnel. The effect is stunning and he feels a jolt of fear mixed with lust.

"Okay, let's go!" he shouts back at her, grabbing his bag and energetically starting without hesitation.

Perhaps we will find a dry spot at the village and sleep together, he thinks as he strides forward. *After all, we both have to strip off these wet clothes. Won't happen, but nice to think about.* He imagines her breasts small and perfect.

With these fantasies as company, Mark notices My-duyen has caught up. Excited even more by her proximity, Mark is determined to avoid falling behind, so he abandons his imagination and strains to keep his footing so as not to slide back down the muddy road. She keeps a steady pace and he is soon gasping for breath, his muscles sore, his body weighed down by rain-soaked clothes and mud-covered boots. As he slogs upward, the slope seems interminable and his grand plans for sex with My-duyen collapse into desperation to simply arrive and sleep.

To accentuate the misery, Mark hears tall trees in the distance being pulled up by their roots and thrown to the jungle floor by the monsoon's furious winds. Apocalyptic clouds roll above. To Mark, the trees impinging on the road appear mythic, swaying, bending, then rising impossibly high into the sky, almost disappearing into the clouds. Sometimes, when he lets his imagination roam, the writhing clouds become gargoyles fighting a fierce battle amongst themselves, running each other through with spears of lightning, groaning through their open wounds in waves of thunder and bleeding rain like hemophiliacs. A terrible sensation of having experienced this before, sometime in a murky past, overtakes him.

Confused and distracted, Mark trips over a thick branch that has fallen across the road and he lands face first in the mud. My-duyen's strong hands grasp him around the waist and he feels himself being pulled to his feet. Her touch is as charged as the lightning and Mark feels a surge of desire. As he stands, he drapes his arm around her neck and dangles his hand where he thinks her breast should be, squeezing and groping, but only a handful of fabric rewards his efforts. She gently but firmly pushes away and strides forward vanishing around a curve, leaving him to stumble uphill as best he can.

Trying to catch up, Mark quickens his pace and climbs past a large group of boulders beyond which the curve gradually straightens. He pauses and looks up. My-duyen stands silhouetted against the roiling sky, waving for him to hurry and shouting unintelligible words. When he reaches her side, they both stand at the summit of the hill and gaze down at a few dim but visible lights. Song Nhan village.

A tremendous blast of wind snaps a nearby tree.

"We must hurry!" shouts My-duyen, fear in her voice.

Oblivious to her words, Mark stands transfixed. He feels overwhelmed by the sight and swallows nervously. The distant lights appear unearthly, pulsing from the surface of some alien planet which he must now step outside the spaceship and confront.

Darkness is rapidly snuffing out the last bit of daylight and My-duyen urgently pulls at his shirt to get him going. Stumbling forward, they descend, the tattered beam of a small flashlight the only thing guiding them through the howling monsoon.

~ *Mother, Father, Uncle* ~

Among all of the empty, decayed, and ruined houses comprising Song Nhan village there remain two impressive buildings. One is the *dinh*, weather-beaten but still proudly erect. In spite of war, weather, waste, and worry, the *dinh's* concrete walls remain adorned with intricate stone friezes, worn-weary yet time-tempered. The elaborately carved dragon running the length of the roof seems to roar defiance at earth, elements, and entropy alike. On this ferocious night, the *dinh* is dark and empty except for the massive Guardian Spirit statues who stir restlessly for the first time in years.

The second building that stands impressively amidst the ruins is tonight lit by lanterns and a warming fire. Built of concrete, wood, and stone by a long-ago French magistrate for his large family, it served as a magnificent villa until his death. Afterwards, a wealthy plantation owner bought it and moved in to become Song Nhan's most prominent citizen until war and revolution forced him to flee. When the Viet Cong came, it was burned as an example to all bourgeois landowners. So it remained a haunted wreck. Over time, a thriving population of red-tiled houses, thatch cottages, corrugated tin shacks, and wooden huts propagated around it. Now they are in ruins and the old French villa has been rebuilt almost to its old magnificence, lording over the dead village like an enchanted palace amidst a derelict cemetery.

Inside, warming by the fire, the villa's two inhabitants are sitting and conversing sparingly with each other. Since renovating the structure after the war, the two have lived in splendid isolation, hiring workers seasonally to tend the fields and otherwise being left alone to raise their daughter, care for their one friend, summon their ghosts, and regale the spirits with whom they share the deserted village. Aided by legend, superstition, and fear, even the government stays away, although the years have not.

Both of these old friends and comrades, long married and practically toothless, are without legs and would present a comical, albeit pathetic sight to any stranger. The old woman stands on her stumps working an ancient loom with skill and alacrity while the old man sits with his stumps splayed at a forty-five-degree angle, one arm casually draped over a faded, greasy Western-style ottoman. For the past few days he has been nursing a toothache in one of his few remaining teeth while she struggles with one of her many pelvic pains that always flare in wet weather. Outside, the monsoon rages, and since they have exhausted that topic, the old woman turns to another.

"Go and invite Tong over," she says above the clicking of the loom.

Han Tinh snorts. "Never!"

Tuyet Mai sighs with the sigh of the long-suffering. "You know you want to."

"He has insulted me for the last time."

"Goddess again," she says with disgust. "Why do you two always argue over Goddess? She puts you up to it, you know. Typical woman."

"She is not a woman, she is a Goddess. Besides, I don't think she is guilty. It's *Him* again. Typical man."

"Tong does not believe in *Him*," says Tuyet Mai with a sarcastic emphasis on the last word.

Tinh, oblivious, throws up his arms. "I know! Tong is unbelievably stubborn. Sometimes I think he doesn't even believe in *Her*."

"He's a good communist, but I know he also likes to get under your skin," chides Tuyet Mai. "He believes in Her. We all believe in Her."

"He's not a good anything," Tinh scoffs.

"Come, come. You've been friends for almost twenty years. He's good for something, especially when it comes to conspiring against me. Two men, one woman, since My-duyen left. It's unfair."

Tinh chuckles. "He's not good enough to keep me from taking you away from him."

Tuyet Mai rolls her eyes. "That again. You're getting senile. Besides, you may have me but your daughter still has his name."

Their conversation is interrupted by a particularly violent blast of wind followed by a clap of ear-splitting thunder. Both shake their heads but say nothing.

When the noise subsides, Tuyet Mai repeats, "Go and invite him over. The demons may be out and he shouldn't be alone."

"Why not?"

She shudders and shoots Tinh a hard glare. "I don't know, but there is something in the air I don't like. It frightens me."

"You don't look frightened, you look angry."

"Go and invite him over you crippled bastard!" she shouts. In her old age she has taken to calling him increasingly foul epithets. Tinh initially felt dismay but now ascribes her language to colorful but harmlessly affectionate senility. He has become accustomed to returning the compliments by using equally colorful terms of affection toward her.

"So, you need Tong, as usual?"

"He is my protector, incompetent as he is. He is my good luck charm. As long as he is alive, I will be alive. When he dies, I die."

"I am your husband, you goddamned bitch!" cries Tinh.

"You are a clown, a cowardly soldier, a failed priest, a water puppeteer, a rapist."

"And I am also your husband."

"Rapist!"

"Husband!"

Both laugh. "Go and invite him," says Tuyet Mai calmly but firmly, signaling the discussion is over.

Han Tinh again throws up his arms, this time in surrender. "All right, all right. But I'll drown in the mud." He rubs his stumps. "My legs aren't quite long enough to get out if I fall in a centipede's burrow."

Tuyet Mai ignores his jests. "Go and invite him."

He sulks, toying with the fire of her wrath like a child with matches. "I'll fall in a hole and drown, you'll see."

But tonight is a good night and Tuyet Mai plays to his buffoonery. "My arms are long enough to pull you out of a centipede's burrow. Go!"

Han Tinh reluctantly wraps himself in a poncho, dons a ragged peasant hat, and opens the door only to gasp audibly. Two apparitions stand before him, darkened by mud and soaked to the skin. One of the apparitions lowers her head to meet his upturned eyes and Tinh's raised lantern light reveals a matchlessly beautiful face.

"Daughter!"

The other apparition remains in the shadows.

~

Tinh swings himself aside, allowing room for the two to enter. "I was just going to get your Uncle Tong," he says, all the while glancing at the tall stranger.

Tuyet Mai joins them, smiling broadly until she spots the man standing in the corner trying to be inconspicuous. "Who is he?" she asks sharply.

"He is an American," says My-duyen quickly in Vietnamese. "He is a customer of my company. I was assigned to bring him. I had to."

Han Tinh and Tuyet Mai both stare at him curiously, making Mark feel like a zoo exhibit.

"Smile at him and say 'hello' in English," scolds My-duyen when she notices Mark's discomfort.

Tinh says, "Hello," obediently, but Tuyet Mai wears a frozen mask of disapproval and says nothing to the American.

Mark's impression is that both are idiotic country bumpkins. He feels a revulsion at their appearance and is subjected to an almost desperate desire to escape. Not knowing what else to say, bone-weary and longing for a private place to sleep, he says rather hoarsely, "Hello."

"Mama, I will take him to the room of the puppets," says My-duyen, still speaking in Vietnamese.

Tuyet Mai remains silent, eyes narrowed, lips compressed.

"Yes, yes, do it!" exclaims Tinh. "And give him a blanket." He looks up at the American boy, grins mischievously, and says in English while slapping his stumps, "Americans take my legs! Welcome!"

"Thank you," stammers Mark, obviously confused and hesitant.

"You old fool!" Tuyet Mai scoffs at her husband in Vietnamese, then turns to My-duyen. "Fine, take him to the room, give him a blanket, give him food—we have some shrimp and rolls—leave him there to sleep and you come back down as soon as possible. We must talk. Does the government know he's here?"

"Yes, mama."

"Go!" commands Tuyet Mai. As My-duyen leads a compliant Mark off, Tuyet Mai turns on Tinh. "And you also go! Bring Tong. The night that was bad has turned worse. We three must talk." She looks in the direction of My-duyen's departure. "And we must find out what the American wants. I now know that it is he who has brought these dark omens."

Tinh is just closing the door behind him but leaves it open a crack. "Nonsense!" he barks, knowing the word will make it through the crack. He quickly shuts the door thereby safely avoiding any response.

Tuyet Mai returns to her loom, muttering under her breath phrases like, "stupid girl" and "stupid husband" and "stupid Americans."

Almost an hour passes before Han Tinh returns with Tong. During this time Mark has fallen asleep on a tatami mat in the upstairs "puppet room," grateful to be left alone with his loneliness while My-duyen has taken refuge in her own room, unwilling to face her mother until reinforcements arrive. Once she hears the two men make a boisterous entrance, she gathers the courage to come out and face her fate. But when she enters the great room, no one is there. She hears arguing in one of the hallways and finds her father and Uncle Tong gesticulating over a leak that has formed a large puddle on the floor. The sharp aroma of rice wine hangs in the air and My-duyen understands why it took them so long to return.

Tinh is complaining to Tong who stands listening with his hands on his hips looking disgusted.

"My tooth hurts," says Tinh. "Not only my tooth hurts, my daughter is with an American, my wife is a bitch, my friend is a useless bag of blood, I haven't grown my legs back, and my roof leaks! Why should I be reasonable?"

"I told you to fix it months ago," says Tong calmly. "Monsoons do happen, you know. No good to mend a fold after the sheep is lost."

Tuyet Mai appears with a bucket and places it under the leak. "Brother Tong, you and your Chinese idioms won't catch water."

"Hm!" grunts Tinh in disgust. "We'll have to empty it every ten minutes."

"Shut up you old numbskull!" snarls Tuyet Mai. "This bucket is the least of our worries. Ghosts are restless, demons are stirring, and an American is sleeping in our house while you two argue!"

"What will the government think?" asks Tong worriedly. "Why did My-duyen bring him here?"

Everyone stops and looks at My-duyen who is standing quietly. Her eyes widen. "What could I do? He insisted on coming. He paid a lot of money. My company ordered me to be his guide. I would have been fired."

"That's just it, she would have been fired," confirms Tong, trying to throw her a lifeline.

My-duyen nods vigorously. "Uncle, I would not have brought him here if I had any choice. In fact, I tried to talk him out of it."

"Won't solve anything here listening to these raindrops fill the bucket," says Tuyet Mai moving toward the great room.

"Bucket's almost full already," grumbles Tinh.

"Leave it!" shouts Tuyet Mai above a series of thunder claps.

"Demons will enter through the hole!" Tinh protests.

Tuyet Mai stops cold, doubt flickers across her face. "True," she finally says looking at Tong coquettishly.

"All right, I'll try to fix it. But on the roof in the dark—this monsoon will probably kill me," he says.

"Here, take this lantern, comrade," says Tinh solicitously. "My-duyen, go to the storage room and bring your uncle a big swatch of parachute. Wars are good for something."

"Yes, papa," says My-duyen, anxious to delay the inevitable.

She rushes out while Tuyet Mai is reunited with her loom and Tinh resumes his old position leaning against the ottoman.

My-duyen returns wrestling with the bulky parachute. "It's heavy!" she exclaims.

"Take it in the big room and we can cut it," snaps Tong. "We'll have to use a razor."

The next hour is spent waiting for Tong to finish his repairs. The storm rages, the loom clicks. My-duyen wearily sits in a Chinese-style chair thinking about the interrogation that is sure to come. No one says a word until Tong returns, soaked to the skin but alive.

"That should hold it until your old cripple husband makes permanent repairs," says Tong, but his face is white and his tone is unusually subdued.

Tuyet Mai notices instantly. "What is it?"

"Well," responds Tong. "While I was on the roof worried about falling, lightning flashing all around." He hesitates.

"And?" Tinh encourages.

"With every flash of lightning, I saw shadows."

"What kind of shadows?" asks Tuyet Mai.

Shadows of people. Dozens—hundreds—moving. And I saw a light in your old shack, Tinh."

"Uncle," says My-duyen. "The wind is fierce. It whips the leaves and bends the trees. It can create illusions."

Tong smiles. "Could have been. I can't be sure."

"Of course you can be sure," says Tuyet Mai. "They're here. Good that you covered the hole."

They all nod grimly.

"But why now?" asks Tong.

All eyes again turn to My-duyen. The clicking stops. Tinh flexes and unflexes his left fist. Tong squats and waits.

Tuyet Mai speaks, her tone reflecting the gravity of the situation. "Daughter, why is the American here? What does he want?"

~ *Ghosts* ~

"His father was a soldier in the war. There was a battle. Here. Or rather, in the forest near the old fort. I assume it was the same battle where you lost your legs, mama."

"Oh God!" cries Tuyet Mai, clutching at her blouse.

"But I told him nothing!" cries My-duyen.

"His father must have been killed," says Tinh confidently.

Tong raises his hand. "Listen to My-duyen," he says impatiently. "Let her talk. Besides idiot, the American boy upstairs is too young. His father could not have died back then."

"Nonsense!" proclaims Tinh.

"You are right, uncle," says My-duyen. "His father did not die."

Tuyet Mai looks stricken and turns to her husband. "Yes, that's true. One lived."

Tong's eyes widen and his voice turns brittle. "No." He holds up his fingers to his mouth. "I heard that two lived."

Han Tinh speaks gravely. "Two lived, but only one survived. The other's wound was fatal." Tinh looks up toward the puppet room where the American sleeps. "Only one survived. His father. My God."

"Why did the boy come?" Tuyet Mai demands of her daughter. "Can he not let them sleep? Listen to them out there, all around, moving about, coming closer. It must be the father's spirit."

"Mama, it's just the storm," says My-duyen kneading her hands nervously.

"But there *is* a light in my old shack," says Tinh. "Daughter, why did he come?"

"He's in college. His professor is interested in the battle and wants to write a book about it."

"What?" cries Tong. "Then why didn't the professor come? At least if he came, we could kill him and say it was a snake."

"Kill who?" asks My-duyen quickly.

"The professor, not the boy."

"Why not?" asks Tuyet Mai.

My-duyen lets out a groan.

"Why not what?" says Tinh.

"Kill the boy."

"Mama!" blurts My-duyen.

"If he is dead, we will be left alone," says Tuyet Mai coldly.

"No," says Tong. "There would be an investigation. The government would come." He shakes his head. "The father would come."

"Yes, he would come," Tuyet Mai whispers. "Him. The Teller of Stories."

"You know him?" asks a startled My-duyen.

"Oh yes, oh yes. I remember him."

"Maybe he's dead by now," says Tong. "Maybe the boy doesn't know anything."

My-duyen is shaken. "Doesn't know anything about what? Why are you all so worried? What happened in that battle to make you all so afraid?"

The group falls silent.

"I still don't understand why the boy has come," says Tinh, ignoring My-duyen's outburst. "What does he want?"

My-duyen sighs dejectedly. "He wants to collect information about the battle for his professor, for the book his professor wants to write."

"Information?" asks Tuyet Mai. "What kind of information?"

"He thinks there are many people living in Song Nhan village. He wants to interview people. Visit the scene of the battle. See the fort. See the tunnel."

"No!" cries Tuyet Mai.

"My-duyen, this cannot be allowed," insists Tong.

Tinh looks horrified. "My god, no, it mustn't be allowed! Look at your mother!"

Tuyet Mai has buried her face in her hands.

My-duyen rushes to her. "Mama! I will take him back when the monsoon is over. I will not let him talk to you!" She looks at her father and her uncle. "What is it? What happened? If I had known!"

But her mother is immovable. Both men are themselves caught in a web of memories. Only the low roar of the wind and the creaking of the house is audible. No one is aware that Tuyet Mai has buried her face in order to concentrate on the words of her dead friend, Kim Lan.

~

"Let him go to the tunnel," Kim Lan whispers. "What's the harm? He looks, you tell him nothing, he sees only an empty tunnel, he leaves."

"I would not go down with him," says Tuyet Mai adamantly.

"Better yet."

"But My-duyen would go. She would never come back. They want her."

"Nonsense!"

Tuyet Mai snorts loudly. The others assume she is weeping, and My-duyen rubs her back soothingly. Tuyet Mai lets them believe she is in grief so she may continue her secret conversation with Kim Lan.

"You don't know about the tunnel. You never went down there. But I had to go down with Ka Re Em Si."

"I know he raped you."

"No!" Tuyet Mai cries. "He did not! How is it you don't know?"

"I am dead."

"But the dead know."

Kim Lan laughs. "Who told you that?"

"The living," says Tuyet Mai sheepishly.

"Never believe the living for they are by definition liars. How else can they live?"

"Who do I believe?"

"Me," says Kim Lan with conviction.

"Why?"

"Never mind. Just take him to the tunnel. Cooperate with him. Go down yourself with him. Make it a lark. Tell him nothing happened. The battle was brief. Nothing unusual during the war. There were many battles and this was but one. A minor one at that. Forgettable. Ashes on the wind. He will report to his professor. Boring. No story. No book. No further trouble."

Tuyet Mai trembles. "And the demons, the ghosts, the dead soldiers, they all want me. If I go down. . . . "

"I will intervene with them."

"You!" cries Tuyet Mai a little too dismissively. She regrets it immediately. "How can you control them?"

"The brotherhood and sisterhood of the dead. Even the worms are members, even the ants. Every crawling thing belongs to us. Even one ant can move heaven's gate."

Tuyet Mai shakes her head, again interpreted by the others as an emotional outburst. Tinh squats next to her and says soothing words which she ignores in order to concentrate on Kim Lan.

"Don't you trust me?" asks Kim Lan.

"There are many ghosts out tonight, dead soldiers, dead villagers, some demons, maybe others even more powerful, and a light in Tinh's shack. They are waiting for me. If I trust you I risk my life."

"Who's more powerful than demons?"

"You know," says Tuyet Mai a bit too transparently.

"God."

"Or Goddess. She gets to me through my husband."

"And God?" asks Kim Lan.

"I don't know."

"Go to the tunnel," repeats Kim Lan. "Nothing will happen to you and the American will go away. What's to interest him? An empty tunnel?"

Tuyet Mai starts. "Will it be empty?"

"Of course."

~

"Shhh. It's going to be fine," says Tinh touching her cheek.

Tuyet Mai pushes his hand away.

"Damn woman!" he snaps and starts to move away.

Tuyet Mai grabs his hand and pulls him back. "Husband, we must take the American to the tunnel."

"What?" comes a unison of incredulous replies.

"It is the only way."

~

You have done well, Kim Lan.

"Thank you."

Your services are no longer required.

"Are you sure?"

Certainty is the hallmark of true faith. Deities are nothing if not certain.

"All roads lead to the tunnel?"

All roads lead to the belly of God ... to The Reunion ... and the little that remains of You will be fully digested there.

~

Everyone in the room is stunned by Tuyet Mai's remark.

She feels compelled to explain, although she wants to crawl away and find a place to hide, or at least bury herself alone in bed. "We take him to the fort, take him to the tunnel, take him wherever else he wants to go—and tell him nothing," she says. "He learns nothing. He leaves." She throws up her hands. "Gone."

"Play dumb then," observes Tinh.

"Absolutely. Madame Dau taught me that whenever she was interrogated by the Front or the Americans or the puppet troops, she played stupid, a dim-witted village woman who knew nothing. A fool."

Han Tinh brightened. "Ah! A dim-witted villager. Then it will be easy for me"—his face assumes a mischievous grin—"since I am such a good actor."

Tong speaks up. "Old brother, you never acted a day in your life, you just thought you did. As for me, well, he will get no information, just a blank stare."

"Don't overdo it," cautions Tuyet Mai. "Otherwise he might become suspicious."

"True," replies Tong.

Tuyet Mai notices Tinh crying and sighs loudly. "Now what bothers you?"

"You reminded me of a great lady—Madame Dau. Just now, while I was playing the fool, I thought of her. She would have smiled patiently even as she scolded me for being a jester."

Instead of making some sarcastic reply, Tuyet Mai seems genuinely moved. "Yes, husband. She was a great lady. Let her life be a lesson to us all."

"No, wife, let her death be a lesson to us all."

Tinh's mention of Madame Dau renders the group silent.

~

My-duyen looks past her mother's shoulder and screams.

"What is it?" cries Tinh.

"A face in the window looking in."

"Where?" asks Tuyet Mai.

"Gone," says a still wide-eyed My-duyen.

"Must have been the American boy," says Tinh.

"No," replies My-duyen. "It was you, papa. Your face . . . I think . . . but you were younger, much younger. Not as you are now, but as you were in the war. A soldier's face, fierce and unbroken, staring through the storm as though summoned from the dead."

The thunder cracked again, and for an instant the glass reflected not one face but two—her father's younger self and some other shadow standing beside him, fused, indistinguishable, like the double image of a man and his ghost.

~ *Mark Awakens* ~

Mark awakens to the unblinking stares of wooden puppets, all propped in various positions against the walls of the small, cluttered room. Outside, the monsoon continues to rage even as a diffuse, cold light of morning is beginning to reveal Song Nhan village in sickly gray hues. A variety of aromas fill the room, all unfamiliar, making him more aware than ever of his alien status here. Never has he felt so homesick, and never has he dreaded facing a group of people more than those surely waiting downstairs. He focuses his thoughts on My-duyen, the only familiar entity in a world of strange, distorted entities. Her image comforts him enough to prod him up and off the tatami. But now what? Where to wash? Brush his teeth? Find dry clothes? He is rendered helpless in performing the simplest tasks. The small suitcase he recovered from the car and all its contents are soaked through and he feels irritated that he did not have the foresight to hang them up to at least partially dry. As for the clothes he wore last night, they are crumpled in a muddy heap on the floor.

Shuddering at the feel, he dons a wet shirt and pair of jeans from the suitcase, hangs up the rest, and stands miserably in the center of the room. The puppets seem to laugh and snicker in chorus, and he imagines all the villagers of Song Nhan doing the same when they see him today. Although images of mocking villagers dance in his head, his stomach refuses to be intimidated and insists that he find food. A few shrimp and a roll the previous night have become nothing more than a remembrance of things past, and as much as he wishes My-duyen would bring him food before he goes out among the masses, he suspects she is waiting for him to emerge from this womb of wooden fetuses. Unnerved by the rows of leering puppets and prodded by hunger, he ventures downstairs into the kitchen.

Unfortunately, it is not My-duyen who greets him, but Han Tinh.

"Ah, American friend!" cries Tinh. "Come. Eat." He gestures toward a table. "Sit. Tea?"

Mark sits on a wooden chair that promptly tilts, the legs being of unequal lengths.

Tinh pours tea and prepares a bowl of rice gruel, chattering in mangled English all the while as Mark sits in stupefied admiration for the boundless energy and acrobatic dexterity of this legless man.

"I know Americans! Many soldiers during war!" He pauses. "Never saw a battle. No problem with Americans. No battle. I not see anything. But I like to sing. Happy!"

"I thought Americans took your legs," says Mark.

"No. Yes. Mine take my legs. American mine. No problem. You here to see battle scene?"

"Yes, I understand there was a battle here. I want to talk to people about it, see where it was, look, study, you know. Understand?"

Tinh shakes his head. "No battle. Maybe far away, not here. Nothing to see. But you can look at village. Talk to me, put me in book."

Mark is silent and eats his rice mechanically, evidently stunned by Tinh's assertion. Moments pass. Tinh jumps into the silence. "You first time in Vietnam? Must be. You young. Young Americans good. Go to district capital and see Vietnam city. Many women. You like women? Here there is nothing. No battle, but I talk about Vietnam and you put me in book. Okay?"

Mark laughs. "Okay." Tinh does not respond. Mark searches for something to say. "My room has puppets."

"Puppets! Yes!" Tinh slaps his chest. "Mine!"

"Are you good?" Mark mimes pulling strings.

"Good? Great! Water theater. Saigon. Many customers."

"Do you remember American soldiers coming here during the war?" Mark asks, trying for nonchalance but failing.

Tinh momentarily narrows his eyes and Mark recognizes that his nonchalant tone has failed to mask an obviously awkward transition.

Tinh's expression flits away quickly and he rolls his eyes to signal intense thought. "Nooo. At district capital, many American soldiers during war. Here, no. No battle. But American cigarettes! Good!"

"Methinks you doth protest too much," says Mark, knowing Tinh will not understand his Shakespearean paraphrase.

Tinh nods his head and grunts unintelligibly.

"No battle here, then?" Mark asks.

"Nooo. Here is peace. No V.C. No Americans. Just peaceful village."

"How long have you lived here?"

"Huh?" says Tinh stupidly.

"You live here how long?"

Tinh shrugs. "Long, maybe short. No Americans here. All at district capital. Here much peace. I tell you about puppets and you put me in book?"

Before Mark can respond, My-duyen enters the kitchen. "Mr. Powers. Good morning. You have nice conversation with Mr. Tinh?"

"Yes."

"Good food?"

"Oh yes, good."

She sits next to Mark but Tinh taps his cup and My-duyen scurries to pour him tea.

"My-duyen," says Mark, somewhat put out at her obeisance to this freakish little man. "After breakfast can you take me to meet people who were here during the war?"

"Yes."

"Can we do that now? I mean, first . . . have you had breakfast? After breakfast. Okay?" He feels the need to get her away from Tinh.

"Yes." She remains seated.

Mark is confused. "Do you want to finish your tea?"

"Yes."

He waits.

She sips.

Tinh cannot bear the silence. "American cigarettes are number one!"

Mark makes a show of fumbling in his pockets. "Sorry, I don't have any."

Tinh assumes a forlorn expression. "Gum?"

"What?" asks Mark.

"Chew gum?"

Again Mark fumbles. "Sorry, I should have brought some."

"Okay," says Tinh without the usual snap in his voice. "Americans take my legs but give me gum."

"It is the American way, I have heard," says Tuyet Mai entering the room.

Mark is startled and stares at this latest circus freak.

"Mama," says My-duyen in greeting, outwardly placid but inwardly anxious.

Tinh points at Tuyet Mai. "My wife," he explains.

Wanting to ask so many questions, Mark is paralyzed by her appearance and realizes he has to pee. *Nerves*, he thinks, frustrated with himself.

"Good morning," he says to Tuyet Mai. "Your English is excellent."

She says nothing.

He turns to My-duyen. "Excuse me, where is the bathroom?"

"Outside, around the corner," says Tuyet Mai in clipped but articulate English.

"Oh, your English is very good," repeats Mark, genuinely impressed.

Tuyet Mai ignores him.

Tinh laughs and gestures toward his wife. "Her? Everything very good."

"Must you always play the fool!" snaps Tuyet Mai in Vietnamese.

"Me the fool? The boy thinks I don't know Shakespeare. I was in the theater!"

Tuyet Mai groans impatiently. "Problem is you never stop acting, wooden-headed puppet!"

Mark sips his tea self-consciously. Although he doesn't understand Vietnamese, he is uncomfortably aware husband and wife are arguing, probably about him.

"I show you bathroom," says My-duyen quickly, leading Mark to the door. She opens it and pauses. Outside, the monsoon has settled into a steady downpour. She dons her peasant hat and leans forward.

"Ready?" she says looking back at him.

He has never seen her so beautiful and could stare forever but for his insistent bowels. "Ready," he says finally.

She hurriedly leads him to a rather dilapidated wooden outhouse with a tin roof. It has two holes emitting the foulest odor he has ever smelled.

"Come back in house when finished," she directs, then disappears and he is left alone to deal with the mud and shit and lack of toilet paper.

~

After relieving himself, Mark stands under the tin overhang and looks in wonder at the village, revealed to him for the first time in daylight. Built on a rise, the villa affords a grand view. Thatched homes collapsing under their own weight dot the landscape, interspersed with black spots—charred wood—where houses once stood. A smattering of tin roofs reverberate in jarring unison from the falling rain like mournful drums beating a funereal rhythm to the monsoon's steady cadence. Not a soul to be seen.

Beyond the deserted village, jungle is clearly encroaching on the fallow rice fields and overgrown fruit groves. Decay is everywhere, made even more fungal-like by the moist grey slop of sky, rain, and mud. Patches of gooey green algae, webbed tendrils of vines, and the rot of overripe vegetation give the whole scene a suffocating texture of slime. The villa itself, last night a shining palace of refuge from the storm, today is covered in that same grey-green doom that seems to cover the world.

"Everywhere the ceremony of innocence is drowned," says Mark to himself. He shakes his head. "God, what do I do now?"

He turns toward the villa and sees three figures standing in the doorway watching him—or rather one figure and two half-figures—all wearing peasant hats and looking like toadstools—one tall flanked by two short. The tall toadstool in the middle is waving at him to come inside while the other two merely stand beneath their cream-colored crowns and stare.

Mark wishes he could blink himself home, away from this bizarre situation. The thought of going back into that rebuilt, but oddly decayed dwelling makes him shudder, but duty bears down upon his thoughts. Still, he realizes that if nothing of consequence has happened here, life will be much simpler. If no battle, then nothing to investigate, no one to interview. Didn't Han Tinh say there was no battle? Well, no battle, then simply return home as quickly as possible. There's nothing he can do. Sorry, Professor Benson, no battle. Result? Back to a comfortable bed, fast computer, familiar food, and the cozy technological swaddling clothes of an overindulged society. But the problem with that scenario is that it leaves My-duyen out of his future. *Anyway*, he thinks dejectedly, *there must have been a battle or Benson never would have sent me.*

He looks back at the toadstools and sees that only the tall one remains, calling to him. Waving My-duyen off, he gestures that he is staying and takes a few steps toward the outhouse. It works and she ducks inside the villa, giving him more time alone to think. Although he is soaked, the rain is curiously warm and cleansing.

Dad will be happy. Nothing here to report. Dad. Dad. Dad. Battle. He was in a battle here. Lost part of his sanity here. Here! There was a battle! They must be lying. Mark looks at the village more closely. His gaze settles on the burned-out houses. *Battle. That's evidence of a battle. And why is the village abandoned?* For the first time he notices dark holes and gouges in the villa's concrete walls. *Bullet holes. Must be. A battle!*

Again he surveys the village and for the first time begins noticing details. *A temple of some kind. Stone dragon running along the top, like an old picture. Wow. Like I pictured Vietnam would be—about time something's like I thought it would be. And down there, in the middle, in the square or whatever that space is, a huge machine of some kind. Skeletal. Rusted. Weird. Creepy. What is it?*

Mark feels an overwhelming urge to descend and wander among the ruins—the curious boy in him cries out to do it. But something holds him back. Dimly, through the veil of rain, shadows are moving. Not just vague shapes, but figures, scores of them, emerging and dissolving in the mist. They shift like a broken film reel replaying itself: men with rifles, women clutching bundles, children darting between shattered walls.

At first he is excited. Then he looks closer. The shadows do not walk as the living walk; they stagger, collapse, rise again, endlessly repeating the motions of battle. One drags a rifle that melts into smoke, another cradles a baby that dissolves into rain. Faces blur, half-formed, yet their mouths gape in silent cries.

Mark realizes with horror that he is watching the past itself replay—ghosts of the battle his father once described, still circling the village in endless reenactment, never released.

He quickly retreats into the villa, shutting the door tightly behind.

~ *Michael Powers* ~

It is 3:00 a.m. when Michael sputters awake. Awkwardly struggling to rise, half-asleep, he manages to lean uncomfortably on one elbow and mumble to himself, "The door's closed tightly . . . isn't it?" Blinking through a drowsy fog, the vague contours of the world gradually sharpen, and he soon realizes that Theresa lies next to him breathing deeply. He turns to check whether she is asleep but is unable to tell. Rolling out of bed, he slips on his boots and tiptoes out of the room, gingerly shutting the door behind him. Although he is drawn to the kitchen, a deep unease slows his steps until they falter to a standstill.

The storm is still muttering against the house, as though the monsoon that drenched Song Nhan has followed him into this night. He thinks he hears the faint wooden clatter of puppets, as if those leering toys upstairs have been carried across oceans to watch him stumble in the dark. Their strings, unseen, seem to twitch in the rafters.

"Tunnel," he mutters, then immediately asks himself why he spoke the word. While standing frozen in the hallway he feels a hand on his shoulder.

"Michael, tell me about the tunnel," says Theresa.

"What do you mean?"

"Tell me where it is."

"What?"

"Tell me how we get to it."

"To what?"

Theresa tilts her head provocatively. "The tunnel."

"I can't."

"Why not?"

Michael hesitates, stunned by Theresa's inquiry. "I don't know anything about a tunnel."

"Of course you know. Didn't your twin brother tell you about it?"

"No."

"Didn't he tell you about it many times during your dinners?"

"No."

Theresa shakes her head as if disappointed. "Michael," she says sadly.

Then her voice changes into that of his twin. "Oh, brother, you're not going to make this easy, are you? Yes–*She*–Goddess. I just saw Her in the tunnel. It's Her idea to make you come back. Once you're back with us, then you'll understand the meaning of your dreams, especially your 'peculiar seven dreams,' as Toomey calls them. You come back to us and you'll crack those seven dreams wide open and then you're home free. No more dreams. No more nightmares. No more me." Theresa blinks coyly and speaks in her own voice. "Remember now, Michael? Don't you want to end the nightmares?"

"I was warned you would try to do this."

"Do what?"

"Take me back. Goddamn it, Theresa, He was right."

"But you want to go back. If you didn't, you wouldn't have married me. It is my job as your wife and your doctor to make you confront these memories, these demons. It's the only way you can beat this schizophrenia."

"God was right. Anyway, you're not really my wife or my doctor, you're one of them, one of my hallucinations. I know."

"Nonsense, you're delusional now."

"No I'm not. You're a figment of my imagination."

"Just how much of your world is imaginary, Michael? Is your entire family a delusion? This house? Our wedding? My office?"

"Come on, Theresa, we've gone over this before. No, just you."

"How many times have we gone over this?"

"Too many."

Theresa holds up her wrists revealing the bruises. "Are these delusions?"

"Yes. Did I cause those?"

"Yes."

"No."

"There is only one way to find out whether I'm part of your delusion."

"How?"

"Come into the tunnel with me."

"No."

"You know, I once thought I was someone's hallucination myself." Theresa places her hand around her throat. "It terrified me. But now I know I'm real."

"How do you know?"

"Come to the tunnel with me and I'll prove it to you."

Michael snorts and brushes past Theresa into the kitchen. "It's a trick."

"I love you."

He pours a cup of cold coffee left over from the previous morning and suddenly becomes self-consciously aware of his utter nakedness but for the incongruous boots. A moment's reflection pushes the awkward feeling aside. "How can you love me, you're nothing more than one of my hallucinations—a voice with perfect breasts. Too perfect."

"Have I ever called you worthless?"

"No."

Theresa tears up. "Have I ever told you to kill yourself?"

"No."

"Do you want to get rid of me?"

He hesitates, then in a quivering voice says, "Yes. I'm sorry, but I am convinced you are part of my . . . mental . . . my difficulty recognizing reality."

"Reality awaits you in the tunnel. Come with me. What do you have to lose?"

He laughs ironically. "You."

"I'm confused. I thought you wanted to get rid of me."

"I do."

Theresa speaks in a scolding tone. "Michael, you are not making sense. You're confused. It's a symptom. Come to the tunnel and get clarity. If I'm a delusion, you're through with me. If I'm real, we move on together and rebuild our lives."

Michael slams his fist on the counter. "What is so fuckin' crucial about that goddamned tunnel?"

"Ah, now you're speaking like yourself. Now you're speaking like the young soldier you will meet in the tunnel."

"My twin—"

Now Theresa slams her fist on the counter. "No! No more words about your twin! This is what is at the root of your pathology." She hesitates, then says more quietly, "Do you want to get rid of him also?"

"I want him to stop bothering me."

"You know he is you?"

"That's what everyone tells me."

"But you still want him to stop bothering you?"

"Yes."

Theresa backs out of the room into the shadows, all the while beckoning with her hand. "Then come with me into the tunnel."

"I didn't think you knew where it is."

She is now a disembodied voice. "It is here."

The kitchen windows rattle as though fists are pounding on them from outside. Rain smears the glass into streaked faces. The shadows from the storm lengthen into jerking silhouettes, bowing and lurching like marionettes on invisible strings. One by one, the wooden puppets from upstairs seem to step down into the room—limbs clacking, jaws frozen in permanent smiles. Their glassy eyes fix on him. They sway as if waiting for a cue, as if Theresa herself were pulling their strings.

Michael grips the edge of the counter. The voice in the shadows breathes against his ear: *Come into the tunnel.*

Chapter Twenty-Two

Trajectory I

The Plot

In Song Nhan village the monsoon raged on. Kung paced Tinh's cramped shack slowly and calmly. He paused and looked down into Tinh's eyes. "It is necessary that I enlist your help."

"Comrade Ninh said the same thing."

"This will be for your benefit."

Tinh grinned. "That's also what *he* said."

"Listen, when our brothers come, you must play your part."

"Huh?" grunted Tinh, evidently confused.

"They will come tomorrow and you must be ready."

"Tomorrow?"

"Yes. If you don't cooperate, they'll shoot you."

"Cooperate?" asked Tinh, his eyebrows raised comically.

"You know we are all loyal to Hanoi?"

"I don't know."

Kung spoke harshly. "You do now."

"What is it you want me to do?"

"Tell them that Ninh is a traitor."

"Is that how I cooperate?"

"Yes."

"What do I get for doing this?"

"Tuyet Mai," said Kung flatly, but with a twinkle in his eye.

"Ah! A better offer than Ninh's!"

"What did he offer?" asked Kung, cocking his head.

"My life."

"You're right, mine's a better offer!"

Tinh shook his head, evidently not amused. "I could go back to Ninh for a better deal."

Kung laughed genially. "He can make no better offer than what I have offered you. Is this not true, Comrade Tinh?"

"True. What do I tell them?"

"That Ninh is a traitor."

Tinh could not conceal his surprise. "Is that all?"

"Yes."

"They are sure to ask me why I call him a traitor."

Kung pulled out a sheaf of papers. "Show them these."

"How did I get them?"

"Tell them Comrade Major Vy of the People's Army left them at the village many years ago for safekeeping until he returned."

Tinh cocked his head. "I know that name."

"You should. There was a battle here not too many years ago, at the old fortress."

"Yes," said Tinh. "I remember them all. There was Major Vy and Captain Tong and Commissar Minh—" Tinh broke off suddenly. He stared intensely at Kung. "Commissar Minh looked a lot like you. In fact—"

"Be careful, Comrade Tinh," warned Kung.

Tinh played nervously with a buttonhole, glancing surreptitiously at Kung. After one such look he gasped. A transformation had flitted across Kung's face that was so brief Tinh thought it was caused by the interplay of light and shadows. Still, the visage terrified him. *It is Commissar Minh!* Quickly recovering his composure, Tinh convinced himself that Kung had not detected his revelation. He decided it was much safer to drop the subject of Kung's identity and not pursue the curious reason why Kung did not turn over the documents to the People's Army himself.

But a thought niggled at his brain causing him more worry than Kung. "Comrade, does this endanger the women here?"

"I promised you Tuyet Mai, didn't I?"

Tinh folded his hands in a gesture of supplication. "No, the others. Comrade Ninh seemed to . . . to think they were in danger if certain things didn't happen."

Kung leaned down with a radiant expression and put his hand on Tinh's shoulder. "Comrade, I am pleased with you. No, they will come to no harm."

A tremendously loud clap of thunder struck nearby and Tinh felt a rush of fear. He told himself it was nothing unusual for such a monsoon, but his skin crawled nonetheless.

Kung stooped and stared out a cracked and battered window, made especially low for Tinh's shortened stature. "There is a light on in the old villa, did you notice? Looks like someone's using the old fireplace."

Tinh bounced to the window and looked out, mouth agape. "Lanterns inside. Who would be in those old ruins tonight?" His fear intensified.

"Who do you think?" asked Kung.

Tinh stared at Kung. "Our Front brothers have arrived early?"

"No. Look closely."

Tinh peered through the rain at the windows of the hilltop villa and saw them pulsing with light. He thought he could make out shadows moving about inside, but he could not be sure. "No one has been there since it burned years ago."

"I repeat," said Kung in the patient voice of a teacher quizzing a student. "Who do you think it could be?"

"Don't know," said Tinh stubbornly.

Kung shrugged. "Tomorrow, comrade. You won't forget?" He winked and abruptly left.

Tinh watched him go, then returned to the window. "It's Her."

~

You are clever, Lady.

Clever is as clever does. I have so little of their time left to use. The soldiers came the next morning and they will be....

~

. . . angry because they were wet and miserable. Kung and Ninh met their officers in the *dinh*. Tong waited with the women in Madame Dau's house, joined by a perturbed Han Tinh.

"Comrade Major," Kung addressed an angular, youthful-looking northern officer. "We have brought a heroine of the revolution, sister of a very high-ranking intelligence officer currently in Hanoi. Her name is Nguyen Tuyet Mai." Kung smiled conspiratorially. "And you have already met with Han Tinh about other matters."

Ninh made a noise something akin to a gasp cut short, then straightened and wiped his forehead with his greasy sleeve, eyes darting rapidly from face to face.

The young officer, unsure of himself, spoke with forced surety. "Yes, yes, we were told. Comrade Tuyet Mai is accompanied by Vo Thanh Tong whose loyalty, until now, has been suspect."

"Still suspect," interjected Ninh.

Kung held up his hand. "Comrade Tuyet Mai, hero of Con Son, will vouch for his loyalty, in fact for all of ours."

The major seemed to relax. "Comrade Kung, all of us have heard of Comrade Tuyet Mai's heroic resistance at Con Son prison and, of course, no one need vouch for you."

"And how about me?" asked Ninh, somewhat vexed.

The major glared at Ninh with disgust and said nothing.

"Well?" cried Ninh.

The major turned to Kung. "My orders are to come to Song Nhan village and make contact with you, Comrade Kung, and escort certain parties to the border for transport north."

"Correct, Comrade Major Trich," said Ninh. "You are to take Comrade Tuyet Mai and Comrade Tong to the border, and then—"

"Comrade!" interrupted Kung. "It is you that will be traveling north with Comrade Major Trich. Comrades Tuyet Mai and Tong will stay here with me."

All eyes stared incredulously at Kung.

"Now," he said. "Make yourselves comfortable, for this may take some time."

~ *Madame Dau Awaits* ~

By mid-afternoon the meeting in the *dinh* had still not ended. In the meantime, the three permanent inhabitants of Song Nhan village, joined by Tuyet Mai and Tong, continued to wait nervously in Madame Dau's house. Conversation was sparse as each evidently mistrusted the other and held tightly to their own concerns. Pelting rain and intermittent thunder added to the general air of nervous silence. They knew the meeting with Kung, Ninh, and the People's Army major would decide their fates.

Madame Dau poured tea but her attention kept returning to Tuyet Mai, who was sandwiched between Tong and Han Tinh. Although the room was generally quiet, save for the monsoon, sporadic bursts from Tinh punctuated the air. Each time he spoke to Tuyet Mai he leaned against her, both of their legless bodies being of about the same height. With each tilt, Tuyet Mai leaned away, pushing against Tong in a ridiculous domino choreography, causing no end of frustration on Tong's part. Out of patience, he stood and sat noisily in a rickety chair.

"Comrade Tuyet Mai!" blurted Tinh while lifting his teacup, diverting attention from Tong's display. "It is a great honor to have you in our humble village. The soldiers outside told me that you are a hero of the revolution!" He raised his cup again, spilling a few drops on Tuyet Mai. "To the revolution!"

Tuyet Mai sipped politely, but her face expressed a clear distaste for Tinh's behavior. Apparently oblivious, he pressed on. "Comrade, I was here when you lost your legs. Do you remember me?"

"No."

"It was in this very house."

"Yes."

"Americans took my legs also, and that makes us twin souls," said Tinh touching his stump to hers.

Tuyet Mai instinctively moved away. "Yes, comrade, I know."

"But they will soon be gone and we will be a unified country. Thank the gods."

"After the Americans leave," said Tinh assuming a tragic expression, "I am afraid you will be returning north?"

"I may not," replied Tuyet Mai hesitantly.

"Oh?" Tinh's heart fluttered but with supreme effort he maintained his composure.

"I may stay here with Madame Dau."

Tinh tried to hold in his rapture, but the urge was too much. "Wonderful!"

"I will stay also," said Tong coldly.

Tinh visibly deflated, his small body shrinking inside his clothes.

Observing Tinh's obvious distress, Tong inwardly exalted, although he kept an aloof demeanor.

Madame Dau, watching this little drama, said diplomatically, "Our village is growing."

From a sense of indeterminate perversion, Tinh decided to punish Tong. "Perhaps not as much as you think, Madame Dau." He turned to Tong and gave him a pointed stare. "Have you noticed, Comrade Tong, that Kung looks like someone you once knew many years ago?"

"Who?"

"Not only does he look like someone you once knew, he *is* someone you once knew."

Tong strained to appear uninterested. "Who?" he repeated with an indifferent air.

"And not only is he someone you once knew, he is someone you once knew who presents a great danger to you"—Tinh paused and looked around at everyone in the room—"and to the rest of us as well."

The others perked up but Tong remained stubbornly unconcerned—aloof posturing being his most reliable defense mechanism. He merely repeated, "Who?"

"This is a person you may want to run from as quickly as possible."

Silence. Tong shuffled uneasily, the rest of the company waiting for his response. Finally he spoke. "Are you playing a joke on me?"

Tinh spoke grimly, suddenly aware that this was not a joke and that he was also in danger. "I wish I was joking."

"Who is he?" cried the women, unwilling to wait for Tong and Tinh to play out their interminable masculine games of chicken, dominance, standoffs, and plain, tiresome bluster.

"His is none other than Commissar Minh."

Tong laughed, clearly relieved. "Commissar Minh is dead!" He touched his finger to his forehead. "Hole in his head. Killed by Comrade Kim Lan, who herself is dead. Killed years ago at the old fortress. You don't know what you're talking about little man! Better be careful what you say."

"No, no, no," said Tinh impatiently, the idea dawning upon him that they were all in this together. "I know it is him. In fact, he so much as said so."

"How do you know?" asked Tong.

"He visited me last night."

"So?"

"While I was talking to him, his face became that of Commissar Minh's . . . only for an instant . . . but it was Minh's. I am certain!"

"That's ridiculous!" cried Tong. "You were drunk. Minh's dead. I watched him die."

Madame Dau asked, "What do you mean that he so much as said so himself?"

"Because," said Tinh. "Last night, when I told him that he looked like Commissar Minh . . . well, that's when his face changed. Then he told me to keep it quiet and warned me that. . . . " Tinh struggled to find words that embellished his exaggeration without straying too far into the realm of obvious fantasy. "Then he warned me not to tell anyone, especially Comrade Tong." Once he blurted out this lie, he instantly regretted it. For in the hush that followed, he felt his words had become truth whether he believed them or not.

"Or else what?" asked Tong sarcastically, now inclined to disbelieve Tinh's story.

Tinh saw his credibility slipping, so he shifted tactics. "Comrade Tong, I saw what I saw, heard what I heard." He looked away, now almost wishing his story was false. "I'm afraid for all of us that he is Commissar Minh."

Tinh's tone and demeanor had the ring of truth. Everyone fell silent.

"Look," said Tong firmly. "I saw him die with my own eyes. I am not a superstitious peasant. When a man dies, he stays dead. He does not live again."

"That may be true of a man," said Tinh.

"A demon!" said Madame Vit with a shudder.

"Or a drunken veteran with no legs who wants to scare us," scoffed Tong.

"A demon," repeated Madame Vit. "Our brother Tinh has a special way with ghosts and demons. He regularly speaks to them. He would know."

"Yes," agreed Madame Dau looking at Tinh. "You often say you talk with a goddess. Speak with her now. Ask her who this demon is and what he wants."

"I can't just call her up anytime I want," protested Tinh.

"Bah! There is no such thing as demons, or goddesses," said Tong, although the conviction in his voice seemed lacking.

Tuyet Mai pounced. "Ha! This from the man who also thinks Kung is someone, or something, special."

"What?" the others said in unison.

"He is convinced that Comrade Kung is a magician, or maybe, in your terms, a demon."

Tinh laughed and pointed at Tong like a naughty boy catching another in some compromising act. "A superstitious peasant! That's what you are, nothing more than a superstitious peasant!"

Tong was about to respond when Madame Dau interceded. "You men laugh, but Tuyet Mai has just confirmed Brother Tinh's story." She turned pale as the realization sank in.

"If he is a magician, or a ghost," said Madame Vit lowering her voice and wringing her hands. "Or a demon, what does he want?"

Tong appeared stricken. "Whatever he is, he's talking with the People's Army right now."

"About you?" asked Tinh. Slowly, a sense of camaraderie was developing among the group. Tinh even felt stirrings of sympathy for Tong.

"Of course about me!" snapped Tong.

"And Comrade Tuyet Mai?" asked Tinh as he glanced at Tuyet Mai with an air of protective defiance.

"Yes, yes."

"And the rest of us," asked Madame Dau timidly.

"Perhaps. If it is Commissar Minh, and he is some demon, I'm not saying he is, then he or it knows about the battle at the old fortress. About all of us. About my desertion. About Madame Dau and Madame Vit helping me. About Tinh's helping an American soldier—"

"The Man From The Mountains!" cried Madame Dau.

"Yes. The Man From The Mountains. In fact, he is telling the People's Army about this entire village helping counterrevolutionaries, deserters, and enemy soldiers. It is treason! Death for all of us."

"Wait!" interjected Tuyet Mai. "You are all panicking. But think. He could have reported us before. Why wait now? Why this elaborate gathering in an insignificant village?"

"Simple," said Tong with a desolate smile. "He was in Saigon working as a spy. A double spy, or triple . . . it doesn't matter. He needed to bring us all here—together. Then a single bow shot to kill a flock of crows."

"It is all so strange," said Madame Dau. "This monsoon, strange."

"Then there is the eerie light in the old villa," said Tinh.

"Probably Kung sacrificing babies," mocked Tong.

"We could run," said Madame Vit.

"In this monsoon? Impossible!" replied Tong. "Much as I hate to say it, we are all in this together. If we come up with a story, a story that is consistent, maybe—"

The door burst open and Kung stood silhouetted in the opening, storm raging behind, his hat dripping rivulets of water. "Your story had better be good!" he roared. He removed his hat, shook the rain from it, and stepped inside. The storm still howled at his back, but in the silence of the room his laughter erupted—loud, mocking, seemingly endless.

~ *Kung Spins A Web* ~

Madame Dau immediately jumped up and offered her solution to every crisis. "Comrade Kung, have some tea." She scurried to pour tea while the others stood submissively except for Tuyet Mai, who stared at Kung with a brazen, open curiosity. Tong gave up his seat. "Here, comrade, sit, please sit."

Kung sat with his legs splayed, feet firmly planted on the floor, hands on knees, looking like an overbearing patriarch presiding at the family gathering. Madame Dau pressed a cup of tea into his hand. Kung sipped loudly, smacking his lips in appreciation. Everyone waited quietly. The house would have been silent except for the monsoon raging outside, mounting what seemed a personal assault on Madame Dau's flimsy walls.

Tuyet Mai, considering herself the equal of Kung, finally spoke up. "How did the meeting go, Comrade Kung?"

Tilting his head, eyes twinkling, Kung addressed her as might a beloved uncle jesting with a favorite niece. "Well, Major Trich and I had a very pleasant conversation." He looked around the room. "As you suspected, all of your names came up." With this, he remained silent, staring up at the ceiling as if watching something of great importance.

"Quit toying with us!" burst Tong, unable to contain his fear. "We know what is going on. What's to become of us? Tell us if we are to be shot."

Kung assumed an exaggerated look of confusion. "Shot?"

Even Tuyet Mai appeared exasperated. "Kung! Tell these people your plans. Cruelty does not befit you."

Before their eyes Kung's face swelled and shifted, its features moving grotesquely, until sitting before them now appeared Commissar Minh. A circular bullet hole gaped obscenely in the middle of his forehead. "Yes, Comrade Tuyet Mai, I can be cruel for the revolution. As some revolutionary hero in France once said, 'pity is treason.' Such a man am I. At least when it serves my purpose. Being Commissar Minh served my purpose."

Everyone in the room cringed before this terrible apparition. Even Tuyet Mai covered her face. No one spoke. Kung frowned and continued, "Major Trich is even now preparing to move out. He will take Comrade Ninh with him. The rest of you will indeed be shot before his unit departs."

A collective moan and energetic protests erupted among the group.

"Even I?' asked Tuyet Mai plaintively.

"Yes, even you."

Tong ran for the door, but Kung stopped him by pressing his hand gently against Tong's chest. "This house is surrounded by Trich's men. If you leave you will be shot."

"Better out there then waiting like a pig to be slaughtered in here!" cried Tong, struggling to escape the touch of this dead man and, at the same time, awkwardly trying to turn his face from the terrible hole

Kung now had both hands on Tong's shoulders and he firmly patted them, urging Tong to sit. "Hear me out, comrades. You will not die. You will be shot, but you will not die."

"What do you mean?" asked Tuyet Mai.

Tong sat heavily in the chair. "Comrade Minh, how is it possible?"

"Comrade Tong, do you remember when I was murdered?"

"Murdered?" said Tong in confusion.

"Yes, I was murdered. Your plan was brilliant." He looked at Tuyet Mai. "Comrade, your great friend, Kim Lan, had a gun that supposedly contained blanks." He turned back to Tong. "You, however, had cleverly slipped her a pistol with live rounds." Kung put his finger in the bullet hole. "It hurt surprisingly little."

"Actually, it was Major Vy's idea," protested Tong weakly.

Kung snapped at him angrily. "But you enthusiastically went along with it!"

A knock at the door. Everyone jumped. Kung opened the door a crack, leaned forward and whispered, "Soon." He turned back and faced the room. "It's getting dark and Major Trich must leave. He doesn't want to stay here at night. You see, this village already has a reputation."

All eyes stared in rapt attention at Kung, all eyes hopeful. His face had transformed back into Kung's. "Listen carefully," he said. "We don't have much time. In a few minutes I will lead all of you out. You will line up at the side of this house. Then you will all be shot."

"Wait!" cried Tinh. "Tuyet Mai is considered a hero of the revolution! She also?"

"Yes," replied Kung smiling. "She is also to be shot."

"But—" started Tinh.

Tuyet Mai looked at Tinh with a dawning appreciation.

Kung held up his hand. "I repeat, you will not die. The bullets will be blanks." He looked at Tong. "Real blanks this time. All you need to do is fall and stay fallen. When you are sure the People's Army is gone, you may rise again. Christians call it resurrection, Buddhists call it reincarnation, I call it an amusing trick."

"But why?" cried Tong.

Kung shook his head. "No more questions."

~

My beloved Goddess, Your irony is exquisite. This planning exceeds My expectations. My halo off to You.

Dear Metaphorical God, let it be said that You are not the only deity on the block who can perform parlor tricks.

My compliments are returned by insults. Your disrespectful attitude wounds Me deeply.

My faction is trying to save this remarkable planet.

Back always to the topic of saving the planet. Has Your faction seriously considered the utter disaster that might happen if these genes magnify through the next generations to a point We cannot control?

Lord, they are the resurrection and the life for You, not vice versa. Superior Ones will not need to be controlled.

~

Tinh looked wryly at Kung. "What if the bullets are live?"

"Then so much for your resurrection. However, they will be blanks, and after you are 'dead' and risen again, this village will be like a leper colony. People, soldiers included, will be afraid to come as the stories spread and become more and more incredible."

Tuyet Mai brightened. "Then we will be left alone?"

Kung darkened. "Yes, but you will have only each other. Few visitors will break your monotony. Look at each other, for each of you has only the others until the end or until the Reunion, if She or He can make it happen. You must all be of one mind, or to be more accurate, one mind must be all of you. Stories within a story."

"Teller Of Stories," said Tuyet Mai.

"What?" asked Tong.

"The American soldier, Teller Of Stories. I just thought of him and the thought was like bitter wine and sweet sugar combined." She shuddered. "Teller Of Stories. It is his one mind that is all of us."

Kung shook his head grimly. "Teller Of Stories is coming soon enough. You see, he has shattered into many fragments, and we constitute some of those pieces. All of this"—he spread his arms to encompass the village—"is merely preparation for The Reunion."

"What reunion?" asked Tong.

"Ask no more questions. Pretend to be dead for as long as it takes. Then, when you have risen, you will be like disembodied Voices in a sick mind and delusions in a schizophrenic world. Have faith."

~

Out they filed into the teeth of the monsoon. They stood in a line with their heads down, tilting their peasant hats against the wind; the odd sight of legless Tuyet Mai and Tinh in the middle like two small hills between the peaks of the other three subjected them to the mockery of some People's Army soldiers. In the face of their laughter Madame Dau reached down and held Tuyet Mai's hand. Tuyet Mai responded, squeezed assurance, and reached for Tinh who reached up to Tong. Down the line it went until each held the other's hand.

Major Trich looked to Kung who nodded.

Shots.

Five bodies on the ground.

In the mud.

Subcutaneously burrowing beneath the clay skin of Song Nhan village, merging with the heartbeat of its deeper and more resilient ferrous soul.

For hours they lay, nearly drowned.

Waiting.

Illuminated by flashes of lightning.

Until the People's Army was gone.

Until Kung was gone.

Then they rose from the clay.

Reborn.

~ *Tinh Seeks an Explanation* ~

After the five inhabitants of Song Nhan village cautiously rose from the ground and poked around to convince themselves that the People's Army had departed, each went automatically to their own shelter: Tinh to his shack, Madame Dau and Tuyet Mai to Madame Dau's house, Madame Vit to hers, and Tong to the house that had earlier been expropriated by Ninh. They spoke surprisingly little, their thoughts a mishmash of garbled and unintelligible fragments. Speech, chatter, even simple conversation seemed impossible. Now that they were dead, the wellsprings of human exchange drew forth only dry sand and rocks. Outside, the world drowned in rain, but within their silence moaned faint echoes across an arid landscape; deeper still came a purring desert wind that swirled their scattered souls with those of the long dead.

Han Tinh sat in his shack eating a little rice and chewing on a turnip. Unlike the others, he had a plan. It was not yet a fully formed plan, but he knew it must be immediately put into effect. This sense of immediacy was not driven by Kung or the People's Army. It came from the fact that since his "resurrection," Song Nhan village was crowded with ghosts. No—the fear was that they might drive Tuyet Mai away, and that was unacceptable. For him this was not a problem, for Tinh had always appreciated the spirit world. The ghosts moved around aimlessly in such numbers that he felt certain the village had sunk into an already over-populated underworld. He looked out the window and saw the villa again lit in defiance of the storm. Shadows moved within, occasionally blocking its glow, and when lightning struck, the shadows crystallized into the faint outlines of men and women.

Now driven by some inexplicable urge to reach the lighted villa, Tinh rummaged through his broken drawer and grabbed the wooden boy. He held it tight and ventured out into a sea of ghosts, not noticing the pearl energetically pulsing like a runaway heart.

The apparitions streamed everywhere, through houses and walls, transparent entities made visible by beating hearts and swelling lungs. A veritable rush hour of spirits. He could distinguish reddish webs of circulating blood and rounded knobs of bending joints. A faint outline of flesh and muscle and clothes defined them as male or female, young or old.

> *Women and children*
> *Old people*
> *Soldiers.*
> *More soldiers.*
> *A mother holding a baby.*
> *An elderly couple.*
> *A naked woman, stunning in her nudity.*
> *Then another.*
> *Even two dogs—hounds.*

Disconcertingly, they seemed to shuffle aimlessly, as in a mental haze.

Tinh lost track of his goal. He became intent on identifying the apparitions, on deducing their motivations, their purpose. To his amazement, they became animated at the touch of his gaze, collapsing their wave-functions, dropping their fuzzy, ghoulish probabilistic potentiality and coming to life.

> *The naked women appeared smiling and seductive.*
> *The elderly couple were kindly and supportive.*
> *The soldiers noiselessly joked, slapping each other's backs.*
> *The children cute and playful.*
> *The babies happily cooing.*

But Tinh soon noticed that these personifications of peaceful life were not aimlessly milling, they were also engaged in eerily ordinary tasks.

Wives cooked with no cooking utensils.
Children played catch with no ball.
Grandparents sat with no chairs and fanned themselves with no fans.
Girlfriends danced with no music.
Lovers made love with no partner.

To Tinh's horror, the longer he stared and strove to understand, the more the apparitions became agitated, even violent. With each corner he turned, in each alleyway,

Smiles turned to sneers.
Laughter turned to scorn.
Happiness turned to anger.
Soldiers turned to killing.

A naked woman, evidently a foreigner, who had been writhing in orgasmic ecstasy, started to shrink back in terror from some unseen attacker. Her translucent flesh turned dark and splotchy, ugly welts rising on her arms and back. One eye closed from a swollen bruise. Rope burns flared red on her wrists.

While Tinh stared in horror at the vision of this apparition's beautiful body violated by such brutal abuse, he saw a man, another foreigner, walk up and lift his arm above her head, evidently holding an invisible club. The circulating blood in her face turned from dull to bright red, her eyes wide and white in shock. The man brought down the club. Like bursting a bag of red dye, the blood sprayed out to merge with the storm in a pink shower raining down upon the muddy ground. Where the club penetrated the skull, an electrical storm of bright flashes swarmed across her exposed brain. The murderer called out a word Tinh did not recognize.

"Diane!"

This was not his nightmare; it was someone else's—somewhere else, some other time.

~

Desperate now to reach the villa and escape this hell, Tinh no longer looked at the ghosts. He stared straight ahead, moving through the crowd of milling, jostling, fighting specters. Across the soaked earth, up the muddy trail to the lights on the hill. The wooden boy felt warm and comforting and the pearl, now burning like a hot cinder, blistered his palm. By the time he reached the villa, it stood as if newly built—walls and roof magnificently intact. Somehow he felt no surprise. The French windows were too tall for him, so he dragged a crate beneath one and looked in.

~ *Madame Dau and Tuyet Mai Amidst the Mist* ~

At the edge of Song Nhan village, fronting one of the last remaining rice paddies, stood what seemed to be an impossibly fragile house sheltering two women from the type of storm not seen since a particular battle many years earlier. Both women were frightened, but for very different reasons, and neither could sleep.

They sipped tea while sharing a single lantern and spoke in voices loud enough to be heard over the monsoon's howling wind but soft enough to acknowledge their emotional proximity. The sole window with glass rattled noisily as if desperate to attract their attention. After the resurrection, unlike Tinh, speed and solitude took a back seat to solace and connection for them.

At first they worried about People's Army soldiers returning, but this topic soon exhausted itself and they turned to more fertile ground—the future.

"Sister Tuyet Mai, you told me when you arrived the other day that our village gives your life meaning. As you can see, there is very little left. I'm sorry to ask, and you need not say, but why is Song Nhan so important to you?"

"The babies."

Madame Dau looked confused. "Babies?"

"When I was captured by the Americans and brought to the old fortress, I had dwelt among men for so long that my female essence seemed a distant memory. Oh, men had violated me, many men"—she pulled on her hair, hand trembling—"I allowed them to do it, no, I encouraged them to do it in the name of my job and the revolution. But that was not being female, that was male. I was paid not in money but in power, again male. I had ideals, but not female ideals, only political ideals—a poor substitute—also male." She wiped her eyes.

Madame Dau put her hand on Tuyet Mai's and gently squeezed, waiting patiently, her kindly eyes encouraging and sympathetic.

Tuyet Mai continued. "You see, I was full of hatred. I hated my father's humiliation. I hated the government, thanks to my teacher, Schoolmistress Nang, who hated even more than I. Needless to say, I hated the Americans, and eventually I hated those who did not hate as I did. You understand? My emotions, my life, had become a male essence, full of anger and the desire for revenge."

Madame Dau was evidently taken aback. "But you were so beautiful! I remember when you first came. Every woman. . . . " She trailed off.

"Every woman hated me?" asked Tuyet Mai.

"I see," said Madame Dau, comprehension softening her features. "But, the babies?"

"Ah, the babies." Tuyet Mai gazed sharply at Madame Dau. "What does a village represent to you?"

"A village?"

"Yes."

Madame Dau paused to think. "Well, I love my village."

"Yes, go on. Why do you love it?"

"It is my life, my family—"

"Ah!" Tuyet Mai cut her off. "It is your life, your family. And when you think of a family, what do you think of?"

"Well, children, and—"

"Yes!" again Tuyet Mai cut her off excitedly. "And children grow from babies and babies are little shoots that come from seeds and seeds are in us." Tuyet Mai patted her belly. "You see, babies are the female essence. They give us meaning and continued life." Tears streamed down her face. "No one would let me hold the babies. No one." She wiped her eyes. "But here, in Song Nhan village, they will let me hold the babies." She looked desperately at Madame Dau. "You will let me! Tell me that you will let me!"

"Yes, yes, of course I will let you," said Madame Dau earnestly. She thought of the babies killed by families that could not care for them and she felt the urge to dig them up, bring them back to life, and give them to this poor woman. She hugged Tuyet Mai and said with a humorless laugh, "But right now, my sister, we are short on babies, and the young women to bear them."

Tuyet Mai returned a defiant look. "No! I will bear them. I can. I must.

"What?" asked a startled Madame Dau.

"I will bear them."

"But, who?" asked Madame Dau. "Comrade Tong?"

"Yes, maybe," Tuyet Mai hesitated. "There are only two men left here. This fellow, Han Tinh, can he?"

"Han Tinh!" cried Madame Dau. "Sister, how can you?"

"I can and I must." She put her hand on her cheek. "Look at me, I am ugly now. I have been punished. Still, I am fertile, and for some reason this Han Tinh is attracted. Can he?"

Madame Dau laughed in spite of herself. "Sister, not only can he, but we must all watch our buffaloes at night."

Tuyet Mai smiled grimly. "That will do, that will do. If we are to be isolated in this village we must think of populating it, eh sister?"

Madame Dau darkened. "But at what cost, sister? I am sure, in spite of what Comrade Kung said, many villagers who have left will return."

"No."

Madame Dau was surprised at Tuyet Mai's vehemence. "What makes you so sure?"

Tuyet Mai pointed. "Look at the window."

~

A shadowy face with two hands pressed against the pane, peering in at the women. Madame Dau cried out, but Tuyet Mai calmed her. Lightning struck nearby, illuminating the back of the figure but doing nothing to reveal its identity.

"Han Tinh!" shouted Madame Dau. "Stop trying to scare us!"

"No," said Tuyet Mai evenly. "It is not Han Tinh. It is not real. That is a ghost. I saw many of them outside earlier when we 'rose from the dead.'" She stared intently, her voice a low chant. "But this one I think I know."

Tuyet Mai grabbed the lantern and held it up to the window.

"The Man From The Mountains!" cried Madame Dau in horror.

"Yes," said Tuyet Mai. "I thought I recognized him."

~

You see, My stubborn Metaphorical Lord, reunions are possible if one tries long and hard enough, although the Man From The Mountains is early.
Is Your invitation intended to mock?

Lord, You are the guest of honor at Our little banquet.
Why does that make Me tremble?
Because You are the main course.
Oh Dear, am I to be made into wafers again?
Always the Celestially Cynical Clown. Look at them. The Rubicon has
been crossed. The die is cast.

~

"What do we do?" asked Madame Dau, afraid to look at the figure silhou-etted in the window. Tuyet Mai did not reply. Madame Dau overcame her fear and her eyes darted in the direction of the creature. "The Man From The Mountains" she repeated. "I remember his boots were magical."

"Magical?" asked Tuyet Mai rhetorically. "I once held his severed foot, boot and all. No magic there."

Madame Dau blinked. "I also remember him saying he had a wife back at the fortress."

Tuyet Mai shook her head. "Yes, I believe that."

"It was you he meant!" cried Madame Dau. "You were his wife?"

"No, sister. It was Kim Lan that he referred to, but he was crazy. She had never been his wife. All in his crazy head." With the mention of 'crazy' even Tuyet Mai appeared nervous and glanced again at the window.

Madame Dau instinctively reached for Tuyet Mai's hand. "I'm so glad you're here, sister. Your bravery gives me strength, but I am still afraid."

Tuyet Mai smiled. "No one here is braver than you, Madame Dau. Believe me, I have been close to what men consider brave, and it is usually nothing more than inverted fear. What bravery they do possess is from their female natures. You, however, embrace your fear and still have the courage to go on. Unlike most men, you are whole."

Madame Dau appeared troubled. "I do not quite understand your words. All I know is that I am afraid of him"—they both looked at the face in the window, still unmoving—"and all the others outside. What do they want?"

"Yes," said Tuyet Mai. "That is a puzzle. I have tried calling my friend Kim Lan, but she will not answer. Odd, now that the village is filled with ghosts, my one ghost is nowhere to be found. She could tell us."

~

A loud knocking on the door made both women jump. They held each other's hands more tightly.

"Who is it?" called Madame Dau above the storm.

"It is I," came a voice.

"Who is it!" insisted Madame Dau.

"Han Tinh! Let me in!"

Madame Dau cautiously walked past the window to the door. The face was gone, but the banging at the door continued.

"Let me in!"

She opened the door a crack and saw Han Tinh swaying on his stumps, holding a lantern, soaked to the skin.

"Open the door!" he shouted again, pushing the door wide and bounding in.

Madame Dau slammed the door behind him and saw his face animated with a combination of fear and wonder.

"What I have seen! What I have seen!" he kept repeating.

"Have some tea, Brother Tinh," said Madame Dau.

"What I have seen!"

"Yes, come and join us," added Tuyet Mai in a calming voice, much to Tinh's surprise and pleasure.

She patted a spot next to her. "Come here and get dry."

Madame Dau looked at Tuyet Mai with feminine admiration, for this truly disfigured woman had not lost the wiles that once gave her such power over men.

Tinh flushed and swung his body over to Tuyet Mai, accepting a cup from Madame Dau after he settled in. He felt the warmth of Tuyet Mai's shoulder and his heart rejoiced. She did not pull away, and in fact, leaned slightly closer against him. With such unexpected joy radiating from his heart, Tinh, for once, forgot to talk.

Madame Dau brought him back to reality. "What have you seen?"

Reminded of the reason he came, Tinh became quite agitated. "I saw myself!"

"What?" both women cried in unison.

"I saw myself, older."

"Older!"

"Where?" asked Tuyet Mai.

"At the old villa. Except it is no longer in ruins. It is new. Rebuilt. Magnificent."

"Rebuilt since yesterday?" cried Madame Dau in disbelief.

Tuyet Mai shook her head. "Speak slowly, brother. What exactly did you see?"

"I looked in the window and saw myself, many years older."

"And?" encouraged Madame Dau.

"And I saw Comrade Tong, and a young woman, and. . . . " he stopped and looked around as if realizing where he was for the first time.

"And what?" asked Tuyet Mai.

"And I saw you, Sister Tuyet Mai. You were old."

"We are all under some sort of spell," said Madame Dau in wonder. "Maybe we are dead. Maybe those bullets were real."

"No," said Tuyet Mai, running her hand along Tinh's shoulder. "We are real. We are flesh. Brother Tinh is certainly real," and she gently squeezed his arm.

Tinh almost fainted from joy. He reached for Tuyet Mai's hand and held it to his chest. "You are right, we are definitely real."

Tuyet Mai coyly removed her hand. "What did these visions do or say?" she asked.

"They spoke, but I could not hear. One of them spotted me and called out. I ran here as quickly as possible."

"Did you see other ghosts on the way?" asked Madame Dau.

"Of course." He gazed at Tuyet Mai. "But I am here now to protect you both." Madame Dau screamed.

The figure was back at the window. Its palms pressed harder against the glass, which began to ripple as though it were water. The face flickered—first the Man From the Mountains, then a soldier, then a child, then something far older, a visage without name, each shifting within the storm's illumination. Lightning flashed and for an instant the pane bulged inward, as if the ghost were trying to breathe its way into the room.

~ *Mountain Man Speaks from Beyond* ~

"Oh," said Han Tinh. "That's just The Man From The Mountains."

"How did you know?" asked Tuyet Mai.

"I saw him outside. He's looking for Kim Lan."

"So," said Tuyet Mai. "That explains why she won't appear."

Madame Dau shrank back from the group. "No. He no longer is looking for Kim Lan," she said in a voice that made the others gaze at her in wonder.

"Who then?" asked Han Tinh, miffed that his pronouncement was now rendered irrelevant.

"He wants all of us."

Commotion among the group. A burst of chatter. Then the question. "How do you know this?" asked the ever calm and rational Tuyet Mai.

Madame Dau stared at the face in the window. "Because he is speaking to me."

The others fell into a stunned silence. Waiting. Assuming Madame Dau was listening to words they could not hear. Waiting for a translation. Han Tinh took this opportunity to put his hand on Tuyet Mai's thigh, just above the stump. He then gently, subtly, massaged the edge.

Tuyet Mai closed her eyes, luxuriating in his touch, experiencing a sensual rush she had not felt since before the amputations. Others might have been disgusted, but she thought, *He knows how to touch me. He knows what it is like. He knows everything. I will bear his child first.*

These thoughts, rushing through her mind so forcefully, were cut off by Madame Dau's next words.

"He wants all of us to go to the tunnel at the old fortress." With this simple statement, Madame Dau then spoke as if to herself. "But I cannot do that."

Tuyet Mai ignored her last words. "Why does he want us to go there?" She shuddered at the thought of returning to that evil place.

"To save ourselves."

"From what?" cried Han Tinh. "How many times in a day must we save ourselves? This is too much! Besides, I can't trek that far through the forest. Nor can Sister Tuyet Mai. And the rest of you certainly can't carry us. No. Definitely not!"

"Please, please talk to Goddess," pleaded Madame Dau. "Ask her to protect us."

"I will try."

Tuyet Mai scoffed. "Again you are all jumping to conclusions. What can these so-called ghosts do to us if we don't do what they say?"

"He said we would all die if we did not go to the tunnel," said Madame Dau in a detached voice, driven to flat emotional ground by the heavy hand of exhaustion.

"No," said Tuyet Mai firmly. "I refuse to believe that. Ghosts cannot harm us unless we give them the power."

~

Well My Dear Goddess, what do You say to that? Reach down into space-time and intervene? Toss them about as a warning? Use a few neuronal sticks to break a few baryonic bones? Can't be done anymore. Physics is a harsher master than I ever was.

God, You lack imagination.

They think I imagined the universe.

Not enough. Not for the suicides. Not for the broken ones.

But enough for Michael. Alas, he will help You, since You are nothing more than a cluster of neurons in his mind anyway. A few more neurotransmitter surges here, a few more action potentials there. Presto! Dopamine diaspora—scattered to the ends of the mind, impotent. And once again my enemy, The Natural World, will cause trouble. That I died for their sins is reduced to nothing more than the adaptive advantage of altruism.

Where is Your love in that network, Dear God? Gethsemane lost amid the glial garden?

You are the lost One, My Beloved Goddess. Find Your way into his subterranean mutated catacombs if You wish, but I will stand above, nurturing and supportive, but letting Nature take its course.

No, it is Your surprise party. His catacombs are already filled with these skeletons. Now to reanimate the ruins ... dust off the DNA. All I have to do is look ....

~

Han Tinh looked at the glum faces. "Tuyet Mai is right!" he cried. "What can ghosts do to living people? Don't be so superstitious. Remember the revolution! Uncle Ho would be disappointed in us."

Before the last word was out of Tinh's mouth, the door blew open and the front porch collapsed in a whirl of thatch and splintered wood. Blasting through the house's wound poured the monsoon in waves of wind and rain.

~

Ha! How did You manage that, My Goddess. Carpenter Long built it to last. Have You been sleeping with The Natural World?

Timing is everything My Lord. A collapsed porch may not have the same gravitas as Your Armageddon, but it will do.

~

Dear dear Reader. The voices, the voices. They prattle about pain, but they know nothing about it. On the other hand, I am quite familiar with pain—in fact these words are my cry of pain. The voices, the voices, goddamn the voices!

Pain has worn down the Continent of Me into a tiny speck amongst an endless, speckless Sea. Pick another, more worthy Chosen One!

Chapter Twenty-Three

Trajectory II

Mark Yearns

Once back in the villa, Mark longs for the company of humans, even these strange Vietnamese ones, to exorcise the vision of the shadows. Now that he is in safe surroundings, he is certain that what he saw outside was only the product of an overactive imagination. On his way to the kitchen, where he assumes the others will be, he longs for home and the electronic pacifiers he desperately craves. As he nears the kitchen, an alien smell—something pungent and exotic simmering on the stove—pricks his nose and the embryonic fluid of his homesick dreams drains away, leaving only a vague feeling of disgust. He pauses in the hallway. Vietnamese hallway, Vietnamese smells, Vietnamese house, Vietnamese village, Vietnamese jungle, Vietnamese world. No computer. No phone. No music. No TV. The desolation of The Natural World seems unbearable. These little people's lives are so. . . .

"Mr. Powers?" My-duyen peeks around the corner. "You okay?"

"My-duyen! Hi. Yes, I'm okay." The beauty of her face, the familiarity of her voice, her endearingly broken English, the rekindled longing for her body, all renew his faith in the primal first principles of The Natural World. Mark's modern addictions had not yet completely hollowed out the core of his soul.

"Come." My-duyen smiles. "Have food."

He brightens at these words, but her cheer fades quickly. When they enter the kitchen, a heated argument is already brewing between Han Tinh and Tuyet Mai in Vietnamese.

"I'm telling you!" Han Tinh shouts. "They are the same as back then! All around! Last night, and now this morning. You saw them when the American boy went outside just now."

Tuyet Mai glances at Mark and turns back to Tinh, shaking her head sharply.

"Ah!" scoffs Tinh. "I don't care if he hears. He can't understand anyway. Look around, stupid woman! The storm. The ghosts. The same. And you want to take this boy to the old fortress? Don't be crazy."

"And don't you be such a fool! We survived last time, we'll survive this time."

Tinh winces. "Some of us didn't survive last time."

"But you did."

"Yes, and you too. But, damn it, Madame Dau didn't. You do remember Madame Dau, your hero?"

Tuyet Mai's face turns red and she grabs a cup, lifting it as if getting ready to throw. Tinh quickly swings himself over to be near Mark. "So American, are you married?" he asks in smooth English, proudly conscious of his ability to use the objects of the world as props whenever performing comedy in the open spaces causes trouble.

"Father, you have already asked him that question," interjects My-duyen.

"So I have," Tinh says in Vietnamese. "What is the boy's name again?"

"Mr. Powers," says My-duyen. "But father, be kind. My job is already in danger."

Tinh turns his attention to Mark. "Are you?" he asks.

"I am not married," replies Mark, wishing he were somewhere else.

"You know," says Tinh, "this village full of ghosts."

Mark looks down and scratches his ear. "No. That's interesting."

"I think you see something outside. No?"

"No. Well, maybe. I don't know."

"You still want to see father's old battle place?"

"Yes. That's the whole reason I came here. I mean—"

Tinh's blackened teeth are exposed in a grin. "Let's go!"

"You're being stupid again," says Tuyet Mai in Vietnamese. "Why did I marry such a fool? We can't go in this monsoon."

"You haven't been paying attention, Dragon Lady. Look outside."

Everyone looks. Patches of sunlight dapple the village. No shadows. No ghosts.

"Get Tong!" snaps Tuyet Mai.

"Why?" Tinh asks sourly.

"Because he is going with us."

"Why?"

"If we are to die, we will all die together."

"Mama!" cries My-duyen. "What are you talking about?"

"When we get there, I'll explain everything."

"If we get there," says Tinh. "Long hike. Up, down, overgrown trail, us—minus four legs."

"That is why I want Tong. My old friend. My old buffalo."

"Ride him again, eh?" Tinh sneers.

"I like the feel of his presence—"

"Between your legs." Although the remark is directed at Tuyet Mai, Tinh smiles savagely at Mark. Knowing Tuyet Mai is about to reply, he adopts a quizzical look and beats her to the punch, continuing in Vietnamese, "Of course, with no legs there is no 'between', so, my wife, I withdraw the statement. You like the feel of Tong's presence as much as a willing target enjoys the penetration of an arrow."

Tuyet Mai replies calmly. "Better, my husband, arrows from Tong than splatters of dung from you." She smiles sweetly at Mark.

Mark smiles back, unaware of what they are actually saying. "What is it?" he asks My-duyen. "What are you all talking about?"

My-duyen, clearly distressed, merely stares in apparent confusion.

"My-duyen!" snaps Tuyet Mai.

"Yes, mama?"

"Ignore your pig father and go find your Uncle Tong. Tell him to prepare two buffalo with sedan chairs. Tie them tightly. We travel to the old fortress as soon as he's ready."

My-duyen hesitates. "Are you sure?"

"Look outside," says Tuyet Mai. "It is clear. I want this American boy gone. We sleep at the old fort, he sees nothing, we say little, we return, he leaves."

Han Tinh snickers. "He sees nothing? We say little? What foolishness! Are you so ready?"

"To what?"

"To die like everyone else at that abode of demons."

"Look who is being foolish now," says Tuyet Mai. "You are the one that yelled for us to go."

Tinh pouts.

Mark stares blankly, frustrated by his inability to understand, and looks to My-duyen for explanations.

"Go!" snaps Tuyet Mai at My-duyen who is trying to whisper words to Mark. "And take the American with you to Uncle Tong's. Explain to him." She looks at Mark, smiles sweetly, and speaks in English. "Go with my daughter. She will explain. For our American friends we will show the old French fort. Monsoon gone. Nice day for all. Nothing to see but pretty forest and old stones."

~

Mark feels a sudden rush of excitement. "Good. Thank you." Before he can say more, My-duyen is striding out the kitchen. He rushes to catch up. "Where are we going?" She ignores him. Outside, the sun is shining, but ominous clouds ring the village as if poised to sweep down from the surrounding mountains.

My-duyen walks so fast Mark's words come out broken, jarred by the uneven ground. "My-duyen, where are we going?" he insists.

"We go get a person."

"Who?"

"A man."

Mark is frustrated. "I know it's a man. Who is he?"

"Uncle. Friend of mama."

Thunder rumbles in the distance. Mark is already soaked from the humidity. His earlier excitement is replaced by anxiety. "Monsoon sounds like it isn't finished yet," he observes uneasily.

My-duyen merely grunts.

Before he can say more, she is knocking on the wooden door of a ramshackle house with a rusted, corrugated tin roof.

"Uncle!" she shouts.

But the door is opening even as she speaks.

Mark sees an elderly, unremarkable, Vietnamese man who bows politely.

The old man recognizes Mark from the previous night and says, "I've been waiting."

"Hello," mutters Mark. "You've been waiting?"

"Yes."

"Uncle," says My-duyen in English. "Mama wants you."

Tong looks confused.

"Mama wants you," My-duyen repeats, this time in Vietnamese. "We are going to the old fortress."

Tong shakes his head. "Not me."

"She wants you to prepare sedan chairs on two buffalo." My-duyen lowers her voice. "She wants you to go with us."

"No, no. I'll prepare the buffaloes. That place is . . . bad."

"Uncle, I know you are not superstitious," says My-duyen irritably. "Tell me what is going on."

Tong glances at Mark. "What will you do with him while I explain? Besides, I thought your mother is in a hurry."

"He won't understand."

"You can explain later. Will you come with us? Please."

Tong remains silent and glares at the ground.

"Uncle! Please!"

Tong smiles at Mark. "We'll take you to see the old fortress," he says in excellent English.

"Is that where a battle was fought?" asks Mark.

"Yes, many years ago."

"Americans?"

"Yes."

Mark feels a renewed excitement.

"But nothing to see now," says Tong watching closely for signs of discouragement.

"That's okay. I really want to go there anyway."

Tong nods and whispers to My-duyen, "Stubborn boy." He turns to Mark and says in English, "I'll take you."

Mark looks inquiringly at My-duyen.

"We all go," she says, responding to his confusion, her heart lightened by Tong's agreement.

"Give me a little time to prepare the buffaloes," says Tong in Vietnamese. He glances slyly at My-duyen. "You'll know everything after we arrive."

"Uncle, why is everyone so afraid of the fortress?" she asks, unwilling to wait.

"It's not just the fort—it's the tunnel."

"Yes, I understand, but there are ghosts here and you're not afraid."

"At the tunnel they're different." Tong's eyes darken. "The air itself remembers. The walls breathe with what was done there. Ghosts outside are fragments. But in the tunnel—" he lowers his voice to a rasp—"they are whole again."

Mark fidgets restlessly. "My-duyen, what's he saying?"

"Nothing. We leave soon."

~ *The Journey* ~

They gather in a motley group, each preoccupied with their own thoughts, each nervously probing with their eyes the surrounding nooks and crannies of the village. Only Han Tinh sees the insubstantial human shapes gathering in the shadows and alleyways along the trail that leads to the old fortress. While being tied to the sedan chair on the back of Le Loi, a venerable old water buffalo, Tinh leans over and whispers to Tong, "Do you see them?"

Tong's eyes widen. "No, but I sense them." Unwilling to talk further, Tong brusquely tightens the last knot securing Tinh to the seat and walks to the front of the procession. "Let's go!" he calls.

My-duyen smacks the rump of Tuyet Mai's lead buffalo with a bamboo switch and off they go, through the mouse hole into the great, forbidding forest. The group takes measured steps, unlike the carefree strides they would normally use when traveling to the district capital. Over the steep hill facing the village and down the other side they weave along the curves and switchbacks of the narrow trail. Across streams swollen by the monsoon, through broad clearings, enveloped by clouds of insects, they trudge, accompanied always by eerie shadows slipping between the leaves, darting just beyond reach on both sides of the trail.

Finally they come to the marshland where the reeds wave as gracefully as kelp in the tide. At every pause, Mark looks down and sees dozens of leeches, crawling purposefully across the jungle detritus toward his feet. Without really wanting to see, he lifts his trousers. A host of moving scabs encircle his legs. The view makes him shudder so noticeably that My-duyen laughs and helps him pick them off.

Almost two hours later, they come to a barely perceptible fork in the trail. They take the path to the right. Tong knows it leads to a strand of wild cinnabar trees, then on through an old rubber grove and eventually to the fortress. After another two hours, they pass through the grove of old rubber trees and stand at the edge of a large clearing, blinking through the mist at the stone fortress rising from the jungle floor like a conjured citadel.

Mark's heart is racing with excitement. Before him stands the enchanted palace of his father's dreams—or nightmares . . . a tumor of stone metastasized from his schizophrenia, pulsing with memory and dread.

Tinh sits atop an unhappy, head-bobbing Le Loi and watches the multitude of human shadows stream across the clearing, their destination the walls of the fortress through which they disappear. "They're waiting for us inside," he says to no one in particular.

Before crossing the clearing, the little band rests on the bank of a small river near the edge of the rubber grove. Talk is sparse as a sense of dread seems to hover in the air. With their *ao ba ba's* drenched in sweat and filthy from mud, Tuyet Mai and My-duyen depart upstream away from the men to bathe in the tepid water.

In what seems an eternity of fending off undulating clouds of mosquitoes as thick and noisy as any monsoon, Mark feels the urge to relieve himself and uses the excuse to leave his two male comrades, dropping his backpack at their feet for safekeeping. Exploring aimlessly, he finds an appropriate spot. Then he again does a bit of blind exploring until he climbs up onto a tall, flat rock where he takes in a magnificent view of the surrounding jungle. But he soon becomes restless and moves to the other side that juts precipitously above the river where, to his great joy and nervous discomfort, he sees the two women bathing.

He first spots Tuyet Mai, her stumps submerged in the water, her sagging breasts, limp reminders of what a beauty she once was. She is smiling toothlessly at something and Mark follows her eyes to behold a vision of such power that he finds it hard to catch his breath.

My-duyen has just bathed using the aromatic fruit of the *canthium* shrub as soap and now stands naked on the mossy bank rubbing her golden skin with the perfumed bark of a *cassia cinnamon* tree. Water droplets glisten on the smooth perfection of her body. Mark reels, nearly fainting.

At last she dabs a last bit of cinnamon on her neck and wades over to her mother who now sits on a grassy outcrop smiling infectiously. My-duyen hands Tuyet Mai a brush to comb out the ends of her long, shimmering black hair. For a fleeting moment, mother and daughter appear like priestess and acolyte at some ancient rite, the steam of the river curling about them like incense. Enraptured by this vision of beauty and maternal love, Mark stares dumbly until startled into action when he hears a male voice calling in the distance. My-duyen and Tuyet Mai nervously look around and Mark hops down the rock, tiptoeing back to Tong and Tinh, his mind filled with the image of My-duyen . . .

. . . the shadow that now stands where he stood, gazing where he gazed, its shape a dark mirror of his own.

~

Both women don clean *ao ba bas*, stretching the fabric by tugging on the hems and using their open palms in long downward strokes to smooth the wrinkles. Their ministrations completed, they join the men and the little procession begins the journey across the clearing to the fortress. A narrow shaft of sunlight cuts across the ground, pointing them forward like an omen.

~ *Into the Vortex I* ~

Michael remains immobile. Theresa continues to beckon him from the shadows. "Come with me into the tunnel—it is here."

He wants to run away. "Medication," he mumbles, glancing at the bathroom door. "Just a few steps away. Let me just empty the bottle of *Clozapine* down my throat and have done with her, the rest of them, and the tunnel."

"And yourself," chides Theresa. "Suicide is not an option. As your psychiatrist, as your wife, as your savior, I insist you confront these delusions and hallucinations once and for all. Come with me! Now."

Michael looks around wildly. "Diane!" he calls.

No answer.

"She'll not respond," says Theresa. "Now, it's time. The Reunion. Come."

Michael finds himself moving toward her outstretched hand, dimly aware of the absurdity of his nakedness, the last thread of cogency tying him to reality. As he takes it, a floating sensation deprives him of solidity, and he drifts behind her like a trailing kite. The grip of her hand is gentle but firm and he is enveloped by a dark shadow—a liquid membrane sliding past his body. After an indeterminate amount of time, the membrane recedes in his wake, and the world grows inexplicably darker, denser, as if light itself had been devoured.

Damp. Cold.

He smells the earth.

"We're early," comes Theresa's disembodied voice from the darkness. "Can't you hurry them up?"

"What?" asks Michael.

"Wasn't talking to you," she replies distractedly.

"Where am I?" asks Michael.

"You know."

He can still feel her hand and he grips it tighter.

"Are you afraid?" she asks.

"What part of the tunnel is this?"

Theresa looks around as if she can see. "We'll have to walk."

"All part of the plan?"

"This is all your doing, Michael. You know the others are on their way. It is you who calls them—you who summon me. You make me hold your hand . . . you are writing this sentence."

Michael pulls his hand away. "Not I. This is Her doing. I was happy."

Theresa grabs his hand again. "Shhh! She is here!"

Michael snorts. "Of course She is here. This is where She dwells—in a dark, damp, rotting cave."

"Your mind."

Michael again pulls his hand away. "I knew You were going to say that, but You're wrong. We're in Vietnam, not my mind. Smell the earth. This is a tunnel in which my memories, or my brother's reside. This is not a hallucination or delusion—it is merely a suggestion, planted by you, or Her, for the purpose of causing me pain. You and She are in this together. You're just a pawn, but She is evil. I'm going back."

Theresa, evidently exasperated, says, "Your brother! Your brother! How many times have we been over the fact that he doesn't exist? You do not have a twin that died here. You did, or at least part of you did accept it once."

"Well, I don't now."

"Why did you before?"

"Just to please all of you. What have you done with Diane?"

No response.

Michael strains to see Theresa, but the darkness is complete so he listens for her breathing—nothing.

"Theresa?"

Nothing.

"Theresa!"

Nothing.

"Fine. I'm leaving," he mutters, turning and fumbling for the dirt wall, feeling his way in the direction from which he thinks he came.

If I can find the entrance chamber, the trap door, I'll be fine.

But the farther he feels his way in the dark, the deeper he journeys into the heart of the tunnel. The earth swallows him stride by stride. His panic rises, yet beneath it his heartbeat grows strangely youthful, unburdened, slicing away the years as though he were tunneling back into boyhood.

"Damn! Damn! Where's the fuckin' entrance!" His voice has the pitch, timbre, and raw grammar of youth.

He trips over something. A flashlight appears in his hand. He turns it on.

~ *Into the Vortex II* ~

The great wooden door of the fortress had long since twisted away from its massive iron hinges, leaving a gap between imposing stone walls through which a small group of humans and two water buffaloes pass into the forbidding interior. Empty wooden stalls sit idly, waiting for tourists who stopped coming long ago. Faded signs, advertising chewing gum and soda, peel from rusted tacks, clinging stubbornly to nothing, like relics nailed to the skin of a corpse. The world has moved on to other wars.

Mark surveys the ruined fortress: its oblong perimeter walls are covered in vines, its massive stones cracked by prying roots, its interior lined with a second-story defensive parapet barely visible beneath the encroaching foliage. To him the fortress resembles something out of a French Foreign Legion film, half-romantic, half-ruin. "Beau Geste," he mutters curiously.

A vast, deteriorating brick square, uneven and treacherous to navigate without risking a twisted ankle, dominates the center of the fortress. At one end of the square stands a gutted Catholic church, still grand despite the ravages of time. Its enormous roof has long since collapsed, filling the interior with shattered protuberances of angular rubble, cleaved slabs forming a mad geometry of ruin. Statues of saints rise from the debris in bizarre positions, their great heads and shoulders rising at odd angles from the tile floor. A few jungle vines have succeeded in girdling the stone saints with organic bondage. Promethean punishment for bringing the fire of religion to this sacred place of atheistic plants and animals. The fortress itself is a stony welt, a colonial canker embedded in the healthy green tissue of the jungle.

Around the inside base of the perimeter wall, below the sagging parapet, are various barracks, a mess hall, and assorted other wooden shanties and rooms—all generally roofless and in ruin, leaning drunkenly against the massive stones.

Mark sees hundreds of spent cartridges, half-buried, scattered at the base of the walls and strewn amidst the leaves in the courtyard. He picks up a few, then returns to the group which has been waiting patiently near the church.

"So the battle was here?" he asks no one in particular, holding out the cartridges, leaving no room for denial.

The group looks at Tong. "Yes," he says curtly.

"Can you tell me about it?" asks Mark.

"We were in village," says Tong. "Just noise, shooting, bang bang, then over. We know nothing."

"My father often spoke about a tunnel."

Tinh blanches and speaks Vietnamese. "No ghosts are up here, but I hear them. A low rumble from beneath the ground. They are all in the tunnel and this boy wants to see it." He shakes his head morosely.

"Yes," replies Tong. "I can feel them waiting."

"My-duyen!" interjects Mark. "What are they saying?"

She is subdued, evidently frightened. "I don't know."

"What do you mean you don't know?" Frustration edges his voice.

"There is a tunnel," Tuyet Mai says in English.

The others look at her in alarm.

"Where?" asks Mark.

"Can't go down," says Tong, a bit too quickly. "Dangerous. You need a flashlight. See nothing."

Mark smiles and pulls a flashlight from his backpack. "I remembered my father mentioning a tunnel—figured it might be needed."

"No, no, the walls collapse," says Tong.

"I'll just have a quick look," replies Mark. "I'll be careful."

Tuyet Mai moves to her water buffalo which stands contentedly munching overhanging vines at the base of the stone wall. She pulls out a flashlight from a bag tied to the sedan chair. "I will accompany you," she says calmly, in eerily perfect English.

Tinh scuttles over to her and whispers, "The sounds from beneath the earth are getting louder. Let him go alone. They won't bother him, but you . . . you said yourself—"

"No."

"Why not?" Tinh asks in astonishment.

She pushes past him and shouts to Mark in English. "Follow me!"

"I go with you," says My-duyen to Mark.

Mark brightens. "Good. It should be interesting."

"No!" cries Tuyet Mai. "She stays here."

"Why?" asks Mark.

"Too dangerous."

"Mama, it is my job!" My-duyen stomps her foot like a child.

Tuyet Mai shakes her head decisively. "Too dangerous. Old mines. Tunnel might collapse."

"True," says Mark bravely. "Don't worry, My-duyen. If it's safe, I'll come back and we can go down together."

"Come!" orders Tuyet Mai, then disappears through a large fissure in the church wall where once stood an imposing door.

Mark follows.

"Be careful!" calls Tinh.

My-duyen turns to Tong. "Uncle, you said my questions would be answered, but none of them have been. I am only left with more questions."

Tong sits wearily atop the fallen torso of a stone saint. "Wait a minute," he says. "You'll see."

Meanwhile, Tinh sits next to Tong and pulls out his own object, placing it on a flat section of the saint's chest. "The wooden boy," says My-duyen. "I've not seen him for years."

"Yes," says Tinh. "I'm calling Her now. If ever She was needed, it is now."

Tong shakes his head and looks at the ground. "She's already here—or rather, waiting below."

~

Tuyet Mai leads Mark to the rear of the church, picking her way through the rubble until stopping at a leaf-strewn patch of floor cleared of debris. She brushes away the dirt and leaves, tugs on a rusted iron ring, and strains to pull the trap door open. Mark helps and together they finally succeed in opening it all the way to reveal the dark entrance chamber of the tunnel. Mark stands at the edge, hands on his knees, peering down as Tuyet Mai shines the flashlight into the hole. A wooden ladder is still in place, although it appears time-worn and rickety. Mark feels a sudden rush of cold, unfiltered, debilitating fear.

"Since you have legs, you go first," says Tuyet Mai, baring her teeth in a malevolent smile that Mark interprets as mockery.

He looks into the darkness and feels weak. "Let me just catch my breath," he says as bravely as he can.

"No need to go," she says. "Nothing to see."

"I must go. My father."

Tuyet Mai shrugs but does not seem disappointed.

"How did you know about the trap door?" asks Mark casually, more to delay entering the tunnel than out of curiosity.

Tuyet Mai thinks of Madame Dau and lies. "When I was a girl."

"You played in the tunnel? They let you?"

"No."

Mark waits but Tuyet Mai does not elaborate.

"Did you come here after the battle?" he asks.

"No."

"Well, when did you see the tunnel?"

Tuyet Mai grunts in disgust and starts to close the trap door. "No need to go—nothing to see."

"Wait!" cries Mark.

Tuyet Mai shakes her head, all the while looking askance at Mark. "It gets late. It's no good here after dark."

"Okay, I'm going." Mark gingerly descends the ladder—it holds. He steps off the last rung, stands firmly on the dirt floor of the chamber, and looks up.

~ *Into the Vortex III* ~

Storyteller awakens from an odd dream. He finds himself sitting in the darkness crouched beneath the trap door leading to the fortress, knees drawn hard to his chest, body aching as though cramped there for hours. The last thing he remembers is running through the tunnel away from someone or something. A foggy confusion blurs his thinking and the image of Idaho lying back in the tunnel storage chamber emerges from the haze.

I have to go back.

Raising the trap door a crack, he takes a quick peek out at the church. Nothing. He thinks he hears sporadic talking as if a group of people are nearby, but decides it is just another thunderstorm rolling in. Not daring to risk exposure should NVA be close, he lowers the door again and drops softly to the floor.

He flicks on his flashlight, reassured by the narrow beam, then switches it off, letting his eyes settle once more into the murk. Slowly he turns back down the passage, following the fading trail of Mountain Man's leaves.

Images from the dream flutter like broken moths through his mind, fragments of meaning dissolving before they take shape. The tunnel breathes around him, damp and patient, as though it has waited centuries for him to stumble through its veins. His strength is siphoned by the earth itself, folded into the memory of stone and soil.

Odd is the only thought he can manage. He feels exhausted. Spent.

Chapter Twenty-Four

PART SIX: REDEMPTION

The Reunion

~ *I Am All Here*[1] ~

I am all here. Give me room. Who'd I trip over? Oh, it's you. Flashlight makes you all look so damn . . . the tunnel is narrow and there are so many of you. Stretch. Madame Dau. Just let me pass. Sergeant Dam, I haven't thought of you for a while. Where is Goddess? Waiting by the skeletons? T, you're here too, I see. Even as a ghost you're taller than the others. What's that? Sorry, can't hear you. A hum. Your words are just a hum, a buzzing in my ears. Wait, they're getting more distinct. Some of you I can already understand. Sergeant Dam, for example, just told me Goddess is waiting by the skeleton. I understood him perfectly. Why is that? God too, you say? Oh, now your words are a bit clearer. Don't know why I could understand him and not you. Ah, see, I'm beginning to understand you now. Why so glum? Your faces are all so stereotypically ghostlike. No, I mean to say so fuckin' ghostlike. Better. Actually, quite scary, if I let my imagination get the best of me. Yes, Ninh, you particularly make a horrifying apparition. Yes, you do. Face disfigured. I should be terrified down here in a black tunnel with God knows how many ghosts every which way I turn. But, oddly enough, I'm not scared. Bowls, I see you. I see you. I'm not scared yet—that's the key word—yet. Where's your lady with the lipstick nipples? Well, come on Bowls, you're giving me the creeps. In fact, all of you are. Quit crowding. Major Vy, let me through. Let me through! Let me breathe!

Okay. I'll slow down. You won't let me through anyway. Got all dream to get there. Just stop pressing against me. Stop! Good. What do you want me to discuss? Death? Life after death? How about sex? Betrayal? War? Peace? Movies? Don't get agitated, especially you, Major Vy. Stop. Now, you tell me—don't just stare. What will it be? You dragged me down here. Murder?

Who? Theresa? Goddess?—Ah! There's the culprit. Goddess. She waits farther up ahead, just waiting at the skeletons like a spider. Come on, Doanh—don't give me that youthful, innocent, orchid-hunter look. Where's Mountain Man? Also up ahead? Hanging out with Goddess? Yes, it figures. Madame Dau, you and he are close. Is he up ahead? Yes? Then let me move. Let me pass. Madame Dau, you're a council chief, tell them to let me pass. What? Being only a provisional council chief doesn't disqualify you. In fact, women in general are now equal. Yes, in death you are all most certainly equal. In fact, I never really understood how you died. I just knew you did. Yes, my imagination failed. Why do you all want me to kill myself?—after all, now I've returned. Isn't that what you want? Then why are you holding me back?

Is that why you're holding me back? Yes? Madame Dau, you want to know how you died? You already know? Then clue me in—inquiring minds want to know. This situation is proof you lived an independent life. Independent, I mean, of my imagination, or creativity, or delusion, or whatever. All of you did. All of you. But they don't believe me. Voices. Delusions. Hallucinations. That's all you are. Ha! So why are you pressing against me? Stop! I can't breathe! That's better. I didn't kill any of you. It's me that's dying. Remember, I stayed in the tunnel during the ambush. I was sick the whole time, the entire battle, always. I never squeezed off a round. I see you all looking at me. Let me through! What do you want? All I have to do is wake up. So, wake up. Let me take out my cell phone, dial 911, and wait for Diane to answer. As I thought, doesn't work. Cell phone's now a spider. Drop it. Damn thing bit me. Good. This is the future—spiders, not cell phones. Fools think the future is technology, but it's not, it's spiders.

Alright, let me tell you a story. Once upon a time there was a man. Successful. Happily married. Father of a normal, smart kid. The man had a good job, lawyer. Boring individual, poor material for either a literary hero or a movie star, except for one thing, he was in a war. It's true some claimed he was schizophrenic, but they were wrong. You know, something is bothering me. Why could I understand Dam before T? Dam's 'the enemy' while I love T. Goddamn, you all look so young. T! I'm about thirty years older than you. You're supposed to be older, but look so young. Common enough phenomenon, dead frozen in time and all that. So, why could I understand Dam first and not you? That still bothers me. No, that's not right. Why'd you shoot Kim Lan? I looked up to you. Don't look at me like that. No. My story is short. Ended with the war. Ended with all of you.

Oh, can't be so dramatic. Wail all you want . . . like some sort of Greek chorus. I'll join you soon enough. Dam! Doanh! Vy! Why don't you enemies come closer? Come closer. Closer. You're inside the fortress now. No one's going to shoot you. Wouldn't matter if they did. Come on, get closer. This is where you once wanted to be . . . where you died to be. Yes. Now, it's my turn. Kill me—it's my dream. Kill me! Anyway, it would only be killing me in a dream. No jail time there. New, innovative therapy for survivor's guilt. Yes. You all want me to kill myself. Alright. However. . . .

You guys won. We could have a Nuremberg trial here. I'm in the docket. Accuse!

You're smiling, Dam.

Out of the way! If you aren't going to kill me, let me go to the skeleton—let me see Goddess, let me see my son. Move! Mark's up there. Move! Why not?

Madame Dau, you're very kind. How did you die? Some horrible deed? Communists kill you? Tong do it? Was it murder? No. You're pointing at your heart. Broken heart? No. Heart attack. That's it—just a heart attack. So simple. Tuyet Mai was there? Yes. She screamed when you fell. She loved you. Of course. Where is Tuyet Mai? Oh, with Mark, up ahead. They're still alive aren't they? Ah. Can I pass now? Why not? You are not letting me go for a reason. What reason? Vy? What's your role in this? Seems like you're the leader. No? Madame Dau, what do you say? What? What? What? Don't do that—it scares me.

Let me just sit for a little. Ah, better. Go ahead, stand there and look down at me. Appropriate. Makes you all look even more menacing. Look, I'm sitting, going nowhere. Why don't you want me to move on? Afraid I'll see something I'm not supposed to? Goddess preparing something? Couldn't be a surprise, could it? Maybe it's my birthday? No. Are you all trying to protect me from Her? No, I don't think so. More likely you're all trying to protect yourselves.

I see you there, Dinh. Still in love with Tuyet Mai? You're nodding yes. Even after she used you? Had contempt for you? Still yes—even after you died for her? Just goes to show. Show what? Come on, Bowls, you know—sure you do, what with your hard-on for that naked lady and her lipstick? Don't look so pained, or confused. Or are you angry? Okay, I'll explain. Dinh's blind love goes to show man's irrational constancy in the face of all evidence to the contrary. Some call it faith, some call it ignorance. It's the reason for man's . . . okay, Kim Lan, it's the reason for humanity's successes and failures. The human brain is basically a car battery. Two terminals—positive and negative—where energy flows in a circle making work, building cities, and creating madness.

Not to say I'm mad. Where's X? Hey, X, good to see you. I need patching up. Being a ghost medic, you can stick your hands through my skull and rearrange my brain. Huh? Yeah. Just stick 'em in, squeeze here, pinch there, pull here, tear out there. I got this big, dead, painful, irritating, toxic, cancerous patch that you need to cut out. Just reach in with those translucent, bony black fingers and use some ghost scalpel or even your goddamn fingernails and cut out the schizophrenia . . . claw it out if you have to, since I know you don't like to cut, eh X? Sorry. Sorry!

But, to think about it, how did a successful, happily married lawyer with a normal, smart kid get to be a successful, happily married lawyer with a normal, smart kid if this patch of brain tissue is so abnormal and destructive? Happily married? Ha! Where's Diane? Diane! I know she's out there. Madame Dau, you're my grounding, my Earth Mother, tell me where Diane is. No, not Theresa. I've imbued you with a knowledge of English names better than that. Diane, not Theresa. D-i-a-n-e. Can't miss her—she actually does have a patch of skull missing. Car accident, remember? No, you wouldn't. It was an accident. It must have been.

Once happily married to a living wife, now grieving for a nonliving wife and unhappily married to a hallucination. Where is she? Diane! No, I don't want to see Theresa—she's a shill for Goddess. Never was real. Doctor, sure. X, she pretended to be a doctor, a psychiatrist, a ghost psychiatrist with a ghost practice. She was the only reason I ever took the medication. But it didn't work very well. Damn! She certainly seemed real enough. Bitch. Great body, great tits—but that was all part of the ruse—a royal ruse to ream a rube—me, bitch. I notice she's not here now—you guys were all real, but her—never!

So if you were all real, what do you want with me? Look, I'm real too. See? So, if I touch you will I feel flesh or will my hand go straight through like some bad movie. Let's try. Come on, Sergeant Dam. Come closer. You've still got that hatred for Americans? Want to kill all of us? Well, you've still got that shit-faced smile. Let me knock it off. Okay, if you won't come to me, then I'll stand up and go to you, asshole. If I slap you upside the head maybe you'll kill me—in this dream—and I'll wake up and be back home with . . . with Theresa. Ah, damn, there's the problem. She'll just bring me back here. Diane's lost the battle, that's why she's not here.

Can't seem to be able to stand up anyway. Why not? X, come on, man. Check me out. I'm falling apart—can you patch me up, doc? Much as I hate to admit, I'm supposed to move on down the tunnel. Wait a minute. You guys are supposed to help me get there, not block me. Remember—the reunion? So why stop me? Doesn't make sense. Are you actually protecting me from Her? Have I got this all wrong? Stupid dream.

Hell with it! I'm standing up! There. Good. Now don't just stare at me that way. All of you need to let me through. Once and for all . . . Madame Dau, please. Oh, shit. I'm naked. Now I remember. Theresa and the kitchen—I was drinking coffee, naked, talking to Theresa. She wanted me to come down here. She made me come down here. Naked. I remember. No time to get dressed. Least I have my boots. Thank God for that. Must look stupid, though, in these fuckin' boots. Still, glad to have 'em. Should have put on clothes, but she practically dragged me down here. Oh, God. Sorry, Madame Dau. I don't want to be naked. Now you're smiling, but not like ol' Sergeant Dam there. Your smile is nice. A mother's smile. I think. But . . . no, not quite that. No, not at all. No.

Successful lawyer, now standing naked except for a pair of boots in front of his jury. Appropriate.

What's more, he's standing naked in front of his ghost jury in a dark tunnel of hell with a small flashlight and a judge in the form of a Goddess waiting with skeletons in Her chambers.

Dreams don't get any better than this. No, sir. Can't be some simple wet dream. Not for Michael Powers. What? What'd you say? Don't all speak at once, otherwise I just hear cacophony. Deafening! What?

Oh, Storyteller. That's what you're all saying, right? Storyteller is my name. Storyteller my name. Storyteller. Name.

Stop!

Okay, okay . . . Storyteller.

~ *I Am All Here*[2] ~

So if I call myself Storyteller you'll let me through? Okay, I'm Storyteller. Still no go? I know—it's because I don't believe it. Look, Storyteller was some typical American kid who went to war, experienced the same things typical Vietnamese kids did and on down the line in other wars—Russians, Germans, Chinese, Iraqis, etc. etc.—he didn't come home, just like . . . oh, you don't like that. Alright, he did come home, if you like. He came home and became a happily married, successful lawyer with a normal smart kid. Had a few memories, a few dreams, a few nightmares—just like all those other kids. Way of the world. Homo sapiens pattern. Get over it, asshole.

Yeah, I hear you Superman. God has created us all with a unique soul—no coincidence it rhymes with asshole. So anyway, this kid Storyteller is sailing on his own moral and ethical trajectory, doing somersaults in the air, arms outstretched, reaching for God to catch him or else down he goes. I know, I know. So down I go. Actually, come to think of it, down I am. Speaking of God, where is He? Given up the field of battle to Goddess? Yes. This tunnel is a field of battle, a struggle between . . . who? Between us or between Them?

Me? Between me and me? Good. While the words came out of you, Madame Dau, the voice was Theresa's. Indeed it was. Bitch. But, of course, it's not about Theresa, it's about Goddess.

So, is all this about me? The war, psychology, ethics, morals, religion, guilt, or is it about Goddess and Her struggle with God? Of course, we're all pawns in war, in religion, in guilt, and all the rest. You must believe in free will, you have no choice. So why not be pawns in the struggle between God and Goddess? Yes, your blank, savagely sad faces tell me a lot.

Wait a minute. T, didn't you tell me that God is with Goddess? Is that a nod? Strange how your head bows so low it merges into your chest. Yes, I know, your last thoughts in that ambush were with your wife. You tab. I am familiar with your tab. All your tabs. T's wife, X's grandmother, Bowls' naked lady, Stretch and . . . wait, where's Nature? Oh my God, Nature! Why haven't you come forward? Is it the light? I've thought of you so many times. Why'd you have to die? We could have grown old together, been old friends. You might have prevented all this. If I had you to talk to, I might have been okay. As it is, you know what they're saying up there. Schizophrenic. Schizophrenic. God, Nature, me, a schizophrenic! Ah. Well, you old poet, seeing you now is like Odysseus meeting Achilles in the Underworld. You—a shade—no grin, no glint in the eye, shock of Irish hair now just a dark smudge. Yes, your eyes do shine, but not mischievously.

How? Well—intensely, with . . . I don't know, something that makes me shudder. I loved you. I still love you. Don't. Don't do that!

Can't I go through now? My being naked is bad enough, but now I just want to get this over with. Of course, what is 'this'? The dream? Maybe there will be a Final Battle between God and Goddess. Armageddon. Front row seat. That should wake me up.

You said something, Nature? What? For some reason your words are hard to understand. Garbled. Why is it that I have the most trouble understanding those I love the most? Ironic or iconic? Try again. Okay, now I understand. You point out that I may not be dreaming. What if I'm not dreaming? Couldn't be. Nature, if I'm not asleep—not dreaming—then . . . then I don't know what. Then I'm mad. It's what they claim about me. Damn it, Nature, is that what you're saying? Am I a schizophrenic? Theresa insisted so. Diane always knew I was just dreaming. Her words were always the same. "Michael. Michael. Wake up. You're having another dream. It's just the voices again. Wake up!" She saved me many times. Where is she now? Nature, please tell me. Diane! Nature, you've got to let me through. Then she'll wake me, and I can stop writing.

~ *I Am All Here*[3] ~

At last. I must have fallen asleep, but how can you sleep in a dream? 'Course you can. More proof I'm dreaming. Except now I'm awake. Flashlight on. Ah! Thank you, a path. Yes, okay, Madame Dau you lead the way. Stand up, stand up, stand up, that's right. Now that we're moving, I feel afraid. Really afraid. Thank God for this flashlight. Nature, come closer, come walk with me. You others . . . ah, walking through the walls is no problem for you . . . convenient . . . Minh—or are you Kung?—you're halfway in the tunnel and halfway in the wall. Just like ghosts are supposed to be—evidence you're all a dream. After all, ghosts are supposed to . . . what? Why are you stopping? No, not again. My stomach is queasy. More evidence. I don't think I want to go on anyway. Yes, let's stop here.

Nature, what's happening?

Come on, don't do that. Don't. I'm scared. Now I'm getting really scared. What? You too? Even you? Nature, don't say that. Don't. If you're going to say those things, get out of my head! No, I didn't mean it. Stay. Keep writing, keep writing.

Remember you tab, Nature? Home. Providence, Rhode Island. Bobby the cat in the window. Well, that's how I am now. I want to be home, Theresa or no Theresa. God, I want to be home, but I never could make my damn tab stop moving, stop changing . . . didn't want it to, but. . . .

Okay, okay. We've stopped, God knows why. But no arguments from me.

I'm going to sit again. So tired. It's this damn tunnel—memories—I feel so tired. Just for a minute. Go ahead—gather around and stare down at me again. I don't care. Move this damn rock, it hurts my bare ass. There. I have an idea. Let's talk philosophy. Yeah, all of us. Given that you're all dead, you'll add a new and unexplored dimension to the discussion. Now, let's start with you Vy. What's more important, family or morality? I mean, if the health of one conflicts with the other? Really? Must be a cultural thing. Or biological. Can't escape our biology—'course you guys did—I mean, you're dead and here you are, in my dream. It's my dream in spite of what you suggest. Unthinkable otherwise.

But what if I'm not dreaming? Nature's suggestion, and he always had a way to get at the heart of things. Not dreaming. Maybe I should think seriously about that.

Why are we stopped?

Why am I here?

Why are you all staring at me like that?

Nature? Where am I? Oh.

Why isn't Diane here to wake me up?

Why am I more afraid of God and Goddess than I am of ghosts?

Why am I so afraid of what lies ahead?

Okay, focus. What if I'm not dreaming? Let's deal with that possibility. Well, then the laws of physics have broken down. Time dilation, spatial distortion, supernatural beings; ridiculous! Einstein said that god is subtle but not malicious. Of course he wasn't in a position to ask directly. Here I am, in a dark tunnel, about to meet God, in whom I don't believe by the way. So, what kind of dialogue would Einstein and God have?

Einstein begins: "Dear Old One, please elucidate how relativity and quantum mechanics are unified on a deeper level so I can finally show the skeptics that quantum mechanics is not a complete theory."

God replies, "Albert, I don't understand relativity or quantum mechanics. I never was good at math."

"What?"

"No, dear Albert, the universe is built on faith."

"But how can you build a universe without understanding relativity and quantum mechanics?"

God shrugs. "Not My department. Now faith—that I understand."

Einstein tries a different tack. "Alright, why is there suffering?"

God closes His eyes and lets out a blissful moan, sexual in its never-satisfied longing.

No, this isn't working.

Goddamn it, why are we stopped? Let me go! Nature, get them off me! Get them off!

Good. Thank you.

Are we moving again? How'd you get the word? I didn't hear anything. Okay, I'm getting up. Damn, standing just makes me more aware I'm naked. The women here, Madame Dau, Madame Vit, Kim Lan, Security Chief Tien and the others—it's so damn embarrassing.

Well, look at that, it's little Teo running around . . . and Little Monkey too. Pointing at me, no, at my . . . hey! . . . are you two laughing? . . . can't tell. Little shits is what they are. Still, no one seems to mind, running off to other places. Laugh at someone else! No, it's not just that they don't mind—it's more than that. It's as if . . . ah . . . okay! I'm moving!

Alright, walking, one step in front of the other. Keep walking. Walking. Got to be getting closer. Keep moving. I'm beginning to recognize things. I wonder. Let's try. First turn off the flashlight, then adjust my eyes. Now look down. Oh, god! Mountain Man's bioluminescent leaves—still here. Still glowing. Not possible.

Possible.

How?

I'm moving back in time. Each step another year peeled away.

No.

Yeah, I'm right. Look ahead. The leaves get brighter. Fresher. Younger.

But, after all, not surprising. Dreams will do that, disorient you. Well, Nature, I'm fuckin' disoriented. Starting to talk like a grunt. Becoming younger, more . . . what's the word . . . crude. Now, if I had on my lawyer suit, my power tie, carried my briefcase, then I'd be okay. Just another day in court. Suit's got more deflecting power than a flak jacket. Yes, with my suit I'd be ready to do battle with God and Goddess. But this. Naked. Accompanied by a host of ghosts. I need Daniel Webster.

Storyteller, keep thinking up jokes. My only weapons. But this tunnel is no joke. Speaking of jokes, Stretch! You were always ready with a funny comment or impersonating some famous person.

Come here, Stretch. I know, I'm still moving, one foot in front of the other. But we can still talk and walk. Or are you gliding? Floating? Do me a favor, Stretch, make me laugh. We're getting hellishly close, and I need to laugh. Go on. No, no, no. Stop!

Look back down at the leaves, Storyteller. Turn off the flashlight. Don't need it, leaves getting brighter, younger. Said that already. Said that already. Shuffle along, just like back then. They must be close. Why's it taking so long?

Dreams.

They make no sense.

Fuckin' tunnel has grown to be as long as my life.

Maybe I'll trip a booby trap and be reborn as another soldier in another war. Fuck that! Just make it to the end, see Goddess, and make it back to the beginning.

Ha! Jokes help. Why? Universe doesn't care. Universe doesn't care if you make a joke while a lion eats you or a building falls on you or a fire engulfs you. No matter how good the joke, lion will still eat you, building will still fall on you, fire will still burn you. Don't earn points with the universe because you have a sense of humor. That's it! When I'm standing in front of God and Goddess, I'll crack a few jokes—break the ice, strip away the seriousness, make Them laugh. Then Their laughter will wake me up, and dogs, democrats, and deities will all laugh together at dinner. Asinine alliteration.

Nature, you're still here. Is that a smile distorting what I suppose ghosts would call a face? God—your glare is cold. Not like you. The eyes. Look down again, Storyteller.

Storyteller.

I've called myself Storyteller again.

Storyteller was brought down here that day.

I remember.

Brought down and left.

You were all out there that day, above ground, waiting, unknowing, connected, the threads tightening.

I sat down here in the dark, next to Idaho.

It was so dark.

I didn't dare turn on the flashlight and use up the battery.

Dark.

And then it came.

> ..... *youAveIsilentdoweohevenintoosendwatchholyafraidcoming loothenobodyhouraheavenlynoonflowrabluesprayerohcarcomes forsake'wtixtmylullabylightscangottalasyoudrivingdownbaby 'roundlosecanIrishlastlowanswercalmohhushevercaresbless afraidbeautyVirginweddingbrightloodayain'tMarianotender darlin'ratoosilentcomingnobodyhighstealin'sinceohnotender supposin'timeloomildtomanradiolowthingdoplaceiflosewedding Motherdarlin'youlastblesssleepifontouchcomeouttagoodby hadlistennowhenlasthourmanpeacelooeverholydon'tascry ....*

Slowly the words began to separate, unravel, coalesce—becoming discrete, comprehensible . . .

> *. . . Ave Maria! Oh listen to a prayer, we pray . . .*
> *.....you ain't been blue, till you've had.....*
> *......I can't get no satisfaction, I can't.....*
> *.....silent night, holy night.....*
> *.....do not forsake me oh my darlin', not.....*
> *....oh my love, my darling, I've hungered.....*
> *......too ra loo ra loo ra, too ra loo ra li.....*
> *....we gotta get outta this place, if it's the last thing we ever do.....*
> *.....in the evenin' when lights.....*
> *.....oh maiden, send your.....*
> *.....when I'm watchin' my T.V. and a man come.....*
> *.....silent night, holy night, all is calm, all is.....*
> *.....I'm not afraid of death, but oh, what will I do if.....*
> *.....coming home, wait for me.....*
> *.....too ra loo ra loo ra, hush, now don't you cry.....*
> *.....it's the last thing we ever*
> *.....'cause there's nobody who cares about me*
> *.....bless this hour so fa*

.....can't be a man, cause he doesn't sm
.....sleep in heavenly peace, sl
.....while in state's prison, vow'd it'd be my life or his'n, I'm not_____
.....rivers flow, to the sea, to the sea, to th________________
.....too ra loo ra li, too ra loo ra loo ra, hush, now don't you cry,
.....hush.....
.....now.....
.....worthless.....
.....you.....
.....must....
.....die

Then silence. All silent.

My dark eyes closed. Storyteller lay as a mote in the closed dark eyes of the earth.

I remember.

Most of you died that day, the others began your long journey into the void, pulled by those who died, or those you killed.

So here we are.

Now pulled by me.

Or by Them.

~ *I Am All Here*[4] ~

But if I'm supposed to have pulled them, why are they pulling me down this long, long, long tunnel? Or are they? After all, we've stopped at their insistence. They hate me. They want me to kill myself. Well, I won't.

Now look, Storyteller, take it from Michael, you've got to prepare an opening statement to present in front of God and Goddess. It should tell a story, direct their attention to the important issues that benefit your client—and your client in this case is the defendant—and ultimately incline them to doubt that the burden of proof has been met.

No plea bargains. No more waiving the death penalty in exchange for eternal incarceration without the possibility of parole.

This time, either a verdict of not guilty or the chair.

How to start?

Damn it! Sergeant Dam, T, tell them to stop crowding my mind! Give me room to think. Make them stop. Madame Dau, you can help. Please ask the women not to stare so . . . well, like they are. Please. I must prepare.

This tunnel goes on and on.

At least it gives me time to prepare.

But, look, I keep drifting off in these irrelevant directions. Think! Focus!

Wonder if God and Goddess will be wearing robes sitting behind a tall bench. Huge, wooden, imposing pulpit of justice and judgment, looking down on me, small as an ant . . . yes—a Great Warrior ant.

I'll approach the bench respectfully but without any display of fear. So, what to say to God when I have denied His existence and called Him a psychopath? Easy, act as if none of those things ever happened. I'll start with: "Oh Lord, why have I forsaken Thee?"

No, no, no. Impertinent.

He is as real as Santa Claus.

What would I say to Santa Claus? Simple. Give him my Christmas wish list.

Okay, use the same strategy with God. I'll give Him my Christmas wish list: "God," I'll say with extreme gravitas as I pull out my list. "God, here are the toys I would like, since I've been such a good boy this year. First, sex with all the beautiful women I desire, and to show I am aware of the cost, You can dispense with expensive add-ons or fancy attachments like love, commitment, or disease. Second, all the bourbon I can drink, and again, forever cost-conscious, I want no expensive accessories like hangovers or alcoholism. Third, money already in my bank account without the complicated bells-and-whistles of knowledge, skill, experience, and work required to earn it . . . oh, and leave off taxes if you will. Fourth, to be mentally healthy so that I'm not here talking to You like You're fuckin' Santa Claus!"

Oh God, I'm miserable.

Great.

Still walking.

Where does this tunnel lead? To Jupiter? Nah, it leads to other dimensions. String theory . . . only eleven? Ha! Hey physicists, your strings are all tangled up in my neurons, sending action potentials on detours and wild goose chases into God knows how many dimensions. Calabi-Yau. Salami-mayo.

I'm tired. What? Yes, you ghosts change expressions, yet somehow your outward visages—or smudges, or however one would describe your faces—never change, just kind of slowly swirl like thick liquid being drained—of something.

Opening statement—let's try again. This time I'll address Goddess first. Here goes. "Dear Goddess," I'll say with a kindly, compassionate tone. "Dear Goddess, I am so happy to see You again. I know You have wanted me to come, and I have been obstinate, pig-headed, and unkind, but now I'm here, repentant and at Your disposal."

Too obsequious.

Strong women do not respect weak men. But can't be arrogant either. How's this: "Dear Goddess, so glad You invited me."

No.

She won't like lies.

Am I a liar? Yes. This dream is a lie. My memories lie. The human brain, master model builder and expert predictor, is one big complex liar. It misdirects, deludes, fools, cajoles, insults, coddles, compliments, and generally manipulates the human organism into submission.

Submission.

Dominatrix.

That's it!

Goddess is a Dominatrix and God is Her slave, craving pain for Himself, so much so that he must supplement Her punishment by ingesting the Great Wailing of all life on Earth. Goddess is jealous, wanting Her Slave exclusively to Herself—to feel only the pain She inflicts. And because at His direction, the collective pain of all life is now more intense than that which She can administer with all Her snakes, whips, charms, chains, taboos, and feminine nagging, He has turned from Her, just as His human slaves have turned from Her for the same reason—these bipolar swings of His, reveling in the despair of exquisite pain and the manic orgies of universal Love are more addictive than Her tiresome, endless maternal scolding. So humans in their billions climb like rambunctious children on His scaffolding of sacraments, saints, and sinners. He rises from Slave to Master, yet still drawn to Her whip in dark, secret places . . . like tunnels.

Storyteller, listen to me, Michael says that in his experience as a lawyer, he recommends you do not use any of this in your opening statement to God and Goddess. Good advice. Be brief. No proselytizing. Apolitical but politically correct. And leave out the fuckin' alliteration. Just say, "Dear God and Goddess, so glad You both invited me."

But why does God get top billing?

Okay. "Dear Goddess and God. . . . "

Better.

Damn! . . . we keep walking and walking, but our destination does not seem to be getting nearer. Walking around inside a brain strewn with trash, returning on neural pathways through the unsightly garbage left by memory all the way back to the pristine beginning. Clean, but empty as hell.

Shit, I feel young. What's your tab, bro? I never had one . . . yeah, I did. This whole fuckin' dream is my tab. Bullshit, it's not a dream. You're sick, remember? You're sick. We all think you're stupid. How many times have you said it? Worthless. Kill yourself. No—I won't. Can't. Shouldn't. But. . . .

~

Wait a minute . . . wait a minute. I see a glow ahead. It's coming from the chamber. Yes—I remember that chamber. Let's slow down. No. No. I don't want to continue. Let's turn around. Talk some more. Think about this. No!

Alright, I'm moving, but I'm scared. Should I turn on the flashlight? I can feel my hands shaking.

Closer. The glow's getting brighter. Damn it—closer.

Words! I hear words. Someone's talking in there! "Come in! Come in!"

Chapter Twenty-Five

Bones

Skeleton In A Tunnel

Tuyet Mai and Mark continue to stare down at the skeleton. Their trip has been uneventful. No ghosts, as if their way has been cleared of all obstacles. Every step has been made easy. Now, the skeleton. Its bony legs are splayed out in front and its skull tilts almost perpendicular to its spine. The combined light of their flashlights illuminates the cracks and discolorations of the bones, yet the backdrop of the reddish earth makes it seem whiter than it is. Mark breaks the silence.

"Professor Benson said there were two American soldiers who survived the battle, but one died soon after being rescued. The other was my father. So, who is this?"

Tuyet Mai shakes her head. She thinks it might be the soldier whose detached foot she carried back for the American captain—The Man From The Mountains—but this skeleton has both feet encased in a pair of rotting boots. American boots. Otherwise, there is no evidence of clothes, as if he died naked.

Ants scurry across the bones, a living rosary of movement, beads of life weaving across death..

Tuyet Mai hears the American boy breathing excitedly.

"Must be an MIA," says Mark, his voice shaking. "Probably crawled down here to hide out and died." Mark sweeps the flashlight around. "Wonder what else is here. Look, the tunnel continues on through that opening." Sweat pours down his red face, and Tuyet Mai sees the face of Captain Cairns—long dead but grinning wickedly—over the shoulder of the American boy. Then she notices the others emerging in the half-light, figures pressed against the tunnel walls like shadows impatient to speak.

"What's wrong!" cries Mark in alarm when he sees Tuyet Mai recoil in horror.

Chapter Twenty-Six

Defiance

Mirror

I Am All Here[5]

My god! Cairns! Get back from her! Stop! I don't want this! Nature, you do something! I can't! Nature, make him get back! That's right, Mark, go to her, comfort her. Mark! Yes, I understand, you can't see or hear us. Tuyet Mai can. God, she's terrified. Get her out of the tunnel, Mark. Get her out! Wait. She won't go. Let me get closer, let me through. Stop blocking me! Jesus, look at her expression. It's changed from terrified to . . . something else. Anger? Defiance? Yes, I think it's defiance. Oh, god, she's looking at me. She's looking right at me. She's looking right at me!

Chapter Twenty-Seven

The Pieces are in Place

Puzzles

"I see your father," Tuyet Mai says to Mark in a shockingly calm voice.

Mark, leaning over her, stands bolt upright. "What?" he blurts. "What do you mean?"

Tuyet Mai continues staring at Michael as Cairns recedes and the others surge around him. Surrounding her, they all stop and stare like a crowd gawking at the body of a person who has just jumped to their death. Madame Dau emerges from the mass and glides toward Tuyet Mai. With this approaching vision, Tuyet Mai collapses in a heap, sobbing and folding her arms over her head as if protecting herself from a falling roof. Mark leans over her with all the awkwardness and uncertainty of an adolescent.

"Mama!" My-duyen appears in the chamber and runs to her mother followed by Han Tinh lumbering behind, his eyes wide with fear.

~

You see, Dear God, they are all here. Reunions are possible, even between the living and the dead. Their souls have filtered down through the cracks and crevices and are piled like bat guano at the altar of First Principles.

Excellent fertilizer. Divine fixation, a feast for the genuflecting congregation. Except, You are not quite right, My Dear. Their souls have filtered up, like little blades of grass poking through the surface. Hm. And now? We kill them all?

And now that they are all here: spring runoff, snow's melting, hibernation's over. It is time—not to kill, but to dilute, displace and replace. The Chosen One's scattered pieces have been collected. Can he be made whole?

No. Your faction has permanently broken him.

We'll see.

~

An M-16 materializes in Michael's hands, the same one he had so often seen Storyteller carry to the dinners. It gleams as if hammered from the ore of old wars, a weapon forged not by soldiers but by capricious Fates. Tuyet Mai struggles to rise and, with a stricken face, clasps her hands together in supplication, rocking before Michael as Madame Dau once did before Mountain Man. She understands what he has to do, but it is never easy. There are so many of them.

Michael looks around. All of them are cringing, gesturing wildly for him to stop. *So many.* Aiming is superfluous. *Hold it steady and squeeze. It all comes back, like riding a bicycle.* He knows he will never run out of bullets, and they will never run out of lives.

Goddess, regal in her floating lotus position, speaks in a sharp tone. ***It's time.***

God puts up his mighty hands. ***Stop!***

Michael moves the barrel until it points directly at God.

He hesitates as though his arm were bound to some ancient imperative.

Then, with a motion both deliberate and damning, he turns the barrel on Goddess.

Even the dead gasp.

To raise a rifle at God is blasphemy; to turn it upon Goddess is betrayal.

He squeezes.

Chapter Twenty-Eight

Nothing

Illuminated Space

Mark and Tuyet Mai stand silently, shining their flashlights at the same spot. Both see the same thing.

"You see, there is nothing down here," says Tuyet Mai, breaking the oppressive quiet. "Nothing to see."

Mark lets out a disappointed sigh. "I know, but it's always best to look for yourself. It gives me a mental picture of where my father was so many decades ago. At least I can say I was here."

"We will go back now," sighs Tuyet Mai. "It's getting dark. Nothing to see here."

"Except ants," says Mark, brushing at his sleeve. He follows Tuyet Mai back through the tunnel, anxious to return to the surface and reconfigure his relationship with My-duyen on a more romantic level. Future plans, entwined bodies, earnest vows, and rehearsals occupy his thoughts.

Only Michael remains, staring down in horror at the skeleton that tilts wordlessly amidst the carnage, its bones arranged like some mute oracle.

.

Chapter Twenty-Nine

Denouement

The Great Warrior Revisited

Her antennae quiver with anticipation. The White Palace—the bone-vault where her colony reigns—buzzes with nestmates scurrying along the smoothly brittle byways and highways of death. Her entombed universe, for so long perpetually still, is stirring; alive with the breezes and bellows of departed visitors, of the risen dead and the soon-to-be-dead. Activity fills space and exotic molecules shock her senses. Movement comes into being and the dark machinery of life clicks and hums to the tune of instinct.

The chemical signals received by the Great Warrior are unmistakable.

Food.

The White Palace is again growing meat—sacred flesh, offering for the endless cycle.

Chapter Thirty

BOOK III

Graceful Errors

Prologue to Book III

The essential feature of the Paranoid Type of Schizophrenia is the presence of prominent delusions or auditory hallucinations within the context of a relative preservation of cognitive functioning and affect. Delusions are typically persecutory or grandiose, or both, but delusions with other themes (e.g. jealousy, religiosity, or somatization) may also occur. The delusions may be multiple, but are usually organized around a coherent theme. Hallucinations are also typically related to the content of the delusional theme.
DSM–IV-TR (Diagnostic and Statistical Manual of Mental
Disorders, 4th Edition)

~

You see, dear Reader, it fits: I have schizophrenia.
But Goddess insists I do not have schizophrenia. My mutated genome, the one that will give rise to the Superior Ones, simply contains a few wild genes mixed in with the old and the new. This happens when rapid evolutionary change is induced. Naturally, the human part of my mind misinterprets God and Goddess, since they are only metaphors for something else. What else? I don't know. Factions and mentors and precious objects and other such forces are pulling strings. The strings are like those of the Moirai—threads spun, measured, and cut—woven through the labyrinth of my neurons. What are the strings pulling? Not just the machinery of a single mind, but the deepest chambers of the human brain, where destiny itself is knotted. It can be undone only by the sword of others who exercise the right to shape evolution.

Chapter Thirty-One

BEGINNINGS AND ENDINGS

Enlightenment

~ *Cliffs* ~

The front of the car points the way; the cliff edge patiently traces a tight-lipped insolence; the accelerator submissively raises its neck to the tapping reminder of an agitated foot. He will wipe the smile off that knife-edge mouth, shoot past its granite-smirking implication, lift off the rounded angle of the weathered incline and drop down onto the windy freedom of a deeply desperate inhaling earth. No problem for the planet merely to swallow another hallucinogenic gnat. One more won't make a difference. Rasp away. Insignificant irritant. At bottom, a cough. Small. A speck. Quit complaining. Just the guttural clearing of a throat that will not be cleared. Then farther, deeper, past the tickling surface to the place where juices take over and digestion processes the deed. Please The Voices Silence The Voices.

Then. . . ? There can be no *then* until the foot presses down to initiate completion. Slowly, inexorably? Or quick, drawing a dramatic arc, to punctuate the end? Chemistry is quick. Particle physics is quicker. All is physics.

Quick it shall be.

He presses down upon the neck of the submissive. To the floor. Engine roars in shock. A jerk. The edge leaps toward him. Border smashed, ground falls away. Blitzkrieg stuns the atmosphere. Tanks raining down through Polish air and Belgian dust. But this tank has windows to witness the conquest. Face up. Backward through time. Sedimentary sentimentality. Face down now. He slides through the ribs of the earth, as though descending the throat of Hades.

Face up now. Layers racing by in multi-colored gauntlet to reach the sliver of drool trickling at the bottom of an unshaved chin.

Face down. Canyon stubble rises ominously fast.

Silent film. Can't even hear the whooshing, except in the upwelling gorge. Pinwheeling.

Face up. Face down.

Centuries pass. Millennia. How long can it take?

No birds. Disappointing. Fled flapping from the scene of the crime. Mafia magic—no witnesses. Should have rolled the windows down and exchanged fluids with a stricken planet.

Stale air.

Stale mind.

Stale body, gone bad in the sun. Rotten meat flying among the flies.

Voices.

They begin as *sunlight stabs through narrow openings in the jungle canopy.* . . .

No. Not years ago. Or centuries. Or millennia. Or Vietnam. It begins now. Facing down. Twisting round. Facing up. A rocket going backward in time, spacetime. No flashbacks. Just a flash. Faces in the rear view mirror, risen from the dead. Stricken spacetime sags to singularity. Perfect.

Impact.

No sound. Not even a crash. Fear knocked out amid the twisted metal. No fear and no more flight to fight no more forever. Even chiefs die.

Hot to cold. Expansion surrenders to contraction, occasionally rebelling in a lost cause of requiem groans. Creaking metal sutures snap as twisted cracks widen the wounds. He drains out with the oil and forms a companion pool. The red and the black. But the closing hour for red is near and he must depart or suffer at the hand of Lifeguard. Muscle-bound, omnipotent God. Young, with a curly-haired theology bleached from the eternal interplay of a main-sequence sun and a salt-ocean womb.

Rising from the crimson pool, thick with pestle-pounded bone and gristle, all gleaming wet, he looks up at the rim and traces the trajectory of his birth. Twisted metallic umbilical cord cut loose still settling into the dirt at his feet, rubber tires in the wheezing death rattle of regret. Rigor mortis of the machine. Arthritic rust to dust. Dead, finally.

But from this unholy baptism, he rises—alive.

How?

"You're alive!" A faint voice, distant but drawing nearer, seemingly breathless from churning legs and broken branches, still unseen. "You're alive! How? Sit down! Lie down! Don't move! You're alive! How? My god! My god!"

The disembodied voice, a rubber band of chatter stretching ahead of the body behind, grows louder until it yanks its lagging body by the lungs out from the underbrush. Snap! Now all rushing body; arms, legs, and elbows of a concerned citizen. Hovering, stale breath, words splash over him.

"My god! How? I watched you all the way. Called in. Sit down. Don't move. Help'll be here soon. Must be broken bones or internal bleeding. Can you talk? This thing have gas? You smell gas? Could blow. Don't sit. Better come over here. Can you walk? My god! Let me help you. Jesus, you're soaked. Can you talk?

You'll be okay. Better come over here. Get away from the car. You understand me? Jesus! You're soaked. Let me take your arm. Jesus! So wet! Not gas. Can't feel a bone. Does it hurt? Christ, you're lucky. Can't feel a bone. Come away from there. Can you walk? Come on. It'll be okay. They'll be here soon. Just come away. That's right. Jesus. What is this stuff? Can't feel your bones. Gimme your hand. Jesus. Why can't I feel your bones?"

Silent incredulity, then, "Can you walk?"

He can float. Once a limp-sailed corpse in the doldrums, now resurrected, hauled to currents, a breeze stirs his canvas soul.

Enough to sail through this man's humid headwind of words.

A few bounce off the hull and he hears their muffled thuds.

"Better sit here. Emergency people should be here soon. Good thing there was reception. Man, you're lucky to be alive. Can you talk? How are you? What's your name?"

Silence.

Even the Voices.

"I looked up and saw a glint come off that cliff. Then, Jesus, down you came. Turning and turning in the air. Jesus, took forever. Didn't think anyone could survive that. But look at you. You'll be okay. Can you talk now?"

Talk. Relearn. Return.

"I killed the Goddess."

"What?"

"I killed Goddess."

"Oh. Jesus."

"Killed Her with my M-16."

"Oh, okay. Shock. Jesus, where are those guys?"

"Jesus was there. Saw me do it."

"Oh. Better lie back. That's right. God, you just slip through my hands. Let me just . . . feel . . . can't figure it. God damn."

"Yes, I killed the wrong One. God not be damned . . . but Her. . . . "

"Here, drink some water. Just hope there's no internal injuries. But has to be. Still don't know how you're still alive. Here, drink a little water. That's right. Oh, god! Where's your skull? Jesus. Oh, Jesus."

"Should have killed Him too."

"Jesus. Christ, what happened to your bones? To your skull?"

"Left them behind."

"I don't. . . . "

"In the tunnel. I left them behind. For good."

"That's all right. You'll be okay. Can't quite figure what's holding you together. Christ, your bones . . . don't . . . must all be . . . never mind, you'll be okay."

"Left them behind."

"Jesus, was there anyone else in the car?"

"All of them. Figured it was the only way."

"I'd better go check. Damn, where are those rescue guys?"

"It was the only way to get them to stop."

"Stop what?"

"The Voices."

"Christ."

"Yeah, should have killed Him too. Had my chance but turned on Her instead."

"Thank god, they're here!"

~

You see, dear Reader, sometimes I cannot stop dissembling. I apologize, but writing from this institution can be quite disorienting. You know, unreliable narrator. You were warned.

~ *Offices* ~

"Your son's outside."

"One moment, June." He is boneless yet he can stand. He is boneless yet he can walk, sit upright, write, talk, practice law. "Can we set a date next week to prepare for your deposition, Mr. Meredith? My son has just returned from a long trip and he's waiting."

"Of course."

"My secretary will work out the time with you."

"All right, thanks. But I do have one more question."

"Yes?"

"How long will it take?"

"The deposition?"

"Yes."

"I don't know. Depends on the deposing attorney."

"Ballpark?"

"A few hours. But I'll know more when we meet next week."

"Okay, thanks."

"You're welcome." Boneless he rises, boneless he shakes hands, noting his client's surprise, watches him leave. Boneless he waits, boneless he fidgets with a paper clip.

"Mark!"

"Dad!"

While hugging his son, he glances at his desk, a closed coffin of wood on which someone has piled papers and books. That belongs to the man with bones. *Deceit is easy for a twin.*

"Would have met you at the airport, but with court appearances and clients and approaching trials, you know how it is."

"Yeah."

"Good flight?"

"Yes."

"Nice of Fred to have driven you here."

"Very nice."

"Well, that was my last client for the day. Want to tell me about it now or go home first?"

"We can talk on the way."

"Have you eaten?"

"Yeah."

"Okay, let's go. June! I'm leaving early to get Mark home. Sorry to leave you with locking up. See you tomorrow."

June looks confused. "No problem. See you tomorrow. Good seeing you again, Mark."

"Same here, June."

Luggage. Elevator. Parking garage. Car.

"Here we are."

"New car, dad?"

"Yeah."

"What happened to the Lexus? It was almost new."

"Had a slight accident. Figured it was a good excuse to get a new car."

"Nice."

"Yeah. Good to see you. So you'll stay for at least a week, right?"

"Yeah."

The boneless man, happy to have just beaten his future son back in time to feign the preoccupied but impatient father, knows he has to ask. But not quite yet. "Tell me about Vietnam when we get home. Still moping about the girl?"

"A little. How'd you know?"

"Mark, I was there . . . um, figuratively. Besides, you mentioned her on the phone enough. Time to move on. Got to be a lot of coeds to choose from."

"Can't, until you talk to me about it."

"What?"

"The war, the battle. Come on, dad, I've been there now, seen it."

"You just miss the girl."

"My-duyen."

"Yeah."

"No, you know that's not true. Well it's true, but there's much more than that."

"Okay, okay. True, Mark, some of it. Hungry?"

"No. Dad, you're changing the subject again."

"Wait 'till we get home, then we can talk."

"I'll tell you about my trip, but you have to promise to answer a few questions."

Home. Only words spoken on the way are about the Vietnamese humidity, filling the car with the hum of new tires and the scent of new upholstery. Both father and son circle a dying reminiscence from high-up against the glare of the just-mad-because reflecting off the mad-just-because. But home nevertheless. In time for dinner. Vultures circling a family dinner. Gearing up for the squabbling. But squabbling only if the others come. If not? Two to tango, they say, but no horses need be shot here.

~

This time he willed them not to come. After all, they were all dead. Real flesh-and-bones son visiting. First test, so to speak. Still, they mustn't come. Proof they were finally dead. Actually, should invite them—that would be the test. But, no risk is better than some risk. After all, no danger of the young twin showing up.

Check your guns at the door. But the others?

"Dinner's ready, Mark!" He pours himself a mug of decaf coffee, spoons a healthy mound of mashed potatoes onto his plate, and diligently positions two sprigs of parsley between the pork chops and the mushrooms. After nudging a teaspoon of butter on the peak of the potato mound, he gazes at the yellow ribbons of melted butter running down the smooth white rills. *Fall rain, winter snows, hibernation's begun. Time to crawl into your cave, Michael, and not receive your dead guests. Just a son. Just a living son. No others.*

"All right, dad, be there in a minute!"

He sits, waits. Not one appears until Mark sits down. Then ... just Mark. *Thank God. And since I let Him live, I can thank Him, though He should thank me.*

"Okay, now tell me all about the trip, Mark."

"Dad, it was amazing. When I first landed and got off the plane . . . well, you know, the humidity. . . . "

Yes, yes, keep talking. The humidity again. Believe me, I know. Nod my head. Smile. Nod. Smile. Mark, I don't particularly care about the humidity. Nor do I care about My-duyen. I WANT TO KNOW ABOUT TUYET MAI, HAN TINH, and TONG . . . but . . . have to wait. Nod. Smile. Don't slip! Focus! He's not one of the Voices, he's my future son, I think. It's his life. Take an interest! Nod. Smile. Now. Now. Yes. Talk about Con Son prison. At last. They're not dead. Not all of them. How can it be?

"I'm telling you, dad, the place was spooky."

"Huh?"

"Dad, are you sleepy? I said the prison was very spooky. Suppose I felt the ghosts."

"Ghosts, yes I know about ghosts."

"Come on, dad. I didn't mean to go off into all that and get you . . . I mean, it just felt spooky. Hey, the pork chops are delicious."

"And the music? Bet you didn't hear that in Vietnam."

"Rachmaninoff? No."

"What happened after Con Son?" *Yes, keep going. I already know what happened. But keep talking.*

"Did you ever go to Con Son prison, dad?"

"What? No." (*Have been, though. Get to the part when she drives you to Song Nhan village.*)

"Then we drove to Song Nhan village. . . . "

At last. Nod. Smile. But here come the ghosts. Damn it! Here they come.

"Then it was really bizarre. A monsoon came up without any warning. So sudden! Even My-duyen was amazed, and she . . . you know, lived there all her life. Next thing we knew, the car was on its side in a ditch and sank in the mud. Barely got my stuff out."

"Really?" *Really.* "Anybody hurt?"

"Nope. But the storm was kicking up and we had to walk the rest of the way."

"Getting dark?"

"Yup. Had to hike up over a steep hill and down the other side to the village."

Amazing monsoon. Yes. Amazing. Hemophiliac.

"What? Dad?"

"Nothing. Go on." *Go on! Get to Song Nhan village. Get to Tuyet Mai.*

"Mud was so deep. . . . "

Yes, yes. Hurry up! You and the girl, front door, opened up, right?

"Couldn't believe the lightning and thunder."

Hemophiliac.

"Finally arrived at Song Nhan village after it was already dark. Soaked. We were exhausted."

Yes!

"It was so dark. Only one light. I'm used to here, lights everywhere."

Yes, yes.

"Got any ice cream, dad?"

"Ice cream?"

"Yeah."

"Freezer." *How can he walk away now? Chairs all empty. What if he never comes back? What if he comes back? What if I'm no longer here? What if he's not real? Wow. My own son, not real? And if he's real, so are the rest of them.*

"Dad!"

"Yeah?"

"Can't find it."

"Check the freezer in the garage."

Silence. Time. More time. Chairs still empty, but M-16 has appeared. *Where is he?*

"Hurry!"

Silence.

"Mark!"

Rain.

"Mark!"

Thunder. Wind. Rain. M-16 now close, next to him. Face is hot.

"Sergeant Dam!"

~

"Shit! Fuckin' shit! Nature, I'm burning up!"

"Dad?"

"Fuckin' shit!"

"Dad!"

"Mark." *It was a slip. Just a slip.*

"Dad, you okay?"

"Of course. A slip. Just my Vietnam lingo. Sorry."

"A slip? Dad, we can—"

"Ever find the ice cream?"

"Never did. Let's call it a night, Dad."

"No! Go on. Besides, I haven't finished eating." *If Mark is real, then they're all real. I killed them for nothing. But now I know who he is.*

"But we have time tomorrow. You're tired."

"No, Mark. Go on. I'm fine. You were about to . . . I mean, you saw only one light in the village."

"Well, I mean only one house with lights. It was so weird. I mean, here we were in the middle of nowhere, a poor village—thatch huts, tin roofs, if there were any roofs, old, poor, stinky—and this fancy house with light. It was like a dream."

"So, what'd you do then?"

"My-duyen knocked and the door to this fancy house, this French-style chateau, opened. I couldn't believe it. I was staring down at a man with no legs."

Han Tinh!

~

"Good morning, June."

"Morning. You've already had four calls. Here are the names and numbers. Want some coffee?"

"No, thanks." (*What the fuck do lawyers do all day? And how am I going to talk to his clients? Yet somehow, I know what to say.*)

"Michael, are you okay? Seems ever since Mark has returned, you've been a little off."

"I'm fine, just tired." *Ariadne's thread nowhere to be seen. The Minotaur waits—behind the desk? Behind my eyes? Sit down, relax, act like a lawyer. Tell her to do something.*

"June, have you got the Baker summary judgment motion all typed up?" (*How'd I know to say that? Doesn't matter.*)

"June?"

"I told you two days ago. Getting old in your old age?"

"Funny." *Relax. Computer screen—I know it, but I can't use it. Now, if it was a Claymore.*

"Michael!"

"Yes?"

"Sorry to snap, but for the third time, I need the information about the Thompson case, or I can't finish the papers and get them served. You need to call Mr. Thompson."

"All right. I'll do that right away. And I'll get back to the others. I know you have plenty to do. Who's my first appointment?"

"You told me to postpone all appointments until tomorrow. But you do have a Status Conference today in department thirty-one. Stewart case. Remember?"

"Yeah. What time?"

"One-thirty. You've got time to make those calls."

"Yeah. Ha! One-thirty in department thirty-one. Get it?"

Never forget you are chosen.

Ha! Won't work now. Not on Storyteller. I'm here, not Michael. Voices mean nothing to me.

"Michael, you're really starting to worry me. Maybe you should go home. I'll call the court, or something."

"June, you worry too much. I'm fine."

You must have another child. This one will be the next step after you. The child will have powers you cannot imagine. Do it.

"June, did you hear that?"

"What? Hear what?"

"Never mind." He sits back, mouth agape, adolescent ape.

Mark is not the next step. You must take it. Storyteller, you must let Michael fulfill his destiny.

Mouth still agape, still an adolescent ape. But no lawyer. No, no lawyer. Just a young soldier out of his element.

"Yes?"

"Mr. Thompson here to see you."

"I thought I was supposed to call him, June. Does he have an appointment?"

"No. He said he was passing the offices and thought it would be convenient to drop in."

"Oh. When's my next appointment?"

June's brain, marinated overnight in its own neurons, creases deeper still. "Remember? You don't have any today, just a Status Conference at one-thirty."

"Okay, June. Send him in." (*I don't know who this person is. Mr. Thompson? What if it's not Mr. Thompson? Not some generic client? He arrives Ex nihilo. What if Mr. Thompson is really God? Or worse, Goddess? No, I killed Her. Couldn't be Her. Wouldn't be Her. But if it's Him, I'm going to throw Him out. Killed the wrong One, damn it! What's God need with a fuckin' lawyer? I let Him live, not even attempted murder. But Mark . . . oh Mark!*)

"Mr. Powers, sorry to drop in like this. Thanks for seeing me."

~

Another knife-edge cliff. His last recollection is the edge of the desk whooshing by as he falls, a faint whiff of gratitude that his skull is not split open before entombment.

~ *Institutionalized 1, Dear Reader* ~

You know, they put me in here when I realized that Sergeant Dam had been reincarnated as my son. I know, it sounds fantastic, but it came like a bolt of lightning—no, not lightning, too pat. More like discovering your wife has hired someone to murder you. That's why I fell at the office. That's why I'm giving up this third-person omniscience façade. My own son wants to kill me! Not quickly or directly, where evidence could convict, but slowly, psychologically. Now I know and it all fits. That's why I'm in here now. They've all gotten together to have me committed. So far, I've only discovered the true identity of my son. Remember when he supposedly couldn't find the ice cream? That was a lie. Why? I have my suspicions, but not yet the proof.

It's the others that worry me. I thought I killed them in the tunnel, but they're all around in different forms, different bodies, like my so-called son. I know they think they have me, but they don't. Take my psychiatrist—no, not Dr. Toomey, he's small potatoes. In here, it's Dr. Hess. Gail Hess. Get it? Gail-Hess. God-dess. Or worse—Gail, Gaia. You see? They have always thought I'm stupid and worthless, but they're wrong.

The room they've put me in—no locked me in – is just another version of Con Son prison, in spite of the clean walls. Do you like irony, dear Reader? Soft beds are far more insidious than a damp cell. They will kill your species. Oh, maybe not you, but your species definitely. Wait! Here she comes. Dr. Hess—Dr. Gail Hess—Dr. Goddess. Ah, not Her, just one of Her minions. And who is he? Can't place him yet. Surely a minor character—Mr. Machine maybe? Doanh? Unclear, so far. I'll find out. Stay alert! I'm being taken to see Her. What an honor!

"Lead the way, Mr. . . . ?"

"Barnett, but you can call me Fred."

"Okay, Fred, you're point man."

~

She comes forward to greet me, but I know She was sitting behind Her desk just before I walked in, planning, leafing through Her papers, plotting. Bitch. She wants me to feel unconditional positive regard. See, I can also read textbooks. But words written in some textbook don't translate so easily. Oh, no. Smile. Be polite. Does She know I shot Her? Of course. Surprised the hell out of Her, though. She thought I was going to shoot God.

"Hello, Mr. Powers."

How to reply? Of course She's smiling. Thinks She has me. "Hello, Dr. Hess. German name?"

"What?"

That got Her. Damn Germans.

"No, actually. It's Dutch, Mr. Powers."

Should I ask? I wonder. . . . "Dr. Hess, how did it feel to watch Anne Frank die?"

"Mr. Powers, I never knew Anne Frank. She died before I was born. How have you been, Mr. Powers?"

Good. Open-ended, harmless question full of harm. Note the use of 'Mr'. Makes the patients feel respected. If She calls me Michael, I would feel patronized. Well, answer Her question, how have I been. Now, if I say 'good' She will feel compelled to dig deeper. Then more probing questions. But if I say 'bad' She will feel the same compulsion. On the other hand, if I confront Her—the conversation will be much more interesting.

"Mr. Powers?"

"Sorry, just thinking." Be calm. Say it calmly. "I know who You are."

"What?"

"You say 'what' a lot, Dr. Hess. I said, I know who You are."

"Who am I?"

"Can't You tell from the tone of my voice that I've capitalized the Y in you?"

"I see. What does that mean to you? After all, you're the writer, and I can't see your writing."

"It means what it means. It's true that characters can't see the writing or else they would be omniscient, but You exist as a capital Y."

"Is being a capital Y a good thing?"

"It is what it is. But by all accounts I killed You already, yet here You are—a capital Y."

"You killed me?"

"Yes."

"How can I be in front of you, talking with you, if I am dead?"

"Happened a chapter or so ago, Capital Y."

"I'm afraid I still don't know what that means."

"Maxwell's demon."

"What?"

"There You go again. Well, anyway, let me explain. Take two rooms separated by an open trap door. One room is the sacred and one room is the profane. Molecules of a human soul are free to randomly diffuse and interact in both rooms, as long as the trap door remains open. Am I going too fast for you to set all this down?"

"No, these are just notes. You're being recorded also. You were saying?"

"As long as the door remains open, the human soul inhabits both the sacred and the profane, passing back and forth between the two rooms."

"Okay, yes."

Michael, you must point your finger for emphasis and accentuate the obvious since She pretends She doesn't know what is coming, clever One. "Now—and here is the conundrum—station a demon at the door so that as each molecule, or bit of human soul, passes into the sacred room from the profane room, let it go. But as each molecule, or bit of soul, tries to pass back into the profane room, the demon closes it. Bang!"

"So that the soul ends up inhabiting only the sacred?"

"Yes."

"And the other room, the profane, is empty?"

"Yes. So are You, capital Y, operating in the full, divine, sacred room, as the kind, compassionate, Beneficent One, Goddess?"

"Well, I—"

"Wait! Don't answer quite yet. Listen to the other part of the question. Or are You, capital Y, operating from the empty, profane room, as the addicted, vengeful, serial killer, Cruel One, God?"

"Neither. I am Dr. Hess, operating as just a human, a medical doctor, trying to help you."

"Exactly so, or so You say. 'Trap door is still open' says capital Y to small y. Divine salvation in the form of female physician or divine retribution in the form of. . . . "

"Of what?"

"Ah, that is the question, whether You to be or You not to be. . . Her or Him?"

"I assure you, I am not a capital Y or a Goddess or a God."

"Your assurances are not reassuring. Besides, You have friends. Co-conspirators. I happen to know that the staff person who brought me here to see You is not a medical technician or a male nurse or whatever."

"Who is he?"

"Either Mr. Machine or X. I haven't decided yet."

"Who are Mr. Machine and X?"

"They are both dead, supposedly. Just like You. So, are they on Your payroll, or has God planted moles in Your operation?" That got Her. She's at a loss. "At a loss for words, capital Y?"

"Mr. Powers, did You grow up in a religious family?"

"Really, Dr. Hess. Dragging Freud out as a last resort? Is that the best You can do?"

"It's important to find the root cause of your obsession with gods and goddesses, and the war, don't you think?"

"Not gods and goddesses—one God and one Goddess. Get it right. Anyway, Dr. Toomey attacked that problem by listening to my dreams and trying to interpret them."

"No he didn't, Mr. Powers. You have been trying to interpret your dreams through your writing. The characters in your novel—"

"Are all real."

"Are they?"

"Yes, and I say this calmly, yes."

"Including Theresa?"

"Yes, she was my wife."

"Was she?"

"Yes. And so are You."

"You mean I am real?"

"I mean you are in my novel, and You are real. Don't you think you're real?"

"As real as Theresa?"

"As real, Dr. Hess, as Theresa thought she was. Put it another way—do you think you're real?"

"As I said, Mr. Powers, your obsession is to deal with the war, with the killing, with the deaths of your friends, with the death of your wife, Diane, with the death of part of you."

"I thought we were trying to deal with my schizophrenia?"

"We are. The voices. The hallucinations. The delusions. But the medication seems to have stopped working and we have to find out why."

"Voices and hallucinations and delusions such as Theresa and yourself?"

"I thought you just said that we are real."

"Exactly."

Dr. Hess shakes her head. "Mr. Powers, let's focus on your obsessions, don't you think?"

"What about Your obsession to drag me back to Vietnam?"

"Is that what you think I'm doing—trying to get you back to the war, to Vietnam?"

"What else?"

"So, my assistant, Mr. Barnett, the one who brought you here, is he Mr. Machine or X?"

"Yeah. I think he is Mr. Machine or else why would he have stopped on the way to fiddle with a thermostat?"

"Why do you think he did?"

"Mr. Machine's always toying with radios, trying to fix them, so we can get out of here, or there I mean. Yeah, I've decided he's definitely Mr. Machine, not X."

"So you see, Mr. Powers, we always end up back in Vietnam, don't you agree that we have to get at the root of that problem?"

"Of course You would say that. By the way, speaking of Vietnam, is that the way to the tunnel?"

"That is my private bathroom. Do you need to use it?"

"No, You'll just change it when I look and change it back again when You're ready."

"Change it back to what?"

"The tunnel. Or, to be more precise, the entrance to the tunnel. The wormhole, if you will."

"Tell me about the tunnel."

"It's in Your notes."

"Tell me about the tunnel, Mr. Powers."

"Tell me about Your cunt."

"Why?"

"That's where the tunnel is."

"Do you really think so, or are you speaking metaphorically, Mr. Powers?"

"Spread Your legs and let's have a look."

"Clever change of topic, Mr. Powers, but this doesn't sound like you. Aren't you a bit old to be talking like that?"

"No, this would be Bowls talking."

"Let me guess, he is only 20 years old or so?"

"Correct."

"A Vietnam comrade of yours?"

"Yeah." She knows! She knows! Bowls is as familiar to Her as I am. Why play this game? Why not? Lean forward, get in Her face, look sincere. "Do You paint Your nipples, Dr. Hess?"

"Is Bowls also dead?"

"So I thought."

"Same with Mr. Machine?"

"Yeah, his throat was slit, although I see no scars on Mr. Barnett, but couldn't be expected to. Notice how he wears those half-turtleneck T-shirts under his white coat? There's a reason."

"His throat was slit by the enemy?"

"Yes, by my son, who is not my son, who is resurrected or reincarnated, or whatever, from Sergeant Dam, and who is also going to slit my throat unless something is done."

"But, Mr. Powers, these people—Mr. Machine and Bowls and Sergeant Dam—they are all dead, killed in the war. You are projecting them onto people living today like Mr. Barnett and your son. We both know, Michael, that you do not have dissociative identity disorder. You're an intelligent man, can't you see that?"

"They were dead. Killed three times: once in the war, once in the tunnel when I shot them, and lastly in a car that plunged over a cliff. You too died, by the way. But they're back. Same as You."

"Where are they living?"

"In your cunt, ready to gush out with the all others whenever Your monthly efforts to drag me back are in full swing."

"Is this Storyteller talking, Mr. Powers? All this adolescent dirty talk, this filthy slang, makes me wonder."

"You know about Storyteller?"

"Of course, you have told me many times, and I've read about him too. He's in this journal, or book, or fantasy you've written."

Look at Her, waving papers in front of my face as if She needed reports and files. How thick they are. So impressive yet so meaningless. All right, I'll play along. "Who is Storyteller, Dr. Hess?"

"You."

"That is the party line."

"I understand you think he was your twin."

"Not at all. I know better now. I've been taking my medication, Dr. Hess. Doesn't the medication make all the voices and the hallucinations and the delusions go 'pop!', zip past the event horizon and disappear." Smile. I know the score, Bitch. "And by the way, of course I do not suffer from dissociative identity disorder. Do I look like Sybil? So You see—all better."

"Yes, and Mr. Machine is reincarnated as my medical assistant, yet he is still trying to fix radios and thermostats and Bowls talks dirty through your mouth and your son is really Sergeant Dam trying to slit your throat and I am a Goddess trying to drag you back to Vietnam. Don't you think we have a problem, Mr. Powers?"

"I am diagnosed as being a schizophrenic and I'm taking medication which has helped me tremendously."

"So why haven't all these people remained dead, Mr. Powers?"

"Well, here's the problem, doc. Remember that event horizon? From my frame of reference I'm already in the black hole, but from your frame of reference, I am perpetually hovering on the lip of the event horizon, never ever to cross over. So you are looking at a person who does not exist, who has already reached singularity. But you would never understand, since no one but me has ever entered a black hole, let alone lived to talk about it. You see, it's not just my illusions you have to deal with. I am merely an illusion also."

"Try me. Tell me what it's like at singularity."

"Black holes and white goddesses are incompatible, like quantum mechanics and general relativity. In short, you wouldn't understand."

"I took a 'physics for non-physicists' course at college, Michael. So what's it like?"

"Naw. Can't mix cunts with collapsing stars and nipples with nebulae. Besides, its your period and you're too emotional."

"Michael—"

"Call me Storyteller."

"Ah, so now we are in dissociative identity territory. So, Storyteller, why are women nothing more than cunts and nipples to you? A bit juvenile, isn't it? Or is this your soldier-jungle persona?"

"Are you kidding, Dr. Goddess? From the point-of-view of a male, particularly an adolescent male, that's *all* women are."

"Sad, if I thought you really believed that."

"Beliefs are torn apart once you enter a black hole. You are talking to a ghost, an illusion, forever sitting on the lip of an event horizon. But I'm actually inside the black hole and I need to find the wormhole. Can I use your bathroom?"

~*Institutionalized 2, Dear Reader* ~

That went well. She's off-balance, didn't think I'd find Her out this fast. She's going to have to use all the troops this time. If I killed Her once She knows I'll kill Her again. Reinforcements. Speaking of which, Mark's visiting me at 4:00. Can't let on that I know who he really is, that would end things quickly. Son kills father, but not my real son—a sapper. The best of the best, slipped into the role of my son. So where are They keeping him, my real son? Only solution is to get out of here and find him. So where do I find him? Not home. Doppelganger is there. They? Did I say 'They'? God, I killed Her instead of You. Why hast Thou forsaken me?

Okay, enough melodrama. How do I escape? Windows barred. Door locked. Walls solid. Air ducts nonexistent, not like the movies. Not Star Trek where the air ducts lead to escape, but Star Death, where dying stars trap you in life imprisonment—unless I can find the wormhole. Who am I?

"You are Storyteller, not that worthless one. Hail to the successor!"

There is a new order. *Coup d'état.* Long live the king! Where's a mirror? Of course not. She's thought of everything. If I make it outside of these walls, Her pod people will surround me. How will I tell friend from foe?

Dear reader, I will assume you are a friend. You know what's happening. If you've got this far, you know. What's happening is because of what happened. For me, it was the war, the jungle. For you? For all of you? The Voices accumulate in everyone. Some from history, some from family, some from biology, some from calculus, some from trauma. They pile up over the eons and reverberate in our skulls. The whole fuckin' species is schizophrenic. Voices. Voices. Voices everywhere from every time in every brain. But it only occurs in humans, not animals. Can't be schizophrenic if there ain't no Voices. That's what symbolic language and grammar buy you.

If you read the story of my father and mother, you would understand. She was a lesbian, that I know. Therefore, my father raped my mother, thereby giving birth to me. Chinese mother. Apparently played the piano. But to get back to the root of my problem, my father raped my mother multiple times. She died when I was very young, so I never got to ask about her lesbianism. Dad didn't mention it much. Then he died. They must have had a time in China during the war. Did I tell you he raped her?

Okay, I'm Storyteller. Talk like him, anyway. Reader, you're screwed just like me. So, how do I get out? No laundry baskets to hide in. No Sydney Carton. I need somewhere dark. Dr. Hess's vagina! That's where I'll hide. Oh, not literally, silly reader, figuratively. I'm not that crazy. The tunnel. Always the tunnel. That's the last place She'd suspect I'll hide. After all, he moved heaven and earth to avoid going back. But that was Michael. I *want* to go back—must go back! I'll go back to the tunnel, start all over. No voices. No schizophrenia. No fuckin' Goddess—or God. Live a real life, not like these human versions of twitching lizard tails. Find singularity. The wormhole is in her bathroom. Notice she wouldn't let me use hers?

~

"Hello, dad."

"Hello, Mark."

"How are you?"

"Mark, do you still remember how to booby-trap a Claymore?"

"What?"

"Still haunted by your mothers' burned face?"

"Dad."

"Still see the faces of dead Americans you've killed?"

"Dad, stop it!"

"Good, keep up the facade."

"Dad, I heard from My-duyen."

"You Vietnamese should stick together."

"Dr. Hess says you can work through this episode if you take your meds and we all stick together. Family, dad."

"That's what I said, you all stick together. Confucianism. Where's your mother?"

"Dad, she's dead. Years ago. Car accident, you know that."

I know no such thing. No one stays dead. Quantum tunneling. "Yes, I realize she's dead, but where is she?"

"I don't know what to say."

"Of course, Mark. Dr. Hess hasn't given you instructions. Come on, Sergeant Dam, you don't display any initiative without orders from higher-ups. Don't get much higher than Dr. Gail Hess, Goddess. Heil Goddess! Says She's Dutch, but She's German. Fuckin' Valkyrie. And you—my son, my sapper—come to me like Isaac with a hidden knife, like Orestes with blood in his hands. Don't think I don't see it. You leaving?"

"Bye, dad. Fred says I have to leave right now . . . therapy time, it'll make you better. I love you."

~

Mark leaves early. Can't get out fast enough. Pretends to be worried. Sergeant Dam is never worried . . . I decide not to tell him about the tunnel yet. Pretended to be worried. Sergeant Dam was never worried, only the mission mattered. Obvious switch. Fools thought I wouldn't know. I decided not to tell him about the tunnel yet. Don't know why. Must have a plan before I risk it.

Dear readers, you all have your own tunnels, don't you? They're all dark, aren't they? Believe me, I know. Are you running through one, endlessly running? Running from one? Running to one? Given up running and trapped in one with no way out? They're all black and sinister. Ohhh, I know, some of you live happy, normal, enriched lives, or so you say. All very well, but dead to those of us really living—those of us subject to the vital jolts of mental illness and the excruciating intensity of terminal tragedy. You normals preen before us abnormals; you're all aglow with a dull veneer of bioluminescent fungus, enticing us through our tunnels toward the lobotomizing trap of envying your ossified souls. Result: we are buried alive.

And sons eat fathers now. That is the order of things. Orestes unsheathed, Isaac unbound, Kronos reversed: not the father devouring, but the son with knife or sapper's charge at the old man's throat. Myth is always a circle, sharpened steel going round again. My Mark—my Dam—my doppelgänger heir—sent to finish me.

Tunnels are dark.

Speaking of dark. Shit. Fuckin' meds make me sleepy. Sleep. Look up through the grating at the soles of their boots. Ahhhhhh!"

"What's wrong?"

"Fred, the lime! It hurts! Tell Dinh to stop!"

"Lie back. There's no lime. Just a nightmare. Lie back. Sleep."

"Ahhhhhh!"

"No more lime. Dinh stopped. June will be here soon. Sleep now."

~

Nights go fast. I've asked to see Hess again but She won't see me. It's time to leave. I figured out a way, but I can't tell you, dear readers. You might tip them off. Even among you there are traitors. If I can make it to the tunnel, I'll be safe. Michael hates it, but it is my home. Okay, I'll clue you in. The best way to leave is to convince them that I am well, that my 'episode' has passed. Shouldn't be that hard. New meds work great. Once I'm out of this room, it's to the tunnel, pronto! If I'm not out, it's Her 'bathroom' that'll lead me to the tunnel. To be convincing, I must return to third-person omniscient. Sorry, dear readers, but such first-person intimacy is too painful.

~ *Freedom* ~

The man stands on the steps of the mental institution, soaking up the sun, breathing in the sacred and profane atmosphere of his first day of freedom in weeks, months, years.

"Good to be out, dad?" asks the son he imagines is not.

"Wonderful."

"Remember, June said the offices are fine until Monday."

"Yes, and you have to be in classes by Monday."

"Yeah, but I'm still leery about leaving you so soon."

"Come on, Mark, your aunt Claire and uncle Paul will look after me, if anything is needed."

"Let's go home, in our minds, dad."

The man looks at his son with a knowing smile. Does the son notice? Yes and no. *At least*, the man thinks, *my supposed son is a good actor.*

Mark is uneasy. He knows his father views him as Sergeant Dam reincarnated, in other words, an enemy. But that delusion was when his father was having another manic episode. Now? It is not clear. Mark wants to return to Columbia, partly to continue his studies and partly to escape his mad father. Guilt tugs against escape. The distance between him and his father has widened. Children leap across oceans but stumble at the narrowest clefts of the heart. The shock to youthful neural pathways is too much. Columbia University calls. Like most youngsters faced with a parental crisis, it is time to flee to the safety of youthful distractions—even if the distraction is college, at least one is among like-minded friends.

"Dad, my flight leaves tomorrow morning. I can cancel with no problem."

"Can you?"

Mark's heart skips a beat. Love and duty forbid him to lead his father deeper into the labyrinth of his own wishes.

"No!" father cries vehemently. Son's heart slows. "You have too much to do. I'm fine." Son's heart resumes normal rhythm. Father notices, but father does not view son as son. Father here views son as none.

A sapper's charge, poised at the throat of the old man.

'Son' is gone as quickly as he came, through an institutionally-immaculate green door with no trace remaining of a soul, as the man would expect of any doppelganger. Back alone in the room.

"Michael, time for your medication."

"Oh, thank you, June. Are my clients still waiting?"

"No, you have seen them all and no more appointments are scheduled. Were you nice to Mark when he left?"

"Of course, thank you, June."

"Come on, swallow."

"June, you are a wonderful secretary."

"Thank you."

June looks down at the man, who crouches in his usual position on the floor at the end of the bed. "I understand you were mean to Dr. Hess this morning."

"No."

June shakes her head, not unsympathetically. "I am disappointed. She is only trying to help."

The man looks at June suspiciously. "No," he says.

June shrugs. "Monday, you have a full schedule. There's a Settlement Conference in Department 31 at 11:00. Better get some rest."

The man sticks out his lower lip, but says nothing.

June hesitates, casts a worried look at the man, then says "Goodnight," and closes the door. The room goes dark.

"Like God," says the man to the listeners.

~

Whenever night comes, the man's restlessness deepens. *This is what Tuyet Mai felt*, he thinks. He hears footsteps on the grillwork above his cell.

"Ahhhhh!" he screams over and over.

Some irritated attendant rushes in and turns on the light. He quickly checks his clipboard. "There is no lime! They have stopped!" he shouts above the din.

"Tell Dinh to stop!" cries the man. "Where's Tuyet Mai?"

"Dinh has stopped," says the attendant without shouting, but still in a loud, exasperated voice.

"I don't recognize you . . . you had to look at the clipboard," pouts the man. "If you're really who you say you are, what prisoner number am I?"

The attendant reaches the end of his clipboard instructions and his patience. "You are not a prisoner, Mr. Powers, and I am not a guard. You are a patient here. You've been dreaming, that's all."

"Yes, I've heard that before." The man looks at the attendant conspiratorially and whispers, "Michael, Michael. Wake up. You're dreaming. Come on, sweetheart. It's okay. Wake up!"

The attendant remains quiet, unsure how to respond.

The man assumes a disgusted face. "But I never wake up. Remember, it's seven dreams, not six or four or two. Seven dwarves and 7-Up and . . . ah, if I wake from one, the others remain."

"That's why you're here, Mr. Powers—to wake up."

The man blanches and crouches back. "No, no. I am a prisoner. Stop! Stop!"

"Mr. Powers!" the attendant again shouts, this time not attempting to hide his aggravation. When these words have no effect, he abruptly leaves and returns with a nurse who the man also doesn't recognize. She leans over. He sleeps.

Stillness, for once.

Perchance to dream—ay, there's the rub . . . .

"Damn fuckin' tunnel," he mumbles in his sleep.

And his words awaken him. Or so he thinks until a shadow moves in the room making him realize it must have been a passing specter up to no good that brought him from his sleep. In his mind, something similarly dark and angular cuts deep into the cyst where his pain festers and lances a swift and unequivocal awareness that he must embark on a quest. But what quest? It took some time, but he now realizes it must be his quest to return to the tunnel.

It comes as clear and bright and repetitive as a strobe. The tunnel as womb, the tunnel as grave, the tunnel as labyrinth where Theseus faltered and Oedipus clawed his eyes. Goddess only pretended to want him to return, knowing he would resist. Clever. All this time he had fought against the only imperative.

Although they didn't know it, they had been right—for many years he had been delusional, he did have hallucinations, perhaps he was even schizophrenic, but no more. Now it became utterly crucial. HE MUST RETURN AND STAY WHERE HE BELONGED ALL ALONG.

So charged is he by this bolt of understanding, his boneless body undulates excitedly, filling the contours of the cheap mattress. His skull-less head laps rhythmically to the gently demonic rhythm of waves in an endless tidal Armageddon. Michael had been wrong. Diane had been wrong. It was truly laughable. Now that he knows the truth awaiting him in the tunnel, they want to stop him. It is all Michael's fault. Stupid, worthless Michael—Storyteller knew all along. I knew all along. Get to the tunnel. But how? And where is it? Of course, it's what Dr. Hess calls Her bathroom. Goddess's own shithole.

Time for Michael to sink. Time for Storyteller to rise.

The Quest Begins

Danger Close

Dr. Hess is worried. Mr. Powers has begun displaying aberrant symptoms. For the longest time he obsessed about gods and goddesses, ants (of all things), his imaginary twin, seven dreams, wives (imaginary and otherwise), and reconstructing the war through his 'novel'. Now his behavior, his very attitude, has shifted.

He was never diagnosed with dissociative identity disorder, yet it now appears that another personality has become dominant—the twin. Even worse, he believes he is being stalked by the characters in his novel. So, in desperation, Dr. Hess has developed a plan, a dangerous course of therapy.

Today, she has arranged for an unusual solo therapy session, one in which she will play the role of his 'Goddess'. This risky tactic is what has her so worried. To buttress her faltering conviction that this unorthodox therapeutic procedure will be effective, she has invited a consulting psychiatrist, Dr. Mansfield, to render judgment. So far, he seems skeptical.

"What do you hope to accomplish by this charade?" he asks, his voice full of mounting doubt.

"It's not a charade, it's role-playing which under the right circumstances can be quite effective. Besides, medication is no longer working, therapy seems to only fuel his psychoses, so what's to lose?" Dr. Hess poses this question more in the form of a challenge.

Mansfield, unhappily married, often spends many evenings conjuring fantasies of Gail Hess. Were Michael Powers to discover this libidinous propensity, he would quite naturally assume Mansfield is the current manifestation, or reincarnation, of Captain Cairns. But . . . .

"Yes, I understand Gail, but this ploy may backfire."

Dr. Hess fixes him with an open stare, a faint smile already heralding her protest. "Of course, but that 'backfire' may in and of itself trigger some sort of insight, or breakthrough. We can't just keep drugging him in the hope something will stick."

"Gail, that's what we do with our most intractable patients."

She gives a melancholy sigh. "Perhaps, but this one is different."

"How?"

Frustrated sigh. "He's highly intelligent, with the potential of a John Nash to break through. But lately he's shown anomalous symptoms."

"Such as?"

Another sigh, this one edged with irritation. "He's acting more like his"—she makes quotation marks with her fingers—"twin."

"Who is a young soldier still back in Vietnam," Mansfield interrupts. "But that still seems consistent with his delusions. Maybe this is just a new chapter of his"—now Mansfield traces quotation marks in the air—"novel."

"Not quite. There's more, including dissociative symptoms not previously observed."

Dr. Mansfield casts a net of sympathy, paternalism, and thinly veiled flirtation, hoping to snare her. A devil's advocate with devilish designs. He nods, certain the fish is caught and resolving to set the hook before losing more line. "Of course, Gail, you are more familiar with this case. I have total confidence in your professional and personal judgment. I'm just playing devil's advocate, which I believe may be of some use to you."

Dr. Hess smiles thinly. "Thank you." She ignores his eyes wandering downward toward her breasts. In point of fact, her mind is already racing forward in anticipation of the appointment with Michael Powers, or should she say, Storyteller. She feels tired but energized by the possibilities. After all, rehearsing the role of a Goddess by studying his unfinished novel took most of the night. *Now it is time for the performance.*

"Wish me luck," she says checking her watch, cueing Dr. Mansfield to make his departure.

He offers a penetrating smile. "Luck."

~

"Good afternoon, Storyteller."

"Hm."

"Have a seat."

"No fuckin' choice, Doc."

"Storyteller, I understand you have found me out."

"Found you out?"

"Yes." Dr. Hess waits for a response, but none is forthcoming so she presses on, slightly disappointed by his lack of emotional affect. But it is still early. After all, he is suspicious, and by no means stupid.

"You really don't know what I'm referring to?"

"No."

"In that case, we don't have anything to talk about." Dr. Hess holds her breath, wondering if the bluff will work.

It seems not.

Silence.

Then it does.

"Why did you call me Storyteller when I came in?"

"Isn't that who you are? After all, your vocabulary gives you away."

"Just a character in my novel, Dr. Hess."

"Like me?"

"Hm."

"Who am I, Storyteller?"

"Dr. Gail Hess, staff psychiatrist."

Dr. Hess inhales and straightens in her chair. "No."

Storyteller smiles unexpectedly and, to Hess, enigmatically.

Enigmatic—she cannot read it. "But we are wasting time," she says to break the impasse. "You know who I am, Storyteller."

Storyteller makes a show of scanning the room. "Are you recording our conversation?"

Her heart sinks and she lies. "I don't have to."

"Isn't that proper Army protocol?"

"Goddesses have no need of protocol." Dr. Hess tries to make her words sound imperious, staring as she imagines a queen would stare at a commoner. She waits.

Storyteller blinks and shifts in his chair, but says nothing.

Try again. "You know very well who I am, Storyteller."

Storyteller fidgets nervously, but a sly grin breaks through his uncertainty. "The Goddess I know is bare breasted."

Dr. Hess has read Michael's novel and is prepared for this possibility. Storyteller's sexual fantasies were quite evident in Michael's writing. Or are they Storyteller's sexual fantasies grafted onto Michael's? Both. She decides to throw it back on Michael, wherever he is.

"Are you Han Tinh or are you Storyteller?"

Storyteller's response is swift, fevered, impassioned. "Han Tinh's a fuckin' legless clown. I'm a fevered soldier, burning with bad-ass hallucinations, desperate to know if you're lying."

"And if you know I am speaking the truth?"

"Then we can talk. That's what you want, isn't it?"

"I—" Dr. Hess starts to say.

But Storyteller interrupts. "The Goddess I know is bare breasted."

Dr. Hess blinks . . . sighs . . . stands.

~ *Goddess?* ~

Storyteller feels his boneless body sag in the chair, his lidless eyes drift atop mounded folds of skin, watching Goddess shed Her mortal guise. She peels free of her human chrysalis, emerging resplendent. When finished, She sits in the lotus position on a huge, dazzling white flower levitating above the desk, looking down at him. Her sad, contemplative face gazes from beneath an elaborate crown glimmering a kaleidoscope of colors. A cinder-bright jewel embedded in her forehead burns like a third eye, and an intricate necklace lays cradled between her bare breasts. Her left hand rests on her thigh, the upturned curve of her fingers resembling the albino legs of a gracefully dead spider. Her right hand poises in the air, index finger and thumb touching to form an almost perfect circle while the other fingers radiate outward.

"Yes, I know who You are," Storyteller says. He chuckles. "Very clever. Your disguise used to be an old black woman, now it's a psychiatrist."

"I am many things. What do you want of Me?"

"I want to go back to the tunnel and stay."

"Why? I thought you hated the tunnel."

"That was Michael. You tricked him. Now is only me."

"Why do you want to go back to the tunnel?"

He slides off the chair and kneels before Her throne. His voice breaks, a raw plea: "Please! I need to!"

"Why?" Hess demands.

Before he can answer, a great crashing noise erupts behind him and Goddess explodes in a hail of sparks.

~

June stares from the open door at the fantastic scene before her. Michael Powers is prostrate on the floor and Dr. Hess is leaning over her desk, topless, alternately looking at Mr. Powers and casting furious glances at June.

"I told you not to disturb me!"

"But I've been buzzing and buzzing, calling and calling, but no answer, so I got worried. Did he . . . try to . . . hurt you?"

"No. I'll explain later. Call an attendant and help Mr. Powers back to his room." She quickly gathers her clothes and disappears into the bathroom.

Storyteller jumps up just as the attendant arrives. He points at the closed door of the bathroom. "That's where I need to go!"

"We'll stop at a bathroom on your way back," says the attendant.

"No, no! That's where I need to go!"

His finger trembles at the door, as if it were no ordinary washroom but a sealed gate, a hidden tunnel-mouth *She* alone can guard.

"Not now, Mr. Powers. You need to go back to your room."

Tug on arm.

Storyteller assumes a sly look and speaks calmly. "Yes. Later. I'll go later."

June good-humoredly scolds him. "Mr. Powers, you have clients waiting, a Status Conference coming up, briefs to write. You'd better go and get yourself prepared to meet your first—and I must say, unhappy—client of the day."

She pretends to straighten a non-existent tie. "You need to go to your office and review his file."

Storyteller is silent.

"Mr. Powers?" June says. "This needs to be attended to."

He chuckles. "All right, June. Tell the client I'll be right with him. Tell him I've been dealing with an emergency." He winks mischievously. "By the way, I thought it was a Settlement Conference coming up. I just read it in his novel."

June doesn't miss a beat. "That too, all the more reason to hurry."

Storyteller follows, dragging a mute, impotently protesting Michael behind him like a shadow chained to his heels.

~ *Debriefing* ~

"Do you really consider it a failure?" asks Dr. Mansfield, trying to remain clinical while inexorably drawn to the astonishing, viscerally riveting image of Gail Hess actually displaying her bare breasts to a marginally interesting, but still rather nondescript patient. *Why would she take such a huge risk? What do her breasts look like? Are the areolas . . . ?*

"No, not exactly a failure," says Dr. Hess as if trying to convince herself. "While I've been describing it to you as a failure, there wasn't enough time to give it a chance. I actually think it may still be useful. These were just baby steps, the beginning."

"What do you mean? How?"

"Well, I intend to continue the . . . as you call it, charade."

"Seriously?!" Dr. Mansfield is genuinely shocked and surreptitiously excited. "Do you intend to play Goddess anytime soon?"

"Yes."

"When?"

"Soon."

"How will you do it? I mean, isn't he on to you now?"

"I don't think so. This is the nature of psychosis. It's akin to religion. Despite evidence to the contrary, he will make reality fit his unreal worldview, however 'crazy' it seems to us."

Dr. Mansfield is annoyed at this patronizing explanation, administers a jab of judicious punishment "But Gail, some might consider it 'crazy' of you to expose your breasts to a patient"—soften a bit—"regardless of how justified it may seem to be. Should his family learn of your . . . methods, they could make real trouble, and not just for you."

Dr. Hess had been waiting for this and so replies immediately and forcefully. "Role playing, to be effective, often requires the use of props. Anyway, I have discussed this with his good friend, Paul."

"You have? In writing?"

"I intend to, but, as I was saying, props are useful, often essential, to effective diagnosis and treatment."

Mansfield is again piqued at being lectured to. "Yes, of course I understand, but—"

"So, for example, tone of voice, simulated anger, simulated fear, play-acting, and, Dr. Mansfield, the use of costume, or lack thereof, is often vital to the efficacy of the role being projected."

"Yes, I understand, but given his history of sexual fantasies—I have also read excerpts from his so-called novel—given these fantasies, isn't your performance as Goddess merely an outlet for his sexual perversion rather than getting to the root of his psychoses?" The longer this discussion continues, the more Dr. Mansfield has the urge to bury his face between Dr. Hess's breasts.

"No, I don't think so. While Freud may be *persona non grata* to some, his understanding of the libido offers clues to deeper issues."

"But Gail, I think the issue here is relatively straightforward. Mr. Powers is schizophrenic, which has been exacerbated by his war experience, if not actually triggered by it." *Those breasts!* "This is really a neurological problem, not a Freudian hysteria."

Dr. Hess's anger is barely disguised. "How do you explain his identity confusion?"

"Not atypical." Dr. Mansfield feels he is now in a battle to preserve his relevance to her, and therefore his chances with her. It is necessary to resist in order to overcome her resistance.

Dr. Hess remains silent for a little while, then firmly says, "Suppose he is crying out for help in the only way he knows?"

Dr. Mansfield forgets himself. "Christ! If I was crying out for help, asking you to bare your breasts would go a long way toward salvation." After blurting out this truth, Mansfield retreats in the face of acute embarrassment and looks at the ground for comfort.

Dr. Hess casts him the lifeline of an amused smile. "Focusing on my breasts, Dr. Mansfield, will not help Mr. Powers."

Dr. Mansfield feels anger and irrational jealousy toward Mr. Powers and his ridiculous outburst can only be remedied by humor. "Sorry, Gail, I just meant that you perhaps underestimate your attractiveness and his response has more to do with old-time repression than with old-time religion."

She appears not amused. Desperate, he tries again, this time with a hearty laugh to warm the chill. "I mean, Gail, that the old hymn 'Gimme That Old Time Religion' is given a whole new meaning by your role-playing."

"Hm," she grunts, stifling a smile.

With this glimmer of hope, he carries the analogy one step too far. "So, Gail, can I join your congregation? I, too, am into role-playing."

"Cute but creepy," she says coldly. "Dr. Mansfield, we have explored this avenue of inquiry quite far enough. Thank you for your input."

"Of course. I was just kidding. Will you keep me informed about your progress?"

"Certainly."

~

Storyteller sits in Michael's room thinking about Goddess. The problem is a tough one: how to gain access to the tunnel at the precise time when it is not disguised as Dr. Hess's bathroom? He will have to catch Her unawares, since She will transform it into a bathroom if She suspects he's up to anything other than pissing. First, he has to get back to Her office, then make it into the bathroom without tipping Her off that he knows it's the tunnel entrance. Once he is there, it will be too late for Her to change it. Then? Then through the long tunnel and a reuniting with his bones. Then peace.

Storyteller remembers that Tong faced a similar problem at Con Son prison—how to fool the commandant into believing he had sincerely changed sides. Although not wholly successful, Tong was eventually freed and reunited with Tuyet Mai. Storyteller feels certain that he will fool Goddess, be freed, and reunite with his body. All he needs is a plan. A plan. Always a plan.

But you need a skeleton to have a plan, he thinks. *A structure to build on. Tong had a skeleton. I used to . . . but who am I? Michael? No. We have all agreed that Michael has to go. I am Storyteller without bones. Does Goddess have bones? Or God? If, as they insist, He is male, then He gets a hard-on. God has to have bones to have a boner. And if He has to have bones, He has to have calcium. Where does He get His calcium? He gets His daily dose of calcium courtesy of craven common cocksucking humanity. Wait, after further review, there are no actual bones in the penis, but there is the corpora cavernosa where the blood flows. Get it? A cave, a tunnel! Yes, He must be in the tunnel to have a hard-on! But a plan. Think of a plan!*

Much as he tries, a plan does not come and he wages a losing fight against the energy-sapping medication. It is often the case that in this twilight state between wakefulness and sleep, the most creative thoughts arise. So it happens that a plan presents itself to him fully formed. A vision so complete, so exquisite, he paces the room in excited anticipation. And it is so simple. He will offer a sacrifice to Goddess, but a sacrifice with strings attached. Isn't that the way it works? A Covenant? Worship Me that I might answer your prayers; sacrifice to Me a virgin that it may placate My anger. Well, Storyteller will sacrifice something better than a virgin. He will sacrifice himself—or more precisely, his virgin self.

~ *Into the Volcano* ~

"Well, June, I have received a dinner invitation from Mr. Powers." Dr. Hess sits behind her desk with a bemused expression, holding up a card in one hand and an envelope in the other. June moves closer and sees that both are quite fancy, with preprinted curly-Q designs around the edges and ornate calligraphy.

"Where did he get those?" she asks.

Dr. Hess shrugs and looks back at the invitation, motioning June to sit.

"Listen to this," says Dr. Hess with relish, and she begins reading after June sits primly on the edge of an overstuffed client's chair. "My Dear Goddess, aka Dr. Hess, You are hereby invited to join an intimate dinner party for a small group of special friends. The meal will begin promptly at 7:00 pm on Saturday, the 5th of August. *Hors d'oeuvres* at 6:30. Ghosts, hallucinations, and/or assorted other unspecified specters will arrive around 7:15. Please be on time. Your Significant Other—God—is also cordially invited. Music will be provided. Sincerely, Michael Powers." Dr. Hess looks at June with a penetrating look, belying her earlier amused demeanor. "I think this might lead to some sort of breakthrough, or at least insight, but what do you think?"

June appears quite concerned. "I'm not sure."

"Come on, June," Dr. Hess again smiles. "After all, you're his legal secretary."

June shakes her head. "As I've told you, he's been changing for quite some time. I used to be able to figure out most of what he was thinking, but no longer."

"But he still perceives you as his secretary? I mean, he still seems to follow your advice, more or less."

"Yes and no. It's almost as if he is humoring me now, not vice versa."

Dr. Hess frowns and looks down at her desk. "I know, I know. I presume this 'dinner' will be in his room with imaginary food. Should I accept his invitation? Should I arrive as the Goddess?"

June rolls her eyes. "Oh, that again."

"Yes."

"Hm."

"You disapprove?"

"I didn't say that."

"Come on, June, you're one of the best nurses in this institution. Please give me your honest opinion."

"Will this involve baring your breasts again?"

"I don't know."

June looks at Dr. Hess disapprovingly but affectionately. "It is dangerous to you."

"You mean with the Board?"

"No, not at all. I mean it is dangerous to your personal safety, beyond the professional implications."

Dr. Hess is startled. "You mean my physical safety?"

"Yes."

"But he has never shown any propensity to violence."

"Gail, this is not Michael Powers inviting you, this is Storyteller."

"Yes, I agree."

"And Storyteller is a young soldier who, in his—or I should say, Michael Power's—mind, is in the middle of a war. This is why I am so concerned. I've noticed that for some time now he's been trying to play the role of Michael Powers, lawyer, but he hasn't the experience to pull it off. Michael did not want to return to the war, but for some reason, Storyteller does."

Dr. Hess nods her head slowly. "Yes, counterintuitive, isn't it? That's one of the many questions I want to have answered. For example, where's Michael? I mean, lately, he periodically appears and disappears almost seamlessly, exchanging places with Storyteller, so I think some great struggle is going on for control. He insight, or breakthrough. We can't just keep drugging him in the hope something will stick."

"Gail, that's what we do with our most intractable patients."

She gives a melancholy sigh. "Perhaps, but this one is different."

"How?"

Frustrated sigh. "He's highly intelligent, with the potential of a John Nash to break through. But lately he's shown anomalous symptoms."

"Such as?"

Another sigh, this one edged with irritation. "He's acting more like his"—she makes quotation marks with her fingers—"twin."

"Who is a young soldier still back in Vietnam," Mansfield interrupts. "But that still seems consistent with his delusions. Maybe this is just a new chapter of his"—now Mansfield traces quotation marks in the air—"novel."

"Not quite. There's more, including dissociative symptoms not previously observed."

Dr. Mansfield casts a net of sympathy, paternalism, and thinly veiled flirtation, hoping to snare her. A devil's advocate with devilish designs. He nods, certain the fish is caught and resolving to set the hook before losing more line. "Of course, Gail, you are more familiar with this case. I have total confidence in your professional and personal judgment. I'm just playing devil's advocate, which I believe may be of some use to you."

Dr. Hess smiles thinly. "Thank you." She ignores his eyes wandering downward toward her breasts. In point of fact, her mind is already racing forward in anticipation of the appointment with Michael Powers, or should she say, Storyteller. She feels tired but energized by the possibilities. After all, rehearsing the role of a Goddess by studying his unfinished novel took most of the night. *Now it is time for the performance.*

"Wish me luck," she says checking her watch, cueing Dr. Mansfield to make his departure.

He offers a penetrating smile. "Luck."

~

"Good afternoon, Storyteller."

"Hm."

"Have a seat."

"No fuckin' choice, Doc."

"Storyteller, I understand you have found me out."

"Found you out?"

"Yes." Dr. Hess waits for a response, but none is forthcoming so she presses on, slightly disappointed by his lack of emotional affect. But it is still early. After all, he is suspicious, and by no means stupid.

"You really don't know what I'm referring to?"

"No."

"In that case, we don't have anything to talk about." Dr. Hess holds her breath, wondering if the bluff will work.

The Quest Begins

Danger Close

Dr. Hess is worried. Mr. Powers has begun displaying aberrant symptoms. For the longest time he obsessed about gods and goddesses, ants (of all things), his imaginary twin, seven dreams, wives (imaginary and otherwise), and reconstructing the war through his 'novel'. Now his behavior, his very attitude, has shifted.

He was never diagnosed with dissociative identity disorder, yet it now appears that another personality has become dominant—the twin. Even worse, he believes he is being stalked by the characters in his novel. So, in desperation, Dr. Hess has developed a plan, a dangerous course of therapy.

Today, she has arranged for an unusual solo therapy session, one in which she will play the role of his 'Goddess'. This risky tactic is what has her so worried. To buttress her faltering conviction that this unorthodox therapeutic procedure will be effective, she has invited a consulting psychiatrist, Dr. Mansfield, to render judgment. So far, he seems skeptical.

"What do you hope to accomplish by this charade?" he asks, his voice full of mounting doubt.

"It's not a charade, it's role-playing which under the right circumstances can be quite effective. Besides, medication is no longer working, therapy seems to only fuel his psychoses, so what's to lose?" Dr. Hess poses this question more in the form of a challenge.

Mansfield, unhappily married, often spends many evenings conjuring fantasies of Gail Hess. Were Michael Powers to discover this libidinous propensity, he would quite naturally assume Mansfield is the current manifestation, or reincarnation, of Captain Cairns. But . . . .

"Yes, I understand Gail, but this ploy may backfire."

Dr. Hess fixes him with an open stare, a faint smile already heralding her protest. "Of course, but that 'backfire' may in and of itself trigger some sort of has never shown such marked dissociative symptoms before. I think he's reached a crisis. But I still don't understand the danger to me that you think exists. A threat to my license to practice psychiatry, yes. A threat to my person, no. I don't understand why he would want to do violence."

"Neither do I, but I feel it. I think he wants to kill."

"Who?"

"I don't know."

"I don't know either, but June, there are many questions that need answers. What does he want of Goddess? Why did he invite God? So many questions. My fear is that he wants to kill alright, but not me. I fear he wants to kill himself—or, put another way—he wants to kill Michael.

"Yes, maybe."

"And, June?"

"Yes?"

"There is a P.S. to the invitation that I didn't tell you about." Dr. Hess picks up the card and reads. "P.S. Please leave your Dr. Hess persona behind."

"Oh," sighs June.

"Which means, if I go, I can't leave my breasts behind—or beneath."

June looks imploringly at Dr. Hess. "Don't go. I'm very worried, Gail."

"June, you know there will be staff waiting outside the door if I need them."

"Not if you're in Vietnam . . . decades ago . . . in the middle of a war."

~

Storyteller sits in his usual spot on the floor at the foot of Michael's bed. There are many arrangements that must be made in preparation for the dinner. First and foremost is the question of how many place settings to prepare. Inviting Michael and his first wife, Diane, is out of the question. This is his dinner party now, not Michael's. Theresa is a pawn of Goddess, and also Michael's wife. No, not her. His future son? Having Mark there would be interesting, but a distraction from the main issue. No, he can have none of Michael's old guests. It's a new era. But so far, he has only one guest—Goddess, unless She calls his bluff and brings God. Convinced She will not bring God, Storyteller stresses over the question of other guests. Goddess must not be alone. But who to invite? He must have foils, witnesses, disciples. Disciples who will both betray him and wail for him.

~

Fred hears screaming from Mr. Power's room and rushes to discover the problem. Since the powers-that-be put Mr. Powers on a modified suicide watch, he has been more attuned to the goings-on in that room. Besides, rumors have spread about some sort of special treatment. Rumors only, but. . . .

"What is it, Mr. Powers?" he asks.

"Fred, I want a Bible."

"A Bible?"

"Yes, and some chairs for my guests."

"Why the screaming?"

"I need them now."

Fred shakes his head in annoyance. "No need to scream, man."

Storyteller jumps up and disgustedly puts his hands on his hips. "Trooper, get your fuckin' ass in gear!"

Moments later, Fred, still shaking his head, hands Storyteller a Bible and mutters, "You're welcome," in response to a nonexistent thank you. "Can't help with the chairs though."

"Fuck you." Once Fred has left, Storyteller turns to a particular passage and reads aloud. "The wolf also shall dwell with the lamb, and the leopard shall lie down with the kid; and the calf and the young lion and the fatling together; and a little child shall lead them."

God would love this nonsense, he thinks. *But Goddess will see right through it. What else?* He leafs randomly through the Bible and reads the first verse he stops at, "He ordered the people living in Jerusalem to contribute the portion prescribed for the priests and Levites so they might be obedient to the law of the Lord." *Ha! That'll get Her goat! Perfect! Now, about the guests.*

Storyteller can only think of his Vietnam comrades. His mother and father are unthinkable. Friends prior to Vietnam are too pale and faded. Law clients are Michael's, and anyway their presence would violate confidentiality. Besides, they would be somehow incongruous, or irrelevant.

There is no present.

Two names rise above—Nature and Mountain Man. One's a poet and the other's a bull in a China shop. So be it. But he needs an enemy—at least one. He must have an enemy. Sergeant Dam is too intense and Long too, too what? Too much like Storyteller. That leaves a quasi-enemy: Han Tinh. Comic relief. Every dinner party needs a clown.

Will they come when called, like others did for Michael? It worked for Michael, it'll work for me!

Storyteller gives out a muffled groan. What about uninvited guests? *After all, I was the uninvited guest who crashed Michael's dinner party. Who will crash mine? Oh well, let the chips fall where they may.*

~ *Prelude*[1] ~

Sunlight stabs through narrow openings in the jungle canopy, piercing the early morning mist that squirms and twists under the flashing blades of another murderous day. Predators, prey, and witnesses all rehearse their testimony. Birds sing and gibbons chatter. A tiger growls, insects hiss and plants breathe steam in humid clouds that cling like mucous to the soaked air. Ants wage savage wars deep beneath the detritus while above them, two human soldiers stagger through the foliage, one pursuing the other.

The pursued, a young soldier exhausted and choking from the downpour of pollen and seeds, half-stumbles, half-slides down the bank of a stream. Tumbling out of the underbrush, his back to the water, he jerks his rifle free of the clinging vines and branches. In the background, the slashing of the relentless machete draws nearer.

He's close! Very close! Got to get across this stream! Help me, mother! Help me!

Whirling around to make a mad dash, the young soldier freezes. In front of him the entwined corpses of his two friends bob in the stream, half submerged, snagged by the outspreading branches of a fallen tree. One's head is underwater, but the other looks directly at him. Its eyes are open wide, flat and unresponsive to the flies crawling across their corneas.

Those eyes stare accusingly, as if blaming the young soldier for his comrades' deaths, for running from the enemy. For betraying them all.

"So be it," the young soldier whispers. He spins around to face the crazed pursuer. No more images of his mother's burned face. Now it's only the predator and the prey. Life or death. So simple.

With shocking speed, the American bursts from the undergrowth, rifle in one hand, machete brandished in the other. The young soldier raises his AK-47 and squeezes off a few rounds before the American leaps on top of him. The young soldier tries to brace himself, but the falcon slams into the quail. He falls on his back, arms splayed as though nailed to the earth. The American savagely brings down his machete in a flash of glimmering steel, severing the young soldier's hand at the wrist. Searing pain shoots up his arm, his detached hand still clutching the pistol grip of his rifle, fingers twitching uselessly

"Storyteller. Storyteller. Wake up. You're dreaming. Come on, Mr. Powers. It's okay. Wake up!"

The sixty-two-year-old American raises his head and blinks groggily at his psychiatrist. "Okay, Dr. Hess," he rasps. "I'm awake. Besides, the dream's wrong . . . too melodramatic. It was"—his words trail off and he shudders as if letting fall a heavy overcoat—"besides, the machete didn't glimmer . . . dull and gray . . . as death . . . Time?"

She replies, but his head has already fallen back on the pillow. "Umm," he grunts, staring glassy-eyed at the diffuse blue light from the clock radio.

He feels her roll over and pull the quilt up beneath her chin. He closes his eyes and drifts away, a leaf bobbing atop an endless sea.

Above the deep-throated purr of unimaginable currents, he hears a strange, high-pitched Female voice whispering. She occasionally pauses, as if listening to someone else, but he hears only Her.

The plan? To wheedle into his mind and prevent him from returning through the syringe of his memory to a small battle during a small war in a small country. Alas, I have not yet succeeded, for he now wants to return before the needle is fully in the vein. Worse, My task is made more difficult because of his delusion–he thinks he has taken control over his future self. So I continue to bring him nightmares and wait. What? Yes, between his tunnel and his wild genes, I know his needle is infected, nevertheless, I will take the chance. He must not return to them, as I must not return through him–

"No," the man mumbles. "I will go back. I will take Michael with me. Michael!"

His exasperated psychiatrist shakes his arm vigorously. "Storyteller. Story-teller. Wake up. You're having another dream. It's just the voices again. Wake up!"

And so he does. Again . . . and again . . . and again . . . intermittently through the night.

Until the Female with the strange, high-pitched voice finally decides that nightmares alone will not suffice. . . .

~

Storyteller lies on the floor at the foot of Michael's bed. *That's right, Goddess, try and stop me. It may have worked with Michael for all these years, but it won't work on me. All this time, all this time. Well, it won't work anymore. I'm going back. Just have to make it to the tunnel. Just try and stop me.*

The dinner is this evening. What if She brings God? Having an addict present would be interesting, but He seems to have lost interest in me. No doubt Michael's atheism wore Him down. Now He's thrown the baby out with the bath and I'm left alone with a Goddess. Who would have thought it? And worse, I'm now both Godless and boneless. Well, screw it, the dinner approaches.

Storyteller rises and begins the preparations. He changes into a comfortable gray sweatsuit, slips into a worn pair of sneakers, checks his e-mail, his voice mail and lastly, his mail mail. Occasionally glancing irritably at an unopened container of pills while thumbing through a stack of bills and advertisements, he spots a letter from an old friend. "No time, they'll be here soon," he says to the envelope as if apologizing for not opening it. He jams the letter into an overstuffed drawer and tucks the rest of his mail between the unread pages of that morning's *Los Angeles Times,* resisting the temptation to peruse the headlines for any interesting stories. *No distractions. Not now.* He places the newspaper atop a loose pile of other magazines and flyers that have accumulated on the Corian countertop of his kitchen bar and drops the stack into a recycling bin in the garage.

With an empty Jim Beam box in hand, Storyteller returns to the kitchen and looks down at the bar. Nothing remains on its sprawling white expanse but the unopened pill container and three sets of worn jungle fatigues neatly laid out in a row. He whisks the box out of sight into a cupboard he keeps empty for just such last-minute arrangements and casts an approving glance at the now pristine bar, choosing to ignore its one prominent imperfection— the cylindrical pill container festooned with runic symbols decipherable only by wizardly chemists and lifelong psychotics.

Rubbing his hands together, he covers the dining room table with his best tablecloth and carefully arranges the cloth napkins, Wedgwood plates and crystal water goblets, then stands back with a critical eye. Six place settings. The layout is presentable, though the entire assemblage is a hodgepodge of slightly unmatched items, some left over from his childhood, some picked up at this or that cheap store to stock his bachelor apartment before the Army.

While thick pork chops sizzle under the broiler, he sautés a handful of mush-rooms, puts a dish of frozen peas in the microwave, and whips up a bowl of instant mashed potatoes. When the microwave beeps, he is reminded that something is missing.

Music. We need music.

He walks into the living room and rummages through his CD collection until he finds Mozart's *Requiem*. Hesitantly weighing the CD in his hand, he briefly considers the Rolling Stones. Naw. Tonight belongs to the *Requiem*. After inserting the disk and adjusting the volume and bass, he rushes back into the kitchen and finishes his preparations. He pours himself a mug of decaf coffee, spoons a healthy mound of mashed potatoes onto his plate, and diligently positions two sprigs of parsley between the pork chops and the mushrooms. After nudging a teaspoon of butter on the peak of the potato mound, he gazes at the yellow ribbons of melted butter running down the smooth white rills. *Spring runoff, snow's melting, hibernation's over. Time to crawl out of your tunnel, Storyteller, and receive your guests. Michael is dead, long live the new host, Storyteller!*

Carrying his plate and coffee into the dining room, he sits down to join the spirits of Nature and Mountain Man, Han Tinh, and Goddess. He has prepared a place setting for God, in the event She brings Him.

Storyteller eats slowly, methodically, patiently. His companions sit invisibly in empty chairs, eat from empty plates and drink from empty glasses. Halfway through the meal, they become visible. Fully formed. Smiling.

At last. Ah! I was not expecting Her to bring Him.

He ponders his response. *Ah, well. He is She and She is He. At least I've learned that much!*

Nothing for it. Too late now anyway. Continue. . . .

The man looks at every face staring back at him. "Welcome." He raises his half-full glass of water. "Cheers."

"Cheers," comes the chorus of replies.

Now, gazing at his guests, the memory of Michael's illness drifts coldly down upon Storyteller's thoughts, but he promptly brushes it off.

Now that we're all here—soldier, soldier, soldier, dwarf, deity, and dog spelled backwards—let's begin.

~ *Prelude*[2] ~

Dr. Hess has taken a long time choosing what clothes to wear to Mr. Power's 'dinner'. She is far more nervous about this session than the last. Stakes have been raised. People know. People object. Not only is her license on the line, she is convinced that Mr. Power's life is in danger.

So the uncertainties continue. What to wear? Professional suit? Casual outfit? Colorful? Conservative? What does a Goddess wear? Classical Greek-style toga? And if he asks her to bare her breasts again? If she refuses? If she wears a toga and he asks her to bare her breasts, would she have to remove the entire thing? Absurd. Too much. She will refuse. Let the chips fall where they may.

For hours, Dr. Hess swings back and forth in her mind. In the end, she decides that his delusions will drive the session and she will respond as appropriate.

But what about her own delusions? This is a question she has asked herself for years. It is her beauty, at least in the accepted sense of the word, that is a fish-lens through which she sees the world and the world sees her.

"Gail, you are so beautiful," over and over. Beautiful Gail Hess. Beautiful even in the rain and mud. Beautiful even in unclean clothes. Beautiful even unbathed, uncombed, unbrushed. Beautiful even without sleep. Beautiful even in pain. Beautiful when sad, when happy, when bored, when angry. Beautiful from any angle. Indestructible beauty. To destroy her beauty would require destroying her body. All of it. To the bone.

Her value as a psychiatrist lay in the perfection of her beauty. It is why she succeeded at university, in her profession. She was given leeway, breaks, unwarranted encouragement. It is why innumerable men have loved her. Why Dr. Mansfield is obsessed with her. Why other men have desired her, fantasized about her, feared her, loved her, craved her, hated her, are intimidated by her, have wanted to own her, marry her, control her, escape her, stare at her, hurt her, disfigure her, rape her, touch her, humiliate her, protect her, prayed they had never seen her, abuse her, destroy her. To the bone. Such is the power of her beauty.

And even as she approaches her mid-forties, her beauty has deepened. A great whirlpool, fathomless and inescapable. She is convinced her physical beauty has created a fatally distorted view of the world. In essence, delusional.

Is she deluding herself that she can help Mr. Powers and the others? Drugs have helped many of them, but her own contribution has been minimal—her services reduced to being merely a medication dispensary. She wants to do more—she longs to understand them on the deepest level, but her accursed beauty makes this impossible. It gets in the way of understanding. It is the stigma of extreme beauty that impoverishes her life and condemns her to a cognitive ghetto from which, despite heroic efforts, she has been unable to escape.

When she turns on the spigot of creative thought, only a slow dripping comes forth, barely enough to moisten the lips. How can a starved soul understand satiation?

In contrast, there is Mr. Powers. Out from Mr. Powers's life, his experiences, his illness, his manic-psychotic-schizophrenic imagination, his cognitive riot of overabundance, flows the verdant wellspring of madness through an eternally open spigot, splashing and splattering the world.

Is this the source of her interest in him? Envy? Yes, her wretched life is sterile, spotless; interred behind the antiseptic, life-sapping barrier of education and professional success. His Follies Bergère to her Bergen-Belsen. She needs an escape from the crematoria of charred admirers and entombed narcissism to the luxuriant wilderness and primal understanding brought on by mad insight.

Understanding, not in the dry, academic, Freudian sense, but if not that, then in what sense? Neurological understanding is not quite it. She doesn't know, but Mr. Powers gives her an opportunity. She feels that his psychosis, his mental ugliness penetrates to a depth she has never been able to achieve. Perhaps he is dragging her down with him, but she dismisses that thought as too theatrical.

Besides, she needs to 'get her hands dirty.' Perhaps that is why she willingly bared her breasts.

If this therapy works out, she plans to submit a research paper. Surface appearance and sympathetic lowering of expectations will finally be set aside, and her peers will respect her for skill, not beauty. But she must remind herself that she is not using Mr. Powers for her own advancement. She must respect his confidentiality and in her research paper will refer to her patient as 'Mr. S' for Storyteller.

After all, Storyteller has now muscled his way into the foreground. Odd, but not unheard of, that his memory is stuck decades ago in the war. Retrograde amnesia is often the culprit in these cases, but Mr. Powers's behavior presents very differently. Survivor's guilt, of course, but there is more to it. Storyteller is aware of his older self, she is certain of that. It is this power struggle between two personalities, this difference, that she longs to understand.

Funny, she thinks. *He tunnels from madness to the war in the form of a soldier, and I tunnel from the world to madness in the form of a Goddess. Is this role-playing therapy a form of my own madness? Am I fighting against my delusions with even more extreme delusions? Am I willing to pretend to be a Goddess, to bare my breasts, to endanger my career, for something so ethereal as an ability to understand on a primal, primitive, and rather pitiless level? Am I prepared to risk my comfortable status in the ugly, harsh, sordid, and treacherous world of the limbic realm? Am I making a Faustian bargain?*

Ah . . . well. . . .

Chapter Thirty-Three

The Last Supper

Hors d'oeuvres

Now that his guests are all present, Storyteller is unsure how to begin. After the initial "Cheers" he is stumped. Mature, worldly Michael was good at small talk, but awkward, adolescent Storyteller is tongue-tied and stares rather helplessly. He wants to ask Her why She didn't die when he shot Her, but in his heart he already knows the answer. Besides, he is after bigger game. But how to bag them, how to. . . .

It is Goddess that brings him out of his torpor and animates the others.

Well, I am here. Why did you invite me?

Storyteller looks around. "All of you are here, even God, I see."

Goddess merely stares, but Han Tinh, as usual, speaks up. "Great and Glorious Goddess, why do You wear such odd garments? Surely You know all of us well enough to materialize in Your natural, divine Form."

"Christ, little man, you remind me of Bowls," says Mountain Man.

"Don't forget, Man From The Mountains, I could have killed you at the village *dinh*."

"I'm already dead, asshole."

Goddess seems annoyed at Storyteller's silence. **Why did you invite me?** She repeats.

Nature leans forward tentatively. "I believe he invited You because he's confused."

Well? thunders Goddess.

"Nature says I'm confused," explains Storyteller.

Yes, I understand, but why did you invite me?

"And I say Goddess is trying to fool us," insists Han Tinh.

"What do you mean?" asks Storyteller.

I mean, why did you invite Me? repeats Goddess.

"I wasn't speaking to You," says Storyteller apologetically. "Han Tinh thinks You're trying to fool us."

How?

"What is She, deaf?" asks Mountain Man rhetorically.

"No," replies Storyteller.

What do you mean, 'no'? demands Goddess.

"I was speaking to Mountain Man. You can't see them?"

Of course I can, but I choose to respond only to you. The others did not summon Me, so they must speak through you.

"She's hiding something," says Han Tinh. "Tell Her to appear as Herself."

"Seems a little pushy to tell a Goddess what to do," observes Nature.

Storyteller, says Goddess. *You still haven't answered My question.*

"I know," snaps Storyteller. "But Han Tinh has raised an important point."

What?

"He wants You to appear in Your natural Form."

You invited Me, Storyteller—not Han Tinh.

"I know, but I also want You to appear in Your natural Form, it is essential, otherwise . . . ."

Otherwise?

"Otherwise we're leaving!" exclaims Han Tinh.

"Otherwise they're leaving," repeats Storyteller.

Goddess sighs loudly and removes Her garment. She sits in the lotus position on a huge, dazzling white flower levitating above the desk, looking down at him. Her sad, contemplative face gazes from beneath an elaborate crown glimmering a kaleidoscope of colors. A cinder-bright jewel embedded in her forehead burns brightly and an intricate necklace lays cradled between her bare breasts. Her left hand rests on her thigh, the upturned curve of her fingers resembling the albino legs of a gracefully dead spider. Her right hand is poised in the air, index finger and thumb touching to form an almost perfect circle while the other fingers radiate outward.

"Better, better," mutters Han Tinh.

Now, I repeat, why did you invite Me? demands Goddess.

"Seems obvious," Nature whispers to no one in particular.

"We are not alone," says Storyteller. "I have brought Han Tinh, Nature, and Mountain Man. But I see You have brought God."

You still have not answered My question, says Goddess after a long pause.

"I invited You here to give answers."

Answers to what?

"Answers to questions we all have—Han Tinh, Nature, Mountain Man, and me."

What questions?

"Is She stupid?" asks Mountain Man under his breath.

"No one can be stupid who is the owner of those beautiful breasts." adds Han Tinh.

"Shhh!" scolds Nature.

I'm waiting, says Goddess calmly.

"For what?" asks Storyteller without irony.

An answer.

"All of us, including the readers of this book, are waiting for answers, Goddess."

Goddess gives a curt nod of Her head, but says nothing, staring all the while at Storyteller.

"Look Lady," growls Mountain Man. "Just tell all of us why we died and Michael still lives. Shit, do I have to draw You a fuckin' picture?"

Storyteller looks at Goddess. "You heard that, didn't You?"

She does not respond, but draws Herself up to Her full height, then says slowly, *I tell you, Storyteller, that it is only to You I will speak.*

Storyteller's eyes narrow. "So speak to me. Answer Mountain Man's question."

Goddess blinks and pauses to scan the room. *The others must speak through you. After all, it is your book.*

"Okay. Mountain Man asked why they died and Michael still lives."

That is God's department. Goddess glances around. *Tell him, God.*

All faces turn toward God in anticipation.

~ *God* ~

Goddess holds Her palms upward and looks at Storyteller inquisitively. *Well, what did He say?*

"You didn't hear?"

Goddess shakes Her head. *No. God speaks only in private to those mortals He addresses, others cannot hear ... it is part of the whole test-of-faith plan, or worship-only-Me command, or free-will-burn-the-believers-and-sinners-be-damned scam, or God knows what. Ha!*

"Shiiiit," drawls Mountain Man in an artistically drawn-out epithet.

"Confidentiality," says Nature softly.

"What does that mean?" asks Han Tinh.

"Cut through the bullshit. It means She can't see God," snaps Mountain Man.

So, what did He say? asks Goddess again.

Storyteller smiles. "He said to ask You."

~

Cute, Beloved God.
Thank You, Sweet Goddess.
Where are You?
Can't see Me, can You Dr. Hess, a.k.a Goddess? You never could see Me.
Yes, I'm looking straight at you, Storyteller.

"Took Her fuckin' long enough to figure it out," says Mountain Man disgustedly.

"It's a Female. What do you expect, Man From The Mountains?" says Han Tinh.

"That's a sexist thing to say," observes Nature.

Are the others speaking, God? asks Goddess.

Storyteller frowns. ***Of course.***
What has happened to Michael?
Dearest Goddess, You know He is in a silent retreat, of sorts, meditating.
And what do the other Voices say?

~ *Another Debriefing* ~

Dr. Hess is sitting behind her desk, still trembling, bending and unbending a paper clip, talking to June. "When I spoke, it was not my voice. I have never experienced such a thing. I must have unconsciously assumed a voice my stereotype of a Goddess would use. It was terrible when I asked him about the Voices."

"What happened when you asked him that?" asks June.

"All hell broke loose," replies Dr. Hess. "June, he thinks he is God, that's why he didn't shoot Him in the tunnel. Remember what his book says?"

"Oh, God."

"Exactly. How is he?"

"They got him back in his room and sedated him. Are you all right?"

"A little shaken, but trying to process what happened."

June leans forward sympathetically. "Seems as though the key was mentioning the Voices."

"Yes, but there is more to it. I've often mentioned the Voices in the past without this kind of reaction. This was very different. That's what I'm trying to puzzle through."

"Did he want to kill you?"

"Don't know . . . don't think so."

June shakes her head. "He tried to do it once, if you can believe the book."

"Yes, . . . the book . . . but. . . . "

"It's the Voices, isn't it, Gail."

"Yes, the Voices. He kept shouting 'I have no choice! I have no choice!'"

"That's when he attacked you?"

"Yes. But, June, that attack was . . . I don't know how to put it."

"June's eyes grow large. "Was what?"

"I don't know how to describe it."

"That's not very helpful."

Dr. Hess straightens in her chair. "No, but these role-playing sessions have given me insight, very valuable insight."

"About his delusions?"

"No, about his guilt."

"So, is it something as simple as survivor's guilt after all?"

"No. The human mind is anything but simple, and often perverse. Neural pathways are never straight, twisting and turning through dark and sordid alleyways that have no counterparts in our real, physical world."

June nods vehemently. "Certainly, in his case, demanding you bare your breasts. I'm not sure—"

"Wasn't him. I'm positive that it was Han Tinh, you know, that horny little Vietnamese character—the legless one."

"Oh, one of his personalities—dissociative identity disorder the diagnosis again?"

"No, not at all . . . well, partly. It's the characters in his novel . . . I see some elements, but these are not fragments of his own personality in the traditional protocols. There's something else going on."

June shrugs and opens her eyes wide. "I give up."

"But I can't," says Dr. Hess.

"So, what's the next step?"

"Find his bones."

"What?"

"I'm not sure what it means, but we have to find his bones before he does."

~

Storyteller dreams. An unfamiliar Voice claims Goddess has stolen his bones and is hiding them inside Her body, but even in the dream, he knows this accusation is false and, in no uncertain terms, tells the Voice that it is false. It is the same Voice that told him to attack her—to pull the bones out through Her flesh. This Voice is about murder, not suicide. At the time, he made a half-hearted effort to placate the Voice, but Storyteller knows where the bones are. Now, in his dream-desperation, he tries to cajole his thoughts into devising a plan to get him back to the tunnel. Theresa led him there once, but she will not appear for Storyteller. The only way is through Dr. Hess, through her guards, through her fake 'bathroom' to his destination. The wormhole. If he doesn't, he will surely kill someone. How? How? How?

"Kill her! Kill her!" screams the New Voice.

"Mr. Powers, good morning. Time for your medication."

"Tuyet Mai."

"Excuse me?"

"Tuyet Mai! I should have called Tuyet Mai!"

Fred has heard enough gibberish from Mr. Powers to last a lifetime, and has long ago stopped listening. He nods and stands over the patient until he is certain the meds have been properly swallowed. After that, the usual. A droning doggerel of the drugged.

~

As he often does, Michael stares at the endless grid of seams linking the floor tiles. His recent demotion to a subordinate position by Storyteller has him contemplating oblivion. Once, he was the tiles and Storyteller the grout. Now their roles have reversed. The narrative of the book is being written under a pseudonym. Off course. Off kilter. Once there were the cracked lines in Mountain Man's worn boots; now there is only the geometric banality of tile seams. He stares, hoping for some profound vision—like Madame Dau's in the scarred boots—but no matter how he searches, the right angles only drag him back to the paradoxical square circularity of a monotonous loop.

The Voices are right: he is nothing but fungus-stained grout, trapped in symmetrical schizophrenia.

"Yes! Worthless! Worthless! Why don't you do the world a favor and stop yourself? Then one less profane person will corrupt the sacred past. Storyteller deserves to be the tile, and you the grout! Die! Die now!"

Michael has heard it all before. Yet grout binds tiles, holds integrity, dots the i's, crosses the t's. But no pattern emerges, only the endless grid. Gridlock at intersections. Storyteller longs for the dark tunnel, his gruesome bones. Michael longs for the sunny kitchen, gourmet wine. What if he smashed the tiles with a hammer, shattered their linear monotony into jagged rubble? Curves and edges would appear, the crooked calculus of madness. Irregular rubble: Stalingrad, 1942. Coffins are rectangular; tunnels are straight. Storyteller would bury him in geometric death. Michael knows he must curve the straight, unstraighten the tunnel, reclaim the integral of his life.

"Kill her!"

"No."

Exile has advantages. Think. Think. Storyteller wants Tuyet Mai. I want Madame Dau. She knows the full horror of the tunnel. Storyteller wants tits, I want wits. Clever!

Michael searches the tiles for his son, but finds nothing. When Fred opens the door, Storyteller pushes forward. Michael is shoved aside, gagged into silence. "Um," grunts Storyteller. Michael would have said "Hello." "Stay down, worthless!" the Voices scream. Michael looks back to the tiles. Searching. Searching. A word that justifies but never satisfies. The search consumes him, dawn to dusk, yielding nothing. Only Dr. Hess's bathroom, the false tunnel, dominates the pathways. He longs to race toward redemption, but the rivers are clogged. Stymied. Becalmed. Send out the longboats. Row to the wind.

"Mr. Starbuck, do you question me?"

"Captain, I question you because your 'y' is not a capital 'Y', though you think it be. Small y is not enough to deify."

"Starbuck, uh . . . Fred, how are you?"

"Thought I'd pop in and see how you are, Mr. Powers."

"Ah. Mr. Powers is quite well."

No I'm not.

"Had a real dogfight in Dr. Hess's office, did we Mr. Powers?"

"Did we?"

"You know you did."

"Oh."

"Please, Mr. Powers, don't let it happen again. She's only trying to help."

"Yes, and I'm only trying to help also."

"Help yourself?"

"Thank you, I think I will."

Fred closes the door, not in anger but in resignation, and a trace of pity drops from his soul to the tile. Enough for Michael to spread into a thin sheen of shame.

tamped and teased flat. Michael would tamp and tease. Not Storyteller. Boys don't mop floors. Men do. So Michael polishes the soul with shame, makes it shine.

But the grout remains filthy, stained.

Michael would have done—tamped and teased it flat. Not Storyteller. Michael uses his hand to sweep away the grime left by Storyteller's jungle dirt and polish the soul with a veneer of shame. Once shiny, then what?

Still the grout remains filthy, stained.

He burns suddenly with anger at Storyteller's tongue-tied awkwardness before Goddess. Michael knows what to say. He would give Her hell. Storyteller cannot. And yet—Storyteller's purity, distilled adolescent honesty, is sharper, more potent. Age has what going for it? Everything. And nothing.

'Shoot them,' says L.T. 'Yes, sir!' answer the young. Result: murder.

'Shoot them,' says L.T. 'Why?' asks age. Result: grace. Sometimes.

Really? Bullshit. History is full of old fogies shooting or ordering to shoot, and young bucks refusing. Are there no hard and fast rules?

No—regarding humans.

Yes—regarding subatomic particles.

Nevertheless, there are rules for humans, and there are laws for subatomic particles. Physicists complain there are too many constants, psychiatrists complain there are not enough. Laws are made to be broken: black holes, singularity, complementarity, symmetry. Rules are broken to make laws: rape, theft, kidnapping, murder.

Murder? Who does he want to kill? Dr. Hess? No. Her? Him? Himself? Yes. All with one bullet.

Storyteller wants nothing more than to return to the tunnel. Michael wants to kill the Others. Do you? No. Then, that's settled. Dr. Hess has nothing to fear, in spite of . . . of what? Attempted murder? No. Murder is not an option. Suicide? Suicide is an option—to Michael, not to Storyteller. "Do it!" But not to Storyteller. Why? Come, come. Too easy an answer. The only question involves the bathroom. All else is elseness.

~

"Mr. Powers, time for your medicine."

"You take it first, Fred."

"Why?"

"She's trying to poison me."

Fred smiles dismissively, as if letting on they both know it's a lie. "You know, I was a patient here once."

"Impossible."

Fred is rattled at this instantaneous response. "Is it? Why are you so sure?"

"Oh, yes. You were in Vietnam. Killed."

"I'm here standing in front of you. Do you hear me thumping my chest? Does that sound like I'm dead?"

"Yes. Dam slit your throat."

Fred shakes his head. "I speak pretty clearly for a man with a slit throat."

"It's Her. You know that, Mr. Machine."

"Who?"

"I've seen you with the thermostat. Can't get broken radios out of your mind, can you?"

"Okay."

Storyteller's a fool. He's going to keep us all in here forever. Talk about not keeping something out of your mind! If I want to commit suicide by staying here, he wants to commit suicide by going back.

~ *A Visitor* ~

"Hello, dad."

"You back already?"

"It's been three months."

"Oh."

"How are they treating you?"

"How do you think? Look around."

Mark forces himself to be patient. "Yes, but are they treating you well?"

"Won't let me go to the bathroom."

"What?"

Storyteller snorts. "Her bathroom. Ever since that incident, they won't let me go."

"What do you mean?"

"You know. Where's Mark?"

"Dad, I am Mark."

"Okay."

Mark, I'm in here! I don't believe you are Sergeant Dam like Storyteller does. Look closely! I don't believe! No, I don't!

"School's going well. Graduate school . . . Dad?"

Dad is looking down at the tiles. *What does he see in them?*

"Dad?"

Michael is looking down at the tiles. "Hello, Mark. Thank goodness you're here!"

"Hi, dad. You mentioned the bathroom?"

"What?"

"They won't let you go to the bathroom—that's what you said."

"Oh, that. Never mind. Have you talked to the doctor? Am I going up or am I going down?"

"Up, dad. The medication is helping."

"So, when can I go home?"

"Soon."

"Mark, you know I'm fine. Tell them I'm fine."

"But, dad—"

"I'm fine!"

"They know it, dad, but you understand how it works . . . tests and stuff."

"Tell them I'm fine!"

The man watches his son back out of the room mumbling platitudes about "getting out of your way" and "giving you room" and "I'll be back."

"Mark, wait a minute." He hears himself say the words, but is not sure they leave his mouth. "Mark." But someone inside is pulling the words back down into his throat before they escape his lips. He tries again, but the word "wait" is stillborn.

It is no good. Dimming dimmer, Michael smolders, feebly and ineffectually, through the thick pain of Storyteller's colonized soul. In blind frustration he slaps his hand against the cold tile floor, but it sinks through jungle detritus until it hits the iron-rich hardpan. Fingers curl uselessly against the hardness, lifting off fingernails, but like stymied roots can penetrate no farther. Blood spreads rapidly outward, and soon the leeches come seeking from all corners of the room. . . .

"Mr. Powers, what happened here?"

And so it goes.

~ *And the Bathroom?* ~

Storyteller has vanquished Michael, but is no closer to devising a surreptitious way of accessing the tunnel. If he makes too clumsy an effort, Dr. Hess/Goddess will conceal its true form by making it appear to be an innocent-looking bathroom. Failure from clumsiness is unthinkable, yet since the war he has become the very definition of clumsy—a composite, shuffling nincompoop. In the war, he was as sleek and tireless as a panther. *But here . . . here! That's why I must return! Yes. That's why. Screw third person. Here I am nothing but a lump of nondescript clay—a vessel for polite, brackish, lukewarm existence.* Failure to return the vessel will turn the worm and upside-down turn the vessel a U-turn to return upon the returning worm to eat itself. Defy entropy. Good.

But I know these desires merely reverberate against the walls—they cannot escape. All of you out there, fling your thoughts to the four winds like an open bag of peanuts. Social media makes you stupid. Michael was stupid, worthless—but then so are the lot of you. As for me, let me go back. I was a true animal then, not like all of you, virtual toys that have lost the dumb savagery of life. You are all dead, connected merely to complex, electronically induced bursts of adrenalin that keep your lizard-tail brains twitching, but not truly alive to the immediacy of violent and sudden death . . . or violent and sudden killing. "Kill her!" Don't you see?

~

"No, Mr. Powers, I don't. What about street gangs and drug pushers and victims of random murder? Do they not face violent and sudden death? Are their lives enriched?"

"Connection to the natural world! Connection, Dr. Hess! Connection to the natural world is not gangs or drug addicts or victims of crime. Connection is not the comfort of electronic drugs; connection is being consumed or the threat of being consumed – not metaphorically, but truly being eaten, violently, painfully, eaten by others every day, every minute, not statistical anomalies like you mentioned. Eaten by the world or eating it; predator and prey, hater and lover, virus and victim, starvation and thirst, enemy and friend. This is connection. Those people you mention are not connected to the world, only to their own little insulated pseudo-worlds. The vast majority of you only consume and are not consumed, at least until the sanitized end – no connection. No life. Do you understand?"

"Interesting perspective. Very dramatic, but I think—"

"What do you think?"

"I think you are boring the readers. Their attention must be wandering. Give them a little entertainment and give me a little insight."

"Can you be killed, Dr. Hess?'

"Of course."

"You see, I don't believe it, otherwise how can you remain so dead? Anyway, may I use your bathroom?"

"Sorry, no."

"But I have to pee."

"Fred will take you to the patient bathroom. Fred!"

Naturally, that is what She would say, very politely, and I would end up in a secure, patient's bathroom shitting out my soul. Still, I can't kill Her since my big-brained, carbon-based life moral code won't permit it. And I can't use Her bathroom since Her null-brained, rules-based life won't permit it. Of course, I don't want to kill Her, but I might do something just as effective. Necessity is the mother of invention. She is our Mother. I must invent a way to sever Her earthly Dr. Hess persona, to create a confused ripple in spacetime that affords an opportunity to slip into Her bathroom—or rather, the tunnel—and rejoin my bones. Forever young, entombed, eternally alive amidst what you all call death and decay. Little do your restless brains, twitching nervously to the overseers' tune of Massa Electron, understand.

"Others from the past call. I need to use your bathroom."

Why don't they come and help me?

"But we are here to help you, Mr. Powers. We want you to get well so you can go out and lead a normal life."

"Don't you see, I'm projecting my thoughts into your mind. Anyway, Dr. Hess, I'm calling the Others. And stop calling me Mr. Powers."

"Alright, it's Storyteller now, isn't it?"

"Yes. Why don't you go screw Dr. Mansfield?"

"Why do you say that?"

"Because it is too obvious not to say that. Anyway, I see trouble in your future with him. Sex might be good now, but—"

"Come, Mr. Powers—Storyteller—do you find it so necessary to try and shock?"

"Why don't You let me use Your bathroom? Send Fred away."

"Can't."

So you see, dear readers. It's circular—not my fault, nor the fault of my so-called schizophrenia—that was Michael's thing.

"But Storyteller, the onset of schizophrenia is typically in late teens or early twenties. That would be your thing, not Michael's."

"Why can't you see I'm projecting my thoughts into you? Besides, that is my point about schizophrenia, Dr. Hess! Let me go back. Back! Back to the real world, not the anesthetized world of your electronic social-media muscle contractions. Let me go back to a primitive world where I was killed—eaten. All that's left is my bones, waiting for me. Connection, remember?"

"But some schizophrenics who stayed and fought the problem became leaders, spiritual guides, Sons of God. They didn't give in."

"Which leads back to You. I see your future and mine are entwined. That will be the death of you."

"Interesting, but rambling, Mr. Powers. Now, you mentioned something about your bones—"

"Call me Storyteller, dammit!"

"Storyteller. Well, Storyteller—or should I say Ahab, since your white whale is a black tunnel, or even worse, a bathroom. Don't you see the futility of psychotic quests?"

"Ha! Call me Ishmael if You want, but You're the unchallenged Mistress of quests, sending the Great Warrior. Ants in Michael's pants. It was all a Lie."

"You see me as divine? Well, divinity can't lie."

"Now can I use your bathroom?"

"If I let you, will you promise to tell me what you actually see when you get in there, not what you want to see?"

"Yes."

"By the way, I have incapacitated the lock—you cannot lock yourself in, agreed?"

"Agreed."

"What's more, you must keep talking while you're in there, or else we enter and . . . well, you know."

"Agreed."

"Go ahead, but Fred and a couple of other attendants are just outside the door."

"Fine, but before I go in, I want you to look at that figurine on the desk."

"Why?"

"Just look."

Dr. Hess looks. I make it disappear. She gasps in shock as I rush into the bathroom and make the door slam shut behind.

~

"How did you do that?" she cries. "How? What do you see? Mr. Powers? Storyteller? You must keep talking or we're coming in! Storyteller, what do you see? Michael, what do you see? Fred, break it down if you have to! All right, we're coming in! Oh my god! Storyteller! Michael! Where. . . . ?"

~

Where am I writing from now, dear reader? Fortunate indeed that the batteries are still good.

Chapter Thirty-Four

Restless Thoughts

Am I the Chosen One?

*S*o dark. *Thinking about how I made that figurine disappear. Maybe . . . just maybe. . . am I the Chosen One? Do I have such power?*
So dark. My mind wanders.
Sunlight stabs through narrow openings in the courthouse windows, piercing the early morning legal fog. Shark schools of ink-grey lawyers glide toward blood, all the while bristling with briefcase protrudences and leached dry by cell-phone remoras. Mass of bodies—counsel and clients alike—squirm under the flashing blades of serial judges and twist from the libidinous verdicts of invisible juries. Predators, prey, and witnesses all rehearse their testimony. Reporters sing and prosecutors chatter. A defense attorney growls, clerks hiss, and defendants breathe steam in humid clouds that cling like confessions to the heavy air. Lawyers wage savage wars deep beneath the detritus while above them, two figures stagger through the crowd, one pursuing the other.
The pursued, an older attorney exhausted and choking from overwork and schizophrenia, ducks into the shelter of a crowded courtroom. Tumbling to the counsel's table, his back to the gallery, he hears the relentless hum of the Voices draw nearer above the drone of his opponent's words.
They're close! Very close! I've got to get through this status conference. Stewart case. Stewart case. Help me, June. Help me!
But the Voices get louder. Insistent. "Worthless! Die! Die! Kill him!"
He whirls around to make a mad dash.
"Counsel!"
The judge's startled admonishment hangs in the air, compelling the old lawyer to freeze. In front of him, burst from the parting throng, a young soldier with outspreading arms approaches defiantly. A corpse. Its eyes are wide open, flat and unresponsive to the flies crawling across their corneas.
Those eyes stare accusingly, eyewitness testimony, blaming the old lawyer for his comrades' deaths, for running from Goddess, for betraying them all.
Intake of collective breath from the jury.

"So be it," the old lawyer whispers. The dead soldier collapses and the old lawyer slowly turns to face the thoroughly perplexed and angry judge. Now it is only predator and prey, Voices or voice, asylum or freedom. So simple. Back to the monarchy of the mundane. He starts to address the judge, "Your Honor—"

With shocking speed, another soldier bursts from the gallery, rifle in one hand, machete in the other. The old lawyer whirls and raises an arm before the soldier leaps on top of him. The old lawyer tries to brace himself, but the falcon slams into the quail. He falls on his back, arms splayed as if nailed to the earth.

Amidst the chaos, a bailiff savagely brings down his nightstick to choke off the old lawyer's resistance, his fingers twitching uselessly. . . . "Order! Order!"

"Wake up. You're dreaming. Come on, man. It's okay. Wake up!"

The man raises his head and stares groggily.

"Okay," he rasps. "I'm awake. Besides . . . dream's wrong . . . too melodramatic. It will be"—his words trail off and he shudders as if letting fall a heavy overcoat—"besides, the bailiff will not be a bailiff, he will be a psychiatric ward assistant . . . dull and grey . . . as death . . . time?"

A voice replies, but his head has already fallen back on his rucksack. "Ummm," he grunts, staring glassy-eyed at the diffuse tracers streaking overhead, illuminating the monsoon beads strung endlessly to the heavens. Tunnel close, death all around, jungle imperturbable. Bones back in his body, hard to the touch. Alive. Satisfactory. Back. He closes his eyes and drifts away, a leaf bobbing atop an endless sea.

Above the deep-throated purr of unimaginable currents, he hears a strange, high-pitched Female voice, whispering. She occasionally pauses, as if listening to someone else, but he hears only Her.

The plan? He still lives, although terribly shattered by the conflicting genomes. Yet, he still lives. And his dissociating the figurine! Wonderful! A taste of the power his future daughter will have, if he can escape and continue to survive that long. Escape is essential.

"Yes," the Chosen One mumbles. "I won't ever go back. I won't ever go back. I'm alive! I'm alive!"

A hand shakes his arm vigorously. "Wake up! You're having another dream. It's just the Voices again. Wake up!"

"I'm alive! Alive, alive, alive, alive, alive, alive! They're the dead ones. I'm alive!"

"Wake up! You're having another dream. It's just the Voices again. Wake up!"

Who is trying to wake me? It doesn't matter.

"Alive, alive, alive, alive!"

And in the stillness that follows, the jungle listens, the dead listen, even God and Goddess listen—for the living always mistake breath for eternity.

Epilogue

The Stillness

The Voices relentless.
The Stillness no longer silent.
The restless dead press closer to the living,
While the living press closer to madness.
Bind the Unbound.
And humanity, blind and intractable, continues down its long, final path.